MONEY, POWER, SEX . . . THEY HAD IT ALL BUT STILL THEY WANTED MORE.

Steve Gilman—He had raw talent and a special way of using it. But in the advertising game, talent wasn't everything.

Libby Gilman—She gave her body to Steve before their marriage. But afterwards, when success became his greatest love, she found that even sex wasn't enough to hold him.

Karen Lawson—She loved Steve in a way Libby never would. But she was driven by obsessive passions that could destroy a man.

Peggy—She longed to satisfy Steve Gilman—with something more vital and enduring than sex.

"A talent for swift moving story-telling is rare, and Mr. Hoffenberg again proves he is one of the best spinners of modern tales among us."

Stephen Longstreet

Other Avon books by
JACK HOFFENBERG

THE DESPERATE ADVERSARIES	29801	$1.95
ANVIL OF PASSION	14076	1.25
FORGE OF FURY	26914	1.75
A HERO FOR REGIS	15701	1.50
REAP IN TEARS	26401	1.95
SOW NOT IN ANGER	25478	1.95
THUNDER AT DAWN	15693	1.25

Jack Hoffenberg

A Raging Talent

AVON
PUBLISHERS OF BARD, CAMELOT, DISCUS, EQUINOX AND FLARE BOOKS

AVON BOOKS
A division of
The Hearst Corporation
959 Eighth Avenue
New York, New York 10019

Published by arrangement with the author.

ISBN: 0-380-00836-X

First Avon Printing, January, 1973.
Fourth Printing.

AVON TRADEMARK REG. U.S. PAT. OFF. AND FOREIGN COUNTRIES, REGISTERED TRADEMARK—MARCA REGISTRADA, HECHO EN CHICAGO, U.S.A.

Printed in the U.S.A.

This Book
is dedicated to

PETER MAYER

whose wisdom and wit
have been a source of
invaluable inspiration

BOOK ONE

Chapter 1

1

Steve Gilman woke at the first ring of the telephone and, as usual in unfamiliar surroundings, experienced a momentary sense of detachment from reality. The bed was strange—wider and roomier than his own—the coverings lighter in weight, the room in total darkness. He could hear none of the customary traffic noises coming from outside. The tone of the bell was more subtle than the shrillness he had come to expect, but equally insinuating. And he was alone.

On the fifth determined ring the fog inside his head began to clear. He reached out with his left hand, which came in contact with empty space instead of the telephone he thought should be there, then rolled over on his right side, touched the cold marble top of a table that shouldn't be there, fumbled for the instrument and found the receiver on the ninth ring.

"Hello."

He heard the brisk, cheerful voice of an operator saying, "Good morning, Mr. Gilman. Your six-thirty call. The outside temperature is fifty-eight degrees, clear, with an expected high of eighty later today."

Voice and temperature-reading returned him to positive existence and placed him in the Beverly Hills Hotel. "Thank you. Room service, please."

"Yes, sir." A moment later, he ordered a tall glass of iced orange juice and a pot of coffee. He threw off the covers, turned on the bedside lamp and screwed up enough energy to go to the floor-to-ceiling windows and draw the heavy double curtains. Outside, the balcony patio was dappled with weak morning sunlight as he squinted up over a cluster of palm trees into the cloudless coppery blue of oncoming day.

Steve Gilman was nearing his thirtieth birthday, growing overly conscious that with each added year it was becoming a bit more difficult to maintain the even 185 pounds that supported his six-foot-one-inch body, and concerned with what appeared to be a slight thinning of his dark blond hair at the forehead. At the back, his hair was neither short nor long, but full-bodied at the collar line without being too sophisticated or too mod. His eyes were deep blue and generally alert, well-spaced over a straight, somewhat arrogant nose and sensual lips.

If he was perhaps vain about his appearance and ultrafastidious in the clothes he wore, he considered this to be an occupational symbol forced upon him by association, as important and necessary as the impression he must make upon his colleagues and clients. In New York, he exercised somewhat irregularly, drank as much as was required of him, smoked too much, and enjoyed a healthy, virile sex life in a world where women were not only very attractive, but available.

After inhaling a few deep breaths of fragrant early morning air, he stirred into activity. He was out of the shower within a few minutes, partly revived from an evening of too much good food and too many drinks, and had almost finished shaving when the orange juice and coffee arrived with a copy of the *Los Angeles Times*. He added a dollar tip to the check, signed it and handed it to the boy, who said, "Thank you, Mr. Gilman. Have a nice day."

"You too."

Steve gave his lean, suntanned face the few remaining razor strokes it needed, patted on some lotion, then returned to the bedroom and drank the orange juice down in quick gulps. The coffee was still hot and he moved out to the balcony where he drank two cups, then dressed quickly and completed packing. He had had no more than four hours of much-needed sleep and felt an overwhelming desire to crawl back into bed and sleep the clock around; and might have done just that if Keith Allard, who had called him from the New York office the day before, had not insisted he would pick Steve up at JFK International Airport on arrival later today.

Last night with the Prices had been a near disaster. Larry had insisted on taking him to the Beachcomber for a farewell dinner—alone—except for Dorothy, Larry's wife. There was no way Steve could refuse this final evening in Los Angeles, during which Larry had consumed very little food and a remarkable amount of Scotch, more than Steve had seen him take on during his month-long stay.

To make matters worse, Larry's conversation had little or no bearing on the problems of today, but kept turning the clock backward to his successes of yesterday, long before Steve's time with the Wm. B. Leary Agency, when the name Larry Price had stood high on the roster of New York's brighter advertising men.

There was, of course, the well-known and oft-repeated Post Tool story in which Larry, the hotshot copywriter of the depression era, had saved the account by coming up with a brilliant suggestion during a copy conference. Post Tool, a manufacturer of tools for heavy industry, was then feeling the effects of a desperate national economy and hurting badly. In that meeting in Chicago between the harried Post and Leary people, Larry, during a painful lapse in the proceedings, suddenly asked, "Look, what about—?"

When the dozen or so men looked, Larry held up a small layout pad on which he had lettered Post's logo, or ad signature:

POST
Manufacturers of Tools for Industry

and beneath which, Larry had added three new, magical words:

and Home Use

For a few moments, everyone stared in silence, which was finally broken when Vernon Taylor, Post's merchandising vice-president, exclaimed, "Hey! Goddamn, that's *it!*"

Within three months, Post Tool was on its way to becoming a leading producer of electric hand tools for do-it-yourself home use and hobbyists; speed drills, hedge, grass and lawn-edge trimmers, circular handsaws, sanders and jig saws; which not only saved the firm from almost certain bankruptcy but became the Chicago branch's most profitable account.

Two years later, Larry Price was brought on to New York and the rest became history. In 1958, Price, then an accountant supervisor, was sent to Los Angeles as backup man to Tom Donnelly, the choice of Wm. B. Leary, Sr.

When, in 1959, Wm. B. Leary, Sr. died and Tom Donnelly retired later that year, Larry automatically stepped in as vice-president in charge of the West Coast branch office.

Now fifty-six and dragging at the heels, it all sounded so damned puerile to Steve, with Price acting like an old ham screen star rummaging through his scrapbook of memories for a disinterested audience, seeking reassurance. But Dorothy Price knew and she recognized that Steve knew. Steve could tell from her tense, tired face, the dead expression in her eyes as Larry rambled on in nostalgic euphoria about this or that coup he had pulled off fifteen or twenty years ago, refusing to allow the dead to remain buried, evading the subject that would face him tomorrow, when he would be sober. Dorothy was placed in the awkward position of having to seem proud of a husband who needed to build himself up in the eyes of a much younger man; and was failing.

During one elaborate, boring recitation, she said meekly, "Larry, dear, I'm sure Steve isn't interested in . . ." Larry turned his glassy stare on her and said in a surly tone, "Dotty, how would you know what advertising men are interested in? Why don't you let Steve speak for himself." Dismissing her abruptly, he turned back to Steve. "Where was I . . . ?"

Tears of humiliation sprang into Dorothy's eyes and Steve, embarrassed beyond words, felt a tremendous urge to reach out and touch her clenched hand in compassion. He had never known this shy woman before, but had seen Larry on several occasions when he had flown back to New York for conferences with Bill Leary, Jr. and Keith Allard. From the agency rumor and gossip mill, however, he knew that Dorothy had been Larry's secretary when he was an account supervisor in the New York office and had married her three years before moving to Los Angeles, after a rather sensational divorce from his first wife, who had named Dorothy as corespondent.

By the time they had dropped Steve at his hotel, Larry was in a near semiconscious state; Dorothy, behind the wheel of the company Cadillac. Larry mumbled something incoherent, something about driving Steve to the airport in the morning, but Steve politely refused, reminding Larry he had to turn his convertible back to the rental agency at the airport.

While packing, recalling the vague details of Larry's

divorce from a minor actress he had promoted into radio commercials and an income that eventually surpassed Larry's, it was inevitable that Steve would turn back to his own divorce from Libby Newell, although the circumstances were totally unrelated, yet no less painful. Libby, who had been his neighbor from childhood and later his first best girl back in Lancaster, Virginia, had simply been unable to cope with New York and . . .

Steve shook Libby from his mind for the moment, closed and locked his three-suiter, then his attaché case, and went to the lobby to check out.

There, at the desk, replacing his credit card in his wallet, came Larry Price, walking toward him—dark sunglasses hooding undoubtedly bloodshot eyes, wearing a gold sports jacket and dark blue slacks, open-throated shirt with a gold-shot blue Ascot tied jauntily around his neck—saying, "Did you, Steve? Jesus, I don't remember you telling me that. Well, what the hell, what kind of hospitality would that be, letting you find your way alone? You can leave the car here. The bell captain will turn it in for you. Here, let me take that bag . . ."

Steve noticed Larry's blue-veined, trembling hand as he reached for the three-suiter, and shuddered involuntarily.

Then, curiously inarticulate until they hit the traffic-packed San Diego freeway—heavily traveled on this bright Saturday morning—Larry began again to ramble on in the past, not once touching on his failures since taking charge in Los Angeles—the loss of Wesco Packing (pet foods), Caltronics, Inc. (electronic components), and Walters-Carr (resort home developers) alone, during the past four years—and he was now facing the very probable loss of his prime account, B & B Coffee, recently billing close to three and a half million dollars annually and accounting for approximately half a million in commissions and collateral profits to the agency.

They were passing the Santa Monica off-ramp when Price suddenly returned to the present, saying, "This B & B thing, Steve, I'm sure you realize it's only a temporary matter. Old Man Bond dying and Perry taking over, I mean. You know how things always appear to be falling apart during a period of readjustment, all the reorganization going on, like a juggler trying to keep a dozen tenpins in the air at the same time. Hell, this was just as sudden to Perry as it was to all of us. He's learning to take command of the situation, getting comfortable in the saddle."

Steve said, "Sure, Larry, I understand." And felt like adding *But why did you wait so damned long before giving the true facts to Bill and Keith? Why didn't you call for help six months ago when things started to go to pot, when they began cutting the budget back?*

Price brightened momentarily. "Give Perry Bond another few months and he'll have things whipped back into shape. I'm sure of it. He's a hell of a bright boy, but he's still got a few things to learn. Once he buckles down"—

Boy, for Christ's sweet sake, Steve thought. *Playboy would be a more accurate description. Give Perry Bond a few more months and there won't be a B & B Coffee Company in existence. Married and divorced three times, playing the Las Vegas circuit, Perry couldn't pull this mess together with the help of witchcraft.* He said aloud, "Do you really think you can count on that, Larry?"

"I'm sure of it, Steve. It won't be easy, no, but he'll come out of it just fine. After all, he was born into the business his grandfather founded back in 1906. Of course, his mother spoiled hell out of him and he's got a reputation for playing around, but all that is changing slowly. He's beginning to realize he has new responsibilities now, for the first time in his life. The reason he never gave a damn before was because Old Man Bond never trusted anybody's judgment but his own . . ."

And with good cause in this case, Steve thought.

"But once he bears down and really takes hold, things are going to be a lot different. I've been playing along, trying to get him straightened out . . ."

This, Steve realized, was pure rationalization, something Larry Price wanted him to carry back to New York to report to Bill and Keith, and Larry's next words bore that point out. "I hope you'll make them understand that in New York, Steve. Three months—four at the most—and everything will be squared away and in good shape."

Over coffee at the airport, there was more of the same from Price, his voice reduced to the whining plea of a man asking—even begging—for another chance, perhaps his last; and Steve felt the pain and uneasiness of Price's personal hell. In no period of his life could he recall a greater sense of relief than when his flight was announced and he finally shook Price's wavering hand and disappeared into the boarding tunnel.

Six weeks before, when Keith Allard first suggested the trip to Los Angeles Steve had leaped at the thought of combining a vacation with business, but when Bill Leary later outlined its true purpose, "to see what can be done to beef up the B & B account Larry Price seems to be blowing," he began to regret his earlier enthusiasm and acceptance. He knew then that Bill expected more than suggestions from Steve to Larry and the B & B creative group on the West Coast. What Bill was proposing, and not too subtly, amounted to a thorough investigation of Price's competency.

After that session with Bill, Steve had again discussed the issue with Keith Allard, indicating his increasing discomfiture with the assignment. "Why me, Keith? Why not Bill, or you?"

"Because you're group head of the GFP account and that's as close as we come to a coffee item," Allard countered. "If Bill or I go out there and find what we suspect may be true, it could come down to firing Larry on the spot. We checked it out with Wade Barrett and he suggested that sending you would be the ideal solution."

"This thing could take a month or more. And what about GFP in the meantime?"

"And why didn't you object to leaving GFP before you talked to Bill? Come on, Steve, GFP won't fall apart. It hasn't before when you've been on vacation. I took a look at your Work In Progress Chart before I talked to Bill or Wade. You're way out in front with your spring campaign plans. Wade can fill in while you're gone and you've got Chuck, Frank, and Reed to help keep the group moving."

"How about Mark Lawson? Won't you need his approval?" Mark Lawson was GFP's director of advertising.

Again Allard grinned, blocking that objection. "Quit stalling, Steve. Lawson can't complain if you're taking a winter vacation, can he?"

"Some vacation."

"Line of duty, Steve. Just bring back a clear picture of what's happening out there. That's all we want, and your responsibility will end with your report."

"Except that I may wind up doing a hatchet job on Price and I own a conscience I have to live with, damn it."

"I'm sorry, Steve. Bill, Wade, and I agree you're the logical choice for the job and it's the only route we can go. Bill doesn't want to pull the roof down over Larry's head without knowing more than what Larry's told him, which was little enough. You've been nominated and elected. How soon can you be ready to leave?"

So Christmas and the New Year had come and gone and now, as he came into the waiting room at JFK, the American Airlines calendar told him it was SAT Jan 10. The clock above it showed 4:12 P.M., a reminder to adjust his watch three hours forward.

The weather came as a shock. The outside temperature registered fourteen degrees and the day was gray and gloomy, made gloomier by the vast expanse of glass that seemed to bring the pewter-colored overcast inside. Through the glass, he could see the powerful jets lined up, waiting for permission from the control tower to take off for destinations around the globe. Towmotors pulled miniature trains of baggage toward the gaping bellies of several gray ghosts, while food service and gasoline trucks discharged their cargoes into other missile-shaped bodies that would soon taxi into the takeoff lines waiting at the runways.

In the leaden, threatening atmosphere, the planes seemed to droop like dull, reluctant birds. How different, Steve thought, from the Los Angeles setting he had left only a little over five hours before, palm trees swaying in the morning breeze, the thermometer already touching seventy-one, with an announced prediction of an eighty-degree high for the day.

Weather was important to Los Angeles, recorded boldly in newspapers, broadcast frequently—almost boastfully—over the airwaves. He recalled his last view after takeoff; sweeping westward toward the broad, endless Pacific, the turn eastward over incredible stretches of white sand beaches, then across the city that never seemed to end; sun-drenched desert and, finally, the sharply ridged spines of snow-capped mountains before rising high over the solid blanket of cotton candy clouds that blocked out the earth below.

He picked up his three-suiter at Incoming Baggage Flight 20 and returned to the waiting room. His plane, with a brisk tailwind, had been early and he wished now that Keith hadn't insisted on picking him up. It would have been more efficient to take an airport limousine into Manhattan and a cab to his apartment, which would also have given him time to arrange his thoughts. He put the suitcase down at the end of a counter, his attaché case beside it. A skycap standing beside a handtruck said, "Limousine, sir?"

"No, thanks." Then, "Could you keep an eye on these while I get a cup of coffee? I'm waiting to be picked up by a friend."

"Sure."

Steve handed him a dollar. "The man I'm expecting is a little shorter and heavier than I am. Gray hair, an older man. You'll know him by a short pipe in his mouth. His name is Allard. Mine is Gilman. Okay?"

The skycap tucked the dollar in a pocket and nodded with mild disinterest. "Allard, Gilman," he repeated laconically. "Okay." Then added, "If I'm here when he comes."

Even with the people milling aound, Steve felt alone. Everyone seemed to be reacting to the weather outside, still huddled inside furs and overcoats, hatted, gloved, and scarfed against the cold despite the warmth in the waiting room, all anxious for the announcements that would send them to their destinations, most of them in warmer climes, he suspected.

Depressing damned place, Steve told himself, barely realizing that the depression he felt came from within as much as from his surroundings. He perched on a stool at the coffee shop counter, choosing one that would allow him to keep an eye on the skycap and his luggage. He ordered coffee from a crisply starched waitress who flashed him the usual mechanical airport smile. He felt certain that once away from the glass-and-steel science fiction surroundings of the airport, his first glimpse of the walled canyons of the city in four long weeks would give him the lift he needed.

Southern California, he mused, was fine; a great place in which to release inner tensions. The seductive warmth, outdoor living, rented convertible, hotel with Olympic-size pool, sauna, open air beaches, golden-tanned girls in nothing swimsuits or micro-minis, the whole ball of wax. One weekend at Perry Bond's pad in Malibu, one in Ensenada, the last in Las Vegas, gambling, enjoying the girls Perry had brought along in his private plane. But somehow, sitting here in New York at a counter over a cup of coffee, none of it seemed real now. An illusion.

Four weeks in the Los Angeles branch had been akin to being sentenced to a warm weather Siberia, lacking the swifter pace and tempo of the New York scene. The casual, enervating, almost "So what?" attitude of Larry

Price had probably filtered down through his account executives and the entire staff of copywriters, art directors, secretaries, clerks, just about every-goddamned-body in the place. Overlong agendaless meetings that were social, rather than business conferences. Never-ending lunches. The inevitable drinking. The four-day fun-and-games swing he'd taken through the territory with Perry and Larry and Perry's current girl friend, who couldn't have been more than eighteen, and was so nauseatingly willing and agreeable.

Out there, the week ground to a screeching halt at noon on Friday, with everyone taking off for Vegas, Palm Springs, La Jolla, a cabin at the beach, a ski cottage at Lake Arrowhead or Big Bear, or wherever the hell else they disappeared to.

Question: How do I handle my report on B & B? And Larry Price? Trim it and protect Larry (and Dorothy) or, in the vernacular of today, tell it like it is?

He swallowed more of the coffee in swift gulps, as though this would bring Keith to the airport sooner, one eye on his luggage. The skycap—and who in hell ever thought up *that* ridiculous name?—had disappeared, leaving the handtruck and his bags unattended. He rolled the last sip around in his mouth. Good, he thought, passing his recently acquired B & B expertised opinion on its body and flavor, with a sense of self-approval.

The waitress, still smiling, returned to refill his cup and eyed Steve speculatively, classifying him. About twenty-seven or twenty-eight, attractive, just returned from some warm climate with a beautiful tan, well-groomed, smooth even features, about an inch over the six-foot mark, too young to be very rich, athletic build, and she decided—with finality—probably good in bed. With his frequent glances toward the entrance, no doubt waiting for his wife to pick him up—*it should only happen to me*. "Anything else?" she said.

"No, thank you. This is fine."

He drank the second cup of coffee more leisurely, and concentrated on the accumulation of notes in his attaché case: a jumble of facts as he had found them, and random jottings of his impressions, some conclusive, others vague. Ad proofs, Xerox copies of upcoming television scripts. How much, he wondered, would Bill and Keith expect of him? He swiveled around, picked up his check, searched for some change and left a tip. At that moment, the skycap materalized, tapped his shoulder and pointed through the glass sheet of door. "That him?" he asked.

Just entering, hatbrim pulled down over his forehead, head tilted to one side, eyes exploring the waiting room, was Keith Allard. His short, crusty pipe, turned upside down to keep out the drizzle, gripped tightly between his teeth, was all the identification Steve needed. Allard was in his middle fifties, about five ten and a half, with the dignity of a Supreme Court Justice. He hunched slightly forward as he looked around for Steve, who was suddenly filled with growing warmth and pleasure at the sight of him. He walked toward Allard, who turned at that moment, eyes and mouth crinkling in welcome.

"Hey, Steve!"

"Keith! Man, am I ever glad to see you. Seems like a year."

"To us, too." Allard's arm curled around Steve's shoulder, gripping it tightly, grinning crookedly, then released his hold. "You look great, Steve. I envy that bogus bronze of yours."

"Bogus? Just wait'll you get a look at my expense account and find out how much that tan cost the Wm. B. Leary Advertising Agency. How is Louise?"

"Fine, as usual. She wanted to come along, but I talked her out of it. Miserable day, eh?"

"Compared with what I left behind me this morning, you couldn't be more right, but it's great to be back. How are things at the shop, Wade, Chuck, Frank, Reed, Peggy? And GFP?"

"Ah, same as usual."

"That bad?"

They both laughed and Allard said, "Well, your buddy, Lawson, has been doing his usual plain and fancy bitching, but I think between Wade, Chuck, and the boys, things are pretty well under control. Nervously, but not too critically. I'm sure Lawson will be happy to have you back again. And Peggy, of course."

"How is Peggy?"

Allard grinned. "I think she'll return to normal now that you're back. It isn't easy for a secretary to ride herd over a crew like yours in the absence of the group head. I didn't tell her or anyone else you were due in today, else she'd have insisted on meeting you and I wanted you alone this afternoon."

"Any special reason?"

The skycap interrupted. "If you gentlemen are ready . . ."

"Oh, yes," Allard replied. "The silver Lincoln just outside the door."

Following the man, tamping fresh tobacco into the bowl of his pipe, he added, "You're not exactly dressed for our weather, Steve. You turn Californian out there?"

He was wearing a medium weight pair of slacks and sports jacket with a combination rain-topcoat, no gloves, no scarf. "It gets to you after the first week. You feel like an Eskimo in Florida if you don't conform. I'll be glad to get into an overcoat as soon as I get to my apartment. Forgot all about it when I left here, the weather was so mild."

Driving toward Manhattan, Allard said again, "Good to have you back, Steve. We've all missed you."

"No more than I've missed you. That L.A. office isn't the easiest thing in the world to take, the general atmosphere, the quality of *mañana.* I'm anxious as hell to get back to GFP."

"No real problems with the work in progress, but you'd better look into your plans for the spring campaign. I think there've been a few changes suggested. Lawson gave Wade and Chuck some rough moments, but they seem to have him tranquillized temporarily."

"And Bill?"

"He's had his problems, too. The market's been playing hell with his nerves, for one thing. Had to straighten out a mess in Chicago for Marty Link. Account exec on the Mid-West Oil account discovered his assistant was undercutting him with the client. Bill had to step in and fire the assistant. A couple of writers and an a.d. quit out there last month, pirated two accounts away from Marty and opened their own shop, but Marty picked up a good $600,000 account that more than offsets his loss. To get back to more pleasant thoughts, I've got your Christmas bonus check waiting for you in my safe."

Steve had asked Keith to keep it for him instead of sending it on to him at the Los Angeles office. That extra windfall would come in handy next April at tax time despite the bite that would go for taxes. "Thanks, Keith, it'll be very useful."

After a few moments, Allard said, "Well, Steve, what's the score out there?"

"You want it off the top of my head or would you

rather wait for a detailed report in writing?" he asked, stalling.

"Well, I don't want to miss any of the details, but skip the written report. Bill wants it faster than that. He is expecting us at his apartment at eleven tomorrow morning for an open discussion over brunch. Nothing on paper, just a frank talk."

"Well," Steve began hesitantly, and Allard was quick to sense his reluctance. "Come on, Steve," he said, "don't hold back. You were sent out there to see what you could do with a badly sagging account. What's with it?"

"Just remember, Keith, it was your idea and Bill's to send me out there, not mine."

Allard grunted softly. "I'm beginning to get a strong feeling that Larry isn't going to come out of this smelling like a rose."

"That's a pretty fair guess."

"So?"

"It's quite complicated. For all the briefing you and Bill gave me, you left out quite a bit."

"We gave you all we thought you needed to know. We tried not to prejudice you too much by prejudging Larry or the situation, but what the hell, you weren't entirely in the dark."

"Then I gather that Larry, as much as B & B, will be the principal topic of discussion tomorrow."

"Since you put it that way, how can we possibly separate the man from the situation? When Larry went out there to understudy Tom Donnelly back in '58, the branch was billing about $8,350,000. Tom was a hustler and a hotshot when it came to digging up new business. When he retired, Larry stepped into his shoes and not only hasn't added a single worthwhile account to his client list, but since '65 has managed to drop some important accounts. Billing is down to a little better than six million and now his prime account, for which he has been personally responsible, has slipped in sales and skidded from third place to seventh in their limited market—"

"I'm well aware of that. Also, that Larry knew I wasn't out there just to soak up some sunshine."

"So he isn't entirely stupid, which we know. And now you know why you, with your experience on Goody Food Products, were chosen to take a hard, cold look at the situation." Allard threw a quick sideglance at Steve, saw his forehead wrinkle into a frown to match the grim line of his mouth. "What's the matter, Steve?"

"For one thing, I don't mind reporting on a slipping account. That's something that can happen here, Chicago, L.A., or anywhere. Also, there is one recommendation I could make tomorrow . . ."

"But—?"

"Well, I don't like the business of pointing my finger at Larry Price. That comes under the head of politics, inter-family politics . . ."

"Steve," Allard broke in quickly, "when an important account like B & B begins cutting back its advertising program drastically, and the fault may possibly—and I repeat, possibly—be ours, it isn't politics, but practical, sensible business logic to get at the cause."

"By firing Price?"

"It may not come to that, but if it becomes necessary, yes. He won't bounce too far if that happens. He'll have thirty years of retirement benefits coming—"

"Keith, the man's in his mid-fifties and over the hill. Even if he's entitled to retirement benefits, it won't be a hell of a lot different from getting fired, will it? What does a man *do,* for God's sake, when he's put out to pasture? It could kill him."

Allard sighed and said, "Steve, most men commit suicide a dozen or more times before they die."

"And in our private jungle, more often than in any other."

"I think you're over-reacting. Advertising has the same faults you'll find in every other profession, in industry, medicine, law, politics, and government. We can't reform them all, nor can we simply abandon the profession because of its inconsistencies or rotten apples. Steve, I've known Larry for a long time. Believe me, I feel for him and I hate to see this happen, but that's life." Again a quick glance at Steve, who was staring straight ahead through the rain-and-snow mixture that had begun streaking the windshield. "And we've got other problems as well, but there's no point in bringing them up now," he added.

Steve remained silent, distant, and unmoved. "All right," Allard said, "let's drop it until tomorrow. By the way, Louise got in touch with your cleaning woman and had her air out the apartment for you. Right now, she's out shopping to restock your refrigerator with the bare necessities. And you're having dinner with us tonight."

Steve stirred then. "Maybe we should skip it for tonight, Keith. I'm so damned strung out I could sleep until Monday if it wasn't for that brunch meeting with Bill."

"Too much fast living in the wild and boozy West?"

"No, but I've been traveling through the territory, flying with Larry and Perry Bond in his private plane, and you've no idea what terror means until you're in a plane with Perry at the controls. Crazy. That overaged juvenile goes through a day as though it were his last one on earth."

"Sure you won't change your mind about dinner tonight?"

"Apologize to Louise for me, will you, Keith? And thank her for having Lorna take care of the apartment, also for the shopping."

"Okay, then, I'll see you at Bill's tomorrow. Eleven sharp."

"Sure. I'm sorry if I've been making noises like a Boy Scout. Maybe I'll feel better after I've had a good, long sleep."

2

There was an accumulation of Christmas cards, gift packages from commercial sources and the usual collection of junk mail waiting for Steve at his apartment on West Fifty-eighth Street. Sorting through the four stacks of letters lying on the table in the foyer with little interest, he put it all aside until later.

He unpacked, undressed and got into fresh pajamas. The bed looked inviting, but sleep evaded him. This was the apartment he had shared with Libby for two years—the entire life of their marriage—before she walked out that last time three years ago, and it all came to a crashing end.

Who was to blame? Where had they failed each other? Questions he had asked himself so many times, and for which he had no answers.

He lit a cigarette to relax himself, then got out of bed and prowled the apartment to refamiliarize himself with his own possessions. Lorna, he noticed at once, had made free with his liquor stock and he made a mental note to replenish what she had either drunk or taken home with her. In the kitchen, he found the refrigerator stocked with fresh eggs, bacon, butter, some cheeses, two T-bone steaks, oranges, milk, and a head of lettuce. There was fresh bread in the breadbox, a pound tin of coffee sitting on the sink ledge, and there were potatoes and onions in the vegetable bin. A penciled note scotch-taped to the door of the refrigerator read WELCOME HOME, STEVE and was signed LOUISE. He stuffed the note into the pocket of his robe as a reminder to reimburse her tomorrow.

The apartment was free of the staleness of nonoccupancy, another sterile reminder of Libby's absence. Lorna had aired it out well. The living room furniture had been thoroughly dusted, and even the pictures, for once, were hanging straight. The small study, originally intended as a guest bedroom before Libby left, and now his favorite room in the apartment, was as he had left it—desk clean, books neatly arranged on the shelves, typewriter covered, drawing table cleared, art supplies, usually in a state of complete disarray, tucked out of sight in the drawers of the Formica-topped art cabinet.

He had had one entire wall lined with corkboard, upon which were thumbtacked a dozen or more ads for GFP's line of cake, biscuit, muffin, cornbread, and pancake mixes, margarine, peanut butter, and salad dressings, all in various stages of completion; rough and comprehensive layouts, engravers' proofs in color, and as they had later been reproduced in finished form for print media. There were half a dozen of the last ads he had personally worked on before leaving for California to look into the problem of Price and B & B Coffee; and now that burr began to scratch at his mind again.

The damned account was in rotten shape from both ends, agency and client. Larry was blowing it badly by letting his copy and art people get by with pure garbage, the evidence of which he had in his attaché case in the form of advance proofs and recently produced ads in print form, plus Xeroxed copies of B & B's television and radio commercials. It was Steve's considered opinion that the material Larry's people were turning out for B & B wouldn't sell liquor to an alcoholic.

On the client side of the coin, the situation was far worse. Perry Bond, in his late thirties, had taken over the family-owned coffee company after John Bond died of a heart attack seven months earlier. Loosened from the tight reins Old John had held on the firm, Perry, the neophyte president, had started B & B on an erratic downhill slide. An only son who had been indulged and catered to by his mother, Perry had been married and divorced three times, gone through two inheritances and was now working on his third, with a coterie of friends to help him.

In Larry Price, Perry had found an ideal drinking companion and another source of interesting, if uninspired and untalented girls, eager for an opportunity to appear in B & B commercials for residual rewards. But with Perry's takeover, the B & B sales staff had become rudderless and directionless. Sales, as well as spirits, plummeted badly and in that fast-paced, toughly competitive market, B & B had been swiftly outdistanced by its competitors.

To make up for the lack of ardor in his sales staff, Perry began an expensive program of giveaway premiums, or outright gifts, to the biggest buyers in the eleven Western states the firm covered; color television sets, elaborate hi-fi systems, all-expense trips to the Far East, cars, cases of liquor, fine cameras; this despite the hot protests of his sales manager, Harlan Weschler. Soon, B & B found smaller buyers clamoring to be included in the payola program for gifts far beyond their importance, complaining they were being discriminated against. Within a short period of time, those key buyers who had been ignored discontinued B & B Coffee from their preferred lists, preventing their individual store managers from ordering the item. Simultaneously, B & B salesmen found themselves caught in a virtual lockout.

As sales sagged, expenses were cut, first among which was the fat advertising budget Larry was unsuccessfully trying to have restored, trying to convince Steve that the slump was a temporary thing. Therein lay the problem.

How to handle it bugged Steve's weary mind. Be tough and give it to Leary and Allard straight, which meant cutting Price's water (or in this case, liquor) off; or play it down to protect the man, who, by the record, had spent almost twenty years with the Leary Agency in Chicago and New York, and over ten more in Los Angeles, most of them productive and profitable. If the former, on whose conscience would Larry Price lie?

But there was one slim hope, if he could pull it off.

A very big IF.

Sudden hunger attacked him and he returned to the

kitchen where he put a pot of coffee on, forked some bacon into a pan, whipped up three eggs to which he added some ricotta cheese, and got out three slices of bread to drop into the toaster as soon as the eggs were ready to be poured into a second pan.

While he assembled his meal, he tried to project himself into Larry Price's position, then into Bill Leary's as owner of the agency; but found that was nearly impossible. Larry Price was older than Bill, the same age as his executive vice-president, Keith Allard, and he had no way of comparing their entire lives in advertising as opposed to his own bare nine. He thought of the cryptic remark Allard had made on the way in, to which, in his depressed state, he had paid little attention, recalling the words now: *And we've got other problems as well, but there's no point in bringing them up now.*

Problems, he thought. How quickly the business problems of an advertising agency became the problems of the agency man. Success and failure walked hand in hand every day, close companions. Steve had seen both; his success in reaching for the job he now held, the failure of his marriage to Libby.

And thinking of men like Larry, Wade Barrett and Keith Allard, who had spent their entire lives in the advertising business, now in their fifties, he began remembering those first days when he stepped into that exciting, confusing world back in 1961.

3

Like certain other momentous occasions, that day in June was one Steve would remember all his life. It was a Monday morning, hot and humid, his diploma from Columbia University only three days old when he came to the Hungerford Trust Building on Fifty-second and Lexington to call on Wade Barrett.

Professor Oscar Sterling, who thought he had detected something special in Steve Gilman, had written a personal letter to his old friend, Barrett, telling him of a student who had what he called

a keen, perceptive mind, a certain talent. Not only with words, Wade, but with an interesting and fresh outlook that intrigues and excites me. This young man is a born writer, but whether his gift belongs to the world of novelists, playwrights, newspapermen or in advertising, I can't say. There's just that feeling I have about him.

You once asked me to keep my eyes open for promising material. I think Steven Gilman's potential should not remain untapped for too long and strongly recommend him as someone who should not be overlooked.

Of this letter, Steve had known nothing. On that morning, he felt alone and naked with a slip of paper in his hand that read:

Mr. Wade Barrett
Wm. B. Leary Advertising Agency
52nd and Lexington Avenue

and with the sure feeling that he could never again return to Lancaster, Virginia, population about 10,700. New York, after four years at Columbia, had crept into his blood. During that time he had spent two summers at home working seriously on his father's weekly newspaper, The Lancaster *Star*. Later, when Grady Gilman died and the paper, in debt, had been sold to a Richmond newspaperman, Steve was determined to remain in New York. During the summer before graduation he had stayed on and worked in the circulation department of the *Herald-Tribune*.

During his final year at Columbia, he had called on every newspaper in the metropolitan area, talked with editors and personnel directors, filled out application forms and left resumés .. and heard not a word of encouragement, received no replies to his followup letters and calls. He had gathered up a dozen of what he considered his best short stories, a novella, and a 120-page outline for a historical novel, and left them with literary agents to be read and judged. The results were cataclysmically negative, although some of the turndowns contained encouraging compliments as to his writing ability.

In desperation, he sought out the man who had encouraged him most, Professor Sterling, who nodded sympathetically, yet held out slim hope; jobs were few, applicants many. But later, Steve became aware that Sterling was taking more than a casual interest in him and his work. Then, on graduation day Sterling called him aside and handed him the slip of paper with Barrett's name on it. "Go see this man on Monday morning. He'll be expecting you. I don't know that any results will come of it, but Wade may be helpful. You'll be meeting a man I've always considered to have an excellent combination of creative ability and keen judgment of talent. If not a job, you may come away with some worthwhile advice. In any event, you have nothing to lose."

It was a thread to hang onto. During the interview, Barrett asked many questions. He was then about forty-five, tall, hair thinning on top, with a bushy mustache, lean, and a heavy smoker. He listened quietly when Steve spoke, discussing his background, college work, and hopes. After three-quarters of an hour, Barrett picked up his phone, dialed three digits and spoke with Keith Allard about "that young man I told you about. Yes, he's here with me now, if you can spare a few minutes. Sure, I'd appreciate it, Keith. Be there in a few moments."

They walked from Barrett's office along a thickly carpeted hallway that led to the plush office of the agency's executive vice-president and creative director, where—once introductions had been made—Barrett excused himself and left.

Keith Allard, despite a desk cluttered with layouts, type proofs, sketches, and several pieces of finished artwork, was extraordinarily patient and gentle. Sleeves rolled up above his elbows, the short-stemmed pipe gripped between his teeth, he asked questions that were not unlike those asked him by Barrett. Steve felt more secure now, giving Allard previously thought-out answers. Until Allard said, "Why advertising, Gilman? What can you expect to give it or get from it?"

For a moment Steve puzzled over an answer that would sound credible, then said cautiously, "I don't really know how to answer that, Mr. Allard," apprehensive for the first time since entering this office, crossing and re-crossing his legs to hide his initial nervousness. "All my life, I've wanted to be a writer, a creator of ideas fit to see print. I've written dozens of short stories, sample news stories, a novella, and an outline for a novel, none of which I've been able to sell, and which doesn't sou like much of a recommendation. Lack of experience is against me, lack of knowledge of the writing markets is against me. All I have going for me is the time I spent working on my father's newspaper, a weekly in Lancaster, Virginia, one you've never heard of. That, and the Columbia School of Journalism.

"As a kid, I delivered the paper to subscribers. During summer vacations, when I was old enough, I learned to type, to write simple items, to handset a stick of type, make up display ads, that sort of general thing. I edited our high-school paper and yearbook.

"Professor Sterling suggested I call on Mr. Barrett, perhaps because he believes my creative talents—such as they may be—belong in advertising. To be honest with you, I can't say they do. If I came to work here, it would be a gamble for both of us."

Allard did not seem inclined to let him go despite the obvious amount of work that lay on his desk, calling for his attention. He took several phone calls and put others aside. Messengers arrived with material they dropped into his IN basket, and emptying his OUT basket. Twice Allard re-tamped his pipe with fresh tobacco and kept relighting it from time to time.

They talked about small towns (Allard was originally from Sharon, Pennsylvania), of business generally, of advertising specifically, before Allard said with a warm smile, "I want you to understand one thing, Gilman. Advertising isn't the glamour business most outsiders seem to think it is, mainly because they are exposed to it every minute of their waking hours, and can't escape it. It's everywhere and people live with it, absorb it, consciously or unconsciously. Advertising is ideas, words, art, and music. And damned hard work. It takes a lot more than inspiration or desire to produce it and get it to where the public will see and hear it.

"Some people condemn it for its seductive effects, urging them to buy more than they need, spend themselves into debt while acquiring and accumulating beyond their means. Some commend it for many better reasons. But one thing is certain, they can't run or hide from it. It's there and the buying public is the Number One target. The question is, for all its good or evil, do you want to become a part of it, direct your creative talents, such as they may be, toward it?"

Without hesitation, Steve replied, "Yes, sir. I do."

"One thing more, and keep this firmly in mind. If you haven't made it to within shooting range of the top by the time you're thirty-five, forget it. Like pro football, basketball, or ice hockey, advertising is for young men. They're always there, like a threat, pouring out of colleges with one or more degrees, not unlike yourself today, ready to take over the world, shooting up from the bottom like toothpaste being squeezed out of a tube, shoving older men aside, up, or out of the way. By thirty-five—forty at the very latest—you've got to be an account executive, account supervisor, or in a solid spot as a department or group head. If you can't make it by then, you'll be out cold. Cold, stone dead, and out.

"Don't look for the milk of human kindness or brotherhood in this highly competitive league. You'll trip and fall, and you'll hit the bull's eye any number of times. You'll be congratulated for your successes by the same people who'll snicker behind your back when you fall on your face. And when you do, don't expect honest sympathy. It is a very rare commodity in this field."

Steve, shocked into silence by those hard words, sat wordlessly. Allard said quietly, "That's about it for now, Steve. I'd like to be able to put you on, but at the moment I can't seem to think of a spot in which to place you. Give me a little time and I'll try to come up with something. If not here, perhaps with another agency that may be looking for a trainee worthy of Professor Sterling's words of praise."

Steve stood up and said, "Shall I get in touch with you . . . ?"

"Why don't you just jot down your phone number and I'll call you when I hear of something useful."

"Thank you, Mr. Allard." Steve wrote his phone number on the slip of personal memo paper Allard moved toward him, shook hands and left, considerably crestfallen.

During the two weeks that followed, he made frantic calls on other agencies, tried again with newspaper personnel men, registered at placement agencies that specialized in advertising men and women; and spent night after night in his room studying current advertising techniques in newspapers and general magazines, wondering how anybody ever got his first job in advertising if experience was the criteria demanded, and with which no one could possibly be born.

And then one morning as he was dressing to go out and make more cold, desperate calls to the list of agencies he had culled from the yellow pages of the phone book, the silent, black monster beside his bed pealed like all the church bells in the city gone mad. He lifted the receiver, fully expecting it would be a wrong number, but the voice said cheerfully, "Mr. Gilman? Mr. Steven Gilman?"

"Yes, this is he."

"Mr. Gilman, can you be in Mr. Allard's office at eleven this morning? That's Mr. Keith Allard, the Leary Agency."

"Yes. Yes, of course. Eleven, you said?"

"Yes, eleven."

"I'll be there. Thank *you!*"

Allard said, "Gilman, I was about to call you to go to the Ford McKenzie Agency for an interview the other day but we've had a little situation change here at Leary that makes a trainee's position available. I'm willing to go along with Professor Sterling's recommendation and Wade Barrett's and my own first impressions and fit you into that spot. If you're willing, of course."

Trying not to appear too eager, "Yes. Yes, I'd appreciate the opportunity, Mr. Allard."

"All right, then. You'll be on probation for six months and attend training sessions two nights each week for the first two months, one night each week for the next four. Report to Mr. Kelso in Personnel next Monday morning at nine o'clock."

Steve had been listening so intently that he hadn't realized the interview was over, that he had actually been hired, until Allard stood up finally and extended his hand for Steve to shake. "Don't be nervous, Steve. You'll find we're a rather closely knit family and get along well together. Mr. Kelso will take good care of you. Good luck."

Bursting out of the Hungerford Trust Building onto the crowded sidewalk on Fifty-second Street, he released the pentup breath he had been holding in his lungs, unable to contain his surging elation as he walked eastward toward Park Avenue. Looking down from new heights with ebullience on passing pedestrians and vehicles, wanting to shout out loud, *Listen, you! I've made it! Made it! I'm on my way!*

Walking without paying attention, heading north in the direction of his room on Morningside Avenue, he thought of many things he hadn't thought about in a long time and, finally drained of his adrenalin-charged enthusiasm, his mind began to plan for the hundred tomorrows that lay ahead waiting for him; all without the barest knowledge of the interior workings of a New York (or any other) advertising agency.

Libby Newell, just then graduating from Sweet Briar in Virginia, pushed into his thoughts, but he put this intrusion aside, wondering what—if any—comforting advice he might have gotten from Grady Gilman if his father were alive today. He could visualize that craggy, lined face, the gentle, proud eyes and smile, even the words: "Son, the whole thing is in your hands now and only you can shape and mold it into success. Or failure. Just don't back away from it. Lean into your new world, learn as much as you can about your chosen craft and use what you learn wisely. I hope I've done my part to prepare you for what lies ahead of you, but that's about as far as I can go. From here on, it's up to you. Don't be afraid. There's nothing to be afraid of once you've made up your mind you're on the right course."

Steve could not assess what his mother, who had died the year following his father's death, would have felt at this moment. For the first eighteen years he had spent with her, they had been no more than intimate strangers living together in the same household. Poor Jenny, he thought to himself, born into a world that never understood her, unable to face a life that had always confused and confounded her.

4

As far back as he could force himself to remember, Steve was conscious of the strangeness, even conflict, that existed between Grady and Jenny Gilman. He recalled only vaguely the earlier tenderness and gentility Jenny had shown him, more strongly the later bitterness and hostility with which she had become infected and was unable to cloak, to the eventual point of withdrawal from husband, son, and friends. From the time Steve was five and enrolled in school, there was an air of perpetual coolness that became more and more marked, puzzling, as time passed. Not until later did he come to understand and accept intrinsic facts.

Grady was almost twenty years Jenny's senior and was generally acknowledged to be worldly and liberal in thought and action. He had been sent to Columbia by his father, who wanted Grady fully to understand certain intellectual, cultural, and political differences that existed between the North and South; and this was followed by a year of travel abroad, a year on the Chicago *Tribune*, another on the St. Louis *Post Dispatch*, and a third with the Washington *Post* before returning to Lancaster to take over the weekly paper and job-printing plant when Carter Gilman died.

Jenny Budlong, on the other hand, was the daughter of a hell-and-brimstone country preacher, who had been raised with strict religious principles that would not sway or bend. When Elijah Budlong died, Jenny was twenty-two years old and virtually destitute. Grady was prevailed upon by a local churchman to give her a job. Apart from her modest salary, he paid her tuition fees at a small business school where she spent her nights learning to type and keep books. From that time on, the *Star* office ran efficiently under Jenny's firm hand.

Two years later, Grady took to his bed with a case of influenza. Jenny not only ran the office, but carried copy between Grady's sickroom and the printing plant, got the bills out, took care of the over-the-counter ads, delivered proofs to advertisers, saw to it that Grady's housekeeper cooked his meals properly, and forced him to take the medicine prescribed by Dr. Murchison. Following his recovery, Grady and Jenny were married. She gave up her job at the *Star*, and six months later, in 1940, Steven was born. Jenny never forgave herself, nor Grady, for having committed a sin against God's commandments and the even sterner principles of Elijah Budlong.

With the same firmness and efficiency she had shown at work, Jenny reorganized the Gilman home, then attempted the same process on Grady. She deplored his Friday night poker games in the back room of the *Star*—a local institution for over twenty years—threw out every bottle of his whiskey, cleared out certain books she declared were obscene, and challenged his public and private opinions on most subjects. She likened the morals of Lancaster to those of Sodom and Gomorrah and spoke out openly against the display of what she called the arrogance of parents who were permissive toward their children, whose conduct was shameful, disgusting, and reprehensible. In Jenny's strongly voiced opinion, modern music, dancing, and movies were an abomination and she publicly accused the local churches of being willfully lax in exercising control over their member congregations. Eventually, Jenny alienated every friend she had ever had. The fact that Grady maintained a business and social life apart from her and away from his sterile home embittered her all the more. She found refuge and consolation in reading her father's Bible every night.

What was most mysterious to Steve and—had he known it—to Lancaster at large, was that Grady Gilman ever married Jenny Budlong in the first place.

Lancaster, during Steve's growing years, was a pleasant valley town which locked onto the main highway that ran to such important cities as Washington to the north and Richmond to the south. Its people were chauvinistic about its rural beauty and only occasionally took trips to those larger cities to shop for special needs not available at home. They were church-going people with simple tastes, deeply involved in their own civic, political, business, and personal problems; a community that depended more on agriculture than on the industries that seemed to be exploding everywhere else during the early, threatening years of the forties. Some war plants were built in other parts of the county—through the political contacts of Barney Newell—but there was no heavy influx of outsiders into the town of Lancaster itself.

Ed Gates, in the post-World War II days, ran his police force the way Mayor Howard Fletcher and the Town Council wanted it run and was seldom troubled with major crime. Grady Gilman's editorials pushed for better paving, more street lights, improved garbage collection and sewers, the elimination of slums, newer facilities to replace the two dilapidated Negro elementary schools, more parks and recreational areas, and the purchase of land for an airport of the future.

Lancaster relied on Washington, Richmond and Norfolk papers for more important national and international news, but remained faithful to its own *Star* for local reportage and merchant advertising. It boasted a commercial center six blocks wide and twelve blocks long, an ancient courthouse, city hall, hospital, jail, and a clutch of other buildings that formed a three-block U with a well-tended park in the center and benches along its cemented walkways. It was proud of its elementary school system and high school—the latter built in 1938—complete with gymnasium, cafeteria, and athletic field. Because it was the only high school, it was integrated, but very few blacks attended, perhaps for economic reasons. There had never been a serious black-white problem during the years Steve had lived there.

Lancaster's most prominent and wealthiest citizen was Barney Newell. The son of a former State Senator and grandson of a Governor, Barney had become titular head of the County Democratic Party, but had no personal political ambitions. He had, however, very important connections in Washington, Richmond and in a number of key Virginia counties, and was satisfied with his role of unobtrusive kingmaker. His wife, Olive, had strong social as well as family-connected political associations in the state, in many cases more prestigious than those of the Newell family. Their son, Marshall, was born in 1935; their daughter, Elizabeth, in 1940.

The Newells lived on a forty-acre estate that fronted on Wilburn Road, with the Gilman home, on six acres, a quarter of a mile beyond it. As Steve grew to school age, it was Grady's practice to drive him into town, stopping at the Newell gate to pick up Elizabeth, known almost from birth as Libby. Marshall, five years older than his sister, preferred to ride his bike to school, to be free of prescribed schedules which the school bus imposed.

Marshall was a young duplicate of Barney Newell; tall, muscular, well-fleshed and as gregarious as his father. Libby was delicate and painfully thin, self-conscious of the braces that imprisoned her teeth, ignored by Marshall during recess periods, and too timid to join in the games of her more adventurous companions. She found escape in books, reading in whatever free time she found, perhaps envying the excitement and joy in which she could not bring herself to participate despite her teachers' urgings.

Until 1954, in his fourteenth year, Steve had paid little attention to Libby Newell or, in fact, any of the other girls he had known all his life. There were, of course, the usual birthday parties, school socials, picnics, casual meetings at Bellinger's for an after-class Coke and hamburger, or school athletic events that brought both sexes together, but in the main, Steve was mostly preoccupied with his own special "gang": Carroll Waggoner, whose father owned the Buick-Chevrolet agency, Ben Tinsley, son of Lancaster's most prominent attorney, Brevard Appleby

(Buzz), Jack and Arnie Porter, David Cameron (Dutch), and Doug Fletcher were his closest friends. Every day, after horsing around at Bellinger's, Steve would head for the *Star* for his ride home with Grady, wandering through the composing and press room, fascinated by the awesome blade of the cutting machine guillotine, watching forms being made up, locked up, the job presses turning out letterheads, envelopes, folders, broadside throwaways and other material.

Wednesday—the day the *Star* came off the presses—was the most special event of the week for Steve, Cal, Buzz, Jack, Arnie, Dutch, and Doug, who handled the home deliveries to earn extra cash to supplement their weekly allowances. Saturdays and Sundays, depending on the weather, were generally reserved for fishing or hunting trips with Grady.

In that year of 1954, Steve was graduated from Sidney Lanier Elementary School and was made aware of his social obligations when he and Cal were appointed to the Graduation Dance and Picnic Committee: the traditional June sendoff before summer vacation, which would be followed by entry into Lancaster High in September. Steve and Cal, Maxine Winkler and Janet Cameron were assigned to work up the invitations, decorate the Gym and prepare the dance programs. This was far less disconcerting than the startling realization that every boy would be required to ask a girl for a formal date, to see that her dance card was filled, that she was served refreshments, that he must remain as her partner for the supper, dance the first and last dances with her, and finally escort her home.

Weeks before graduation, groups of boys and girls were herded into the gymnasium where Mrs. Norman Bates, the music teacher, conducted a special class in basic dance steps that would have been more familiar to their parents; this was also the traditional and accepted method employed to promote social awareness, intended to eliminate shyness in the selection of partners for the Big Night.

Two weeks before graduation exercises, Steve was heavily engaged in discussion with Cal and Ben on the question of whom they would ask to the dance, ending, as usual, in fruitless indecision. He arrived home later to find Olive Newell visiting with Jenny and Grady. It was dusk and Olive's smart new convertible, its top down, stood in front of the house, causing Steve to wonder. He could never remember seeing Olive Newell in the Gilman house and the sight of her, regal in a bottle-green linen suit, with hat, purse, shoes and gloves to match, made him pause at the doorway into the living room.

"Ah," Olive said with a smile, "here's Steven now," a remark that only added to his bewilderment. "Hello, Steven."

"Uh—hello, Mrs. Newell. How are you?"

"Fine, thank you." A brief pause, then, "Steven, I have your father's and mother's permission to ask a special favor of you."

"Uh—yes, ma'am?"

"I'd like to ask if you would escort Elizabeth to the graduation exercises next week."

"I—uh"—

"Mr. Newell and I would appreciate it very much, Steven. You know how shy Elizabeth is with strangers and we'd like to be sure she is with someone she knows well and with whom she will feel comfortable."

"Well, you see, we were . . ."

Again Olive interrupted, which not only annoyed Steve but prevented him from giving his reason for turning her down. "I've talked with Elizabeth, not about you, of course, but about people in general. I know she feels much closer to you than any other boy, having known you for so long."

Steve looked at Grady, his last court of appeal, but received no help from that quarter. No use looking toward Jenny who, in her own silent way, seemed absurdly amused, perhaps at hearing the social arbiter of Lancaster and grand lady of Wilburn Road humbly asking a favor of her son.

"Well, Steven?" Olive Newell asked.

No help came from any source. He said, "Yes, ma'am."

Olive smiled and stood up. "Thank you, Steven, that's very gentlemanly of you. Incidentally, Elizabeth doesn't know of this visit, so I'm sure you won't mention it to her."

"Then—uh—how will she know?" he asked.

Olive's face broke into a patient smile. "Dear boy, you'll telephone her tomorrow at about this time and simply invite her. I'll have Thomas drive you that evening in one of the cars. Mr. Newell and I will arrive later and, afterward there will be a small party at our home for a few select couples. Is that a satisfactory arrangement for you?"

"Yes, ma'am. If you say so."

That last phrase caused Olive to stare at him for a moment. She said, "And you'll be sure to phone Elizabeth—?"

"Tomorrow, this time," Steve replied, adopting her manner of interrupting.

"Thank you, Steven. I'm sure you'll have a delightful time. And goodnight, Jenny, Grady. Thank you again."

Grady and Steve followed Olive out and Grady saw her into her car. When she drove off, he rejoined Steve on the porch. "What's wrong, son?"

"What's *wrong?* Holy *cow,* Dad. I was going to ask Irma Powell. There's gonna be a dance afterward. I don't want to drag that drip."

"Then why did you say yes to Mrs. Newell?"

"Because she didn't give me a chance to say no."

"Nonsense. Of course she did. If you had a chance to say yes, you had an equal chance to say no, didn't you?"

"Oh cripes, Dad, you know what I mean."

"Well, maybe what you're trying to say is that it's difficult to say no to a determined woman."

"I guess so."

"Well?"

"What do I do now?"

"Have you asked Irma to the exercises and dance?"

"Not yet. I was talking to Cal and Ben this afternoon. We were going to make our dates tonight."

"Well, I'm afraid you won't be able to do that now. What you'll do is what you promised Mrs. Newell you'd do."

"Dad . . ."

"Steve, you can't beg out of a promise you made knowingly. You'll call Libby tomorrow evening. You'll be attentive and make sure she has every dance, with you or with one of your classmates. Understand?"

"Geez, Dad, *braces* on her teeth!"

"It was your decision to make and you made it. If you'd said no, that you had made other plans, that would have been another matter entirely."

"Well, I hadn't really made the other plan yet, but . . ."

"No buts, Steve. You're committed. Don't offend Libby. This isn't her fault. She's a shy, sensitive girl and you could hurt her for the rest of her life. It's important that you understand that."

Glumly, defeated, "Yes, sir."

On the evening of the graduation exercises, Thomas, dressed in his black driving-uniform, arrived to take Steve to call for Elizabeth Newell. Carrying an acetate box that contained a camellia corsage which Grady had brought home for him, nervously awkward in blue jacket and cream-colored slacks he was wearing for the first time, Steve formally presented himself at the imposing Newell home. Olive sent a grinning Hattie to tell Miss Elizabeth that Mr. Steven was calling for her and within a few minutes, she came walking down the stairs in a white dress, much like a somnambulist, no less flustered than Steve. For this evening, her braces had been left off, her hair arranged differently, and she wore a faint trace of eye makeup and lipstick. The effect was somewhat less than spectacular.

Steve bowed stiffly. "Good evening, Libby," he said, and handed over the corsage. She took it and replied, "G-good evening, Steve-Steven. Th-thank you v-very much," and followed by the benevolent smiles of her parents, they walked out through the door held open by Hattie.

"We'll see you there in half an hour," Olive called from the veranda, and Thomas, showing two rows of huge white teeth, opened the door to the black limousine for them.

The auditorium was packed with parents, relatives and friends and—lacking air-conditioning—the hour and a half of ceremonial speeches, diploma awards and receiving line for congratulations were an enervating experience for all. Grady was present but Jenny, as usual, hadn't been "up to it," her excuse for avoiding public appearances. Olive and Barney Newell, having performed their duty, left with the other parents and guests. Chairs were removed, an orchestra made up of members of the school band began to play, and the dancing began. Two teachers, the principal and his assistant, served as chaperones. There were cakes, cookies and punch, supplied by various parent-donors and later, a supper was to be served. But at ten-thirty, Thomas returned to drive Libby and Steve back to the Newell home for the private party. Marshall Newell, now 19, hadn't gotten back from the University of Virginia.

A few couples, carefully screened by Olive, made up the private party. They danced to records until midnight when a breakfast was served, and shortly thereafter the party was over. Guests were called for by some parents or dispatched in Newell cars, driven by Newell servants. Steve, as escort to the hostess, was last to leave. He thanked Olive and Barney for their hospitality and Libby saw him to the door.

On the porch outside, alone together, Steve said, "Goodnight, Libby. I had a very nice time. Thank you."

Libby said, "My mother asked you to escort me, didn't she, Steve?"

"Uh—what makes you think that?"

"I know my mother. Besides, nobody else asked me," Libby volunteered frankly.

"Listen, I wanted to take you," Steve lied.

"That's okay, Steve. I know."

"You don't know anything of the kind."

"All right," she said, smiling faintly, "thank you anyway. You've always been nice to me. I'm glad you asked me."

That might have ended it, but a curious, self-imposed guilt pressed him on to a new commitment. "Libby," he said, "will you go to the class picnic with me on Sunday?"

She hesitated for a moment, then said, "Are you sure you want me to go with you?"

"Why else would I ask you?"

"To be nice. So I won't have to play sick because nobody else asked me."

"Libby, cut it out, will you. You're just feeling sorry for yourself. I thought you were very pretty tonight. And you dance swell."

She reached up and kissed his cheek swiftly, a quick, light brush of lips he scarcely felt. "Thank you, Steve. You're very nice. I like you better than any boy in Lancaster." And turning suddenly, Libby ran into the house.

There was no car left and he walked across the lawn to the path, then along Wilburn Road to his own house. Grady and Jenny were in their separate rooms, the house dark except for the porch and hall lights. Steve undressed slowly, brushed his teeth, and went to bed, wondering where, at this very moment, Cal and Ben were; if they were still with their dates and if so, were they making out.

Within minutes he was fast asleep.

5

The Sunday picnic was the last official school event. It was held at Forest Lake, a resort developed by Barney Newell shortly after World War II had come to its end. There were lakeside homes and cabins, larger homes on the hillsides overlooking the lake, and there was a public area of stores, shops, eating places close to the beach, a dance pavilion, and docks where small boats could be rented. There were also picnic areas with benches, tables, and brick ovens for outdoor cooking, as well as numerous hiking trails.

Steve and Libby rode up with Cal and Maxine Winkler, Ben and Laurie Fletcher, driven by one of the Waggoner shop mechanics, in order to escape the thirty-mile round trip in crowded school buses. As usual, Libby was quiet and spoke only when a question was directed at her. The day, spent by most at games, swimming, hiking, and overeating, was almost a total loss to Steve, and he wondered now whether his act of personal sacrifice had been worth the effort. Libby would not participate in any activity except the group singing and by nightfall Steve was grateful the day had come to its end.

On Monday morning, Libby left Lancaster with Olive for Richmond and her annual round of visiting with family, which would be followed by a trip to New York for shopping, with the balance of the summer to be spent with Olive's family at their home in Virginia Beach; this while Barney was touring the state mending political fences for the upcoming elections in November.

Steve spent the summer in Lancaster, his first full term of work on the *Star*. He began with two weeks as an apprentice in the back room, cleaning presses, type forms, operating the proof press, learning to set and sort hand type, improving his typing when Miss Essie Hancock was busy with other duties. Later, Grady set him to the task of proofreading. where he learned the special shorthand system that only a printer can understand, marking copy, and carrying proofs to advertisers.

The week before Labor Day, Lancaster was shocked by the front page news in the *Star* that brought tragedy home when Marshall Newell was killed in an automobile accident near Annapolis, Maryland. The girls and a nineteen-year-old male companion were seriously injured when Marshall's car missed a turn in the road, struck a tree, overturned, and rolled downhill into a ravine.

Those were the simple details published in the *Star,* but the Washington papers were somewhat more explicit. All four, according to one of the survivors, had been drinking rather heavily.

Barney Newell went to Annapolis to claim Marshall's body. Olive and Libby returned from Virginia Beach and went into seclusion. The funeral, four days later, was held in private with only members of Olive's and Barney's immediate families present. Other than a formal notice, nothing else appeared in the *Star,* despite lawsuits that followed and were quietly settled out of court.

In September, Libby entered Lancaster High, more alone than ever before; and again, it was Steve—by Grady's suggestion, and now by his own strange sense of protectiveness for Libby—who became more or less a constant companion, trying to ease her pathetic loneliness.

At the end of their sophomore year, Olive Newell decided that "something must be done" about her sixteen-year-old daughter. The sorrow left behind by Marshall's death spurred her into action and she took Libby off to New York to seek specific remedies.

Tiny miracles began to work when various establishments there took the problem in hand. Entered in a school that catered to eliminating awkwardness by replacing it with charm and grace, Libby endured three months of physical exercises, beauty, diet, and mental therapy. She attended classes designed to correct social attitudes, studied dancing and acting. The braces came off for all time. Her hair was cut shorter and restyled. A completely new wardrobe replaced the old, and by the time she returned to Lancaster in September, Elizabeth Newell was hardly recognizable as the Libby Newell who left there in June.

Olive, enthused by the visual results of her efforts, continued the promise by giving a series of parties at the Newell home, and two at the country club, all of which included Steve who, despite the physical changes in Libby, continued to see her as the shy girl he had dated twice.

On her own, Libby did her best to live up to the promise of those three months spent in New York. She decided to become involved in at least one extracurricular school activity and after considerable thought applied for a staff assignment on *Sound Off!*, Lancaster High's bimonthly newspaper, whose editorship very logically fell to Steve Gilman.

Steve was more than agreeable to her joining the staff. He tried patiently to teach her to write news items, but she was quick to admit failure in that department. He encouraged her to try her hand at photography and after several hundred dollars spent on a camera and other necessary equipment, this proved to be too technical for her. In a stroke of brilliance, Steve offered her the job of advertising manager. Until then, *Sound Off!* had been carrying four or five ads from local merchants that occupied less than half of one of its four pages.

"I don't know a thing about advertising, Steve," Libby protested. "Maybe I should give the whole thing up."

"Don't do that, Libby," he pleaded. "I know this is right for you and I'll help you with it. You know everybody in town and if we can build up our advertising revenue, we'll be able to run six or even eight pages instead of four. With that extra money we can do things this paper couldn't do before. Come on, be a sport and stick it out."

"Well—I'll think about it."

"Do me one favor. Talk it over with your father before you decide, will you?"

"Okay. I promise."

Barney Newell listened to Libby and later, laughingly remarked to Olive, "By God, that Steve Gilman is a cute operator. With Libby out soliciting ads from the list of merchants I make up for her, and after I've made a few phone calls, that little old school paper just might outshine the *Star*."

"Maybe," Olive suggested, "you ought to keep an eye on him for the future."

"And maybe, " Barney replied, "you're not just kidding."

On Libby's first excursion, dressed in a smart blue jumper dress and frilly white blouse, she returned with more ads than *Sound Off!* could possibly handle, with contracts signed for the full school year. The paper went to eight pages and, for the first time in its history, showed a profit.

Socially, Libby's life had become full and complicated, with more demands on her time than she knew how to handle. Between school and her work on the paper, free time was at a premium, trying to schedule after-school lates, movie dates, Saturday night parties, multiple-couple dates at Forest Lake, football games and an occasional trip to Richmond or Washington.

Cal Waggoner began showing a concerted interest in Libby, which began to pose a personal problem for Steve, whose own interest in Libby had begun showing signs of increasing. If anyone had asked Steve who his closest friend was, he would have answered, "Cal Waggoner, I guess," despite the fact that Cal and he had had four fights at various stages of their childhood. Cal, always aggressive, was competitive by nature, and had developed a need to assert his leadership, although most of their acquaintances naturally gravitated toward Steve. Therefore, it was logically assumed that Cal would do his utmost to move in between Steve and Libby. It was, in fact, a wasted effort. Libby gave Steve every opportunity to first claim on her time, and on several occasions—without Steve's knowledge—had broken dates with Cal, and others, to accept one with Steve.

With Marshall's death on their minds, Olive and Barney were well aware of the dangers that mobility and speed could bring and felt that Libby was better off with Steve than with Cal, who already owned a flashy Buick convertible and had too much money to spend. And, as Olive pointed out, "It's a young world, Barney. We can't give her the means to enjoy life and hold her back from taking part in it. We've got to rely on her own sense of what is right and what is wrong."

6

During their junior year, they became consciously aware of many problems in life and living, problems heretofore not fully understood, and therefore easily dismissed.

Alcohol and marijuana were no longer mere words but actualities, today, here, and now. Student pushers appeared on campus. Harry Beal and Junior Devers were arrested on drunk driving charges, several others for driving after their licenses had been revoked. A sophomore was robbed and raped while walking home from the house where she had been babysitting. Vandals broke into the high school and senselessly ran faucets and firehoses at full force, wrecked the principal's office and storeroom and scribbled obscenities on a number of classroom walls.

Mr. Joyce, a history teacher, had his car stolen and two students, a boy and a girl, were picked up in it while driving toward Forest Lake, under the influence of marijuana, with more marijuana in their possession. These were not entirely new incidents, but were suddenly brought home with emphatic force because those involved were their own contemporaries; classmates, neighbors, lifelong friends. Some laughed it off, some accepted the new behavior as the "now thing," others were mildly dismayed, and still others expressed envy at the daring it took to jump into the new scene.

Betty Jean Cartwright was quietly hustled off to visit her grandmother in Macon, but the story was being voiced around that she had been made pregnant by Paulie Ferris, who suddenly dropped out and was next heard from by Dutch Cameron, his cousin, in a letter from the Marine Recruit Depot in San Diego. Tremors of scandal rocked the community when it was discovered that Harry and Sarah Ellen Pease and Bob and Maryann Howell, who had pitched in to buy a cabin at Forest Lake, were not only sharing the cabin, but each other.

But the real shocker came when Miss Andrea Lormond, a young, attractive English teacher recently imported from Norfolk, and easily the most popular member of the teaching staff, fell from grace. On a Friday night, Miss Lormond was picked up in a raid on a house on the outskirts of Lancaster—shared by two construction workers—along with two men and another woman, and charged with lewd and lascivious conduct while under the influence of narcotics, resisting arrest, and using obscene language.

By Monday morning, the story had spread throughout Lancaster. At school, boys and girls knotted up in separate groups, whispering excitedly while the teaching staff tried heroically to keep aloof from the subject, with little success. Steve, who felt a special rapport with Miss Lormond, a member of the advisory board of *Sound Off!*, and had been accused by Cal, Ben, and Buzz of harboring an erotic crush on her, refused to engage in the discussions. At noon, he cut the rest of his classes and walked to the *Star* building.

"What happened?" Grady asked. "School holiday of some kind?"

"No. I just didn't feel good."

"Something you ate?"

"No."

"Or something you heard?"

Steve looked up into Grady's eyes, knowing that Grady knew what it was that was tormenting him. "Come on, Steve, let me buy you a Coke."

"I don't want a Coke."

"Want to talk?"

"No. I just want to hang around."

"Okay. Here's a short news item I just wrote. Why don't you go inside and handset it for me."

"Sure."

He worked at the item for half an hour, tied the type form, pulled a proof, read it, found and reset the errors, pulled another proof, and took it back to Grady. "That's fine, son. You're getting pretty good." After a moment, "Some day when you're running this paper, you'll hear all kinds of stories about people you've known all your life, people you'll have to write about. You'll learn they're good and evil, charitable and miserly, warm and cold. But mostly, you'll learn they're all human beings with the same hangups, frailties and frustrations we all live with. How they overcome them, if they do, how they fail to resolve them, that's all a piece of the world we're a small part of. We live with happiness and sadness, with or without a decent sense of values, but we live until we die. That's my world, your world, everybody's world." He added softly, "And Miss Andrea Lormond's world, too."

For the next week Steve went through a period of personal depression over the Lormond affair, refusing to engage in the many discussions, arguments, and debates that concerned her, even after she had been dismissed and given a floater out of town with orders never to return. Cal, Ben, Jack, Arnie, and Buzz tore at the subject like a dog at a bone, exploring its erotic implications in minutest detail. It remained a prime subject among the girls, whose whispering huddles fell into awkward silence at the approach of a teacher or any boy. The *Sound Off!* staff kept starchily aloof, as though Andrea Lormond had never existed.

And, in time, although occasionally remembered, that incident, too, passed out of their lives.

The Junior Prom was different from any they had known. At seventeen, they had achieved a certain social maturity and awareness of each other as individuals, rather than as members of various cliques or groups.

Some owned cars, and sported gasoline credit cards and increased allowances. They dressed casually except for special occasion dates. Smoking pot was "in" and a few boasted of having experimented with stronger stuff, obtained from student pushers who received their weekly supply from a Washington runner named Big Augie. Two seniors, George McAfee and Lou Battasio, were picked up through an undercover student, Frank Alessio, and expelled. From that day, Frank was marked "poison" and no one would speak to him. He became the school's first pariah.

Steve's interest in Libby Newell continued to grow. Working together on *Sound Off!* brought them in close contact and he helped her with ad layouts, and occasionally gave her a news assignment which he published under her own byline—an act of favoritism, he knew—justifying his action by the belief that he was helping her gain confidence in herself. They had movie dates on Friday nights, weekend dates, studied together, and were invited to parties as accepted steadies.

On a Saturday before the Junior Prom, they double-dated with Cal and Maxine and drove to Forest Lake, which had opened for the summer season that weekend. There they met and joined up with Ben and Janet Cameron, Buzz and Jack Porter who were with the Murchison twins, Ann and Margaret. They swam, dressed again, hiked through the woods, ate the picnic food the girls had prepared, and later danced at the public pavilion. Cal and Maxine drifted away first, then Ben and Janet, followed by Buzz and Ann. Steve and Libby wandered out of hearing of the four-piece band toward the lake, skirting its shore, avoiding the small fires that had sprung up along the sandy beach, arms encircling each other's waist.

Steve suddenly thought of Andrea Lormond, then wondered about Cal and Maxine, who were reputed to have a thing going—to which Cal only grinned slyly, admitting nothing. Steve knew Ben and Janet were sexually involved, but Ben had told him, under oath, that he and Jan were planning to be married as soon as they were graduated which, somehow, made it seem all right. Steve suspected others were engaged sexually and had had proposals from still others to visit the red light district on Race Street, the dividing line between the white and black areas, but had never succumbed to what was variously known as Trash Alley or Chancre Square.

"What are you thinking?" Libby said after a while.

If you only knew! "Nothing much," he replied.

"I was thinking of the Prom next week."

"What to wear?"

"No. Who to go with."

"Aren't you going with me?"

"Well, Cal and Dutch have asked me."

That shook him for a moment. "So did I. Just now."

She laughed teasingly. "I thought you'd never ask."

"You knew I would, didn't you?"

"Yes, but I don't like to be taken for granted."

"Oh, hell, you *knew*. What did you tell Cal and Dutch?"

"That I was going with you."

"Suppose I hadn't asked?"

"I would have sent my mother to ask you, the way she did that time at Sidney Lanier."

He laughed at the reminder, again seeing the scrawny, frightened girl of fourteen—a complete and total stranger to the full-blown beauty of seventeen—who had known all along he had been coerced by Olive. They turned away from the shoreline and walked northward into the woods, silent in the dimness of oncoming night except for the crunch of small branches under their feet and the soft rustling of leaves in the warm wind. "You'll be going away for the summer again, I guess," Steve said.

"I don't want to, but I suppose I'll have to. Dad will be traveling around the state as usual and it's the only chance Mother ever has to get together with her own family and friends."

The thought depressed him. "It'll be a long summer."

"Yes. What are you going to do?"

"Work at the *Star*. Dad's going to let me dig into the writing end more than before."

"You'll be good at it. I wish I could stay in town. I'd like to help you the way I have on *Sound Off!* Traveling around with Mother can be a real drag most of the time."

"Well, we could use a good ad salesman. Summer is pretty slow in that department."

She stopped and said, "Let's sit a while. I'm getting tired."

They sat on the soft new grass and Libby brought out a pack of cigarettes and a book of matches, lighted two, and handed one to Steve. "I'll miss you, too, Steve. I wish we could go off somewhere for the whole summer, just the two of us, like gypsies."

"Hey, now, that's the brightest idea I've ever heard you come up with." He exhaled and said, "You know what that would mean, don't you?"

"Of course I do. I've thought about it a lot."

We're getting closer to it, he thought, feeling his heart pound at a faster rate. *How do you get to it? It just doesn't happen by itself. Somebody has to start the ball rolling. Do you just ask, or go ahead?* He fell to wondering if what was going on inside him was going on inside Libby's mind and body. How could it not?

Libby stubbed out her cigarette in the grass and began talking, but he was no longer hearing her voice, only the soft laughter between the words. He thought of her as he saw her in his erotic dreams and unselfconsciously reached out and touched her upper thigh. Her dress had moved upward and his palm cupped the smooth flesh, firm and warm to his touch, and she moved then, closer to him so that his hand was forced higher by the movement. Her other thigh closed over his fingers and held them tight, and he realized then that she had stopped talking. It was only her breath he heard now, coming in short, soft bursts.

He felt her face touch his and their lips met, firm and hard upon each other, and in the darkness that had enveloped them he could feel himself growing enormous. One of Libby's hands touched him there and remained, so that all he could think of was the vision of themselves coupled in the act itself. Then, unable to contain himself, he moved over her, his weight forcing her to lie flat on her back, feeling her squirming body beneath his own. He raised his head and whispered, "Libby, Libby . . ."

She lay still, her body rigid and unmoving, as though at the last moment, permission had been revoked. He rolled off and lay on his back beside her, unable to predict what would happen next, his mind a blur of confusion, feeling an urgency he had known many times while fantasizing the act with Libby. And with Andrea Lormond. He sat up and put his arm around her. "Shall we do it, Libby?"

"I don't know . . ."

"All the kids are doing it. You know that."

"I know, but . . ."

"Afraid?"

"No. Not afraid. I know about it. I've read a lot about it. I hear the girls talk about it all the time. I know some who are doing it—they go through hell afterwards, worrying about being found out, getting pregnant, other things —I don't want to live with that." When Steve said nothing, "I'm sorry. Are you angry with me, disappointed?"

"No," he lied. "I'm sorry I asked you. I was out of line."

"But you won't ask me for any more dates, will you."

"Of course I will. I don't like you any less. If anything, more," he said unconvincingly.

He lighted cigarettes for them and they smoked in silence until Libby turned to him and said, "If you want to, Steve, I will."

The magic spell, however, had been broken. The thought of taking her in fear . . . "Now who's being nice to whom?"

"I'm not saying it just to be nice to you. I mean it."

Suddenly, he stood up, dropped the cigarette, and ground it out in the grass. "Come on, Libby, let's go back."

"You're angry, aren't you?"

"I'm not. I swear I'm not, but if we stay here any longer, I'll change my mind and I don't want to do that. Not now."

"Then will you kiss me?"

He took her into his arms and kissed her, felt her lips open, her yielding body against his own; and was again tempted. But reason—or fear—overruled urgency. He drew back and the moment was over. Arms linked together, they walked back to the pavilion area, Steve feeling a peculiar sense of having forever lost an experience he very much wanted, yet with something like a halo of nobility floating over his head.

7

The summer was unending. When Libby returned after Labor Day to begin their senior year, they were like eager strangers, willing and wanting, yet standing off to see which would make the first move. He wondered now, as he had through those hot, dull months, if she had met and liked someone new and different enough to have gone through with what he had so gallantly—or out of cowardice—turned aside. And because during that summer he had taken his first introductory step into the sex act with a girl he had never known before nor seen since, he was more determined than ever not to expose Libby to the urgent rage he had felt during the act. Not yet.

The last year in high school flew by with remarkable swiftness. Steve was appointed to the senior editorship of the Year Book and Libby became an associate editor. They worked on *Sound Off!* together and dated every chance they got. He spent less time at the *Star* than in any other period he could remember, feeling an added sense of guilt for his abandonment of the Saturday fishing and hunting excursions with Grady. It seldom occurred to him that of all his thoughts, so few were spent on Jenny.

Nearing eighteen, he became more interested in the world outside Lancaster, outside the United States. He and Grady would often discuss and argue over civil rights, international situations that seemed to be drawing America into more direct involvement throughout Southeast Asia, South and Central America, and the rest of the world. Complex as that world was to Grady, at his age, it was that much more enigmatic to Steve at his.

There were other questions, equally perplexing to Steve, for which he sought answers. One day, fishing together, Steve said, "You're always so sure about everything, Dad. How do you know when you're right?"

"About what, for instance?" Grady asked.

"About anything. What you write in the *Star*. You write an editorial, your opinion about a law, a man running for office, or the new sewer project. You say we need to start thinking about an airport. Mr. Fletcher, Mr. Lawrence, Mr. Benton, and other people say it isn't needed, that Lancaster is too small, the tax cost will be too high, we're years away from needing an airport . . . who is right? If you are, how do you *know?* And how do you know they're wrong?"

As a senior at Lancaster High and an editor in his own right, Grady knew that Steve was subject to criticism for just about everything that appeared in the *Star*. Controversial subjects that would cost the taxpayers money; an increase in pay for teachers, for which Grady had fought strongly, if ineffectively, for years; building a new elementary school; reasonable integration; buying up land to put aside for parks and recreation before prices skyrocketed out of sight; suggesting condemnation of certain properties that were rapidly creating a slum area on the periphery of the business district; and, of course, his dream of the airport of tomorrow.

"Well, Steve, I'll try to give you an honest answer," Grady said. "You think about it, project today into the future, decide what's best for the greatest number of people, knowing it will hurt some while the majority benefits. And when you've spent enough time dreaming about it, discussing it with knowledgable people, researching, reading, and learning as much as it is possible to learn about the subject, there it is, clear as this stream we're fishing. When that happens, you take a stand for or against it.

"If clearer minds than yours can make you see a viewpoint better and wiser than your own, you accept that and change your view. If they can't convince you, you stick with your own judgment, no matter what anybody else says about it, regardless of the pressures that are brought against you. That's called having the courage of your own convictions and no man can be an editor or spokesman without it."

"But the guys in school say . . ."

"Steve, what the guys in school say is mostly what they've heard their parents discussing at the supper table, people who generally haven't taken the time and trouble to learn all the facts, or look at more than one side of the question, and who can see progress only as long as the cost doesn't come out of their own pockets. That's what makes it hard to fight for, when something important has to be gained. The man who turns his back on a problem or remains neutral because he's afraid to fight for his honest beliefs, is the real coward. That's what confronts every newspaper editor, whether it's just a country weekly or a metropolitan daily."

Always, when Steve had come to him for advice, Grady made him understand that it was not mandatory that he accept what was offered without first thinking it over carefully. In order to encourage him to make his own decisions, Grady, wherever possible, had always tried to give him a choice. Either, or.

On the subject of college there was such a choice to be made between Columbia—Grady's alma mater—and the University of Virginia, where Jenny's father had studied. Even then, Grady tried not to exert undue influence on Steve. "How," Steve asked during his junior year at Lancaster High, "can I know if I'm making the right choice?"

"That's something, son, you've got to think out and decide for yourself. Don't limit yourself to one or two colleges. Write and get as much information as you can from several others. Check with your adviser at school. Turn the question over in your mind and take a good hard look at it until you see for yourself which college will benefit you most in what you want to do, and become. When you've got all the facts in front of you, we'll discuss it."

Steve's uncertainty persisted. "When you're faced with taking an important step in your life, Steve," Grady told him, "you've got to accept the responsibility that goes with it, whether you succeed or fail. Like any other problem, work the solution out for yourself. Ask yourself, 'Is this the right way to go? Do the advantages outweigh the disadvantages?' The answers to those questions will answer the bigger ones: 'When I've done it, will it have been worth the effort? Will I be proud of what I've done, feel that great sense of satisfaction in accomplishment?' And finally, 'Will anybody suffer by what I do?' "

At that moment, Steve felt a gnawing desire to ask a question he had often wanted an answer for, one he could not ask: Whether Grady had asked those very same questions of himself before he married Jennie Budlong.

When the time came, as he had known all along he would, Steve chose Columbia, knowing it would please Grady, and equally certain his choice would in some way hurt his dour, taciturn mother, from whom he had received so little, to whom he had given so little. Libby's application to Sweet Briar, her mother's alma mater, had already been accepted.

The weeks, days, and hours before departure into strange new worlds were exciting to both Steve and Libby. For Libby, it meant new clothes, a trip to Sweet Briar with Olive to become acquainted with her new home during the next four years, letters to write to the daughters of Olive's friends whom she would be meeting at college, choice of sororities to make and the new car Barney gave her for a parting gift. For Steve, new clothes, selection of luggage for his very own, hours of discussion with Grady over which courses of study would benefit him most.

On the Saturday before Steve left, he and Libby drove to Forest Lake in her new car. It was a brilliant sunny September day and they brought a picnic basket along with their bathing suits. Before lunch, Steve rented an outboard in which they cruised the lake, leisurely, until they came to a deserted cove where they beached the boat and ate their meal. When they were finished, they changed into swimsuits, using clumps of bushes for privacy.

"Do you like it?" Libby asked as she emerged from the protective thicket wearing the most revealing two-piece suit he had ever seen her in.

"Wow! It's beautiful!"

"Well, don't just stand there staring."

"Your mother really let you buy it?"

"Not without a battle. Do you really like it?"

"How could I not like it? I'm glad you're going to an all-girl college."

"If you think I bought this for the benefit of other girls, Steve Gilman, you're sadly mistaken. Sweet Briar isn't exactly a convent, you know."

"I almost wish it were."

"You're not really worried, are you?" she teased.

"No, but you're giving me a lot to think about while I'm away."

"From what I hear, New York isn't much of a retreat for monks."

"You know how much I'll miss you, don't you, Libby?"

"No more than I'll miss you."

He embraced and kissed her. "I love you, Steve," she said.

"We . . . we've got such a damned long way to go, haven't we."

"It's not forever, and there'll be holiday vacations and long summers . . ."

"When your mother will drag you off to Richmond and Virginia Beach while I sweat it out on the *Star*."

"Maybe I'll start putting my foot down next summer. I'm not a child any more."

"As any fool can plainly see. You think you can convince your mother, though?"

"We'll see when the time comes. Let's swim, shall we?"

They were strong swimmers and worked off their energies by racing to the near center of the lake, where they floated on their backs for a while, then swam back at a slower, more even pace. They dried themselves with large beach towels, then spread them on the grass out of range of passing boats and lay down to rest, head cradled on folded arms, staring up at the sky.

"Steve," Libby said quietly.

His head turned toward her, their eyes only inches away. "What?"

"Do you remember last summer up here, just before the Junior Prom?"

"I remember."

"I want to do it, Steve. With you."

He swallowed hard, staring directly into her eyes, voice muted by the implication of her words. "Don't you want to?" she asked.

"You know I do. You know that. What about—what if—?"

"I get pregnant?"

"It's something to think about. I don't have anything with me."

"Then you'll marry me and we'll live happily ever after. But I won't, Steve. I know what to do."

"You're sure?"

"Yes, yes."

He put his arms around her and drew her toward and over himself, feeling the strength in her eager, violent embrace. Then she drew back, sat up, and untied the thin strap that held her bra in place, slipping the skimpy panties down over her hips and along her legs, and tossing them to one side. With trembling hands, Steve slipped out of his swim briefs and turned to her, seeing the intense look as her eyes explored the evidence of the urgency that overwhelmed him, roused by the sight of her nakedness.

They came together nervously, lying side by side for a while, kissing, fondling, discovering each other as though for the first time, although never before so intimately. Teeth and tongues met and lingered. Libby burrowed under him, twisting her hips to indicate her readiness. She was small, so there was some difficulty in entering her and she squirmed, whimpered, and said, "I don't know a damned thing about it, for all I've heard and read about it. Do you, Steve?"

"A little. Not much more than you. It's something we have to learn together."

It was awkward, but they managed somehow, and once they were joined he moved gently—not without some difficulty—until with a sudden and startling thrust, Libby moved her hips upward with force, winced, gasped, and then fell back, totally impaled. They lay quietly together until the moment passed, neither speaking, Libby's eyes closed tightly. Then Steve began to move slowly, feeling her response, probing, exploring, until both went into a frenzy of thrust and counter-thrust that brought them to the final explosion of climax. There were tears in Libby's eyes and Steve had no way of knowing whether they had been brought on by pleasure or pain, happiness or regret; until she smiled and said, "That was wonderful, Steve. I'm so glad it was with you."

"I hope it will always be with me, Libby."

"Do you?"

"Yes, of course."

She laughed lightly and said, "You've never once told me you loved me. I know you do, I can feel it, but you've never said the words, *I love you, Libby.*"

He said them, stifflv, unnaturally, "I love you, Libby."

"Not like that. You didn't say it, you recited it."

"Libby, I don't know how to say it except in those words, *I love you, Libby*. I mean it."

"I think you do, but you make it sound so formal, like you were forcing it."

He lay back, thinking, *When you don't practice saying it, how else can it sound?* and it occurred to him then that he had never heard those words spoken between Grady and Jenny, between himself and his parents. He had read of love in books, heard and seen it on movie and television screens. He had felt and understood it, if it was the same as love for a pet, for nature, or for his work on *Sound Off!* and the Year Book; but to actually speak the words meaningfully to another person was a novel experience.

"Four years from now," he said, "when we're both home again for good, will you say *yes,* when I ask you to marry me?"

"Of course, silly, if you don't change your mind by then."

"What about you changing yours?"

"Try me."

"Are we engaged—really, Libby?"

"I guess we are, unofficially. We'll have to keep it to ourselves, Steve, our own secret. Right now, Mother would turn blue. Will you write me often?"

"Every chance I get. I'm going to work hard, Libby. I want to study writing the way a med student studies a body, its physiology, bones, muscles, nerves, arteries, flesh, and skin, and the pharmacology it takes to make a sick person well again. I want to write things other than news stories. Books, maybe plays. A novelist or playwright can live anywhere, go anywhere in the world as long as he keeps writing, and that's what I'd like to do. Write, and keep moving from country to country until I've seen 'em all."

"Golly, Steve! I never knew you were that ambitious. What about the *Star?*"

"I've thought about that, too, but by the time I'm out of college, I'll have a better idea about what I want to do, what I *can* do. If I can make it, I'll come back to the *Star*, but not forever. Maybe a year or two. I'll make my final decision by the time I'm twenty-five or twenty-six."

"Are you including me in your plans?"

"Of course. It wouldn't be much fun doing it without you. Now that we're engaged, I can talk about it with you. How do you feel about it?"

"It all sounds so wonderful. I'll be a big help to you, Steve. Maybe do your research for you, and type your manuscripts. Golly, I'd better add a typing class to my courses."

Steve's exhilaration, discussing plans he had kept secret for so long, even from Grady, mounted. "Hey!" he exclaimed, "we're really with it, aren't we?"

They discussed the merits of the novel form over playwriting, the countries in which they would prefer to live for a year or two at a time, the possibility of a hit play or novel being bought for the movies, which turned the conversation to Broadway and Hollywood.

And, as dusk began to fall, they made love again, intensely and more satisfactorily this time, then dressed, returned the outboard to the public dock, and drove back to Lancaster. But neither wanted to go home and Libby phoned Olive to tell her she would not be home for dinner. They had steak sandwiches at a roadside restaurant, then went to a movie, held hands, and kissed frequently. After the show they drove out to a diner for hamburgers and Cokes. They rode aimlessly, adding new thoughts and ideas to previously discussed plans and, sometime after midnight, pulled off onto a narrow dirt road and made love again. It was nearing two in the morning when Libby dropped him at his home and continued along Wilburn Road to her own.

Steve was surprised to find Grady awake, reading in his study-workroom. "Hi, Dad. Not waiting up for me, are you?"

"No, just catching up on some neglected classics. You have a nice outing with Libby?"

"Sure. Just great. I'm beat, though. I think I'll hit the sack."

"Sure. Run along, Steve, and sleep well."

In those few moments, Grady had observed a difference in Steve and wondered—if he had guessed right—how much happiness Steve and Libby had enjoyed this night. And how much sadness it might bring them in the future. But there was little doubt in his mind that the phenomenon of sex was no longer a mystery to Barney and Olive Newell's daughter Elizabeth.

On Monday morning, Grady nudged Steve awake, saying, "Come on, son. It's a beautiful day and a whole new world is out there waiting for you."

He dressed and ate breakfast with Grady. Jenny, following her usual custom, had not come down yet. Nor would she until Grady had left the house. Steve went to her room and knocked. "Come in, Steven," she said in her low voice.

He went in and looked down upon her, lying in bed, hollow eyes staring up at him. "I've come to say good-bye, Mother. Dad's driving me to the bus station so I can catch the noon train out of Washington."

Without any display of emotion or sentiment, she handed him a Bible she had bought in town. "Good-bye, Steven," she said. "Read this when you can, and behave yourself. Don't give them any trouble up there. And don't drink, gamble, or run with those women."

What she did not add, but what was implied in her implacable tone was, "Like your father."

Nor did she kiss him.

He would always remember that silent ride into town with Grady, unlike any other of the many they had taken together. Never were his senses more attuned to this morning of his leave taking, alive to the wondrous odors and beauty of its tree-lined roads, homes, gardens, streets, buildings, and people imprinted on his mind as if for the last time, abandoning everything familiar for exile in an alien land where he would live among strangers, exchanging the known for the mysterious unknown.

He was passing into a new life, with the promise of Libby Newell waiting to share it all with him one day.

Chapter 2

1

Sometime during the night Steve was awakened by the pounding of rain against the four windows that faced Fifty-eighth Street. He stirred restlessly, feeling the piercing night cold, then switched on his reading lamp and checked the time. 4:35. He had lowered one window a mere two inches from the top before going to bed and now was forced to get up and close it. He lit a cigarette, got back into bed, turned the thermostat control of his electric blanket up several degrees, and by the time he stubbed out the cigarette and turned the light off, felt its comforting warmth. Within moments he was sound asleep again.

The phone woke him at 9:30. It was Louise Allard, asking him to come over for coffee before the meeting. "Yes, thank you, Louise. I'll be there as soon as I can shave and dress, if that won't hold us up."

"There's plenty of time, Steve. Come as soon as you're ready."

The room was pleasantly warm and he felt refreshed after his long sleep. He got out of bed and began preparing to face the day that lay ahead.

Showering, shaving, and dressing, his mind was on Larry Price, seeing again the faded remnant of a once-prominent creative executive with nowhere to go but down. And out. Having observed him with near-microscopic clarity for a full month, Steve had seen only deterioration, a man victimized by the times, as much as by himself. *What the hell,* he thought now, *he's just another guy who didn't know how to handle success. The world is full of them. Why am I feeling so damned guilty about what's happening to him? He had his chance and blew it.* And then, *But I wish to God I didn't have to blow the whistle on the poor, sad bastard.*

He got out his wool-interlined raincoat, scarf, gloves, and hat and rode the elevator down to ground level, hoping against hope for a passing cab. At that moment, one pulled up to discharge an elderly couple and he held the door for the woman while the man paid the driver. He got in, and gave the driver the address on Sutton Place, thinking, *A little luck to start the day.*

Louise Allard, dressed in light-blue slacks and dark-blue topper, greeted him with a warm hug and kiss. "You look simply marvelous, Steve, so tanned, and positively brimming with health. I wish Keith and I had taken the trip with you."

Instead of me, he thought. "It's all still out there, Louise," he said. "I don't know why you and Keith don't slip away for a week or two, just to soak up some sunshine, particularly now with the weather as lousy as it is here."

Allard came into the room, knotting his tie. Hearing this last bit of exchange, he growled, "You trying to wreck my happy home life, boy?"

Steve insisted on reimbursing Louise for the cash outlay to resupply his kitchen needs, but Louise protested that it was a homecoming gift. Toyo, the Allard houseman, served coffee in the breakfast room while Louise questioned Steve about California. He told them of his visit to Perry Bond's beach house at Malibu, the weekend in Ensenada, the hair-raising experiences of flying with Perry at the controls, the trip to Las Vegas, keeping as far away as possible from the subject of B & B Coffee and Larry Price.

"How were Dorothy and Larry?" Louise asked finally, and Steve said simply, "I saw Dorothy only once, at dinner the night before I left. They both seemed fine." He was aware that Louise had known the Prices here in New York, but since that had been before his time, he felt some relief in knowing he would not be called upon to make comparisons. Still, the question recalled the desperation he had seen in Dorothy's face, the weight of Larry's questionable future burdening her.

After their second cup of coffee, Keith said, "Time to go, Steve. Excuse us, darling," and went to get his outer coat and hat. Louise exacted a promise from Steve to return with Keith and that they would later have dinner together. The houseman held an umbrella for them, which he placed inside the Lincoln, and dashed back into the house. The rain was mixed with snow now, the car heater a comfort as they drove north to Sixty-third Street, then east toward Fifth Avenue where Keith turned the car over to the apartment-house doorman.

The Leary duplex was a cooperative, purchased by Bill and Donna for a reputed eighty thousand dollars at the time of his marriage in 1959, its value almost trebled now. Donna, and their daughter, Angela, were spending the weekend with Donna's widowed father in Old Lyme, Connecticut, Keith told him.

In the nine years Steve had been with the agency, this was his first visit to the Leary apartment and its size and beauty almost staggered him. The entrance foyer alone, two stories high, with its silk-covered walls and black-and-white marble floor, was nearly as large as his own living room. The man who admitted them said, "Good morning, Mr. Allard, Mr. Gilman," and had no doubt been instructed that Steve would be coming. Allard said, "Good morning, Reese," while Steve remained speechless, momentarily dazzled by the opulence of his surroundings.

Reese took their hats and coats, then led them past a huge formal living room into a smaller room whose walls were tastefully done in tan-leather blocks, each about two feet square. The table top, chairs, and sofa were upholstered in matching leather—very definitely a man's room. The table was set for three, and after Allard had lighted his pipe, and Steve a cigarette, Bill Leary—in purple smoking jacket and wine-colored trousers—joined them. He nodded to Allard, favored Steve with a smile and handshake of welcome, then said, "You look fit, Steve. Let's have some breakfast, shall we? I'm starved."

Reese served eggs, bacon, sausage, and kippers from the sideboard, while Bill poured and passed the coffee. They talked of general matters in which Steve scarcely participated, hearing Bill's petulant complaints about the Chicago situation, the market, tight money, bits of pertinent information about varous agency clients, and the familiar run of advertising street gossip. Bill was to leave for Chicago in two weeks to attend an important presentation by Marty Link to a drug manufacturer, one that might increase billings by close to a million dollars, but there was much competition and Bill was generating no enthusiasm for the success of his mission.

Eventually, Reese cleared the table and brought a fresh pot of coffee. Bill said, "Well, Steve, what's the story out there?"

For all the thinking he had been doing, searching for a way to break the news gently, Steve blurted out, "We're in deep trouble with B & B, Bill. We're going to lose it within the next two or three months, perhaps sooner."

"Why?" Bill asked with surprising calm.

"Because of a number of things. Taking them one by one, I would say Perry Bond is mainly responsible. He took the company over, the way he takes delivery on a new car, boat, or plane. Use it for pleasure, burn it out, and walk away from it. He couldn't care less for the company, except as another toy. He and his mother are very well fixed for life, no matter what happens, so B & B isn't really that terribly important to him."

"And what about the people who were with the company while his father was alive? Some of them go back as far as his grandfather's time. Aren't they important enough to count for something, for God's sake?"

"Bill," Steve said, "are you aware that Harlan Weschler, B & B's sales manager for over twenty years, quit about three months ago?"

Both Bill and Keith looked up quickly in surprise. Bill said, "No, I didn't know that and I'm damned sure Keith didn't know it either." Here, Keith nodded in agreement. "Larry—for some reason—seems to have neglected to mention that item in his progress reports or in our telephone conversations. Like so many other bits and pieces that keep turning up. Maybe he didn't think that was important enough to pass on."

"Well," Steve continued, "Harlan Weschler, as I understand it, tried to hold the company together as best he could after John Bond died, but knowing Perry, he must have realized he was spitting into the wind. Last August—or September—there was a serious blowup between them and Weschler quietly sold his stock in the company and resigned in October, to accept an offer from Cal-General. By the end of October he'd taken the best of his salesmen into C-G with him, and B & B's balloon started ripping apart at the seams.

"Then Perry brought in a friend to fill Weschler's shoes—a guy named Sanders—but other than his reputation as a hotshot brokerage man, he'd had no practical business experience worth mentioning. Morale was shot to hell, sales began slipping, and the handwriting was there on the wall for anybody to read. I got most of this on the q.t.

from Dave Chesler, Larry's account executive on the B & B account."

"And what were our people doing to help the situation?" Bill asked.

"Well, there really wasn't a hell of a lot they could do about a purely internal problem, was there?"

"Come off it, Steve," Bill said, showing his first sign of irritation. "You know better than that. The least Larry could have done was to read the same handwriting on the wall and let us know what was going on. What's more, I've seen some of the material his people have been turning out for B & B recently. That was our purpose in pulling you off GFP and sending you out there to take a close look."

"All right," Steve said, "I'll agree the quality of their material during the last few months has been less than great, even substandard, and it should have been picked up sooner by Larry. Or somebody. Not that I think it would have helped the situation as far as Bond and Weschler are concerned. When it started slipping . . ."

Bill interrupted then. "You're right to some extent, but we've had other important problems to concern ourselves with here. It was Larry Price's job, Dave Chesler's job, either to do something about it or to keep us informed fully and accurately back here. The question is, what in hell has happened to Larry Price? Why was he so damned secretive about what was happening to his principal account? Why didn't we hear about it until B & B started slashing its budget?"

Steve hesitated, using the time to reach for a cigarette and light it, hoping for some way in which he could further avoid placing the blame. He was grateful when Keith spoke up and took the burden from his shoulders.

"You know what it is, Bill," Allard said calmly. "Larry's been up to his old tricks. It always happened back here whenever he ran into a brick wall. Peace at any price, and the client is never wrong. For a long time, things went along smoothly after Tom retired, but he was rolling along on Tom's foundation. Then he lost Wesco, Caltronics and Walters-Carr. We should have stepped in then and done something about it. Now, with John Bond gone and Perry in charge, Larry was in deep trouble again and the bottle was his best way out of the bind. Isn't that it, Steve?"

Steve didn't answer that charge and Bill said, "The next question is, what can we do to salvage the account?"

Both men were looking directly at him and Steve said,

"From the agency's point of view, nothing very much that I can see. Even if we sent in a whole new team on a crash program, I don't think it would help the internal sales problem in the least. Besides, the budget is no longer there. If it were the advertising alone I'd say we might pull it off, even handle the account from New York on a temporary basis until it got back on its feet. But with a slashed budget and Perry riding high for the first time in his life, it's pretty much a dead issue. I don't see how advertising can overcome a disorganized sales situation."

Bill's upper teeth began biting his lower lip, always a sign of extreme agitation, which Steve recognized at once. Bill said, "Keith was opposed to my father's choice of Larry for the West Coast job in the first place, but Dad overrode him. Later, when Tom Donnelly retired, he was still against Larry as his replacement, but I was in charge then and I thought we owed it to Larry, for old time's sake, to let him have his chance. Well, this is one of those things I'll have to handle myself, much as I dislike it. Goddamn it, this could mean the end of the branch itself, the jobs of sixty or seventy people if we have to close up that shop." He looked at Keith and said grimly, "Well, any suggestions?"

Keith said, "If there are any, they'll have to come from Steve at this point."

And now Steve recognized that this was Keith's way of subtly reminding him he had mentioned a recommendation he could make, while they were on their way in from the airport the day before.

"Steve?" Bill said.

He was no longer sure of himself, but knew he must speak up. "Well, it's just an idea I'd been toying with during the last few days out there. At this moment, I don't know if it can work, but if we could pull it off, we might be able to offset our loss and it might even give us a substantial profit."

Bill grabbed at that straw. "What is it?"

Steve took a deep breath and plunged. "It occurred to me that the only possible way we can save the B & B account is to take it completely out of Perry Bond's hands."

Bill looked perplexed. "I don't understand you. How can we do that?"

"I know it sounds crazy as hell, but I thought if . . .

well, it crossed my mind that B & B would make a great new item in the Goody Food Products line."

Keith and Bill both sat up straight. Keith got up then, walked to the sofa, and dropped into it, knocking the dottle from his pipe into a huge metal ashtray. "Think of that," he said almost to himself. Then, as Bill remained thoughtfully silent, "Go on, Steve, let's hear more."

More sure of his ground now, Steve continued. "GFP, over the years, has brought in new items like margarine and mayonnaise and peanut butter, and those—despite some earlier doubts—now account for a sizable share of their sales. From time to time they've experimented with new items, dropped some, kept others. I know that this is on a much broader level, but what if we went to Herschel Goodwin and told him the story of B & B, had him put his legal people to work to sound out Perry Bond and his mother on the possibility of selling the company?

"B&B's stock has been dropping and I think a valid case could be made for a buyout. I'm sure that sooner or later some competitor or conglomerate will begin nibbling at their heels with the same sort of proposition. If GFP were to come up with a reasonable offer right now, we'd stand a good chance. If it works out, we could introduce the new item nationally and use both names, call it GOODY'S B & B COFFEE and not lose the identification it now has in its own Western market, however limited. Give it a big opening shot nationally as a new member of the GFP line. Not only would we save the account but increase its billing on a national, instead of sectional scale. Both the agency and GFP would come up with a profit on the deal."

Again there was silence, but a different kind. Steve knew that while he was talking, Bill's and Keith's minds had been racing well ahead of his voice, and had come to the same conclusion. It was a chance, one only Herschel Goodwin could decide. But at Goodwin's age, the question was whether he would want to become involved in a matter as big as this, commit time, energy, and necessary financing to a new and somewhat unrelated product.

Keith broke the silence. "Why not? It's worth a try. Hell, GFP is a natural for it and the item is a natural for GFP—" He looked toward Bill, whose eyes were glittering with suppressed excitement. Bill said, "You think the Bonds would go for it, Steve? You know B&B has been a family-owned company since Perry's grandfather founded it."

"Bill," Steve said earnestly, "If I weren't sure in my own mind, I'd never have introduced the subject." Warmed now by Keith's unquestioning approval, "There's only Perry and his mother, and Cornelia Bond spends half a year traveling abroad, the other half at her home in Santa Barbara. From my own reaction, and what I've been able to pick up from others, I honestly don't think it would mean a damned thing to Perry except to get a growing problem off his back and save him the humiliation of losing the company through possible bankruptcy proceedings some time in the near future. I'm sure that if a sound offer were made, he and Mrs. Bond would at least entertain the idea."

Allard said, "A hell of an interesting proposition. If we don't explore this further with Herschel Goodwin, we should have our heads examined. I'm for it all the way. What do you think, Bill?"

For the first time since the discussion began, Bill smiled. "I think we should call Herschel and set up a meeting for later in the week," he said. "Meanwhile, Steve, I want you to give me what information you have in writing so that I can properly present the case to Mr. Goodwin."

Inwardly elated, Steve said, "Sure. I'll get started on it in the morning. I can have it on your desk by Tuesday evening at the latest."

"What about Mark Lawson?" Bill asked. "You think he might be a stumbling block, taking pot shots at a revolutionary idea brought in by the agency?"

"I doubt that very much, Bill," Steve offered. "I think Mark will want it, because it will improve his own image and importance."

"Yes. I think you're right. I'll want to include you in the meeting, Steve."

"I'd like very much to sit in on it. Also, I think Wade should be there. After all, he's supervisor on the account."

Bill hesitated for a moment. "Well, we'll decide that later."

Which was a new note for Steve to consider. Why would Bill even hesitate to bring the GFP account supervisor into so important a meeting with the client? Well, that was out of his province and Steve decided not to mention Wade Barrett's name again at this time. Instead he said, "If this goes through, how will Larry Price figure in it?"

Bill shook his head negatively. "That's something else we'll decide later," he said evasively.

"At this moment, he's pretty close to Perry. That might be helpful to our cause."

"Perhaps. I'll take that into consideration," Bill replied conclusively. "Thank you, Steve, Keith." It was a dismissal and Keith stood up and said, "If that's all, Bill, Steve and I will run along. We've got a dinner date with Louise."

In the car, Steve said, "He's really down on Larry, isn't he, Keith?"

Keith said, "Well, how long does a pitcher last on a ball team after his arm goes? I think Bill's had it with Larry this time."

"Don't you think he owes Larry something more than forcing him into involuntary retirement?"

"And what does Larry owe Bill, to hit the bottle every time he's faced with a difficult situation? And why do you have to feel so damned defensive about him? If you hadn't found out what you did, don't you think someone else would have pointed the gun at him?"

"I realize that, Keith, but every man has his strengths and weaknesses. With his experience, I think it would be a waste to just toss him out. If we pull the B & B deal off, Wade could probably use him in the Western or Mid-Western area . . ."

Allard wagged his head from side to side and smiled bleakly. "You're going to learn about it sooner or later. Wade's been having his own troubles with McCreery and the Chevalier account, but that's not your problem. All right, Steve, if this deal goes through, I'll do what I can to save Larry from the fate of retirement, but I can only go so far. I'll talk to Bill, but not until something shows with the B & B people. Okay?" He turned and saw some sense of temporary relief in Steve's face.

"And incidentally," he added, "I'm proud as hell of you for coming up with that proposition, even if it doesn't go through."

2

Monday morning was as bleak as Sunday and Saturday had been, overcast, temperatures dipping slightly below twenty degrees, and Steve, for all his earlier rationalizations felt an understandable longing for the sunshine and warmth of Southern California. He fixed his breakfast of pancakes and bacon, drank two cups of coffee while reading his *Times,* then dressed for the outdoor cold and picked up his attaché case. In the hall, he ran into George Maczerak, his next-door neighbor who worked for a large toy importing firm and traveled to the toy centers of the world seeking new items for the American market. George was a breezy, rotund Czech in his mid-forties, married to an extremely attractive Swedish girl whom he referred to as "the little toy I picked up in Stockholm." Inga Maczerak worked as an interpreter with the Swedish mission to the United Nations, a job she had taken because of George's frequent absences abroad.

"Hey, Steve! When did you get back?" George called from the bank of elevators.

"Hi, George. Got back on Saturday."

"Nice trip?"

"I enjoyed it a lot. A nice change from this lousy weather we're having. You in town for long?"

"Another week, then I'm off for Tokyo. Inga is raising hell, as usual, but I've got a lead on something that could be big for us. Incidentally, she missed you. Seems she's run out of cake mixes and hates like hell to pay for anything she can get for free."

"I'll bring some home for her. How is she?"

"Like I said, raising hell. I go everywhere, she goes nowhere. You've heard the words and tune before. Look in on her while I'm gone, will you?"

"Sure."

On the ground level, George said, "Going to your office?"

"Yes, of course."

"Let's grab a cab and I'll drop you off. I've got to get over to our lawyer's office on Lexington to check out a couple of contracts."

Steve got out at Lexington and Fifty-second and entered the side lobby of the Hungerford Trust Building, a thirty-five story brownstone edifice whose age and interior comforts—along with certain inconveniences—was its charm. Built in 1900 and remodeled several times since, the lobby floors and walls were of imported marble, the modernized elevators paneled in walnut, and carpeted in soft green material. The building housed its principal tenant, Hungerford Trust, on the ground, second and third floors, with lawyers, accountants, architects, civil engineers and a miscellany of other tenants from the fourth to the thirty-fourth floors. The thirty-fourth and thirty-fifth floors were occupied solely by the Wm. B. Leary Advertising Agency, somewhat crowded for space by 224 men and women who were responsible for producing $32,950,000 in advertising for its national, sectional, and local clients.

In Chicago, the Leary office directed by Martin Link employed 120 people, who handled seven industrial accounts for approximately $22,000,000 in annual billings; while Los Angeles numbered sixty-six people, billed (now) some $6,050,000 and handled certain television productions for New York and Chicago as called for. However, with the big switch in recent years from network shows to spot commercials, both New York and Chicago were producing more and more of their own filmed and taped commercials, except where California-based personalities were involved.

On his way to the thirty-fourth floor, Steve greeted and was greeted by several familiar faces, some of whose names were lost to him, just as his might easily be lost to many of those who worked in the Leary complex. The thirty-fourth floor had no corridor entrance. Arriving employees stepped from the elevator directly into a large reception area and queued up at a long L-shaped desk to sign in on a series of lined pads held in departmental clipboards, a special color designating each department.

The walls here were of dark-green grasscloth and displayed the recent print media output for its eighteen clients behind unframed sheets of clear glass, conveniently arranged so that changes could be made as new replacement material appeared. GFP, Lovell Cosmetics, Chevalier Cigarettes, Norwood Distillers, Miyazaki Automobiles, Nagano Cameras, Prestige fashions, Penn Health and Life, were the stars of the show, surrounded by less prestigious accounts. On the side walls, similarly framed and spotlighted, was the output of the Chicago and Los Angeles branches. The one thing they had in common was the rich look of professionalism: dignity with flair, and humor with grace. Interspersed among the ads were dozens of silver- and gold-mounted plaques awarded to Leary copywriters and art directors over a period of many years.

As a group head, Steve was not required to sign in. His secretary, Peggy Cowles, would inform the reception desk of his arrival the moment he reached his office. He went through a door on the left and stepped into a wide corridor where he met the first faces he knew well; Sam Abrams, account executive for Prestige Fashions, was talking with Norman Adrian, senior copywriter for Chevalier Cigarettes, the latter already in shirtsleeves ready for work, and Sam, as usual, dressed in a slender-waisted, flare-bottomed jacket with matching flared trousers, a high-collared orange shirt with a wide blue-and-orange striped tie. They welcomed him back to, as Sam put it, "the World," and after a brief exchange, Steve continued on to the suite of offices where the advertising of GFP was planned, created, written, designed, and where its production was supervised.

The area given over to the GFP team consisted of an outer office, presided over by Peggy Cowles, the large office that was Steve's private domain, a smaller adjoining office for Chuck Baldasarian, his assistant, and another office shared by Frank Hayden and Reed Baker, the two account representatives. Beyond these was a large open area, banked on two sides by ten smaller rooms, each glass-walled from waist-high up, and occupied by copywriters, art directors, a Television-Radio assistant producer, and a production liaison man. In the open area between those offices was an arrangement of desks for three secretaries, three typists, three clerks, and a messenger-trainee. All other assistance required in Media, Merchandising and Marketing, Television-Radio, Art and Production, was furnished by those special departments on request from Steve or, in his absence, from Chuck Baldasarian.

Lovell Cosmetics ($5,460,000) and Chevalier Cigarettes ($3,800,000) operated similarily, with independent teams, while the balance of the agency's accounts—running from $250,000 to $1,500,000 each—were handled by various account executives functioning under account supervisors, or creative and group heads responsible for two or more accounts; in the same way that Wade Barrett was in control of GFP ($11,260,000), and Chevalier. In this way, theoretically, it became more difficult for an account executive with higher ambitions personally to control an account so completely that he could pirate it to another agency, or use it to start his own shop. However, this system carried no sure guarantees, and piracy among agencies was not only common, but an important part of the overall games they played.

In the outer office, Peggy Cowles—about twenty-six, with the lean, clean looks of a post-debutante—had begun her day by readying a thirty-cup coffee urn that sat on its own special table surrounded by a dozen china cups and saucers, and a tray that held sugar bowls and containers of powdered cream. She had just plugged the urn in when Steve entered and said to her shapely back, "A hell of a cold reception for a returning hero, I must say."

Peggy whirled around quickly at the sound of his voice, abbreviated skirt flying upward to reveal a pair of spectacular upper thighs, her face animated with pure joy. "Steve! Where in the world did you drop from? Why didn't you let me know—gee, it's great to have you back! You look wonderful! Am I allowed to kiss the returning warrior?"

He grinned, pleased. "One a day, just to keep up your morale." Peggy rose on her toes, embraced him warmly and kissed his lips. "You're back earlier than we expected. What happened out in Fantasyland?"

"Not too much. I ran out of problems and defected back again. And glad to be home again. What's the good word, if any?"

He watched her face closely as she spoke, the upcurl of her lips, twinkling eyes, the familiar movement of her head to right, then left, indicating an inner excitement that stirred him with unexpected warmth. There had been times in their association when he was sorely tempted to broaden their close relationship into something more meaningful, but he had always been held back by the suspicion that it could lead to a serious disruption in what had become a perfect working arrangement. "Not bad, not bad at all," she said. "Everything is more or less still glued together. There's a stack of mail on your desk—yea high—but we took care of the business stuff and left the personal things for you." Accusingly, "Including a foot-high stack of Christmas cards."

"Don't let it boggle your mind, princess. I sent cards to all my personal friends from L.A. The rest are probably business acquaintances who know I've been away. Anything else?"

"First, thanks for the gift you left me, and you missed your dental checkup last month. I couldn't confirm another date without knowing when you'd be back."

"I'm back, so take care of it, huh? How does the WPC look?"

"If you can find it on your desk, it's up to date as of late Friday afternoon."

She took his outer coat and hat and followed him into the inner office without further comment. As he entered, he came to an abrupt halt and stared at his desk, which was littered with proofs, newspaper and magazine tear-sheets, layouts, and other materials he did not recognize as his own. He stared at the disarray for a moment, then said, "Just what the hell is this all about?"

Peggy said sweetly, "Oh, that."

"Yes, that."

"Well, a few days after you left, Chuck decided it would be more convenient to work at your desk instead of his own. He and Katie moved in, and—well, don't blame me. I told him . . ."

"Is he in yet?"

"Yes, he's out back checking something with Lew Kann."

Crisply, "Get him in here."

Peggy went out and Steve was tempted to sweep the entire mess onto the floor, but that moment of childishness passed. He reached beneath the clutter and pulled out the Work In Progress chart, an institution that dated back to the days of the late Wm. B. Leary, Sr. It consisted of a pad of large square sheets, ruled off into blocks into which were recorded the day-by-day progress flow of each job currently being prepared for a specific client. By this means, those responsible for the account were kept posted on its current status. He noted that the last entries had been made on Friday, January ninth.

Steve was sorely annoyed at Chuck Baldasarian's presumption, but knowing him so well, felt he should have expected something of this sort. Chuck was not a man to sit still when an opportunity presented itself to put himself forward.

Baldasarian was one of the agency's infrangibles, with a life support system reinforced by blood relationship to Martin Link, head of the Leary office in Chicago, and Link's brother-in-law, George McCandless, a Chicago attorney high in the ranks of the Democratic party there and in Washington, an influential dispenser of political patronage and—for Marty Link—an important source of new business.

In length of service on the GFP account, Chuck was senior to every member presently working for that client, excluding Steve. Prior to that assignment, he had worked on a variety of lesser accounts as art director, but personal conflicts, obverse attitudes, and a unique sense of values required shifting him about. The last move was accompanied by a veiled warning from Norman Axelrod that the next move would be the final out. Thus, Chuck had moved up to his present position as Steve's principal assistant by seniority alone, and not at all by Steve's desire, nor to his liking.

Peggy came back with Chuck at her heels, a tentative smile on his lips. "Hey, Steve! Glad to see you back. How come you didn't let us know?" He extended a hand which Steve took, and dropped immediately.

"Hello, Chuck."

"How was it out there?"

"Great. How is it here?"

"Oh, fine. Hey, give me a few minutes and I'll get Katie in here and have this junk of mine cleared off your desk. I hope you don't mind my moving in here. It was a hell of a lot easier than running back and forth, okay?"

"Okay. I'll have some coffee with Peggy while you get this squared away. Then I'll want to check out the WPC with you."

"Sure. Give me ten minutes."

Steve and Peggy went to her office while Chuck and his secretary removed the evidence of their temporary occupancy. The coffee wasn't ready and Peggy offered to get some from the Lovell group down the hall. "No," Steve said, "I'll wait. Go through the mail if you like."

"I've already been through it. Nothing critical or exciting."

Steve lit a cigarette. "How did Chuck get on while I was away?"

She threw a glance toward the doorway behind which Chuck was working at clearing Steve's desk. In a lowered voice, "Like he'd inherited the throne and crown. You know. Chuck is—well—Chuck. He got along fine with Mr. Barrett and Mr. Allard, but he and Frank had it out one day. And there were a couple of run-ins with Reed Baker, but all of that blew over. I don't know about Frank, though, and I don't know too much about what happened at GFP between Mr. Lawson and Chuck, but take a good hard look at some of the latest entries on the WPC. I think you'll find some changes were made from the original schedules for the spring campaign."

The coffee was ready, and Peggy poured two cups. Steve sipped at his thoughtfully, wondering about those changes, then recalled his first abrasive encounter with Chuck, which had concerned Peggy, only a week after Steve had chosen her to be his secretary. Chuck, always on the alert for opportunity, said to Steve, "Hey, man, what about that chick in the front office?"

"Which chick?"

"That Peggy broad."

"Chuck," Steve said shortly, "Peggy Cowles isn't a chick, nor a broad. She's my secretary."

"Okay, so are you ballin' her yet?"

"No, you slimy-minded bastard."

Grinning lewdly, "So if she won't put out for you, you mind if I take a crack at her?"

Growing angrier, Steve said, "Let's settle that point once and for all. I don't give a good goddamn what you do outside this office, Chuck, but on the job, she's *my* secretary, period. You've got your own. Does that answer your question?"

Chuck grinned, unabashed. "Yeah, but yours looks like she was a girl before she became a secretary." A moment of hesitation, then, "You know something, Steve, for a nice, bright guy, you're quite a *schmuck*."

Fortunately, there were no further problems in that direction. Peggy's reaction to Chuck Baldasarian was patently negative.

The door opened and Chuck came in, a broad smile on his face. "All set, Steve. You're back in business."

To Peggy, Steve said, "Keep yourself free this afternoon. I've got a thousand or two notes to whip into a report for Mr. Leary."

At his own desk again, Steve said to Chuck, "Any problems with Mark Lawson?"

"Nothing I couldn't handle."

"How about Frank and Reed?"

"Oh, they did okay, I guess. No complaints, but there wasn't a hell of a lot for them to do, really."

To question Chuck further about Frank Hayden and Reed Baker, would—he knew—point a finger at Peggy, and Steve decided not to pursue the matter for the moment. "Then everything is in good shape."

"Well, I'd say yes, but you know how ornery Lawson can get. You haven't seen the WPC yet, have you?"

"Just a brief glance. Let's go over it, item by item."

Peggy came in with a fresh cup of coffee for Steve. "Chuck?" Steve said, and Chuck replied, "No, thanks. I had some out back." Peggy turned and went out, and Chuck, eyes following her, said, "You know, that dame's got a bad case of virginity that needs curing. You ought to do something about it, Steve."

"If you couldn't, Chuck, there's no hope for me. Let's get on with it, shall we?"

Item by item, they started through the WPC from the top line, and half an hour later nearing the bottom of the sheet, Steve looked up and said, "What is this, Chuck? I don't remember . . ."

"I've been waiting for you to come to that. These are the changes in the spring stuff we were working on when you left."

"What about it? Who made the changes?"

"Don't get all sweated up . . ." Steve waited, feeling a chill go through him, staring at Baldasarian through narrow slits. "About the middle of December, Wade and I made a call on Lawson at his request—Lawson's, I mean—with the roughs you approved before you took off. Lawson looked them over and turned them down, then gave us some pretty definite ideas about what he wanted for the spring campaign."

"And whatever it was, you bought it?"

"Don't lay it off on me, man. Barrett was the dude in charge."

"But you were there, too, weren't you?"

"Okay, so I was there, but I couldn't take the ball out of Barrett's hands, could I? He was the . . ."

"I know what he was—the man in charge. What happened?"

"Well, Lawson pulled out a stack of ads he'd clipped . . ."

"That's an old Lawson ploy, Chuck, using last year's competitive ads to shake us up a little, you know that. Hell, you've been there with me when he's pulled that, and you saw how I talked him out of it."

"Okay, so I know. But Barrett got uptight from the word GO, and the more Lawson talked, the more enthusiastic Wade got about the whole thing, kissing his ass right down the line. Nobody asked me a damned thing. I was out of it, period. When we left about two hours later, we were practically committed to every change Lawson suggested."

"The hell you say!"

"The hell I don't say. You'd better check our Call

Sheets for that day and the two calls I made alone after that."

"You went along, instead of putting up a fight?"

"Steve, I tried to shut the faucet off that first time, but after Wade bought it, what could I do? Hell, I've never seen anybody so eager not to make waves . . . just sit back and take it!"

"What kind of crap did Lawson roll out this time?"

"It's pretty lacy stuff, as you'll see. These weren't any competitive ads, but a lot of fancy, frilly, sex-oriented cosmetics and fashion ads he'd dug up from somewhere. You know, flowers and gauzy broads reeking of perfume and springtime in the county. That's the effect he wants."

"Oh, for Christ's sake! Barrett actually went for that swill?"

"You'd better believe it. Swallowed it hook, line, sinker, and reel."

Steve waited for a few moments, trying to sort out his muddled thoughts. "Listen, Steve," Chuck said, "that Barrett is a very worried guy. He's changed one hell of a lot in just a month."

"All right, give me the rest of it."

"Well, the Chevalier situation isn't as healthy as it might be and the word's out that he's having domestic problems, which doesn't help matters very much."

"And that's the rumor making the rounds?"

"It's not just rumor. Bob Freeman, Paul Nicholson, Kay Berry, and a couple of others on Chevalier have been showing their books around. Norm Adrian has been having trouble keeping them in line."

Freeman, Nicholson and Kay Berry were copywriters and art directors on Chevalier. Their "books" were personal portfolios of published ads for which they were responsible and which were treasured, not unlike a model's book of photographic samples, as references when applying for a new job with another ad agency or job placement service. In the uncertain world of advertising, creative personnel showing their books around is a clear indication that the agency's grip on a specific account is shaky. Soon the word hits the street, and competing agencies, like sharks smelling blood, begin converging on the client in question.

The Slipping Account is Fear Number One in the agency world. It affects the agency in the same way that the rumor of Asian plague might affect an entire community.

The reverberations in the concerned shop reach from the top of the organization to the mail room, its first symptoms showing in nervousness, short-fused tempers exploding over the most minor incidents, apprehension, mild desperation, and—to those directly concerned—the pandemonia of threatened job loss. When a major account is lost and the news announced in trade and daily papers, the security of the agency's other accounts is threatened. Clients ponder the "why" of a major account's change of heart, and the relationship between those clients and the account men begins to suffer.

To the account supervisor, to senior and junior members of the lost account group—creative and noncreative alike—the loss is immeasurable. The higher the level of operation, the longer they will be out of work—in most cases, a year spent in the ranks of the unemployed—unwilling to settle for a salary less than what they had previously earned.

In the case of Chevalier, the agency's income ran to some six-hundred-thousand dollars plus collateral profits. About a dozen high-priced account men, writers and art directors were directly concerned with its output for every known media, and some thirty others indirectly. The one beneficial result of such a disaster is harvested by the manufacturers of aspirin, sedatives, painkillers, and sleeping pills—and, quite understandably—the liquor industry.

"All right, Chuck, let me think about this for now," Steve said. Chuck shrugged his massive shoulders and went out. Steve resumed scanning the WPC and the computer printout on the GFP budget, from which each committed expenditure was subtracted to show an accurate running account of where the money was being spent and how much was left for projects yet to come. The changes Lawson had asked for were not yet completed and therefore not reflected in the printout, leaving Steve in the air as to just how much money was involved.

The door opened and Wade Barrett came in, one hand extended, smiling. In his other hand he held a sheaf of beige forms which Steve recognized by their color as Call Sheets, formal reports of interviews with client personnel that were required to be filled out following any conference or contact between agency and client. These reports were Xeroxed and distributed to all concerned persons on both sides, and one copy went to the agency's Traffic Control. In the month he had been away, Steve noted that

Barrett seemed more tired, a little grayer, leaner from loss of weight. Or was it fear? His face was pinched with deeper lines, eyes narrowed down to a squint.

"Steve, how the hell are you?" Barrett boomed. "I just got in and Vanessa told me you'd checked in. We missed you during the Christmas festivities around here. Christ, you look great. Just great. I wish I could have been out there with you. Good vacation?"

"Are you kidding? I was up to my you-know-what in work from early morning until late at night. How are Sylvia and Carol?"

"Oh, Carol's fine. I saw her over the weekend." Steve could not ignore Barrett's omission of Sylvia in his reply and changed the subject quickly, pointing to the beige reports.

"I haven't had a chance to catch up on my Call Sheet file. Anything important?"

"Yes and no. If you're swamped, it can wait for this afternoon."

"Tomorrow afternoon would be better. I've got a report on my trip to get out for Bill and Keith. Bill's anxious to see it."

"It's not that pressing as long as we can get together before you see Lawson."

"Sure. How about lunch tomorrow?"

"I'll check my calendar and have Vanessa call you. I'm up to my ass with McCreery and Hugh Benson. Contract expiration on July 15, you know, and we've got a presentation to work up, with Ted and Norm still at each other's throats."

"Rough going?"

"With the new contract coming up, you've no idea how rough it can be. Something's got to give. How did you find things, out on the Coast?"

"So-so. A little on the rocky side, but I think it might work out."

Barrett grinned owlishly. "Don't con me, Steve. I know a little more about it than you think. I sat in on a couple of discussions with Bill and Keith before you went out there. In fact, I was the one who first suggested your name to Bill."

"Thanks, pal," Steve said, his tone larded heavily with sarcasm.

"Was it that fouled up?" Barrett was still grinning, as

though he had fully expected everything would be fouled up and would have been disappointed if it hadn't been.

"I'll have to go over my notes and line it out in my report before the whole thing can be evaluated," Steve said evasively. "You'll probably get the whole story from Bill or Keith."

"Sure. By the way, how was old Larry?" and before Steve could reply, "We saw some high old times together before Larry went out there. Did you know it was a tossup between Larry and me for that job? When Bill, Senior picked him, I was feeling kind of low about it. I was tied in too closely with Chevalier and GFP at the time. The way things are now," he mused, "I'm almost glad he won out, although I'm sure it would have worked out differently if I'd been out there in his place."

Steve remained silent, reserving his own opinion on that score. Barrett said, "Tomorrow then, if we can make it for lunch?"

"I'll look forward to it, Wade."

Barrett left and Steve rang for Peggy, who came in carrying a fresh cup of coffee. She put it down on his desk and said, "You'd better drink this. I think you need it."

"Then you know what's been going on here."

"Oh, sure, but what could I do?"

"Where are Frank and Reed?"

"I think Frank is still here. Reed is at GFP."

"Ask Frank to come in, will you?"

Frank Hayden, young, smoothly likable, came in frowning and slipped into the visitor's chair. "Long time no see, boss," he said, taking a cigarette from Steve's pack and lighting it.

"From what I hear, too long."

Frank grinned, exuding charm. "What else do you hear?"

"What I hear is why I asked Peggy to get you in here."

"Look, Steve, I've got enough problems on my hands just keeping alive. All I can say is, I'm damned glad you're back."

"Chuck?"

"That's another name for it."

"What happened?"

"For one thing, I found it a little hard to walk around here, or down at GFP, with his foot sticking out, tripping me."

"How about getting down to specifics."

"It's hard, Steve. Nothing I can point a finger at, but that bastard has a way of putting me down in front of Mr. Lawson, Tom Jewell, Dan Tyson, even their secretaries and clerks, that makes it hard to take. Not only me. He did it to Reed, too, time after time. It's as though he resented us being with Lawson or any of the other people we've been seeing there, trying to give the impression we're only errand boys doing his bidding."

Steve waited for more, and Frank sighed. "Look, Steve, I've enjoyed working with you, more than I can tell you. I've learned a hell of a lot, but I don't think I can take much more of this sort of thing from Baldasarian. Reed feels pretty much the same way I do. We know the fault isn't yours, that he's got an angel back in Chicago who protects him through one foulup after another, but stomping a couple of juniors isn't making him more lovable to either of us."

Steve said, "Frank, you and Reed were hand-picked by me for your jobs, and you've been doing very well at them. What I'm asking of you, and Reed, is not to bring anything to a head at the moment. If things get out of hand I'll step in, I promise you, but right now I need you both on the job. Will you trust me that far?"

"Sure, Steve, anytime, but—well—we'll see."

"Thanks, Frank. I'll talk to Reed when I get a chance."

Frank smiled and went out. Steve picked up his coffee cup and walked to the window with it, sipping slowly. Outside, Fifty-second Street was being blanketed with a new layer of snow, cars bleated their way eastward and tiny figures, bundled up in heavy coats, scurried in both directions. Peggy came in again. "Everything okay, Steve?"

"Yes, for the moment. Let's get this mail cleared away first and hold all but the important calls . . . wait, I'd better talk to Lawson first. Get him for me, please."

She dialed the number on the direct outside line while he came back to his desk and sorted through some thirty or forty envelopes, scanning those that had return names and addresses. Peggy hung up after a few moments of conversation, saying, "This is your lucky day. Mr. Lawson and his wife are snowbound at his father-in-law's home in Wyecliffe and he won't be in today."

"All right, let's get on with the mail."

Most of it, as Peggy had told him earlier, was unimportant; notes and letters from time and space salesmen—

network people; from Ed Friedman, an editor at *Advertising Daily* asking for an article; a Chicago premium-house vice-president requesting an early appointment; a letter from an executive placement service asking him to fill out a registration form and submit a resumé; and a note from his accountant regarding an adjustment in his estimated income tax. He dictated several replies and told Peggy in general terms what to reply to the rest.

"And the Christmas cards?"

"That can wait for the moment."

"You interested in the local gossip?"

"Should I be?"

"Well, some of it hits pretty close to home."

He leaned back in his chair and cupped his hands behind his head. "All right, you've got two minutes. Let's have it before you burst."

"There's some talk going around about the Chevalier account . . ."

"You mean with McCreery and Adrian at each other's throats?"

"Well, it's gone a little beyond that. There's some suspicion that Ted McCreery is fed to the teeth and might be looking around for an out."

"You mean, walk out with the account?"

"Well, I don't know if it's gone that far, but there's talk."

"Hell, Peggy, there's always that kind of talk in this business, you know that."

"I know, but Marie Chardis, Ted's secretary, has been acting kind of strange lately, not communicative at all . . ."

"So the word from the water-cooler gang is that she's probably getting ready to move out when and if Ted does, eh?"

"Don't knock it. It can happen. It has before."

"Anything can happen, and usually does. Or doesn't."

"Okay. The other thing is that Mr. Barrett is having trouble with his wife again. He's been spending his nights and weekends in town instead of suburbia."

"Well . . . some other time, Peg. I want to get into that report of mine. Be a good kid and run along now, will you?"

"Sure. Let me know when you're ready for a rough draft."

"I'll whistle." Wade and Sylvia crossed his mind when Peggy left and he began riffling through the Christmas cards again—some commercial reminders, many from friends to whom he had sent cards from Los Angeles—dropping them into his wastepaper basket after a mere glance at the names and personal inscriptions: from the Brevard (Buzz) Applebys and their two children; one from the Arnold Porters and daughter; from Eli Tinsley; another from the Benjamin Draper Tinsleys and sons; all vivid reminders of Lancaster.

There was none, of course, from Congressman and Mrs. Carroll Waggoner.

Mrs. Carroll Waggoner, the former Elizabeth Newell Gilman.

There was little time to dwell on the past and he returned to the task of sorting out the notes that had accumulated and must be organized before attempting to coordinate them into the formal report for Bill Leary. He worked steadily until Peggy returned, her face freshly made up, ready to leave for the day.

"You look like you're back in full harness, as though you hadn't been away," she said.

"What time is it?"

"Time to quit and restore your energies for tomorrow."

"God, I'm bushed. Sit and talk to me for a few minutes, let me unwind."

"If it's therapy you need . . ."

"Hell, no. I've been wiring myself back to California with this damned report Bill wants. Just seeing you, hearing your voice, brings me back home again."

She sat down, crossed her legs, and said, "Everything looks normal with you behind your desk instead of Chuck."

"I almost feel normal with my nose pressed to the grindstone again." He lit two cigarettes and handed her one. She drew on hers and exhaled slowly. "I learned something new about you while you were away," she said.

"You run across my criminal file in my desk?"

"Something more interesting. I didn't know you had writing ambitions other than advertising."

He looked up quickly, almost embarrassed. "You been rooting through my desk?"

"Not out of curiosity. With Chuck working in here, I wanted to make sure nothing was displaced."

"So?"

"So I ran across a very intriguing outline for a historical novel by Steven Gilman."

"Amateurish kid stuff. I did that back in college, a million years ago."

"I thought it was great, the idea, the characters; but then, I've been a Civil War buff ever since *Gone With The Wind*."

"Come on now, Peggy, that's pure, unadulterated flattery."

"I think it could make it. Big."

"And I think you're off your rocker. That thing was turned down by at least four agents."

"In its unfinished form, I can understand why. What I can't understand is why you never expanded it into a finished novel."

Steve tapped the report notes lying on the desk before him. "For the simple reason that the job comes first, period. Do you have any idea what it takes to beat your brains out creatively all day long, then go home and sweat over a typewriter for four or five hours every night, working with a whole new set of fictional characters and situations? Or over the few undisturbed weekends when I can't shut out the work waiting for me on Monday morning? No chance."

"But you'll do it someday, won't you?"

"I doubt it."

"Then why do you keep it lying around?"

He laughed wryly and said, "Just to impress nosy and impressionable secretaries."

"Steve, it's a pure waste of good talent."

With a shrug of dismissal, he said "Talent is what I need for Leary and GFP and the bread it brings in to allow me to live in this overpopulated jungle we call a city." He stubbed out his cigarette and added, "And that draws the curtain on a long, tiring day. Come on, sweetie, I'll walk you to the subway."

3

Steve spent the summer following his freshman year at home. Libby returned from Sweet Briar more beautiful, more desirable than ever, and he had seen her every day and most nights for two whole weeks before Olive took her off to Europe, where Barney would meet them sometime in August. Meanwhile, Cal, Ben, Jake and Arnie Porter, and Buzz were home from college and the six old friends spent their first few weeks with those girls who were also home from college and available. Later, Steve began to spend more of his daytime hours at the *Star* with Grady.

Jenny, when he saw her on the first day of his return, seemed to have aged by ten years, her face gaunt and lined, eyes deeper set, moving about with difficulty. She permitted him to kiss her cheek lightly, replied that she was, with the help of God and His mercy, alive and ailing, but generally well. Beyond this, there was little more. She asked no questions except, "How did you get along up there?" and was reassured when he told her he had done very well.

During his absence, Grady told him later, Jenny had been under Dr. Murchison's care for an undetermined ailment. She had, from time to time, fallen into catatonic lapses, withdrawing from the small part of life in which she participated, and seldom leaving the house. Melinda, the Gilman's three-day-a-week cleaning woman and sometimes cook, had been installed in a room on a full time basis as housekeeper-nurse, but at infrequent intervals, Jenny would rouse herself for a day at a time and clean the house with a furious burst of energy, then return to her bed or sleep or read her father's Bible for days on end, quoting passages loudly to herself.

When Steve went to her room to see her every morning, Jenny would sometimes recognize him and smile wanly; sometimes lie and stare at him with glazed, unseeing eyes. After a few minutes her eyes would close, as though signaling him to leave.

In March of his sophomore year, Steve experienced his first personal tragedy. It came in the form of a phone call from Eli Tinsley early one morning, with the shocking news that Grady was dead, victim of a heart attack. Steve caught the first train to Washington, then a bus to Lancaster. He took a cab to the house on Wilburn Road where, to his complete surprise, Jenny was up, dressed in black, and as fully alert as he could ever remember seeing her. Melinda was nowhere in sight.

"Where is Dad, Mother?" Steve asked, after kissing her withered cheek.

"He's gone to his reward and God's punishment," Jenny replied with stony calm.

In that moment of intense grief, Steve became angered

by her tone and words. "Nobody is going to punish my father," he said harshly. "Where is he?"

"At Moseley's Funeral Parlor. Mr. Moseley is waiting for you to make the arrangements for his burial."

"And you couldn't do even that much for him? Why isn't he here, in his home, where he was born?"

She turned on him and said waspishly, "Because he didn't die here, in his home, where he was born. He died in the house of a prostitute on Durban Street. His friends brought him home out of shame, so it wouldn't be known."

"And that's all that matters to you, appearances? Are you planning to go to your husband's funeral?"

"It will be expected of me. You were so much closer to him, I thought it would be more fitting if you made the arrangements."

"Mother, for God's sake! You were married to him for almost twenty years. Is this the most you can feel for him?"

She stared at Steve and said simply, "He was a godless man."

He inhaled deeply and exhaled slowly, trying to maintain some sense of equilibrium. "What right have you to judge him, me, or anyone else? He was a good man who had many friends. He loved people and helped them. They loved him. Maybe the reason he went somewhere else was because he couldn't find what he needed at home."

She said icily, "He drank and gambled and whored with his good friends who loved him. He raised you in his own image and when I tried to guide you in righteous ways, he . . ."

"Oh, for Jesus Christ's sake, Mother! Listen to me this one time, will you? You've lived an entire life of lonely, dreary, self-made isolation and drudgery. You cut yourself off from husband, son, and friends in order to bury yourself in your father's Bible and become eligible for the next world—one you don't even know exists—ignoring every human pleasure this one offered you. Is that what your God wants for His children on earth?"

He saw tears of anger and frustration welling up into her eyes, hands trembling as she contracted them into small tight fists, showing white across the knuckles. "Mother, I'm sorry, terribly sorry to hurt you like this, but he was my father and I loved him very much. I can't stay here and listen to you malign him. I'm going to see Mr.

Moseley. I'll tell him I want Dad buried tomorrow. I'll come back and let you know the time."

He waited for her reply, but there was none. He turned and left the house.

The funeral had been tentatively scheduled for the following day by Eli Tinsley, he learned from Mr. Moseley, subject to Steve's approval. Steve agreed after hearing that most of Grady's friends had already been notified. From there, he walked across the street to see Eli Tinsley in his office.

There, he received his second shock. Eli told him that the *Star* was sorely in debt. Grady had borrowed from the bank to buy a new press and other equipment two years before, and Steve recalled his own and Grady's enjoyment as they watched the factory mechanics complete the installations and turned the press on for its test run. More recently, Eli added, Grady had borrowed more money from Barney Newell to pay his mounting paper and ink bills. "Your father, I am sorry to say, had been drinking rather heavily, Steve. The paper was being held together by his friends. He missed you a lot, boy."

"The way I miss him now," Steve said. He turned away with misted eyes and walked toward the window, staring blankly down at the street. "I appreciate everything you've done, Mr. Tinsley. You were one of Dad's oldest and closest friends. I feel—I—"

"I hope you'll always feel the same way, son. Anytime you want to talk to me about anything, I hope you'll write or telephone me."

"Thank you, sir. I'd like to ask you a question you may not want to answer."

"Well, you ask, and I'll see if I can handle it."

"My mother told me how my father died, not in his own house or bed. Is that true?"

"Yes, substantially. I wasn't there, of course . . ."

"When did it start, the heavy drinking, I mean?"

"A short time after you went off to college. Last summer, before you came home for your vacation, he quit and didn't start up again until you went back. Don't take it to be your fault, Steve. He was a lonely man living in an empty house with your mother the way she's been since you were born. You know what his life was like at home, so . . ."

Steve turned back to face Eli, to get him off the subject. "Did you mean the paper is gone? Bankrupt?"

"Well, it's not all that bad. I think we can salvage something from it. Barney Newell and the bank hold all the outstanding notes, so they've got first liens on it. Here's something else I don't think Grady would've told you."

Some months earlier, Eli told him, Grady had had an offer from a Mr. Paul Marcus, a Richmond newspaper executive who was being retired and wanted to live in a small community and run a weekly paper. Grady had turned the offer down and Eli now saw this as a way out of total financial distress. He had discussed the matter with Barney only recently, and Barney had agreed, assuming that Paul Marcus was still interested.

"I'll phone Marcus the day after tomorrow. If it works out, I think we can adjust the price so your mother can come out a few thousand ahead. The house on Wilburn Road is free and clear and I assume your mother will continue to live in it. Your educational policy should see you through college, so there's no problem there. There are two life insurance policies intact, one for twenty-thousand dollars and another for seventy-five hundred dollars, so she'll have enough to live on until you're out of college, can even keep her woman on if she wants. That's about it, Steve, except for your plans."

"I hadn't really made any, Mr. Tinsley. I'd hoped to come back and work with Dad on the *Star* for a while, give him more time to relax, take things easy. That's over now. I'll have to start working on some new plans."

"I don't want to be presumptuous, Steve, but . . ."

"Go ahead, please."

"I hope you'll plan to come back here. Too many of our young people been running off to the bigger cities."

Steve shrugged. "What do you suppose I could do here?"

"Well, you might think about a place on the *Star,* for one thing, if Mr. Marcus is still interested in buying. I could make that a special point when I discuss it with him—"

"I don't think he could afford what I would want—would need—in order to settle down in Lancaster."

"Well, ah, there are other courses."

"Like what?"

"You could consider a good marriage to the right girl."

Steve smiled bleakly. "With my great prospects?"

"You've still got 'em, son."

"What prospects I had died when my father died. What girl, the right girl, couldn't see that?"

"Uh—I was talking to my Ben. He tells me you and Libby Newell were—uh—kind of interested in each other."

"Mr. Tinsley, I'm barely nineteen and only in my second year of college. Libby is nineteen, with her own education to complete. That wouldn't be much of a start for either of us, would it?"

"Well . . . just a thought. Just a thought. Didn't mean to butt in on your private affairs, you know."

"I appreciate that, sir. I know you want only the best for me."

Grady Gilman's life had touched most of Lancaster's inhabitants and the funeral was the largest anyone could remember. Most of the town's business establishments closed down for it, court was recessed, and civic affairs put aside for a few hours. Moseley's chapel filled up and the overflow waited outside in the cold until the service was over, then drove or walked to the cemetery for the interment.

Steve stood beside Jenny at Grady's graveside, hearing the brief sermon, the shortened eulogy most had not been able to hear in the chapel. Jenny stood stiffly, hands clenching a black handkerchief, relentless, unyielding and stern, still refusing to forgive, or accept the words of love and reverence spoken over her husband's coffin.

When it was over, the crowd broke up slowly. People were remembering the many intimate glimpses they had shared with Grady Gilman, wondering if Steve would remain now, and take over the *Star*. At the house on Wilburn Road, they came in a steady flow that evening to pay their respects to Jenny, whom few knew well enough to be other than formal, and to Steve, whom they had known throughout his life. By ten o'clock the last visitor had departed and they were alone.

It was then that Steve told Jenny of his earlier conversation with Eli Tinsley, the portion that concerned the state of her financial affairs. She nodded, stood up and said, "Thank you, Steven. I'll go to bed now. I'm very tired."

"Then I'll say good-bye now, Mother. There's no purpose in my staying on. I want to catch the early bus to Washington."

"Yes. I thought you would. Good-bye, Steven."

"Mother . . .?"

"What?"

"Please, Mother, don't be so bitter. There are people here who would be your friends if you'd only let them."

Jenny stiffened. "I don't need them," she said firmly. "I really don't need them. What I needed, I never had. Your father had a son. I had nothing." She turned quickly and went up the stairs.

Steve sat in Grady's favorite chair remembering back to when he was a child, the vagrant memory reawakened by his mother's final words: *Your father had a son. I had nothing.*

When he was nearing his fourth year, Grady and Jenny had a terrible row over him. Grady declared that, by God, his son was going to be raised as a boy and not a girl. The break came later, one day when Grady, remembering he had left an unfinished editorial at home, came back to find Jenny out shopping and their laundress hanging the wash on the line. Among the items, he saw several dresses and some feminine undergarments that could only fit Steve, who was in the house playing with his dog.

In a rage, Grady swept the small garments up in his arms, stormed into the house, and threw them into the wood stove, then put Steve in his car, took him down to Lynd's barber shop, and had Joe Lynd give him a boy's haircut. From there they went to Angriff's and had Steve outfitted in boy's clothes, buying an adequate supply to complete his wardrobe. He waited at home until Jenny returned and made it clear to her that never again was she to put a dress on their son.

What had previously been a rift between Grady and Jenny now became an uncrossable gulf. Jenny turned from Steve while Steve grew closer to Grady. Later, on his way to the paper every morning, Grady would drop Steve off at school, and afterward Steve would walk to the paper where he would amuse himself until Grady was ready to take him home.

On the morning of his return to Columbia, Steve decided he would look in on Jenny before leaving, but when he knocked on her door, she was still asleep. He came inside the room and stood watching her for a few moments, then went downstairs and wrote a note to her, which he gave to Melinda to deliver. On his way out he found a letter in the mailbox addressed to himself. It was from Libby, away at Sweet Briar, expressing her sincere condolences.

He never saw Jenny alive again.

4

During the spring of 1960 Steve wrote Jenny he would be staying on in New York that summer to look for a job. She did not reply to his letter. He found a job in the circulation department of the *Herald-Tribune* and although it did little to further his ambition to work on a metropolitan daily as a writer, he was able to pay his way without having to call on Jenny for additional funds. Some day when he became a published, by-lined writer, the thought occurred to him that his biographical sketch would include a brief mention that he had once worked on the prestigious *Herald-Tribune.*

In July, he was surprised by a phone call from Libby, alone in New York to see a few shows and do some shopping. She was staying at the Sherry Netherland for a full week—a gift trip from Olive and Barney—before taking off on her usual visiting rounds with Olive.

Libby's presence posed a monetary problem for Steve. Jenny had never inquired into his financial needs, nor had he written her about them, now more determined than ever to pay his own way over and above what his educational policy provided. He was living in the same rooming house on Morningside Avenue, within walking distance of the University, and possessed less than fifty dollars in cash. Fortunately, his wardrobe, such as it was, was still presentable.

Steve took Libby to an inexpensive, out-of-the-way Italian restaurant that first night, and it was quite apparent to Libby that he was wretchedly preoccupied. After a while, she asked, "What is it, Steve? You look like you're miles away. Aren't you glad I'm here? I came up especially to see you when you wrote you couldn't come home for the summer. Is it another girl?"

She looked so gloriously tanned, smartly outfitted, ravishingly attractive; all of which emphasized the width and depth of the chasm between them. He said, "Libby, there's no other girl. There couldn't be, but I don't think you should waste any more time on me. I've got this nothing job with barely enough to scrape through on, each week, let alone entertain you the way I'd like to, and as much as I want to."

"I know, Steve. Dad hinted how things might be with you, but don't let it bother you for a minute. I brought along enough for both of us, more than enough."

"Libby, you don't understand. This isn't a high school party with the girls furnishing the food while the guys rustle up the wheels. We're adults now and I can't sponge on you. I've got to make it on my own, by myself."

"Steve . . ."

"Libby, I'm a man now and I've got to *be* a man, to live like one. When I can do that, I'll be able to accept favors, but only as long as I can afford to return them."

She put down her knife and fork and stared at him across the table. "Does that mean we just say good-bye and forget each other?"

"No, of course not. It only means that I need some time. A lot of time."

"And what am I supposed to do while you're taking your time to find what you need to make you feel you're a man, sit and wait?"

"Libby, please. I'm just asking you to understand."

"I understand, and I know the situation, but if you're too proud or stubborn to accept help, I can't understand that. Come back to Lancaster, if only for the rest of the summer. I'll refuse to go to Richmond and Virginia Beach with my mother. My father will help you. He's in real estate, politics, he owns . . ."

"Libby, I'd die there, taking charity from your father."

Again she stared at him in silence, uncomprehending, then said, "I love you, Steve. I thought you loved me."

"I do, Libby, but I can't . . . goddamn it, I can't *use* you."

"Isn't that what we've been doing for the past three years, using each other by not seeing anyone else?"

"Call it whatever you like. I felt we were sharing something. But that was while my father owned the *Star* and I could see some kind of a future ahead of me."

"Steve, please, you ought to come back to Lancaster and see what's happening there. They're talking about a big plastics plant moving in. Dad says there'll be jobs for everybody who wants to work. They'll bring in new families and need homes and stores and cars and clothing, food, everything else. Mr. Marcus, the man who bought the *Star,* will need more people. He's planning to bring in some new men and turn the paper into a daily. Dad's working on a project for a big new shopping center out on Pleasant Road and he's talking with out-of-town real estate people who represent chain stores interested in starting branches there. Mr. Marcus would give you a job. My father . . ."

"There we go again. Your father."

"Why are you being so damned superior? What gives you that special right? My father is no different from other fathers who help their children get started. Listen, I'll even quit college and get a job if that will make you feel any better about it."

"Libby, I can't let you do that any more than I could quit college right now. We'd hold it against each other for the rest of our lives." He paused for a moment, then said slowly, "What it comes down to is, I'm not ready for marriage. I can't say right now when I will be."

She began to cry softly and he knew of no way to comfort her. Even the waiter, hovering nearby, began to show visible hostility toward this *tanghero* who was making her weep.

"Libby," Steve pleaded, "please don't cry."

"Take me back to my hotel, will you?"

"Libby . . ."

"Please, Steve . . ." She stood up, picked her jacket off the hook on the wall behind her and walked toward the door. Steve asked for the check, paid it with a tip he couldn't afford, and followed her. In the cab, Libby was icily silent and at the hotel, she got out without looking back and said, "Good-bye, Steve."

"Will I see you tomorrow? Listen, I'll take the day off."

"No, don't bother. I'm going back in the morning."

"Libby, look at me."

"No, Steve," she said without turning. "When I do, all I can see is your mother. Hard and cold as marble."

5

In his senior year, Steve received his second call from Eli Tinsley. Jenny Gilman had died quietly in her sleep.

The call came as the Easter vacation was beginning, and again he caught the Pennsy to Washington, and the bus to Lancaster. This time he arrived at noon and Eli met him at the bus depot. He hadn't been home since

Grady's funeral and, curiously, he noticed that the streets in the commercial area had been made one-way to accommodate the traffic, now heavier than he had ever known it. He saw a tall sign over the rooftops of the commercial buildings, somewhere bordering the river, marking the location of a new motel. Many store fronts were dressed up in modern facings, with new signs. Progress had, as Libby had told him, come to Lancaster.

From Eli's office windows he could see the *Star* building and the changes the new owner had made. The front had been sandblasted, the red brick painted white, a canopy erected over the entrance, the sign rejuvenated by the addition of a single fine line of neon.

Tinsley said, "That fellow, Marcus, you know, he brought some new men in from Richmond and Baltimore. With all this new industry booming, the *Star*'s going to become a daily next month."

So Grady's dream, postponed until Steve would be graduated, had finally come true. Paul Marcus's dream now. His own, shot to hell.

Jenny's body lay in an open coffin until he could see her for the last time. "She must've known something," Eli said quietly as he stood beside Steve. "Left a note tucked in her Bible that once you'd seen her in this—thing—the cover was to be put on and not removed."

Steve, not surprised in the least, nodded. Jenny would not want to be stared at by the curious. He said to Mr. Moseley, "You can close it now," and he and Eli went out again.

All he could think of were Libby's words, her last. *Hard and cold, like marble.*

He asked Eli to put the house and six acres up for sale, but Eli advised against selling at that time. "Land values are moving up, Steve. You wait it out and in a few years you can count on double what it would bring now. Even triple. Meanwhile, I can find you a tenant who'll give you a steady monthly income. Your mother left a little over eighteen thousand dollars in cash, so you won't be hurting."

Steve agreed.

At Jenny's funeral next day there were less than thirty people present, and those—Steve knew—had come out of respect for Grady's memory and friendship for himself. Barney and Olive Newell were there and although he knew Libby was home for her Easter vacation, she was absent from the services.

Later a few of his friends dropped by the house to pay their condolences, but by nightfall they were gone and he was alone. Libby hadn't come and this was a source of deep regret. He wandered through the house but felt nothing more than deep depression. Other than the furniture, nothing remained to remind him of Grady. His books, fishing tackle and hunting gear, treasured photographs, civic awards and trophies had all been removed. It was as though Grady had never existed in this house where he had been born; that Jenny had lived her life here alone. In her room, her clothing hung in the wardrobe, her comb and brush and other personal articles were on the bureau, her father's Bible on the nightstand beside the bed.

He went downstairs to the kitchen to prepare something to eat, and found eggs and bacon in the refrigerator, the least difficult to prepare. Jenny had never drunk coffee in her entire life and he found none there now. He disliked tea, and the milk had turned sour. After the meal, he washed it down with water and decided to go to bed and catch the early bus to Washington after calling on Eli again to ask him to dispose of whatever would be in the way of the new tenant. Partially undressed, he heard the doorbell ring. He rebuttoned his shirt, went down to the door, and found Barney Newell there, alone.

"Can I come in, Steve?"

"Of course, Mr. Newell."

Seated in the gloom of the ill-lighted living room, Barney puffed a fresh cigar into life and said, "Steve, just thought I'd drop in to ask what your plans are. Don't take offense, son. Grady and I were close friends all our lives. I've known you since the day you were born . . ."

"No offense taken, Mr. Newell." Barney settled down more comfortably in his chair and waited. "I'm planning to leave for New York in the morning, to go back to school."

"You'll be graduating in June. What then?"

"I'm hoping to get a job in New York."

"You want to live up there, make your life there?"

"If I get the job I want, yes."

"You wouldn't consider coming back here?"

"I don't think so, sir. There's nothing to come back to."

"You mean the paper, don't you. Well, there are other

jobs, you know, but if you want one on the *Star,* I'll be glad to talk with Paul Marcus. He's a fine gentleman and indebted to me . . ."

"I wouldn't want it that way, Mr. Newell. It wouldn't be the same."

"I know, Steve, but like I said, there are other things, even better than the paper."

"Such as?"

"Well, politics, for one thing. People here know you, like you. Your name would be a big asset. With a little help, you could go a long way in a short time. Richmond, Washington, someday even the United States Senate. The people I know in the right places, Olive's connections . . ."

"I'm afraid I couldn't make it in politics, Mr. Newell. I haven't the feel or desire for it, or the drive it takes"—

"All right, Steve, maybe politics isn't for everybody, but I'm dealing with some big people in industry, trying to convince them to locate in Lancaster. I'm sure I could . . ."

"Mr. Newell," Steve said, "I've got definite plans for my future and I can't see that any job here would help me reach my goal. That's something I've got to work out on my own."

Barney stirred restlessly. "Well, then, there's something else. I'd hoped I wouldn't have to bring it up, but you're forcing me."

"What?" Steve said, knowing exactly the new turn this discussion would take, and showing his own discomfort.

"Libby," Barney said simply. Then, "I don't know what happened between you in New York last summer. Libby wouldn't talk about it to Olive or me, but we know that whatever it was, it hit her hard. I'd like to try to straighten that out, if I can. Steve, she's our daughter, our only child with Marshall gone. What can I do to bring you together again? You're turning down the help I want to give you as far as a job is concerned. Is it money?"

Embarrassment turned to resentment. "It isn't a job and it isn't money," he said with rising anger. "It's just that Libby made the same suggestion you've been making, that I come back to Lancaster where you could use your influence and money to help me. Us. I don't want that kind of help, Mr. Newell, not yours, or Mrs. Newell's. I want to do what I've got to do on my own. If Libby can't understand that, there's nothing to be done about it."

"Don't be too sure, Steve. I'm sure she loves you. Do you love her?"

He had known Barney to be a forthright, outspoken man, and the bluntness of the question did not surprise him, although it left him speechless for the moment. "Do you?" Barney asked again.

"I don't know, Mr. Newell. I thought I did. I was sure last summer, but I don't know now. I think that if we loved each other I would be talking this over with Libby, not with her father."

"Don't get any wrong ideas, Steve. Libby doesn't know I'm here with you. She'd raise the roof if she knew or suspected. I'm doing this on my own because I want my daughter to be happy, no matter what it costs. If you're what it takes, I want that for her."

"I'm sorry. I don't know what to add to what I've already said."

"Steve, she's here in Lancaster. You're here. Go see her. Talk to her and give it a chance. For myself, I don't beg anything from anybody, but for Libby . . ."

Steve remembered back to the Sidney Lanier graduation dance. It had been Olive then, it was Barney now, running interference for Libby. What would it be like if he and Libby were married, living in Lancaster? How big a part would Olive and Barney play in their lives, their privacy, choice of home, furniture, cars, children, their entire future? For Libby, they would turn the world upside down. His world. His life.

"I'm sorry, Mr. Newell," he said finally.

Barney stood up slowly, his face flushed. "Steve . . ." he began, then turned slowly and walked heavily out of the room. Steve heard the front door close and knew that a curtain had been drawn over an important part of his life.

Chapter 3

1

When Steve Gilman reported to Frank Kelso on the morning in June that followed his graduation from Columbia, the climate was hardly as cheerful as it had been on his two previous visits to the Leary agency. Or as pleasant.

Kelso, head of Personnel, was a dour, cadaverous man of about fifty, who gave off all the warmth of an empty, abandoned refrigerator. Steve was required to fill out a formal application, giving the usual vital statistics, social security number (which he would obtain later), educational attainments, marital, draft, and health status, next of kin (he wrote Eli Tinsley's name in that block, assigning the fictitious title "Uncle" to him), experience, under which he listed the Lancaster *Star* and *Herald-Tribune* (the latter with two fingers crossed).

He listened as Kelso's rasping voice droned on, outlining employee benefits such as paid vacations (when he would become eligible); health, accident, and medical insurance; and the firm's retirement plan (also when eligible). There were certain rules of conduct to which he must adhere; rules when dealing with the Almighty Client (if he ever reached that level of competence), rules concerning vendors of time and space, chains of command to follow, gifts he must refuse from all vendors; punctuality, the requirement of all new employees to attend training classes, and many more do's and don'ts to remember.

The session came to an end when Mr. Kelso handed Steve a booklet that covered each subject in more explicit detail. He was then turned over to an attractive young Negro girl who took him on a brief tour of the agency to familiarize him with its physical layout, while giving him a quick history of its birth and growth. From the executive area on the thirty-fifth floor, which housed the agency's ranking administrators, account supervisors, and staffs, through the thirty-fourth floor and the working divisions:

from Copy, Art, Production, Media, Marketing and Merchandising Research, and Television-Radio, into Reception, then along a wide corridor of offices occupied by the agency's account executives, each with its outer office for a secretary, and more offices for the staffs under their control. He saw more attractive females during that tour than he had noticed in all of New York during his four years at Columbia.

"Some of our account executives, particularly those assigned to our largest accounts," the young messenger-guide explained, "work in groups, or teams, so they are quartered apart from the others. For instance, Goody Food Products, Lovell Cosmetics and Chevalier Cigarettes operate almost as independent agencies within the Leary Agency—"

"Why?" Steve asked.

"Why? For efficiency, of course. The people on those accounts work very closely together, art directors with copywriters, account representatives with account executives. When they need additional help for a sudden increase in activity, the group head calls on the executive creative director or art director for more manpower. It takes some getting used to your first time around, but you'll get onto it pretty soon." She smiled, and added, "There's still a lot I don't know about it, but you'll catch on."

"I hope so," Steve breathed prayerfully.

He was assigned to an anonymous cubbyhole among many similar cubbyholes that reminded him of cells. It contained a small desk that took up the full width of the room and faced a window that looked out upon a brick wall. There was a table along the right wall that held an ancient typewriter. There was a wastebasket, a chair, and a coatrack. There were some shelves over the desk and along the left wall, but these were empty. In the desk were several type books and a few paper samples. On the wall over the typewriter table, a previous tenant had neatly lettered the legend:

TOO MUCH KNOWLEDGE OF THE CLIENT'S PRODUCT IS DANGEROUS

and beneath that:

BE WISE, BE KIND, BE FAIR (BEJESUS)

On the left wall was a bumper sticker which had originally read:

WE SHALL OVERCOME

but had been altered to now read:

I AM OVERCOME

It was obvious that no client ever saw this section of the agency.

"This is all mine?" he asked facetiously.

"All yours. For the time being. Until somebody notices you're working here," the girl replied.

"Ah, luxury," he sighed. "What do I do in the meantime?"

"Somebody will come by pretty soon and fill you in," she replied. "Good luck."

"Thank you. What is your name?"

"Letitia Anderson. Most people call me Tish."

"Thanks again, Tish. My name is Steve. Steve Gilman."

"I know," Tish smiled. "I hope you make it, Steve."

That parting shot, however friendly and well-intentioned, sounded ominous. Steve readily assumed that many before him had not made it, including the occupant of this very stall, who had been overcome. An hour later, as he sat at the sterile desk riffling through the *Employees' Manual* given him by Mr. Kelso, a voice like a bear's growl startled him awake. "Hey, you Gilman? I'm Chuck Baldasarian."

"Hello. How are you?" It almost came out as *Who are you?*

"Off your ass and on your feet, man. I'm supposed to fill you in on something called Departmental Indoctrination. A fancy title for a crock of shit."

So, self-consciously, began the career of Steven Gilman in the world of Advertising.

Departmental Indoctrination was no more than a closer look into those areas that came under Wade Barrett's supervision, labeled "Barrettsville" by Baldasarian, and including the Chevalier Cigarette and Goody Food Products accounts, with vague explanations of what the personnel in those departments were doing—or supposed to be doing. The tour was hardly enlightening and only contributed a greater sense of confusion to Steve's already clouded and perplexed mind. Baldasarian introduced him to several art directors and copywriters who were then engaged in nothing more important than taking coffee and cigarette breaks, exchanging pleasantries, or involved in working bull sessions. None showed the slightest interest in Baldasarian or the too obviously new trainee he had in tow.

During that brief tour Steve learned that Chuck had been with the Leary Agency for fifteen months, the first four spent in the mailroom, the next six in Production, and the last five in the art directors' bullpen working on various small accounts. His ambition, clearly stated, was to become creative group head on a major account, and some day take over as the agency's creative director.

His name was Charles, he hated Charlie, and preferred the breezier, less formal Chuck. By his own account, he had been an outstanding sophomore quarterback at Purdue, but late in the season received a knee injury that ended what might have become a brilliant future as a pro, and cut his college career short. (Again, Chuck's version.)

In those two guided hours, Steve learned much more about Chuck and little about the Leary Agency, except how to get around various rules, certain upper-echelon excutives to whom he must cater, those to avoid, "and keep your eyes on this sonofabitch" pointing to a door plaque that read:

NORTON AXELROD
Assistant Controller

"he's the hatchet-man in this joint. The Axe. If you get a call to come to his office, start packing your stuff because that'll be your last day here."

With growing distaste, Steve observed Baldasarian's gregarious, and patronizing behavior, as well as the oversized chip he carried on his shoulder. He was ingratiating toward the senior creative members they encountered, offensively pompous and rude to those of lesser stature, to whom he referred with contempt as "fucking civilians." He swaggered, and boasted, was profane and vulgar, and pointed out various girls with whom he had allegedly "scored." Steve felt a deep sense of relief when the tour was over, and an even greater comfort later when Chuck was suddenly reassigned from Barrettsville to the Lovell Cosmetics account as a junior art director. That he could hold *any* position of worth in the agency was a never-ending puzzle to Steve.

He saw nothing of Keith Allard or Wade Barrett during the next two weeks. After his "operational tour" it came as a surprise that one of Baldasarian's early predictions had failed to materialize. He was not assigned to the mail room. Nor was he given a special assignment, no opportunity to knit words into fanciful, pithy, eye-catching phrases, or arresting headlines that would light up the sky and start a rush of money-bearing consumers toward the nation's stores to buy up the merchandise he was hustling for Leary clients; no brilliant or witty paragraphs for which the print media and readers of America waited with bated breath.

Instead, he was given a chair at a long table in the agency's library, where he began to study the organizational and structural makeup of Leary, familiarizing himself with the agency's history, its accounts, and the men who controlled and serviced them. It came as a complete surprise to him that Leary supported a branch office in Chicago, and another in Los Angeles, each responsible for its own clients while indirectly servicing the accounts of the other branches when applicable.

Indoctrination also included interdepartmental tours to learn how work was initiated and passed on to the next pair of hands until it reached its ultimate agency goal—Production—where he would begin his practical training. There were night lectures twice each week, conducted by various department heads; Ethan Loomis, Production; Alexis Kent, Executive Art Director; Martin Elias, Norman Adrian and Sam Chase, Copy. There were talks by Account Supervisors Wade Barrett, Ian Wilcox, and Roger Meade, and by various account executives and their assistants, each discussing his particular specialties, duties, and relationships with the client. Frequently, network, newspaper, magazine, and other specialists with whom Leary dealt were invited to lecture.

During those first weeks, Steve took brief side-trips to a broadcasting studio, a printing plant, newspaper and magazine offices, an engraving plant, a composition house, and an organization that produced television commercials. Back in his own cubbyhole, he skimmed over endless pages of new and unheard-of type faces, only a few familiar from the sparse type cases and linotype magazines in the composing room of the *Star;* dozens of sizes in each face; light, medium, bold, heavy, extra-bold, extra-wide, italics, and phototype.

Paper samples, he learned, came in 14-, 16-, 18-, 20-, and 24-pound weights, meaning that amount of weight to a ream of five hundred sheets. Wondering, unwilling to ask, *What about 15-, 17- and 19-pound papers?* There were plain bond, rag bond, book, newsprint, litho, sulphite, and enamel papers, that were uncoated, coated one-side, coated two-sides, deckle-edged, and God only knew what the hell else.

Lithography, multilith, letterpress, silkscreen, etcetera, etcetera, etcetera. In the Art Department, he was introduced to line and wash drawings, pencil, stipple, scratchboard, crayon, water colors, oils, pastels, and charcoal; and their reproductions in line, halftone, halftone with dropouts (there, too?), combination line and Ben Day, four color process, and for God's sweet sake, where would it all end? And when, if ever?

And finally, to his immense delight and relief, and to the utter disgust of Chuck Baldasarian ("That punk! I broke him in, for Christ's sake!") and envy of his fellow trainees, his first tryout on a live account. Solo flying, man. Sweating it out, preparing himself mentally.

He sat in his cubicle staring at the typewriter, that ancient, venal piece of equipment loaned to him for the purpose of producing words. Not just *words*, but salable copy. Wondering how he could write about a product of which he knew absolutely nothing; how it was made, designed, or put together.

Strange and weird thoughts assailed his mind while the blank sheet of paper in his machine stared back at him. How to start? Where? He conjured up—of all things—a cellulose sponge, although this was not related to the product with which he was concerned. Did it grow? How was it fertilized, harvested, formed, and packaged? Take whiskey. How does a copy writer write about whiskey? By the amount he has consumed? What makes TWA a better or safer plane to fly than United, Eastern, American, when most major airlines buy planes from the same source, Boeing, Douglas, etcetera, and are under regulations that require the utmost in maintenance and care? So safety is out as a gimmick. Fares are the same. Okay, let's sell the food, the girls. Sell smiles. Don't talk about delays, loused-up schedules, your arrival in L.A. while your baggage flies on to Hawaii, or Tokyo. *Ac-cen-tuate the posi-*

tive. Eelim-in-ate the negative. Don't screw around with In-between.

Start *some*where. Anywhere.

He began writing. One word, two words, then a flow of words. Shearing, pruning, polishing a single paragraph until every one of the fifty-seven words gleamed and glittered, knowing it was right. Right, hell, it was perfect!

He knew, of course, that the assignment was a test. The copy was neither for GFP, Lovell, or Chevalier. Nor for Wade Barrett. Like a minor league baseball player, he had been farmed out to Rita Mannion, senior writer on the Prestige Fashions account, which was handled by Sam Abrams. Steve rechecked and retyped those fifty-seven words half a dozen times without finding any means to improve upon them, then typed the final draft, unwilling to trust this precious child of his brain to the typing pool. He clipped it to the layout, walked it around to Mrs. Mannion's office, and left it with Abrams's secretary.

Back in his cubbyhole, he waited, going over rough notes he had taken while touring the Television-Radio department, checking notes on storyboards, I.D.'s, sixties, thirties, zooms, answer prints, pans, dollies, interlocks, voice overs, tight c.u.'s, b.g.'s, medium shots, long shots, all so strange and mysterious to Steve, so uncomplicated and clear to everyone else. And he waited.

Two days later, the call came from Sam Abrams's secretary. Entering Sam's office, he found Keith there with Abrams, seeing him for the first time since that second meeting, when he had been hired. The offending layout and his copy lay on the desk blotter in front of Sam.

"Come in, kid," Sam said. "Sit down." Indicating a chair with a daggerlike finger, his expression giving nothing away. Allard was calmly tamping his pipe, lighting it, sucking on the stem to bring it alive.

"Ah—hello, Steve. Nice to see you again," Allard said. Sam picked up the copy and handed it to Allard, who scarcely glanced at it. "I dropped in to visit with Sam and he showed me this." He sucked at his pipe again, and relighted it. Belching smoke. "Ah-h. This copy for Prestige. Clever phrasing. Catchy headline. The whole thing reads very smoothly." He glanced at the copy sheet again, then looked back to Steve. "Unfortunately, it doesn't sell anything."

Steve blinked and swallowed hard, thinking, *I've blown it. I'm dead.*

Sam Abrams looked on with patient tolerance. Allard smiled softly and said, "You've hit the product fairly well, but you've missed your audience by a country mile. What this needs is a different dimension. It lacks credibility." When Steve sat in silence, "The thing you've got to ask yourself every time you sit down at your typewriter is, *Who am I trying to reach? Who is going to read this piece of copy?*"

What Steve asked himself was, *Where did I miss?*

"This ad," Allard continued, "is part of a clothing manufacturer's kit used to guide department stores and specialty shops in writing *their* ads for *their* prospective customers. If we come up with a direct hit, they will use the ad as we reproduce it in the kit. What you've written here is an excellent hundred-twenty-five-dollar ad for an eighteen-dollar-and-ninety-five cent buyer."

At once, it became clear to Steve where he had gone astray.

"Steve," Allard went on, "advertising is full of bright, clever young men and women, but they're of little use when they start chasing rainbows instead of customers. This is a tough, competitive business we're in, not a rest home for dreamers. You've got to study, learn, and know your product and market before you put your first word down on paper. If you're ever in doubt, ask. Never guess."

"Yes, sir," Steve said, mollified. "May I take another crack at this one?"

"Of course. That's why you're here discussing it."

He went back to the library and studied the past advertisements of Prestige, reluctant to check back with Mrs. Mannion. He worked and bled for hours to find what Allard had urged him to find—his audience—the target. There was no comment on his second effort, and Steve took tremendous pride some time later when he saw that very ad included in the Prestige Fashions Ad Book, his first professional effort, and still later, seeing it incorporated into ads bearing more than a dozen different signatures of department stores and dress shops around the country. It became the first clipping for his "book."

He began working on various spot assignments in the same manner; a trial piece for Chevalier, a shot at a dealer broadside for GFP, a wispy, fanciful piece for a

Carribean Cruise folder, a shot at a billboard slogan for Norwood Distillers. Only three of a dozen of his efforts were accepted and only after he had had to revise them. He managed a three-base hit when Lovell was in need of a name for a new suntan lotion and he submitted two: SurfTAN and SwifTAN, which threw Ian Wilcox into a veritable dilemma because he liked both and couldn't make up his mind which one to use. Chuck Baldasarian, then one of the Lovell art directors, sat in on that meeting and it was through his persuasion that the latter name was chosen. From that moment, the word began to spread that Chuck had coined the name, and Steve never refuted his claim.

In time, Steve was permitted to participate in certain account discussions, sitting quietly in the background absorbing information on upcoming projects and presentations, budgets, media selection, merchandising programs, and promotion plans. He listened to the barrage of what at first sounded like double talk between copy men and art directors, between group heads and account executives. He heard ideas hurled across conference tables and desks, tasted, digested, regurgitated, and discarded. There were wild suggestions that might have come from outer space and rational ideas proposed after much deliberation, and he saw them replaced by new suggestions within seconds; but not without much wrangling, shouting, arguing, bickering, even cursing; much like a contest between *them* and *us*: the men who knew what they wanted, versus the account rep or exec who knew—or felt he knew—what The Client needed. Sparring, compromising, holding out for strong, effective emphasis; hard sell versus soft sell; and finally coming to understand that much of what he heard was guesswork. Guesswork based on previous experience. Which Steve, at this time, lacked.

Admitted to a client-agency conference as an observer, he heard Smith Parnell, advertising director for AmerChem Products read off a list of names the agency had submitted for a new detergent.

"Come on, fellows, you know you can do better than this," Smith complained with a tinge of scorn edging his voice. "I want a name that shouts out loud, a good, zingy name with some zip in it."

And in a subsequent meeting about a week later, Steve heard Mike Drew, a copywriter, suggest blandly, "Smitty, how about ZIP for that new detergent?" stopping Parnell in his tracks.

"Perfect!" he exclaimed. "Perfect! I knew you could come up with something better. All you've got to do is put your minds to it."

As in most agencies, there were the "Leary Legends," stories of those who had served their time and gone on to other agencies to create more legends, or out of the business before Steve's arrival. Some few remained as living evidence of their fame or notoriety.

The creative element lived in a strange and different world and were often referred to by the more conservative, noncreative staff members as the "crazies"; while they, in turn, were referred to as "those goddamned stupid civilians," generally with mild contempt. Frequently, when a "civilian" crossed swords with a "crazy" by venturing an adverse opinion toward the "crazy's" creative effort, a conflagration could be expected. As in the case of Harry Penn, an art director with less than three months tenure, and Gene Ardleigh, an account executive with eight years behind him.

Ardleigh came into Penn's cubicle one day and stood watching as Harry Penn finished off a full page newspaper ad for Chum Pet Foods. Ardleigh's presence as a voyeur caused Penn's temperature to rise considerably, but when the account exec picked up a soft lead pencil and struck out a word in the headline, Penn leaped up, grabbed a pair of scissors and stabbed Ardleigh's hand, inflicting a small wound. Penn then chased the alarmed account exec down the hall, screaming, "You sonofabitch! You ever make a mark on a layout of mine again, I'll cut your goddamned heart out!"

Ardleigh ran down the stairs to the sixteenth floor before he felt safe enough to take an elevator the rest of the way down. He went home and refused to return until he was assured that Harry Penn had been fired.

There were other similar moments of excitement from time to time that built up an unhealthy respect for, or outright fear of, the crazies by the civilians, who treaded softly and gave them a wide berth. There was six-foot-four George Dennison who, in heated debate with his five-foot-six account executive, suddenly got bored with the argument, picked the little man up, and carried him to the window with the stated intention of dropping him thirty-four floors to the pavement. Frustrated in the attempt by other members of the copy-art conference, Dennison picked up a letter opener and viciously scarred the polished surface of the long, oval table, then returned to his office and completely wrecked it.

Jerry Finney was a copywriter who would argue a point only so long with an account man, then stuff all available pertinent data and worksheets into a briefcase, check into a hotel and complete the job there, and in *his* way—which generally proved to be the best way.

Al Wordsmith, another copywriter (what else, with that name), possessed the most marvelous vocabulary of foul, obscene words, many of his own invention, but could produce beautiful copy that would have won awards from the PTA or Legion of Decency. Al, of course, was seldom permitted within artillery range of a client.

Wally Greenrich, who hated all clients as well as the account men who represented them, had been in analysis for three years. One day during a copy-art conference, while the account man was reviewing plans for an upcoming campaign of major importance, Wally grabbed the account exec's briefcase, which was filled with precise notes, and dumped it out of the thirty-fourth floor window. Wally, however, couldn't be fired, for the simple reason that the client was thoroughly sold on his copy style.

On the eve of a most important policy meeting of the Agency Plans Board, Obie Caltrop and several of his colleagues from Production, removed every fluorescent tube and light bulb from the thirty-fifth floor while the Board was out for a premeeting dinner. The meeting was canceled because the records to be discussed were in the files on the darkened thirty-fifth floor and all the file-cabinet locks had been jammed.

Charlie Mellinger, a Miyazaki copywriter, refused to use a typewriter because once, in anger, he attacked it with his fists and broke three fingers. From that day on he sat in his own private barber chair with a drawing board in his lap, and wrote all his copy with a pencil.

Gil Berends, a meek and calm Nagana Camera art director, never argued with anyone. He worked off his frustrations by phoning a particular adversary's secretary, leaving astonishing messages for him, using his considerable talent as a mimic to disguise his voice. Among his favorites, "This is Joe Bladgett. Tell Mr. Axelrod the abortionist he used last time had to blow town, but if he wants the address of a new one, to call me back."

Or, "This is Mr. Jensen's Happy Time Service. The call girl he had last Tuesday can't make it for four o'clock today. If he can get away at 2:30 today, okay, otherwise he can have one of the others. Tell him to call me back."

Or "This is Lieutenant Dickerson, Seventeenth Precinct. When Mr. Melnick was released on bail last night, he forgot to claim his personal belongings from the Property Officer, he was in such a hurry. . . ."

Eventually, Gil's secretary, who despised him, sent an anonymous note to Mr. Axelrod, who invited Gil up to the thirty-fourth floor for a chat. Exit Gil Berends.

Almost anything within reason was permitted as long as The Client was protected. Outright murder, understandably, was frowned upon.

There were, among the two-hundred-twenty-four Leary employees, several men who maintained offices and secretaries on the Executive Floor, and whose positions and duties were almost as anonymous as the men themselves. At any given moment, James Fanning, Hartwell Woodward or Andre Chalfonte might appear suddenly, and without invitation, at an art-copy conference, a preview showing of Television commercials, a discussion concerning an important campaign, or they might drop in on an agency-client conference in progress. No one ever questioned their right to be present and, generally, they offered little more than their presence. To some agency personnel, this could be unnerving; to others, more experienced, it was a test of personal courage. It was generally assumed that these somewhat mysterious gentlemen controlled certain valuable accounts by family, social, or political contact, knew little or nothing about advertising *per se,* and happily collected their weekly salaries as long as the client remained content.

Least mysterious among them was Norton Axelrod, who held the title of assistant controller and who was held variously in awe or fear by executives and subordinates alike. Privately wealthy, coldly urbane, evilly suave, Axelrod was known as The Axe, The Chopper, or the Hit Man. A summons to visit with Mr. Axelrod for a chat invariably meant dismissal. The merest hint from an account supervisor or department head, of dissatisfaction with an account executive, copywriter, art director, secretary, or clerk, and Norton Axelrod virtually leaped at the opportunity to display his special ability with finesse and fervor. It was a task that Bill Leary abhorred, but one that Axelrod relished. Very often, a telephone message to appear in his office at a certain time, usually near the closing hour, was ignored; the victim in question would merely go directly to the personnel ofice, submit his resignation, collect his severance pay, and clear out, thus eliminating the embarrassment of verbal dismissal.

Steve worked very hard. He listened, absorbed, and sweated, but there was always so much to learn. He read with a voracious appetite, studied current advertising journals, as well as every newspaper, magazine, and trade paper he could lay his hands on. He discovered, by this means, how to differentiate between good taste and bad. He wrote secretly in his room at night, then destroyed those infantile efforts almost at once, chagrined by his lack of skill and technique in translating informative notes into acceptable, publishable copy.

He learned what he accepted as The Truths:

Advertising creates Desire.
Desire creates Sales.
Sales create increased Production.
Production creates Jobs.
Jobs create Purchasing Power.
Purchasing Power creates Economic Strength.
Economic Strength creates National and World Power.

Ergo, *Advertising is the savior of Natonal Economy, Strength and Power.*

This, then, became the Image, the official portrait of Advertising. It supported the nation's newspapers, magazines, printing establishments, radio and television-broadcast networks, and stations, and paper mills. It created tens of thousands of jobs in many subsidiary industries apart from the advertising profession.

It also supported the Wm. B. Leary Advertising Agency.

2

He saw Wade Barrett and Keith Allard only occasionally, now approaching the end of his probationary period with a feeling of mild apprehension and without any true indication of how his contributions to a meager scattering of accounts had been received. Other than that his work was being well received and the rejections were fewer, he had no way of knowing what reports were being sent back to Barrett and Allard; yet both men, in passing, were pleasant and friendly in greetings and manner.

About ten days before Christmas, Vanessa Enright, Barrett's secretary, stopped Steve in the hallway between Art and Production and said, "I have a note on my desk to call you, Steve. Mr. Barrett would like to see you in his office this afternoon at 4:30."

"I'll be there," Steve replied and at once began wondering how his Christmas holiday would be spent; joyously on GFP, Chevalier, or Lovell—even a lesser account—or making the rounds of employment agencies in search of a new job. But Wade Barrett's warm smile gave him comfort and confidence.

"Sit down, Steve. Sorry I haven't had much time to spend with you lately. Your name came up in a discussion I was having with Keith Allard at lunch the other day and I think we ought to get this thing settled now."

What thing? Steve lighted a cigarette and waited.

"I've been getting some very favorable comments about you and your work," Barrett continued, "and what brings this about was a request Keith got from Ian Wilcox on Lovell and another from Rita Mannion on Prestige. I think both would be happy to have you working for them on a permanent basis. Also, Norm Adrian hinted to me he'd like to have you on Chevalier."

Steve flushed with pleasure. "That's very gratifying and I'm flattered, Mr. Barrett. I—uh—don't think I've really contributed very much to any of those accounts."

Barrett smiled slowly. "Steve, let me give you a piece of unasked-for advice. Copywriters and advertising artists are the forgotten men in our profession. Unlike authors, or fine-arts painters, they're the anonymous people of the creative world. They write their hearts out, design, draw, paint, and are known only within their own craft, so when you receive praise for your achievements, accept it, even boast about it graciously. Apart from a promotion or raise, that may be the only recognition you'll ever get until you retire and write your memoirs." That speech, to Steve, was a reward in itself, and full confidence was restored. Barrett said, "How do you like us, Steve?"

"Sir?"

"Working here at Leary."

"Oh, great. Wonderful, Mr. Barrett."

"Then as of now, your probationary period is over. Congratualtions, and with that, your salary will be increased as of your next pay check."

"Thank you, sir. I appreciate that very much."

"While we're at it, let's come to a decision. Among Lovell, Prestige and Chevalier, which would you choose if that choice were yours to make?"

Without hesitation, Steve said, "Chevalier, with Norm Adrian."

Barrett nodded, pleased. "Good choice. Adrian is one of the best creative copy men in the business. Let me think about it."

In mid-January, Steve moved from his cubbyhole into the section set apart for the Chevalier Cigarette group. As the most recent addition to the team, he felt the aloneness and insecurity of the novitiate among professionals, like a medical student checking in for his first day as a hospital intern. He reported promptly at nine o'clock that morning and sat cooling his heels in Vanessa Enright's office until Barrett arrived at a quarter past ten. "Oh, Steve, glad to have you aboard. Sorry I'm late, got held up by Hugh Benson on my way in. Let's see, suppose I take you around to meet Ted McCreery before we turn you over to Adrian."

Walking along the corridor to McCreery's office, he felt much as he had some six months earlier when he had first called on Barrett; dry-mouthed, a curious tightness across his chest, his muscles like steel bands about to snap with strain. He had seen McCreery several times—an aloof man at best—but had never been introduced or spoken to him. McCreery was busy on the phone when his secretary showed them in. At his desk, McCreery was the epitome of what Steve had come to believe an account executive should look like; about twenty-eight or twenty-nine, not quite as tall as Steve, sandy-haired, brown-eyed, smartly dressed from shirt collar to alligator loafers, with nails meticulously manicured. His voice was strong and self-assured on the phone as he casually waved Barrett into the empty visitor's chair and totally ignored Steve. His desk was almost entirely covered with four full-page magazine layouts, a number of separate color proofs of art and type, and progressive color proofs of the artwork alone.

As he spoke with a peculiar tone of irritation, his brown eyes flashed with indignation and Steve remembered a remark Chuck Baldasarian had made about account executives in general one day when the subject of their relationship with the client came up. "Account execs," he said, "hell, you can recognize one the minute you see him. They've all got brown eyes."

Steve knew the remark called for a *why*. "Why?" he asked, playing straight man.

Chuck grinned and drew a finger across his forehead. "Because they're all full of shit up to here."

McCreery concluded his conversation with, "Okay, then, Eth, send somebody in here to pick these up. I'm not going to show them until I've got complete proofs. I've told you people a hundred times that Benson won't okay partials or pasteups. For Christ's sake, get your people on the goddamned ball, will you?"

On introduction, Steve could feel McCreery's eyes examining him carefully, slowly, as though he had forgotten to zip up his fly. After the first brief amenities, McCreery smiled flintily and said, "Well, Gilman, do you think you can fit into the slot?"

"I hope I can," Steve replied. "I'll certainly give it my very best effort."

"That will help. Do you smoke?"

"Why—yes."

"Which brand?"

"Chevaliers." Almost expecting to be asked to produce proof, Steve unconsciously began reaching for his inside left breast pocket. "At least," McCreery said snidely, "you've learned that much." Abruptly, he turned to Barrett. "Wade, I'm due over at Benson's office. I'll have to stall him until I get complete proofs on these ads. Would you mind turning Gilman over to Adrian?"

"Not at all, Ted. Come along, Steve."

As they walked the few yards to the stairs and down to the thirty-fourth floor, Barrett said, "Ted can be a little short at times, but he's great with Benson, Chev's ad director, and the Gilmore people. On the q.t., his uncle, Jim Dandridge, is chairman of the board."

Which explained matters more clearly and acted as a mild warning that Ted McCreery would be the man to please.

Norm Adrian, who headed the Chevalier creative group, appeared to be in his late forties, a large bear of a man who reminded Steve of the photograph of Heywood Broun which had hung on the wall in Grady's cluttered office among his collection of favorite newspaper personalities. He was a shirt-sleeve worker with thick, hairy arms and the shoulders of a wrestler. His reddish brown hair was unruly, with collar opened at the throat and tie pulled down several inches, the complete opposite of McCreery in appearance. He sat hunched over the desk examining a large, impressive chart that resembled the logistic plan for an army about to embark on maneuvers, with lines and arrows running from one box to another.

"Norm," Barrett said, "you know Steve Gilman, don't you?"

Adrian looked up and smiled. "Of course, Wade. I asked to have him assigned to Chevalier, remember?" And to Steve, "Glad to see we made it. Ready to join our happy little family?"

"If you're willing to put up with me," Steve said.

"Fine. I'm up to my ass with this evaluation analysis chart from Hugh Benson's office which Marketing sent to Ted, who bucked it down to me because nobody can understand the damned thing, or what it's for, but somebody expects an answer of some kind."

Barett laughed and said, "Give it to me, Norm. I'll either figure it out or lose it somewhere. It doesn't belong here, anyway. Forget it and get acquainted with Steve."

"Thanks, Wade. And tell Ted to stop loading us up with these corporate brainstorms so we can get our work out."

Barrett picked up the elaborate chart and said, "Good luck, Steve. I leave you in good hands," and went out.

Adrian laughed. "That McCreery. Anything his bird brain can't understand, he sends to me marked 'For immediate attention and action.' Well, with that off my hands"—he stood up, rolled his sleeves down and picked up his jacket. "Come along and let's have some lunch. We'll do better in less formal surroundings, if you can call this formal."

By the time they returned, Steve had a fair knowledge of the parent Gilmore organization—as well as that of its subsidiary, Chevalier Cigarettes—and the names of those with whom the agency was primarily concerned: Hugh Benson, director of advertising; Glenn Chamberlain, president of Chevalier; and the corps of men and women in the client's advertising department on Fifth Avenue.

He met Sandy Gerson, Adrian's secretary, the three copywriters, two art directors, a television and radio producer, production liaison man, typists, clerks, and a messenger-trainee who labored solely for the benefit of Chevalier. Over coffee later, Adrian said, "Well, Steve, what do you think?"

"As of right now, I'm overwhelmed with what I've seen, and the professionalism of the people I've met, but I want the chance very much, Mr. Adrian."

"It's Norm, Steve, and you'll get your chance. In a little while you'll feel more at home, get to know our people better, but for starters, you'll be doing chore work, filling in here and there, a little bit of everything as called for. We operate on a team basis with this account. A copy man and art director working on an assignment together makes a hell of a lot more sense than working separately, then trying to fit the work of one to that of the other. The communication between them cuts down on the rivalry and helps both. You'll catch on quickly."

During the following six months, Adrian's prediction came true, although Steve had the idea that the big creative head was sparing him, shielding him from Ted McCreery's occasional intemperate outbursts; yet he felt he had become a fully accepted member of the group as he began working with Noel Barrano, a talented young art director who was almost as new at the agency as himself.

McCreery never came down from his lofty suite to the operating area and other than an infrequent conference with Adrian, which always took place in McCreery's office, communication was generally limited to written memos or verbal messages delivered by messenger. It hadn't taken long for Steve to learn that a deep-seated animosity existed between Adrian and McCreery.

Norm had, after brief excursions with several other agencies, been tapped by Keith Allard when the Chevalier account first came to Leary, which gave Adrian considerable seniority leverage over McCreery. He was forty-six, Steve learned, the father of a son and daughter.

McCreery, at the time he joined Leary, was twenty-six. On graduating from Dartmouth, he had gone to work for the Gilmore Corporation, of which his uncle, James P. Dandridge, was chief executive. After a year, Ted was moved into the Chevalier Cigarette division's advertising department as Hugh Benson's assistant at a salary of $11,500, the top figure the job called for. A year later, at a time when the account was up for contract renewal, Hugh Benson suggested to Bill Leary that Mr. Dandridge would be uncommonly pleased if Leary were to offer Ted the job of account executive on Chevalier, thus further cementing their long and pleasant relationship and, without doubt, insuring automatic renewal of the contract that was being avidly sought by competing atencies.

Bill Leary needed no large screen picture projected for him. He phoned Ted, invited him to lunch at his club and made the proposal, which Ted quickly accepted. Shortly thereafter, he moved over to the Leary Agency at $25,000 a year, with all the fringe benefits and privileges of a full-fledged account executive. The current account man, Bob Fletcher, was offered another account, which he refused, resigning to accept a position with another agency.

Until McCreery joined the Leary organization, the relationship between Fletcher, Adrian, and the rest of the group had been one of warm, friendly harmony, with Adrian the cornerstone of the team. He was a brilliant copy and idea man who could pick up a mere thread and weave it into a dream. If his nature had been other than that of a patient, satisfied laborer in the fields, he may one day have joined the ranks of the legendary figures of his profession; but Adrian had no greater ambition than to be left alone to do his job; which he did well.

So, with Fletcher's departure and McCreery's entrance, the entire complexion and character of the group changed.

From the very start, the relationship between the two top men was patently abrasive. McCreery held long, senseless conference meetings with the creative group to pass on "The Word" from client to agency, adding nothing new, different or beneficial. McCreery soon became aware of Adrian's insouciance and at one regular Monday morning meeting, stopped suddenly and said, "Norm, would you mind repeating what I just said?"

Adrian replied, "I wasn't aware that I was in a classroom, Ted, and as for your question, the answer is, I can't repeat what you said because I haven't the faintest idea what you've been talking about."

The group tensed up, waiting expectantly for what had to become a showdown of major proportions, obviously relishing the next explosion. Ted said, "Just what in hell do you think these meetings are for, an excuse to drink coffee?"

Blandly, Norm replied, "To tell you the truth, Ted, I've been trying for three months to figure out just why we have to sit here every Monday morning for an hour or so listening to a monologue we've all heard many times before. In those three months, I figure we've wasted over a hundred man-hours per man, times eight, that's about eight hundred hours that could have been put to productive use. I'll ask you the same question: Why?"

"Goddamn it, Adrian, I've been sitting here quoting some very important statistics . . ."

"I'm not interested in meaningless statistics when I've got a lot of work to do," Norm said, "but since you are, here's one for you. The Queen Mary takes five days to come from Southampton to New York. Therefore, five Queen Marys should be able to make it in one day. Think it over."

McCreery's face flamed over the involuntary giggle of Sandy Gerson. Adrian stood up and said, "Excuse me. I've got work to do," and walked out on the meeting.

The word spread through both floors of the agency like wildfire, but the expected showdown never materialized. Keith Allard heard about it. Bill Leary got it from Keith. Norton Axelrod prepared himself mentally for a confrontation with Adrian. Wade Barrett had the word passed on to him by Vanessa and waited nervously for McCreery to come bursting into his office. But McCreery, so new on the job, backed off for the moment. There were, however, no more Monday meetings called in his office.

From that day on, McCreery assuaged his damaged feelings by finding fault with every piece of copy he recognized to be Adrian's, bucking it back with memos that read, "Who wrote this piece of garbage, some eighth grade kid?" Or, "Not suitable." "Not acceptable." And, "Can't show this to HB until it's cleaned up to make sense."

Adrian bore his burden well, bucking the copy back with notations reading, "Suggest you give me a new lead to take the place of this." "Checked this out with Keith Allard. Please note his initials of approval." In time, the boil became a simmer.

A threatened newspaper strike did little to improve the

McCreery-Adrian situation. In a general staff meeting at its outset, there was a consensus that it would be settled within a week. Adrian took exception to that opinion on the basis of his belief that the publishers would prolong the strike in order to weaken the union financially and force a more favorable compromise. McCreeery strongly rejected that point of view. "The publishers can't afford to lose the advertising revenue," he stated firmly. "I doubt if the strike will even come off."

Adrian said, "The publishers can stand the loss of revenue a hell of a lot better than the employees can stand the loss of wages, or the union its dues, in a prolonged strike. This one is going to be long and dirty."

Allard broke in at that point. "Norm, if you're right, what suggestion can you offer to get around the situation?"

"Speaking only for Chevalier, I'd take our local newspaper money for the next three months, maybe four, and put it into additional papers in nearby New Jersey, Connecticut, Philly, Boston, Washington, and Baltimore. Those are the papers New Yorkers will be reading during the strike. Also, I'd shift a good deal of the money into local TV and radio spots, in and around news and sports broadcasts."

Don Bryce said, "If we're going that route, I'll have to get cracking. The stations will be programming more news coverage and a long line of time buyers will be forming."

"Ted, how about it?" Bill Leary asked.

"I'm not going to be panicked by a loose guess from one of my copywriters, Bill. I'm for standing pat."

"Liz?" Elizabeth Berton, head of Media, took a passive stand. "I'm afraid I can't second-guess this one. I've heard a lot of talk on both sides, and one seems to cancel out the other."

McCreery bounced to his feet. "Regardless, I hold to the belief that my intuition is just as reliable as that of anyone else. The strike will be over in a week, probably less. If it takes place at all."

A few others went along with Ted, but most bought Adrian's theory. And after convincing Hugh Benson, who went along with his protegé's opinion, Chevalier coasted into the strike situation totally unarmed.

That strike lasted one hundred forty days and Chevalier suffered through the period valiantly, with McCreery stubbornly refusing to move into other newspaper areas. As predicted by Bryce, additional television and radio time were almost impossible to buy. Chalk up another victory in the Adrian column.

On a later occasion, McCreery took it upon himself to add an entire paragraph of twenty-two words to a piece of Adrian's copy that was already tight and which would have necessitated scrapping the expensive full color artwork in order to accommodate the additional space required. Adrian sent the ad back untouched, adding a memo that read:

What you are asking for here is a blivet.

N.A.

to which McCreery replied, also by memo:

Please explain the meaning of the word BLIVET, *a new term to me.*

T.MCC.

And Adrian's reply:

A blivet, Mr. McC, occurs when one tries to cram five pounds of horseshit into a three-pound bag.

N.A.

A furious Ted McCreery stormed into Keith Allard's office to demand that Adrian be fired or removed from the Chevalier account.

"I can't do that, Ted," Allard said. "Adrian has been with us, and on the account, for as long as we've had it here. The fact that you don't seem able to resolve your petty differences with him makes him no less valuable to us, or to the Chevalier account. If we replace him, not only will we lose a damned good man, but Chevalier will suffer by it."

"No man is that indispensable, Keith."

"I agree, but the loss would be a hardship I don't like to think about."

"Keith, I'd hate to go over your head."

"Your privilege, Ted, and don't let me stand in your way, but I think Bill will agree with me."

"I'm not thinking of Bill Leary."

"Then I take it you're talking about your uncle, Mr. Dandridge."

"And/or Hugh Benson."

"All right, you do just that. I think we've earned sufficient leverage with Mr. Dandridge to subject ourselves to a test of strength. Be reasonable, Ted. You're young, and I understand that. What you're overlooking, perhaps, is an opportunity to learn from a man who has a lot to teach. Come down off your pedestal and give yourself that break."

"What if the account is in jeopardy?" Ted asked.

"We're not children, Ted, and I refuse to be threatened. J.P. Dandridge is not a child, either. Besides, our present contract has a long way to run. Do you want to live at war with Adrian for that long?"

Through pursed lips, McCreery said, "All right, Keith. You've made your point. Let's see what happens between now and then."

Despite the atmosphere of divisiveness, Steve progressed and grew with the account. He took his writing assignments seriously and there came a day when hardly any of his copy was being returned by Adrian for rewriting. Eventually, he found himself rewarded by learning that an ad he and Noel had created had been entered in *Advertising Daily*'s Annual Awards Show, and had taken first prize for copy and second prize for art.

Adrian and Barrett were delighted. Steve and Noel were summoned to Bill Leary's office where—in the presence of Keith Allard, Adrian, and Lex Kent, the agency's executive art director—both were presented with framed copies of their ad, with their awards included. The original artwork and complete ad were then hung in the reception room among previous award winners, with a brass plate acknowledging its authors. Ted McCreery's ungracious reaction came later. "Well, you two boys have got something to shoot at now, so don't let this go to your heads."

Steve, gaining more assurance, worked harder than ever, polishing, honing and paring his copy down to barest essentials, struggling for perfection without sacrificing the all-important message. The pressure was on him to compete with every copywriter in the group, in the agency, in the city, to hit the mark of excellence with every shot fired; a tough goal to achieve.

And one day, not too long after, he ran afoul of Ted McCreery. He had written a headline then discussed it at great length with Noel, who produced a layout to fit the theme: a young couple in a richly appointed den, the man sighting down along the barrels of an expensive shotgun, his wife looking on as she held the shotgun's twin in the crook of her arm while lighting a Chevalier. The cigarette pack lay on the table between them, prominent in the foreground.

At right center of the page were ten ruled lines to indicate the copy to come from Steve, and at the bottom, the standard signature or logotype: a pack of Chevaliers with four cigarettes extended at dissimilar lengths.

The layout before him, Steve wrote:

> The better things in life are those from which we derive our greatest pleasures—from fine, hand-tooled guns, sports cars and boats, down to the cigarettes we smoke and enjoy. Like Chevaliers. They are mild, but give you the rich, flavorful, flawless satisfaction you demand. Chevaliers cost no more, yet give so much more. They are obviously for you who enjoy the very best things in life. Try them today.

He pulled the copy sheet from the typewriter and studied those seventy words carefully, checked his type book, and decided they would fit the copy block perfectly in ten-point Bookman regular, with sufficient leading between lines to make it readable. He gave it to Noel, who read it, and handed it back with the traditional thumb and forefinger circled to signify Okay.

He dropped copy and layout in his OUT box to be picked up by the messenger and passed along to Adrian for his approval. Two days passed before he received a call from Sandy, telling him Adrian wanted to see him. "Sit down, Steve," Adrian said, and as he slid into the side chair, saw his piece of copy clipped to Noel's layout, a pink interoffice memo attached to it. He made no effort to read the upside-down message, but saw the printed heading clearly. *From the desk of* THEODORE H. MCCREERY.

"This copy," Adrian began, picking it up and placing it on top of the memo. "I like it, Steve. Ties into the headline . . . better things, also that touch . . . the guns. Beautiful. But . . ."

Steve swallowed hard, waiting for the blow to fall.

"But *el maestro* kicked it back to us."

"Mr. Benson, or Ted?"

"It hasn't left the building. Ted."

"Any comment I can go by, Norm?"

"Well, comment is something you seldom get from *el maestro*. Criticism, yes, but it's never objective. That's one of the problems here. Ted isn't a writer, so he doesn't understand writers. For that matter, he isn't a very good advertising man, but he's great on contact, and his job is to keep the client happy, which is what he does best. I'm sure Benson would pass this without objection, but Ted has to like it before he'll let Benson see it."

"May I see Ted's comments?"

Adrian grinned. "Well, Ted isn't exactly noted for his tact or diplomacy."

"I'd still like to see what he wrote."

"Okay, if you insist, but it won't help much and don't take it to heart." He pushed the memo toward Steve, who picked it up and read

Who's turning out this slush? Come on, let's get with it. We're not shooting for subway riders. Let's aim for the Cadillacs and Rolls Royces. The're our target!

T.H. MCC.

"Christ," Steve said, "Don't subway riders smoke Chevaliers? Adrian laughed. "You'll learn, Steve. The people at Gilmore like to think of Chevaliers as their big prestige brand. Benson is as big a snob as McCreery, so the snob appeal is their thing. Personally, I'd like to shoot for the mass market and move Chev up on the hit parade, but what the hell, I'm not the guy who aims the cannon.

"What probably irked Ted about this ad is the phrase, *cost no more,* which pulls Chev down to the common level."

"I can rephrase that sentence, Norm."

"Sure you can. That's what this is all about. Okay, take another shot at it. We'll hold it for a couple of days and Ted won't even remember why he killed it in the first place."

As Adrian predicted, it happened exactly that way. Ted submitted the ad to Benson with the offending phrase deleted. Benson okayed it without comment, and Steve guided it through to final production. When the color proofs came through, he saw Wade Barrett's and Ted McCreery's initials in their respective blocks, silent voices of approval. Steve kept a copy for himself to add to his growing "book" of successes.

3

Steve's salary jumped to twelve thousand five-hundred dollars and with the security of permanence consolidated he moved from his rooming house on Morningside Avenue into an unfurnished apartment on West Fifty-eighth Street, dipping into his private funds to buy good pieces of furniture he would one day move into a larger, better-located address. Moving in, arranging his new possessions with the help of friendly neighbors, the Maczeraks, and agency and outside friends, he found himself thinking more and more of Libby. Time had been of small help in trying to forget her and now he felt a desire to remember her more clearly. At work, at home, at parties, she had become a persistent wraith that hovered over his mind. As her birthday approached, he sent a card with what he believed was a properly formal sentiment, but there was no response. Nor had he really expected there would be one.

The six-month period that followed was exciting and self-rewarding. He was working well with Noel, and receiving favorable reaction and comment from Norm and Wade Barrett. Occasionally from Keith Allard. He saw McCreery only at rare briefing sessions, each one with increased dislike for the querulous man, coming to regard him with contempt as a "civilian," an errand boy between client and agency, throwing the weight of his relationship to the board chairman of Gilmore around in a most patronizing and disagreeable manner.

The work itself, the discovery of power in meaningful words, absorbed and fascinated him, writing, sensing, feeling the *drama* that poured out onto the sheet of paper in his typewriter, knowing that much of what he wrote was still superfluous, redundant, and would need to be cut severely; yet unable to stop the creative flow.

Steve had spent two evenings with the Barretts, neither enjoyable, since it was obvious that Wade was not getting along very well with Sylvia, a caustic, vinegary woman who seemed to be in no mood to entertain a lowly Leary copywriter. On another occasion he met the Barrett's daughter, Carol, who was in town for a holiday from an upstate college where she was a psychology major. Carol was nineteen, attractive and appealing, but her stay at the office was too brief for more than an exchange of introductions. More pleasant and rewarding were the two visits to Adrian's apartment for dinner, where he met Norm's wife, Lisa, and their two children; and Steve began to understand how the pressures of the day could evaporate in the happy atmosphere of the Adrian home. He had, in turn, taken Norm and Lisa to dinner and a show.

As time passed, Steve came to welcome the hood of anonymity that included him as a member of a select intellectual group and was pleased with his acceptance by his peers. He adopted the trade jargon that belonged uniquely to the advertising fraternity and soon began to speak a language that, to the outside world, could have been the code, or mystic gibberish, of a secret society.

His manner of dress was influenced as well, changing into the same quiet and unobtrusively smart styles worn by the trimly tailored account executives rather than the wild and garish accouterments affected by those he held most in awe, the creative element; he was now able to afford what pleased him by virtue of the money left him by Jenny, and the rental income from the house on Wilburn Road, occupied by an executive at the plastics plant.

As another year went by, he came to the astonishing realization that nothing about him was unusual, different or outstanding; he was a carbon copy of a thousand other young advertising men who were doing a satisfactory job. Satisfactory. No more, no less. And so the days, exhilarating and exciting at first, began to repeat themselves and became photocopies of a long string of similar days in which even the faces of those involved were not unlike. Soon, he picked up the knack of seeming to listen with interest while his mind was miles away; the ability, when asked an opinion, to come up with the correct stock phrase which might fool the uninitiated, but not another member of the advertising clique.

Steve's social activities increased. His apartment was large enough for entertaining and there were attractive people everywhere; at the Leary Agency—and others where he had made friends—in broadcasting studios and in offices. There were minor artists, writers, actors and actresses, and newspaper and magazine people whose careers were in the same initial stage as his own, and whose after-hours company he enjoyed. He saw shows, movies and athletic events with gift tickets sent him by men and women who sold advertising space and time to the Chevalier account. He spent a winter of weekends learning to ski, summer weekends at Long Island and New England beaches, fishing, swimming, and learning to sail. And despite the fact that there were more activities in which to participate than there was time in which to accomplish all of them, he felt no real sense of permanence: victim of the rootlessness that infects most outlanders living as transients in Dream City.

In this nomadic jungle, Steve began a series of quiet affairs, but found most were unsatisfactory after the third or fourth encounter, when it became apparent that more was expected of him than he was willing to give. Determined to skirt deep emotional involvement, he turned to one-night stands, which brought on periods of abstinence, followed by periods of over-indulgence, neither of which he found satisfactory.

During this period of self-adjustment he made several attempts to complete the historical novel begun while at Columbia. He restructured the beginning, which he believed was weak, wrote long and over-elaborate descriptions of its principal characters, then chapterized the complete outline. But when he reached the point where he must commit himself to the full first draft, the pressure of agency work increased and he put the whole project aside once more.

He began to miss Libby desperately. Always, at play, in his work, or in the arms of another woman, she was present in his thought processes. He had begun a hundred letters in his mind, and several on paper, but for a man who had always known he would make his living with words, he could find none he felt could successfully explain why, at this early stage of an uncertain career, he should ask her to renew their old association and accept the risks of marriage. And now, with a secure cushion of funds in the bank, a more than modest salary each week, and a monthly income from his Lancaster property, he could not bring himself to crawl.

So he climbed aboard the merry-go-round and took what pleasures he could find in the camaraderie he found in such bars as Emil's, Wonder Bar, Charlie's, P.J.'s and his favorite, a singles bar on Third Avenue named O'Malley's, which was owned by a man named Hornstein and where drinks were christened Hangover Special, Bloody Awful, Brain-splitter and Rum Abominable; but the food was good and without pretentiousness. Here came the chic and drab lonely to find their counterparts; secretaries, clerks, young executives, all seeking companionship, temporary romance, even love, and often finding it. They were bold, shy, casual, brassy, quiet, and loud, but were drawn to O'Malley's by the same need; to avoid the emptiness of four walls, the appalling loneliness of streets crowded with strangers, the drab boredom of self. It served a need, a purpose for the moment, and he added names to his address book that within a short time would become difficult to match with faces. Which was Nancy, Sally, Margaret, or Andrea?

Steve found that people everywhere, on learning he was "in advertising," began showing magisterial interest, and voicing solemn opinions about his chosen profession. He knew his reaction was defensive toward such "attacks" but later felt that, like all other professions and businesses, advertising was in need of considerable defending. And in time, he began to question his own role in advertising, and the role of advertising itself; the artificiality of prose he committed to paper to describe the sweetness of ripened tobacco he had never seen ripen; the fullness of flavor he himself could not taste; the supreme satisfaction he had never derived from pack after pack of Chevaliers; for the only true benefit he received from the product he was huckstering was purely financial, in the form of the salary check he received every Friday and the cartons of cigarettes that were supplied free by the client.

And so he began to see his world as one of soap bubbles, clouds, cardboard skies and paper moons, living so intimately with lies of his own manufacture that the real and artificial could not be told apart. Thus, sentiment became pure corn. Honest emotions were square. Reality was something unclean, to be hidden away from sight. Truth was an obstacle to be circumvented within limits set by the FTC. Graciousness had become synonymous with impotence, "guarantees" and "money back offers" something thrown indiscriminately at the public, whose supine attitudes reflected affluent indifference that presupposed they were going to be "taken." The insincerity of the used and new car dealer, tire salesman, television repairman, the merchant who promoted spurious "sale-priced" goods and similar gimmicks, only reinforced his feeling that Integrity, and not God, was dead. Cynicism became his thing.

He came to understand more. That after fruitless years in pursuit of recognition, the advertising man learns that his reward can only be measured by promotion within the establishment and the oblong pink, blue, green, yellow, or beige check he receives for his labors, with infrequent increases and bonuses to remind him that his work is not unappreciated. That he would live well, generally, but seldom within his means because there would always be the need to show his superior status to neighbors, friends, and others outside the world he inhabited. And eventually, in order to avoid total anonymity before death, he might once again be spurred to try his hand at a novel or play that would, hopefully, bring him public acclaim he could gain in no other way. He would have walked so long with frustration that the normal frustrations of an average life would seem inconsequential and surmountable by comparison.

His gravest obstacle would be the man immediately ahead of him on the ladder upward, yet he must keep a sharp eye on the man one rung beneath, trying to climb over him.

4

In March of 1964, Keith Allard invited Steve to his home for dinner, his first visit to Sutton Place. Louise Allard, he judged, must be in her middle forties but could easily have been taken to be ten years younger. Energetic and vivacious, warm and friendly, she gave Steve the immediate feeling of having known her for years. Over a martini while Keith finished dressing, he at once succumbed to her charm and the comfort of his surroundings.

The old house was rather narrow and long, but the rooms were surprisingly large, with high ceilings, and the decor was in excellent taste. Among the paintings in the living room Steve noted a Miro, a Chagall, and a pencil drawing by Picasso. The furniture was a charming mixture of periods that ranged from Victorian to Swedish modern, yet everything seemed to fit elegantly into place, even to the Japanese houseman, Toyo, who served them.

Keith came in, apologizing for having kept them waiting. "Sorry, Steve, I got hung up in a last-minute conference with Wade and Bill." To Louise, "Time for another drink or shall I have it at the table?"

There was time, and Toyo poured fresh drinks. A few minutes later they followed Louise into the dining room. Louise kept the conversation free of business talk and alive with the news of the day: the theater, a friend she had visited in the hosital after minor surgery, and an invitation to Westport that weekend to visit an author friend who had had his eighth novel published and needed a celebration blowoff before leaving on a promotional tour sponsored by his publisher. Steve somehow felt involved in every subject; and relaxing with the Allards, he discovered in them the very special human quality that had been so desperately lacking between Grady and Jenny Gilman.

After dinner, Louise excused herself, and Keith led Steve to his second-floor study, a large room with a desk, two comfortable sofas, side chairs, a lighted fireplace and three book-lined walls, which made Steve promise himself, *Someday I'll have a room exactly like this one*.

They sat in facing leather chairs placed on either side of the fireplace. Toyo brought a tray of coffee and brandy, then moved the logs so that they flamed up, brightening the area and driving out the chill of the March evening. Keith began the conversation with the almost expected question, "How are things going with you, Steve?"

"Very well, sir. I haven't had any complaints from Norm about my work."

"And Ted?"

Steve laughed. "Well, I don't really see much of Ted."

Keith smiled knowingly. "Wade and Norm are high on you, which is what counts most. As a matter of fact, you were the subject of the discussion I had with Wade and Bill this evening."

Steve's eyebrows raised, but he remained silent. "I think you may be due for a little change," Keith continued, "if you are agreeable."

"I—don't know what to say. Could I hear a little more about it?"

"Of course. You know the GFP account, don't you?"

Steve's pulse began to race. GFP, Leary's largest and most profitable account. And one of its oldest. "I know of it, yes, but not too much about it."

Steve waited until Allard filled and lit his pipe. "You know Jack Henderson, I'm sure," Keith said finally.

"Only by sight. He's the senior writer on GFP, the man who took over from Cliff Sorensen when he left."

Keith nodded. "Jack is leaving the agency. Gave Bill his notice two weeks ago, going over to Franklin, Kenyon and Hale. He'll be leaving on the first of the month."

The excitement in Steve began to rise the way it had when he had first been assigned to Chevalier. GFP. A chance any copywriter with much more experience would leap at. Allard said, "Andy Makyrios will move up into Jack's spot, Jim Whipple into Andy's. Leaves us a man shy in the writing department. Do you think you could fit into that slot?"

"I'm sure I can. I know I can," Steve said quickly. Then, "If you think I can do the job."

"If I didn't think you could handle it, you wouldn't have entered into consideration. All I want to make certain of is that you're sure of yourself. You're young and you've still got some learning to do, but I think you can cut it. Wade was a little hesitant about taking you off Chevalier, but since GFP is also his responsibility, it won't be as though he's losing you, merely a shift from one of his accounts to another." *Then*, Steve realized, *I was chosen by you and not Wade.*

Keith's low baritone voice rolled over this thought. "I sold Bill and Wade on the idea that you're the right man for it, Steve. I think you have that certain talent, an analytical approach to advertising that could be very useful with GFP. On the other hand, there are men senior to you who deserve a crack at that spot and would jump at it, which means I'm sticking my neck out quite far by offering it to you. Would you want a few days to think it over?"

"No, sir. I'm sure I can handle it. I'd like that chance."

"All right. Keep this to yourself until I make the official announcement. Before I do that, we'll have to cool Norm Adrian off, but I'm sure he won't want to stand in the way of your progress. Meanwhile, use every spare minute going over the GFP material in our library. I'll have Gail get together their past budgets, company policies, call sheets, copy style book and any other data you might find useful. Take it all home with you and study it there during the next week.

"Wade will arrange with Mark Lawson, GFP's director of advertising, to send you over to their main plant in Harrison, New Jersey, for a week of indoctrination. You'll study the operation firsthand, how their products are manufactured, quality control, packaging, shipping, see their test kitchens, lab facilities, new product research department, the works.

"You'll meet Mr. Herschel Goodwin, the president of GFP, over there. The plant in Harrison was the first of GFP's four and Mr. Goodwin spends most of his time there. One of your jobs will be to sell yourself to him. He's a fine old gentleman and likes to meet everyone who works for GFP, including our agency people who service the account. All our key personnel have gone through that part of the job. After Harrison, you'll spend about two weeks at GFP's headquarters office on East Forty-second Street where you'll get to know Mr. Lawson and the procedures of working with the client.

"I want you to learn—as quickly as you can—the internal politics there, then stay clear of it. Mark Lawson is Herschel Goodwin's nephew by marriage . . ."

Steve did his homework well. By the time he was ready to report to his new assignment, he knew as much as it was possible to learn from its past advertising and a careful analysis of its budget breakdown. The initial visit to East Forty-second Street was a mere formality to signal his introduction to the advertising director, whom he didn't get to see. Nor his assistant, Bob Davies. Instead, a handsomely structured secretary examined him briefly, took his business card and smilingly said, "Oh, yes, Mr. Gilman. Mr. Lawson was expecting you, but is tied up in conference. You're to report to the Harrison plant and ask for Mr. Behrman, the superintendent. Do you know how to get there?"

"Yes, but I was told to see Mr. Lawson first."

"I'm sorry. I think Mr. Lawson will be tied up for most of the day."

"I see. Thank you."

It was a two-hour drive despite the absence of heavy traffic. He drove his rented car along the Henry Hudson Parkway, crossed the George Washington Bridge, and picked up Route 4 through Paramus and on to Harrison where, half a mile beyond the town proper, he came upon several acres of well-tended lawns and signs of new construction to the left of a headquarters building four stories high, surrounded by a series of single-storied buildings that housed the pilot plant. He parked the car behind the administration building and after identifying himself to the receptionist, waited for half an hour until Mr. Behrman could be located.

Behrman was a man of perhaps fifty, gray-haired, dressed in white trousers and jacket that resembled a doctor's garb. "Yes, yes," Behrman said, peering over a pair of steel-rimmed spectacles, "you are expected. I will send for someone to show you around. You will change into whites and not speak to anyone who is operating a machine."

"Will I meet Mr. Goodwin in the plant?" Steve asked.

"Yes, yes, you can be sure of that. Mr. Goodwin will find you." Behrman grinned toothily from beneath a walrus mustache and added, "Sooner or later."

While he waited for his escort, he spoke with the receptionist and learned there was a motel in town where he could stay during his visit and she telephoned to make a reservation for him.

For three days, he toured the maze of buildings where GFP's various food products were manufactured, where raw materials were received by rail and by fleets of trucks that arrived in a never-ending stream, were later shipped by the same means in tightly sealed cartons throughout the United States, Canada, and abroad. And this, he knew, was only one of four large plants, the others newer and larger than the one in Harrison.

Having been under escort for three days, he later retraced his steps on his own through vast weighing and blending rooms where stainless steel vats received and prepared the flour and other important ingredients that would be packaged to make the baking chores of hundreds of thousands of housewives lighter, and produce more perfect biscuits, cakes, cookies, muffins, pancakes, pie crusts, toppings, and other products. Various foremen explained what he saw, but the complexity of the massive overall operation was too great for him to absorb with full clarity in so little time. Items like mayonnaise and margarine were manufactured in one of the other plants, he learned.

He went through the long glassed-in laboratory where several men and women were examining product samples in test tubes and through microscopes. In this sacrosanct arena, hardly anyone noticed him. In clean white trousers and jacket, he was just another of many employees similarly dressed. Beyond the lab were the test kitchens and he stopped long enough for a cup of coffee and a sampling of fresh coconut cookies.

It was an amazing revelation, this meticulous factory, as clean as a hospital dispensary, with its chemists, technicians, operators and mechanics busily engaged in their duties, manufacturing the products he would soon be writing about. Everyone was dressed in white, men and women alike, the latter wearing unflattering hairnets for sanitary reasons. Batch testers. Sanitation and exterminator crews. The "gas chamber" where all paper and cardboard were fumigated with a deadly cyanide gas to kill off parasites before introducing the material into the assembly rooms. Fork lift and towmotor trucks moved cases of cartoned packages from assembly lines to the shipping department, each piece of equipment spotless and sparkling.

Sipping coffee while looking out through the broad sheet of thick glass, Steve heard soft footsteps behind him and before he could turn, a voice said, "You are the new man from the Leary Agency, eh?"

Steve turned and looked into the bright, intelligent eyes of a man he knew instinctively was Herschel Goodwin. He was tall and spare, his face showing his years: iron-gray hair, shaggy eyebrows, beaked nose, thin-lipped mouth; in all, a face that showed strength with gentleness, and was smiling quizzically. He wore the familiar white suit, shirt, and a pale blue tie that conformed with the general color picture. He reached into a pocket and pulled out a pack of cigarettes, offering one to Steve. "Only in here do we permit smoking," he said.

Steve took the cigarette and snapped a lighter into flame for its donor. "Thank you, Mr. Goodwin. I'm Steven Gilman, from the agency. I'm new on the GFP account."

"Ah, yes. Tell me, Mr. Gibson . . ."

"Gilman, Steve Gilman," Steve corrected.

"Yes. Gilman. Tell me, Mr. Gilman," Goodwin said with that same curious smile, "are you here because you want to be or because you were sent?"

Steve had the notion that Mr. Goodwin, away from more serious work for the moment, was toying with him. "Both, I suppose, Mr. Goodwin, but if I hadn't been sent, I should have asked permission to come."

"Why?"

"To learn what I can about your business."

The smile broadened. "I have been working as a baker now, in this business, all my life, and I haven't learned all there is to know about it. Tell me, why do you want to learn about our business, Mr. Gilman?"

"I suppose so that one day when I begin to write about your products, it will be from personal knowledge of the people who manufacture them, the care they take, and the pride they show in their work. If I can feel the way they do, the way you do, maybe I can make the public feel it."

"You believe you can do that with words, Mr. Gilman?"

"I can try my best. Honest enthusiasm can often be transferred, Mr. Goodwin, just as I have become enthusiastic by what I've already seen here during the past few days."

"Honest," Goodwin repeated. He looked up from under his shaggy eyebrows and said, "Are you an honest man, Mr. Gilman?"

"I hope I am, sir."

"Let me tell you something." Goodwin's English sounded harsh and carried with it a distinct old country accent that all his years in America had been unable to eradicate completely. (The word *something* came out as *somesing*, his *w* as a *v*, *th* as *z*.) "I know you have been here for four days now. I have talked with my people and they tell me the questions you ask them. Good questions, the kind that show interest. You talk and look like a bright young man."

"Thank you, sir."

"*Nu, nu.* I don't know what you can do, Mr. Gilman, what you can write, but I believe you are honest. I try to be honest, too, to give the best for the least cost, but the costs get higher and higher all the time." He sighed, put out his cigarette and stared thoughtfully through the glass wall into the assembly area. "I began my life as a baker in Germany with my father and brother, *alov hasholem.* Ah, that was such a long time ago. When my father died, Zalman and I came to America and became bakers here.

"Today, nobody wants to bake the way they did in those days. Quick mixes. Instant this, instant that. Anything to save time. Or maybe they are afraid their own baking won't be so good. The love of baking in the home, the art, it is gone with the women of my generation. So today they pay more and complain about the high cost. I try to give them what they want, what they don't know how to make themselves, in their own kitchens. Quality, and good taste. The best. You believe that, Mr. Gilman?"

"I believe it, Mr. Goodwin."

The old man gripped Steve's arm and smiled again. "I think you do. Anna would like you."

"Anna?"

"My wife. After Zalman and I sold the bakeries—twenty we had—she helped me start this business. Then Zalman and his wife died—ah—you are married, Mr. Gilman?"

"No, sir."

"You should be. You will. A man needs a wife like my Anna. Now she can't help me any more, but I know one thing. If I can please Anna, I can please any housewife. She is my first and best customer for anything new we make here." Herschel Goodwin looked at his watch and said, "Time for lunch. You will eat with me?"

"I'll be happy to."

He spent the full week in New Jersey then returned to New York, where, after checking in with Barrett and Allard, he reported to Mark Lawson who, after a few minutes devoted to bare identification, turned him over to Bob Davies, dismissing him with, "Show this fellow the ropes, Bob, but don't let him waste too much of your time."

Davies, Steve soon discovered, was a man whose principal function was to serve as a fence between Lawson and the rest of the staff: Dan Tyson and Tom Jewell, two young product managers; Lance Cardell in Sales Promotion, Lloyd Benziger in Marketing, Orrin Killian in Merchandising, and Reed Steinhorst and Valerie Harris in Purchasing. It soon became apparent to Steve that there was little love lost between Lawson and Ward Hardwick, the director of Sales, a GFP executive of over twenty years tenure, too tough and experienced in his job to brook interference from Lawson, and important enough to maintain his position of strength with Herschel Goodwin. Once, within Steve's hearing, Hardwick referred to Lawson as that "goddamned professional relative," a remark that was received with quiet glee among Hardwick's associates.

Steve's interest here was in learning the advertising operation from the client's end, primarily how it meshed with its national sales promotion and sales efforts. He worked along with Dan Tyson, who was concerned with the mixes and toppings, then with Tom Jewell, whose area of interest was in margarine, mayonnaise, and peanut butter. Most of what he learned was superficial, relying on the Sales Statistical Analyses punched out by teletype machines and the daily reports on production, sales, and shipments delivered on computer printouts.

In Purchasing—a huge department that occupied an entire floor—he became interested in that section which dealt with the purchase of printed materials; the colorful packages for each item, labels, shipping cartons, forms, and stationery, all designed by the Leary Agency but bought by GFP on the open market. At the end of each day, Steve took a number of computer printouts with him to study at home.

A week later, prior to his return to the agency, Steve was astonished when Lawson sent for him and asked him out to lunch. Expecting a quiz session on what he had learned during his two weeks with GFP, Steve was further surprised that such was not the case. Lawson, in an affable mood, engaged him in a discussion about the theater and football, doing most of the talking himself, then began asking a number of personal questions that Steve resented as being too intimate, and did his best to avoid, without giving offense. He had the distinct impression that Lawson wanted him to understand he was dealing with a super being whose favors were much in demand.

Satisfied that Steve was duly impressed, Lawson returned to the subject of advertising. "I expect two things in my advertising, Gilman. One, I want the housewife to *taste* the product she's reading or hearing about, make her tongue tingle when she licks her lips. Two, I want her to realize how much time she saves in the kitchen by using our products. Give me that, kid, and you and I will get along. Just don't try to con me with the same kind of tired old bullshit your people keep trying to make me swallow from time to time."

Steve flushed with chauvinistic resentment, but held himself in check. "I understand," he said.

"Good. Let's get back to the office." The check lay on a small tray beside Lawson. As they rose to leave, Lawson said, "Pick up the tab, kid. The agency springs when we work together."

Steve paid the check.

During that final week Steve had seen Wade Barrett on one occasion when the account supervisor came to call on

Lawson and take him to lunch. Following that, he was permitted to sit in on a discussion when Andy Makyrios and Jim Whipple called with a series of color proofs of two magazine ads, and copy for a new thirty-second television commercial, which gave him an opportunity to see Lawson in action.

Lawson gave both men a rough hour, but since he had previously okayed the ad copy (and was shown his initials on the earlier layouts), he was held for no gain at the line of scrimmage. The television copy was new, however, and Makyrios and Whipple took the full brunt of Lawson's profane criticism.

"Jesus H. Christ," he exclaimed, "this is the same kind of shit I was telling the kid here about just the other day." He turned to Steve and said, "Wasn't I, kid?"

Steve was in a quandary. To say "Yes" would be tantamount to agreeing with Lawson's opinion on the caliber of the copy as well as the principle point about which he had made his obscene reference. To say "No" might be an even greater disaster as far as his somewhat unstable relationship with Lawson was concerned.

Makyrios saved him by saying, "Suppose we take this back and rework it, Mark."

"Why the hell can't you do it here, now?" Lawson demanded churlishly. "Goddamned waste of time, bicycling this crap back and forth."

"Because I need a quiet place to think over the changes you've suggested," Andy replied diplomatically, which almost caused Steve to burst out laughing since Lawson hadn't suggested anything except that he was unhappy with the copy in general. His only contribution had been his customary carping.

"Oh, for Christ's sake!" Lawson snarled. "Okay, okay. Take it back, but for my money, the kid here could do it with one hand tied behind his back."

When Steve finally reported back to the agency, he spent an hour with Wade Barrett, who told him he had passed the acid test with flying colors; Lawson had agreed to have him on the account.

Makyrios and Whipple, when he checked in for his first assignment, were eager to have him in the group and greeted him warmly. Whip said, "Welcome back from Siberia, comrade. From now on you'll be working with us peasant serfs instead of that fascist bastard genius."

Mack said, "For a multimillion dollar account, we have

to take a certain amount of crap, but screw Lawson, he wouldn't know shit from Shinola if they were served to him on the same platter. If the sonofabitch didn't scream bloody murder five times a day, nobody would ever know he was alive. It ain't easy, Steve old boy, but it ain't bullets, either. The sooner you learn to hate the bastard, the easier you'll find it to live with him."

And then it was June. Vacation schedules had been made up for the group by Makyrios and since Steve was the newest member of the team. he had no choice in the matter and had been marked down for the second and third weeks of the month. *Question*: Where to spend those two weeks?

During the preceding week, Steve made a dozen plans, but the pull was toward Lancaster, with Libby the magnet. He left on a Friday, reached Washington early in the afternoon and, still deliberating on the wisdom of Lancaster, checked into the Shoreham for the night. At nine o'clock, having had his dinner and walked through the grounds for a while, he returned to his room and put in a person-to-person call to Miss Elizabeth Newell.

Olive answered the phone and asked the operator who was calling. When Steve spoke up, there was some hesitation on the other end of the line, then Olive told the operator to hold for a moment. After a while, Libby came on and Steve found himself virtually tongue-tied.

"How are you, Steve, where are you calling from?"

"Washington."

"Are you there on business?"

"Uh-no. Vacation."

"Are you spending it in Washington?"

"Well—no. I haven't decided yet."

"You mean whether to come to Lancaster?"

"Something like that."

"Well . . ."

"Uh . . ."

"What?"

"I—nothing. I was thinking about you . . ."

"Steve, if I asked you to come down . . ."

"Will it be all right—I mean, could I see you?"

"Of course, silly. Why not?"

"I'll be down in the morning."

"There's a nine o'clock bus."

"I know. I'll catch that one."

"I'll meet you."

"That'll be great. Listen, will you get me a reservation at that new motel?"

"Of course. No problem. See you tomorrow, then?"

"Sure. Yes, of course."

Libby, beautiful as ever, met him at the bus station. Both were hesitant and shy and only a handshake passed between them. Barney, Libby volunteered at once, was away on business at the moment and she and Olive were supposed to leave for Richmond and Virginia Beach on Monday.

"I'd forgotten about your annual trek. Another couple of days and I'd have missed you," Steve said.

"I really don't want to go, but there wasn't anywhere else I wanted to go and Mother insisted she wouldn't leave me here alone."

"Well, at least there's today and tomorrow."

"Tomorrow we'll be packing."

"Do you have to go on Monday, Libby? What if Olive went down and you follow in a couple of weeks?"

"I—don't know, Steve. I'll try." They found her car on the parking lot. Steve dropped his suitcase in the back and Libby pulled out, heading toward the river.

"Libby, don't go with Olive on Monday."

"I said I'd try, Steve. What decided you to come back so suddenly?"

He said quietly, "It didn't happen all that suddenly, and the answer is, you."

"I thought that was all over."

"It's never been over. I told you back then that I needed time. We were both in college. I was practically broke . . ."

"And so damned independent."

"About taking help from your father, yes."

"And now?"

"I've got a good job and equally good prospects. I've got some money in the bank, a cushion. I'd like to tell you more about it if you'll listen."

"I don't know if I should. I've had a hell of a time, Steve, almost a breakdown."

"I'm sorry, Libby. I didn't know."

"I got through it somehow. I just don't know if I can . . . I don't . . . I couldn't stand that same . . . thing again."

He said quickly, "I love you, Libby."

"And I guess . . . I guess I love you, too, Steve."

"Then we can make it work."

"I'm . . . I'm a little frightened. You're different, something about you has changed."

"We're both different, older, maybe even a little wiser."

They arrived at the motel and Steve's room was large, bright, and overlooked the river. To one side was a swimming pool. The day was hot and a number of guests were already at poolside soaking up the sun. Steve removed two suits from his bag and hung them in the closet. "Do you still carry your bathing things in your car, Libby?"

"Of course."

"How about a swim, some sun, and lunch?"

She hesitated, and Steve said, "Get your things while I change, then you can have the room to yourself."

"Okay. I'll be back in ten minutes."

They swam, had lunch, and talked about the future. Steve drew a layout of his apartment for her, located the streets nearby, and the stores in which Libby would shop. He described in detail the people he worked with, the Allards in particular, his friends.

"What about your writing ambitions, the novels and screenplays, the Broadway plays we once talked about?" Libby asked.

"Darling, all that changed when my father died. We're talking about today, tomorrow. I've got my job to think about, and the rest, the writing part, that may come later, but it's not for now. You understand that, don't you?"

"Yes, Steve, I understand."

"Look, Libby. In two weeks, I'll be back in New York. I'll talk to Keith and make necessary arrangements. When do you think you can come up?"

"I can't say at this moment. I'll have to discuss it with Mother and Dad."

"You won't have any problems there, will you?"

"None I can think of right now, but I'm sure they'll want the wedding here in Lancaster."

Steve stirred. "That might be a problem. This is my vacation. I don't know if I can get the necessary time off for a big . . ." . .

She said quickly, "It won't be big, Steve. I'll insist on that. All you'd need would be a weekend and we'll save the honeymoon trip for later."

"How soon?"

"I'll have to work that out. Steve, I want to, very much, but please be patient with me, will you?"

"Of course."

They returned to his room at four-thirty and, without many preliminaries, made love. They bathed, dressed, and had dinner with Olive at the Newell home, then went to a movie. Olive had been her usual cool, serene self and Steve knew that Libby would have no easy time convincing her mother when the subject would come up between them later. When the show was over, Libby asked, "Don't you want to see any of the old crowd, Steve? It's still early enough . . ."

"Not tonight. All I want to see is you."

They returned to the motel and made love again, and Libby left him there shortly after midnight.

In the morning, Libby phoned to tell him Olive was leaving for Richmond shortly after lunch. Alone.

"Great. Swell. What about our plans?"

"I'll stop by as soon as she leaves and tell you all about it."

When she arrived at two o'clock, all smiles, she described her talk with Olive at breakfast and Oilve's final blessing. However, it would take a while before Olive would see Barney and make the arrangements for their wedding.

For the next two weeks, Libby and Steve relived their earlier lives in Lancaster. They saw Buzz, Arnie, Jake, Maxine, and the Murchison twins, spent days and several nights together at the Newell cottage at Forest Lake, called on the family who lived in the Gilman home, and explored Barney's new housing developments and shopping centers. Steve called on Eli Tinsley at his office, but couldn't bring himself to visit the *Star*. He went alone in Libby's car to the cemetery, to stand between Grady's and Jenny's graves and marvel to himself that these two, so distant from each other in life, could be so peacefully close together in death.

Libby was like a woman renewed; twenty-four, alive, and fully alert. She dressed in a new costume each day, and changed every evening into something fresh. They dined at the motel, or in town, and were invited out by the Applebys, Porters, Camerons, and Fletchers.

When he mentioned Cal Waggoner, he learned that Cal was doing some political legwork for Barney in Washington, and when he inquired more deeply into what Cal was doing for Barney, Libby dismissed it with, "I really don't know, Steve. He's just another one of Dad's many errand boys."

Life, Steve assumed, was filled with "civilians."

5

They were married in a quiet home ceremony during the Labor Day weekend in Lancaster, with Keith and Louise Allard their only guests from New York. On Monday, Barney and Olive drove Steve, Libby, and the Allards to Washington to catch the train for New York.

In November, they received word from Olive that Cal Waggoner had been elected to the House of Representatives, replacing Sherman Collier—incumbent for seven terms—who had decided to retire from politics and return to his law practice in Lancaster. But Steve and Libby were too caught up in their new life together to give the news much thought, beyond sending a telegram of congratulations to Cal.

The months that followed were the happiest in their lives. Libby, with the help of Louise Allard, rearranged and redecorated Steve's apartment completely. Olive came up for a few days and bought a number of pieces of furniture, expensive cabinets, a sofa and matching companion chair, an antique desk. Inga Maczerak took Libby on a tour of introduction to the neighborhood shops and became her kitchen instructress. Inga, a pennywise housekeeper, made most of the new curtains from fabrics she and Libby selected at a wholesale house, to which Inga had an entrée.

Soon the Gilmans were entertaining, and being entertained by, many of Steve's agency colleagues and friends, and they were hard pressed to know what to do with the many gifts that, surprisingly, kept arriving from sources hardly known to Steve: television and radio stations, publications and printers, and television production houses that served the GFP account. The payola aspect disturbed Steve considerably, but Makyrios and Whipple put him at ease. He accepted the television set, three radios, a tape recorder, a substantial stock of records and tapes—among others—after a brief struggle with his conscience, and allowed Libby to send thank-you notes. The gifts from Bill and Donna Leary, the Allards, Barretts, and other agency people were duly acknowledged with invitations to dinners and cocktails.

They dined out frequently, saw the top shows, and visited many night spots during the first two months, which were followed by a period of natural weariness. They spent their first Thanksgiving holiday in Lancaster with Barney and Olive and the Christmas-New Year week skiing in Vermont. Barney and Olive came up for a week in March, but Steve could spend little time with them because of increasing work pressures. When they left, Steve discovered that Libby had acquired an entirely new wardrobe and some expensive pieces of jewelry from her parents, and was sorely annoyed: but at this moment of Libby's happiness, he could hardly protest.

In May Libby went off to Lancaster alone, to attend Carol Fletcher's wedding, which surprised Steve because Libby and Carol were three years apart in age and had never been remotely close. From there, Libby was carted off to Richmond to the wedding of Sara Chapman, a distant cousin of whom Steve had never heard. In July, Steve's three-week vacation fell due and he and Libby flew off to London and Paris, an all-expense-paid tour—courtesy of Barney and Olive—from which they returned in a state of virtual exhaustion.

They did not really settle down until after their first year of marriage had passed and Steve's job began making heavier incursions on his time. Makyrios and Whipple, as well as Wade Barrett and Keith Allard, had been more than patient and understanding, but as the GFP workload increased, Steve was forced to pick up and carry his share of the load.

Now there was less time to devote to Libby. Very often he worked at night, returning home after midnight to find Libby fast sleep, leaving her in bed to rise early to get to his office for an important conference. Libby complained but, at this stage of his progress, his work came first.

Alone much of the time, Libby began to feel a sense of disillusionment with big city life. She found Inga Maczerak —and others in their apartment house—incredibly provincial and narrow in their views. Except for two trips to Europe (the second with Barney and Olive when Steve could not spare the time), most of her travel had been confined to brief visits to Lancaster. She began to dread New York's subways, was intimidated by cab drivers, overwhelmed by traffic, and panicked by pedestrians who crowded her. Shopping in unfamiliar stores, served by disinterested—even hostile—clerks, dismayed her. Newspaper stories of increasing crime threatened her. She was unwilling to be examined by a doctor or accept a new dentist, and used these excuses to return to Lancaster.

At first, it had all been a grand, new, exciting lark, but now the gregarious, outgoing people they knew, their small talk—brazenly intimate conversations in mixed company—somehow brought back her childhood shyness, and made her unable to compete. The complex jargon of advertising talk that rolled off their tongues so easily only added to her confusion, for she was ignorant of its terms, unable to grasp its full meaning, and unwilling to learn. She felt excluded, and embarrassed, even hurt. She endured parties they were required to attend by protocol, but by the time they reached home, she was often in tears. Nor was she able to explain any of this to Steve.

Louise Allard, herself a product of small-town life, recognized the problem and tried to help by inviting Steve and Libby to small parties and quiet dinners for no more than six, but these more intimate gatherings left Libby with an even greater feeling of inadequacy. Her favorite topics—Lancaster, Barney and Olive, and her friends—soon wore thin.

Steve, busier than ever on GFP, was of little help. Libby spent her days in complete boredom, writing endless, newsless letters to Olive, unwilling to brave the teeming city to explore the richness of what lay outside her door, waiting for Steve to return from work. His news, necessarily concerned with advertising, evoked little interest in her and soon she gave up trying to understand what it all meant.

When Steve made his first trip to GFP's Canton plant, Libby packed a bag and went home to Lancaster. She remained there for a week beyond his four-day absence. Well into their second year, those visits home became periodic musts: a checkup by Dr. Murchison, dental work by Dr. Pritchard, a hurried call from Olive to meet her in Washington to do some shopping, family engagement parties and weddings in Richmond, Fairfax, Norfolk, and Virginia Beach; all trips she made alone.

Back in New York, Libby became a neurotic weeper. She wept when it rained or snowed, when she found a small stain on a dress, if the once-a-week maid failed to show up, or if Steve was late for dinner or skipped the meal because of a late conference. She became hysterical when she thought she was pregnant and was inconsolable when she learned from Dr. Murchison that she was not.

Their physical need for each other seemed to decrease with the frequency of Libby's petulance and tears and, finally, they began to talk separation; that it might be beneficial to both if Libby were to go home for a month or two. Libby leaped at the suggestion and when she left the following week, Steve felt as though a heavy weight had been lifted from his back and mind.

He was twenty-six then, but those two years with Libby in New York seemed longer, himself much older. In her absence he began to notice that the field of choice had become much broader and far richer. Coming home to an empty apartment to find an occasional letter describing her complete joy and contentment in Lancaster, the absolutely grand fun she was having visiting her friends there, was anything but enjoyable for Steve, who now found himself fighting the temptation to stray.

During the third week of Libby's absence, Steve felt he had entered his post-graduate course in advertising and there was no end to the detail he encountered. He was included in every copy-art conference, generally held on Monday mornings. These were frequently attended by Wade Barrett, occasionally by Keith Allard, or Bill Leary when the problem reached a higher magnitude and required a policy decision. Steve sat in on discussions following a call on Lawson by Barrett, Makyrios, or Whipple, but had not been permitted to make a call at East Forty-second Street since his initial indoctrination period. He took part in budget discussions and conferences with personnel from Media, Marketing, Merchandising, Research, and Television-Radio, contributing little more than his presence, this for the purpose of thoroughly familiarizing himself with the overall operation for GFP. With his colleagues, he viewed miles of video tape and film, and made careful notes in anticipation of the discussions that would follow.

There was another yardstick by which he could measure his personal success: He began getting calls from agency placement service organizations offering him jobs at larger agencies "if you are in a position to take it, of course, Mr. Gilman." And he began receiving phone calls inviting him to lunch with other agency men he had met. When he accepted, they invariably began talking about advertising accounts in general, slipping into the usual street gossip, then leading up to the Big Question: "Are you happy at Leary, Steve?" or, "How would you like to come over to our shop? I think we've got a spot opening up soon that you could fill. Probably get you a couple of thou more than you're getting at Leary." He derived a certain satisfaction out of these encounters, each a new ego trip, but in the end turned the propositions down. For the time being, he was perfectly happy with the progress he was making where he was.

Steve overslept and arrived late for a copy conference one Monday morning, and Makyrios slyly grinned and said to Whipple, "Why don't we let Steve get his feet wet with this one?"

"Sure," Whip agreed, "why the hell not?"

Steve asked, "What's the penalty for being late this time?"

Makyrios handed him a note that had been scribbled hastily and which he recognized as Mr. Lawson's. "A special request from On High," Mack said. "The Master wants a new tagline in place of the one Whip suggested for the new spring series. Claims he's seen it somewhere before, or something like it, but can't remember where, which is a crock of shit. Whip must have stepped on Lawson's toes the last time he saw him."

"Okay," Steve said confidently, "I'll take a crack at it."

Another half hour passed and the meeting came to an end with fresh assignments handed out to Don Berman and Arnie Cook, the senior art-copy team. Steve went back to his desk to re-read the note, which gave him no direction to follow, then asked the group secretary for the file of duplicate copy sheets on the new series.

He found the tagline originally suggested by Whipple:

You'll do it Better—and Quicker—every time
with GOODY CAKE MIXES

He remembered the ads, full color, full page, scheduled to break in every important magazine for women, plus the prominent newspapers and Sunday supplements, and the spring editions of two magazines for brides. Television and radio spots had been closely geared to the ad themes and would break simultaneously across the nation. He had worked on various parts of the campaign from the start, watched it from the creation of rough and comprehensive layouts through Lawson's acceptance, then the finished art and photographs, type selection, composition, and engravings. He had suffered as much as the rest of the staff over Lawson's quibbling and questioning this word or that and now—in its final stages—insisting on a new tagline. Steve began making notes on a fresh layout pad.

By noon, he had torn up the third sheet of brainstorms and he went to Emil's for lunch, where he ran into Makyrios and Jerry Fellman, a space salesman from *McCall's*. Mack invited him to join them and Steve did so. Fellman, riding a solid schedule for GFP, was talking about his magazine's big spring issue, its increase in circulation and ad pages; all of which Steve (and Mack) had heard from other space salesmen about their own publications.

"How are you doing with that new tagline, Steve?" Mack asked.

"Great. I've drawn a total blank so far," Steve replied.

"Keep something extra in reserve. Be a good idea to do two and show him the best one last, the prick."

"Lawson?" Fellman said knowingly.

"The Man Himself," Mack replied. "You seen him lately?"

Fellman laughed. "Hell, no. What a miserable bastard. I used to call on him once in a while, just to touch bases, you know. No more. He had the most wonderful way of making me feel as though I were the garbage man come to collect the office trash."

Mack said, "Yeah. You don't have to be a prick to be a client, I guess, but it helps. Man, I've seen some tough ones in my time, but they never made me kiss the royal ass before. Jack Henderson damn near quit six times before he caught on. Used to deliberately spell a word or two wrong just to give Lawson something to pounce on." He turned to Steve and said in a pitchman's voice, "Tell you what I'm gonna do, son. You come up with that tagline, I'm gonna let you take it to the Genius himself, in person. How's that for a show of old-fashioned brotherhood?"

"Thanks a lot, friend. You think I'll live through it?"

"What the hell, you're young and tough. Time you began taking a few scars and earned yourself a battle star or two."

"Okay, Mack, if I'm going to be bloodied, it might as well be by an expert."

Back at his desk, he toiled over his layout pad trying to coin new phrases, reaching for something eye- and ear-catching, something different. He stared again and again at Jim Whipple's offering: *You'll do it Better—and Quicker—every time——with* GOODY'S CAKE MIXES. It wasn't the greatest by a long shot, but it did roll off his tongue easily and he wondered why Lawson had picked it to chew on. Headlines, or body copy were more easily changed, but a tagline, once chosen, might run for the full life of the campaign, and even on into the next. It was an important assignment, the most important he had been given so far on GFP and Steve didn't want this one to get away from him.

His wastepaper basket was almost filled with crumpled effort by the end of the day and inner tension began to overcome him, hung up and strung out as he was on one simple sentence that refused to come. He ate a solitary dinner at a nearby restaurant and went into a movie house in the next block to catch a new foreign film and rid himself temporarily of everything connected with GFP. On his way home, trying to concentrate on the film, a montage of Lawson and GFP ads nagged and niggled at him.

There was a letter waiting for him from Libby. Cal Waggoner was down from Washington, the Congressman himself, the local boy who (with Barney's help) had made good. There were parties everywhere for him and she sent Steve regards from Cal, Buzz, Arnie, etc. etc. etc. Before falling asleep, a thought popped into his mind and he jotted it down before turning the bedlamp off. In the morning he re-read the note, nodded a silent *Maybe*, and tucked it into his shirt pocket.

Later, at his desk, he pulled the note out, polished and pared a word here and there, then typed the sentence on a clean sheet of copy paper:

People Who Use GOODY MIXES
Mix With The Best People

He studied that for a while, let it cool, read and re-read it more than a dozen times, then refined it down to read:

People who Mix with GOODY'S
Mix with the Best People!

He retyped that sentence on a fresh piece of copy paper and clipped a routing slip to it with a large question mark on it in red, then took it to Mack's office. Mack was out and Steve left it with his secretary.

After checking with Production and Traffic control about a job he had put aside to work on the tagline, Steve returned to his office to work on the current assignment, a series of ads for a test campaign on a new item, a coffee-flavored mix with a cinnamon-nut topping. The area chosen for the test was Washington, D.C. and the surrounding bedroom communities in Maryland and Virginia. Marketing had made the selection on the theory that with so many people living there who came from every state in the union, the buying reaction of all fifty states would be measured in this one shot at a single high-density population center.

"How's it coming, Steve?"

Busy poring over his work progress sheet on the test campaign, he hadn't noticed Mack as he came into the room. "Fine, Mack. The print media and display material are in. All I'm waiting for now are the video tapes due from Ascon tomorrow morning."

"Great. We'll check the whole deal out with Barrett tomorrow afternoon. If it's okay with him, we'll be all set to go."

"I think Mr. Barrett will like it. Whip has been checking me out on it every step of the way."

"Swell, but after Barrett, Allard is the man we've got to satisfy." A pause, then, "You've never handled one of these test campaigns before, have you?"

"No, this is my baptismal fire."

"I think I'll suggest to Wade that you go to Washington with the field unit and follow through on it."

"What will I do there, Mack?"

"You'll observe and learn, buddy, see what it's all about outside the office. You'll have people with you. Art Thalberg from Marketing, Frank Castle from Merchandising, along with their counterparts from GFP. Give you a couple of days away from your desk. You'll enjoy it, at least for the first time."

"I think I'd like that." It suddenly occurred to him that he might slip away to Lancaster and spend a full day and night with Libby.

Until then, Makyrios hadn't mentioned the new tagline. He said, "Okay, Steve, you've earned it. I'll talk to Wade and Allard about it." He sat on the edge of Steve's desk and added, "I saw that new tagline of yours. I like it a lot. Much better than Whip's."

Steve felt a glow of warmth spreading inside him. "Thanks, Mack. You still want me to do another to show Lawson before I let him see this one?"

"Hell, no. This one ought to grab him by the balls. You uptight about calling on him by yourself?"

"I don't know. That'll be another first."

"Well, hell, why not? Some day you'll have to bell the cat and you might as well start with this tagline. You know the bastard, so you've already had the first bite taken out of your hide."

"Is he really that tough, Mack? I didn't see too much of him while I was down there breaking in."

"I'll let you make your own judgment. Hell, maybe you've got charisma. If it works out, we'll expose you to him more often." He took a cigarette from Steve's pack, lit it, and said, "Give that tagline to Lex Kent and have him dress it up. Get him to mount it on the color proof. I'd like to see it in a sexy kind of hand-lettered script with the name GOODY's the way we always use it, gothic, in the same orangy red. Let me see it before we show it to the brass, eh?"

"Sure, Mack."

"Nice going, Steve. I think he'll buy it."

"It was just a lucky shot."

Makyrios laughed. "Don't be so fucking modest and stop backing off from a credit you've earned. It's the only way you'll ever move up, you dumb bastard."

6

Mark Lawson stared at the tagline at the bottom of the color proof with pursed lips that told Steve nothing. He leaned back in his oversized chair, pinched his lower lip between thumb and forefinger, then leaned forward to examine it again. He looked up at Steve, sitting in the side chair to the left of the desk, then back at the tagline, lips moving as he read it over to himself once more.

"Whose," he said finally, "is this?"

Now it comes. "Whose?" Steve asked with arched eyebrows. "The Leary Agency's, of course."

"Oh, for Christ's sake. I mean who wrote *this*. This

tagline. Mack, Whip, Barrett, or the Almighty Allard himself?"

"Oh. I did," Steve said, and added silently, *I, with my own brain and typewriter, I killed Cock Robin.*

"Is that why they sent you down here with it?"

"No."

Then Lawson smiled for the first time and said, "I like it. It reads well, even sounds good. *People who mix with* GOODY's *mix with the best people,* he quoted. "Right on target. Congratulations, kid. You really lucked in on this one."

"Thanks," Steve said, then suddenly, feeling reckless and made bold by Lawson's approbation, "The name is Steve, Mr. Lawson. I've been with Leary since 1961 and this was no lucky accident."

Lawson stared coolly at him, then with a widening grin, "Hey, you've got guts. You know, I think you and I are going to get along." He initialed his "Okay, M.L." on the proofsheet and said, "Come on out to lunch. I'll pick up the tab this time."

Steve came back to the agency on a cushion of air and was congratulated all around, with a special smile from Barrett, who added, "You may become one of our important contacts with GFP, Steve. Keep up the good work."

Steve made the trip to Washington as an observer. In the club car, Arthur Thalberg and Frank Castle excluded him from their lofty conversation that dealt with consumer reaction analysis, marketing, merchandising, and general statistics. Steve was grateful for the exclusion and watched the New Jersey, Pennsylvania, Delaware, and Maryland countryside roll by.

It was February, and everything beyond the square of window looked dead or asleep. Bare branches, stiff, spiky, colorless grass, ice-rimmed rivers, leaden skies. Smoke from industrial plants befouled the air. Trucks and cars sped along broad highways and crept over secondary roads exhaling noxious vapors.

He thought of Lancaster again. And Libby. He hadn't asked Barrett for a few extra days off to spend with her, but since the test would be over on Saturday, he could easily run down for an overnight stay and come up to catch the early train on Monday morning without upsetting the office routine too much. He would call Libby from Washington. Or should he go on down and surprise her?

She might even return with him. This might even give him some time with Eli Tinsley, to learn whether land values were sufficiently high to sell off the old Gilman place and acreage. When he had last seen Eli, the weekend of his wedding. the attorney had advised him to hold onto the property.

In Washington, after checking in with the others at the Statler. he called on the *Post, Star,* and *News,* and found the GFP ads ready to break on the following afternoon, the *Post*'s in the morning. He next visited the television and radio stations on the schedule to make sure everything was in order, then returned to the hotel. The GFP people were in the lounge gathered around a table in discussion: Bob Davies, Orrin Killian and Lloyd Benziger from GFP, teamed up with Thalberg and Castle. Moments later, Robin Ford, who was in charge of the field demonstrators hired for the Thursday-through-Saturday campaign, joined them.

Robin, whom he had never met at GFP since most of her work was done out in the various territories, was an extremely attractive woman who, Steve guessed, was about his own age, perhaps a year or two older. Dressed smartly in a warm woolen suit, a fur-trimmed coat over one arm, her personality sparkled as she greeted and spoke with the group. Steve took particular notice of the gleaming black hair that fell to near-shoulder length, the curve of her body lines and long. exquisitely formed legs. Equally important, she had an excitingly vibrant manner and a quality of ease that could come only with experience and total self-assurance. It was more than a meeting as they were introduced; it was the performance of a woman who knew exactly how to use a combination of ability and beauty. Steve wondered if she were married; and if not, he asked himself, why the hell not?

They broke an hour later to dress for dinner, met in the lobby and half an hour later were sharing a table at a seafood restaurant along the waterfront. The conversation, quite naturally, was along business lines, with each giving an account of his own contributions to the test campaign. Bob Davies, Steve took particular notice, showed an annoyingly proprietary interest in Robin, seating her beside himself, and turning to her frequently with a question or remark. From across the table, Steve watched her, turning away only when she looked up to find him staring at her.

Soon, normal curiosity gave way to physical interest. He understood from her conversation that she had been through many similar test campaigns, which were no longer an exciting novelty in her life. By ten o'clock, with a full day ahead of them, the party drove back to the hotel and again, Davies guided Robin Ford into his cab. Steve rode back with his colleagues feeling a definite sense of loss. At the hotel, it was Davies who called the time to turn in and escorted Robin to the elevator while Steve went back to the bar for a lonely nightcap. It was not until an hour later, as he was getting into bed, that he remembered about the call to Libby, and decided it was too late.

On Wednesday evening, the first ads broke, the commercials hit television viewers and radio listeners, transit cards appeared on buses, banners were pasted on the windows of every major chain outlet, and the stores were well-stocked with Goody's Cinnamon-Nut Cake Mix; all waiting for the response of the buying public.

Steve did not see Robin that night, nor the next, but on Friday night the group had dinner together at the hotel. Robin was very tired and went to bed early. As she stood up to leave them, Bob Davies said, "See you tomorrow, Robin?"

"I'll be getting a very early start, Bob," she replied.

"Breakfast, then?"

She shook her head negatively and smiled. "Don't count on it. I'll be up by six and gone by six-thirty."

"Tomorrow night, then. Don't knock yourself out."

"Thanks. I think I'll be all right."

Davies left a few minutes later and Benziger said, "Since when did he appoint himself Robin's watchdog?"

Killian laughed. "When Bob represents GFP, he represents."

"Insufferable jerk," Benziger commented.

On Saturday, having driven his rented car through Northwest Washington and the Arlington suburban area to check various retail outlets to see how the aisle displays had been set up and how the demonstrators were handling shoppers, Steve returned to the Statler at five-thirty and went to the bar for a drink. There he found Robin with Thalberg, Castle, Davies, Benziger, and Killian. He joined them for a drink and soon after, Thalberg left to call his wife, and Castle went to his room to check out and catch the next train to New York. The GFP personnel followed suit soon after, leaving Robin behind with Steve.

"Why the sudden exodus?" Steve asked over his drink.

"That's all there is, there is no more," Robin said. "The campaign, for all practical purposes, is over. The generals have left the field and gone back to their headquarters to wait for the results of the battle."

"And Davies, too?"

"And Davies, too. There's no more for anyone else to do here. Thursday through Saturday, and this is Saturday."

"Then why aren't you fleeing with them?"

"Because I've still got work to do."

He wondered what else there *was* to do and why her appointed watchdog, Davies, was leaving her to get it done alone. "How did it go?" he asked.

She threw him a lively smile and shrugged. "It generally goes well with a nicely planned campaign and plenty of good advertising to back it up. You agency boys did a very handsome job. The action was heavy and the sales were great everywhere I was able to check."

"Which is what I found, too. That should put it in the bag, shouldn't it?"

"Not quite. There's a lot more to it than that. With a hundred or more demonstrators pushing the item, almost force-feeding it to the shoppers, it was bound to sell. The real test comes during the next two weeks, the re-orders. On Monday, the salesmen will begin reworking the territory, with Cinnamon-Nut at the top of their lists, while I'm checking with the distributors and calling on store managers to make sure the item hasn't been swept away with the debris of the battle."

"How long before we get a real indication?"

"We should know the score in about two or three weeks, maybe a month. After that, we'll break it in the Mid-West and if the results are good, we go nationally with it. And that's enough business talk. I'm up to here with Cinnamon-Nut."

"I agree."

"Then you'd better pack and get back to New York with the others. Washington can be the dullest city in the country on Sunday."

He smiled and said, "I hadn't planned on going back tonight. I thought I'd take in some of the sights I haven't seen in years. Also, I have the address of a very fine Italian restaurant Jim Whipple told me to try, and I haven't been there yet. Are you booked for dinner?"

"No, and I hate eating alone."

"I shouldn't have thought you'd ever have to do that."

Robin laughed prettily and said, "You know, I like you. You're very nice."

"I've always gotten an A in the being-nice-to-stranded-girls department. Especially beautiful girls."

"And in other subjects?"

"If you divide my waist measurement by two you'll get an approximation of my I.Q. Shall we change for dinner?"

The restaurant was overly crowded and they sat at the bar for almost an hour before Steve's name was called. Robin wore a close-fitting black dress that showed every line of her finely molded body and the perfume she wore all combined to drive Steve frantic with the urge to touch and possess her. They had a superb dinner and enjoyed themselves thoroughly and Steve became intrigued with the possibilities that lay ahead. Libby was driven out of his mind completely. Before he could notice, the restaurant was practically empty, the check on a small tray beside him and his watch told him it was nearing midnight. "Shall we?" he said and Robin rewarded him with a bright smile and an affirmative nod. He got their coats from the checkroom and they walked along Connecticut Avenue until an empty cab came along.

At the hotel, he suggested a nightcap in the bar and they sat and talked for almost another hour until Robin said, "There's got to be something more comfortable than these chairs."

Steve said, "I've got a very comfortable sofa in my room."

"And I in mine."

"Toss a coin?"

"I don't think I have one with me."

He reached into his pocket and withdrew a quarter, handed it to her. She spun it into the air, caught it and placed it on the table, her hand covering it. "Heads!" Steve called. She raised her hand and revealed the classic Washington profile. "Your choice," she said.

"Your room."

Arms locked together, swaying slightly from the accumulation of Scotch, wine, and brandy, they crossed the lobby to the elevators, got out on the ninth floor and went to her room. As he closed the door behind him, she turned, and he took her into his arms and kissed her. Her lips were warm and their eagerness matched his own, drowning out all thought of Libby, GFP, Cinnamon-Nut, Leary, and the world. Only Robin and himself. Robin all to himself.

She drew away from him with an abrupt move and said, "Steve—"

"What?"

"Maybe this isn't such a good idea."

"I can't think of a better one."

"I . . . I honestly think we shouldn't get . . . involved. It wouldn't be very smart."

"I've had a sneaking suspicion we're already involved." He kissed her again and felt response in her body.

"This could lead to trouble . . ." she began, but he kissed away the rest of the sentence. "What's wrong, Robin, are you married?"

"No, it isn't that."

"Then what are you afraid of?"

"Us. You and me. We could get awfully hurt."

"Come off it, Robin. We're two, grown, fully adult people."

She paused in a moment of indecision, staring up at him, then said, "All right, Steve. You're a very attractive man. There's a nice style, a flavor about you." She turned her back to him, kicked off her shoes and unzipped her dress, removed it and laid it on a chair, and then pulled off her stockings. She took three backward steps toward him and motioned him to unfasten her bra. "You're lovely," he said hungrily.

She laughed, and said, "The current word is stacked, isn't it?"

"Perfect would be more appropriate." He took her into his arms and crushed her, kissed her, feeling her full breasts against his chest, trembling with anticipation. "You're not still afraid, are you, Robin?"

"I'm not afraid of you, if that's what you mean."

In bed, they merged into one being and he recognized at once that she was easily as expert as he and it was all he could do to restrain himself from driving at her with the lust that had mounted in him, driving him demented with the need for her; but he allowed her to set the pace, until it came to an end in a shattering burst that drained him completely. They lay close together in tight embrace, recovering.

"Oh, God," Robin breathed against his chest, "that was wonderful, Steve."

"You were marvelous. I don't know what in the world you were afraid of."

"There are some things you don't—can't understand."

"How can I if you won't tell me what's bothering you?"

"Oh, let it go."

"I wish you'd tell me. I'd like to know."

"There's nothing I can tell that would reassure you. Or me."

"You're hinting at something."

"Well . . . let it pass." Abruptly, she turned the subject away from herself. "You're married, aren't you, Steve?"

"Yes."

"But not happily, I take it."

"You could say that at the moment."

Wisely, she did not pursue the question, but turned the subject back to herself. "I've been married twice. The first time, I was seventeen. That one ended in an annulment. After that, I came to New York and found a job with a public research firm—taking polls—that kind of thing. Then I studied shorthand and typing at night and went to work inside as a secretary. I quit to marry a bright, upcoming research analyst who turned out to be an infant who should never have been cut loose from Mama's apron strings. It lasted only a year and ended in divorce. That's when I went to work in GFP's marketing and merchandising department. I've been there three years, a little while in town, a little while on the road, doing what you've just seen me do. It gets boring and awfully lonely at times, but it pays well and I do a good job. Besides a man would cost them a lot more than they pay me."

They had finished their cigarettes, and Robin reached up and turned off the light. In the darkness, as she drew closer to him, his hands became his eyes, running over her neck, breasts, and thighs, lips caressing her partly opened mouth, hearing her small gasps of pleasure at his touch. They came together with breathtaking desire, attacking, devouring, finally drowning in each other's bodies.

In the morning, Steve went to his room long enough to shower, shave, and change his clothes. Robin met him in the lobby. They breakfasted together and he thought she was lovelier and more desirable than ever, with most of the eyes in the dining room following them to and from their table.

"You weren't really going sightseeing, were you, Steve?" Robin asked when they returned to the lobby.

"Not until you mentioned that you weren't going back to New York."

She smiled in that infectious way and said, "You do have a way of flattering a girl directly or indirectly." And when he said nothing, but returned her smile, "What about your wife, won't she be expecting you?"

"My wife is down in Virginia, visiting her parents."

"Well, as I told you before, Washington can be deadly on a Sunday, except for other sightseers on the prowl."

"I find the prospect of a dull day in Washington very exciting. With you."

"Let's get my car from the garage and take a ride. A long ride."

Steve gave an exaggerated groan. "The only ride I want is by elevator to the ninth floor."

"Don't be so tunnel-visioned. The ninth floor will be here when we get back."

They drove into the Virginia countryside, bleak and cold at this time of year, then turned around in Middleburg and came back. Robin had no objections to the ninth floor, and there they spent the afternoon making love, napping, and awakening at nightfall. They dressed and had dinner in the same seafood restaurant where they had gone on the first night of their meeting, and then returned to the hotel where they spent the night in Steve's room.

In the morning they had breakfast in the coffee shop and Robin drove him to the station to catch his train. "When will you be back in New York?" he asked while waiting for the announcement that would separate them.

"That depends on how it goes here."

"You're being evasive."

"All right. By the end of the week. But Steve"—

"I'll call you."

"You musn't. I won't take the call."

"Then at home. Where do you live?"

"I won't tell you."

"Robin, you're not telling me this is all, are you?"

"It could be difficult there, Steve."

"You keep saying that, but you can't really mean you want to end it here and now."

"I can't tell you more than I have already. I don't want us to interfere with my job, for one thing. There are complications. For another thing, there's your job. And your wife."

"My wife will be out of town for another month, perhaps six weeks."

"Unfortunately," Robin said, "my spare time is accounted for."

"To whom, for what?"

"I can't tell you any more than that."

He could see her perplexity in her wrinkled forehead, her eyes, trying to come to some decision. She said finally, "Let me do this my way, please, Steve. I don't want anything to tip the table over, that's all."

"All right, but only if you promise to call me."

"I will. When I can."

On his way back to New York he began to wonder if Robin might not be right; that it would be safer all around if they didn't see each other again.

And then he began to wonder about himself and Libby, and what had become of their marriage.

There was a letter from Libby waiting for him with the same newsy, yet newsless, details of her days and nights in Lancaster and—*oh, Jesus!*—she had been planning to spend the last weekend in Washington with Olive and Barney at a reception given by the British ambassador in honor of an arriving dignitary from London! The same weekend he had just concluded with Robin. For a moment he experienced pure fright, then put it aside. The reception, he was certain, would have been at the embassy and, as he read on, he found that he was right. The Newells had stayed at the Shoreham. Cal Waggoner had been with them . . . He crumpled up the letter and threw it aside.

The test campaign had gone well and Cinnamon-Nut was being expanded into Ohio, Indiana, Illinois, Michigan, and Wisconsin, which comprised the East North Central market. He assumed Robin was out in the field doing her job as she had done it in Washington, and waited impatiently to hear from her, but no call came, no letter.

He made two calls on Mark Lawson, bearing copy and artwork for approval and was pleased, as were Mack and Whip, that Lawson okayed everything with a minimum of changes. He made a third call there with Barrett, at the latter's request, to discuss some change in the budget, which Lawson accepted without a qualm. On his next call, Bob Davies told Steve that Lawson had been called away to Detroit and Chicago to check on the progress of Cinnamon-Nut there, and Steve went through a period of extreme envy that bordered on jealousy. He worked with one of the brand managers for three hours and returned to his office in a state of despondency.

Libby returned from Lancaster three weeks later and for a brief period everything went so well that Robin Ford dimmed in his memory. But after a month, Libby began to behave as though she had been in New York on a visit from home and could hardly wait to return to Lancaster. She chattered endlessly about Olive and what great things Barney was accomplishing, of Cal Waggoner's latest speech or bill in the House, of Buzz, Maxine, Arnie—*ad infinitum.*

Spring came early and Libby began showing signs of nervous restlessness. She and Steve bickered and argued over the most ridiculously minor incidents: a dress returned from the cleaner a day late, Steve leaving the morning *Times* crumpled on the breakfast table, his need to check out GFP's television commercials at home when she wanted to see a certain program and, as before, his frequent lateness for dinner. It seemed that no meal they shared could be concluded without some outrageous disagreement. They stopped accepting invitations and did no entertaining. Bed became a place for sleeping only.

Steve began to yearn for Robin, and as they went into May, had twice found comfort and relief in the arms of a GBS programming assistant and once with a girl he picked up at O'Malley's. Then Robin came back to town and during the week that followed before she left on another trip, he spent three stolen afternoons with her in various hotel rooms, and the entire weekend, telling Libby he would have to be in Chicago on business.

Then Libby began to suspect his infidelities. There were telephone calls to the apartment that broke off suddenly with, "Sorry, wrong number," or went totally dead when she answered. When Steve took some of those mysterious calls, the one-sided conversation was always brief and sounded more like a guarded, coded report from a CIA agent to his bureau chief in the presence of an enemy listener.

There followed a brief period of accusations, tears, recriminations, and reproach. Deadly silence. And guilt. Steve's work began to suffer and eventually he was forced to confess to Keith Allard that he and Libby were on the verge of separation. Or divorce. Keith urged patience, but could give no further advice. He had seen divorce among agency employees—victims of the profession—too many times.

Early in July, Steve came home one evening to find Libby gone, two suitcases, cosmetics case, and clothes with her. Taped to the full-length mirror in their bedroom was a hastily-scrawled note:

STEVE

I think we will both be much happier this way. I won't be back. All I ask is that you will please not contest the divorce or make things difficult for me.

LIBBY

During the latter part of August he received word from Eli Tinsley that Libby had obtained an uncontested divorce in Juarez, Mexico.

All Steve could feel was relief.

Chapter 4

1

With Libby out of his life and Robin out of the city, work became Steve's antidote for the nothingness left by their absence. He suspected that Allard had conspired with Barrett to pile as much detail on him as he could carry, and with Mack and Whip giving him more than a normal share of creative responsibility, the summer and fall months sped by. Despite the efforts of the Allards and others to take up the slack time in his life, he felt something akin to failure and anxiety about the breakup of his marriage. During those months he had seen Robin twice, in from territorial swings, and as Christmas neared, he began to dread facing that holiday alone.

Robin wrote from Houston that she would be spending the season of goodwill to all men with her parents in Denver. He was at his lowest, most desperate point when Keith and Louise invited him to share their Christmas–New Year vacation at Grandview, New Hampshire, where Louise was determined to learn to ski and insisted that Steve teach her. He accepted at once.

The days on the ski runs with Louise were exhilarating (Keith refused to risk a broken arm or leg and spent his daylight hours hiking or reading) and the nights were given over to sitting around a man-high fireplace in the public room over pleasant conversation and hot drinks with the other guests. There were enough singles to make the days and nights interesting and Steve participated in the social life to the extent that he was able to put both Libby and Robin out of his mind temporarily, along with the GFP account.

New Year's Eve fell on Friday night. In place of the record player, the management of the Grandview Hotel had arranged a party for its guests, importing a six-piece band and providing a late supper and favors. The Allard table grew from three to an even dozen. Steve paired with Trina Rogers, a young writer from New York who was terribly excited about her first big assignment, an upcoming trip to Europe at the magazine's expense. The party blazed into the next year with champagne flowing and Steve awoke to the new year in Trina's room.

The revelers began leaving late that afternoon and by the next day, Steve and the Allards were virtually alone, having taken their rooms until Monday morning. Steve saw Trina off after lunch on Sunday, then he and Louise took one final turn on the near-empty slopes while Keith napped in his room.

After dinner, Louise excused herself to start packing while Keith and Steve sat alone in the warming comfort of the blazing fireplace, sipping brandy. "Steve," Keith said after a while, "when we get back you'll be moving up a step. Before we left New York, Andy Makyrios turned in his notice."

"Andy quitting?" Steve asked in surprise.

"He's going over to Hayes, Stanley, & Coleman as account executive. Jim Whipple will take over from Mack and we'll bring in a new man to fill your slot. Okay?"

"Of course, Keith. I assume Wade knows all about this?"

"Naturally. I didn't think you'd have to ask that." He threw a quick glance at Steve and said, "You're not having any problems with Wade, are you?"

"No. No, it's just that as close as I've been to Mack, he never let on for a single moment."

"Then you haven't any reservations at all about it?"

"None at all. I work very well with Whip."

"That's fine, then. Bill and I discussed it with Wade and he was particularly pleased because you and Lawson get along so well."

"Does that mean I'll be doing most of the contact work?"

"Let's say you'll be dividing it more equitably with Wade and Whip."

"Hell, Keith, you know Wade avoids Lawson the way he would the bubonic plague."

Allard laughed lightly. "Other than top policy calls, you're right. I don't know why that should make so much difference."

"Except that I don't like the idea of giving up the creative end of the work to become an executive errand boy for Lawson."

"Don't let that worry you. There'll be plenty of creative

work for you and Whip to handle, besides overseeing the rest of the group. Also, you'll be stepping up from eighteen-thousand to twenty-two thousand, five hundred, plus your regular bonus."

Which closed off any further objections Steve may have had in mind at the moment.

Steve's workload—sharing full creative accountability with Jim Whipple—increased tremendously in volume. Apart from current assignments and supervision of the overall work in progress, he spent much of his free time planning future campaigns while Whip concentrated more on current copy for the print and electronic media. His smooth relationship with Lawson continued and there were fewer biting and unjustified criticisms. Even Barrett began relying more on Steve to substitute for him in making routine calls on Lawson, devoting more of his time to the Chevalier account, which had been having its own share of problems since the Surgeon General's report on smoking was released, with the industry fighting the clamor that cigarette advertising be suppressed. Steve was also aware that Barrett was having increased domestic problems with Sylvia, from whom he had twice been separated and reconciled. Having gone through the divorce procedure with ease himself, he was certain that such would not be the case with the Barretts.

2

It was a Friday, late in the morning, when he next heard from Robin, using her maiden name, Grainger, suggested by her on one or two occasions when they had checked into a motel for the weekend. Nancy, standing beside his desk while he ran through a report she had brought him a few minutes before, took the call.

"It's a Miss Grainger," she said, holding her palm over the mouthpiece. "Do you know her? She sounds spooky."

"Grainger?" It took him a few seconds to remember the alias. "Oh, of course," he said and reached for the phone. "Miss Grainger? Steve Gilman here."

"Steve," he heard her shaky voice, "is it safe to talk?"

"Just a moment, please." He pushed the report toward Nancy and said, "This is okay, Nancy. File it please."

When she went out he said, "Robin, where are you?"

"Steve, I need help," she said fuzzily.

"What is it, Robin, where are you?"

"I can't tell you about it over the phone." Now he could hear the soft sound of sobbing behind her words. "Can you get away, Steve? Please, I need you."

"Are you at your apartment?"

"No. No. Can you get away?"

"Yes. Where are you?"

"At the Madrigal on West-thirty-fourth Street. It's a . . ."

"I know where it is. What's your room number?"

"Let me get my key. Wait." A moment later she came on again. "It's room 607."

"I'll be there as fast . . ." He heard a gasp on the other end of the line. "Robin, are you all right?"

There was only the *click* of the receiver as she hung up, and he felt sudden terror. Robin's voice, but strange, even weird. He went out, pausing only to tell Nancy he would be gone for an hour or two, trying to act casually about it.

"Any place where I can reach you if something comes up?"

"No. Stall anything you can. If I'm not back in two hours, I'll call in."

He hurriedly walked the block to the Summit where he caught a cab and gave the driver the Thirty-fourth Street address, lighting a cigarette to dispel his nervousness. He had never heard a voice so filled with fear, speaking brokenly, crying softly. And why the Madrigal, of all places—a small midtown hotel of questionable character—for someone like Robin?

He paid the driver, entered the hotel lobby, and went directly to the elevators. An old man took him to the sixth floor and he turned right, following the arrow indicator, and found 607. He put his ear to the door and heard water running, then silence. He knocked and got no answer, then knocked again, harder; and this time he heard some movement, a shuffling across a carpet, then her low voice. "Steve?"

"Yes, open up."

The inside lock grated and the door opened a mere slit. Her eyes confirmed his presence and she stood aside to allow him to enter. Robin was in her bra and a half slip, wearing stockings but no shoes. He stared at her face and saw no marks there, only an ugly purplish bruise just beneath her left breast, another on her thigh. Her relief at the sight of him was immense and she came into his arms and clung to him, trembling.

"Robin, Robin, for God's sake, what is all this about?"

"Give me a cigarette, please. I'm all out."

He lit one for her and placed it between her lips, and she went to the bed and sat on its side. The room was shabby, its furniture cheap, scarred, the entire atmosphere shoddy. Her dress lay crumpled on a chair, her purse on the night table was open, half of its contents spilled out: lipstick, loose change, a billfold, an empty cigarette pack, and a book of matches. She puffed on the cigarette for a moment, then said, "Thank you for coming, Steve. I feel so much better now with you here."

"What happened, Robin?"

She said simply, "Mark Lawson happened."

"Mark Lawson? What in hell—what has he to do with this?"

"Oh, Steve . . ." she began, then stopped. "You didn't know it was Mark? You never even suspected?" When he looked blankly at her, "Remember that time when we were in Washington? I told you then there were things you couldn't understand, things I couldn't tell you . . ."

He felt a dull ache sweep over him, akin to stupidity for having failed to realize that Lawson had been the other man in her life, to realize why she had been so persistent in not allowing him to contact her, refusing to tell him where she lived. "Why, Robin?"

She drew deeply on the cigarette and exhaled slowly. "We had a blowup. We've been falling apart lately. I recognized the signs and asked for a showdown. I knew it was another woman, but he's been through those before. Except that this one was lasting longer than the others. Not that I minded so much, except that he was actually taunting me with her. Last week he started hinting that I'd be going out on the road for a much longer time than usual. Out West. I told him I wouldn't do it. I wouldn't let him get rid of me that easily.

"He threatened to fire me and I got angry and told him I'd go to his wife and tell her all about us. He quieted down then, and last night he asked me out to dinner to talk it over. We drove out to the Island to a little out-of-the-way restaurant where we wouldn't be seen. On the way back, he told me he wanted me to leave town for good, that it was over. He handed me an envelope with a thousand dollars in it and said he'd expect me to resign and be gone by Sunday, that he'd already found a replacement for me.

"I told him he couldn't buy me off that easily and we argued the rest of the way back to town. When I brought his wife into it again, he struck me and lost control of the car. It sideswiped a parked car and he and the owner exchanged cards, but his car couldn't be moved because the fender had crumpled into the tire. We left it there on Thirty-fourth Street and started walking to find a cab, when he started accusing me of being the cause of the accident. I told him to go to hell and started walking away from him, but he struck me here"—she indicated the bruise—"and knocked me down, then walked away. A passing couple helped me up and I limped in here and checked in. I'm frightened, Steve. He's a madman, a lunatic."

"Oh, Jesus. You're lucky it wasn't a lot worse."

"It's bad enough."

"Do you think he may have broken a rib?"

"I don't think so. It just hurts like the devil."

"Let's get you dressed and I'll take you to your apartment. We'll talk about it on the way."

"That's what I'm afraid of. He has his own key. He may even be there. I don't want to see him again, ever."

"I doubt if he'd be there this time of day. To hell with him. We'll risk it, pack your things, then take them over to my place."

"I can't let you do that. I don't want you to get involved."

"Then what can I do? Why did you call me?"

"For one thing, I needed someone. I've never felt so alone in all my life. The clerk was suspicious enough when I checked in without any luggage, like some hustler who'd walked in off the street. All I want to do is get home and pack what I need, and leave. For good."

"Where to?"

"I don't know yet. Wherever a thousand will take me. The West Coast, maybe. All I want is to get away from him."

"I doubt if he'll do any more, Robin. He can't afford to have a thing like this explode into a police matter. Hell, if this hit the papers he'd be dead with his wife and job. Get dressed."

"But only to pack and leave. I've had it with Mark and New York."

"And me?"

"You don't even enter into it any more, Steve. I mean that. You can't, particularly now. It's messy enough as it is. Please help me."

"Get dressed."

It was the first time he had seen her apartment and he understood why she had been reluctant to give it up. It was furnished in beautiful taste, and he was momentarily surprised that Lawson would pick up so expensive a tab for exclusive rights to Robin. Or any woman.

Yet there was something unnatural, Steve thought, in the way Robin went directly into the bedroom and began emptying drawers and the closet, piling dresses, suits, undergarments, stockings, and shoes on the bed, selecting only those items she intended taking with her, and leaving the rest. It seemed as though she might be doing this for someone else instead of herself. Steve got out a large and a small suitcase and helped her pack. Into an overnight cosmetics case she dropped a collection of bottles, tubes, toothbrushes, and finally, an assortment of costume jewelry, with one or two more expensive pieces among them. She looped a double strand of pearls around her neck, put two rings and a brooch into her purse, then removed the ten one-hundred-dollar bills from the envelope and tucked them into her wallet, replaced it in her purse, and was ready—even eager—to leave. As he closed the door behind them and lifted the suitcases, the telephone began to ring, but it was as though Robin was deaf, striding toward the elevators as though she had heard nothing. It occurred to Steve that she was walking out like a transient leaving an overnight hotel room, as they themselves had left the Madrigal, without sentiment, or a single look back.

"You won't come to my place, Robin?" he asked again in the elevator.

Without looking at him, she shook her head from side to side. "No, Steve, I won't." And, somehow, he knew she was right. He couldn't afford the risk of which she had been keenly aware from the start, no more than Lawson could afford public exposure in an affair of this kind. At the moment, he knew it was over between himself and Robin, just as it was between Robin and Lawson, and beneath his disappointment, he was conscious of a deeper-seated feeling that could only be relief.

"Where to?" he asked.

"Just put me in a cab. I'll go to a hotel and spend the night. In the morning, I'll get a plane reservation and leave. What I need right now is some sleep."

The doorman whistled up a cab, a look of mild surprise—perhaps suspicion—on his face at the sight of Robin in the company of a stranger; and Steve, feeling his stare, turned to one side so that he would not be recognizable in case Mark came asking questions. Steve saw her into the cab, her luggage distributed on the front seat and rear floor. She offered her cheek, and he kissed it tenderly.

"Good-bye, Steve. I'm sorry. I wish it had been you first," she said.

"Will you write?" he asked.

"Maybe. I've got so much to think about first."

"Good-bye, Robin. I hope you'll be happy wherever you are."

She started to reply, but the words choked in her throat and tears came into her eyes as the cab pulled away.

Steve walked to the corner of Third Avenue, a feeling of tightness in his chest, the dampness of sweat under his arms, conscious of a shortness of breath. It was pure anger for Mark Lawson, he knew, an inner rage that was all-consuming, and he wondered how he could face him again without accusing him of his vileness toward Robin, and toward his wife. To himself? *Bastard* was what Andy Makyrios and Jim Whipple had called Lawson so often. *Evil sonofabitch* was how Steve classified him, a man who deserved every known suffering.

He had walked south on Third Avenue from Seventy-sixth to Fifty-second Street and turned west toward Lexington. At the entrance of the Hungerford Trust Building he stopped, then crossed over and walked the block to the Summit, got into an empty cab and gave the driver the address of his apartment. It was three-thirty when he reached home, and instinctively he picked up the receiver to phone Peggy to tell her he wouldn't be back today, then cradled the receiver, went into the kitchen, and got out a bottle of Scotch. He removed his jacket and tie and began drinking.

Some time later he heard his doorbell ring and became aware that dusk had fallen. And that he was quite drunk. He turned on a lamp and heard the bell ring again. When he reached the door, thinking—even hoping—it might be Robin returning to him after having second thoughts, he heard footsteps retreating as he opened it. She turned and came toward him again and, as she reached him, he saw it was Inga Maczerak, George's Swedish "toy."

"Steve . . ." she began, staring at him with curiosity.

"Inga. What?"

She giggled. "You are drunk, Steve? Something is wrong?" Not too many years away from Sweden, her accent was still fairly pronounced.

"Wrong? N—no, nothing wrong. Do something for you, Inga?"

"Only to see can I borrow some coffee? I work late today. I forget I am out of coffee. George is in Frankfurt . . ."

"Sure. Come in an' he'p yourself. Anything you want."

"You have eaten?"

"No. I been drinking."

"Alone is no good to drink."

"I know. Had a rough day."

"Ah, poor Steve. I tell you, you need a wife."

He laughed grimly. "Already had one, remember? Why do I need another one to share all the beauty of my life? Why do I need to be tied to somebody who will walk out on me again? Tell me, Inga."

"Ah, Steve, you joke with me. Why do you talk hate when you should talk love?"

"Inga, you Swedes see life differently from the way we do here. You look at it with open, realistic eyes. You take love less seriously than we do. Why can't we accept it as a natural phemom—phe*nom*enon, for what it is, instead of something to be shackled to with a lot of mystical, superstitious words mumbled by another man who is probably just as humanly error-prone and horny as any other man?"

Inga giggled again. "Ah, you Americans. You look for purity in a wife while you go with another woman or run to prostitutes and feel shame. From childhood, you are Pur—Pur—what is the word, Steve?"

"Puritans," he supplied.

"Yes, Puritans. You grow up feeling guilty for your thoughts of little girls, then of big girls. In Sweden, we think freely of such things. I have no guilt that I wanted to go to bed with a man when I was thirteen, fourteen. I knew my first man when I was fourteen. After that, there were boys in school. In England, I knew other men and I was happy with them."

"Why did you marry George?"

"Because I wanted to come to America," she said simply. "George was older, but he said he would marry me. And America I always dreamed of."

"Inga . . ." he began, then broke off shortly and said, "Let's get your coffee."

In the kitchen, Inga said, "You are sad over something. A woman, I think." She turned to face him and added, "I will fix dinner for us. To drink alone and not eat is bad, yes?"

"Yes," Steve agreed, unwilling to see her leave, to spend the evening alone thinking of Robin and Mark Lawson. Of Libby.

"Good. You go and take shower."

"All right. Can you find everything?"

"I know where it is. You go now."

He took a shower leisurely, then decided to shave, the effect of the Scotch beginning to wear off. He wondered about Robin, where, in which hotel she was hiding, nursing her bruised body and mind. He dressed in slacks and a sports shirt and smelled the appetizing odors coming from the kitchen and his mind turned to Inga's thinking and liberal talk that had caused considerable suspicion and gossip about her among the other occupants of the apartment house.

Inga had fixed a zesty stew and salad, and opened a bottle of wine. They dined and talked until Steve's spirits were lifted out of the earlier morass of depression. Afterward, they sat in the living room over cigarettes and cognac, talking of Inga's earlier life in Sweden, of her sisters and a brother, about whom—and all subjects—she was equally frank and honest, which caused Steve to marvel that so much of his own life lay buried and unshareable with others; his life, Grady's and Jenny's, his earlier fear of marriage, and now its death. And then it was eleven o'clock and Inga wanted to hear the late news and see Johnny Carson who followed. Midway through the program, the effect of the cognac took over and Inga fell asleep on the sofa where she had been lying. Steve, himself well underway again, shook her awake. "Time for bed, Inga," he said.

"I am tired. I sleep here," she mumbled.

"Come on, Inga. Home and to bed." He pulled her up into a sitting position, one arm around her for support. She looked up at him and smiled. "It is not good to drink alone or to sleep alone. With someone you like, it is much, much nicer."

"Inga . . ."

"Put me to bed here, Steve."

He got her to her feet and she swayed against him. He put his arms around her to steady her. "Inga, don't tempt me."

"Then what was all this talk for, Steve? A woman can be lonely too, no?"

He stared down at her blond crown and little-girl face, flushed with sleep, her body warm and yielding, inviting. "And George?"

"Ah, George. If he does not know, will he be unhappy? And in Frankfurt, there are no women to make him not lonely?"

And as he held her, wanting her, temptation wrestled with conscience and lost. He led Inga to the door and said, "Goodnight, Inga. Go home and dream peaceful dreams."

She looked up at him and smiled again. "Ah, you are a foolish man, Steve. But a very nice, foolish man."

3

So another year passed and Steve began to feel a stronger sense of professionalism he hadn't experienced before, even though he relied heavily on Whip's cool brilliance and Allard's long years of experience to guide him over the remaining few rough spots. He began to evade Barrett, not only in work, but the carelessly dropped invitations to visit him and Sylvia, assuming they had once again reconciled their differences. And he adopted a policy of avoiding any entanglements with any of the many attractive women who worked at the agency. His entire social life was spent away from the area of his work now.

In July of 1967, Jim Whipple announced privately to Steve that he was resigning as of the first of September, which gave Steve the distinct feeling of having been suddenly set adrift without a rudder. Whip, at thirty-nine, had saved some money and had had a remarkable bit of luck in the stock market. Now he wanted to take two years off to write the novel he had been quietly outlining during the weekends and holidays, and needed at least six months of research in Europe, and another eighteen months to do the actual writing. Jim's wife, Frances, who wrote magazine articles, had encouraged him in the move and, as Whip put it, "If I don't do it now, I'll end up like every other sad sonofabitch who couldn't decide to break away when the time was right. Do me a favor, Steve, keep this under your hat until I spring it on Wade and Keith."

"Count on it," Steve replied, not without a great deal of envy for Whip's courageous move.

In August, in his sixth year with Leary and his third on the GFP account, Keith invited Steve to his home for dinner, and this time, Steve knew the reason for the invitation. Usually, when he was asked in for social get-togethers, the invitation would invariably come from Louise. This, then, would have to do with Whip's resignation, and Steve felt an overwhelming sense of uneasiness he had never felt before.

After dinner, Louise excused herself and kissed Steve goodnight, adding, "I know you men want to talk business, to which I can contribute nothing. Don't stay up too late."

Keith wasted no time getting to the point. "Has Whip said anything to you about leaving at the end of the month, Steve?"

"Yes," Steve admitted, "he mentioned it to me."

"You think you can handle the top spot?"

"I don't know, Keith. I think this is one shot you're going to have to call for me."

Allard grinned slowly. "First time I've known you to shy away from a direct answer." When Steve maintained silence, Allard said, "I think you can do it. I know damned well you can. I'd hate to bring someone else in from the outside to put over your head."

Which moved Steve to reply, "Keith, I know the account as well as anyone in the group, with the possible exception of you, Wade, and Bill. I've sat in on every budget and worked on every campaign and presentation since before Mack left, but you're practically asking a sort of glorified copywriter to take over a hell of a big and important account with an account executive's responsibility."

"Don't you agree that's one way of getting there?" Keith said. "I know, because I went through the same thing years ago. Steve, there's always an important time in a man's life, the moment of decision, when he must choose for himself which direction he will take. You've seen two good men do that within two years, Mack and Whip. Now it's your turn. You're what, twenty-seven, twenty-eight?"

"I'm twenty-seven, but at this moment I feel twenty-one again, like the first day I walked into Leary asking for a job."

"Come on, Steve, you're a mature adult with six years of good hard work and practical experience behind you. Lawson likes you and I know he'll be pleased with the news that you're taking over. You'll have plenty of help from this end and Wade and I will be working closely with you until you are sure you can go on your own."

"What about Bill, how does he feel about it?"

"When I told Bill about Whip, yours was the first name he mentioned as his first choice. Let's see, you're getting twenty-two thousand five hundred dollars now. This will jump you to Whip's level, twenty-five thousand dollars. In another year, if all is going well, we'll talk about more money."

"That part of it is fine, but . . ."

"What is it then, afraid of the responsibility?"

"No, of course not . . ."

Keith waited for a moment, then said soberly, "Your decision now could be most crucial to your career, Steve. There are two or three men I can think of who would be more than happy to take over the job. Roland Thompson in Chicago, who's been asking for a shot at New York and has offered to take less money to get it. And of course, we could shop around. But where would that leave you? Among other things, Steve, don't lose your sense of balance, and values. You've done very well here and I'd hate to see you toss away that kind of seniority, even though your job wouldn't be in jeopardy if you turn this opportunity down.

"I know Bill would be as disappointed as I am, and the other thing to consider is that—here, or elsewhere—who would put a man in charge if the man in question didn't feel himself secure enough to handle the top spot?"

Steve said contritely, "I'm sorry if I've given you that impression, Keith. And then again, maybe it's just that I'm unconsciously afraid the job is too big for me, the responsibility of carrying so much of the load on my shoulders . . . I just don't know . . ."

"Try it. You haven't got too much to lose and a hell of a lot more to gain. At worst, you won't get fired. Anything else bothering you?" Steve looked thoughtful but remained silent and Keith said, "Steve, we've brought you along pretty fast and perhaps that was a mistake, but I'm sure I haven't been that wrong. Besides, I think you owe us a little something, don't you?"

Steve felt himself bristling. "Just what do you think I owe the Leary Agency, Keith?"

"Shall I mention loyalty, for one thing."

"That's a pretty scarce commodity in this business, from what I've been able to see."

"It does exist, you know."

"I'm sure it does, in some special, isolated cases. Like yours."

"And yours, too."

"I wasn't particularly aware of it until you brought the subject up. I guess I've gotten to think of loyalty in abstract terms, like integrity."

Allard smiled. "You make it sound like a dirty word."

"Am I supposed to revere it? Take a look at the number of accounts that switch agencies every year. Try to count the number of account reps, execs, copywriters and art directors who change jobs in any given month. How much loyalty does that add up to?"

"How about looking at the brighter side of the coin, Steve. The Leary Agency hasn't lost a major account in over nine years, not since Charlie Weatherford walked out of here with the Lincoln Brewery account and used it to start his own agency. At least we have a good reputation for client loyalty and only because we've had good, talented people doing damned good work for them, and they get the highest pay checks in our profession."

"All right, Keith, let's say I'm satisfied if you are. I'll give it my best, I promise you."

"That," Allard said quietly, and with some satisfaction, "is all I've ever asked of you or anyone else."

4

On Friday, September 1, 1967, Steve Gilman sat in Wade Barrett's office with Keith Allard and Bill Leary present. He listened carefully as Wade outlined his responsibility to the GFP account. "Of course, Steve, I'll be in overall command," Wade said needlessly, "and you'll have everything you need to backstop you. However, since you will be in direct contact with the client, you must realize that the success or failure of our largest and most profitable account will rest largely in your hands. We'll give you every possible assistance in every department here, but what happens between you and Mark Lawson will be most important to the client-agency relationship. It won't be a light load, carrying nearly ten million dollars in billings, and we know that.

"Lawson—you already know—is the man you've got to live with, but the needs of the account are much more important than the whims and erratic moods of the man. You understand that, I'm sure."

It was a pompous speech, coming from Barrett, and Steve didn't know if it had been intended for himself or for the benefit of Bill and Keith, neither of whom seemed the least impressed. Steve nodded. "You've made that perfectly clear, Wade," and then with a stroke of perversity added, "but I have a question. At what point do we say to Mr. Lawson, 'If you want an agency that will roll over and play dead for you, find yourself another boy'?"

Bill Leary jerked upward to his feet, his face showing frank annoyance, "Never," he said in a brittle tone. "If it comes to that, bring the problem to me and I will relieve you of all responsibility. Let's not have any misunderstanding on that score, Steve. I'm satisfied with Wade's and Keith's recommendation that you take over the leadership and contact work on the account. Until this moment, I was personally pleased, but your raising that sophomoric question clouds my opinion somewhat. You seem indecisive and I don't like that in anyone about to take over an important job. I want an affirmative answer from you right now."

Steve saw Wade turn his gaze upward toward the ceiling and in turning toward Bill, caught the wince on Allard's face. He said, "You have it, Mr. Leary. I will do nothing to offend Mr. Lawson, no matter how wrong I may believe him to be."

Leary hesitated for a moment, then said, "I'll accept that. I might add, too, that I have never believed the client's okay makes a campaign or an ad a good one, but I expect the man in charge to be diplomatic enough to overcome any objections to a well thought-out program or ad by reasonable suggestion."

"Yes, sir."

In Allard's office later, Keith said, "I suppose you know

you were within an inch of blowing it, back there. A couple of seconds more and you might even have received an invitation to have a little chat with Norton Axelrod."

Steve grinned sheepishly. "I sort of experienced that same feeling."

"Steve, is there something bothering you about this that you haven't told me about? You're acting as though you've got some kind of a death wish about this whole thing. Is it something to do with Lawson?"

"It's nothing, Keith," he replied. "Just jitters, like my first day at Columbia."

"All right. Wade is phoning Lawson about the assignment now. He'll try to set up an appointment for you to see Mark on Monday or Tuesday morning, to give him the weekend to mull it over. That is, if Mark gives it any thought at all."

On that first Tuesday of September, Steve cabbed directly from his apartment to Mark Lawson's office, carrying his attaché case and a large envelope of color proofs that would appear in the Christmas editions of the major general and women's magazines and Sunday newspaper supplements. Lawson's welcome was friendly, as usual, but he made no mention of Steve's change of status with the account as Steve spread the proofs out on the desk and Mark examined them. Moments later, Lawson threw him a quick side-glance and Steve saw the smile he had come to recognize as one of approval. "Nice," Lawson said. "Very nice. New background, isn't it? I don't remember seeing this in the comprehensive."

"It's the same background, Mark, but we decided to use a special screen technique over it. You'll notice that by dulling the background a bit, the packages and cake illustrations are more strongly emphasized, almost third dimentional."

"Yes, you're right, they do stand out better. Let me show these to Bob." He pushed a button on his desk intercom and Davies's voice came back to them at once. "Yes, sir?"

"Come in here for a minute, Bob. I want you to see these Christmas ads. And, oh, if Miss Garvey is there, ask her to come along, too."

As the seconds sped by, they waited in silence, and then the door opened and Bob Davies stood there holding the door open for a young woman Steve had never seen before. "Come in, Sue," Lawson said with a broadening smile.

She was about Robin's height, a piquant, lithe-bodied girl in her early twenties, her hair the color of ripened wheat. She wore a short, double-breasted jacket over a pleated white blouse and a dark gray skirt that ended about two inches above her kneecaps. Her head was tilted slightly to one side, a smile on her face that indicated complete ease and the knowledge that she would be welcome.

"Miss Garvey," Lawson said, "I don't think you've met Mr. Gilman from our advertising agency. Steve, Sue Garvey. Sue took Miss Ford's place when she resigned."

Resigned? You bastard! Steve thought as he examined Robin's replacement, taking the hand she offered, and wondering if Miss Sue Garvey was occupying the apartment Robin had vacated so suddenly on the day she left New York, months ago. Sue's hand was firm and strong. She was beautiful and young. The texture of her skin was smooth and flawless and other than a touch of lipstick, she wore no makeup which was recognizably unnecessary. He could see the look of possessive pride in Lawson's smile, that of a man showing off a new and expensive trophy. "A pleasure, Miss Garvey," Steve said, releasing her hand.

"I've heard a lot about you from Mr. Lawson, Mr. Gilman," she replied, "mostly complimentary."

"Thank you."

Lawson said with magnanimity, "Let's cut the formality, shall we? Since we're on the same ball team, it's Sue and Steve, okay?"

She smiled and Steve acknowledged it with one of his own, but could hardly avoid the erotic surge that was prompted by the certain intuition that Mark and this girl were sharing more than their days together. They gathered in a knot behind the desk and scanned the proofs carefully. Sue's approval came quickly and Davies said, "Not too much trouble with the copy on this one, eh, Steve?"

Beyond a simple "A merry, tasty Christmas," showing in delicate white script through the dark green grasscloth background, the entire GFP line was spread across two pages in an oval. There was no more copy, not even the usual signature, since each package, with its individual wedge of cake in the foreground, the jars of mayonnaise, and peanut butter, packages of margarine, and toppings, were clearly recognizable as GFP products and served as identification.

"No," Steve said casually, "what we do in this case is charge each copywriter with a week's vacation."

Sue said, "They look marvelous to me, but if you'll excuse me, please, I've got a lot of last minute details to check over before I leave for Cleveland tomorrow."

She left and a few moments later, Bob Davies went out. "Sit down, Steve," Lawson said when Steve offered his pen for the initialing ceremony. "Leave it for the time being. The old man is upstairs with Curt Fitzjohn. I told him you'd be in this morning and he wants to see you."

"Fine. I haven't seen Mr. Goodwin since that first time at the New Jersey plant."

"Okay. What's all this about Whipple? Barrett phoned me on Friday that you were taking over."

"With your approval, of course."

Lawson smiled, toying with him. "I told him I'd think it over."

Steve squirmed. "Well, have you?"

"Yes." He stopped there, waiting.

"Mark, if there's any doubt in your mind, I think we should talk it out right now, don't you? After all, it isn't as though I were coming to GFP out of the blue . . ."

Lawson flagged a large hand at him, waving the question aside. "I'll let you break the good news to that snotty bastard, Barrett. When you get back, you can tell him you're in. And to relieve your own mind, I haven't any doubts at all, or I would have told him then and there. I held back to shaft him a little."

Steve smiled over Lawson's churlish explanation, yet not without some relief. He said, "Mark, I appreciate your confidence, but I've never understood this thing, whatever it is, between you and Wade. Even more so now, I get the feeling I'm trapped in some kind of crossfire between you and one day I'm going to get cut down by bullets flying in from both sides."

"Well"—Lawson began—then laughed. "It looks like you and I are going to be working a lot closer from now on, so I don't mind telling you I like the idea a hell of a lot better than having Andy Makyrios around me, looking down his goddamned nose like a dog sniffing another dog's ass. I don't like intellectual snobs, especially Whipple, with his fucking Phi Beta Kappa key dangling from his watch chain. Shit, imagine a guy wearing a vest all year round so he can show off that goddamned key. Or Barrett, who once told a space rep my head had as many brains in it as a kid's circus balloon. Or, for that matter, Bill Leary and Keith Allard, always running to the old man over my head when they think they can't sneak something past me. Is that enough for starters?"

Steve nodded and Lawson swiveled 180-degrees to point to his wife's picture on the cabinet behind his desk. "When I married Karen and took over this spot from Sid Roth, Leary and Barrett were the most patronizing sonsofbitches I'd ever met in my life. They shafted every goddamned idea I ever came up with and I've been shafting them back every chance I've had. Of course, the old man is still in the saddle here, but someday I'm going to ream them where it's going to hurt most. What's more, I don't appreciate . . . oh, the hell with it. You're in, and that's that. We'll work well together, won't we?"

"Sure, Mark." At that moment, Steve's curiosity got the best of him. He said, "What happened to Miss Ford, did she really resign?"

Lawson looked up quickly. "Did you know Robin?"

"Yes. I met her some time ago in Washington, on the Cinnamon-Nut campaign."

"Something, eh?"

"Uh—she was very attractive, as I remember."

"You can bet your sweet ass she was, but she got too pushy and I had to get rid of her. I'll tell you one thing, though, just between you and me. She was one hell of a thing to see in bed. Hey, that's confidential and strictly off the record, remember."

Steve nodded again, remembering that morning at the Madrigal. Lawson said, "Now let's get something else out of the way. You and I are going to be living in each other's laps, more or less, and I want to be damned sure that, other than pure business, nothing else, rumor, gossip, or whatever, gets back to the agency. Leary, Allard, and Barrett in particular. We'll be taking trips out in the field once in a while, too, and whatever you see is strictly on the q.t. Is that understood?"

"I understand." But what he understood most of all now were the complications that must have been plaguing Robin during their initial and later encounters, keeping Mark from finding out about her outings with himself. "I appreciate your confidence, Mark. For a while, I'll be busy day and night getting used to this account on a much higher level."

"Sure, sure, but we'll work it out." He picked up his pen and scrawled his initials on each proof sheet just as Herschel Goodwin walked in unannounced. Steve stood up and waited for Goodwin's recognition.

"Mark," the older man said in greeting, then to Steve, "Ah, Mr. Gibson. Keep your seat, keep your seat. I'll only stay a minute. I'm glad to see you again, Mr. Gibson."

"Gilman," Steve said, "and thank you, sir. I'm happy to see you looking so well."

"Nu, I could feel better, but I'm getting along, getting along." He dropped into the chair beside Steve and said, "How long ago was it when you came to see me in Harrison?"

"It was March of 1964, I think. Three and a half years ago. A long time."

"Ah, time. How slowly it moves for the young, how fast for the old. You have done well in your work, eh?"

"I hope I have, Mr. Goodwin."

"And now you are the—what do you call it in your agency, Mr. Gilman?"

"The group head. Or account executive, take your choice."

"Ah, yes. And these ads, you did them?"

"Not alone, sir. All our output is teamwork, copywriters and art directors working together."

"Yes. Yes." Goodwin stood up and glanced down at the two-page spread, seeing it upside down from his point of view. "An expensive Christmas card, no?"

"It's more than that, Mr. Goodwin. It's an expression of thanks to the millions who buy and use GFP products."

"Yes, I know. And how much will we spend on advertising this year, Mr. Gilman?"

"Very close to ten million dollars."

"Ten million dollars. *Guttenu!* Well, as long as Mr. Fitzjohn tells us we can afford it . . ." He broke into a chuckle, shaking his head from side to side. "Ten million dollars," he whispered in awe, "just to show pictures of what we make and say 'Merry Christmas.' *Rebenu shalolom."* He moved back and extended a hand to Steve. "Good luck, Mr. Gilman, and stay well. When you find time, come to Harrison to see me. In three and a half years, we have made many changes, many improvements."

"Thank you, sir. I'll do that the first chance I get," Steve promised.

"And you are married yet?"

Steve hesitated, then said quickly, "No, sir." He shot a quick glance toward Mark, who started a broad grin at his denial of marriage and divorce.

"You should, you should, Mr. Gilman. It's not a life, living alone." He turned back to Lawson. "And you, Mark? We'll see you and Karen in Wyecliffe this weekend?"

"Of course," Mark replied offhandedly. "We wouldn't miss yours and Anna's anniversary for anything."

5

He had crossed the invisible meridian from Indian to Chief and there were only a few problems in realigning his department. As he had been second-in-command to Jim Whipple, the move to head the group was well-received, even to a congratulatory dinner tendered him by the entire team, organized by his two principal assistants, Frank Hayden and Reed Baker. And a new piece of grafitti for his office wall; a portrait of himself in the center of a bull's eye with THIS IS THE ENEMY! WATCH IT! lettered boldly at the top of the outer circle.

When he had taken over the large office previously tenanted by Cliff Sorensen, Jack Henderson, Andy Makyrios, Jim Whipple, and others beyond his recall, Wade Barrett solemnized the occasion with a complete new leather desk set and three bottles of champagne. Bill Leary's contribution was an offer to have the office repainted and redecorated, and Keith sent him a new attaché case with his initials in sterling silver. Telephone calls and letters of congratulations came from those on the outside who profited most from GFP's output; television and radio networks and stations, magazine and newspaper reps, printers, billboard houses, and other suppliers. From Mr. and Mrs. Andy Makyrios came flowers and a note.

After getting settled in, Barrett asked, "Made your choice of a creative group head yet, Steve?"

"No, but I've got a couple of good people in mind."

"Ah—before you do anything about that, I'd like to make a suggestion."

"Who?"

"Chuck Baldasarian."

The proposal stunned him. "Chuck? What the hell can he contribute to the job? Christ, Wade, Chuck is the last person on earth I—look, suppose I were knocked out for some reason, can you see Chuck taking over? I'd lose my best people in no time at all. Frank Hayden, Reed Baker . . ."

"Steve, I know Chuck isn't the most lovable character and if anything happened to you, I'd be there to step in. Give him a try at it."

"Why don't you shove him off on somebody else? And you don't have to tell me any more. I've got a good idea he's screwed up on Lovell and I can't see myself manufacturing a job for him. Why not Chicago, with his what's-his-name uncle?"

"Marty Link?"

"No, the other guy who's shoving him down our throats."

"You mean George McCandless. Well, it seems neither George nor Marty wants him in Chicago and Chuck wants New York."

"Wade, he spells trouble and I don't want him."

"He's done well for Lovell."

"Then why not leave him where he is?"

"Something did happen there. Steve, I'm not doing this entirely on my own. I wouldn't be pushing him onto you, except that Bill Leary personally asked me to see if I could fit him in."

"Oh, shit." Deeply annoyed to be placed in the position of refusing this first request from Bill Leary, "What did he screw up this time?"

Barrett grinned idiotically, sensing victory. "It's one of those little stories that become advertising legend. Happened just the other day. You'll hear about it before long. I've got an appointment, but I'll send Chuck along to talk to you."

He heard about it before the day was over.

Lovell had been Chuck's first real opportunity to display what creative talent he possessed. Ian Wilcox, the account exec on Lovell, had given in to Chuck's urgings and the results were surprising to Wilcox and Loris Chambers, the account supervisor. Chuck moved into the account as an art director, warhead in place, and A-OK to go. He was soon shot down by the more experienced copywriters and art directors and fell into a normal slot. Much of his early efforts were rejected, and at one time Ian was about to send him back to the bullpen, but with grim determination Chuck hung on and began submitting passable material.

What marked him for the firing squad eventually was the incident that occurred during a meeting that took place between the Leary staff and Lovell people, its purpose to come up with a name for an entirely new item in the Lovell line: a vaginal hygiene spray deodorant. Not unmindful of the delicacy of breaking a campaign for so intimate an item on the public, the Lovell ad director, Barbara Kirk, spent half an hour impressing on all concerned the need for extreme subtlety and scrupulous good taste in the choice of name and the advertising pattern to follow.

Names submitted had been chalked on the large blackboard in the Lovell conference room, then discussed, considered, scratched through, and others added. After an hour, only seven possibilities—most of them suggested by the agency personnel—remained: *Femine, Suave, Delicado, Fleur, Milady, Charm,* and *Allure,* with no marked enthusiasm for any. Baldasarian, bored with the entire proceedings, sat at the oval table doodling little obscene sketches on the yellow pad in front of him. Then Charles Lovell, president of the cosmetics firm, dropped in to see what progress was being made, but the fountain seemed to be running dry at that point.

Mr. Lovell glanced over the names on the blackboard and "hm-m-m-ed" for a moment, then turned to Barbara Kirk who, in turn, desperate for a way out, said to Ian Wilcox, "Any further suggestions, Ian?"

Baldasarian came out of it then and interrupted. "Ian, I think I've got a natural for you." Without waiting for a reply, he stood up and, with every eye in the room focused on him, strode to the blackboard, picked up a stick of chalk and wrote large and bold:

UP YOURS!

on its surface.

Barbara Kirk's face flamed and Ian Wilcox gasped. There were a few sounds of indrawn breath at this piece of flagrant audacity as Chuck added, "I think that puts it where it belongs, right between . . ."

With a withering glance, Mr. Lovell turned and stalked

out of the room. Mrs. Kirk said, "I think that will be all for today, Mr. Wilcox. Perhaps another time."

The entire Lovell group rose as one and left the conference room. Wilcox turned to Chuck and said, "You cruddy sonofabitch, you're through."

But, considering the influence of George McCandless and Marty Link, it was apparent that this was not the case. And so, with topside pressure behind Barrett's request, Steve added Chuck Baldasarian to the group roster, not without some misgivings. He was pleased, however, to discover that Chuck's proximity to disaster in the Lovell matter had toned him down considerably. Steve assigned him to the small office next to his own with the title of assistant creative group head, to the complete surprise and dismay of the other members of the GFP team.

Excluding Bill Leary, Keith Allard and Wade Barrett, the GFP team now consisted of Steve as its head, and Frank Hayden and Reed Baker as account executives, bright young men who called upon Dan Tyson and Tom Jewell, the brand managers who worked under Bob Davies's supervision at GFP.

The creative group was composed of Alan Grant, Randy Ellis, Bennett Archer and Jon Hartman on copy, Arnold Cook, Lyle Keller and Norris Bardo, art directors, with Gary Parris as Television-Radio producer and Lew Kann for production liaison.

Peggy Cowles became Steve's secretary, new to the group, replacing Jim Whipple's secretary who resigned to be married. With a stenographer, secretaries for Hayden, Baker, and Baldasarian, clerk-typists and a messenger-trainee, the group now totaled twenty-two in number.

It was a young and spirited team with a fairly strong orientation toward food advertising. Each member had been carefully screened, some retained, others brought in from the outside to fill a particular need or specialty. By the time six months passed and they were moving into 1968, the team was functioning as though they had been working together for years.

Steve's private complaint was that he was being forced to pay more attention—as group head—to administrative, rather than creative duties, but he soon discovered that overall supervision brought him closer, into more direct contact, with every phase of the operation, with particular emphasis on television. At the start of that year, the television schedule supported a full one-hour prime time variety show, one half-hour games show, along with a full schedule of twenty- and thirty-second spot commercials and I.D.'s. In time, Steve assessed, television expenditures would surpass the outlay for print media advertising, and he began to allocate more funds to that department, which pleased Don Bryce, vice-president in charge of Television-Radio.

It now fell to Steve to isolate and define policy and objectives, to plan ahead for the future while supervising the work of the present, to draw up orderly courses of procedure, delegate assignments to his staff, and sweat out the final execution of each program; and, finally, to bear full responsibility for its success or failure. With so many eyes watching his every step, he began to feel the uneasiness that had become an integral part of his job.

On a mildly ashen morning in February, Ethan Loomis, longtime head of Production, who had the strong good looks of an Ossie Davis, dropped in on Steve. "Got a few minutes to spare, Steve?"

"Sure, Eth. Pull up and sit down. Peg?"

"I know," Peggy said. "How do you take your coffee, Mr. Loomis?"

"Natural." When she went out, Steve said, "What can I do for you, Eth? Usually, it's the other way around."

"Got a little problem you might be able to help me with, Steve."

"Glad to help, if I can."

"Well, this nephew of mine, he went to UCLA, an art major, three years Army, last two in Vietnam. Discharged honorably, a Bronze Star and Purple Heart. Right now, he's in New York, footloose, confused, and needs a job. Been here about five-six months and can't find a thing to fit his talents. Mopes around, anti-establishment, antiwar, antiwhite, anti-me, the works. Moved out on us and took a place in the Village and we hardly see him, but I talk to him on the phone once in a while."

"What can he do, Eth?"

"He's a hell of an artist, but in a kind of special field. Did a lot of cartoon stuff out in California—some published—then on the Army paper when he wasn't in combat. Good sports cartoonist, great on action, and does the kickiest caricatures you ever saw. He's not only good, he's fast."

"How do you think he'd fit in here? I could talk to Lex Kent—"

"I could do that myself, but I don't think he belongs in an art department bullpen. Too regimented. He's too free-spirited to be a mechanic."

"Then where else, Eth, art director on GFP? A cartoonist?"

"Well, it came to me just last night, Steve, been bugging me ever since. I don't have much to do with Don Bryce in TV, but I thought Lennie'd make one hell of a storyboard artist—you know—where he sketches the scene-changes for commercials. I know Bryce has Charlie Walls doing his storyboards, but I also know Charlie wants to move over into Lex's department. I thought if you could talk to Bryce . . ."

"No sweat, Eth. I'll be glad to see him and put it up to him for you. What about your nephew, what's his name?"

"Lennie Hawkins, my sister's boy. He's down there in the Village, beard, beads, the whole art bit. He's a good-looking enough boy . . ."

"This anti-thing of his. Is he a dedicated revolutionary?"

"Maybe just on the verge. Gets it from those alley cats he hangs out with and makes the big talk that can scare hell out of me sometimes, but mostly, I've got the notion it's just talk. I'm sure a good job with a weekly paycheck would be enough to bring him back into this world . . . convert him."

Steve smiled. "Into an Uncle Tom?"

Eth grinned back. "Maybe into an Uncle Eth."

"Okay, Eth. Tell him to come in and see me, bring some samples of his work with him. I'll have a talk with him, then set him up with Don."

Lennie Hawkins was about six feet tall, a few shades lighter in color than Ethan Loomis, broad-shouldered, slim-waisted, with powerful legs that strained the cloth of his skinny-legged black trousers so tightly that the emphasis fell on his genitals. His hair was cut in modified bush style and Eth had evidently convinced him to shave off his beard and mustache and do away with the beads. Over thin lips and a wide, bridgeless nose, a pair of strikingly alert eyes flicked from side to side to take in the unfamiliar surroundings. He wore a gold-colored jacket, a light-green shirt and a crimson neck-scarf. In all, his appearance was something less mod than some of the younger employees at Leary, particularly those in the art field who affected long hair, beards, and mustaches, and rather wild touches of color and style in their dress. He carried a familiar black art portfolio with him.

His hand, when he took the one Steve offered, was moist and limp, perhaps from nervousness or reluctance, belying the almost fierce stare and grim line of his mouth. "I'm Lennie Hawkins," he announced, withdrawing his hand quickly. His voice was low, his words enunciated clearly. "Mr. Loomis . . ."

"I know, Lennie," Steve said. "I talked with Eth about you last week."

"Well"—looking around with affected casualness—"I'm here."

"Sit down. Get comfortable."

"I'm comfortable," Lennie said, then realizing he couldn't remain standing for the interview, dropped into the chair Steve indicated for him. "Did you know I was his nephew?" he asked.

"If you're asking if I knew you were black, yes," Steve said. "Did you think it would make any difference?"

"It always has. You talk to somebody on the phone, it's one thing. When you show up in person, the whole ball-game starts all over again."

"Lennie, let's not get off on the wrong foot. Your uncle has been here in a top job since long before my time. He knows what he's doing and he's admired and respected for the job he does. If you've got a chip on your shoulder, it won't help one damned bit and can only hurt your chances. Color doesn't make a bit of difference here at Leary, only your ability to do a job. If you get it. Does that get through to you?"

Lennie nodded, although he didn't look convinced. "Okay. Do I call you Mr. Gilman, or Steve?"

"Whichever you feel most comfortable with."

Lennie thought for a moment and decided to use neither. He lifted the art portfolio from the floor and untied the strings. "Samples," he said, then took out about forty sheets of art board and laid them on the desk. All were in black ink, pencil, or crayon, some sprayed with a protective fixative, others covered with Cellophane. Some were sports cartoons, some combat scenes reminiscent of the Bill Mauldin style, a few were political in tone, but they had one thing in common—a unique sense of lively motion—action with subtle humor. There were a scattering of printed reproductions from papers in which some had appeared. Lennie waited, drawing deeply on his cigarette while Steve examined each piece.

"What about color?" Steve asked. "Have you worked in color?"

"Sure, quite a bit. Water color and pastels, no oils. I didn't bring any along because none of them had been reproduced anywhere. These were mostly for newspapers, college, and Army."

"Have you tried the papers here for a permanent job?"

Lennie's smile was grim. "No way, man, no way. They've got somebody locked into every slot." Steve remembered his own efforts to land a job on a paper and could appreciate Lennie's difficulty with total sympathy. At that moment, Peggy came in with a memo for Steve which she dropped into his IN basket. "From Mr. Barrett, Steve, the thing he called about this morning."

"Oh, yes. Peggy, say hello to Lennie Hawkins. Peggy Cowles, my secretary, Lenny."

"Howdy, Miss Cowles," Lennie said, lumbering to his feet.

Peggy said, "We met, a few minutes ago."

"Peg, take a look at these," Steve invited. She looked down at the sheets that were spread out on the desk, then came around to Steve's side to examine them closer. "Golly," she exclaimed with heightened interest, "these are great, absolutely marvelous!"

"Thank you," Lennie said.

"That's a beautiful talent you've got, Mr. Hawkins," Peggy said. "I wish we could use some of it for GFP."

"Not our bag, Peg," Steve said. "Will you get Don Bryce on the phone and ask him if he can spare fifteen or twenty minutes."

"Sure." It hit her then. "Storyboards," she said.

"Storyboards, but don't mention it to Don."

"I'll get him right away." As she turned to leave, Lennie said, "Miss Cowles," and she stopped and came back to the desk. "Yes?"

"Miss Cowles, I—uh—I'd like you to pick out any one of these you like and take it with you."

Her eyes widened. "Why, I'd love to have one, but there are so many beautiful things here, I'd hate to have to make a fast choice. May I make it later?"

"Sure, anytime."

"Thank you, Mr. Hawkins. If you autograph it to me, I'll have it framed to hang on my wall."

"You're welcome." When she went out, Steve said, "Well, you've made one person very happy," and when Lennie did not reply, "I think Bryce will buy, Lennie, but if he does, you understand you'll be on probation."

Lennie smiled for the first time. "Man, don't I ever know it. I've been on probation since the day I was born."

"I'm not talking about that kind. I mean the kind I went through, the kind everybody who works here goes through until he proves he can do his or her job."

Lennie said, "Okay, I get the message. I guess I owe you an apology. I'm sorry. It's a kind of carryover with me. I've got to learn to get past it."

"That being the case, suppose you start by calling me Steve."

"Sure—Steve. What I don't want is for anybody to know about Uncle Eth and me. I want to make it on my own without the family clout on my side."

"You'll make it, Lennie, I'm sure of that."

The phone rang and it was Peggy, with word that Don Bryce was in and could spare the time to see Steve. "Okay, let's gather these up and beard the lion in his den."

On the following Monday morning, Charlie Walls reported to Lex Kent's art department and Lennie Hawkins moved into the art cubicle in Bryce's department to begin his career as a television storyboard artist.

6

Early in May, Mark Lawson invited Steve to accompany him on a five-day "swing around the territory, a kind of goodwill mission among certain big distributors and retailers in the field. It will give you an insight to our relationship with our customers." Steve checked with Barrett first, then Allard, and both approved the jaunt if only for the sake of maintaining his friendly relationship with the client.

They covered Pittsburgh, Cleveland and Detroit in two days, then flew into Chicago where they were met at the airport by a man whom Mark introduced as Pete Channing, "one of my oldest friends." Channing drove them to the hotel where Mark had reserved a suite. From the start,

Steve suspected that this portion of the trip would be more social than business in purpose.

The three lunched together at the hotel, during which Steve gathered that Pete Channing was a principal supplier of GFP's printing needs and, at some time in the past, had been Mark's employer. Later, after arranging to meet Pete at their hotel, Mark and Steve made two brief calls on prominent food distributors. They had dinner with the president of a large supermarket chain and returned to their hotel to find Channing waiting for them in the bar with three girls, as obvious as they were attractive. At midnight, Pete and his girl bid them goodnight and left; leaving no doubt that the other two intended spending the night with Mark and Steve. After another round of drinks, Mark said, "It's been a long day. Let's hit the sack."

The girls were pleasantly agreeable. In their suite, they had a nightcap and Mark led the blond, Sherry, to his bedroom after suggesting to Steve that he sleep late. "We don't have an appointment until after lunch."

The dark-haired girl, Jo-Ann, began turning off the lights in the sitting room while Steve finished his drink and a cigarette. When the last light was out, Jo-Ann said, "You don't like Mark much, do you?"

"Is it that noticeable?" Steve asked, not without some concern.

"Well, I don't know, but there's something, something I can't put my finger on. As though you disapprove of him. What kind of a boss is he?"

"He's not my boss. I handle his advertising."

She shrugged and said, "Same thing, isn't it? I sort of get the feeling you're not with it, like you left something, or somebody, behind in New York."

She was fully undressed now, and as she talked, he noticed that she was an extraordinarily lively young girl with a marvelously shaped body, lovely oval face and loosely flowing dark red hair, almost black. Through a mildly alcoholic haze that increased his ardor, he said, "Sweetie, save the ESP for somebody else. We've got things to do besides delve into the psychogenic, haven't we?"

She laughed merrily. "Hey, what are you, some kind of an intellectual?"

"In a situation of this kind, Jo-Ann, my intellectual level drops to an absolute zero." Removing his clothes, he asked, "What kind of man is Pete Channing? Have you known him long?"

"Pete? He's okay. I've known him for about a year."

"And Mark?"

"First time I've ever seen him."

"Is Pete from Chicago?"

"New York, but he's out here on business five or six times a year, as far as I know."

Jo-Ann, he decided later, no matter what the cost to GFP, was well worth the price that would somehow appear in Mark's expense account under another category.

At ten-thirty next morning, the phone woke them. It was Mark, up and ready to start the day. He had ordered breakfast for four sent up. Steve and Jo-Ann dressed and were ready by the time the rolling table arrived. Mark seemed fresher, more gregarious than ever. He charmed the two girls with anecdotes and jokes and at the conclusion of the meal, handed each a crisp one-hundred-dollar bill and said, "Beat it, kids. We'll see you again soon."

They visited the headquarters of another chain in Evanston, took the head buyer and his wife to dinner and returned to their hotel well past midnight and too tired for more than a single drink before going to bed. Next morning they had breakfast with Channing and Pete offered to drive Mark to keep his two appointments for the day. Steve, with Mark's permission, spent the morning at the Leary office, had lunch with Martin Link and one of his account supervisors, then returned to the agency to meet people he had known only by their names on the organizational chart, some of whom serviced GFP's advertising and promotional activities in the Mid-West area.

By five-thirty, after declining an evening on the town with two Leary men, offering Lawson as his excuse, he was back at the hotel. Mark hadn't returned and Steve lay down for a brief nap. When he woke next it was nearing seven o'clock and there had been no word from Mark. He showered and changed into fresh clothes, left a note on Mark's dresser, then went to the dining room for dinner. Outside in the balmy May air, he walked until he came to a movie house that was showing a picture he had missed in New York. He bought a ticket and thoroughly enjoyed two hours of escape from the cares and problems of the world at large, including his own.

At midnight, he was back at the hotel and found no sign that Mark had returned, his note untouched. He tore the note up, undressed, showered, got into bed and fell asleep at once.

He was startled awake by a chilling shriek and sat up in bed, fully alert, nerve-ends tingling. For a moment he thought it had been a dream and started to fall back on his pillow, but then he heard a whimpering cry and a muffled voice pleading, "Don't—please don't—I didn't . . ."

He switched on the lamp beside his bed and saw the time on his watch, 3:20. Outside, the night was black and starlit. He threw the light cover off and went into the sitting room, found the wall switch and turned the overhead light on. Now the sounds were more distinct, the voices coming from Mark's room, one weak, the other strong with anger.

"Goddamn lousy whore-bitch, I oughtta . . ."

And the girl's plea, "Don't hit me again, Mark, please . . ."

Steve ran across the room to Mark's door and opened it. Jo-Ann, Steve's girl of the first night in Chicago, was cowering in a corner fully dressed, one hand to her cheek, the other extended outward as though to ward off Mark, who stood in a drunken crouch before her, wearing only the bottoms of his pajamas. There were traces of blood, a thin trickle dribbling from Jo-Ann's mouth. A chair had been overturned and Mark's trousers, jacket, and shirt were lying on the floor near the wall.

Mark was very drunk, weaving toward the terrified girl like an animal about to attack. Steve leaped forward, grabbed his shoulders and wrestled him off his course. "Mark! For God's sake, Mark!"

"Get the hell away from me," Mark snarled, stopped for the moment by Steve's rush, which had spun him completely around and off balance. He straightened up and turned, began staggering toward Jo-Ann, who was cringing between a chest of drawers and the television stand. "He's crazy drunk, wigged out," she groaned. "Get me out of here, Steve, please."

Mark was struggling ineffectively to get past Steve and Steve said, "Mark, what the hell is going on here? You'll bring the police down on us, for Christ's sake."

Mark stopped then, threw a baleful glance at Steve, eyes glazed and disoriented. "Police," he said, then, staring at Jo-Ann, "This lousy bitch," he muttered. "We're out with Pete and Sherry, got back here an' went to bed. Woke up a li'l while ago, she's all dressed, goin' through my wallet, for Christ's sake, rollin' me."

"I wasn't. I wasn't," Jo-Ann wailed. "All I was doing . . ." but her explanation was lost on Steve.

"Mark, let her go. You can't afford it. My God, if this breaks into the papers, you're dead."

Mark glared first at Steve, then at Jo-Ann. "Yeah, sure." He was breathing heavily, moving unsteadily. "Yeah. Okay, Steve, okay. Just get her the hell out of here, lousy whore." He wobbled back to the bed and sat on its edge, snarling at Jo-Ann, "Go on, get the hell out of here before I knock your fucking teeth out."

Steve went to Jo-Ann, took her arm, and led her to the sitting room. "Wait here," he said, placing her in an armchair.

She refused to be left alone and followed him into the bathroom. "I'm afraid. He's crazy wild. He'd passed out cold. All I wanted was my hundred, that's all. That's all I took, I swear it. Let him check his wallet and he'll see."

Steve dampened a washcloth and wiped the blood from her mouth and chin, patting it dry with a towel. "Lord," Jo-Ann moaned, "I thought he was going to kill me."

"Why didn't you stay the night?"

"Well, it was kind of silly. I couldn't do him any good, he was so drunk, and he couldn't do me any good, so I just decided I would take off instead of lying there listening to him snore. I swear that I wasn't rolling him."

"Next time you play with loaded revolvers, keep your finger away from the trigger."

She blinked. "What?"

"Never mind. Did you get your hundred?"

"Yes. I was putting the rest of it back when he woke up and . . ."

"Do you think you can make it on your own now?"

She got to her feet, weaved unsteadily from side to side, then stood more erectly. "I'll make it. And thanks, Steve. If you ever come back to Chicago . . ."

"Forget it." At the door she stopped and asked, "Did he mark me up much?"

"Not much. You've got a red mark alongside your mouth, but it should wear off in a day or two."

"Oh, Lord . . ."

Fortunately, there was no one in the hall at that hour. When he closed the door, he got his cigarettes and lighter from his room and went back to Mark's. Mark was still sitting on the edge of the bed, elbows on knees, face buried in his hands. He looked up and said drunkenly, "Thanks, kid. I mighta killed that pocket-pickin' whore. Get me a drink, willya?"

"Don't you think you've had enough for now, Mark?"

Anger flared in Mark's face. "For Christ's sake, don't try to be my nursemaid. Get me the goddamned drink and knock off the lecture. I can see it on your face."

Steve poured an inch of Scotch into the water glass and handed it to him. "How about you?" Mark asked.

"No, thanks. It never solves anything, just covers it over for a little while."

"C'mon, don't pull your fucking priest act on me, buddy. Your wife didn't divorce you for cutting out paper dolls, did she? And don't forget, I've seen you drink."

"But not for the same reasons."

"So we're in for some psychological crap, are we?"

"No," Steve said shortly.

"Well, stop looking down your goddamned nose at me."

"All right, Mark. I hope you'll feel better in the morning."

"Wait, wait. Don't run out on me now."

"I thought you'd had enough company for one night."

"Siddown, siddown an' don't be so goddamned touchy. Don't let those tramps throw you. They're all alike, hustlers. Treat 'em rough, they come back for more. Treat 'em like ladies, they roll you."

"I wouldn't know that much about it," Steve said.

"No, I guess you wouldn't, comin' up the easy way. Well, lemme put you straight, boy. I came up the hard way. Nobody ever made anything easy for me. I climbed out of the lower East Side an' knocked around plenty, workin' for nickels an' dimes, takin' jobs in between to keep the wrinkles out of my belly."

Mark's chin jutted out, shafting the world in defiance. He stood up, staggered to the table and emptied the last of the Scotch into his drinking glass, then went back to the bed and took a hard pull at his potent drink. "You don't know," he muttered to himself as much as to Steve. "You just don't know." He put the glass on the floor, eyes half closed, staring down into the glass.

"You think I got it made, don't you? Big job, beautiful wife, everything a guy could want. Yeah. Solid." He burst into a short, derisive laugh. "An' a goddam ring through my fuckin' nose with a steel leash on it. She pulls it, I follow. She says, 'Jump!' an I say, 'How high, baby, how high?' Boy, you just don't know . . ."

Mark's head, like a tether ball on a string, fell sideways, and his limp body followed it downward on the pillow. One foot kicked the glass of Scotch over, the fluid staining the carpet. His eyes closed and, mouth open, he began to snore.

Steve picked up the glass and replaced it on the table beside the empty bottle, then placed the overturned chair where it belonged, wondering how much, if any, of all this had been heard by occupants of the suites on either side of theirs and whether they had phoned the desk to report the disturbance. He lifted Mark's legs and swung them around onto the bed, covered him, and turned off the lights. He left the clothes on the floor where they lay, and Mark's wallet—bills partially exposed on the table where he had thrown it, hoping it would serve to remind Mark of the near calamity that might have brought the police and destroyed him with publicity—perhaps to vindicate Jo-Ann. He returned to his own room and lay there until the coppery dawn lightened the sky, before he could fall asleep.

Steve had left his door and Mark's open and he woke when he heard Mark's rasping voice as he ordered a pick-me-up, some aspirin, and coffee from room service. Steve got out of bed, shaved and showered unhurriedly, then took his time dressing in order to give Mark time to recuperate more fully. When he was dressed, he walked across the sitting room and found Mark sipping coffee, dressed, and apparently ready to face the day. It was twenty minutes to noon.

"Hi," he said cautiously.

"Hi," Mark replied. "Have some coffee. There's plenty, and it's still hot."

As he poured a cup for himself, Steve said, "How do you feel?"

"Okay. I've felt a hell of a lot worse. What happened to that broad of yours?"

Now she was Steve's, no part of Mark. "She got away safely."

"How about that bitch, rolling me like that?"

Steve said, "I don't know, Mark, but you sure do take some long chances."

Mark grinned sourly. "What the hell, we're a long way

from home. Just remember, this is strictly between us. And thanks."

"Don't mention it. What about cutting this thing short?"

"I was thinking the same thing. You hungry?"

"Not terribly."

"Okay. Let's book the next flight back and check out."

On the return trip, Mark slept all the way back to New York.

The following morning, Steve didn't get to his office until ten-thirty. He checked out the Work Progress Chart with Chuck and Peggy, then went up to see Keith. Barrett was spending the day with McCreery at Hugh Benson's office. Seated in Keith's comfortable office, drinking coffee and watching Allard tamp his pipe full, puff it alive. Steve felt at home again and grateful to be there. "Well," Allard said, "how was the trip?"

Steve had already decided to omit the seamier side of his experience and replied, "Not too bad. I didn't learn a hell of a lot that I didn't know before."

"And that was all?"

"That's the sum total of my adventures. Mark put on a performance for a few buyers, but I don't know how profitable that will turn out. I've just checked the WPC and everything here seems to be in order."

"Yes. I looked in on your group a few times to help Wade, and to give Chuck a leaning post in case he needed one."

"Thanks, Keith. How's Bill?"

"Eh? Oh, Bill. He's all right. Left him only a few minutes ago. He's already talked with Lawson."

"Did he call Mark?"

"No, of course not. The other way around."

"What kind of rating did I get from the Almighty?"

"Better than passing. I'd say an A-plus with a bit of *magna cum laude* thrown in. Bill was, to say the least, very pleased. Something about your spirit of cooperation and—uh—alertness and perception to conditions and problems in the marketplace. Quoting Lawson, of course."

Steve grinned. "Thanks. I've got some notes. I'll dictate a formal report for Bill as soon as I get the chance."

"Skip it," Allard said with a conspiratorial wink. "Bill's heard all he needs to know from Lawson. Spend the time justifying your expense account and don't be too modest.

GFP will pick up the tab. And if you aren't too worn out by Saturday, Louise would like you for dinner."

"Love to, Keith. I'll mark it on my calendar."

7

Back at his desk, Steve found Lew Kann, his production assistant thumbing through a sheaf of magazine reprints that were to be sent out to the GFP distributors for display on windows and inside the retail outlets they served. Lew, normally an easygoing, placid man who guided the work of the group through every stage into production, was very perturbed.

"What's up, Lew?" Steve asked.

"These reprint samples," Lew replied, pointing to the stack he had laid on the desk. "They're so crummy I feel ashamed to see them go out into the field."

Steve looked through the scattered reprints. There were four separate sets of advance ads, each centered on an oversized sheet of enameled stock, each ad reproduced exactly as it would appear in the nation's top women's and general magazines. Each reprint carried the additional legend in bold type: *As Advertised in,* and the list of publications in which it would appear.

They were printed badly and Steve could understand Lew's negative reaction. Not only were the colors slightly out of register and muddy, but the back of each was smudged with ink where it had rolled off the delivery end of the press onto the one that had preceded it.

"Who the hell's printing these?" Steve asked.

"Bennington Press, out on Long Island," Lew replied. "And this isn't the first lousy job they've turned out, either. Some of the point-of-purchase display material they've printed in the past has been just as bad, some even worse."

"Have you talked with Mrs. Harris at GFP about it and asked her to cut Bennington off the list?"

"Hell, I've talked to her a half dozen times personally and asked the account reps to nudge her, too. She keeps telling us she'll get after them and for a while, everything runs smoothly. Then, up pops the devil, something like this screwed-up crap."

"Okay, Lew, I'll take it up with Lawson next time I'm

there. Let me have one each of these to take along. Peggy, don't let me forget about this, will you?"

Peggy made a note and gathered up one each of the reprints and Lew took the rest back to his office. Later that day, Steve needed to check on a piece of artwork he had asked Lex Kent to do as a special favor, necessary for a television slide. As he left Lex's office, he ran into Ethan Loomis in the corridor.

"How you coming along, Steve?" Loomis said. "We peons in the back room don't get to see much of you since you grabbed the brass ring."

"Fine, Eth. Your boys are doing such a good job for us, there's no need to bring you any complaints."

Loomis grinned, exhibiting two rows of large white teeth. "Man, you don't belong here. You ought to be in the diplomatic corps."

"That's all they need down there in Washington, another huckster. Hey, how is Lennie getting along? I haven't seen him since he got the job."

"Great. Just great. He's doing some fine work for Mr. Bryce."

Steve nodded. "I did see a couple of the storyboards he's done. A big improvement over Charlie Walls's work. Is he happy?"

"Well, I don't hear so much about burning down the establishment any more. Everything all right with GFP?"

"Pretty much, Eth, but now that you mention it, I wouldn't be surprised if I get rapped for some of the lousy printing jobs we're putting out for them."

"Oh, oh. You mean that last bunch of reprint samples we got in from Bennington."

"How'd you ever guess it? They damn near ran Lew up the wall."

"Well, Lew ain't the only one, but don't you take the rap and don't lay it off on us. If GFP squawks, you can pin it right back on them, where it belongs."

"What's the score there, Eth?"

"Well, sometime before you took over, we used to handle all their printing through the agency. Then it started taking up a lot of our time—you know—the specification details, letting out the contracts, sitting on every job, and so forth. Mr. Leary complained to Mr. Roth that our service fee didn't cover the cost, so Sid Roth decided they'd handle the printing end themselves. Okay. After that, all we did was write and prepare the copy for camera and turn it over to GFP. They handled the rest of it out of Forty-second Street. All we got were the samples of each job from the printer. No problems.

"Then Mr. Roth retired and Mr. Lawson took over. Not too long after that, Bennington Press got into the picture and began taking job after job away from Argo, Dunstable, and Marquis Press until there's only Bennington and a couple of other printers, both smaller than Bennington, who gets the lion's share, the packages in particular, where the heavy bread is.

"When Bennington began getting slipshoddy, I put up a howl and their big man at the plant came to see me and practically told me to stop bugging him, and if I didn't like it, go holler to Lawson. Which I did. After a while, I gave up, but Lew Kann never got the message."

"What message is that, Eth?"

Loomis laughed. "Come on, man, you ain't all that naïve you need me to spell it out for you."

"Try me."

"Well, if you want it in living color, somebody down on Forty-second Street is getting paid off by somebody on Long Island and I'm not talking in nickels and dimes. With about a million dollars a year or more floating around, the cut comes to something more than chickenfeed."

"Lawson?"

"I can't name any names, Steve, but in my book, this guy Channing's either sleeping with Lawson or Mrs. Harris."

Steve gulped. "Who did you say?"

"Lawson or Mrs. Harris. She handles all the print buying in Purchasing, but Lawson sits on top of her. They got all the say in handing out those big jobs."

"I don't mean them, the Bennington man."

"Channing. Pete Channing, Bennington's sales manager."

Chicago flashed back into Steve's mind. Pete Channing. Mark. Sherry and Jo-Ann. Channing picking up tabs for dinner, drinks, supplying cars, girls . . . "A man about thirty-five or so, showing a little gray around the edges, heavyset with bushy eyebrows?"

"That's your cat, Steve. Nothing'd make me happier than getting rid of that bum."

"You ever pass this along to anyone else, Eth? Mr. Barrett, Mr. Allard, or Mr. Leary?"

"I once mentioned it to Mr. Allard, a long time ago,

but you're the first one to pop that question at me since. We don't hand out the jobs, so it's no skin off our noses."

"Okay, Eth, don't voice this around, will you? I'll try to see what I can do through Lawson."

"Sure. Good luck, man."

Steve took the reprint sheets to GFP on his next visit and stopped off in Purchasing to see Mrs. Harris before going to the floor above to Mark's office. He remembered her as a mousy woman during his very first visit on being assigned to the account, but in the time that had since elapsed, she had blossomed out considerably. In her private office, wearing a smart navy-blue suit and white blouse, she removed her glasses, lit a cigarette and said, "Well, Mr. Gilman, it's been a long time, hasn't it? How are things at the agency?"

"Fine, Mrs. Harris, except for a little problem I think you might be able to straighten out for us."

With a sweet smile and slightly raised eyebrows, "If I can I'll be happy to do it. What's the problem?"

Steve opened his attaché case and spread the reprint ads out on the desk before her. "These reprints. We've had a number of complaints about the sloppy jobs we've been getting and the result is that retailers refuse to display them, which doesn't help our overall sales picture very much."

"That's strange," Valerie Harris said. "I haven't received a single complaint from the field, Mr. Gilman."

"Only because there's the general belief that the agency is responsible for any and all printed matter GFP produces. Which printer did this job?"

Blandly, "I really don't know offhand. I'll have to check back and see who got the contract."

"Maybe I can save you the time. Bennington Press?"

She flushed and said, "You must be clairvoyant."

"It was an educated guess. My production people tell me that this sort of work is characteristic of their output. I think Lew Kann and Ethan Loomis have talked with you before about this, haven't they?"

Mrs. Harris stiffened. "Mr. Gilman," she said, "I run this department and I do it efficiently. I'm not going to allow your Mr. Kann or Mr. Loomis to dictate how I operate. If you have any further complaints, I'd advise you to take them to Mr. Lawson."

"And not Mr. Steinhorst, Mrs. Harris?"

The color quickly drained from her face at the mention

of the vice-president in overall charge of Purchasing. "I wouldn't do that if I were you, Mr. Gilman. Mr. Lawson was responsible for bringing Bennington Press into the picture. I think he would be very upset if you went over his head to Mr. Steinhorst."

"Well—suppose I were to drop the whole matter here and now, Mrs. Harris. Would you see what you can do with Bennington to improve the quality of their work?"

"I'll get on it at once," she replied, her expression reflecting a measure of relief. "I promise you."

"Thank you. In that case, I can see no need for taking this any further. I'll just leave these samples with you to show the Bennington people."

As he left her office, Steve was more than satisfied that Eth Loomis had guessed correctly. There was obvious collusion between Valerie Harris and Mark Lawson in which both were undoubtedly sharing financial rewards from Pete Channing.

In the time it took Steve to reach Lawson's office, the word had been relayed ahead. After a quick greeting, Lawson said, "What's the beef with Mrs. Harris about, Steve?"

Steve told him, minimizing the importance of the matter and without mention of his suspicions, but added, "If you'd like to see the reprints for yourself, ask Mrs. Harris to send them up. I left them with her."

"Never mind, I'll look into it myself. And lay off Pete Channing in the future, understand?"

"I read you loud and clear, Mark."

"Then see that you remember it. Pete is my friend. I want to keep it that way."

Lawson himself had pinpointed the culprit.

BOOK TWO

Chapter 5

1

On a bitterly cold day in December of 1910, a German ship with the imposing name, *Drachenfels,* arrived in the port of New York where it unloaded its cargo of freight and one hundred and sixteen men, women, and children passengers. Cases of tools, crates of machinery, and other goods were unloaded and stored in dockside sheds and warehouses to be claimed by their proper consignees while the haphazard human cargo was transferred to Ellis Island to be laboriously examined and processed by health and immigration officials, then released to friends, relatives, or a sponsor agency.

Among the arrivals were Zalman and Herschel Guttmann, ages seventeen and ten, wearing large identification tags attached to their heavy overcoats, and carrying their worldly possessions in one large suitcase and a small canvas sack. After the rough winter crossing from Bremen, no amount of inconvenience or monotony could further dampen their sagging spirits, deeply depressed as they were by the realization that they were aliens in an alien land. Of the two, the younger, Herschel, had some small smattering knowledge of English which he had learned in school. Zalman spoke only German and Yiddish.

The bleakness of Ellis Island was not the fairyland they had envisioned from legends told over and over again in their small *shtetl* in the old country, and Zalman, as much to keep his own courage up as to lift the gloom from his younger brother, repeated these oft-told tales, recalling passages from letters sent from the New World describing the wonders of New York which, to them, had always been synonymous with America. They had four days of interrogation, appraisal and waiting to endure; time to recall the deaths of their mother, Shorah, and of their father, Karl, within a year of each other; of the Guttmann bakery that had been sold to an uncle, Jacob, whom both detested.

Uncle Jacob, with three sons of his own, was more than pleased to be rid of Zalman and Herschel, and when the subject of America was first introduced, wrote a letter to Josef Behrman, a distant cousin whose trip to New York eighteen years earlier had been financed by Karl Guttman at a considerable sacrifice. Josef, now the owner of a prosperous grocery-delicatessen on the lower East Side, responded at once, eager and willing to help the unknown sons of the man who had been his generous benefactor.

Zalman's and Hershel's excitement heightened when Josef, finally notified of their arrival, came to claim them. At the Behrman home, tearfully grateful for the warm welcome they received from Josef's wife, Sarah; the Behrman sons, David and Morris; and daughter, Dora, they were finally installed in their own room in the Behrman flat above the store on East Houston Street. Here, with one hundred and fifty marks sewn into the waistband of Zalman's trousers, and with the knowledge they had acquired from their father—a master baker from his youth until death—the two brothers began a new life.

For Zalman, big and strong at seventeen, Josef Behrman found a job in the bakery that supplied his store with bread, rolls. bagels, buns, and cakes. Herschel was enrolled in school the following fall, meanwhile studying English with a young *Yeshiva* student as tutor, and with Morris and Dora Behrman to help with his studies at night.

When he was fourteen, Herschel began working beside Zalman at the bakery after school hours and during summer vacations, happy in an atmosphere familiar to him from birth. Zalman, at twenty-one, proud of Herschel's ability with the new language, began to pick it up as they worked side by side and at night. Together, they scrimped and saved toward the day when they would open their own shop, encouraged in that ambition by Josef and Sarah.

That dream came true in 1919, at the close of World War I, when Josef backed Zalman in his own shop on the corner of Essex and Rivington in a building owned by Harry Rosen, a wholesale food distributor of considerable wealth, and one of Josef's principal suppliers. Within two years, the Goodwin brothers (their name Americanized on arrival) had outgrown their ability to supply the demands of a continually growing clientele. Josef and Harry Rosen proposed they expand into a second shop on Stanton and Avenue C. The second store went into operation with Herschel in charge and, when they had cleared up their indebtedness to Josef and Harry, they began planning a third shop. So began the pattern for even further expansion.

By 1927, Goodwin Brothers had become a flourishing chain of twenty-one shops, operating daily delivery service that spread east, west and north, to supply homes, groceries, delis, restaurants, and sandwich shops with their tasty products. In December of that year, Zalman and Herschel received an offer to sell out to Penn-National, a large commercial bakery complex operating in Pennsylvania and New Jersey, and anxiously seeking retail outlets in the lucrative New York area. With Rosen and Behrman advising them, negotiations began.

In April of 1929 Penn-National came up with a take-it-or-leave-it offer of one hundred and eighty thousand dollars for the Goodwin Brothers name, inventories, accumulated properties, vehicles, and goodwill, with the provision that the brothers would not engage in any bakery operations in Manhattan or its environs. Goodwin Brothers ceased to exist as a firm.

Despite fabulous fortunes being made in the stock market that year, the brothers, drawing upon Old World economics learned from Karl Guttman's conservatism in financial matters, resisted the advice of Josef and Harry to plunge into an adventure in which neither had experience or understanding, more concerned with the more perplexing problem of finding a business in which they could invest their fortune in cash.

Herschel, at twenty-nine, and Zalman, at thirty-six, had never known the meaning of a vacation and now, with ninety thousand dollars each, Zalman placed his share of the bakery sale in a neighborhood bank and announced that he would take a trip back to Germany to visit what family remained there. Herschel, however, had no such desire for travel. He encouraged Zalman to make the trip—even find himself a bride—while he, Herschel, remained in New York to make a concerted effort to find some business in which they could invest within the limits of the restriction placed upon them by the agreement with Penn-National. In order to keep his cash readily available, and recalling the bank failures of the early twenties,

Herschel took his ninety thousand dollars uptown and rented a safety deposit box.

To fill his days out, Herschel allowed Harry Rosen to persuade him to take a temporary position as a salesman, thus permitting him an opportunity to observe grocery store operations at firsthand. Harry had another reason in the back of his mind, one he did not disclose to Herschel: his daughter, Anna, who was twenty-six years old.

Herschel was aware of the subtle pressure being put on him by Sarah Behrman to marry Dora Behrman, a vivacious, friendly enough girl, some five years his junior, but living in close proximity with the Behrmans for so long, Herschel had come to regard Dora with no more than brotherly affection. Anna Rosen, however, was another story.

Anna, motherless, attractive, and intelligent, ran the Rosen household for her father with firmness and adoration. She was a pleasant, unpretentious girl who had refused to go on to college after her mother died of cancer, and whose prime concern was looking after her father and their home. Without the constant companionship of Zalman, Herschel was more than willing to visit the Rosens and partake of their hospitality.

Despite his desirability as a catch, there appeared to be no possibility of a match between Anna and Herschel, so far apart were they, intellectually; but with Anna's growing curiosity spurred by her father's deep interest in his protégé, inquisitiveness eventually blossomed into a need to take a hand in Americanizing the man she had come to think of as a displaced immigrant.

Herschel, thus taken in charge, began to see another side of New York life. Together, he and Anna explored theaters, movie houses, uptown restaurants, nearby beach resorts and, occasionally, a speakeasy. He learned simple dance steps, bought a new Chevrolet sedan, began to patronize better men's shops, and even heeded Anna's advice in the selection of shirts, ties, and shoes to complement his growing wardrobe. Further, Herschel forced himself to pay close attention while Anna expounded classical theories, not with any particular interest in the core of her philosophical utterings, but simply because he had fallen in love with her from the start.

At the end of October, the collapse of the stock market crashed down on America and Herschel suddenly realized that while all around him was crumbling, his ninety thousand dollars in cash, despite the number of bank failures, was safe. Zalman's money, on deposit with the small East Side bank, was swept away in the debris when its doors closed and two of its principal officers, unable to face the horde of vacant-eyed, accusing depositors, committed suicide. Zalman's was a sad homecoming in mid-November.

The depression that followed left its cruel imprint of devastation everywhere. People stared in bewildered, helpless anger as factories and stores were shut down, jobs disappeared; bread and soup lines began to form and expand. Harry Rosen's business fell off to such a degree that more than half of his warehouse space was empty by the following summer. Trucks were taken out of service and stored in the yards, and employees were dismissed. The atmosphere became so oppressive that Rosen began to remain away from his work, relying on Herschel to look after what buying, selling, order-filling and delivery needed to be done. Doors had to be doubled-barred and night-watchmen were hired to prevent burglaries which many food stores and warehouses were suffering. Herschel put Zalman to work as a warehouse foreman in order to keep his older brother from going insane over his loss.

"What good," Zalman moaned, "is it to work? We worked so hard for so long and now . . ."

"Zalman, for now, we will work. I still have my half of the money, ninety thousand dollars. We both have jobs. Half of what I have is yours. When this craziness is over, we will find something together."

"When, Herschel? When will it be over?"

"I don't know. Nobody else knows. But when the time comes we will be in another business together."

"In the agreement, it says we can't be bakers."

"*Nu*, so we will find something else. The world needs more than bread. If we keep looking, we will find something. Think how much better off we are than thousands of others, millions."

"Ah, Herscheleh, for you the sun still shines. To everybody in Germany, I was a rich man, a somebody, a *mensch*. Today I am a nobody, a *kabtzen*."

"You talk like a child. If it will make you happier I will go to the bank tomorrow with you and give you half the money, forty-five thousand dollars. You won't starve and you'll have a place to live."

"*Mischugener*. The money is yours. Mine I lost. You

will need it for your wife someday, your children. I can't take from you."

"Zalman, we are brothers. You brought me here, took care of me. What would I be without you?"

"No. You are what you are and I am what I am, an *aüslander* who can't even speak good English, who works in a warehouse, but a *schnorrer* I am not."

"It will be over soon. It can't last like this and we will have another chance."

Zalman sighed. "How many chances does one man get in his life, Herschel? We came here as boys nineteen years, twenty years ago. We worked hard and made a good living. We got a lot of money for the business we built from nothing. We were rich. Now the world has gone crazy. It won't be over so soon." For Zalman there was no future in which he could believe.

Herschel continued with his job for Harry Rosen, who now looked upon him as an adopted son. As time passed, Rosen confined his interest to inside operations and put Herschel in charge of the sales force. Zalman buried himself in his work, taking on additional tasks to keep from brooding. At night, they discussed the possibility of finding a business of their own, but with conditions as they were, it seemed a hopeless thing at the moment.

In 1931, Herschel finally generated enough courage to ask Anna to marry him. It was mid-summer and they had driven out to a beach park on Long Island where, after they had bathed, eaten, and listened to a band concert, they sat in Herschel's car overlooking the Sound as night began to fall.

"Look," Anna said, pointing to the sky, "the first star. Make a wish."

Following the line of her arm, hand, and index finger, Herschel said, "Does it have to be a new wish?"

"No. Any wish will do."

"Then," Herschel said slowly, "I wish a girl named Anna Rosen would marry me."

Anna's hand dropped. She turned toward him and said, "What took you so long?"

"I was afraid."

"Of what?"

"That a girl named Anna Rosen would say *no* to a greenhorn like me."

"Oh, Herschel. Silly Herschel. Twenty-one years in

America and you can't forget the ten you lived in Germany."

"Then you'll marry me?"

"Of course. If I don't, my father would probably kill me."

2

The wedding was set for October and there were lengthy discussions over where they would live. The apartment Herschel shared with Zalman—who declared he would move into a room nearby—was too small. Harry Rosen was opposed to their moving into his roomy house, which had been Anna's first suggestion. Harry voiced his objections emphatically. "A couple starting out in life should live alone. I lived with my in-laws for two years before your mother and I had a home of our own and those were the worst years of my married life. Besides, I have been a captive of this girl ever since her mother *alov hasholem* died. I think I'm entitled to some freedom and peace in my old age."

"Look at him, Herschel," Anna retorted. "Not yet fifty and he can't wait to get rid of me so he won't have to go out to meet his *nafkehs*. All right, Daddy, you can have the whole house to yourself. We'll find one of our own."

"You see, you see, Herschel? She even spies on me!"

"Oh, Daddy, what kind of a stupid girl do you think you've raised."

"All right. All right. So find a house. My present to you will be to pay all the cost of furnishing it. All right?"

Although he loved Zalman and Harry Rosen, Herschel was immensely pleased at the thought of having Anna all alone to himself, and set himself the task of finding a suitable home for his bride, one that would be far enough away from the overcrowded lower East Side where he had spent the last twenty-one years.

Through a broker he found a house on East Eighty-fifth Street that had been vacant for three years, its owner in deep financial distress. Within two weeks, he bought it with a five thousand dollar cash down payment and a comfortable mortgage on the balance. Anna fell in love with the four-storied granite-faced house and at once began planning how she would furnish and redecorate it. All at Harry Rosen's expense.

Although Anna invited Zalman to live with them in the new house, he refused, and insisted on remaining alone in the flat he had shared with Herschel since they had started their first bakery together. No amount of persuasion could move Zalman to change his mind. His habits were too well set: By day, he had his warehouse job to occupy him; at night, he ate a simple meal, read the Jewish newspaper, then went to bed. One day was the same as the one before, except for Saturday, which Zalman, after years of neglect, spent at the nearby synagogue. On Sundays he rose early, fixed his own breakfast and spent the entire day walking. Observing. Brooding.

Herschel and Anna were married in mid-October in a banquet hall that was filled with relatives, friends, and business acquaintances of the Rosens, Behrmans, and others acquired by Herschel and Zalman during the past two decades. Some four hundred people had gathered for the occasion and Zalman, out of sheer bewilderment or distress over his temporary loss of his younger brother, got roaring drunk and passed out cold. At the height of the festivities, Anna and Herschel slipped away and barely made it to the station in time to catch their train to Miami Beach.

Two weeks later they were back in New York, Anna busily engaged in completing the furnishing of her "uptown mansion," opening, classifying, exchanging, or otherwise disposing of hundreds of gifts that had accumulated in their absence. She added one touch of heretofore unknown luxury, a permanent live-in Negro couple—to cook, keep house and act as occasional chauffeur—Eric and Leona Jackson.

Herschel resumed his work with Harry Rosen, calling on the grocery trade to spread goodwill, solve minor problems, and simultaneously check on the activities of his salesmen. One day while making a routine call on a grocer whom he had known for quite some time, he happened to notice an item on the shelf, which, while vaguely familiar by sight, he knew very little about. It was called Reddi-Bake, a blend of flour and a few simple ingredients that would purportedly produce a vanilla-flavored cake simply by adding water, placing the mixture in the oven, and allowing it to bake for the stated length of time. Presto.

As a former baker, the idea intrigued Herschel. "Sam," he called to the grocer, "what is this *chazzerai?*"

Sam, busy stocking canned goods on a shelf, shrugged.

"Who knows? They asked me to put in a couple of cases on trial, *eppis* a favor I should do them."

"You're selling it?"

"How many boxes do you see on the shelf?"

"Seven."

"So in ten days, maybe two weeks, I sold forty-one boxes."

Impressed, "You'll reorder?"

"You wouldn't? It sells, so I'll reorder."

"I'll take two boxes."

"You? What for?"

"So Anna can bake me two birthday cakes, what else?"

He brought the two packages home that evening and in their kitchen after supper, Herschel and Anna, with Leona looking on curiously, followed the simple instructions, worked the batter into a lightly-buttered pan, waited the required time as it baked, allowed it to cool, and then tasted the results, expecting little for their expended effort. Sampling the plain cake, they drew quizzical glances from each other. Leona and Eric were called in, given a slice to try. Their reaction was favorable.

"Well, *mayvim,*" Anna said finally, "what do you think?"

"Since when did you stop telling and start asking?"

"Not bad," Anna said. "It's not really home-baked, of course, or as good as what Goodwin Brothers turned out in their own bakeries, but good enough."

"You think people will buy it?"

"Didn't you?"

"Only to see what kind of cake can come out of a box."

"So what do you think, expert?"

"I think we could make it better. A lot better. It tastes so *thin*—it needs maybe an egg"—

"And more varieties. A full line. Chocolate, orange, coconut, devil's food. And it should come with icing and nuts to give it a *tahm.* Herschel, what about cookies, biscuits . . ."

"Yes, yes. Anna, *liebschen . . .*"

She could see the glow of excitement in his eyes, heard the rise in his voice. "So when do you start?" she asked.

Taking courage from her smile, her implied consent, "Right away. Listen. I'll look into this a little more, then I'll take a place, and put in one oven. We'll have to experiment, work out a line, try out different ingredients for each mixture, and learn which needs milk or eggs to be added instead of just plain water. We'll keep it simple enough so that even the biggest *dumbkopf* can make a cake she can be proud of. We'll tell her on the package how to make it in layers, with different icings. Anna, what do you think?"

Anna smiled. "I think we're in business. It won't be a bakery, but the grocery stores will buy and sell the packages. No more stale cake to throw out. Women will keep the boxes in their pantries and make cakes when they want them, small or big ones. Herschel, if you can do it, Papa will carry the line. And if he does, other distributors will carry it."

"And Zalman. I'll need Zalman. He knows more about this than I'll ever know. I'll take him out of the warehouse and we'll be in business together again, Anna."

Zalman, after rejecting the idea as ridiculous, finally became infected with the enthusiasm of Herschel, Anna, and even Harry Rosen; also, it could become his escape from the warehouse routine that had reduced him from his former status as bakery-chain owner to common laborer.

Herschel devoted his efforts to locating a small building and the necessary basic equipment, and a printer to produce a package with an individual design to attract the eyes of women buyers. In the meantime, the experiments—under Zalman's critical touch—began. He developed various blends and test batches, baked them, discarded many, began again and again, seeking perfection. The cinderblock building Herschel had rented in Harlem was too far from where Zalman lived and Anna persuaded him to move in with them so that Eric could drive them to work every morning instead of wasting their time on the subway.

Soon after, Anna announced that she was pregnant and Herschel redoubled his efforts to get into production, but Zalman was adamant and refused to be hurried. Then, as if to celebrate the arrival of Anna's son, Robert, Zalman, after long months of trial and error, came up with four satisfactory items. Herschel at once installed more expensive automatic mixing equipment and hired a crew of women to blend, weigh, and package the four cake mixes. Men packed the boxes into shipping cartons, stenciled, and labeled them. A local delivery service was engaged to make deliveries to Herschel's list of individual stores.

The items moved slowly at first, but they were *moving*, and that was all Herschel needed. From experience gained with Harry Rosen, he knew that with any new grocery item, the initial purchase was very important, but no more than a test. It was the re-order that was vitally essential.

Of all the suggestions Herschel and Anna labored over—forbidden to use the name GOODWIN BROTHERS—they finally shortened the name to GOODY and a trademark was born. Anna came up with GOODY'S *for* GOODNESS SAKE, which was adopted as the company slogan for Goody Food Products.

They were not, of course, the first. Other food companies whose advertising and promotion were at work changing the baking habits of a nation began pulling Goody Cake Mixes along with them. Rosen Distributors did its share to promote and sell the items and, as predicted by Anna, other distributors and food brokers took up the less expensive and competitive GFP line. Before long, the building in Harlem became too small to accommodate production needs.

After much deliberation, Herschel decided on moving the operation to Harrison, New Jersey, where—God willing—there would be adequate room for even further expansion. Land and building costs were cheap, and labor was plentiful in those distressed times. Overhead was held to a minimum and Goody's prices continued to remain lower than the competition. In the tight circle of their localized markets, they were able to hold their heads well above water.

Harry Rosen argued that what the fledgling GFP needed was a regular program of advertising to expand into a larger operational area with widespread distribution, but the costs of advertising to compete with the giants of the industry were frightening to Herschel, who put off the question and soon began to see his sales curve dip. For the next year or two, it was touch and go.

Meanwhile, Zalman began to emerge from the darkness into which the depression had plunged him. With an entire plant—a factory!—to oversee, he became interested in equipment to make the work flow more smoothly. To be closer to his work, he moved into a room in Harrison so that he could spend more hours planning, devising, and organizing his labor force. Herschel opened an office in New York from which he could direct the sales and purchasing efforts, but in time it became necessary for him to spend more time in Harrison, and he resented those days and nights when he could not be with Anna and his son, Robert.

On weekends, Zalman came back to the house on Eighty-fifth Street. The old apartment on the East Side had been given up, all his possessions moved in with Anna and Herschel. And then, Anna undertook a project of her own; to get Zalman married off.

Sophie Hartog was an excellent seamstress who carried on a modest business from her flat on West Tenth Street and had done considerable work for Anna before she was married. Sophie served a neighborhood clientele, styling, fitting, sewing, and remodeling dresses and suits, which helped support her fatherless three-year-old daughter, Karen. She was thirty-two years old and had come from Russia with her parents, Max and Rachel Kirsch, as a child of fourteen. In her twenty-fourth year she married a man much older than herself, who died a few years after Karen was born. Sophie was a plump, good-natured woman, a meticulous housekeeper, and a more than competent cook. Zalman, once again financially secure, began enjoying his first real contact with a world other than his work.

A few months after Anna had begun inviting Sophie to the Goodwin home to do some remodeling and sewing, Zalman's interest in Sophie developed, and encouraged by both Anna and Herschel, he proposed marriage to her. After several months, they were married. Zalman found a house in Harrison, and the happy couple and Sophie's daughter, Karen, moved there. Within a brief period, Sophie became pregnant, and in her sixth month aborted. They were further saddened by the doctor's statement that she would never bear another child. But there was Karen. Sophie agreed to her adoption by Zalman and her name was legally changed from Hartog to Goodwin.

3

Early in 1938, when America began showing small signs of having shaken off the worst of the depression, Herschel received a visit from a bright young man who introduced himself as Wade Barrett, and who looked to be no more than twenty-four years old. Barrett's imitation engraved card represented him as a member of the Kortner, Abelson, Simon and Hutner Advertising Agency of Manhattan, with the impressive—if meaningless—title of vice-president.

Actually, the agency was known in the trade as "the house that KASH built," one with a miscellany of small retail and industrial accounts far less impressive than its name. Wade Barrett was, in fact, a new business-getter who was paid a miniscule salary against a commission on any new business he brought in; in which case, the account would then be taken over by one of the four principals and Vice-President Barrett sent on his way to birddog another account.

But young Mr. Barrett yearned for a decent account of his own, to hold, service, and cherish with a reputable agency; which KASH was most certainly not.

"Why me?" Herschel Goodwin asked with a smile. "I am small, a nobody."

"Because," Barrett replied with statesmanlike diplomacy, "nobodies don't engage in a business that can compete with the biggest names in the country. Only men with courage and vision attempt that, Mr. Goodwin. Your company is small, yes, but small is a comparative word. I've sampled your products and I like them. They are far superior to most of the others and, even more important, sell for less. All your company lacks is the advertising it needs to strengthen your line in its local market and expand it into national prominence and acceptability. Not all at once, but area by area, step by step."

"The cost . . ."

"Will be self-liquidating by the sales your advertising will generate. Let me explain in detail." Whereupon Mr. Barrett, flushed with nominal success in the initial buttering-up process, explained in erudite Princetonian tradition, and in somewhat vague detail, the process by which small manufacturers become large manufacturers through proper advertising and sales-promotion methods; this, at what he suggested would be a modest cost at the outset, yet which seemed staggering to Herschel Goodwin. Herschel gasped, gaped, then said, "Let me think it over, Mr. Barrett."

"Do that, Mr. Goodwin. Meanwhile, without any cost to you, I will work up a practical program and give you something concrete to discuss with your associates. Absolutely no obligation on your part."

On his return to the KASH offices, Wade Barrett, as required, filled out his Daily Call List, necessary in order to collect his outlay of cash for transportation and telephone calls. Deliberately, since the GFP lead was his own discovery, he omitted the visit to Harrison, deciding to gamble the cost of his bus fare out of his own meager funds. Later, from an outside pay phone, he called an acquaintance, Keith Allard, who had been his classmate at Princeton and who had been with the Wm. B. Leary Agency for nearly two years as a copywriter-layout man.

"Keith? Wade."

"Hello, Wade. Long time no hear. How's everything at KASH?"

"Lousy. In fact, pretty damned desperate."

"Jesus, Wade, I'm sorry. I wish we had an opening here, but it's rough going right now. Not hurting, you know, but . . ."

"I know. Listen, I've got onto something that could change the situation for both of us. How about dinner?"

"Sure thing. You sound as hot as a two-dollar pistol."

"I am. Even hotter. I'll meet you outside your building. Six?"

"Six will be fine."

They met and discussed the project over their meal, but Allard was not overly impressed, nor was he enthused. "We could be putting in a lot of time for nothing, Wade, if they can't come up with the money to back it up."

"I know it's only on spec, Keith, but I've got a strong hunch about this one. We can work up a tight plan, hold down the costs as much as possible for openers, and show it to Goodwin. What I want him to see is the projection into the future more than anything else. It's a pure gamble, sure, but I've got this feeling he wants to go with something. He *needs* it, Keith. I could see it written all over him."

"All right, suppose he buys and comes up with the money. Where are we then?"

"All right. Then we take it to Mr. Wm. B. Leary and hand it to him on a silver platter. I handle the contact, you get the creative end, and we're both in solid."

"Hold it, Wade, let's back up a minute. Just where does KASH enter into this?"

"Screw KASH. I'm doing this all on my own. They'd

run a thing like this into the ground in no time at all. There isn't a decent advertising man in that whole borax organization worth the powder to blow him to hell."

"Well—"

"Keith, it's a step up for both of us. KASH doesn't have the slightest idea about this contact. It's all mine and it's a virgin. Let's do it. We'll both make out, and so will Leary."

"All right, Wade. Let's spin the well-known wheel and see where it stops."

At the end of each day for an entire week, plus a full weekend, Barrett and Allard met in Keith's small apartment and came up with a modest kickoff campaign, including a radical change in package design that was certainly more appealing, pictorially attractive and professional. The projection "into the future" was pure genius on Allard's part, portrayed in a manner designed to whet any prospective advertiser's appetite. As Barrett said when he first saw it, "Sheer seduction."

Armed with a borrowed Leary flip chart, Barrett returned to Harrison and made the presentation to Herschel Goodwin, who hadn't noticed the sleight-of-hand change from KASH to Leary. When Barrett went back to the city, leaving a typed outline along with the flip chart for Goodwin to study, he was more certain than ever that he had made a successful pitch. Again, Goodwin had said, "It makes good sense, Mr. Barrett. Let me think it over. I like it."

"When shall I call you?" Barrett asked.

"Give me three days. Call me on Wednesday."

That night, Herschel brought the presentation to Harry Rosen and discussed it with him, enthusiasm larded with doubts. If he borrowed the money and lost, it would not bankrupt GFP but . . . well, it was still a major gamble on something so vastly indefinite. Was it worth that?

Harry Rosen said, "It looks good, Herschel. What's more, it's reasonable. Herschel, listen to me. You gambled on coming to America with Zalman, again when you started your first bakery, when you expanded, and when you sold out. Also, you gambled when you married my Anna, and when you went into this new business. Your whole life, mine, Anna's, everybody's, is a gamble."

"But I gambled on what I knew, my own brains, my hands, my money. Now I'll be gambling money that is not my own, with somebody else's brains."

"It's all the same thing, Herschel. Henry Ford did it all with his own money? General Motors? General Foods? Do it. It's right for you, I know. Tomorrow we'll go to my bank and arrange the loan."

On Wednesday, Barrett called. Herschel said, "Mr. Barrett, I like what I see and I have arranged for the money, sixty thousand dollars, but . . ."

"But what, Mr. Goodwin?"

"You are, you should excuse me, so young. I would like to talk to somebody, maybe . . ."

"Mr. Goodwin," Barrett said excitedly, barely able to catch his breath, "of course, of course. Let me arrange to bring Mr. Leary to Harrison to see you. It will take a day or two, Mr. Leary is a very busy man. I'll call you tomorrow."

Next morning, while Harry Rosen was checking out the Wm. B. Leary agency, Keith Allard and Wade Barrett were sitting in Mr. Leary's office explaining what they had done to bring a new client into the agency. Mr. Leary, sober and urbane, cleared his throat and said, "While I appreciate your motive and zeal, Mr. Allard, and respect your ingenuity, Mr. Barrett, I find this a very unorthodox method of creating new business."

"Sixty thousand dollars, Mr. Leary," Barrett reminded him gently.

"Ah, yes. As I have said, I can't condone raiding another agency's clients—"

"GFP is not a KASH client, sir," Barrett replied quickly.

"A technicality. However . . ."

"It will build up, Mr. Leary," Allard interjected. "GFP is only getting started."

"Very well. As you say, GFP is not a KASH client at this time. Shall we say Friday, Mr. Barrett?"

"Friday. Yes. sir, I'll phone Mr. Goodman and make the appointment."

Mr. Leary was suave and impressively businesslike. In the presence of Herschel Goodwin and Harry Rosen, he reviewed the brief Allard-Barrett outline, expanded, elaborated, and embroidered it into what rapidly became a comprehensive Leary Agency presentation, incorporating merchandising and marketing along with media. Goodwin and Rosen listened respectfully and with deep interest.

Barrett and Allard, who had accompanied Mr. Leary to Harrison, received their first important lesson in proper agency approach, sitting in speechless wonder as they watched, listened and absorbed; equally mesmerized by Leary's mellifluous flow of scholarly cognition of business operations and his skillful handling of probing questions by Goodwin and Rosen. The outcome was never seriously in doubt. Four hours later, GFP became a client of the Wm. B. Leary Agency.

On their return to New York, Wade Barrett made one stop at the KASH Agency where he resigned, took what little pay he had coming and cleared out his desk. He then journeyed to the Hungerford Trust Building and joined the Leary staff as contact man on GFP under Mr. Leary's personal supervision. Keith Allard was made responsible for its creative output.

By 1940 GFP had made brilliant progress and further expansion was necessary. Russell Charles, who was Harry Rosen's attorney, became attorney for GFP and it was on his advice and through his offices that Herschel paid a visit to Kevin Almond, a Wall Street brokerage executive. Almond made a careful study of GFP's financial structure, then visited the plant in Harrison. After considerable investigation, he proposed incorporation and a stock issue.

The first issue was for 250,000 shares at a par value of $2.50, of which 130,000 shares were held in reserve. The remaining 120,000 shares were quickly bought up by Harry Rosen, Russell Charles, and Wm. B. Leary, Sr., who took five thousand shares each, the rest spread among Kevin Almond's private list of subscribers.

Zalman, who refused an outright partnership as charity, was named a vice-president of the corporation and given ten thousand shares of stock by Herschel. Another five thousand shares went to Sophie and Karen jointly. Zalman, happily busy in his role as production superintendent, kept aloof of management problems, devoting his entire time to the business at hand. Work, which he had known all his life, had become his salvation. Titles meant nothing to him. At home, there were Sophie and Karen. He needed little more.

Herschel made another move that year. Anna wanted to get away from the city and the travel time from East Eighty-fifth Street to Harrison caused Herschel to be on the road two hours each way, every day. It was Russell Charles who suggested they buy eighty acres that were available next to his estate in Wyecliffe, only fourteen miles from Harrison, which would give Herschel easier access to the plant and provide the country living Anna wanted for Robert, Herschel, and herself.

It was a lovely weekend when they drove to Wyecliffe, first stopping at Harrison to leave Robert with Sophie, Zalman, and Karen. They stayed with Faith and Russell Charles and at once fell in love with the countryside and the McComb property that, for a quarter of a mile, bordered the Chatham River. There were ample woods and the crumbling two-hundred-year-old McComb house had some vague historical reference to the pre-Revolutionary period, which Anna wanted to explore, perhaps even restore. They spent Saturday and Sunday riding and walking over much of those eighty acres and decided to buy. In the ensuing week, Charles negotiated for its purchase and an architect was employed to design the new house. By mid-1940, construction began.

When it was completed in October of 1941, Herschel, Anna, and Robert moved to Wyecliffe. Sophie, who hoped to move back to New York someday, urged Zalman to buy the house on Eighty-fifth Street from Herschel and Herschel sold it to Zalman for the outstanding mortgage balance, leaving most of the furnishings behind.

Immediately prior to the outbreak of World War II, GFP completed a new, larger building in Harrison that was given over to producing components for Army field rations. GFP stock had risen from 2½ to 7½ and by the time the attack on Pearl Harbor took place, moved upward to its greatest high, 18.

The war years were fraught with problems of transportation and labor, building materials and supplies, but with government priorities they managed somehow to keep production rolling, and even expand their facilities, When the war was finally over and GFP returned to civilian production, cake mix sales soared. It was a period when the public demanded more leisure time to enjoy war-swelled affluence and to try to forget the miseries that major conflict had brought to so many. Instant and frozen foods were in great demand to give housewives more time away from their kitchens. GFP was ready, and began broadening its lines by acquiring other related food items. In 1948, GFP stock split at 34, then gradually rose from 17 to 30¼. In 1950 it climbed to 44 and split once more.

The death of Josef Behrman in 1947 plunged the Goodwins into deep grief and a year later, they again stood sadly together as the coffin of Sarah Behrman was lowered into the grave beside that of her husband. David, Morris, and Dora Behrman, their wives and children, Dora's husband—Sidney Roth—and son Julian, went into mourning for a second time within a too-short span.

By the end of that year, David and Morris were at odds with each other and shortly thereafter, David bought his younger brother's interest in the family business on behalf of Dora Roth and himself. Morris, after six months of casting about for some new field of endeavor, went to Zalman and Herschel and was offered a job in the Harrison plant as Zalman's assistant.

In that same year, Dora's husband, Sidney Roth, lost his position as assistant sales promotion manager with a manufacturer of pharmaceuticals in Trenton. At Dora's confidential request, Herschel asked Sidney to call on him. The result was that Sidney was made assistant advertising manager of GFP, under Norman Katz, at its Forty-second Street headquarters. Two years later, when Katz resigned to heed his doctor's advice and move to Arizona, Sidney Roth was elevated to fill the vacancy.

In the year that followed, Harry Rosen suffered a massive stroke and before Anna and Herschel could reach his bedside at the hospital, he was dead. Anna, and his grandson, Robert, were his principal and immediate survivors. With the aid of Russell Charles, Herschel sold the Rosen business to another food distributor and Anna and Robert inherited the one-and-a-half million dollar estate.

So Zalman and Herschel's earliest friends and benefactors in America were gone. Nostalgic memory and tragedy drew the Goodwins closer together to the children and grandchildren of Josef and Sarah, and in time, after many family gatherings, birthday parties, *bar mitzvahs,* graduations, and weddings, even David and Morris were reconciled, although Morris remained with GFP in Harrison.

Chapter 6

1

When Karen Hartog, born prematurely, was removed from her hospital incubator and brought home to West Tenth Street, she was kept in virtual isolation from the rest of the world, a prisoner of Sophie's smothering parental love, constant attention, and deep concern. Ever conscious of the near loss of her first-born and her own agonizing prenatal experience with pain, nausea, sleepless nights, and pure fright, each disease of early childhood, every minor cold, cough, scratch, or bruise became cause for major alarm.

Ephraim Hartog, a gentle, sickly man who was fifteen years Sophie's senior, had little voice in the matter of raising his daughter. An immigrant plodder who eked out a bare living as a presser for a pants' contractor, Ephraim had lost whatever status he had in his home with the arrival of Karen into their lives.

By the time his daughter had reached her third birthday Ephraim had coughed his way out of this world into the next. Once he was buried, Sophie returned to the business of dressmaking which she had given up in her fifth month of pregnancy and, within a few months of activity it was as though Ephraim had never existed.

In that depressed period of the thirties, old customers returned to have dresses and suits repaired, refitted, and remodeled; thus Sophie was able to support herself and Karen comfortably. And, with Ephraim gone, there was more time to devote to her daughter's needs and care: the slavish, meticulous routine of bathing, feeding, and dressing; the daily ritual airing in clement weather, and regular checkups by Dr. Morstein, as well as the constant sewing to maintain Karen's elaborate wardrobe of dresses, coats, and play clothes.

When—almost two years after Ephraim Hartog died—Zalman Goodwin was introduced into the household through Anna Goodwin's matchmaking plan, Karen's reluctance to acknowledge him was instantaneous. Zalman, as opposed to the delicate, soft-spoken, unobtrusive Ephraim, was a gruff, bearish man, loud of voice and rough-handed. In time, since his presence was an accomplished fact by virtue of his marriage to Sophie, Karen came to accept him as necessary to her mother, but remained distant to his overtures to win her over. Too young to understand, or object to, adoption, the subsequent change of her name from Hartog to Goodwin had no effect upon her.

Her closest companions became Robert Goodwin, her new cousin, and Julian Roth, both the same age as herself with only a few months separating them. Of the two, she preferred Robert, perhaps because of the closeness and more frequent visiting between the two households; or perhaps it was because she adored Anna.

Karen was ten years old when Zalman and Sophie moved to Harrison, a town she detested immediately, because it was so far removed from everything familiar and comfortable to her. During those years of war, Harrison boomed with cheap restaurants, beer taverns, liquor stores, pool halls, shoddy amusement centers, nightclubs and jerry-built movie houses that were open around the clock to accommodate night-shift war-plant workers. The crime rate rose, drunkenness in public was a common sight, prostitution proliferated, and gambling increased. The local newspaper duly recorded the behavior phenomenon of Harrison's war-born society along with the war news, both deplored from every pulpit.

Karen's schoolmates were a new, audacious breed who came from many distant states and cultures, their parents lured by the highest labor pay rates they had ever known or dreamed of. Their children were brazen and unruly, possessed of an adult, earthy knowledge of life, heretofore unsuspected by the pre-war Harrison community, whose population doubled, then trebled as the war pace increased. In most cases, both parents were at work, either on a day or night shift, their children left alone to find ways and means to keep themselves occupied.

There were rumors of activities too mature for Karen's understanding, made more explicit when concerned teachers, alarmed by the growing rate of venereal disease, quietly began discussing the subject of prevention methods with small groups of girls of vulnerable age. It all became even more explicit when, not too long after, police raided several houses near the school and arrested twenty men and a dozen women on charges of prostitution and lewd conduct. Among the "women" arrested were four sixteen-year-old high school students, and two sisters aged fifteen and fourteen. Within a short time, the action had moved into another house on a nearby street, almost without interruption.

When peace came in 1945, the situation had become commonplace and by the following year there was some improvement when most of the war-geared plants—small suppliers of components to larger manufacturers—closed down. Trailer parks were deserted by their gypsy occupants, who drifted away leaving their debris behind. Much of Harrison took on the appearance of a ghost town as the pool halls, taverns, movie houses, and night spots faded into oblivion. A considerable number, however, remained to take jobs in the expanding GFP operation, now the single largest and most important industry in Harrison.

In 1946, Karen reached her fourteenth birthday, beset by certain biological changes that were taking place in her bodily functions, ignorant of the causes, and disturbed by the lack of communication between herself and Sophie. In desperation, she turned to her closest friend, Marilyn Zeiss, one year older than Karen, whose father, Paul, was an attorney and member of the Harrison City Council. Marilyn's mother, Hannah, was a civic activist who looked toward a brilliant political career for Paul.

Marilyn, a warm, friendly girl, was not only knowledgeable in the matter of growing from girlhood into young adulthood, but at once produced reading and pictorial material that went far and beyond mere explanation. It was, in fact, explicit to the point of pornography and resulted not only in a long verbal discussion, but oral experimentation. And finally, into a relationship between the two that resulted in a complexity of excitement and guilt for Karen. The affair was broken off by Karen when Marilyn proposed that they extend their experience into a more mature arrangement with two boys, with whom Marilyn had begun dating surreptitiously.

During the following summer, Karen became infatuated with Gilbert Eisman who, at sixteen, was already a senior at Harrison High and had won a scholarship to Harvard. His father was president of the local synagogue and a close friend of Zalman. Gilbert taught Karen to play tennis and to swim, his two outlets from study, and within a short time they were dating steadily. Before the summer came to an end, Karen finally gave in to Gilbert's persuasions and engaged in the ultimate act of intimacy.

The experience was far from what she had expected. Not only was Gilbert inept but her own fears prevented a satisfactory conclusion, or the exhilaration she had known with Marilyn. In September, Gilbert went off to Harvard, his departure heralded by the local press. Karen felt only relief and heavy guilt. The summer had been broken by several visits to Wyecliffe and return visits by Anna, Herschel, and Robert, to which Karen had looked forward; but now, in her sophomore year, she looked forward to a bleak winter.

2

Anna Goodwin, who adored Karen, had very early recognized certain dangers in Sophie's and Zalman's neurotic preoccupation with Karen's health and welfare, and now observing Karen's nervous restlessness and seeming lack of social awareness, decided to take matters into her own hands. And to Karen, on those infrequent visits, Wyecliffe had become a means of escape from her parents' constant vigilance and questioning; also escape from Marilyn, and—more recently—from Gilbert.

There were eighty acres to explore at Wyecliffe, the swimming pool, tennis courts, stable with two horses, and the kennel with Robert's four Irish setters. And Robert. The Goodwin estate was several miles beyond residential and commercial Wyecliffe, referred to locally as The Village, and, encouraged by Anna and Herschel, offered Robert's intimates all the advantages of a junior country club.

Nor was Herschel unaware of Anna's purpose in trying to wean Karen away from Harrison. "You know what you're doing, Anna?" he asked one day after the Harrison Goodwins had left for home.

Anna laughed quietly. "Now we both know, don't we?"

"Be careful. Sophie is so possessive and Zalman is . . ."

"An old-fashioned, old-country tyrant where Karen is concerned," Anna concluded.

"So? He is her father."

"Her stepfather," Anna corrected.

"He adopted her legally. He is responsible for her."

"Which doesn't give him the right to be her jailer, does

it? That poor girl is a prisoner, dying for companionship with children her own age. She's in a concentration camp —without barbed wire."

"Anna, we shouldn't interfere."

"Herschel, I can't stand by and watch them ruin that child's life. If you can, you're no better than Sophie or Zalman."

Herschel sighed deeply. "I'm not trying to stop you, only don't create wounds we won't be able to heal, eh?"

"You believe I would be stupid enough to do that?"

"No, no. All I'm asking is that you be cautious."

In May of 1948, Anna and Herschel drove to Harrison on a Sunday for dinner, bringing Robert with them. Later, while Robert and Karen walked over to a nearby park, Anna broached the subject to a shocked Sophie and Zalman. "For the whole summer?" Sophie asked in astonishment. "No. It's crazy. She is a child."

"Look again, Sophie," Anna urged. "Karen is growing and a growing girl needs boys and girls her own age to grow with. The few friends she has here will be going off to camps, or on trips. Karen will become a woman long before she has had a chance to be a girl."

Sophie said painfully, "Anna, she is happy with us and doesn't need camps or trips. Why should we send her away?"

"Because she needs some change in her life, and Wyecliffe isn't the end of the world, it's only fourteen miles away. She needs what we can give her, and you can see her on weekends. What does she have here in Harrison, among *goyische* plant workers and their children?"

Now Zalman spoke up, defending Sophie's point of view. "She has us," he insisted sternly. "She is a child and a child should be with her parents. I don't want to push her out of her own home."

"Zalman, Sophie," Herschel interjected for the first time, "the same world that is pushing us is pushing Karen. Look around you. Children aren't the way we were when we were her age."

"Sixteen years old, she's already a woman?"

Herschel smiled patiently. "You and I became men when we were *bar mitzvah*, only thirteen."

"Yes, yes, but we were different."

"Everything was different then. Today, Karen reads books, magazines, newspapers, listens to the radio, things we never had at her age. She knows more and wants what other girls her age want. How can you say *no* to her?"

"I don't say *no* to her," Zalman said explosively, "only to you and Anna for this . . . this foolishness you ask."

"So why don't we ask Karen what *she* wants?"

"She wants to stay here with her papa and mama."

Anna said, "Then it won't hurt to ask her, will it, Zalman?"

"So ask, ask. You will see. She will say *no* and that will be the end of it. Call her, Sophie."

Karen and Robert came in together. Zalman said confidently, "Karen, *liebschen,* your Aunt Anna wants you should go to Wyecliffe to stay for the whole summer when school closes."

Karen's eyes widened with excitement. "The *whole* summer?"

"The whole summer, Karen," Anna said, "until school starts again in September. Would you like that, dear?"

"Oh, yes, yes, yes!" Karen ran to Anna and hugged her tightly. "I'd like it so much, so very much!" Turning to a disconcerted Sophie and Zalman, "Please, please, may I?"

Thus, the pattern for that, and other summers, began.

They were Robert's schoolmates and friends, these children of Anna's and Herschel's contemporaries who came from Wyecliffe Village; the Rosenbergs and Lerners (attorneys), Freitags (insurance), Bernsteins (accountant), Wallensterns and Caplans (merchants), the Lindstroms (physician), and others. They ranged in age from fourteen to sixteen, all with youthful zests and appetites for active living, and made a huge playground of the Goodwin estate.

Beyond the swimming pool was a guest house with four bedrooms for overnight guests and to one side, a series of cabanas for dressing-rooms, with outdoor showers. All summer long there were impromptu parties, cookouts, games, riding, and hiking, and there was the old McComb house to explore.

They played tennis, softball, basketball, volleyball, one-wall handball and pingpong. They consumed tons of hamburgers, hot dogs, steaks, salads, and fruits, and drank gallons of pop, lemonade, and milk. Besides Eric and Leona, there were Giacomo, the gardener, his wife Betta, laundress and helper with the heavy housecleaning, their eighteen-year-old son, Mario, who had just completed high school and served as handyman, and other help brought in as necessary during the three months of summer activity.

To the non-Semitic community, the Goodwins were known as those "rich New York Jews who got Russell Charles to buy the old McComb place for them out on Thorpe Road." There was, of course, a silent understanding that no Goodwin (or Rosenberg, Lerner, Freitag, Bernstein, Caplan, Wallenstern or Lindstrom) would ever be permitted, wealth notwithstanding, to join—even enter as a guest—the hallowed halls of the exclusive Wyecliffe Country Club; and that none could expect to be included on certain party invitation lists.

Apart from that mildly annoying fact, the Goodwins found suburban living much more involved than life in the city. And far more pleasant. They became absorbed in those small community activities which they were permitted—and eagerly sought after—to participate in; the small orthodox synagogue and larger conservative temple kept them busy, attending services at the former, contributing generously to both, serving as board members, or on Brotherhood and Sisterhood committees, involved in every charity function, on school, hospital, and library committees, and often heading numerous fund-raising drives.

In this atmosphere, Karen spent her first memorable summer away from Harrison. Herschel bought her a yearling to add to Robert's stable and Robert let her choose one of his Irish setters for her very own. Anna drove her into the Village to outfit her with a summer wardrobe that surpassed anything she had ever owned, including her first Western jeans, riding boots, and bathing suits.

In Anna, Karen found easy, comfortable companionship, gentle understanding, wisdom, and true affection; a far departure from Sophie's and Zalman's suffocating intrusions and unwanted togetherness. And here—as the summer came into full swing—surrounded by boys and girls to whom she became a partner in every activity, she soon found that her experiences with Gilbert and Marilyn were growing dimmer and dimmer.

3

At sixteen, Karen's body had fulfilled an earlier promise, having lost its flat boyish charm, and having now developed into definable, graceful curves. She was more exotic-looking than beautiful, with a lean face, high Slavic cheek structure, and a gentle slant to her eyes that gave her an almost Oriental look. Raven-black hair with feather bangs spilled over her smooth forehead to add a *gamine* quality to her patrician nose and sensual lips. Anna noted happily that a spirited competition for her company had festered between Alan Caplan, Johnny Bernstein, Kenny Lindstrom and Ben Rosenberg.

That summer, Sidney and Dora Roth came up to spend a weekend at Wyecliffe, bringing their son, Julian, whom, with Robert, Karen had known as far back as she could remember. Anna invited Julian to stay on after Sid and Dora left on Sunday afternoon, and Julian accepted with alacrity.

Although Julian felt completely at home with Anna, Herschel, Robert, and Karen, he seemed out of place with the Wyecliffe crowd of boys and girls. His city ways and manners, even the clothes he wore, marked him as different, and participating with and among them, he often became inarticulate and physically awkward. A full head taller than Robert, he was a mediocre tennis player, worse at handball, clumsy at basketball despite the advantage of height, and little better at volleyball. His greatest joy was in swimming, at which he was expert, and spent a great deal of his time in the pool. During his two-week stay, he openly courted Karen, which brought about considerable amusement and teasing, not without some embarrassment on Karen's part.

Within a week of his departure, he disappeared completely from Karen's mind. Labor Day was approaching and she and Robert became involved with planning the summer's biggest party, the last before they would all be returning to school, and Karen to Harrison.

Guests began arriving on Friday and the Goodwin home took on the atmosphere of an army encampment. The main house and guest house overflowed onto the grounds, where some were assigned to sleeping-bags laid out on the edge of the woods. All meals were planned to be taken out of doors on planked tables and benches that Mario and Giacomo had knocked together. It was—as had been planned—a marvelous blowoff to end the summer, and on Monday night, after an enormous steak cookout, the guests left for their homes, calling out their thanks, good-byes and see-you-next-summers, although some would be meeting again shortly at Wyecliffe High. When the last had departed, Robert got out his car to take Eileen Lerner home.

"Don't be too late," Karen warned him. "You've got to drive me to Harrison early tomorrow morning."

"I'll be ready when you are," he called back.

Zalman and Sophie, as usual, had missed only two weekends at Wyecliffe that summer; the one preceding the Fourth of July, when they drove Sophie's parents, Max and Rachel Kirsch, from their home in the Bronx to Ventnor, New Jersey, where they rented a small cottage for the summer—a custom for some years—and the Labor Day weekend, when they returned to Ventnor to drive the Kirsches back to the Bronx. Karen could already anticipate the pattern of their questions: What did you do? With whom? You're so thin, didn't you get any sleep at all? to which she would reply with short, ready answers.

In her room, Karen felt the weariness of the long weekend overcome her. She lay on the bed, hearing the sounds and voices of Eric, Leona, Giacomo, Betta, Mario, and the three hired men from the Village as they cleared away the debris left in the wake of the party. She heard Anna call out to Leona, and Leona's muffled reply. And then she heard nothing but her own private thoughts coming through and began to anticipate the sadness of her own departure in the morning.

She thought of the oncoming fall, winter, and spring in Harrison, three seasons of the year without Anna, Herschel, and Robert, except for infrequent weekend visits. Especially Robert, with whom she was certain she was in love; and with equal certainty, was sure he was in love with Eileen Lerner. She envisioned them together at this moment, in Robert's car, parked somewhere on a dark side road, in each other's arms, injecting every erotic implication her mind could conjure up; and again felt the agonizing pain of jealousy she had tried so hard not to show all summer. She had used Ben, Alan, Johnnie, even Kenny, who was only fifteen but big for his age, to awaken interest in Robert other than the brotherly affection he displayed for her, but nothing had worked. Not even when Julian Roth had pursued her so assiduously.

She tried her best to remain awake to hear his car return, but it was only a little past nine and she had so much lost sleep to recapture. At least, she thought as she undressed and was brushing her teeth, I'll have him all to myself in the morning.

She got into bed and was asleep by the time her head touched the pillow.

The call came shortly before ten o'clock. Anna was still out on the grounds giving last-minute cleanup instructions to Eric and the other help. Herschel, shoes off, a cool drink on the table beside his favorite reading chair in the small study, was relaxing when the telephone rang. He listened for a while before he could identify the voice of Max Kirsch, weeping brokenly as he tried desperately to tell Herschel the unbelievably tragic news. Then someone else came on the line and identified himself as a New Jersey State patrolman, and gave it to Herschel with the crispness for which State patrolmen are noted.

At four o'clock that afternoon, Zalman and Sophie had gone down to the beach for a last dip before starting the drive back to New York. Sophie, running in ahead of Zalman, dived under a huge incoming breaker. Zalman waded in after her and was drawn out by the strong undertow. He began to struggle fiercely, unable to sight Sophie, and began swimming to the point where he had seen her last. Max and Rachel Kirsch, fully dressed and watching from the beach, began screaming for help and several bathers came running. Two lifeguards plunged into the heavy combers as did two or three of the men in the crowd that had gathered quickly at the scene. To no avail.

Lights were set up and the watch continued. Shortly after eight o'clock, Zalman's body was sighted and brought in. An hour later, Sophie's body was recovered.

When Anna entered the study, Herschel had hung up, his hand still gripping the receiver, the blood drained from his face, tears streaking his cheeks. "Herschel! What is it?"

"Ah—ah—h—h . . ."

"Herschel, tell me!"

"Ah—where—where is Karen?"

"In bed, asleep. What's happened? What . . .?"

"Zalman. Sophie," he groaned. "Dead. They're dead."

"Oh, my God! How? Where?"

Slowly, brokenly, he told her what he had learned from Max Kirsch and the State patrolman.

"God, God," Anna cried softly. "How can we tell Karen?"

"No. Not now. Let her sleep. Tomorrow will be soon enough." Herschel began rocking back and forth in his chair, beating his left breast with his right fist, reciting, "*Yisgadal v'yiskadash, shmey rabbo . . .*"

"Stop it, Herschel! Stop it! I can't stand it!"

Momentarily, he returned to his senses, still weeping. "Why?" he asked. "Why? Why Zalman, why Sophie?"

Arms around him, Anna said, "We don't know. We never know why."

Herschel began a broken-voiced rambling about Zalman's and his own boyhood in Germany. Growing up, school, the bakery they had built into a chain together, and sold. He spoke of Zalman's marriage to Sophie, of incidents long forgotten, and remembered now in stress.

Robert returned shortly after midnight, surprised to find his parents still awake, Anna, entering the study carrying a pot of fresh coffee. "Hey, what's up? Tomorrow's a working day . . ." He saw Herschel's reddened eyes brimming with tears, and the strain on Anna's face. "What is it, Dad, Mom, what's happened?"

Anna told him.

"Oh, good God! Poor Karen!" Robert slumped into an armchair. "Does she know?"

"Not yet. She's asleep."

Robert leaped to his feet again. "What happens now? What do we do? We can't just sit here like this doing nothing, can we?"

"Robert," Anna said, "the best thing you can do is go up to bed and try to get some sleep."

"How can I sleep, Mom? We've got to go to Ventnor, bring them back . . . funeral . . ."

"Not you. And not Karen."

Now Herschel bestirred himself and began pacing back and forth. "In the morning, I will go to Ventnor. I'll take Eric with me. I'll do what has to be done. I want you and your mother to stay here with Karen, break the news to her when she wakes up. Both of you should go to bed now."

But neither made the move to leave him. Sometime after three o'clock, Robert fell asleep in his chair. Anna woke him and led him off to bed. For herself and Herschel there would be no sleep that night, kept awake by their own anguish.

After Herschel and Eric left for the airport early next morning, Anna sent Leona to Karen's room to wake her.

When she was dressed and came down to breakfast, she at once sensed the troubled air. "Where is Uncle Herschel?" she asked. "I'm all packed and ready to go home. Is Robert up?"

"Uncle Herschel had to leave early," Anna replied. Robert came in and sat at the table, showing no interest in the food that Leona, also teary-eyed, placed before him.

"Something is wrong. What is it?" Karen said.

"Please, darling, eat your breakfast."

"I know something is wrong. I can see it on Robert's face, yours, Leona's too. Why are you crying, Aunt Anna? *Tell me!*"

Anna moved her chair closer to Karen's and told her. She looked up, the color totally drained from her face, but there were no tears. "They're—*dead?* Mama and Papa are *dead?*"

"Yes, darling. I'm so sorry to have to tell you this way, but there's no easy way to tell someone—someone— Uncle Herschel and Eric have gone to Ventnor . . ."

Karen stood up and said, "Excuse me. I want to go to my room."

"I'll come with you . . ." Anna began.

"No. Please. Alone."

When she left the room, Robert said, "Oh, Christ! Isn't there *some*thing we can do for her, Mom?"

"Just wait, Robert. That's all any of us can do."

"I feel so damned helpless, useless."

"So do I, but we'll have to wait until she comes back to us."

Anna went to her own room then and slept, her strength depleted by her nightlong vigil. Shortly after one o'clock she woke when Robert knocked on her door to tell her Herschel wanted to speak to her from Ventnor.

"Karen?" she asked.

"She's still in her room."

On the phone, Herschel outlined the plans he and Max Kirsch had made for the funeral in Wyecliffe, and Anna told him she had not yet discussed any details with Karen. When she hung up, she sent Robert into the Village to talk with the rabbi and arrange for two gravesites beside those she and Herschel had chosen for herself, Herschel, and Robert.

"What about Karen?" Robert asked.

"I'll try to talk with her while you're in the Village. I think you'd better ask the rabbi to reserve another gravesite." Robert nodded, knowing it was meant for Karen. "Go now," Anna added. "I've got other phone calls to make."

Anna showered quickly, dressed, and went to Karen's room. When she knocked, there was no answer. She tried the knob, found it unlocked and entered quietly. Karen lay on the bed, curtains drawn. She was fully dressed, eyes wide open and tearless.

"Karen?"

No answer.

"Karen, darling, we've got to talk to each other."

"I don't feel like talking now," Karen said, staring up at the ceiling.

"Darling, listen. Uncle Herschel is bringing your mother and father . . ."

"He isn't my father. He was never my father. My father died a long time ago. He is my mother's husband."

"Then your mother . . ."

"I don't have a mother either. She's dead."

"Karen, please. I know how difficult this is for you, but you must understand. They're both dead and we must bury them. We—your uncle and I—want to bury them here in Wyecliffe."

Again there was total silence.

"Look at me, Karen. I have something important to say and I want to be sure you understand."

Karen's head turned and Anna saw her tearless eyes through her own mist. "Darling, listen. No one can say why this tragedy happened. Only God knows why. We want your mother and—her husband—buried here so they will be close to us. You must remember that Zalman is Uncle Herschel's brother, no matter what you felt for him. Do you understand?"

Karen nodded. Anna said, "You'll live with us now and we will be your father and mother, and Robert your brother. We want you because we love you so very much, as much as we love Robert. You'll be our daughter in every sense of the word. You won't even have to change your name." Anna felt her voice breaking and paused; then, passionately, "Oh, Karen, we want you so much. We've always wanted a daughter. We'll go into court and adopt you."

Karen said, "I was adopted once. I don't want to be adopted again. Because my mother's husband was Uncle

Herschel's brother, you can be my aunt and uncle. You can't be my father and mother."

"We'll talk about that later. Meanwhile, we'll take care of everything. We'll close the house in Harrison and bring your things here. Will that be all right for the present?"

"Yes."

"I'll have Leona fix some lunch for you."

"No, please. I couldn't eat. I'm very tired."

"Then sleep, darling. We'll talk again later."

Herschel and Eric returned late on the afternoon of the following day, driving behind the hearse that bore the bodies of Sophie and Zalman. After a stop at the Rodman Mortuary in Wyecliffe Village, they came home to find Rabbi Kinsman and his wife with Anna, Karen, and Robert. Herschel and the rabbi went into his study to discuss arrangements for the funeral the next day. The phone rang constantly. Anna answered each call, speaking briefly, giving the time of the funeral and, in some cases, directions for reaching Wyecliffe and the address of the funeral home. Earlier, she had made the necessary calls to those close to the family. The Kirsches had gone home to the Bronx to prepare themselves for the ordeal of tomorrow.

Karen went up to her room and Robert followed her. "It's funny in a way," Robert said. "Not funny, odd, I mean. We've always been able to talk about so many things, people we know, school, sports, everything we do. Well, almost everything, anyway. Then something tragic like this happens, something really big and important, and we don't know how to talk about it."

"I know," Karen said. "Nobody likes to talk about dying. Everybody has to die someday, we know that, but it's as though it's a secret everybody knows, but nobody is prepared for it."

"Like when my grandfather, Harry Rosen, died," Robert went on. "I was nine or ten years old and wasn't even allowed to go to his funeral. I loved him very much and I know he loved me, but when he died, it was over like a shot and I wasn't even a part of it."

"I remember. We were at your house when everybody came back from the cemetery. All those people. I asked my mother if there was always a big party when someone died. All week long people came and brought food, cakes, and wine. They sat around and talked, and even told stories and jokes. I really thought it was a party. I didn't know. No one ever told me. Mama never explained anything to me. About most things. Until I started spending my summers here in Wyecliffe I was the dumbest kid in school or out." She paused, took a deep breath, and let it out slowly. "I guess it will be the same thing all over again now."

"Are you going to be all right, Karen?"

"I think so. It's something a person has to live through."

"I'll be there with you. And afterward."

"Thank you, Robert."

"Don't thank me. You're my sister now. Look, Karen, I know it's going to be hard on you, a big change in your life, but we'll make it up to you. Mother and Dad love you, you know that. I never had a sister and you never had a brother, so that much will be different for both of us."

"It won't be much different, Robert. I know you've always thought of me as a sister, but I've never thought of you as my brother. I—I love your mother and father. And you. I think I'll like living here, going to Wyecliffe High instead of Harrison . . ." Her voice broke then and she couldn't go on. Robert touched her shoulder. She looked up at him and he leaned down and kissed her gently, a mere touch of his lips across her cheek. "Julian phoned this morning," he said. "He'll be here tomorrow with his mother and father. The offices and plants will be closed, too."

Karen said nothing.

Next morning, the Kirsches arrived in the chauffeured limousine Herschel had ordered for them. Max Kirsch's eyes were red and moist, Rachel shriveled into a state of near collapse. They drove into the Village to the mortuary together. The chapel was filled with friends and business associates from New York, Harrison, and the other plants in Syracuse and Elgin, Illinois. The executive staff from the New York office was present as were a number of executives from distant cities who had flown in the night before. As the funeral got under way, others were still arriving. Practically the entire Jewish community of Wyecliffe filled the chapel and overflowed into the hallways.

Karen became the central object of sympathy from old friends of Sophie and Zalman; the Behrmans, Roths,

Rosen relatives, bearded old men who had known Zalman from those earlier days at the East Side *schul* he had attended, and many others she could not remember or recognize. People inched forward to offer condolences, pressed her hand, teary-eyed. voices strained. She sat in the front row between Anna and Robert while Herschel spoke a few last words with Rabbi Kinsman.

Then the services began with a prayer, first in Hebrew, then repeated in English, most of which escaped Karen. She echoed "Amen" when the word swelled into a low roar from the many responding voices and, looking to her left, saw Russell and Faith Charles, a *yarmulka* on Russell's head, and a scarf over Faith's. She saw Julian sitting with Sidney and Dora, surrounded by young friends she had come to know during her summer visits to Wyecliffe, and others who had come with their parents from Harrison.

Rabbi Kinsman gave the eulogy and spoke of the humble man and woman who had come separately from their native lands to eventually meet in America, marry and make a good life together. He did not mention that Sophie had lost her first husband earlier or that Karen had been the product of that first marriage. He recounted incidents in their lives—no doubt supplied by Herschel and Anna—that had been heretofore unknown to Karen; so that, at times, it was as though he spoke of two people who were strangers to her. He talked about the depression, their marriage, hardships endured, the outbreak of World War II, the success and happiness they shared in the years that followed, the love they poured out upon their daughter, only to be taken at this moment in time by God's will and reasoning, which could not be questioned.

From the chapel, they drove to the Wyecliffe Memorial Cemetery, led by two uniformed officers on motorcycles. The sky was heavily overcast, gray and threatening. Someone remarked at the large number of cars in the procession, but no one else turned to look back. The Kirsches and Anna sat on the rear seat of the limousine, Karen and Robert on the jump seats, Herschel beside the driver. The cars formed a large circle on the concrete driveway and Karen got out, Robert beside her, and she saw the double-width oblong hole with fresh raw earth peeping out at the edges of the carpet of synthetic grass that covered the mound. Herschel and Anna were weeping quietly, Rachel

Kirsch wailed hysterically, Max Kirsch hunched forward, sobbing, crushed, defeated.

The rabbi's voice was clear, considerably louder in the open than in the chapel, where he had had the advantage of a microphone. Karen tried to follow his words, but most were meaningless to her as she gazed in fascinated horror into the hole and saw the two caskets lying side by side, trying to remember Sophie as she had seen her before they departed for Ventnor, eager and expectant at the prospect of their annual holiday, only a few short days ago. She averted her eyes and stared at the sky, wondering if Sophie was somewhere up there looking down upon this gathering.

Good-bye, Mama, she whispered.

There was the *kaddish*, the mourning prayer, spoken softly by the rabbi, louder and brokenly by Max Kirsch and Herschel, while Karen tried to repeat the Hebrew words that Robert spoke close to her ear. Then the men formed a double row for the family to pass through and they were once again in the limousine. As they left the cemetery grounds, cars behind them peeled off at intervals in various directions and they were finally alone on Thorpe Road, heading for home.

The Kirsches would not enter the house until a vessel of water was brought outside so they could rinse their hands in orthodox tradition. And no sooner were they inside than people began to arrive to pay their respects and form the *minyan* for the first of the afternoon and evening services. In their absence, the Rodman people had brought half a dozen special mourning chairs, legs shorter than the others, and a large, gold-shaded *yahrzeit* candle that would burn throughout the mourning period. Trays of food had also arrived, sent by friends in order to eliminate the necessity of the family preparing food during that sorrowful time of *shiva*, but Leona had already cooked more than was necessary to accommodate the family and the expected visitors.

Max and Rachel Kirsch were uncomfortable in a house that was not, according to their religious standards, truly orthodox, and Herschel ordered the limousine to return them to their Bronx home where they could conduct their own *shiva* period of mourning.

Julian, Sid, and Dora Roth were among the first guests to arrive, followed by David and Morris Behrman, with their wives and older children. Most of the GFP people followed, paid their respects, and left soon after to catch planes or drive back to their home bases. The local people came in time for the first service, led by Rabbi Kinsman. Late that night most had gone, but Julian remained, taking over one of the bedrooms in the guest cottage. However, with the constant flow of visitors during the next few days, there was little time he could share alone with Karen and, under the circumstances, there was little point in trying to be alone with her.

On Friday afternoon, the ritual of *shiva* was over, the extra chairs, mourning candle, and prayer books were removed by the Rodman people, and some sense of order was restored. With the constant flow of visitors, up early for the morning service and to bed long past midnight, there had been hardly a moment for close, intimate family talk and, as Herschel had observed with grim humor, "Not even a time for mourning."

Karen had gone to bed late in the afternoon and did not waken until Saturday morning just as the sky was beginning to lighten. She dressed in comfortable slacks and a shirt and came downstairs to the kitchen to find Leona up and preparing breakfast. "Good morning, Miss Karen. You up so soon?"

"I slept the clock around, plus. May I have some coffee?"

"Sure. Here, or in the breakfast room with your uncle?"

"Is he up?"

"Up and waiting for his breakfast. You want more'n coffee, honey?"

"Just coffee, please."

"Go in and sit with Mr. Herschel. Eric'll bring it to you."

Herschel was glancing through the morning paper when she entered. He put it aside and said, "Sit down, Karen. You slept well?"

"Yes, thank you. Are you going to the plant today, Uncle Herschel?"

He smiled and said, "The plant can wait until Monday. I'm going to *schul* this morning. How do you feel?"

"I don't really know. Tired, confused a little. It's been a long, tiring week."

"Yes, it always is. Anna and Robert didn't get to bed until after midnight."

"Uncle Herschel . . ."

"What, darling?"

"Thank you for everything, what you and Aunt Anna have done . . ."

Herschel said, "He was my brother. Sophie was a sister to me. What we did, Karen, that's what a family is for."

"I know, but . . ."

"We are still a family, Karen. Remember that. Always."

"I will."

"Monday, I will be going to Harrison. What do you want to do about the house there?"

"I don't know. I only know I don't want to go back there."

"All right. I'll find somebody to sell it to. And your clothing and other things?"

"Can I have them sent here to me?"

"Of course. And your father's and mother's things, clothes?"

"I'd like to give the clothes to charity, someone who can make use of them. The personal things, those can be sent here, too, can't they?"

"I will take care of everything for you. You won't have to go back there if you don't want to."

"I can write for my school records."

"Yes. The reason I am asking you these questions is that I want you to understand that you are a grown girl, an independent person with your own decisions to make about certain things. You understand that, Karen?"

"Yes, I do." The food arrived then, and Karen's coffee with it. After Eric left them, Herschel said, "You have talked with your Aunt Anna, Karen?"

"Some, yes."

"So. You have lost your parents. I have lost a brother and sister-in-law whom I loved very much. Your Aunt Anna's loss, believe me, is as great as yours or mine. So now we have buried them and they will rest in peace and we will keep on living because we must. The four of us. You, Anna, Robert, and I. A family, living together and for each other. You understand, Karen, it isn't because of laws or customs, but because we love you, want you, and need you. You know that?"

"I understand, Uncle Herschel."

When Herschel left to attend morning services in the Village Karen went outside and walked along the path past the play area to the guest cottage. The door to Julian's room was open and, peering in, she saw it was empty. She opened the clothes closet but there was nothing to indicate his presence. The shelf over the bathroom sink was devoid of shaving gear, toothbrushes, after-shave lotion. She thought it curious, with the weekend just starting, that Julian would have gone back to New York without saying good-bye.

She returned to the house and refused Leona's second offer of breakfast. "I'll wait for Aunt Anna and Robert," she said, and went to her room. Standing at the window, she stared out at the woods beyond the guest cottage. To one side, Giacomo had begun working in the garden, dressed as usual in denim overalls. She watched as Mario joined him, carrying an armload of newly cut stakes, and both men began driving them into the ground at regular intervals. Every evidence of the summer's activities had been cleared away: tennis, volleyball, and basketball nets stored in preparation for the oncoming fall and winter. From the kennel, she heard one of the Irish setters bark shrilly, answered by another, then a third. From afar came the faint whistle of a train, and she wondered idly why she had never heard it before.

Death, she thought, comes to seasons as it does to humans, except that the seasons return each year and the person is gone forever.

She shuddered at the thought and felt sudden fear, recalling a conversation she had once had with Robert. It was a subject, like many others, that was seldom discussed in her presence; a thing to be hidden from the young, unmentionable as though it were obscene. Now it had touched her life intimately and she was frightened by it.

It occurred to her then that so much of her sixteen years had been lived with a shield around, built by Sophie and Zalman to protect her. How many times, she wondered, had she asked questions that were put aside or evaded, so that she appeared to be foolish, or naive, about many subjects that were discussed so freely and openly by her contemporaries; the shock she experienced when Fran Hollander told her only a few weeks ago that Robert and Eileen Lerner were "doing it," which she refused to believe. And now, she asked herself, what reason do I have for not believing it?

She saw Betta, Giacomo's wife, come into the garden. Mario called out to her, straightened up and went with her into their house, probably to have his breakfast. Betta was a tall, heavily framed woman with powerful arms and legs, yet not unattractive. Giacomo put his arm around Betta's waist as they walked along, both smiling. Betta spoke to him and he laughed, then replied, slapping her playfully on her well fleshed buttocks. Betta dodged, laughed, then canted her head toward the house. The play ended then and they went inside their cottage.

They were, Karen guessed in their middle or late forties, but acted so much younger. She had seldom seen any similar indication of affection between her mother and the man she had married, and the memory of her own father was too dim to recall. If anything occurred between Sophie and Zalman that could be construed to be intimate, it was in the privacy of their bedroom, never in the presence of others, even herself; no kiss, never a caress. How different they had been from Anna and Herschel, who always kissed on parting in the morning and on his return in the evening. They often walked the grounds together as she had just seen Giacomo and Betta doing, holding hands, arms around each other's waists, an act Karen couldn't even imagine taking place between Sophie and Zalman.

And now, in this critical mood, came fresh guilt to add to other, older guilts; the strange, inexplicable thing with Marilyn, the disappointing affair with Gilbert.

How many times in the years past had she wished to be free of Sophie and Zalman's constant *presence*; wished she had been born to a mother and father who were intellectually able to understand and respond to the needs and dreams of a growing daughter instead of giving her obsessive over-protection; wished she were the daughter of Anna and Herschel and could live with them permanently in Wyecliffe.

Had she, in fact, ever loved Sophie?

Certainly she had never wished their deaths. But now, she reasoned, by what other means could she possibly have been free of them except through death? Had she then, subconsciously, willed them to die?

The thought disturbed her and she turned away from the window, examining her room. It would be hers now. It was a beautiful room, with its own private bath, a luxury she hadn't known until she first came to Wyecliffe. When she came to spend that first summer, Anna had had it completely redecorated for Karen and even allowed her to choose the material for the curtains and draperies, the wallpaper and furniture, which had given her a sense of ownership. The closets with built-in drawers held her own clothes and it was as though she had never lived anywhere else, Harrison was already beginning to slowly fade in her mind.

She heard footsteps in the hallway, and a pause outside her door. Anna, no doubt, listening for some movement to indicate she was awake and stirring. In this house, unlike the one in Harrison, privacy was respected; no one opened a door without first knocking. She could remember nights when she would awaken suddenly to find either Sophie or Zalman in her room, adjusting a window, drawing a cover up over her, or merely hovering over her bed to be sure she was alive and breathing; remembrances from earliest childhood. In the darkness, she had learned to identify each by individual odor; Sophie's cologned scent, Zalman's musty factory smell that could never be bathed away.

She moved across the room toward the door, heard a faint rap, and Anna's voice called softly, "Karen?"

"Yes. Come in, please."

Anna, wearing a light silk robe over her nightgown, entered. "I thought I heard you moving around. Up and dressed so early?"

"Up, dressed, and I've already had coffee with Uncle Herschel before he went into the village for the morning services."

"Robert wanted to be wakened, too, but he got to bed so late, I decided to let him sleep." Anna stood off a few paces and stared at Karen, smiling. "You're a beautiful girl, Karen."

"Thank you."

"Yours is a wonderful age," Anna continued. "Soon, you'll become a beautiful woman with a full life ahead of you. Think about that, Karen. College, a career of your own choice, travel, marriage, children . . ."

"I can't think of those things now. I'm so confused about everything, Mama . . ."

Anna put an arm around her. "Remember them, of course, darling, the way we all will, the way I remember my own father. Time will pass and we'll be here to help you when you want or need us. We'll try to lessen the pain of their deaths, but we'll have to think of the future, too. Your future."

"I know. You've done so much already."

"We love you, Karen. We'll try to advise and guide

you, but we'll never interfere. I promise you that. You will make your own life and I hope we can always be a part of it."

"You will be. You're the only family I have. I love you and Uncle Herschel and Robert." She burrowed her head against Anna's breast and said, "I didn't want them to die, Aunt Anna, I didn't—"

"What a silly thing to say! Of course you didn't. And keeping to yourself isn't good for you. Now let's go and have breakfast with Robert. He's waiting for us. Oh, I forgot. Julian drove back to New York last night. He asked me to say good-bye for him and give you his love."

It was as though she had been reborn as a young adult. Anna took her off to New York for a few days and returned with a new fall wardrobe. They had experimented wildly with a new hairstyle and cosmetics, explored bookstores, and had a dozen or more volumes of Karen's choice sent to Wyecliffe, visited museums and art galleries, stayed at the Plaza, lunched and dined in smart restaurants. Among her new possessions, those that excited Karen most were the charge and credit cards and checking account in her own name.

Karen entered Wyecliffe High as a junior, the transition from Harrison made smoother by friends acquired during the summers spent here on vacation. Each morning after breakfast, she drove to school in Robert's new car and drove back with him every evening, which nettled Eileen Lerner somewhat and pleased Karen very much. The table talk at dinner was far from the sterile mealtime discussions she had felt completely excluded from in Harrison. It was lively with stories from Herschel, with relating their experiences of the day at school, all received with interest. Karen and Robert studied together at nights, a great advantage for Karen, since Robert was a straight A student. On Friday nights, they went off to the Village for a movie or to a party at one of their friends' homes. Weekends, they rode their horses, went for drives, saw high school football and basketball games together, and frequently double-dating with Eileen and one of the numerous boys who had attached themselves to Karen. In time, Karen came to share Fran Hollander's opinion that Robert and Eileen were more than mere "steadies."

Well into winter, she met an outsider to their crowd, Pierce Nieland, a senior, the leading scorer on the Wye

High basketball team, who began taking a strong interest in her. Pierce was, Karen decided, the most excitingly handsome boy she had ever known. Tall, slender, with dark blond hair, deepset blue eyes and the classical look of an All-American campus athlete. And a *goy*.

Pierce's mother had died shortly after his birth and his father, Howard Nieland, a partner in the New York brokerage firm of Cranston, Packard & Nieland, had allowed Pierce to remain with his grandmother. Mrs. Carolyn Pierce Nieland lived in Wyecliffe on what remained of her considerable estate with only Pierce and her servants. The late Commodore Howard Case Nieland had sold more than half of his land to a group that then developed it into what was now the ultra-exclusive Wyecliffe Country Club, of which Mrs. Nieland was a lifetime member of the board of directors.

Life suddenly became marvelously exciting for Karen. Parental restraints aside, she became interested in extracurricular school activities, participated in class elections, served on the Student Government Committee, joined a sorority, became a member of the Thomas Paine Literary Society and the Drama Club. She ran for the office of Class Secretary, organized a campaign with Robert as her manager, and won hands down.

When her year of mourning was over she began dating regularly, and among those more prominent in her life was Pierce Nieland. There were no objections from Anna or Herschel when she began inviting Pierce to their home along with her and Robert's other friends, and Pierce became a frequent visitor. Karen saw every basketball game that Pierce played in, cheering him on vociferously.

The following summer, Anna invited Julian Roth to spend the month of July with them, perhaps to counteract Karen's growing interest in the Nieland boy, and Julian accepted readily. Shortly after his arrival, Pierce left for a two-month trip to Europe with his father, a graduation gift that would precede his entrance into Princeton in the fall.

On the Saturday before Julian was due to return to New York, he and Karen double-dated with Robert and Eileen for dinner at a lake resort in the northern part of New Jersey. Of the four, Julian seemed least to be enjoying himself, taking little part in the gay conversation of the others. They returned shortly before midnight and Robert dropped Karen and Julian at the Goodwin house before taking Eileen home. Julian showed little inclination to go to his room in the guest house and Karen went to the kitchen to fix two Cokes for them. Julian followed her and removed the caps from the bottles while she got a tray of ice. "What's wrong, Julian?" Karen asked. "You acted as though you weren't with us tonight."

"I don't know. Maybe it's because I'll be leaving in the morning. I hate to see this come to an end."

"That's silly. You can always come up on weekends."

"I know, but I can't help feeling what I feel, or showing it. I'm not like the others, I guess. Like Robert, Ben, Johnnie. Or that new guy, Pierce."

Karen laughed. "Are you saying you're jealous?"

"I guess so. Sure, I'm jealous as hell."

"Now that's *real* crazy. They're just friends, boys I go to school with."

"Sure. And grow up with, go to college with, and marry . . ."

She turned so suddenly at that word, that she almost dropped the two glasses she was holding. "Julian . . ."

"Listen, can't you see I'm in love with you?"

"Oh, Julian, don't say that!"

"It's true. I mean it. I'm serious. I want you to think about it."

"Think about what?"

"About marrying me." Seeing the honest shock in her stunned expression, "I don't mean now. Later, when we're out of college."

"Julian, you're out of your mind. That's five whole years away."

"I always look ahead. I told you I wasn't like the others. Do you like me, Karen?"

"Yes, of course I do, but . . ."

"Then think about it, will you? I'm not asking for anything more than that now. Karen . . ."

"What?"

"I've never kissed you. Really kissed you, I mean."

"Yes you have. The first time was at your *bar mitzvah*."

"That was kid stuff. I mean since we've grown up."

"You've never really tried, or even asked."

"I'm asking you now."

He was standing close to her and putting his arms around her waist, drew her close to him. Karen allowed him the kiss, a gentle press of lips, then more firmly. "All right?" he said.

"Yes. That was nice."

"You've been kissed before, haven't you?"

"Of course, but not seriously, like this."

"Does it bother you, being kissed seriously?"

She giggled softly. "I don't think so."

"Will you think about it, what I said before?"

"I'll think about it if you want me to."

He kissed her again, more relaxed now, feeling some response in her, and he moved one hand up to caress her breast. "Julian, don't . . ."

"Karen, I love you."

She broke away from him. "Julian, please don't . . ."

"It was only a touch. Don't be afraid . . ."

"I'm not afraid. It upsets me."

"That's a good sign. You're responding to me."

She wondered how *he* would respond if he knew about Gilbert. She shook her head negatively and said, "No, Julian."

Julian laughed and said, "I think we've just proved something."

"What?"

"I'm sure you love me, too."

Karen put the untouched Coke down on the kitchen ledge and said, "Goodnight, Julian. I'm going to bed. I'll see you in the morning."

Love or fear? What was it she had felt at the first touch of lips, that initial probing hand over her breast? The thought of finding herself in intimate embrace with Julian, as she had with Gilbert, repelled and disgusted her now. She had, since coming to Wyecliffe for the summer, often wondered what it would be like with Robert, but Robert had been conditioned to think of her as a sister, and would under no circumstances violate the bounds set by family tradition. This feeling with Julian, in a serious mood, the thought of marriage behind it, chilled her.

There was, of course, the fear of long ago, burned deeply into her mind by Sophie, ignored when she became involved with Gilbert. Sophie's preachments on the dangers of allowing any boy to touch her intimately. Disease. Pregnancy. Shame. Dishonor. Even death. Like the Ten Plagues recited annually at the Passover feast. And yet, how could anything so pleasurably exciting be wrong and harmful?

Julian seemed more cheerful at breakfast and later, was unable, in the presence of Robert and Anna, to say more to Karen than "Good-bye. You'll remember, won't you?"

"I'll remember," Karen replied softly.

And later, when Robert asked, "What did Julian want you to remember?" she replied, "Oh, it wasn't anything."

She remembered for a day or two, then put it out of her mind as, in the final weeks of the summer holiday, activity increased. Pierce Nieland returned from Europe, but they saw very little of each other because he had so much to do before leaving for Princeton.

4

Her senior year at Wye High was one of restless discontent. When it began in September, Herschel surprised her with an MG sports car with a right hand drive, and although she was tremendously pleased at first, it soon occurred to her that Robert had been freed from their morning and evening ritual drive to school and that this gave him those afternoons to spend with Eileen and his male companions. It took very little to imagine how he and Eileen spent that time together.

Pierce wrote frequently. He had made the Princeton freshman basketball team and invited her down to several home games, but understanding as Anna and Herschel were, Karen knew she would be risking their displeasure if she accepted a weekend invitation away from Wyecliffe with a boy. Next year, perhaps, when Robert would be at Princeton, she might be able to work it out.

For herself, she had chosen Smith College in Northampton, close enough to forestall familial objections, far enough away to permit complete freedom. Anna and Herschel, happy she had given up her earlier suggestions of USC in Los Angeles and UC at Berkeley, voiced their approval.

Pierce came up for the traditional Nieland gathering in Wyecliffe for Thanksgiving but was only able to get away for one evening to see Karen. They drove out into the countryside on that crisp, cold evening. Karen again explained why, at seventeen, she couldn't spend weekends with him at Princeton and Pierce was disappointed, but picked up when she said, "Robert will be going to Princeton next year. Maybe then."

They were parked beside a lake, watching the path of moonlight that divided it in two. Pierce lighted two cigarettes and handed her one. "What about now?" he said.

"What do you mean?"

"Don't be naive. I mean you and me. Right here, now."

"Pierce . . ."

"Don't you want to, Karen?"

It was the first outright, undisguised pitch he had ever made to her and her voice shook with emotion. "Ye—I think—yes, I do, Pierce, but I'm not going to."

"Why not, if you want to?"

"Because I don't know how to handle . . . the situation. If anything happened . . ."

"Don't let that worry you. I've got a thing with me."

"I've heard they sometimes don't work, and even if I did, I'd still be alone here and you'd be in Princeton. And if it didn't work, I'm sure you wouldn't rush back to Wyecliffe to marry me."

"Oh, come on, you're making too big a thing of it, you know."

"Maybe, but no. Not now."

The "not now," even though stated positively, somehow held the promise of the future, and Pierce did not press her further. They kissed and fondled each other until Pierce achieved an artificial climax, then drove back again.

She was met by curious glances from Anna and Robert on her return, but there were no questions. No prying.

Christmas came: the new year of 1950 was born. Karen and Robert were working hard to keep their grades up, social activity died down considerably, and soon it was spring again. Exams were over and their grades placed them well above the margin of safety. The weather turned mild and outdoor life, after a harsh winter, became pleasant once again.

They were graduated from Wye High in June, looking happily forward to the summer that lay ahead before parting to go off to college. But on June 24, some sixty thousand North Korean troops, spearheaded by more than a hundred Russian-built tanks, crossed into South Korea and shattered the blissful days to which they had looked forward. Gloom was heightened when Arnold Freitag and Johnny Bernstein, who had graduated with them less than ten days before, left notes for their parents early one morning, caught the first bus to New York, and enlisted in the Marine Corps. For a while there were tense suspicions that Robert and others of his friends might follow Arnold and Johnnie, but as the weeks passed Robert became less uptight about the war, less inclined to leap into the flaming police action.

Pierce, after a week in Wyecliffe, went off to New York to spend some time with his father and begin his apprenticeship in the brokerage business. He hadn't pressed Karen beyond their previous mild intimacies, and a promise that, with Robert at Princeton, Karen would come down for a few football and basketball games. Pierce was reasonably certain he would be given a spot on the varsity team.

And, after Karen had long forgotten Julian Roth, he suddenly appeared to spend two weeks at Wyecliffe. Karen was hard put to find ways to tell him she was not interested, without hurting him. Julian tried valiantly to reintroduce the subject, but Karen was determined not to give him that opportunity.

The Fourth of July fell on Tuesday. On Monday night, Julian asked Karen to drive into the Village to see a movie. "I'd like to, Julian," she said, "but with all the company we're having tomorrow, I should stay here and help Aunt Anna."

Anna said, "We've plenty of help for what needs to be done, darling. Go on to your movie and enjoy yourselves."

Robert had already left for a date with Eileen and Karen could find no other way to escape. In Julian's car, his mood became cheerful. "You know," he said, "this is the first minute I've had alone with you since I got here."

"That's not so," Karen objected.

"I said *alone*. There's always somebody around, Robert, your aunt and uncle, people dropping in."

"Julian, I can't be with you exclusively and ignore my family and guests, can I?"

"I had a crazy idea I was a little more than just a guest. To you, I mean."

When she didn't answer he said, "Have you given it any thought, Karen?"

"What?"

"You know what. What I asked you to remember last summer."

"Oh."

"Just 'oh'?"

"I thought about it. I don't think it would be right for us to get that serious."

"Why not?"

"Because—well—because we're not old enough. At least, I'm not. I've got four years of college ahead of me and so have you. I haven't even begun to make up my mind about what I want to do, to be . . ."

"Why not Mrs. Julian Roth?"

She went completely limp at the thought. "I—Julian, don't push me. I can't look ahead to four years from now."

"Are you saying you don't love me?"

"I think I'm saying I don't know what love really is, what it's all about. I like you, yes. I like other people, too, and . . ."

"Pierce Nieland?"

"And Pierce and Ben and Kenny, but I don't like one to the exclusion of all others."

"Then there's still a chance, isn't there?"

"What chance there is will have to wait until I know something more about myself, my own mind. Oh, Julian, I can't even say the right words, how to explain, I'm so mixed up."

"Okay, Karen, I won't pressure you, but I'm not giving up, you understand?"

The movie, which she really wanted to see, was a total loss. When they returned home, she pleaded weariness and the day that faced them, and went immediately to her room and to bed.

After breakfast next morning, Julian managed a moment alone with Karen. "Listen, I was pushy and I upset you last night, didn't I? Will you forgive me?"

She smiled brightly. "Of course. There's nothing to forgive."

Julian grinned. "If you'd given me half a chance, there would be."

Karen returned the grin. "Then I'm glad for both of us that I didn't. That way, there's nothing to be sorry for."

"Okay, but don't write me off. I still mean it."

This time she turned away without answering.

An hour later, their guests began arriving, Pierce Nieland among them, up from the city for the day without his grandmother's knowledge. Pierce monopolized Karen most of the day at the pool, at tennis, and was her partner in the impromptu basketball game. Later, they saddled horses and rode off for an hour, and on their return at five o'clock, Pierce thanked Anna and Herschel, and left for the city.

Julian, in a fit of depression, moped in his room in the guest house and when Karen, having changed back into a swimsuit, came down to the pool, she found Robert alone and dropped into the chair beside him. "Where's Eileen?" she asked.

"Helping Mother and Leona with the food for the cookout."

"And trying to prove what a good daughter-in-law she'll make?"

"Come off it, you pinhead. What about you? You gave Julian a rough time, running off with Pierce."

"That's Julian's problem, not mine," she replied.

"You're getting to be something of a little bitch, you know."

Karen grinned impishly. Robert said, "You're going into the Village with Julian for the fireworks, aren't you?"

"I promised I would, if he still wants me to go with him."

"He'll want, bet on it. Hey, you're pretty far gone on Pierce, aren't you?"

"And you're getting to be pretty nosey, aren't you?"

Robert shrugged. "I don't think I'd get too interested if I were you, pussycat."

"No?" she said loftily. "And why not?"

"That should be pretty obvious by now, even to you. His grandmother, for one thing. Very rich, very snooty, very class-conscious. She wouldn't approve of Pierce marrying the niece of those rich New York Jews who bought the old McComb place. That's how she and the others in their clique refer to us, you know."

"I think you're a bigot. Pierce isn't like that, Robert."

"Pierce is . . . well, as long as you don't get too serious about him, I guess there's no harm."

"And if I did?"

"Then, baby, you're going to get very damned hurt. If, for instance, Pierce got serious enough to want to marry you, he'd stand a good chance of being disinherited, and nice or not nice, Pierce isn't going to do anything that'll cost him a big slice of the fortune she'll leave to him and his father."

"I see." Robert saw the cloud that shadowed her face.

"Hey, you haven't—uh—had anything going with Pierce, have you?"

"Not what you mean, no."

"As long as we're in this deep, and I know it's none of my business, what about Julian?"

"He wants to marry me."

With open surprise, "Julian? He's that serious?"

"Yes."

Robert whistled. "Jesus. He's a deep one." When Karen said nothing, "How do you feel about him?"

"Julian?"

"Of course, Julian."

"I don't know. I like him, I guess. I've known him forever."

"Well, with that much enthusiasm, you've answered the question. Does he know where he stands?"

"I've tried to get it across to him, but he won't listen. Let's drop it, shall we?"

"Sure. Swim?" He stood up, reached for her outstretched hand and pulled her to her feet. Karen ran to the deep end of the pool and dived in. Robert followed, and paced her for four round trips. The subject of Pierce and Julian was shelved for the time being.

At six o'clock Eileen came walking by, ringing an old-fashioned farm bell, calling everyone to dinner. Herschel, chef's hat jutting upward and to one side, served the steaks from the grill. Eric and Leona dished up the salads, baked beans, hot rolls, while the guests fanned out to select tables and partners for the meal. Julian came up and joined Anna, Herschel, Robert, Eileen and Karen at their table. The subject under discussion at the moment, as it was being hurled from table to table, was Korea, the drive south by the North Koreans, the effort of the United States, as usual, to come from behind and push the enemy beyond the thirty-eighth parallel.

Herschel, in an effort to turn the subject aside said, "So you'll be going away to Princeton in September, Robert. You and Julian, eh? And little Karen to Smith. Ah, how the time flies."

Robert said, "Well, I'm all for it, but Uncle Sam might very well make a decision that could upset our plans. Anyway, I don't think I'd mind too much. I'd like to get a piece of the action."

"The war," Herschel stated pontifically, "will be over before Thanksgiving. I have a feeling about it."

Robert laughed and Julian joined in. "I know a lot of guys who'd be awfully relieved to hear that," Robert said.

"So you have my permission to quote me. I think that next summer you should take a three-month trip to Europe. Would you like that?"

"Again," Robert said, "if Uncle Sam doesn't come up with another set of plans for my future."

Karen said, "If Robert goes to Europe, I want to go with him."

Anna looked up quickly. "We'll talk about that some other time. And if you're all going into town for the fireworks celebration, let's finish up here so that the help can clean up and go, too."

Herschel said, "At least, that's one plan Uncle Sam won't be able to interfere with."

Anna and Herschel, after a long day of playing hosts, elected to remain at home. At dusk, they saw everyone off, then returned to the house. Karen was paired off with Julian, Eileen in Robert's car with another couple. Julian was in the same black mood that had plagued him during the day and as they became one of the cavalcade of cars along Thorpe Road, he said, "My God, this is the very first minute I've had you to myself all day."

"You always say that and you know very well that I can't ignore our other guests. It wouldn't be fair."

"And how about all the time you spent with the *goy*?"

She said angrily, "Julian, don't you ever let me hear you call him that again. Pierce made a special trip up from the city to spend a few hours with us . . ."

"With *you*."

"Whatever. It was his holiday as much as it is yours or mine."

He said, grumbling, "They ought to call this place you live in the Wyecliffe Hilton."

"Don't be so grumpy. It doesn't help things."

"You don't seem to want to help things, either. Have you forgotten that I want to marry you?"

"Oh, Julian—" she said wearily.

"I'm serious, Karen. I know I'm pretty much of a square compared to guys like Pierce and Robert, but I want to get a good start so that when we're married, we'll be . . ."

"Don't, Julian. You keep making plans as though everything is settled between us, and it isn't. I don't want to hurt you, but I've told you before, I can't even begin to think of getting married. I'm barely eighteen . . ."

"Do you know how many girls get married at eighteen or under, Karen?"

"No, and I'm not interested in the statistics. I'm looking forward to college and everything that goes with it."

"You could still go to college . . ."

"It wouldn't be the same, married, maybe even pregnant."

"Now that's a very beautiful thought."

"Not for me, and not for now."

"All right," Julian said with resignation, "but keep my application on file, will you? I still want to be Number One in line."

The Fourth of July spectacle was an annual event sponsored by the Wyecliffe Senior and Junior Chambers of Commerce, the Business Men's Association, the American Legion, the Veterans of Foreign Wars, and other civic groups. The townspeople of Wyecliffe and surrounding communities turned out to fill every seat in the small stadium, and chairs were set out for the overflow. There were four competing bands, pompom girls, flags, banners, marching groups, as well as speeches by Mayor Cass Hazlett and State Senator Albee Thurston.

At nine-thirty, three small cannons boomed repeated salvos as all lights were doused and a huge American flag burst into flaming glory while the four bands combined to play the *Star Spangled Banner*. For the next hour and a half the sky was shattered with all manner of rockets, flares, sunbursts, pinwheels, and bomb flashes, to the complete delight of the spectators. At eleven o'clock a massive frame was lighted to depict America's fighting men in action in Korea. Along its upper edge, the words appeared one by one, WE SHALL WIN! The crowd applauded, whistled, howled, and roared.

As if this were a prearranged signal, it began to rain. People scurried out of the unprotected stadium as thunder rumbled and lightning split the skies. Within moments it had become a heavy downpour and the audience, protected only by programs and newspapers over their heads, raced toward the exits and to their cars for shelter. It took a long time to get through the narrow exit tunnels and gates. Many of the spectators were bunched up and trapped inside the tunnels that led to the parking areas, making passage through almost impossible. In the crush,

Karen became separated from Julian and the others of their party, and was pushed along with the crowd. The concrete parking lot held less than half the cars, the rest having been parked on grass and dirt lanes surrounding the stadium, all of which had now become a sea of churned mud.

Karen felt a hand clutch her shoulder, turned around, and saw it was Robert. "Where's Julian?" he called, circling an arm around her wet shoulders.

"I don't know. We got separated. Where's Eileen?"

"Lost in the shuffle. Jesus, what a mess. Come along—this way—I'm parked over here."

With his arm supporting her, Robert plodded through the loose underfooting until they reached his car, its windows down and the seats wet. Robert found a small rag in the glove compartment, but it became uselessly soaked after a few wipes. Karen raised her skirt and tried to remove her half slip. She stumbled against him. "What are you doing?" he asked.

Someone from the car beside theirs wolf-whistled as she said, "Trying to get my slip off so we can wipe these seats dry. Here, hold my skirt up."

He held it above her waist and she was able to loosen and remove it. Robert said, "Hey, that's quite a sight. Beautiful." Admiring howls came from the car beside them as well.

She handed him the slip. "Dry the seat, sonny. You've seen more of me in a bathing suit. And of Eileen, too, without a bathing suit, I'll bet."

"Yeah? How much has Pierce seen of you?" Wiping industriously.

"Wouldn't you like to know."

"I can guess."

"Well, guess again and get the seats dry, will you. It's chilly out here, and I'm soaked."

"It's okay now, as dry as I can get them. Get in and let's go." She got in, kicked off her wet shoes, and pulled her skirts high up. Robert started the motor and turned the heater on, but they were still blocked in and helpless to move. Robert cracked the side vents to give them some air, looking out on both sides for anyone from their party. "See anybody?" he asked.

"I'm on the blind side. I can't see anybody or anything."

Here and there, cars began to move, but it was half an

hour before a path opened up and Robert was finally able to inch the car toward an exit. None of the cars that remained were recognizable in the driving storm and they gave up the search for Julian, Eileen, or the others. Shortly afterward they came into the Village, through it, and onto Thorpe Road. "What about the others?" Karen asked. "Do you think we should try to find them?"

"Are you that anxious about Julian?"

"No, but I thought you might be about Eileen."

For a moment he said nothing, then, "Screw Eileen. We're through."

"What happened?"

"She's getting engaged to some guy from Chicago she met. He goes to Michigan State, and she's going there too."

"I'm sorry, Robert."

"I'll get over it. No use trying to find the others. They'll probably get lifts with someone else. Jesus, what a climactic finish."

"The celebration, or Eileen?"

"Listen, forget Eileen, will you? I said it's over. *Fini*."

"Okay, *Fini* Eileen."

Robert depressed the accelerator and the car leaped forward. Within minutes they reached the house, but Julian's car was not there. The lights had been left on, but Anna and Herschel and the servants were asleep.

"Hungry?" Karen asked.

"Ravenous. Let's get into something dry, then look for something to eat."

"There's plenty left over. Give me ten minutes."

They changed into slacks and sweaters and returned to the kitchen. Karen made some roast beef sandwiches while Robert got out a tray of ice cubes and some Cokes, then went into Herschel's study and returned with a bottle of Canadian Club he had taken from the bar. He poured two Cokes, then added a liberal jigger of Canadian Club to his. "You want a warmer-upper?" he asked.

"What's good for you can't be bad for me."

"You've had it before, haven't you?"

"Of course. What am I, a child or something?"

"A child, no. Something, yes." He poured a jigger of whiskey into her glass. "When did you start drinking?"

"I've tried it a number of times, but not at home in front of nosey relatives."

"Pierce?"

"Pierce, yes."

"Anything else you do away from the curious eyes of your nosey relatives."

About to cut the sandwiches in half, she paused, aiming the knife point at his chest. "Now let's not get *too* nosey, Mr. Princeton-to-be."

"Just curious."

"Well, to satisfy your curiosity, I've taken a drink or two now and then and what's more, I like it. I've also shared a joint or two—"

"Where? With whom?"

"Keep your voice down, you idiot."

"I'm interested. No, intrigued. When?"

"Last winter and this spring."

"I'll be damned. Our first family hashhead."

"Relax, Big Brother. All it did was nauseate me."

"Then why try it the second and third time?"

"Because it was there and I sort of went along with it. All the kids do it. Haven't you ever tried it?"

"No. Hell, no. Listen, is that the extent of your experimentation with life?"

She smiled and said, "Are you inquiring into the state of my virginity, Big Brother?"

He shook his head, "No, hell no. I'd be the last guy in the world to butt in on somebody else."

"Why, because you and Eileen . . . ?"

The question, unfinished, brought him up short. "Just how much do you know, or think you know, about me and Eileen?" he asked.

"Only what I've heard . . ."

A car pulled into the front driveway, then ground its way to the back of the house. Robert turned on the outside rear lights and a moment later Julian burst into the kitchen, shirt and slacks soaked and wrinkled. "Wet your pants, sonny?" Robert asked.

"Big joke, funny man," Julian snapped, and to Karen, "Where'd you get to? I was worried."

"I was in safe hands." She indicated Robert with a toss of her head, who said, "Change your clothes and grab a sandwich, Julie."

"All my stuff is in the guest house. I'll only get soaked again coming back here."

"Okay, we'll make some more sandwiches and you take them there."

While Karen sliced more roast beef and prepared the

sandwiches, Robert found two raincoats, put one on, and gave the other to Karen. He brought along several bottles of soft drinks and the whiskey. Karen covered the sandwiches with waxed paper and they ran down the bricked path to the guest cottage. There, Julian changed into dry clothes while Robert fixed a stiff drink for him, and more for Karen and himself. They sat in the living room eating, talking about the celebration, and the debacle of its conclusion.

Julian said he had picked up Roy Bernstein and Al Harris, then Eileen Lerner, and had driven them to their homes. "Eileen," he added, "was telling us she's changed her mind about Sarah Lawrence and is going to Michigan State."

"That's right," Robert said. "What's more, she's practically engaged to a med student out there. Did she tell you that, too?"

"No, but—Jeez, Robert . . ."

"Let's have another drink."

The conversation lagged then and they sat listening to the rain, now driving with greater intensity against the side of the cottage and windows. Karen said, "I love the sound of rain. It makes me feel warm inside, sleepy."

"That whiskey you're lapping up wouldn't be helping out, would it?" Julian said sarcastically.

"Oh, Julian, shut up. You're a worse nag than . . ."

Julian put his glass down and stood up, offended. "Oh, shit," he snapped, then, "I'm sorry. It's been a long day and I'm beat. Why don't we call it a night."

"Go ahead," Robert said. "We'll go up as soon as it lets up a little."

"Okay, goodnight. See you in the morning." Julian went out and down the hallway to his room. Karen stretched out on the sofa, a pillow under her head. She sipped at the last of her drink and then said, "I feel fuzzy. But nice and warm."

"You should," Robert said. "That's your third drink."

"You counting, Big Brother?"

"No, but—want to make a dash for the house?"

"And get soaked all over again?"

"We've got the raincoats. It's only a hop, skip and a jump."

"Uh-uh. I want another drink."

"One more and I'll have to carry you!"

"Oh, come on. You're beginning to sound like Julian."

"Poor Julian."

"What about poor Karen, and poor Robert?"

He fixed another drink for her without comment, then poured one for himself. He brought it to her and sat beside her on the sofa. "This is the last one, so enjoy it."

They clinked glasses and drank. Karen put her glass on the floor and closed her eyes. Robert said, "Hey, how about it? You'll sleep a lot better in your own bed with all that booze in you."

"I think," she said woozily, "I'll sleep right here. I'm too comfortable to move."

"Come on. Mother'll be worried, you sleeping down here."

"Because of Julian?"

"Maybe."

"What would she say if I slept here with you?"

"All right, knock off the jokes and let's go, huh?"

He leaned over, put his arms under her and raised her up. As she came up, Karen wrapped her arms around him and kissed him full on the mouth. Full and hard. He pulled back for a moment, then returned the kiss firmly. "There," he said, "is that what you want?"

"Yes. Didn't you like it?"

"Sure. Now come on . . ."

"No. I want to stay here with you. That's the first time you've ever kissed me that way. Like you really meant it."

Robert laughed. "Little girl, I think you're drunk."

"May—maybe just—enough, but I'm not a little girl, damn it."

"Knock it off, will you? Julian's only two doors away."

"Oh, screw Julian. Who cares about old Julian, anyhow."

He held her for a moment, not knowing what to say to her in this strange mood, now suddenly conscious of the warmth and contours of her body. "Hey," he whispered, "let's go. You're working me up."

"Good. That's what girls are for, or haven't you learned that from Eileen?"

"Karen . . ." he began warningly.

"Don't you like me as much as you like Eileen?"

"Let's drop the subject of Eileen, will you."

"All right. You said it before, so screw Eileen."

"Goddamn it, you're getting to be a real dirty-mouth."

"And you're a moron, a blind idiot." She lay back, eyes still closed, a smile playing mischievously on her lips.

Robert bent over and whispered, "Karen, listen Karen . . ."

She opened her eyes and put her arms around his neck, drawing him down closer. "Robert," she said, "I'm serious. Please love me, love me—"

"Karen, this is crazy. Real crazy!"

"Robert, please. I want it to be you . . ."

When he tried to pull back and upward, she came up with him, her head buried against his chest, holding him tightly. He could feel the softness of her body, braless breasts against him, and his hands moved over her, then under her sweater.

"Robert, Robert," she whispered, "please. I don't want Julian, I don't want Pierce, or anybody else. I want you so much. Please."

He stood up as though to leave, but her arms caught at his thigh and held him. "Please, Robert . . ."

Robert kneeled beside her, seeing her as he had never seen her before, sweeter, more desirable, so eager. "You know what you're saying?"

"I know. I know, Robert. Please, don't make me beg any more."

He reached for the wall switch and turned off the light, then the lamp on the table beside the sofa. In the darkness that followed, hearing the rain pounding on the roof and running down the spouts, he pulled off his shirt, trousers, and socks. Karen was sitting up and he could hear the rustle of her slacks as she tugged them off. He helped her get the shirt off, inhaling the perfume of her body.

Then they were lying together on the sofa, kissing, embracing naked flesh, eagerly responding to each other's touch. She moved away and lay flat on her back and he slid over her, caressing and kissing her young, firm breasts as she reached for him, found, and guided him into her. "Does it hurt?" he asked.

"No. It's fine—fine . . ."

She could feel him grow larger inside her and moved her legs apart to accommodate him, then moved up convulsively as he drove downward. She gasped and held him tighter, but he made no move then, waiting for her shuddering tremor to subside. "Don't stop, Robert, don't . . ."

She remembered the sensation, remembered Gilbert out of the past. Something different was happening, a new feeling exhilarating her beyond recall and she whispered, "Robert, oh, Robert—" She uttered a cry then but he smothered it with his lips, and when she subsided, "Julian!"

he cautioned, and she compressed her lips to hold back any further sound, driving, reaching . . .

And then, unaccountably, Robert stopped and went slack inside her.

"Go on, Robert, go . . ." she urged.

"I can't—I . . ."

"Robert, *please* . . . don't stop now!"

"It—it's not—working . . ."

"What's wrong?"

He slipped out, uselessly limp. "I don't know—I—it's wrong. I can't make it with you."

"You made it with Eileen, didn't you?"

The mention of Eileen angered him. "All right, I did. That was different. This—this—goddamn it, Karen, with you it's incest."

"That's ridiculous. It can't be different. We're not even related. If we wanted, we could even get married."

"For Christ's sake, you must be out of your mind. You're—I'm crazy. Jesus, what I've done to you? I must be out of my stupid skull . . ."

"I'll help you." With her hands, she found him and tried, but Robert could not achieve an erection. "Stop it, Karen. It's no damned use," he groaned. "It just won't work."

She released him then, turning on her side away from him. Robert moved closer to her, touching her nakedness, one hand sliding along her thigh until he reached the magic triangle. Karen's thighs opened, then closed on his fingers. "Do it that way," she said.

He began his manipulations. Karen turned fully toward him, moving in concert with his hand, but without result. And finally she rolled over and away from him, exhausted, silently admitting her failure to achieve orgasm. "I'm sorry, Karen," he said.

"Don't be sorry. We'll try again later."

"The hell we will. Not later, not ever again. We shouldn't have started . . ."

"Don't say that. We'll go back to the house."

"I tell you, it won't work between us. We're too much like—like brother and sister."

"We're not, damn it!" she snapped.

"Keep your voice down, will you? And get your clothes on. We're going up to the house."

"No."

"Come on, damn it, it's way past two o'clock."

"Stay here with me."

"With Julian only two doors away? You're crazy."

He dressed and heard her movements in the dark silence. He saw her shadowy figure as it crossed in front of the window. He picked up the raincoats and tiptoed after her. On the porch, she shrugged into one of the coats, but when Robert took her elbow, she pulled away angrily. "I don't need your help now," she said, and ran up the path to the house.

5

In his room, only two doors beyond the living room where he had left Robert and Karen, Julian undressed, slipped into pajama bottoms and went to the bathroom to brush his teeth. He could hear their voices faintly above the sound of the rain—a small burst of laughter from Karen—and wondered what Robert had said to make her laugh; something he had seldom, if ever, been able to achieve with ease. When he and Karen were alone, Karen might laugh *at* him, never *with* him.

Why? he wondered. Why can't we joke or tease? It came so easy for Robert, for others. And for that *goy*, Nieland. And why had Robert come up with that crack, *Wet your pants, sonny?*, a bitter reminder.

And why had he said he was tired and needed sleep, when what he wanted most to do was to stay up all night long—with Karen—but not with Robert sitting there, the two of them drinking, smoking, kidding around, showing him up as a sober clod.

The *what* of the matter was as old a story as Julian himself, who had known personal catastrophe most of his remembered days. It was the *why* that confused and confounded him.

From his earliest childhood until two years ago, when he was sixteen, Julian had been a chronic bedwetter. After a reasonable period that followed his infancy, Dora had at first been concerned, then alarmed. She had taken him from doctor to doctor, from clinic to clinic, but no one could discover anything organically wrong. Dora conscientiously followed instructions and saw to it that his intake of liquids was limited to barest necessity after a certain hour, but even that did not help. Julian slept in rubber pants on a rubber-covered mattress and the only result was that Julian cried out in discomfort and Dora was forced to get out of bed every night to change him. Nor did it help when Sidney, a man of short-fused outbursts of temper, complained bitterly that *her* son was not like the sons of other parents.

"He can't help it, Sid," Dora protested in tears. "He's delicate."

"Delicate, my ass! I'm delicate? You're delicate? So why should this little *pischer* be delicate?"

"Six doctors, four clinics . . ."

"Doctors, clinics, what he needs is to have his water cut off for a few days."

"And let him die of thirst?"

"So pamper him, spoil him. What the hell happens when he starts going to school?"

Eventually, it reached that worrisome and problematic stage. In school, away from Dora's eternal vigilance, Julian came to understand the meaning of pure humiliation; that he was different from other children. On his very first day in class, he became suddenly aware that the thing he most dreaded was happening. He began squirming in his seat, unwilling to call attention to himself, and finally, in desperation, raised his hand to attract the teacher, engaged at the blackboard, her back to the class at that moment. Too late. He felt the gush of warm wetness he could not control. A small puddle formed under his seat which was soon noticed and set off hoots of laughter from the boys, and giggles from the girls.

When Dora met him outside the schoolyard at noon, Julian was in tears. He handed her a note from his teacher which advised her to "look into the matter." It took every means of persuasion (and finally the tight rubber pants he detested) to induce him to return to class.

But the damage had been done. The lower East Side was notoriously tough and intolerant of weakness, and once the word had spread about Julian Roth's watery infirmity, it all came down to a matter of personal survival. None could be more cruel than his own contemporaries and Julian was jeered at and taunted in class, and ridiculed during recess and after school. He became the target for abuse from older, tougher boys, and the one accomplishment he could claim was the ability he achieved as a runner, expert in the art of escape. On several less notable occasions, however, when flight was impossible, he was trapped and beaten, and his nose was once broken.

Julian grew up in a state of loneliness, unwanted by his peers, a social outcast with no friends other than the children he came in contact with through close family connections; principally his Behrman cousins and the Rosen and Goodwin children. There was one compensation, though this would not become apparent until much later; Julian, with little else to do with his spare time, lost himself in study and became an outstanding scholar.

In time, by intense concentration, he learned to control his bladder weakness in school, but at night, approaching his fourteenth year, it was still necessary to wear those hated rubber pants to bed; his sleep interrupted every night by the necessity to get up and change into dry shorts and rubber pants. During the next year, he suffered the hell of severe acne. More doctors, more clinics, greasy ointments, constant warnings to keep his fingers away from the infected areas, all adding to his deeply depressed state. Nor did it help matters when, at Dora's urging, Sid began to lecture him on matters of youthful indiscretions in sexual matters which, in Julian's frame of mind, seemed rather inappropriate, even ridiculous, leaving him with the feeling that there was something else important that was lacking in his life.

As he approached his sixteenth year, the acne disappeared as suddenly as it had come. And with it, the bedwetting miraculously ceased. Emerging as though newly born as a young adult, Julian scarcely knew how to begin his new life. Enforced shyness had left him without intimate friends. Other than family affairs, he had never been to a purely social party, had never learned to dance, and he knew no girls he could invite to a movie or simply walk, talk, or study with.

Sidney Roth, with his job at GFP going well at this point, decided to move uptown to an apartment on Riverside Drive. In new surroundings, a new school, among an entirely new group of schoolmates, Julian began to discard old fears and ties to the lower East Side and made a determined effort to expand socially. He became an enthusiastic exerciser, took on some weight, and was soon no longer a gangling boy. Because of his height he was sought out for the school basketball team, but discovered he had an aversion to any sport that entailed body contact. Swimming became his *tour de force*, which gave him a sense of accomplishment apart from his studies and helped in his physical development.

In time, he joined one of the school's social clubs, learned a few dance steps, picked up a swingy patter and began dating. There were girls—he discovered in that year of 1947—who had achieved emancipation of a sort during the war years, some older than himself, some younger, all more sophisticated. Some engaged in sexual exercises for pure pleasure, others for the material benefits sex offered. With a more-than-adequate allowance from Sid, Julian took the latter course, thus eliminating any complicated emotional alignments or attachments. Too, there were no complaints over his failures, which were all too frequent.

Then, in his sixteenth year, he rediscovered Karen Goodwin and a certain hope began to blossom within Julian Roth. In Karen, he saw the ultimate desire of his heretofore unremarkable life, his one chance for happiness. At this early age, Julian had discovered the meaning of love.

He returned to his bedroom. Karen and Robert were still in the living room waiting for the rain to let up. He was tempted to slip on a robe and rejoin them, but lay on the bed instead and tried to imagine it was he, not Robert, with Karen; talking, even drinking the whiskey he disliked, Karen laughing at his witty remarks.

He began to wonder about Karen and Robert, and their closeness brought about by the death of Sophie and Zalman. He wondered if they were closer in private than met the eye, but dismissed the thought at once, knowing that Robert was too far gone on Eileen Lerner, and began to feel the heat rising in his loins as he invoked the image of Robert and Eileen naked, locked together.

Sleep eluded him. Desire for Karen punished him.

He wondered if they were still in the living room and got out of bed, opened the door, and listened for their voices over the sound of the rain. The light from the living room threw a warm shaft of yellow into the hallway, but he heard no voices. And then, suddenly, the light went out. Julian waited there, expecting that they would come out and make a run for it to the main house. But all he heard, except for the rain—was silence.

He crept down the hallway to the entrance to the living room and stood there, numbed by his own thoughts. And heard movement. Movement and breathing that were all too familiar to him. Then voices. Karen's. Robert's. Muffled. . . .

Then he knew torture and cried silently, "You bastard! You no-good bastard! My girl—she's my girl!"

He held onto the doorpost to keep from bursting into the room and exposing them, then turned and went back to his room, weeping silently into his pillow. He knew there would be no more sleep for him this night. He got up, dressed in the dark, packed his suitcase and shaving kit and sat in the chair with his agonizing knowledge and bitter thoughts. How long he sat there, he didn't know, but after what seemed to be hours, he got up, carried the bag and kit out to his car, and started to drive back to New York.

To hell with Karen. To hell with Robert. To hell with the whole goddamned world and everything and everybody in it. Who needed them?

6

Early next morning Karen awoke from a restless sleep, feeling panic, uncomfortable, with an unaccustomed pain in her upper thighs that brought back the events of the night before. Outside, it was still raining. She heard a car start and wondered if it could be Herschel on his way to the Harrison plant, but it was too dark out, and much too early for him. She heard the car move out and then the sound of its motor was lost to her. She fell back into a daze and when she awoke again it was nearing ten o'clock.

She got up, ran a bath, and lay in it soaking up its warmth, relieving some of the nervous tension she felt. The rain was still coming down, but not as hard as it had the night before. By eleven, she was dressed in slacks and loafers and went to the breakfast room, wondering what her own, and Robert's reactions would be when they next met.

Anna was at the table having a cup of coffee. Leona brought some orange juice for Karen, took her order for toast, jam, and coffee. Anna said, "Did the rain spoil the celebration last night or was it over before the downpour started?"

"Only the last display got rained out. We had an awful time getting away, everybody pushing and milling around like cattle."

"Did you and Julian enjoy yourselves?"

"Yes. Everybody did for most of it."

The toast, jam, and coffee came, and Leona, assured that nothing else was needed, returned to the kitchen. Anna said, "Karen, did Robert say anything last night to you about driving into the city early this morning?"

She experienced a spasm of fresh guilt. "No. Isn't he here?"

"No. Julian too. Julian left earlier, without breakfast, before Robert was up."

"Didn't he say why—Robert, I mean?"

"No. I was in my room. He called to me and said he was leaving. I thought he might have said something to you."

"I don't know why," Karen said. "Neither one said anything about it last night."

On the following morning, Anna received a phone call from Tim Hendricks, a service station operator in the Village, telling her that Robert had left his car there the morning before, with instructions to notify her this morning. Disturbed, Anna dressed quickly and asked Karen to drive into the Village with her. At the station, Tim handed her an envelope with a note and the car keys inside. She read the note and handed it to Karen, her face white. "Does this make sense to you?" she asked.

DEAR MOTHER

I hope you, Dad, and Karen will forgive me for running off this way. When you hear from me next, and it will be soon, I promise, you will understand why I couldn't discuss my action with you beforehand. I love you all very much and please, please don't worry.

ROBERT

Anna drove the Cadillac home with Karen trailing behind in Robert's car, her mind in a state of total turmoil.

Later in the day, Karen phoned the Roth home in New York, but Dora said that Julian had returned unexpectedly and had gone off to a beach somewhere until Sunday night. Karen asked Dora to have him phone her as soon as he returned.

On Monday, when Julian hadn't called, and goaded by

Anna's and Herschel's distress, she telephoned again and reached him at his home. Julian told her he was very busy and couldn't speak with her at the moment, but would call later that evening. His voice was strangely brittle, abrupt, and surprisingly cool.

Julian did not return the call.

Herschel, Anna, and Karen went through eight more days of desperate anxiety until they received Robert's first letter. It was postmarked from Parris Island, South Carolina.

"I have joined the Marine Corps and am in training here at Parris Island. I would have written sooner, but was unable to find a spare moment until now. I know this has caused you a good deal of unhappiness and for that, I ask your forgiveness, but it is something I felt I had to do. The training is very rigorous, but physically rewarding. There is nothing I need that the Marine Corps doesn't provide. I only hope you will not worry about me. I'm very sorry I couldn't discuss this openly with you before.

"I love you very much, Mother, Dad and Karen, and will write when I can."

Julian, after three weeks of silence, came to Wyecliffe on a Saturday afternoon. He, too, had received a brief note from Robert and told Anna and Herschel he had had no previous knowledge of Robert's intention to enlist. He mentioned that he had slept in the guest house the night of the Fourth of July and had started back to New York very early, before anyone in the house had risen, but gave no reason for having cut his visit short by several days.

He declined Anna's invitation to stay over, and later, found Karen alone and waiting in the guest house. He entered quietly, startling her when he spoke. Karen said angrily, "Why didn't you call me back as you promised, Julian? It's been three whole weeks."

"Don't you know why, Karen?"

"No, how could I?"

"Karen, don't play your games with me."

"I'm not playing games . . ."

"The hell you're not. Look, I know I'm no great bargain, but I'm not as stupid as you think."

She remained silent, staring at his darkly flushed, sullen

face. He looked away from her, then walked to the window and looked out over the deserted pool. "It was always Robert, wasn't it? And all the time I thought it was Pierce Nieland you were so hot for."

"What are you talking about?"

"More games. Why the hell don't you stop trying to kid me?"

"Why don't you stop talking in riddles?"

"All right, I will. That night—you know—here, the Fourth of July. When I went to bed and left you here with him . . ."

She knew then that Julian knew, and her face reddened. "You spied on us!"

"I didn't. I didn't need to. You were both drunk, and you forgot all about me, didn't you? I couldn't fall asleep, thinking of you, how much I loved you, wanted you. I got up after a while to come back and talk. Just then the lights went off. I stood in the hall beside the door. I heard you—and him—all of it. I didn't need any light to know what you were doing. You and Robert . . ."

"Julian, don't, don't! It—it just happened. We'd been drinking . . ."

"Oh, come off it. Don't use that as an excuse, for Christ's sake. You've always been in love with him, admit it."

"Julian, you're trying to punish me. And yourself. I never once said I loved you, did I?"

"No, but Karen—Karen listen to me." He came back to the sofa and sat down beside her. "Listen, will you? I've tried to stay away from you, even hate you, but I can't. Despite what happened between you and Robert, I don't give a damn. I still love you. I didn't mean to tell you I knew about it, it just spilled over, but I'm willing to blot it out of my mind. Marry me. I promise I'll never bring it up again."

She saw tears forming in his eyes and her own began misting with pity for him. Or perhaps with self-pity. To cover her deep embarrassment, she stood up and walked to the window, then to the door. When she turned back to look at Julian he was sitting on the edge of the sofa, an abject figure, chin resting on his chest, eyes on the floor, arms resting on his thighs. She said, "Julian, I'm sorry. I really am, more than I can tell you. I never wanted to hurt you, but you were asking more of me than I could give you. Please believe me."

She went out quickly, before he could look up or answer, then ran across the porch, down the three steps, and up the path toward the house. She waited in her room until she heard Julian's car start up and drive off, and with a sense of relief lay on her bed and began to cry.

During the following month there were three brief notes and one longer letter, then a one-pager from Camp Pendleton in California where Robert was being readied to ship out, giving an APO number for his future destination.

It was a brilliant summer, marred only by the monumental gap left by Robert's absence, one that could in no way be filled. Herschel went off to Harrison each morning, frequently to New York, and occasionally to visit one or another of the GFP plants when his presence was required. Anna and Karen tried to busy themselves with some minor decorating after a while, then became engrossed with shopping to get ready for Smith in September. Between times, they waited for a letter from Robert.

In mid-August, Anna and Karen drove to Northampton to arrange for her living quarters. They found a new, modern apartment building not too far off campus, but the only furnished unit available was a two-bedroom affair, tastefully decorated, and outrageously expensive. Anna persuaded Karen to take it rather than live in a dorm or rooming house, reasoning that there would be room for herself and Herschel should they decide to visit for an occasional weekend. Anna wrote a check for the first two months and the last and signed the lease. They drove through the college grounds, explored Northampton's shops, restaurants and points of interest, spent the night in a motel and returned to Wyecliffe the following day.

There were several trips to New York to complete Karen's wardrobe and these helped revitalize Anna's interest and keep her mind busy with everyday living.

Early in September they received four letters from Robert, evidently written aboard ship en route to Korea and describing his life as a Marine, his excellent state of health, hardened body, and improved strength and endurance. Two days later there was another letter, lyrically descriptive of the strange country he found himself in, totally lacking in any information about the war itself.

Herschel's study became a war-game room with a large color map of Korea on the wall. Each evening after dinner, he and Karen checked *The New York Times*, took notes from Walter Cronkite's news program, then brought the map up to date, using various colored pushpins and strips of ribbon to differentiate between allied and enemy troops, marking each advance and retreat from their notes.

Then it was time for Karen's departure and a new sadness for all. Herschel had turned in Robert's and Karen's cars for a new Jaguar and Anna gave her her first important pieces of jewelry: a diamond-and-emerald cocktail ring with matching watch-bracelet. The weekend prior to her departure sharply reawakened memories of Robert. She had driven into the Village to pick up a pair of riding slacks at Freitag's, listened to Benita's account of her summer trip abroad with little interest, then started toward the curb where her bright new Jag was parked. A familiar sports car braked sharply, pulled into the space immediately behind, and Pierce Nieland called out, "Hey, beautiful! Hold it!"

In navy-blue turtleneck shirt and gray slacks, patrician features sun-bronzed to perfection, Pierce looked wonderfully fit. Princeton and Manhattan had matured him remarkably since she had last seen him. He vaulted his long, rangy body over the side of the car without bothering to open the door and came to her. "Hi, Princess, how are you?"

"Fine, Pierce. You look sharp, just great."

He winked and smiled. "Sun lamp and handball courts at the New York Athletic Club three times a week. Some weekend golf and sailing, too."

"How is the brokerage business?"

"Fabulous. I do most of my work at the club, in restaurants, or out on the Sound. Grandma Nieland's been raising hell with me for neglecting her, so I came up for the weekend. How was your summer? Did you get away at all?"

"No, just hanging around Wyecliffe."

"How's Smith?"

"Fine, from what I saw of it one weekend. I think I'll like it a lot."

"Well, then, how about dinner somewhere tonight?"

"I don't think so, Pierce. There's so little time left to be with Uncle Herschel and Aunt Anna."

"Oh, come on, now, I know it's been rough as hell with Robert taking off like that, but you can't shut yourself away from the world and stop living. Put the package in the car and let's have a hamburger. I'm absolutely starved."

"Okay," she conceded. The package disposed of, they walked the block to Rector's and ordered hamburgers, a Coke for Karen, and a beer for Pierce.

"You get more beautiful every time I see you," he said.

"Coming from a Princeton superstar, that's quite a compliment. You must be very much in demand, socially."

Pierce grinned broadly. "I'll be damned. You sound almost jealous."

"Don't be silly. Tell me all about the exciting life a varsity basketball star and brokerage expert leads."

"It's not as glamorous as you think. When I graduate, that'll be it. No more jock-strapping. I'm going in with my father's firm. Hey, what about coming down for some of our big games? You never have, you know. Or maybe when we play Yale or Harvard, you could come up to New Haven or Cambridge."

"I don't know, but I'll think about it."

"I'll send you a schedule as soon as they're printed. Now what about dinner tonight?"

"What about your grandmother?"

"Darling, she's eighty-three. She has her dinner every evening at five o'clock and goes to bed by six-thirty."

"Pick me up at seven?"

"Sure thing." He reached over and kissed her cheek lightly. "I've missed you."

"You could have come up before this, you know."

"Karen, you've no idea of the demands that are made on a guy just breaking into the brokerage business. It's as much social as anything else."

"Tell me all about it tonight."

The eve of Karen's departure was a busy one, involving Anna, Leona, and Eric. Even for Herschel, who was preparing a duplicate of their war map for Karen to take along. A trunk, cartons of books and odds and ends, skis, tennis racquets, ice-skating shoes, and other impedimenta. Endless promises to write and phone often. For Karen there was an exhilarating sense of escape, yet not without a certain feeling of loss for so much that was familiar, and the memory of Robert. But above all else, there was the intriguing challenge of being entirely on her own in a strange new world, completely independent.

The initial adjustment period kept Karen gratefully busy, too much so to dwell on the deep personal problems that beset her. Meeting girls from almost every state in the Union, as well as from abroad, reviewing schedules and courses she would be taking as an art major, learning to identify the various buildings and locations of her classrooms, finding her way around the campus, meeting with counselors and faculty members, acquainting herself with endless rules and regulations, choosing the right sorority: far too many activities to think about herself.

Her apartment, by comparison with the dorms, sorority, and rooming quarters shared by most of the students, was a distinct luxury. Karen fully stocked the kitchen and learned to prepare meals when she had the time, eating out only when there was little of it to spare. At first, she welcomed this privacy, but as the weeks wore on and her workload fell into place, she missed having company. She began to invite classmates in for dinner, and to spend the night. Some brought dates, the dates brought food, wines, and liquor, and before long the apartment took on the atmosphere of a social center.

The most interesting of her classmates was Rachel Reeves, who was nineteen. Rachel was a rather large girl who came from Texas, had spent a year abroad "to get a feel for life and living," as she explained it, "before becoming entombed in a damned nunnery." She was blond, witty, goodnatured and outspoken. Her clothes, casual as they were, were well made and expensive, and bore the labels of some of the better known European couturiers, a good number of them from Neiman-Marcus. As Rachel herself put it, "I'm not really pretty, but I'm properly packaged in all the right places, and that's what counts with men."

Rachel undoubtedly came from a wealthy family, although she never mentioned her parents. For the time being, she lived in a motel and drove a Cadillac convertible, "one my old man had lying around that needed exercise." Rachel was an indifferent student, and it puzzled Karen that she attended college at all. And then, one day after classes, Rachel caught up with Karen on the way to the parking area.

"I owe you a feed, Karen. How about having dinner with me?" she invited.

"I've got half a roast left over from Sunday. Follow me home and we'll get rid of it."

"Okay, but I'll never get out of your debt this way."

After dinner, Rachel examined Karen's paintings, two

of which were in the unfinished stage. "Hey, you really serious about this art jazz?"

"Well, I enjoy it very much. I'd like to keep on with it if it seems worthwhile."

"As a living?"

"If I'm good enough to be a professional, fine, but not necessarily—in which case, I'd do it as a way of life. What about you?"

Rachel laughed easily. "All I'm doing is taking up space here. I want to get through liberal arts and graduate. After that, I'll be on my own and nobody to account to, my own woman."

"You know, you're something of a mystery to all the girls. They're terribly curious about you, Rachel."

"That's their problem, not mine. Listen, I've been trying to find a decent spread, but I checked in too late to get anything like this. How'd you like to let me move in and share expenses?"

"I don't know. My aunt and uncle might come up to visit . . ."

"So I'll bunk in with you when they do or spend the night somewhere else. That motel is getting a bit too much, with every transient joker on the make and every date mooching around for a shackup."

Karen was agreeable and a decision was made, but before Rachel left, she told Karen, "I think I ought to bring you up to date on Rachel Reeves so there won't be any ugly surprises later on."

"I don't think I understand."

"Well, I'm not planning to go rash, but let me put it on the line so that if you decide you don't want me for a roommate, we can call it off now without any hard feelings. I'll tell you something else. With me, you can live your life and I'll live mine, no questions asked."

She told Karen. She had dropped out of the University of Texas in her freshman year after an affair that resulted in an abortion, then spent a year in Europe getting over it. Her parents were divorced, both remarried, her mother to a man not much older than Rachel. As she got deeper into her story, she said, "Look, kid, I'll level with you, but keep it to yourself. I'm not exactly what you'd call a sterling character. I've been hooked on the hard stuff, knocked up, aborted, and I spent a year in a Swiss sanitarium getting unhooked and analyzed, having some of my plumbing removed, and just about everything that can happen to a woman in fifty years, except that I did it all in eighteen.

"My old man was a wildcatter who fell into a hole one day and came up spitting an ocean of oil, you know? A Texas oil millionaire. Up until that time, we'd been as poor as churchmice. All that money coming so suddenly blew my old lady's stack and she took off like something out of a rocket launcher. I was fourteen when she started sampling what was lying around waiting to be sampled. She was maybe thirty-eight, my old man around forty-five. After he made it to about the same number of millions, Mama walked out with a young stud, got herself a Mexican divorce, and settled for something like ten or fifteen million dollars.

"Daddy was a drinker from way back and was doing some sampling himself. One day when I was about sixteen, he came home with this chick who was about twenty and introduced her as my new stepmother. That's when things really went to hell. And that's about it, so if you want to change your mind, now's the time."

But Karen's decision, already made, was firm. "I don't want to make any changes, Rachel. I think we'll get along just fine."

As promised, she drove home for the Thanksgiving holiday and to a joyous reunion with Anna and Herschel, bringing Rachel and another friend, Sharon Phillips, with her. Sharon was from New Orleans and had a boy friend at Columbia, who came up from the city with a boy for Rachel. The weather was brisk, sunny, and perfect for riding. For a while it was like old remembered times, but the jolly cheer of the young only emphasized the ache Anna and Herschel felt. The Goodwin home rollicked with tales of parties, football games seen, faculty teas attended, and just about every subject except studies. The weekend was a huge success, with Anna and Herschel the perfect hosts. They were impressed with Sharon and delighted with Rachel, and invited them to return.

Karen went to New Haven for the Yale-Princeton basketball game that was played on a Saturday afternoon. Yale won and Pierce received permission to stay behind for the weekend. They drove back to Northampton where he and Karen had dinner and returned late that night to her apartment. Rachel was out on a date of her own. They had several drinks and Karen found herself seriously tempted to give in to Pierce's persuasions and allow him to spend the night; but confusion and doubt overcame her and at the last moment, she used Rachel's imminent return as an excuse.

"How about my motel?"

"Not now, Pierce. Not tonight. I couldn't."

Wisely, Pierce did not press her, feeling a certain advantage in her lukewarm refusal. There would be other games, other weekends. Patience, he decided, would bring its own rewards.

Regularly, she received photostatic copies of Robert's infrequent letters from Anna and kept her own war-map current from daily news reports, this with Rachel, who somehow had been caught up in the game. Most of the letters, after the bitter winter set in, were grim, but reassuring. Robert was in good health, but details of any action were either lacking or censored.

Strange names, Pusan, Seoul, Inchon, Yalu, Hungnam and Pyong-yang had become as familiar as Jersey City, Trenton, Paterson and Harrison. United States troops (white) and South Koreans (blue), struggled against North Koreans and Chinese (red). Ribbons and pins moved up and back to mark each new advance and counterattack. The following spring, came the news that white and blue had pushed red across the thirty-eighth parallel and Karen's spirits were on the upswing. Telephone calls to and from Wyecliffe brought joyful reactions. Robert had been promoted to the rank of sergeant "because there was a vacancy and my company commander comes from Newark. His wife uses Goody's mixes."

And then on the first day of May, Herschel telephoned Karen and she knew from his voice that his preliminary greeting was the forerunner of evil tidings. When she said, "What is it, Uncle Herschel, please tell me," he replied, "Karen, can you come home for a few days? Anna needs you. It's important."

"It's—it's Robert, isn't it?"

"Yes. Robert. Please come home."

Rachel helped her pack a bag and offered to drive her to Wyecliffe, but Karen insisted on going alone and started immediately. She arrived in the pre-dawn hours and found the lights on, and Anna on the verge of collapse, Herschel pacing back and forth in their bedroom. He handed her the telegram without comment.

Sergeant Robert Goodwin had been killed in action on April twenty-eighth, his body as yet unrecovered from an enemy-held sector. A Bronze Star would be sent from Washington at an early date. Regrets, etcetera.

The war-game was over. Karen took down the map from the study wall, carried it out behind the guest cottage, and burned and buried the ashes there, weeping bitterly.

Friends came to pay condolence calls. Telegrams and letters arrived by the score, one from Eileen Lerner away at Michigan State. A wire came from Julian, at Princeton. Pierce wrote Karen, "I know how deeply you cared for Robert and that he loved you as much as a brother could have loved a sister. I wish there were some way I could console you, but such personal tragedies must, unfortunately, often be borne alone. My thoughts are with you in this sad moment and I hope that time will bring you comfort and heal your great loss."

That sense of loss, to Karen, was immense, even as great as that of Anna and Herschel, submerged in their own grief. She wept over the thin packet of letters Robert had sent, the five or six snapshots of himself in uniform; and the Bronze Star and Purple Heart that arrived on the eve of her return to Northampton. And over the agony of her very private, insurmountable guilt.

I drove him to it.

I killed Robert.

When she returned to her apartment she found that Rachel had thoughtfully removed her own map, the collection of news clippings, and all the trappings that could remind her of Korea. Only the framed photograph of Robert remained.

In June, she packed and went home, not yet certain she would return. Rachel was spending her summer in Europe and pleaded with Karen to come along, but she knew that Anna and Herschel needed her more than ever now and refused to consider leaving them alone.

On her first Sunday in Wyecliffe, Leona came to her room at noon to tell her that Herschel wanted to talk with her. She took a few minutes to brush her teeth, comb her hair, and slip into a robe. Anna was still in bed after a wakeful night, and Herschel waited for her in the breakfast room.

"What is it, Uncle Herschel?"

"I was lonesome for you." Leona brought orange juice

and coffee. "That's all for me, Leona," Karen said and turned back to Herschel. "What is it, Uncle Herschel?"

"I don't like to bring up anything to make you unhappy so soon after you got here."

"Then what?"

"Robert," he said.

Karen felt her heart twist. "What about Robert?"

"His official papers. When he went to the Marines, he made out his insurance papers to you, ten thousand dollars."

Her hands began to shake and she clasped them in her lap, tears welling into her eyes and threatening to spill over. "I don't want it. I don't deserve it."

"Nonsense," Herschel said. "He wanted it that way. You were like a sister to him. He loved you."

"Oh, Uncle Herschel . . ." She was sobbing openly now. Herschel went to her and put his arms around her. "*Shah, shah, liebschen.* Don't cry. He would be unhappy if he knew this would make you sad."

"I can't help it . . ."

"So cry, but don't be sad. He gave this to you so you would remember him, but not with tears."

She dried her eyes on her napkin. "Even without it, I could never forget him."

"Good. But remember him with happiness, eh?"

"Do you remember him that way? Aren't you and Aunt Anna sad when you think about him?"

"Well—yes. Sometimes. And sometimes, when we remember other things about him, no." He sighed deeply and said, "A child buries a parent, it's more natural, to be expected. But when parents must bury a child, it's—something they never get over."

"What about his body? Was it ever recovered so we can bury him in Wyecliffe?"

"I have written, five, six times. He hasn't been found. But I will keep trying."

"I hope they can find him."

"Enough. Here is the check, the papers." He withdrew the documents from his breast pocket and handed them to her, along with his pen.

"Please, I don't need this. I've more than I need in my checking account."

"So endorse it and I'll put it into something for you." She did so, then sighed the receipt.

"Karen," Herschel said, "there are only three of us

now. You know how much we love you, we need you more than ever now."

"I know. And I love you and Aunt Anna very much."

"Thank you." He paused and said, "This summer will be a lot different from other summers. I would like it very much if you and Anna would take a nice long trip to Europe. She has never been outside the United States, neither have you. You could see London, Paris, Rome . . ."

"Would you come with us?"

"I couldn't, darling. There's so much to be done here, expansion, new equipment, installations."

"Aunt Anna wouldn't go without you."

"She told me already. But if you ask . . ."

"No. It wouldn't be a happy trip for either of us so soon after—after . . ." She broke off, then added, "Maybe another time. Next summer."

She saw few of her old friends from Wyecliffe. Most were off on extended vacations or had taken summer jobs. She turned down invitations to visit classmates in various parts of the country and for a moment, after reading a long, newsy letter from Rachel—in Paris at that moment—regretted having turned down her invitation. She encouraged Anna to ride, drive, and swim with her, and enticed her to accompany her to New York to help with some shopping problems. Anna saw through Karen's little schemes, but admitted to herself that she was better able to hurdle her own grief with Karen there to help.

Julian Roth did not come to Wyecliffe, nor did he attempt to get in touch with Karen. Herschel told her, when she inquired, that Julian had taken a summer job with GFP's purchasing department in the city and was doing an exceptional job for a beginner. She saw nothing of Pierce, busy building his career of the future with Cranston, Packard & Nieland.

7

Pierce telephoned excitedly the week before Christmas to tell Karen that a virus epidemic had struck half the team and their schedule had been canceled until after the holidays. He and several couples were planning a skiing holiday in New Hampshire and he pleaded with her to come along. Karen had gained enough confidence on nearby shallow slopes and the idea appealed to her very much. She told Pierce she would phone Anna and call him back.

Moments after she hung up, she remembered her promise to Herschel to come home for that holiday and was struck with second thoughts, but Rachel urged her to go. "You owe something to yourself, too. You've been hitting this art jazz pretty hard and there'll always be enough weekends you can spend with the folks at home. Go ahead, pack your diaphragm and cut loose for once."

As always, Rachel's frank, indelicate way of expressing herself brought laughter to Karen. "I don't even own one and besides, it's not that way between Pierce and me."

Rachel threw her a knowing smile. "Look, baby, it's that way between any man who calls to invite a girl on a skiing weekend and the girl who is just as anxious to go. Give yourself a break with Mr. America before somebody else cuts in on you."

Karen phoned Anna, who tried to contain her own disappointment, and assured Karen she would use her own special tact and diplomacy to placate Herschel. "Go and enjoy yourself and be careful not to take any risks," she added.

"That aunt of yours," Rachel commented, "is a real prize."

"What about your holiday, Rachel?"

"Don't waste your thoughts on me, baby. I'm heading for New York and the bright lights. I'll probably come back weighing ten pounds more than I do now."

"Rachel . . ."

"I said, don't worry. I won't do anything to get myself kicked out of this nunnery. If I bust out of here, I couldn't buy my way into another college in the whole country."

The party was comprised of six couples, driving in tandem. On arrival, Karen became acutely aware that two of the couples had checked in as man and wife. Karen shared her twin-bedded room with Susan Long, a vivacious girl from Boston who was Bart Liggett's date. No sooner were they in their room unpacking than Susan said, "What arrangements do you want to make about the boys?"

"What do you mean?" Karen asked.

Susan eyed her quizzically. "I hope you're not putting me on."

"I'm trying not to."

"Well—I mean visiting privileges. You and Pierce, me and Bart. I don't want to walk in on you accidentally . . ."

"You won't have to worry about that, Susan."

Susan threw her an "are-you-for-real" look. "By the same token," she said pointedly, "I don't want you walking in on Bart and me."

Karen said evenly, "Then keep the door locked and do it in your own bed."

"Well, for Pete's sake, Karen . . ."

"And don't patronize me, please. You do what you want and I'll do what I want."

"Suit yourself. If the door is locked, knock three times and wait ten minutes before you use your key, okay?"

When they all met in the common room for drinks before dinner, there was that accelerated exuberance of a group about to embark on a long holiday away from class routine, far from supervision and observation. After dinner they sat toasting themselves in a large circle before the roaring fireplace, already on first name terms with other guests, discussing temperatures and the condition of the slopes they would attack after breakfast. Their host, Fred Durkin, a robust outdoorsy man who, at seventy, looked like a weathered fifty, reassured them that skiing conditions were perfect. He contributed his share of local anecdotes and bought several rounds of drinks for his appreciative audience. For another hour they danced to radio music and records and by eleven o'clock the informal party began breaking up with bets offered and taken as to which couple would be out first and ready to go in the morning. Of their own group, only one couple remained, the rest had gone off to their rooms. Susan and Bart had disappeared earlier and when Pierce took Karen to her room, she remembered Susan's warning and tried the door. It was locked.

"Christ," Pierce said with a grin. "The least they could do would be to put out the DO NOT DISTURB sign. Well, back to the bar."

"I don't think I want any more to drink," Karen said.

"Then how about my room until . . ."

She said, "Did you know it was going to be like this, Pierce?"

He shrugged. "Hell, Karen, people do what they want,

even at Smith, don't they? Nobody's guardian to anybody else's conscience."

They walked down the hallway to the room Pierce shared with Bart, entered, and sat in the two chairs. Pierce said, "If I'd known you felt so strongly about it, I'd a lot rather we'd gone off by ourselves somewhere."

She went to the bed nearest her and sat on its edge. "I don't think that would have made any difference, being alone. We'd eventually get around to—to . . ."

"Where we are now," he concluded for her. "What are we fencing for, Karen? You knew what my intentions were when I asked you to come along for this week."

"Yes, I knew."

"We've been close to it before, but I didn't want to overpressure you and take the chance of losing you. You're a very special person to me."

She studied him quietly for a few moments, his loose, relaxed stance and soft, smiling self-assurance. "I like you very much, Pierce. We've done some things together that prove that, but I—I don't know if I'm ready for the big jump into bed with you."

"Okay, I can understand your feeling that way. It has to do with the way you've been raised. What you need is to shed some of your middle-class morality."

She flared angrily. "Now that's a smug sonofabitch of a patronizing remark, isn't it?"

"Don't blow your cool. It's a common ailment," he said, coming to the bed and sitting beside her. "How about that drink now?"

"After that, I think I need one."

While he dug into his kit bag and came up with a bottle of Scotch, Karen came to the realization that the alternative to her constant refusal to go to bed with Pierce was losing him. She heard him say, "There's water in the bathroom, but no ice, except what's on the windowsill."

She got off the bed, took two glasses to the window, raised it, and scooped some of the glistening snow into both. Pierce poured the Scotch. They touched rims and she said, "To fate, and what it brings."

"Amen." They drank and Pierce poured the second drink. "Let me know when it starts getting to you," he said.

She giggled and replied, "By that time it will be too late." She lay back on the bed, Pierce stretched out beside her. She drank half her drink, feeling its warmth spreading through her, then sat up, handed her glass to Pierce, and removed her outer sweater. When she lay down again, she turned him and said, "You've had a lot of girls, haven't you, Pierce?"

"I don't know what you mean by a 'lot of girls.' I've never gone in for comparative figures with anyone."

"I said that badly, didn't I?"

"Maybe because it wasn't what you really intended to say." He kissed her, and she reacted happily, returning his kisses. Moments later she said, "Maybe you're right. May I have another drink?"

"Sure." He got up, fixed it for her, and lay down beside her again. "Damn it," Karen said, "why am I so uptight?"

"First time stage fright," he suggested. "Drink up. Scotch is a great loosener-upper."

"Or a temporary coverup for our true feelings."

He laughed and said, "It would take a hell of a lot more than this to cover what I'm feeling right now." He took the glass from her when she finished the drink and put it on the table, then took her into his arms. She kissed him, moving against his hard, athletic body, and felt his hand under her skirt caressing her thigh, then move up to fondle her breast. "Pierce?"

"What, darling?"

"Let's."

"That's not the Scotch talking, is it?" he said softly.

"Darling," Karen said, "to paraphrase somebody or other, nobody speaks for Karen but Karen. Please turn off the lights."

At first, she experienced the sensuous pleasure of naked, physical contact and gave herself utterly to Pierce's deft precoital lovemaking, then to the act, responding to his smooth, expert probing; but as they progressed, she felt little more than the collision of their bodies pressing against each other. She tried valiantly to concentrate and cooperate with his every movement, but the initial feeling was dissipated. Twice, Pierce stopped to ask if she felt she was ready and she thought to herself, *Ready for what?* and finally, in desperation, she said, "Yes, I think so," and although Pierce tried to bring her to peak, could feel that something was lacking. He could hold back only so long and was forced into eventual climax. As they lay side by side, he could find no way to alleviate her unspoken distress. She said dully, "I had a feeling it wouldn't work for me."

"Don't blame yourself. It could be the liquor. Or over-eagerness, the first time."

"It wasn't the first time, Pierce."

"Well—I'll be damned."

"Are you shocked?"

"No-o. A little surprised."

"End of confession. No questions, please."

"I'm not prying, just . . ."

"Just what?"

"Did it happen the same way those other times, no climax?"

"Yes. At least, it worked for you, so all is not lost."

"Karen, get this through your head, will you? I'm not an animal. The greatest part of my pleasure is the pleasure I can give you. Sex isn't a one-way street, but something two people share equally."

"I'm sorry, Pierce. It simply doesn't work that way with me."

"Then you need help. Psychiatry, perhaps."

She recoiled. "I couldn't. I'd die of shame."

"Oh, Christ, Karen . . ." he reached up and turned on the bed lamp, "you can't go through life with this hangup. It's too important to living."

"How really important is it?"

"That's a question too goddamned stupid to come from a girl as intelligent as you. Ask Susan, Cheri, any of the other girls. Ask your own friends at Smith. For God's sake, men have committed suicide because they couldn't make it with a woman."

Robert flashed into her mind, another bitter reminder. "And what do women do?" she asked.

"I don't know, but if it's serious enough, they should be smart enough to look for help, turn to psychiatry."

"Or to each other and become Lesbians?"

He didn't answer. The room had grown chilly and she drew the blanket over her exposed shoulders. "I'd better get dressed and go back to my room. Bart . . ."

"Bart will stay shacked up with Susan as long as nobody knocks on the door."

"Shall we sleep here, then?"

"Why not?"

"What about the others?"

"You can be awfully naive about some things, can't

you? What they don't know, they'll suspect, and it doesn't matter a damned bit anyhow."

She went to the bathroom and returned a few minutes later. Pierce then went to the bathroom and when he came back, got into the narrow twin bed with her. "Won't you be more comfortable in the other bed?" she asked.

"More comfortable, but more alone. I love being close to you."

She moved to give him more room. "Then you don't dislike me for it, not being able to . . ."

"Don't be silly." He switched off the bedlamp and embraced her. She kissed his mouth, chin, cheeks, and neck, felt eagerness in his response, the growth of his erection. Within seconds, she guided him into her body and again there was that initial sensual exhilaration.

"Hey, are you making it?" he asked.

"Go on—don't stop!"

Firmly, strongly, he drove pistonlike into her flesh, but as had happened before, the first excitement became lost and she fell back exhausted. He paced his movements, hoping to recapture the first excitement she had felt, but it was useless. "Go on, Pierce," she said, "finish." He came then and it was over. This time, there was no discussion. Both lay in silence and both felt a strong sense of failure.

In the morning, they joined the others at a gargantuan breakfast. Of their own party, three couples were alert enough to get out on the slopes, the others obviously in need of more sleep; but an entire week lay ahead of them with plenty of time for outdoor activity. There was a general holiday mood, boisterous, good-humored and stimulating, in which Pierce and Karen joined.

Susan dropped into a chair beside Karen while Pierce went out to get some cigarettes. "If you want," she said, "I'll move my things into Bart's room." It was a question rather than a simple statement and Karen said, "Don't bother, Susan. I'll move mine in with Pierce."

Susan smiled with a sudden show of friendliness. "All of a sudden, I'm beginning to have a little more respect for you Smithies. You catch on fast."

The move was made after lunch. Karen and Pierce went out for an experimental trial on an upper slope, then went back to their room to continue their experiment of the night before. It was a long week, disappointing and fruitless for Karen in her quest for an answer she could not find.

8

On her return to Northampton, Rachel filled her in on her New York holiday, but Karen responded so reticently to Rachel's casual questions that she cut off any deep discussion. Karen spent the next three weekends in Wyecliffe doing penance for having gone off with Pierce when Anna and Herschel had expected her home. Between times, she concentrated on classroom work by day, stood at her easel at night, refusing to go out for any reason, coffee, a movie, or visiting mutual friends. The atmosphere in the apartment had grown silent, even severe.

One evening, Rachel found Karen staring at herself in the bathroom mirror, examining her face closely, massaging the circles under her eyes, the result of restless, sleepless nights. As she entered, a spasm shook Karen, doubling her up over the sink. Rachel took her arm and said, "What in the world is ailing you, anyway?"

"I'm all right," Karen replied, pulling out of Rachel's grip.

"The hell you are. You've been acting like somebody about to receive a visit from Mr. Death himself."

"It's nothing."

"For something that's nothing, you're sure making a big scene about it. Everybody's noticed."

"I don't give a damn what anybody notices. It's my problem and it's very private. You understand privacy, don't you?"

It was a childish display toward the best friend she had ever had among her own sex and she regretted her sharpness immediately, but Rachel had walked out and gone to her own bedroom, closing the door—which, in itself, was an unusual act. Later, while Karen was washing her brushes in a special basin in the kitchen, Rachel came in, went to the refrigerator, and poured a glass of milk. "Want some?" she asked.

"No thanks," Karen said.

Rachel started out, then turned, and came back to the sink. "Karen," she said, "I don't know what I've done to offend you, but if you want me to move out, I'll find another place to live."

For a moment, Karen was shocked into muteness.

'Well?" Rachel said.

"No, Rachel, please, no. It's nothing you've said or done. It's me. I'm . . . I've just discovered something about myself and I can't get used to the idea."

"You know," Rachel said, "the worst possible thing in the world, in a situation like that, is to keep your thoughts and feelings all bottled up. I'm not applying for the job of confessor, and I respect your privacy as much as you respect mine, but if you want to talk it out, just remember, you'll be talking to a friend."

"I know that, Rachel, and I can't tell you how sorry I am that I've been such a thoughtless bitch since . . . the past few weeks. Please forgive me?"

"Sure, but if you need a sympathetic ear and a closed mouth, mine are available."

"Thank you." She kissed Rachel's cheek. Rachel went out and Karen returned to her brush-cleaning chore, crying softly as she worked.

Later, when she passed Rachel's room, the door was open, Rachel in bed watching a movie on her television set. When Karen paused, Rachel said, "Come in. Turn that damned thing off, will you? It's bad enough to watch but not bad enough to put me to sleep."

Karen turned the set off, then lay on the bed beside Rachel. Again, she apologized for her recent behavior, a prelude to a full disclosure of what had happened between herself and Pierce, and her inability to achieve the ultimate pleasure in their encounter. And, having told that much, she went deeper and related her experiences with Gilbert and Marilyn Zeiss and the tragic result of her seduction of Robert.

Rachel listened without interrupting and when Karen had concluded, said, "Baby, you're sure carrying a hell of a load on your mind. I'm no psychiatrist, God knows, but—do you have any feel at all for it—sex?"

"Yes, I'm sure I do. I think about it a lot. I like the feeling at the very first, but then something happens and the feeling disappears and I'm not with it. I feel as though I'm being used, a common whore lying there to serve somebody else without sharing the full pleasure, the thrill everybody talks and writes about. I've read about frigid women and it scares me near to death."

"Forget it. If you were frigid, you'd never get that close to it in the first place. I've had all of it explained to me in that funny farm in Switzerland. Frigidity, Lesbianism, nymphomania—listen, do you know the meaning of nymphomania?"

"Not generally. Are you suggesting. . . . My God, that *can't* be. I'm not chasing every boy I see, trying to get him into my bed. You know *that* much about me."

"No, no. I'm not suggesting you're a nympho, only some of the causes. What do you think a nympho is?"

"How should I know? I'd say a girl or woman who enjoys sex and needs it more than the average girl or woman, an easy mark for any man they run into or pick up in a bar, on the streets, wherever."

"Wrong. The way I had it explained to me, she's someone who needs it, looks for it, but doesn't necessarily enjoy it because she seldom, if ever, has a climax. Most professional whores are nymphos."

"That's pretty horrible, frightening. My God, to go through life like a cripple—a wheelchair paralytic."

"Hey, now, don't go taking on symptoms you've only heard about. I had a similar problem and I don't have it any more."

"How—what?"

"Okay. When I started sleeping around, I was screwing everybody and anybody on campus and off. What's more, it didn't do a damned thing for me except get me pregnant. I was a dumb kid, doing it because it was the thing to do. Later on, after I'd gotten aborted, hooked on the needle, and shuffled off to Switzerland by my old man who was glad to get rid of me, I started learning things. This shrink explained *why*, which was the most important step I took to getting over it. It wasn't easy, all that hypnosis jazz and all—"

"Well, why?" Karen asked.

"Most of it comes from hostility, resentment, call it hate if you want. I hated my mother for running off with her stud, I hated my old man for marrying a girl only a few years older than myself. I hated them all every day, particularly my old man when I knew he and that chick of his were in bed screwing, which was like all the time. I hated so many things that I flipped. I missed the affection I never got any more and went out to find it on my own. It took a whole year at that funny farm to straighten me out to where I knew what it was and could enjoy it."

"Who straightened you out, finally?"

Rachel laughed and winked. "My shrink, who else? I

learned more in his bed than I did on his goddamned couch."

Karen pondered over that conversation long into the night, in her own bed. *If* hostility was the reason for her failure, it all became suddenly reasonable. She had lived with hostility as far back as memory could take her. Hostility for the man who had replaced her father, hostility for her mother's over-protectiveness and nagging possessiveness. Hostility had become an everyday part of her life, for which she was now paying dearly.

For several weeks, she haunted the library trying to find any material on the subject, but there was hardly enough to satisfy her need. The local library was not much better. She ordered certain text books from local bookstores and buried herself in them, acquiring knowledge and understanding, but Rachel, the pragmatist, pricked her intellectual balloon.

"Baby, all the reading in the world won't help," she said one night.

"You think a psychiatrist is the only answer?"

"Maybe yes, maybe no, but you can't find out by yourself. For instance, you told me you tried it with him"—pointing to Robert's photograph—"but nothing about him, how it got started. Were you in love with him?"

"I don't want to talk about Robert, Rachel."

"Baby, that's your hangup, the things you can't bring yourself to talk about, where it all begins. Until I opened up with my shrink, and it took months, I was all wrapped up like an Egyptian mummy. Once the stable was unlocked and the wild horses freed, the *why* I hated my mother, *why* I hated my old man, then it all began to fall into place. Of course," she added, "I don't hate either of them any less, but I learned to live with it."

"Rachel, I don't hate anyone now. My mother and stepfather are dead. Robert is dead."

"Karen, hate isn't funny about who has it, or who it's for, and it doesn't have to be as of now. And sometimes, it can be self-hate, the same as guilt. Maybe if . . ."

"If what?"

"I wonder what would happen if you just took off into the wild blue on your own, met somebody, a total stranger. No Pierce, nobody connected or related to anybody you ever knew. Just you and some man you never saw before . . . oh, hell, I'm just babbling. I still think you need a good shrink."

But the idea of opening her mind and heart, disclosing her innermost feelings to a psychiatrist in a sterile room, under clinical conditions, hour after hour, week after week, month after month, dredging into her childhood, exploring her relationship with her mother, father (brought back by deep hypnosis), stepfather, Gilbert, and Robert, going back to her first awakenings to sexual urge, all gave her a feeling of mental, almost physical, enfeeblement. And if she became involved in psychiatry there would have to be some explanation to Anna and Herschel about the cost. Perhaps, even, the need.

However, another thought implanted by Rachel lingered in her mind for weeks, taking firm root. Early in May, she took that step toward self-discovery.

Or whatever it might lead to.

For that adventure she chose Springfield, not too close, not too distant from Northampton, a city she had never visited before. Driving through Holyoke, she considered the risks, imagining and examining situations that were purely novelistic, even fantasy, half-determined that when she reached her destination she would probably lose courage, have a quick lunch, and return. But before that thought solidified in her mind, she was there. She came off the highway onto a street in a commercial section, and wandered aimlessly until she found herself along the river road. A factory whistle somewhere in the distance behind her announced the arrival of noon and as she curved left with the tree-lined road, she saw the large sign of CRANE'S PRIDE MOTEL, a sprawling arrangement of modern one-storied barracklike buildings flanking a two-storied central structure.

The open parking lot was more than half-filled and there were a dozen or more cars parked at various private entrances to the one-storied buildings, which were obviously guest rooms. Karen pulled into a space in front of the main building, marked: *15 Minutes Parking Only*. She went into the wide, comfortable lobby, approached the desk, and asked the clerk if there was a room available, almost with the hope that there would be none. The clerk nodded, giving her a swift look of appraisal. "For how long, miss?"

"Just overnight."

The clerk smiled for the first time. "Yes, miss. We'll be sort of crowded by tomorrow night, a sales convention coming in for Monday, but we can take care of you for tonight. Would you like something in this building or . . ."

"This building will be fine."

"Yes, miss." Turning the registration card holder toward her, he reached behind to the long row of mail compartments for a key, "Room 232, double bed, nine dollars single."

"That will do nicely," Karen said, inscribing the name Carol Hartog, 133 Elm Drive, Worcester, on the card. The clerk, reading as she wrote it, said, "I'll have someone bring your luggage in, Miss Hartog."

"Don't bother. It's only a small overnight case."

"No trouble, Miss Hartog. I'll have the boy park your car nearby and put your bag in your room, and your car keys will be in your mail slot when you want them. If you'd like to have lunch . . ."

"I'd like that. Thank you."

"Far side of the lobby, to your left. I hope you enjoy your stay."

There was a bar to the left of the dining room, which was filling up with early arrivals for the convention; men in groups of two, four, and more, all wearing large white lapel cards with the word PICOT printed in red letters, individual names written in ink on the line beneath. In the lobby behind her was a desk with a sign over it reading: PICOT *Representatives Register Here.*

Karen chose a stool at the bar, the middle one of three empties. Most of the bar tables were occupied by properly badged Picot men, most in their forties and fifties, a few younger. She ordered a daiquiri from the barman, who eyed her with a smile. Or leer, perhaps, classifying her as an early arrival among the professional hookers who worked conventions as a career. Halfway through her drink she felt, rather than saw a man mount the stool on her right, and concentrated her full attention on the glass in front of her.

She heard him order a bourbon and soda, which the barman placed in front of him. She heard him say, "May I?" then saw his hand, slim and firm, as it reached for the ashtray in front of her. She pushed it toward him without looking in his direction. In the backbar mirror, tinted blue, she could not make out his features except that he was slender.

When her drink was down to the quarter-inch mark, she opened her purse and took out a pack of cigarettes. Before she could come up with her lighter, she saw the flaring light held an inch away from the tip of her cigarette. She accepted the light with a smile, and said, "Thank you."

"My pleasure," the man said. She saw his face then, eyes smiling expectantly, lean jaw, black hair, full lips, firm chin; an executive type, not young, not old, about thirty-five, she guessed, in his smartly styled suit, neat tie, and crisp linen. "Nice town you have here," he said genially.

"I'm not from Springfield," Karen replied. "Just driving through. I got tired and decided to spend the night."

"I'm from Detroit, here for the convention. My first time in Springfield, even though this is our headquarters."

She said, "What does PICOT stand for?" pointing to his lapel badge.

"Now I know you're not from Springfield. Couple of miles back is the big Picot plant, and a local man, Orville Picot was the founder."

"If it's not a state or military secret, what does Picot make, or do, or grow?"

He laughed pleasantly. "I wouldn't want the Russians to overhear us," he said, leaning toward her, speaking in a low, conspiratorial whisper, "but we manufacture oil burners."

"How quaint."

He laughed again and said, "You know, that's exactly what my wife said a long time ago when I brought home my first commission check. 'How quaint,' she said."

"How long ago was that?"

"About fifteen years."

"I assume all that has changed by now."

"You can bet it has. I'm out of the commission and selling field now. Division sales manager. What about you, married?"

"No."

"How quaint," he said, and they laughed together. To the barman, "Another round here," and Karen said, "This one and no more."

"Okay. What then?"

"Then I go into the dining room, have lunch, go to my room and have a nap."

"Too bad. I've already had my lunch. What is your room number?"

Moment of decision. She turned toward his smiling, eager face. It was warm, goodhumored, and gentle. If she said, 'That's a top secret' or other discouraging words, she knew he would accept the turndown without question. Hesitating only slightly, she said, "Room 232. Why?"

"I thought you might like some company."

"What about your convention?"

"Today and tomorrow are check-in days. We don't get down to official business until Monday morning."

She said, "An hour?"

He checked his watch. "One hour."

At two o'clock he knocked on the door. Karen sat up in bed, naked, almost startled, certainly nervous. She could remain quiet until he went away or— She shrugged, slipped on a light, knee-length robe. He knocked again and she called out, "One moment," then went to the door and opened it. He came in, carrying a brown paper sack. The curtains were drawn, and for a moment he hesitated to allow his eyes to become accustomed to the dimness.

"Hi, beautiful. I brought along some refreshments. Shall I get some ice? There's a machine at the end of the hall."

"Only if you want it."

"No. I don't need it."

"I don't, either."

"Well—shall we?"

There was little need for further preliminaries. They each had one drink and he began to undress. She watched as he removed each item of clothing and folded it neatly on the chair beside the writing table. When he turned toward the bed, she looked away, heard his shuffling steps across the carpeting, felt the weight of his knee on the mattress, the tug at the top sheet as he raised it and crept in beside her. He took her into his arms and kissed her, and for a moment she thought of leaping up and locking herself in the bathroom. He was whispering words in her ear, eager words, but what he was saying was lost to her, for she heard nothing but the thunderous clamor rising in her body and mind, obliterating everything else.

He was enormous and she felt a shock wave of pain as he entered, clinging to her, getting himself set, then driving into her like a machine. Feeling his full weight upon her, she twisted and turned from side to side to evade his precisionlike attack; and then it came to her, like a delayed reaction, the feverish desire for more, more, more. She rose up to meet each thrust with counterthrust, holding him firmly, riding with his eager body, reveling in the press of his flesh against her own, panting, and open-mouthed, biting at his shoulder, wet with the perspiration of her own body and his, outside, and finally, wet with mutual orgasm inside.

Now, the pounding inside her was not of fear or tension, but of pleasurable exhaustion. It was over and she had performed in what Rachel would undoubtedly call the classic manner. Evidently the strange man lying upon her had received the same sense of satisfaction, for he lingered over her, unwilling to part, and when she felt him out of her, she could feel the hammering in her head, in every nerve end. And an overwhelming sense of embarrassment. She wanted him gone, to be alone with her new, electrifying discovery.

"Hey," he said, "you're something. A real tiger."

She lay still, saying nothing.

"How long you going to be around?"

Silence.

"Hey, you're not angry about anything, are you?"

"No."

"Then come on, say something. You enjoyed it, didn't you?"

"Yes."

"How about if I come back later, around five, okay?"

"Yes. All right."

He got out of bed and began dressing slowly, methodically. "Listen, honey, you mind if I bring a friend? A hell of a nice guy, my territorial supervisor. He'll take care of you, too."

Suddenly, embarrassment turned to shame, anger. She sat up, drawing the sheet over her naked body. "Why not the whole convention?" she said. "Post a notice on the bulletin board . . ."

"Hey, now, look, that's what you're here for, isn't it? Christ, I didn't rape you, did I?"

"Just go away, please."

"Okay, okay." Disgruntled, he belted his trousers, zipping them. "What the hell, you want to run your business that way, it's okay with me. How much?"

"How much?"

"Yes. How much do I owe you?"

"Nothing. It was free. A sample."

"Listen, I'm no cheap John, for Christ's sake. Tell me how much." Wallet in hand, riffling through some bills.

"Will you please just go away? I'm not a whore."

He picked up his jacket and tie, and stared at her while moving toward the door. "Well," he said, "you sure as hell could have fooled me. Thanks for the sample." He was gone.

She went to the bathroom and took a hot bath, then came back and lay on the bed, glowing with the realization that it had finally happened to her, that she could react to normal intercourse. A sensational discovery. But why only with a total stranger? Why not with Gilbert, Robert, or Pierce? She rolled over on her stomach and fell into a light doze, then into a deeper sleep, thinking, *Rachel was right. Rachel was right. Bless Rachel.*

At a quarter to five, the telephone startled her awake and when she heard his voice, she recognized it immediately. "Say," he said, "I wonder if you changed your mind?"

"No." She hung up abruptly, dressed, checked out, and started driving back to Northampton to report her success to Rachel.

Rachel beamed like a proud mother. "I didn't think you had the guts, but you did, and it worked. You saved yourself a lot of money and maybe a year of couch time."

"Rachel, you'll never know how indebted I am to you."

"Anything for a friend, but don't let it stone you. You've got to learn how to handle it and not burn yourself out."

"Tell me, Rachel. I want to know."

"A girl with your looks and body packs a lot of power, baby, the kind men embezzle, cheat, divorce their wives, lose their homes, even commit murder for. They say all cats are gray in the dark, but a cat who knows how to handle the power she's got can have the whole world on a string for her private yo-yo. Just be smart."

"How, smart?"

"Like playing it cool. You've got it, they want it. That gives you the upper hand no matter who, what, when, or where. Promiscuity is the one thing that can wreck you. There are jillions of diamonds lying around for almost any price, but there's only one Kohinoor, one Hope. Hold out for the best. Keep your eyes out for a winner and stick with him, forget the field."

As time went on, Rachel became her mentor. She chose her friends with extreme caution, double-dated occasionally with Rachel, took her sexual exercises only at a safe distance from the campus and seldom played return dates. Neither she nor Rachel ever brought a man to their apartment. Karen became engrossed in dramatics as well as painting and dutifully spent occasional weekends at Wyecliffe, bringing Rachel with her.

That summer, Karen remained at home, working seriously at painting and sketching. Pierce Nieland, having graduated, was living in Manhattan permanently, busily engaged in his father's brokerage firm. Karen didn't see him the entire summer, although she spoke with him twice on the phone when he called. She dated a few of her Wyecliffe acquaintances, but permitted no liberties beyond mild kissing and some mild fondling above the waist, recalling Rachel's sage advice, giving no reason for anyone to suspect she was anything other than what she appeared to be.

In the fall, Rachel Reeves failed to return to Smith. She wrote Karen, telling her of the summer she had spent in Honolulu and other islands. She had her credits transferred to the University of Hawaii, where she intended to finish her college education. It was a sad blow to Karen who, out of sheer loneliness, chose another roommate, a quiet, serious student, Gwen Herschfeld, from Medwick, Pennsylvania, whose father was a professional painter and whose ambition was to spend at least two years in Italy and France after she was graduated from Smith. Gwen, a motherless loner who was comfortable to be with, became attached to Karen and life fell into a strangely placid routine.

That Christmas Karen received a brief note from Rachel, who had picked up "the kickiest beach boy you've ever laid eyes on" and was living on Niihau with an experimental communal group.

So much for Rachel's wisdom and advice.

Chapter 7

1

In June of 1954, Anna and Herschel drove to Northampton for Karen's graduation exercises. Her parting from Gwen Herschfeld was tearful, but only on Gwen's part, for she had inevitably become a trying bore and Karen was happy to say good-bye and send her on her way to Europe for a two-year stay.

At home she received two splendid surprises: a magnificent rope of pearls from Anna and, since her last holiday visit, Herschel had had the back bedroom in the guest cottage converted into a studio, fully equipped with easels, art cabinets, framed and unframed canvasses, tubes of paint, brushes, sketch pads, and a skylight.

It was a time for refamiliarization with an era of the past, one that could never be brought fully back to life. The Irish setters and horses had grown older, as had Eric and Leona, Giacomo and Betta; even Anna and Herschel. Mario was gone. Arnold Freitag was a rotting corpse in Korea. Johnnie Bernstein, with a bullet in his spine, was an invalid in a distant Veterans Administration hospital. Others were missing from the scene, many were either away for the summer, had moved elsewhere to begin careers in the professional or business worlds, or were married. With the few who remained, she found little in common. She was tempted to take her long-dreamed-of trip to Europe, but could not, at this time, feel she could leave Anna and Herschel alone. Not yet.

Pierce Nieland, now a full-fledged customer's man with Cranston, Packard & Nieland, wired flowers, and came to Wyecliffe on her first Sunday home, but when she refused to leave Anna and Herschel, he left early in order to be in Washington the following day, for he was involved in the projected merger of two airlines in which his father was the principal negotiator. Julian Roth, graduated from Princeton, had moved into GFP's purchasing department on a permanent basis, she learned from Herschel. Julian made no effort to get in touch with her.

Anna took Karen off to New York for a round of shopping, shows, visits to museums, and art galleries; and home again, Karen was faced with the problem of what, in her twenty-second year, to do with her life. Sooner or later, she knew she must make the break away from Wyecliffe, from Anna and Herschel, and into a life of her own. Meanwhile Karen spent much of her time in her studio, painting, sketching, reading, and playing her collection of records. Riding and driving alone became tiresome and Anna had grown less inclined toward such activities. Conversation, after their first few weeks together, grew more and more difficult. It was a long, unrewarding summer.

As fall drew near, Karen realized that she must begin taking her first steps toward freedom. She drove into New York and phoned Pierce, who put aside an appointment to take her to lunch. He was now very involved in his work. Howard Nieland, he told her, had been turning more of his clients over to Pierce in order to devote himself to the role of the firm's chief negotiator in the numerous mergers and buyouts that were taking place in American industry.

"You've no idea what's going on," Pierce explained. "When you have inside information before a merger or a buyout takes place, fortunes can be made almost overnight. Conglomerates are springing up everywhere. Corporations are trying to diversify. Single product companies are getting into subsidiary lines, buying into anything they can get their hands on. Everybody wants in on computers and data processing. Some specialists are getting fat on finder's fees alone. I took a flyer on one deal and pulled out two months later with a sweet twenty-two thousand dollar profit."

"Is that your big heartbeat now, making money fast?" Karen asked.

"You're not knocking it, are you? What else is there? All my life I've lived on my father's money and what Grandmother Nieland gave me. In a little more than a year I've made better than fifty-five thousand dollars on my own, and I'll top that this year."

"Why the big rush? One day you'll inherit your grandmother's fortune . . ."

"Karen, you don't understand. It isn't the same. This is

money I'm making on my own, money I don't have to account for to anyone but Uncle Sam. That's power."

She thought of Rachel's definition of power and said, "Is that what you need, power to make you feel important?"

"Why don't you ask your uncle that question?"

"My uncle doesn't do what he does for power, Pierce. He does it because he loves what he's doing."

"No more than I love what I'm doing."

"But not for the same reasons."

"Look, Karen, I don't even know why we're discussing this. God knows, I've seen so little of you for so long."

"It's not because I haven't been available."

"I know, and I'm sorry I've been too tied up to get away, but now that you're back, we can make up for lost time. I'll have more time on my hands now."

"How nice for you. Meanwhile, I'll go back to Wyecliffe and wait until you can find a weekend or two to share with me. When you aren't seeing your grandmother."

"Karen, what is it with you? You're different, changed."

"I don't know. I suppose I thought that once college was over, the whole world would open up for me. Frankly, I'm bored to death. I paint, read, ride, swim, but mostly, I'm alone. I'm even bored with painting. Everybody I know has left to take a job, find a career of some sort, travel, or do *some*thing. Or they're married. I'm just vegetating. My biggest moment is coming to the city to do some shopping or have my hair done."

"Then why don't you move to the city?"

"I'd have a fine time selling my aunt and uncle on that idea, wouldn't I?"

"Others have done it, why not you? Get a job, take an apartment, go out on your own. One of our clients is a publisher, Sherwood Press. I'm sure I can get you a job there."

"Doing what?"

"Whatever you've been trained to do. Secretary, reader, maybe a junior editorship. It could be exciting, don't you think, meeting authors, sitting in on book conferences long before they're published."

"Do you think you could do that, Pierce?" she asked, excited by the very thought of the suggestion.

"If I can't, I'm sure Dad can. Walter Entwhistle has been his client for years, and Entwhistle is chairman of the board. Let me give it a try."

Excitedly, she said, "Do it for me, Pierce, please?"

"I'll get on it first thing in the morning. Will you move into town if you get the job?"

"I'd have to. I'll use it as my reason for moving out of Wyecliffe. That's a brilliant idea, Pierce. Thank you so much."

"Shall I try to find an apartment for you?"

"Later, maybe. After I have the job."

"Hey, that's great. We'll have a ball together."

Lunch over, he urged her to stay overnight at his apartment, but despite his pleading, Karen put him off. "I can't, Pierce. I want to get home and begin planning my strategy."

"Karen, I haven't been with you since that trip to New Hampshire."

"I know. We'll make up for it when I move to the city."

She drove back to Wyecliffe in high spirits. Rachel, despite her illogical alliance with a Hawaiian beach boy, had been right. She was beginning to experience the power of sex by withholding it from Pierce.

2

It wasn't easy, nor had Karen thought it would be. For the first time in her memory, Herschel and Anna were prepared to deny her something she very much wanted. After her initial announcement, and her rejection of Herschel's suggestion that she take a job with the company in Harrison, an embarrassing coolness developed that made previous easy conversations almost impossible. There was a new and strange awkwardness between Anna and Karen by day, both unwilling to pursue the discussion, and each knowing how strongly the other felt. At night, with Herschel present, table talk was constricted, stilted, and limited.

Karen was aware that her aunt and uncle were holding constant private conversations and their unhappiness over her decision to move to Manhattan left a depressing gap nothing seemed able to bridge.

Three uneasy weeks passed before Pierce phoned to tell her an appointment had been arranged for her to see Morris Mitchell, senior editor at Sherwood Press, in his office on Eighth Avenue and Fifty-fifth Street. Karen phoned Mr. Mitchell, whose secretary confirmed the appointment for the following afternoon.

She knew, from the reception she received, that Morris Mitchell had had his orders from a superior to treat her with care. Admitted to his office at once, she saw a rather stern man of medium height, perhaps in his late thirties, with thinning black hair that was offset by extremely heavy eyebrows and a myopic stare through black-rimmed glasses. He was standing as she entered the room, pulling on a jacket over his light blue buttoned-down shirt. There was a tentativeness in his greeting as he said, "Good afternoon, Miss Goodwin, will you take this chair, please." She felt an immediate sense of importance when he picked up the phone and said into it, "Hold my calls, please," and suspected that this was a device to give nervous visitors a feeling of confidence or reassurance.

She sat in the hard, worn armchair and tried to guess how many famous authors had sat here before her, discussing their manuscripts with Morris Mitchell and his predecessors. Sherwood wasn't Doubleday, Random House, or Simon & Schuster, but it could claim an excellent list of impressive authors and had recently bought a reprint house to market paperbacks.

The room, apart from its three windows that looked out on Eighth Avenue, was small, made smaller by the incredible number of books that filled three walls of shelves to overflowing with Sherwood's and other publishers' books, foreign editions, folded galley sheets stacked in piles, manuscripts held perilously together with wide rubber bands. There was a door leading to his secretary's office and another that was either a closet or bathroom. In the immediate center of his desk was a manuscript he had been working on, a long ruled pad beside it with penciled notes. Along the forward edge of the desk were more manuscripts, several hardcover and paperback books, miscellaneous proofs, promotional material, a dictating machine and tape recorder, all without any sense of order.

He smiled apologetically for the disarray, then leaned back in his chair to examine her more closely. There was a certain charm about him that made up for his lack of good looks. His skin was swarthy, though not from exposure to the sun, and she was again conscious of the sparseness of his hair; his face, thin and long, was hollow-cheeked, with deepset brown eyes behind those oversized glasses. His hands showed strength as he toyed with a wooden pencil.

"I understand you've had no previous experience in the publishing field, Miss Goodwin," he stated flatly.

"Nor in any other, Mr. Mitchell," Karen admitted quickly. "I was graduated from Smith last June, an art major. I can type fairly well, but I'm nowhere with shorthand. If it helps at all, I've been an ardent reader most of my life and my marks have been high . . ."

Mr. Mitchell smiled bleakly. "Yes. Well—let me see. We're rather fully staffed in our reading department and are well taken care of as far as typists, stenographers and secretaries are concerned. However . . ." he paused, put the pencil back in the tall beer mug that held a dozen or more like it, and added, "I think we might be able to use an assistant to help with some of the innumerable details that come across my desk. Would you be interested in something of that sort?"

"Yes. Very much," Karen replied.

Mr. Mitchell looked disappointed. "Then suppose you give me another week to arrange it and make room for you. You've met my secretary, Mrs. Holliday? I'll turn you over to her for processing and so forth. There's a small room next to hers that we've been using as a storeroom of sorts. I'll have her put that in order for you. Let's say a week from today, shall we?"

Outside, she phoned Pierce, but he was not in his office. She had lunch, bought a suit, two dresses, and a short jacket, then drove to Wyecliffe to break the news to Anna, who finally accepted the fact that further discussion about Karen's plans would not only be useless but reckless. Later, Anna called Herschel at the plant and forewarned him.

Two days later, Karen moved into a small, quiet apartment hotel in New York to begin her new life.

The job, she discovered at the outset, was a far cry from what she had expected. Mrs. Holliday, a curt, efficient woman in her late forties, set her to doing the menial tasks of the office, "to acquaint you with the routines." She helped open and sort the mail for Mr. Mitchell, distributed letters intended for other members of the editorial staff, checked through manuscripts to see that all pages were numbered and in proper order, checked on galleys due in from printers, saw that they were returned on schedule by the authors, brought coffee to Mr.

Mitchell, who consumed inordinate amounts of the stuff during the day, and made luncheon reservations for him and his callers. Mrs. Holliday, she learned, was far more than a secretary. The widow of a former editor, she acted as Mitchell's buffer, knowing who would be permitted to talk with him or see him and who must be denied that privilege and shunted to another editor, this in a manner that would not be offensive.

During her second week at Sherwood she saw Pierce twice, once at lunch, the second time at dinner; and on that second occasion, spent the night at his apartment. This encounter was a surprising pleasure for both, their sexual bout normal and eminently satisfactory in every respect. "God, you're marvelous." Pierce crooned, "absolutely fantastic. What's happened?"

"One learns as one grows," Karen replied cryptically.

She spent each weekend at Wyecliffe and tried to squeeze in several luncheons with Anna, in town for shopping, but found that an hour gave them little more than time to simply eat together. But she gave every appearance of being happy in her work and Anna and Herschel soon came to accept her absence, as they did her visits.

Her affair with Pierce was resumed on a regular basis now and he became her constant escort, despite the numerous opportunities Sherwood Press, and New York in general, offered her. They dined, saw shows, visited night spots together and shared each other's bed at least three times each week. Pierce's efforts to interest her in his complex work, however, failed. Karen professed little knowledge of the market, mergers, or intricate financial deals. "In fact," she admitted, "it's all I can do to balance my checkbook every month."

Pierce, who was completely involved, was persistent. "You're twenty-two years old, Karen. Isn't it time you were handling your own financial affairs?"

"Why, Pierce? My uncle does that for me and I see no need to bother my head with all those details."

"That's childish. Everyone has the right to know where he stands. You don't know if you're worth a hundred thousand or a million, do you?"

"That doesn't worry me in the least," Karen replied. "When I need money, it's there. It always has been. I don't have to know more than that."

"Well, you should do something with it instead of letting it just sit there."

Karen laughed and said, "Pierce, I don't have to do a single damned thing about it. Whatever it is, whatever it amounts to, it's where it belongs, and it's safe."

Exasperatedly, he muttered, "Oh, Jesus, Karen, you talk like an idiot."

"So I'm an idiot and let's not discuss it any further, okay?"

When she returned to Wyecliffe that weekend, Karen found an occasion to mention the subject to Herschel, out of Anna's hearing, asking how GFP stock had fared in the recent drop in the market. "That interests you, Karen?" Herschel asked with a smile.

"I hear so much talk about the market at the office."

"Well, maybe that's good. GFP closed one-quarter off at forty-one on Friday. That's six points down from its high for the year, but there's nothing to worry about. It will come back and go higher."

"I'm not worried, but since I do own some it of, I'm interested, let's say, curious."

"So. Maybe it's time for you to show some interest in the company, eh? Let me see. Zalman and Sophie, *alov hasholem*, had fifteen thousand shares. Split twice, it has now become sixty thousand shares. At forty-one—" he pulled an envelope and pencil from his pocket and made a few broad, slashing figures on its back—"your stock is worth two million, four hundred thousand dollars. Plus"—he scribbled more figures. talking as he wrote—"the investments I have made with your dividends. Treasury bonds, commercial paper and blue chip stocks. Also, there was Zalman's and Robert's insurance, and the cash, the house you own on East Eighty-fifth Street . . ."

"I own the house?" Karen said. surprised.

"Yes. Don't you remember, I sold it to Zalman? It's yours now. So, let me see. Roughly, I would say you are worth close to four million dollars, maybe even five. If you want, I can have my people draw up a financial statement . . ."

"That isn't necessary at all." After a moment, "What about all the money I've cost you since . . ."

Herschel smiled. "Cost? You cost us nothing, darling. Whatever it was, you have repaid it a hundred times over with what you have given us in return."

"Uncle?"

"What, *liebschen?*"

She went to him and kissed his cheek. "I love you and Aunt Anna very much," she said simply.

"For this?"

"No, not for this. For being who you are and what you are. You mean a lot to me and I'm sorry if I've made you unhappy in any way."

"Ah, Karen, Karen, you should only be happy, marry, and raise a happy family of your own. That's all we want for you."

"I know you want only what's best for me, you and Aunt Anna." She returned to her chair and said, "Uncle Herschel, do you like Pierce Nieland?"

His face grew solemn. Shaking his head from side to side slowly, he said, "I can't answer that. I don't know a man I have seen only a few times and have never spoken to him except to say 'Hello' or 'Good-bye.' "

"Is it because he isn't a Jew?"

A slow smile broke over Herschel's craggy face. "Maybe it's because you *are* a Jew."

She frowned, puzzling over the way he had turned her question around, then said, "You think his father and grandmother would object to me because I'm Jewish?"

An expressive shrug. "You don't?"

"I honestly hadn't thought about it very much."

"Then think, Karen, before you make false dreams in your pretty head."

It was a Sunday in February when Pierce brought up the subject of her worth again, and this time Karen made a point of outlining her financial status in greater detail. "Four or five million! God, what I could do with that!" he exclaimed. "So many opportunities lying around at this moment that would . . ."

She cut him off short. "I'm not interested, Pierce. I live well and I don't need more than I have."

"But, Karen . . ."

"Pierce, what about us?"

He frowned as though puzzled. "What do you mean, what about us?"

"Just that, what about us? Do we simply go on the way we have, with no more than a telephone line between us, an occasional dinner and a night spent together at your apartment or mine?"

"Karen, aren't we getting far away from our original subject?"

"Not at all. I think they're the same subject. My money is my future. I am my future. Therefore my money and I are one and the same."

"That's a peculiar algebraic viewpoint, isn't it?"

"I don't see anything peculiar about it at all. Pierce, let's stop these childish evasions, shall we? Do you have any intention of ever asking me to marry you?"

He turned, came back to her, and sat on the sofa facing her. "I can't, Karen," he said. "I honestly wish I could, but it—just isn't possible."

"Why not?"

"I think you know that without forcing me to tell you."

"Tell me, Pierce."

"All right, since you insist. For one thing, neither my father nor grandmother would approve or permit it. For another, I want a family, and children to succeed me and carry on the Nieland name. It's expected of me, and I can't let my family down. I'm the last of our line. With you, that simply isn't in the cards."

"In other words, my being a Jew is the stumbling block."

"You didn't hear what I said."

"I heard what you meant."

"Karen, I . . ." He threw his hands upward and outward in a gesture of helplessness. "I don't know what I can add to what I've already said."

"I don't need any more than that." She stood up. "Thank you, Pierce. You've explained your position thoroughly and I accept it. Will you please go now?" She turned and walked out of the room and Pierce's life.

3

Stanley Bridges and Evan Ross, two bachelor editors at Sherwood Press, helped tremendously to fill the gap left by Pierce, and she became a jewel of a find to them; a delightful young woman of some mystery. They went to lunch with her on a share-alike basis, frequently used her hotel apartment as a midtown stop on their way to other engagements, took her to dinner, the theater, little out-of-the-way "in" spots, and shared frequent potluck meals put together at her place at a moment's notice.

Through Stan and Evan, she met authors with whom they worked, and other men and women of the literary, theatrical, and musical worlds. She entertained at little impromptu parties and, in turn, was entertained by a widening circle of people she found very interesting and exciting. She became more and more interested in the theater and dropped a few thousand dollars as one of a group of backers in two off-Broadway shows and, against Stan's and Evan's advice, allowed herself to be bilked out of seven thousand five hundred dollars by an engaging, smooth-talking entrepreneur who had mesmerized four other gullible investors into backing a Broadway play from a beautifully written script in which he owned no rights whatever. But despite that loss, she felt compensated by the fact that almost every waking hour of her life was occupied with interesting activity.

Karen missed the physical contact she had enjoyed with Pierce and not too long after, in a moment of quiet desperation, she ignored one of Rachel Reeve's basic rules of sexual conduct. She made herself available.

Stan Bridges, only two years her senior and a brilliant editor, thoroughly charming and equally ambitious, was the first to take Pierce's place in her bed. Evan Ross, on discovering this, retreated and left the field of battle to the victor. The affair ended a few months later when Stan resigned his position suddenly and went to Mexico to write a book on his own. Within a short time, Karen resumed her friendship with Evan, older, wittier, and more amusing than Stan; but Evan, she soon learned, was deeply immersed in a heretofore undisclosed domestic problem; he was separated from his wife, and far behind in his alimony and child-support payments.

Karen, on Evan's advice, had previously taken a five thousand dollar flyer in a Broadway play, *Penny For Your Thoughts*, produced by Aaron Riggs, and had not only gotten back her original investment, but made a two hundred per cent profit and was still running. When Evan suggested that he was entitled to half of that profit, Karen wrote a check without protest and broke off the relationship.

A month or two of boredom passed during which she resumed her weekend visits to Wyecliffe and, as another summer came to a close, accepted a weekend house-party date in Easthampton with Jay Flannery, a novelist she had met through Stan Bridges. The party, scheduled to end on

Sunday night, became an orgy that lasted until Tuesday, complete with marijuana, hallucinogenic, and hard drugs.

When she returned to work on Wednesday morning, Mrs. Holliday eyed her coldly. Her attitude indicated total disbelief in Karen's story that she had been taken ill while in Wyecliffe. Mrs. Holliday said, "I don't think you'd be wise to use that story on Mr. Mitchell, Miss Goodwin. He's waiting to see you."

The sudden change from "Karen" to "Miss Goodwin" should have been the tipoff, but the full shock came moments later when she learned from Mrs. Holliday that Jay Flannery was married to Morris Mitchell's sister, that they were separated, and that Mrs. Flannery had been having Jay under surveillance by a private detective agency for several months.

Karen didn't see Mr. Mitchell then, or later. She picked up her bag and walked out.

For a full week she debated whether or not to look for a new job. She busied herself with shopping and lunching with various friends, but the nights were long and lonely. Later, she called on several publishers, only to discover that the sixteen months she had spent at Sherwood qualified her for no more than a junior clerkship, a job generally filled by girls just out of college, willing to work very hard for small salaries, with little opportunity to elevate themselves into positions of importance. For a while she was tempted to ask Herschel to place her in a position at GFP's Forty-second Street headquarters, but that would not only be an admission of failure but put her under certain restrictive controls.

Then one day, emerging from a Fifth Avenue beauty salon, she ran into Julian Roth. Five years had made a number of physical improvements in Julian, who was elegantly dressed, carried his height well without an extra ounce of fat, and with more self-assurance in his bearing. For a moment they stared at each other without speaking, then Karen smiled and said, "Julian. How nice to see you again. You're almost a stranger."

"Hello, Karen. You look wonderful. Beautiful."

"If I don't," she quipped, "I've just thrown away forty dollars."

He actually laughed, a rarity in Julian. "A pure waste of money," he said, "gilding the lily."

"Thank you. How are Dora and Sid?"

"They're fine. Dad's still at GFP, advertising director, you know."

"And you?"

"I'm there too, in Purchasing."

"Do you enjoy your work?"

"Oh, yes, very much. I've always liked that part of it. Sales bring in the money, of course, but the decisions on where, how, and on what to spend it, watching it being disbursed, is what makes the difference between profit and loss so much of the time."

"How interesting. I've never thought about it that way."

"I hear you're living in the city."

"Yes, for over a year and a half now."

"I—are you in a hurry, or could we have lunch?"

She checked her watch, considering the invitation, wondering how far they would, over lunch, go back into the past. "I'm free until 2:30," she said finally. "There's a show at a gallery on Fifty-seventh Street I want to catch."

They walked the two blocks north and had lunch at the Plaza. There was nothing that reminded Karen of the Julian of five years ago—the sullen boy who sulked when he was displeased—yet she could not help remembering their last meeting; the revelation that he had known about herself and Robert and had still insisted he wanted to marry her. But there was no mention of that meeting, nor of Robert. Or Pierce. Julian talked of himself, and his job, and asked questions about herself that were easily answered.

On parting, he asked if he could see her again and she gave him her address and phone number, which he dutifully recorded in a small memo book. A week later, Julian phoned, and asked her to dinner and a show for Saturday night. She accepted, and asked if he had chosen the show yet. "No. I thought I'd ask your preference."

"Have you seen *Penny For Your Thoughts*?"

"Not yet. It's still playing to a capacity house, but I'll try . . ."

"Let me do it, Julian. I can get the tickets."

"On only two days' notice?"

"The producer is a friend of mine."

"Oh. Well—fine—that's great."

They had a drink at her apartment, dinner at a nearby restaurant and saw the show, Karen's ninth time, but as enjoyable to her as an investor as it had been on opening night. They met Aaron Riggs in the lobby between the second and third act curtain and he invited them to his apartment later, where his wife, Leah, and he were entertaining some people from Los Angeles who were negotiating for the motion picture rights to *Penny*.

Julian took it all very calmly, even when he learned that Karen owned a piece of the show. He took no part in the jocularity that flowed so easily between the others, but became totally interested when the talk turned to budgets, production costs, possible returns, and projected profits. He soon learned the difference between proposal and fact, when Aaron later dismissed it all as an exercise in Hollywood gymnastics. Aaron already had a firm offer for the rights that far exceeded any offer made that night.

On the way to Karen's apartment he was vocal in his perplexity. "If Riggs had this firm offer, why let these other people go on and on without any possible hope?" he asked.

"Because this business isn't conducted like any other, Julian," Karen told him. "These are games they play because one never knows when a studio will change hands, a producer will be fired, or someone will take advantage of an obscure escape clause and back out. Every time Aaron listens, it's like having another iron in the fire."

"Crazy," Julian said. "Absolute lunacy."

"But interesting, isn't it?"

"If you like to play Russian roulette, yes."

Julian saw Karen in, refused a nightcap, and left without indicating that he would call her in the future. During the next week, Anna phoned and asked Karen to come up for the weekend. When she arrived on Friday evening she learned there was to be a dinner party the following night: the Freitags, Rosenbergs, and Lindstroms. Also, Sidney, Dora, and Julian Roth had been invited. Karen knew then that the word was out that she and Julian had seen each other and that a possible *shiddach* was in the making.

Saturday evening went off very well. Herschel, Max Freitag, Milton Rosenberg, and Dr. Lindstrom went into a huddle to discuss the new Hebrew School building fund, of which they were the planning committee and principal contributors. Their wives were involved in plans for social activities that would engage the Jewish community in full force, deciding in their own wisdom how much each family could, or should contribute.

Julian and Karen, after dinner, escaped to Herschel's small study, feeling no part in these familiar sessions, an ancient story to both. Julian refused the brandy Karen offered and selected a group of records from Anna's collection of symphonies which he stacked on the stereo player, then sat on a small sofa facing the one opposite Karen, watching as she sipped her drink. After a few minutes, "Karen, are you happy?"

The unexpected question caught her by surprise. "I'm not unhappy," she replied.

"I suppose that's an answer of some kind."

"Let me ask you the same question. Are you happy, Julian?"

He smiled. "*Touché*. I suppose all happiness or unhappiness is a matter of relativity. I enjoy what I'm doing very much. I'm even happy in it, but . . ."

"But you're not very happy away from it, are you?"

The smile faded. "Not very."

"Poor Julian," Karen said softly.

"That's how you've always seen me, isn't it? Poor Julian."

"I didn't mean it that way and I'm sorry. Let's change the subject, shall we? I don't think either of us is comfortable with this one."

"Karen, what happened five years ago, that's long done and over with. We were no more than children then. I'd like to make a fresh start with you."

"That almost sounds as though you were forgiving me for something."

"No. There's nothing to forgive."

"But you'll never let yourself forget it, will you?"

"I've forgotten everything except that I was in love with you then and I still am."

"Oh, Julian . . ."

"Poor Julian?"

"No. It's just that . . ."

"What?"

"So many things have happened since then."

"What difference does that make? Things have happened to me, too, but they haven't changed how I feel about you. I'm older, better able to understand life, responsibilities, a lot of things I couldn't understand then. I would like you to consider a serious proposal of marriage, without the excuses of youth and college we used when neither of us was ready for it."

Karen got up, went to the bar, and poured more brandy into her glass. When she returned to her chair Julian said, "I'm not pressing for an answer tonight, Karen. All I want is for you to think about it for now. I've waited this long, I can wait a little longer."

"Thank you, Julian. I'll think about it."

"Seriously?"

"Seriously."

"Will you see me in the meantime?"

"Yes, if you won't make this an issue when we meet."

"Agreed." He stood up, smiling. "I think I'd better start urging the folks to leave. It's a long drive back to the city."

4

Julian called Karen two weeks later. They went to dinner and the ballet. Two more weeks passed before he called again, and this time, Karen prepared dinner at her apartment. Then his calls came with weekly regularity. She put him off once or twice and he accepted these turndowns graciously and without complaint. He sent flowers on her birthday, and dropped her cards when he went out of town on business.

On visits to Wyecliffe, Karen became aware, from the number of times Julian's name was injected into her conversations with Anna and Herschel, of growing interest in their progress. It was subtle prying, but prying nevertheless, and she played it as a game, giving them little or nothing to go on.

Then there came a Sunday morning when she had had breakfast and began thumbing through the pages of the *Times*. She saw the item, one among many on the page, the picture of a radiant blond above it; and learned that Mr. Pierce Nieland had been married to Miss Amelya Dart Cranston, daughter of the senior partner of Cranston, Packard & Nieland on the previous Sunday at the home of Mrs. Carolyn Pierce Nieland of Wyecliffe, New Jersey.

On the following day, Karen booked a flight to Europe and remained away for two months. London, Paris, Rome, Florence, Venice, Nice, back to Paris, then home again. She phoned Anna, got her car out of storage and drove to Wyecliffe with gifts for Anna, Herschel, Eric, and Leona, and spent the entire week there with them.

She had spent two months of restless movement without allowing the past to catch up, the perfect purge to rid herself of her memories of Pierce. And now there was a need to fill the void that remained. On her return to the city, she telephoned Julian.

They were married in October of 1957 in a quiet affair in Wyecliffe with only those few members of the family close to them present. Rabbi Kinsman performed the ceremony and after the wedding dinner, Karen and Julian drove to New York and went aboard ship for a month-long cruise to the Caribbean.

On their return in November, Karen decided to open the house on West Eighty-fifth Street. She contacted a firm that specialized in home renovation, and after examining several houses they had restored and renewed, signed the necessary contracts. Work began immediately. The house was emptied, furniture and fixtures removed, exterior stone sandblasted, wide casement windows installed, the entire front modernized with a pierced-screen façade, and a wall of cast concrete blocks built up to add beauty and provide a sense of privacy. A single wide slab of polished oak replaced the original double doors and large planters flanked the steps, from which Italian cypresses rose to almost second-story height.

Inside, the house received a thorough transformation. Walls were broken through to enlarge the master bedroom, which now included a private bath, sauna, and fully equipped exercise room. The ceiling was lowered in the second-floor study, plastered with accoustical tile, walls paneled in walnut and soundproofed for the high fidelity stereo equipment installed.

The fourth floor, other than one section to be used for storage, was closed off. The third floor became Karen's studio; completely open except for a bathroom and dressing room. Behind the frosted glass ceiling, endless tubes of fluorescent lights turned night into day, with supplementary spotlights for added brilliance when required.

The front of the basement was converted into a servants' apartment, and the kitchen was modernized. Furniture and furnishing began to arrive by the truckload and Karen and her decorator were on hand every day to see that the carpeting, rugs, and draperies were properly laid and hung, and chairs, sofas, cabinets and other appointments correctly placed. By May the house was ready. Karen had interviewed a dozen couples and finally chose Max and Gerda Meyers, a middle-aged Swiss couple, as housekeeper-cook and houseman. In June, she and Julian moved into their new home. The cost had come to eighty thousand dollars, which Julian considered profligate. Virtually the only part he had played in the entire project had been to audit each invoice against original projected prices, complain, and threaten to take the contractors to court; and then show petulance and dismay when Karen simply laughed and sent the bills to Herschel to be paid.

5

It would only be a matter of time, Karen admitted to herself a few months after they were settled in their new home, before her marriage would come to an end. Nothing had worked as she thought it would. Despite everything else, her home was run meticulously. Max and Gerda were expert and efficient in their duties, freeing Karen from all domestic problems. Julian went off to work every morning, leaving her to sleep well into midmorning. At first, shopping, visiting galleries, working in her studio, meeting old acquaintances for lunch, and dropping in for an occasional matinée with former student friends from Smith took up the rest of her days. In odd moments she would slip away to Wyecliffe to visit Anna and Herschel and on infrequent weekends the Goodwins would come into town to see her and Julian, and to marvel at the changes that had been wrought in their first home.

Dora Roth began a weekly, then daily, telephone ritual that drove Karen frantic. Julian invited his parents for Friday night dinners until Karen put her foot down firmly, refusing to be held to what was rapidly becoming a weekly commitment, which caused a minor rift in that relationship and brought on a period of sulking on Julian's part.

Karen had never fully understood Julian's sensitivity in their earlier years and understood him less now. At times he was shy and grateful, like a child granted a very special favor or given a toy; at other times, for the most minor reasons, he became distantly remote and unreachable.

Apart from his work, Julian had few outside interests, and fewer friends. Most evenings at home, he spent in his study, endlessly poring over reports, projections, and a miscellany of papers he brought from his office. He regarded time spent at the theater, a concert, or the ballet an utter waste of time.

Before long, marriage had become a huge, glaring bore to Karen.

They hadn't yet adjusted sexually, and although Karen supposed this condition would rectify itself in time, six months passed and there was little improvement. Julian remained shy, clumsy in his overeagerness, leaving her unsatisfied, lying awake long after he had fallen asleep more often than not. That situation caused frequent spells of irritability in her and she began planning evasions. She would go to bed before Julian was ready, feigning sleep when he came up from his study to join her. Or, when Julian was ready for bed, she sat up reading until he had fallen asleep. At other times, she pleaded exhaustion, or period irregularity.

For days, she spent much of her time in her studio, going through pencil and charcoal sketches that dated back to her years at Smith, but found nothing to interest or stimulate her into transferring those efforts to canvas. She began wandering through the Museum of Modern Art, Whitney, Guggenheim, Metropolitan, Cooper Union, private galleries, and the permanent displays in Greenwich Village. At Castagna's, on Sixty-seventh Street just off Madison one day, she came upon a showing that intrigued her, of the works of a Lee Chandler; flowing landscapes, bold portraits, and figure sketches that came brilliantly alive by his mastery of brush strokes.

Luis Castagna, noting Karen's rapt attention, approached unobtrusively and stood quietly beside and behind her. "Interesting, are they not, Mrs. Roth?" Luis said after a while.

"Very," Karen replied. "Who is he? I've never seen any of his work before."

"In a year, two years, he will become well-known. In ten, even famous The prices will go sky-high then."

"I can believe that, Luis. Who is he?"

"My very own discovery. I found him on the pavements in the Village. He is young, vital, with much in him yet to come. You agree?"

"I do. I love this portrait of the boy. And I can't decide

between these two," indicating a landscape and one of the lower New York harbor under misty fog.

"I advise you with all sincerity, Mrs. Roth, take all three."

Karen thought for a few moments. "I think I will," she said and wrote a check for nine hundred and seventy dollars. "Luis," when the transaction had been completed, "do you think Mr. Chandler would take me as a pupil?"

"He has had pupils, yes, but now"—a shrug—"I could ask for you, if you wish."

"Will you, please? If he is interested, send him to me. I would also like his advice on how to frame these properly."

"I will be pleased to do it, Mrs. Roth."

Two days later, Lee Chandler came to the Eighty-fifth Street house. He was in his late twenties, just under six feet tall, boyishly slender with light brown hair, alert, with bright eyes that took in everything with an air of surprise. He wore a mustache and beard, trimmed neatly as was his rather longish hair, adding a certain maturity to his delicate features that reached a point of near-effeminacy; but his musculature was prominently displayed in a form-fitting knit shirt, tight black slacks, and a similarly body-hugging jacket.

Lee, she learned, had been born in Italy, of American parents. His father had been in the service of the State Department as an aide to the commercial attaché. Lee had studied in Florence, then Paris, and had gone back again to Rome. When his father was transferred to Argentina, Lee came to the United States and found his way to the Village, where he had labored hard and long for the recognition that was only now becoming his reward.

Only very recently, he admitted over coffee, had his work been discovered by Castagna, who had given him his first gallery show. In fact—he admitted further—Karen's was only the second sale of his work from the gallery and he was deeply grateful.

"I would like," Karen said, "to show you my studio and become your pupil."

"I would like very much to see your studio, Mrs. Roth."

"Then you must call me Karen."

"If you will call me Lee."

Not until after he had examined the surprising studio and the examples of her previous work would Chandler consent to take her on as a student. During the following month, Lee came to Karen's studio three times each week. Under his instruction, she showed pleasing progress. Lee improved her greatest weakness, basic drawing, then focused on perspective and proportion. He taught her patience in mixing and blending color, which became rich, clear, and definable without any trace of its former muddiness. He worked on her brush technique and showed her how to develop facial and body structure, to place subtle emphasis on outstanding characteristics and keep nonessentials from detracting from the central core or theme of her work.

During their third month together they became lovers, and in this, Karen found Lee to be equally patient, deliberate, passionate, spiritual, and eminently satisfactory. He seemed to sense in her those moments when she needed release and, as meticulously as he had applied himself to work, paused in his labors to accommodate her in love.

Julian, of course, knew that Karen had become deeply involved in her painting again and found the change in her personality gratifying, although he understood little of what she produced on canvas; and had the wisdom to refrain from commenting adversely on her efforts. Karen, on the other hand, allowed Julian infrequent intimacies and no longer expressed her open dissatisfaction with his sexual inadequacies. And then, one day in the eighth month of their marriage, Julian came home before noon to pack a bag for a sudden three-day trip to the Ohio plant. He let himself in with his key, and seeing Max in the living room, aproned, duster and cleaning cloth in his hands, asked, "Is Mrs. Roth home, Max?"

"Yes, sir. She is in her studio."

"Fine. I'll want you to drive me to the airport as soon as I pack a few things—say—half an hour."

"I will be ready, sir."

Julian ran up the stairs to the third floor. He flung the door to the studio open, calling, "Karen, I've got to . . ."

He saw them then, lying together on the sofa, torn apart by his abrupt entrance. Karen leaped up, naked, hair disheveled, mouth open, eyes glazed, as though struck by a burst of brilliant light, completely disoriented. Julian was only vaguely aware of the man lying on the sofa, a blur behind Karen.

"Ju—Julian . . ." her voice quavered nervously.

"My God—oh, my God—you—you *whore*—you filthy, whoring bitch . . ."

"Julian—don't . . ."

He stood facing her trembling body, outraged, defeated, lips moving soundlessly. He never allowed her to finish the sentence she had begun, hit her across the face with the back of his hand, then grabbed her arm, held it, and hit her again. She sagged toward him and he saw the trickle of blood that ran from her nose down over her lips and chin. The man had gotten off the sofa and pulled his trousers on quickly, standing white-faced, waiting in doubt for the inevitable assault; but Julian pushed Karen toward him and Lee caught her as she was about to fall. "Take her!" Julian shrieked. "Take her and keep her! She was a whore then, and she's still a lousy whore!" He wheeled, ran out and down the steps. He stopped on the second-floor level in a moment of decision. On the lower floor, Max stood—hat in hand—waiting.

Julian went to the bedroom, gathered up some clothes at random, cleared his shaving gear from the bathroom and carried the single suitcase down to the first level. Max approached him hesitantly, apprehensively. "You want . . .?"

"Never mind," Julian snarled. "I won't need you. I'll send for the rest of my things later."

Two months later, after Russell Charles had held several meetings with Julian's attorney, Karen left for Mexico to pick up her prearranged divorce. The sudden end of her marriage came as a violent shock to Sidney and Dora, as it had to Anna and Herschel, who took the breakup very hard, but were sympathetic and understanding to Karen's meager explanation. From years of practiced restraint, they stood by her loyally, knowing that any interference on their part would create an unbridgeable gulf.

The divorce had no effect on Sid Roth's job as GFP's director of advertising. Julian, however, after a closed meeting with Reed Steinhorst, accepted a transfer to the Ohio plant as supervisor of purchasing there.

Freedom became a heady tonic for Karen with Julian out of her life, but she lost Lee Chandler. Even though the way was now clear, he never returned, nor would he return Karen's calls. She took off for Florida for a month and returned with a renewed zest for work, finished off several paintings, and once again became absorbed in the theater when she received a call from Aaron Riggs.

Aaron had taken an option on a drama by Stuart Everett, a play called *Love Bind,* and invited the same group of investors who had backed *Penny* to an informal reading at his apartment. At the moment, considering her profits from *Penny,* it was something in which Karen wanted participation.

On the night of the reading, Aaron moved among his guests exuding charm and confidence. When Karen noted Leah's absence to Edwin Bassett, she learned that in the time that had elapsed, Leah Riggs had gone to Las Vegas, divorced Aaron, and that the settlement he had been forced to make was hurting him badly. This was confirmed by two other investors, Alan and Shirley Koppel, who suggested that Aaron had picked up *Love Bind* in an effort to work his way out of financial desperation.

After drinks were served and the potential backers introduced to the tentative cast, Gordon Washburn, the director, arrived with the author, Stuart Everett, and got down to the business of the moment. The cast were placed in a semicircle while Aaron's guests sat on the dozen folding chairs facing them. Washburn arranged the lights so that all but the cast were in semidarkness.

Stuart Everett was about thirty, cadaverously thin, bearded, and wore a suit that bordered on shabbiness. He outlined the story briefly. Its principals were a wife, husband, and the younger brother of the wife. The rest of the cast consisted of a parent of the husband, mother and father of the wife and brother, and several neighbors and friends, an even dozen in all.

In the actual reading, the play became a rather dreary exposé of an enforced marriage and incest, in which there were numerous bitterly witty lines, a preponderance of sexual permissiveness, and a dearth of entertainment value. Karen found much of it discomfiting and discovered that more than half the other potential investors felt as she did.

The reading over, Aaron, Washburn, and Everett took turns discussing the possibilities for the success of the play over a buffet supper, and at its conclusion, only three believers agreed to purchase single units. Karen left without committing herself and although she felt far less enthusiasm for *Love Bind* than she had during the reading of *Penny* there was an urge on her part to become involved with the project.

Thinking the matter over the next day, visualizing the cast as they read through their parts, she remembered most clearly the man who had been chosen to play the part of the weak husband, David Brandon, but could not recall his real name. Martin—Mark—Mark-Something, whose stage wife, Nora, had restored to sexual intimacy with her brother, Warren, who was David's business partner, and who, desperate over his impotence, eventually took his own life.

Mark-Something was still on her mind when, a few days later, Aaron phoned her for an answer. He told her he was making excellent progress and with one or two more affirmative replies, would be ready to schedule rehearsals. Karen asked him to send her a copy of the play to read before giving him her answer, and Aaron had the script delivered to her that same afternoon by messenger.

In cold type, the play showed no more promise than it had during the reading. It was, in fact, too reminiscent of incidents too closely related to her own life, too close for comfort. She learned, however, that David Brandon's real name was Mark Lawson. When Aaron phoned the following morning to ask how she liked the script, Karen agreed to buy two units at ten thousand dollars each.

Once the cast was decided upon and signed, Karen began dropping in on rehearsals at the Helen Hayes Theater on Forty-sixth Street and even when, under Gordon Washburn's competent direction, they became a company well-versed in their parts, she saw no conceivable reason why the play should last longer than a few weeks on Broadway, or a month, at best.

Mark Lawson, she learned, was playing the most important role of his erratic stage career and seemed well-suited against Ann Lucas, as Nora, who had gained some minor prominence in a succession of lesser roles. During the third week of rehearsals, Karen invited Ann and Mark to have lunch with her. A few days later, she had Ann, Mark, and Leigh Page in for dinner at her home. Then it was Harry Collier and Mark. And finally, on a Sunday, it was Mark alone.

He was an easy and amusing conversationalist and within a short time it was obvious that he had worked very hard at becoming an actor since dropping out of NYU during his second year, due to financial difficulties when his father—a printing salesman—died of a heart attack in 1942. Mark, who was Morrie Levinson in those days, went to work for his father's firm, Bennington Press, escaping the draft when it was discovered he had a heart murmur.

In 1945, his mother died. Morrie moved out of the rented flat into a small two-room apartment he shared with Abe Anselman, a numbers runner by day and a student at the Macaban School for the Living Theater at night, operated by Jeanne Macaban in a nearby loft. Morrie, visiting the school with Abe, who was registered as Andrew Armour, was at once intrigued by what he saw and became infected with the acting virus. On a subsequent visit, he enrolled as a student.

Morrie's voice was good and he showed a natural flair in the small parts Jeanne Macaban assigned him. A quick study, he was responsive to Jeanne's patient coaching. He read the many plays she loaned him, and soon he began stealing time from his selling job to drop in on matinées.

"You were sleeping with her, weren't you?" Karen said.

"Well, eventually, yes. Do you mind?"

"Not in the least."

"Then why make a particular point of it?"

"When I hear a story, I don't want the important details left out. It's distracting."

"The next episode should be more interesting to you. I got a part in *Journey Into Murder*, a small part in a minor play that closed after two weeks, but during its short run I made a fan who . . ."

"A woman fan, no doubt."

He ignored the interruption. "Who lined me up with an agent, and I wound up in *Hope For Tomorrow*."

"I didn't see it, but I remember it."

"Which ran for six months on Broadway and another year on road tour. Paramount bought it for the screen, but none of the original cast was chosen to go to Hollywood. You can still catch it on the late, late show once in a while, when they're desperate for material."

"What next?"

"Ah, then the lean years. A couple of months on the beach, bugging my agent, calling on producers known and unknown, back to Bennington Press, one summer with a stock company in New England, another in upstate New York. Off and on that way until my agent called me to read for *Love Bind*."

After dinner, Mark and Karen lounged in the library over cigarettes and cognac, listening to soothing music, his long, sensitive fingers keeping time against his thigh. "This is a very lovely setup you have here," he said.

"I find it comfortable."

"Nice. Very nice."

They listened to the symphony for a while longer and he turned to her and asked, "What do you think of *Love Bind*, Karen?"

"I invested in two units," she replied. "That should tell you something, shouldn't it?"

He smiled. "For you, that's like buying a new engine for a toy train set. What I mean is, how do you *really* feel about it, way deep down?"

She was sitting on the sofa, long legs curled up under her, one arm stretched negligently along the back, almost touching his shoulder. She said, "I think it has a fair chance, don't you?"

He shook his head slowly, negatively. "I shouldn't say this to an investor, except that I like you. It'll bomb out. The day after the reviews come out, it'll be as dead as a month-old newspaper. Any theater party advance sales Aaron has lined up will be cancelled, and that will be it."

"If you feel that way about it, why are you in it? A failure can't do very much to further your career, can it?"

"Two reasons. One, I'm a basket case when somebody comes along with an offer for a Broadway part. Two, even that short exposure could get me seen, maybe a good review for my part. I'm a complete optimist. Or maybe a wishful thinker. A part on Broadway, once you've tasted it, hell, there's nothing like it. It's the pot of gold at the end of the rainbow you keep searching for, even though you know the gold will turn out to be nuts and bolts when you finally find it. Maybe it's because I've never been close enough to the big, big break."

"So you keep on chasing after it?"

"Yes. I'm hopeless, I guess. But to be honest with you, Karen, I don't believe *Love Bind* will ever make it. If that comes as a disappointment to you, I'm sorry."

She said, "It isn't my first venture and it won't hurt too much. Besides, I've made a substantial profit on Aaron's *Penny For Your Thoughts*."

"It's nice when you can take it so philosophically. A bath for twenty thousand would put me under permanently."

"Mark, does the theater mean that much to you?"

His mouth broke into a wide, pleasant grin. "It's my life's work. My hobby is selling printing, but without my hobby, I couldn't support what I sometimes laughingly refer to as my career."

"It all sounds so—destructive and wasteful, and insecure. I wish I could help you in some way."

"You helped Aaron a lot. If you hadn't come up with your twenty grand, the show wouldn't have gotten off the ground. You were the key to the whole thing."

"That delicate a thread?"

"Karen," he said, "most of Broadway is held together by those thin, delicate threads. If Aaron wasn't as broke as he is, he'd never gamble on this turkey. His divorce from Leah just about cleaned him out, and he was hungry."

She said suddenly, "Were you ever married, Mark?"

"No, not even close. You?"

"Divorced."

He grinned. "Left you with plenty, didn't he?"

"Wrong. It was all mine before I met him. It's still mine."

"Bad guess. You off the hook for good?"

"No. I suppose I'll remarry some day. When I find the kind of relationship I think will be compatible with my way of life."

"That shouldn't be so hard, with a combination of all this, beauty, warmth, everything any man could want. I can't understand the problem, if there is one."

"No problem. It's just a matter of time. And timing." She stood up, went to the bar, and poured herself another drink. "A refill, Mark?"

"Not right now." He came to the bar, sat on a stool, and reached across the polished counter to touch her hand. "You're a very lovely woman, Karen. I wish I could fill the bill."

She smiled appealingly. "Let's not dwell on that subject, shall we?"

"I'd like to pursue it further."

"Not now. I'm not in the mood for making decisions."

"All right. I'm not one for pushing my luck."

"Will you have that drink now?"

"Sure. Hemlock on the rocks."

"Come off it, Mark. You can't be serious. You don't even know me."

"How much does anyone have to know in order to get hit by lightning?"

She poured the cognac into a snifter and pushed it toward him. He twirled the liquid in the glass, dipped it, staring at her over the rim. "Penny?" Karen said.

"What I'm thinking has just been classed off limits."

"There are other subjects, aren't there?"

"I've already told you the story of my misguided life, complimented your food and wine, discussed the weather, and the play. Tell me, do you play a good game of checkers?"

Karen laughed prettily. "If that's all we have left, why don't we call it a night?"

He stood up and grinned. "That caps the bottle. See you at rehearsal?"

"Maybe." At the door she offered her cheek for a brief kiss.

On the following day, she remained away from rehearsal. That evening when Mark telephoned, Gerda told him Karen was out and that she had no knowledge when she would return. Karen, listening on an extension, was pleased by the disappointment in Mark's voice then, and by his two subsequent calls.

She remained away for three days and, dropping in on the fourth, watched Mark almost break up in his eagerness to rush through his part to sit beside her. When the rehearsal ended, he followed her out and they went to a little bar on West Forty-sixth Street. "Where in hell have you been hiding?" he asked with petulance and concern.

"I took a trip up to Wyecliffe to visit my uncle and aunt," Karen lied smoothly. "What are you so upset about? I found half a dozen messages from you when I got back late last night."

"My God, don't you tell your people where you're going when you take off for days at a time, or when you'll be back?"

She sipped her drink slowly, then said calmly, "Mark, if we're going to be friends, you've got to understand one thing about me. I don't like anyone to adopt a proprietary interest in where I go, what I do, or with whom."

"Is that your big hangup?"

"Just one, among many."

"Fill me in on a few more. I'm interested."

"That might take more time than either of us can spare."

"Try me."

"Well, for one thing, I'm young, but not immature. I believe in a universal standard of conduct for men and women alike, equal rights, equal freedoms."

"What it all boils down to is sex, doesn't it, sexual equality?"

"Read it anyway you like, but mostly it's my need for personal freedom without interference. I've had too much of that in my life."

Mark grinned and frowned simultaneously, which gave him the unique expression of doubtful awe and amusement. "Lady, that's really laying it on the line."

"Where it properly belongs."

"If I read you in the clear, that's a hell of an ultrasophisticated concept of friendship. Or marriage, isn't it?"

"Does the concept bother you?"

"Well . . ."

"Equal rights, equal freedoms. Let me try to make it clearer. The reason I live alone is that I can come and go as I please, do as I please, without having anyone to account to. I despise overpossessiveness. In any friendship or relationship I form, I expect to continue the same pattern of freedom. It's that important to me."

"That's clear enough, but aren't you asking a lot of tolerance and understanding from another person?"

She gave him a raised-eyebrow look. "Why? I would expect that person to exercise those same freedoms."

"Without question?"

"Without question."

Mark regarded Karen with a silent stare for a few seconds then said, soberly, "Are you really that enlightened, Karen, or are you putting me on?"

She reached for her purse. "Let's just drop it, shall we?"

Mark caught her arm to prevent her from rising. "Hold on, will you? Give me a chance to think."

She sat back in her chair, smiling. "I thought the theatrical world was one of the greatest sophistication. Am I to take it you find my attitude so unreasonable?"

"I don't know. It's too much like eating your cake and having it."

Still smiling, "Well, for heaven's sake, what's so terribly wrong with that, Mark?"

"For a Jewish boy who was raised on the lower East Side, it takes a bit of getting used to."

"I didn't always live on East Eighty-fifth. I was born on West Tenth."

Mark's forehead wrinkled. "And that's about the sum total of what I know about you. West Tenth, East Eighty-fifth, an aunt and uncle somewhere in New Jersey, you were married and divorced, and can blow twenty thou on a dog like *Love Bind* without blinking an eye."

"That's something else I enjoy, being a mystery woman."

"Look, I . . ."

Karen glanced at her watch. "Mark, I've got to run now."

"When will I see you again?"

"When is your next free night?"

"No rehearsals tomorrow night."

"Would you like to come for dinner?"

"Love to. What time."

"Eight o'clock, then?"

"I'll be there."

Freshly showered, barbered, and manicured, Mark Lawson wore his best dark-blue suit, a white shirt, and pale-blue tie for the occasion. On his way to Karen's he toyed with the thought of bringing flowers, then canceled that out in favor of a bottle of wine that was highly recommended to him by the proprietor of a shop that catered to gourmet tastes. And, for the first time in memory, he felt a sudden and strange shyness to find himself in the act of courting a woman, reluctant to admit to himself that he was on the verge of falling in love; or stood on the brink of an affair in which his partner, for once, would be the stronger of the two.

Karen had left no doubts in his mind. Precisely, explicitly, she had spelled out her position and, affair or something deeper, Mark knew she would be holding all the cards. His own, as usual, would amount to an inside straight he had never been able to fill in his thirty-three years. And yet, if he played his cards carefully, running the bluff and giving what she seemed to be asking for. . . . But whatever came of this night, he was certain it would be on Karen Roth's terms.

He was more than curious about her background and the source of her obvious wealth, which supported her in luxury. His numerous fleeting affairs had been with theater people and hangers-on. Once, there had been a widow in her middle-forties who had taken a strong interest in him, and led him to believe she would back a play for him. That came to naught a few months later when her attorney-business manager called on him in his dreary Village room to inform him that his sponsor couldn't spend a cent beyond her immediate personal needs without consent of the bank that administered her estate, which he represented; consent that would under no conceivable circumstances be forthcoming.

And now, Karen Roth. Nine years his junior, attractive, and willing. And most assuredly, loaded.

The dinner was excellent, the wine perfect for the occasion. They discussed the progress of rehearsals and exchanged views on various members of the cast, some complimentary, some critical. Mark's anecdotes about his experiences on the straw hat circuit were new. alive, amusing, and perhaps inventive. He felt he was holding up his end of the evening with remarkable success.

Karen was wearing an ankle-length hostess gown of soft pink chiffon which, on her elegant body, seemed incredibly feminine. As they left the table, Mark said, "That's a perfect color for you."

"I've seldom worn pink. It's always seemed so delicate."

"You should wear it more often."

"I'll remember that. And how well you look in blue." She led the way to the second-floor library where she put on the Prokofiev Symphony No. 5 with Eugene Ormandy conducting. Mark went to the bar and poured two snifters of brandy, then returned to the sofa beside Karen. After a second drink, she lay in his arms quietly until the symphony came to an end, when she disengaged herself, shut the instrument off and said, "Well, Mark, shall we?"

So the moment was at hand; put up, or throw in his cards. He came up off the sofa and said, "What about your people downstairs?"

"You needn't worry. Come."

In the stillness of her bedroom, Karen slipped out of her gown in one quick, easy movement. Mark's eyes became glazed at the sight of her graceful figure, so much smaller undraped, yet perfectly proportioned. The tip of his tongue flicked out to wet his lips and for a moment he stood motionless, staring in anticipation. Karen smiled then and held out a hand toward him. He came to her like a man walking in his sleep; expecting the lovely vision to vanish at first touch; but the lovely vision began tugging at his tie, then realistically unbuttoned his shirt while he held her as close to him as was permissible without interfering with what she was doing. Karen moved toward the bed and he removed the rest of his clothes. She lay between the covers watching as he finished disrobing. His unclad torso seemed larger than when clothed and his equipment, at this stage, was impressive. She turned the dial on the rheostat on her night table and the room lights dimmed to a peach-hued softness.

In bed together, Mark approached Karen as though he were about to perform the most important role of his career. With tender passion he began the love-play intended to bring her to a state of unbearable stimulation, then drive her into a frantic, rewarding third act curtain. The part called for a certain amount of genteel restraint at the start, taking his cues from her reaction to his ministrations, then. . . .

But inexplicably, the expected reaction was not forthcoming, and he wondered if he had in some way managed to come up with that phenomenon of phenomenons—the unresponsive, frigid woman; perhaps that was the reason for her divorce? He sensed some withholding on Karen's part, then, finally, faint response; and with a valiant last effort, drove for the climax which, for Karen, did not come off. A total disaster. Karen lay back silently, reproachfully. No cheers, no applause, no curtain calls. He moved to take her into his arms, but she turned on her side away from him without a word.

"I'm sorry, Karen," he said. "I know it was bad, but we'll try again as soon . . ."

"I'd rather not, Mark," she replied. "Let's forget it."

"Please, Karen. You've been there before. You know there are times when . . ."

"Mark, just lie quietly, please."

The golden opportunity was slipping away fast. Mark got out of bed and began to dress quietly and she made no move to stop him. He went to Karen's side of the bed, leaned down over her and said, "I'm leaving, Karen."

"Goodnight, Mark. You can find your way out?"

"Sure. I'm sorry, Karen. I wanted it to work."

"It may have been my fault, Mark. Maybe another time."

Another time. Hope. He touched his lips to her forehead.

"Next time," he said.

In his own room he puzzled over the mystery of his failure with the one woman who meant more to him than all others before her, the woman with whom success could have meant so much.

Class barrier he wondered? The princess and the goatherd? Bullshit. The inhibiting hangup, whatever it was, was hers he was sure, and not his; but the need to overcome it must remain his. Next time.

And there was a next time. It came on the night before the cast left for the Boston tryout. This time, after the first awkward stage, Mark was certain it was going well. He began pacing himself carefully, alert to any sign of response from Karen and, just as he thought she had reached her peak, she stopped moving beneath him and lay inert.

"Karen?"

"I can't, Mark. You go on."

"Oh, Jesus, Karen . . ."

"Go on. Finish, and get it over with."

That did it. He felt himself go limp and withdrew. "Karen," he said, "you've got one hangup you've never told me about. This."

"Maybe."

"No *maybe* about it. You were ready. I could feel it. Then—nothing."

"All right, let's say it's not your fault and I'll take the blame. Something happens to me when we do it this way."

"What do you mean, *this* way?"

"There are other ways, you know."

"You mean. . . . For Christ's sake, Karen, I'm no queer."

"That's nonsense. Husbands and wives practice it all the time. When two people enjoy doing the same thing together, there's no harm or shame in it."

"How do you know so much about it?"

"Mark, I'm not a child. I've read a lot on the subject, and I've known couples who practice it. It works."

"Karen?"

"Do it for me, Mark."

It was up to Mark and he accepted the new role. Awkward at first, he improved slowly, then performed flawlessly, pacing himself, stroking more forcefully as he became aware of Karen's intense satisfaction, guiding him with both hands, elegant legs flung over his shoulders, locked around his head, driving herself upward to meet his accelerated thrusts. And, finally, falling back in exhaustion as climax overtook her.

Mark needed no reviews to tell him his performance had been superbly received.

But what was more surprising to him was that sometime during the night she awoke and stirred restlessly against him. He cradled her in his arms, kissed her, and felt her response. He said, "More?"

"Yes. More." And when he began to move lower down on her body, "Not that way, Mark. Let's try it the normal way."

This time, everything worked as he had thought it would the very first time and, thoroughly lost in postcoital exhaustion, Karen slept in his arms.

He realized then that what she had put him through had been a test; that she had deliberately withheld herself from climax in order to prove her certain superiority over him. On her terms, his to accept or reject. The humiliation he felt kept him awake until nearly dawn, when his anger reached its height. He dressed and slipped out of the house, went to his Village room and packed for the trip to Boston.

6

Love Bind never reached Broadway. It opened in Boston to negative reviews and Producer Riggs, Director Washburn, and Author Everett labored heroically to correct its deficiencies. Philadelphia was the next stop, where it was met with icy disdain. In Washington one week later, the *Post* critic dismissed it briefly with a suggestion that the producer apply for government assistance as a disaster. In mid-week, Riggs folded the show.

In a fit of understandable dejection, Mark returned to New York with the rest of the humbled cast. Leigh Page decided to give up the ghost and return to Buffalo to marry a real-estate dealer she had left three years before to make it on Broadway. Warren Best's agent had an "iffy" offer for him to audition for a small role in a television pilot. Ann Lucas planned to take two weeks off before making the rounds again. Harry Collier played gin rummy with Jerry Burke and spoke of no plans at all. The others merely stared out of their windows in silence.

Mark's agent, John Dietrich, had nothing on tap. It was a bad season. The critics were merciless, howling bastards. Ticket prices were rising, audiences weren't responsive, shows were folding like umbrellas after a shower, and backers were timid. "I hear Aaron is talking to Alex Kirov," Dietrich said. "Some kind of a co-production deal, but I can't get to Aaron at this point. It's all supposed to be very hush-hush."

"Nothing on Broadway is hush-hush," Mark said. "Aaron hasn't said one damned thing about another show."

"Why don't you go around and sound him out? Kirov's got a couple of things on ice, but he needs a front man like Aaron to get him off the ground. Backers."

"Oh, shit, John, Aaron's fresh out of backers after this bomb and if he's as tight-lipped as you say, he won't tell me anything."

"Well, that's about all I can tell you. If I hear anything, I'll call you."

Don't call me, I'll call you. It was three-thirty and Mark had nothing to look forward to but his depressing room. He made several phone calls, none of which gave him the barest hope and, in desperation, phoned Karen. She was home and invited him to come around to tell her of the formal death of *Love Bind.*

He learned that Karen, as an investor, could salvage something from the débris that lay scattered between Boston, Philadelphia and Washington by writing off her twenty thousand dollar investment as a tax loss. The information did little to comfort Mark or diminish his personal loss in terms of time and waste of effort.

"What next?" Karen asked.

"I don't know. I went around to see Dietrich this afternoon. All I got from him was a complete rundown on how many shows have opened and closed in less time than this dog. That, coming from an agent, is what's known as total understanding and compassion."

"Nothing else in sight?"

"After that cold shower, I called the sales manager at Bennington Press and got some equally good news. Business is down and they've had to let several salesmen go. I'm behind in my rent by a month, I've got one hundred and twelve dollars in the bank and three dollars and some odd change in my pocket. Also, a questionable gold *bar mitzvah* watch, three suits, a sports jacket, and three pairs of slacks. Will you marry me?"

Karen laughed impishly. "How can I possibly afford the luxury? With all your worldly goods, you'd throw me into a higher income tax bracket."

"Seriously."

"In your moribund condition, no."

"Okay." He stood up. "If you want to get in touch with me, leave word at the Skid Row branch of the Salvation Army."

"Sit down. We'll work something out."

"For instance?"

She studied him for a few moments, then said, "I want you to take a trip with me this weekend."

"Where to?"

"Wyecliffe."

"New Jersey? Aren't the Indians still taking scalps out there?"

"Stop clowning. I want you to meet my uncle and aunt."

"Oh? To pass a physical?"

"I want them to get to know you. They live a very quiet and respectable life and I don't want to startle them with any wild tales about show business, all right? You're a nice Jewish boy who works for a printing firm. Do you think you can play the part?"

"Of course, but why?"

"Because I want you to."

"Good enough. Because you want me to. Yes, ma'am."

"And you'll play it straight, no ad libs, no departures from the script."

Karen phoned Anna on Friday afternoon and after their normal exchange of greetings and inquiry into matters of health and well being, Karen said, "Would you like some company this weekend?"

As always, Anna's response to that question was immediate and affirmative. "So you feel you need to ask? Of course, darling, anytime."

"I'll be bringing a guest."

It was the first time Karen had suggested bringing someone with her since she had been living in Manhattan and Anna at once made a sharp guess, but kept it to herself. "This is still your home, darling. Bring anyone you want."

"This is a man I met a few months ago, Aunt Anna. I want you and Uncle Herschel to like him."

"If he's your choice, Karen, I'm sure we will. Come early."

"See you tomorrow."

There were questions in Anna's and Herschel's minds that neither wanted to ask of each other. Divorced seven months, and a new man for whom Karen was asking approval. A considerable departure from her usual need for privacy. "Well," Herschel said after a while, "what do you think?"

"Who can tell until we see him?"

"So?"

"So we'll wait and see and talk with him and we won't ask any questions that will annoy Karen."

"I'm worried."

"Like a father, like a mother, we're both worried. What could be more natural?"

"Ah-h-h . . ."

Within an hour of their arrival, Mark seemed to have won them over with a commendable performance of modesty, shyness, and good manners. He was duly impressed with the grandeur of the New Jersey countryside, made proper comments of appreciation toward the Goodwin home, grounds, stables, pool, and guest cottage, and displayed a keen interest in the original McComb house with some knowledge of that historical era, having been previously coached by Karen.

Anna's and Herschel's joy at entertaining Karen and "her young man" made the simple occasion into a family affair, and Karen indulged her aunt and uncle by playing out her chosen role. Herschel, genial, but with natural caution, took Mark for a walk through the gardens after dinner and subjected him to mild, subtle questioning that touched on Mark's family background, occupation, interests, and, indirectly, his prospects. Throughout the ordeal, Mark displayed a remarkable sense of dignity and aplomb and when they left on Sunday afternoon following lunch, felt that the reviews would be more than satisfactory, a fact that was corroborated by Karen.

"I'm really astonished, " she said. "I hadn't realized how talented an actor you actually are."

"Baby, if we'd had this script on the road instead of *Love Bind*, we'd have racked up every award in the book."

"Don't let it go to your head, you ham. I just hope you didn't overplay it with Uncle Herschel out in the garden."

"Forget it. He was my best audience. I was more worried about your aunt. Why didn't you tell me he was the Goodwin who owns Goody Food Products?"

Karen smiled. "I make it a habit never to overplay a part, either."

"I think you did this time."

"How so?"

"Come off it, Karen. I'm way out of my league. I don't fit into this kind of action."

"You could if you'd apply yourself."

For the first time, Mark realized that their affair, small as it was, the weekend trip, the present conversation, was developing into a viable situation. "Okay, Karen, let's have it in the clear, shall we?"

"All right. We each have something the other wants. How much, to what extent, who knows? I've already made one very big mistake and I don't want another. You've asked me to marry you. I haven't quite made up my mind either way, but one thing I must insist on. It will be with the approval of my aunt and uncle, or not at all. I've hurt them once and I won't let that happen again."

"Why? Do they control your money?"

"Yes, but only because I want it that way, where it's a lot safer than in my hands."

"Okay, so what comes next?"

"A few more visits to Wyecliffe, a certain amount of tact on your part, and we can both have what we want."

"Go on. You're beginning to get to me. I know you've got some terms in mind."

"Conditions. First, you'll have to stop chasing after a Broadway career. Second, I'll see to it that you're offered a well-paying job at GFP that will give you some direction in the business world."

"I'm more interested in you and me."

"We'll do well together, Mark, but it won't work if we don't help it. Third, we will sign a prenuptial agreement that in no case can what I now own ever be considered community property or joint ownership. Uncle Herschel will insist on that, as he did with my first husband."

For the next few minutes, Mark kept his hands firmly on the wheel of Karen's car, eyes on the road. He said finally, "In short, I'll become an employee of both Herschel Goodwin and Karen Goodwin Roth, is that it?"

"Not exactly. You'll become an employee of GFP and the husband of Karen Goodwin Roth."

"On your terms."

"On conditions I have outlined as openly as I know how. The rest is up to you, Mark."

There was another long silence before Mark said, "Goddamn it, I don't know if I understand it, or you, but it's crazy enough to interest me into buying it."

"You're not buying anything, Mark, only accepting."

"And you're serious about this?"

"To use a business term, it's a firm offer."

"Okay. Do we just shake hands, sign a contract, or seal it with a kiss?"

She smiled and said, "As soon as we get home, we'll make it properly official."

There were more visits to Wyecliffe and several from Herschel and Anna to New York before Karen was sure Mark had won their approval. At Karen's request, Herschel had Russell Charles prepare the prenuptial agreement which Mark signed in Charles's office. The forthcoming event was formally announced in the Wyecliffe *Register*. Four weeks later, Karen and Mark were married in a quiet ceremony that took place in Rabbi Kinsman's study with only Anna, Herschel, Mrs. Kinsman, and a handful of the Goodwins' Wyecliffe friends present. After a luncheon celebration at Heritage House, Karen and Mark drove to New York, then caught a plane to Paris to begin a month-long honeymoon.

Herschel, who had given Mark one thousand shares of GFP stock for a wedding gift, began to think of some position into which a former printing salesman could fit without creating disruption in the organization. On Monday morning, he made one of his infrequent trips to the Forty-second Street offices and sent for Reed Steinhorst, his vice-president in overall charge of Purchasing, who had been with the firm for over twenty years.

With an organizational chart of that vital division spread out before him, Herschel studied the subdepartment that purchased all of GFP's printed material; the millions of colorful packages, coupon inserts, shipping cartons, endless record forms, letterheads, envelopes, magazine reprints, brochures, display material, recipe books, annual reports, all the way down to individual memorandum pads. In all, a vast expenditure in the annual budget.

"We could," Steinhorst suggested diplomatically, "make room for him in Plant Equipment or—something more important—like . . ."

"No," Herschel said, "we will put him where he will be comfortable. He knows printing better than construction, engineering, or equipment, better than flour, sugar, chocolate—tell me, who is in charge of buying our printing?"

"A very bright young man, Ken Muir. In fact, he was Julian Roth's classmate at Princeton. Julian brought him in to us."

"Any problems?"

"None at all. I can promote him into—let's see—here, fork lift and towmotor equipment, buying and maintenance. That will leave Mark with an open field and a good assistant, a well-trained staff . . ."

"Good. Keep Mr. Muir on the job until Mark can take over from him. How much does the job pay?"

"Eleven thousand. I'll have to give Muir a slight raise when I move him up to Mr. Douglas's department."

"So. We will pay Mark eighteen thousand. Eleven thousand from Purchasing and seven thousand from—ah—Advertising, eh?"

"Yes, sir. I'll find a way to work out the payroll problem with Mr. Fitzjohn, but Mr. Roth won't like the idea of paying out seven thousand from his advertising department."

"Leave Mr. Roth to me, and I'll mention the other thing to Mr. Fitzjohn. Get started now so everything will be ready by the time Mark and Karen get back."

"Yes, sir. I'll talk with Ken Muir this afternoon, then have Mr. Douglas in. And I'll see Mr. Fitzjohn first thing in the morning."

7

Upon their return, Mark's job was waiting for him. Under Ken Muir's tutelage, Mark began to study GFP's purchasing policies, procedures for preparing specifications, receiving bids, awarding contracts, methods of checking delivery receipts for shipments of printed matter to various plants and the Forty-second Street offices, and payment of invoices, which he must first approve.

Mark was quick to learn despite the curious attitude of Ken Muir who, for some unfathomable reason, had taken an immediate dislike to Mark. Mark was also aware that much of the burdensome detail of the department passed through the hands of Muir's capable assistant, Valerie Harris, who looked to be about fifty, was widowed, and had a daughter in her first year at NYU. Mrs. Harris had been on the job for twelve years.

He had also been warned by Mr. Steinhorst that Mrs. Harris might prove somewhat hostile toward a new, inexperienced sub-division head, and on the day when Ken Muir moved over into his job, Mark called Mrs. Harris in for a general discussion of the department's procedures. She entered his office with a decided chip on her somewhat sagging shoulder, and left an hour later with a beaming smile on her face.

By pre-arrangement with Mr. Steinhorst, Mark authorized an annual raise of six hundred dollars for Valerie Harris, an additional week's vacation with pay and, in a masterful bit of strategy, suggested he would have her open working area enclosed as a private office, out of sight and hearing of the rest of the clerical staff. Later on, he heightened Mrs. Harris's prestige by permitting her to handle certain small contracts entirely on her own, and frequently consulted with her before finalizing decisions he had already made.

Within a remarkably short period, every person on the staff would have agreed that Mrs. Harris was in Mark Lawson's hip pocket.

At home, Mark was ardent and thoughtful. He played the game by the rules Karen had established without complaint. Karen was permitted to sleep in every morning, with Mark required to get up, dress without disturbing her, have his breakfast alone, and be driven to his office by Max. When Karen worked in her studio Mark must not interrupt her. If she decided to drive to Wyecliffe to visit Anna, she might or might not ask him to accompany her.

But these were exceptional incidents. They were entertained by, and in turn entertained friends at small parties at home or at a restaurant. They attended plays, visited night spots, played bridge and spent occasional weekends at the shore or in the mountains. When Mark first told Karen of Mrs. Harris's resentment toward him, she was pleased by his clever handling of the situation and told him so. When he remarked at Ken Muir's hostility, she said, "Leave Ken alone, Mark."

"You know him?"

"I've met him several times. He was one of Julian's closest friends and Julian didn't have many of those."

"By the way, where is Julian now?"

"You don't know? He's at the GFP plant in Canton, Ohio."

"And his old man is still advertising director?"

"His *father*," she said, stressing the word, "is a very capable employee, Mark, and an old friend of my uncle's family. Don't get involved in something that doesn't concern you. You won't win."

Mark recognized the warning tone and let the subject die.

But Sid Roth, the word filtered down to Mark, had complained bitterly about carrying seven thousand dollars worth of deadwood—that share of Mark's salary being charged to his department—during a staff meeting. With a sharp reminder from Curtis Fitzjohn, GFP's comptroller, that the decision had been Herschel Goodwin's, Roth cut short his objection; but from that day, neither man communicated with the other except indirectly. Sid became the first real enemy Mark had encountered.

Mark's salary of eighteen thousand dollars was a more than reasonable figure, he considered, since it was the greatest amount of money ever paid him for services rendered, and because he was not required or expected to contribute a penny toward the expense or upkeep of the household. With ample funds of his own, he sought ways to please Karen with occasional and unexpected gifts, but soon learned that it was impossible to titillate a woman who literally had everything; except, perhaps, rare jewels, furs, or paintings that were beyond his reach.

As time passed, however, Mark began to feel the pressures of his live-by-the-rules agreement. Max and Gerda's attitude toward him was redolent of the practiced tolerance one would show a guest who had overstayed his leave, an outsider, not a member of the household. They carried out his requests silently, and with Swiss correctness, but with little show of warmth, and only when his orders did not come in conflict with Karen's.

Certain patterns of conduct that emerged after a while began to annoy, and later infuriate him. Having breakfast alone was the least of numerous irritations. Karen's lack of interest in his work, the discipline of having to be at his desk by nine o'clock every working morning while Karen lay abed, gnawed at him like an open wound. Soon, Mark was forcing himself to interpret Karen's inexplicable moods before even attempting to engage her in conversation. There were times when, in the middle of a story he was relating, she would suddenly yawn or leave the room in boredom. Often, when he would enter a room while she was in the midst of a telephone call, she would end it abruptly with, "I've got to hang up now. I'll call you tomorrow."

And there were those times when, without explanation, Karen would take to her third floor studio for several days at a time, sleeping there, having Gerda bring her meals to her, denying him admission, refusing to answer the house phone. Then, suddenly, she would reappear in the role of warm, loving wife. At other times, she would simply disappear for a day or two, a weekend, leaving word that she was visiting an old schoolfriend, seldom letting him know where. On her return, she gave only vague (or no) explanations and Mark understood he was expected not to ask questions beyond a casual, "Have a good time?"

Mark began circulating among old show world friends, infrequently spending a night or two away from home. When he discovered that Karen did not appear to notice, he was certain that she was as serious now as she had been at the very start about equal freedoms: a fact he had not been able to fully accept as true before. The frequency of his nights out increased, but he could not help being bothered by Karen's own "freedom trips." As he had said earlier to her, *For a Jewish boy who was raised on the lower East Side, it takes a bit of getting used to.*

In their eighth month together, Mark invited David Groley, a young London producer he had met at a party, to their home for dinner. Groley had had three fairly successful shows in London, then came to Hollywood to produce and direct his first feature picture. Before long, he ran into a brick wall of studio restrictions, financial backers, union regulations, and the demands of his sulky female and male stars. In its final stages, he learned to his dismay that he would have neither voice nor part in the editing phase of the picture. The completed film bombed out and was hooted by the critics before it got out of the preview stage. Whereupon, David Groley took his money and decided to lick his wounds in New York, hoping for a try at the Broadway stage.

Groley was an intense man of thirty-three, ruggedly built. With the exception of a few scars, honorably received, a nose that was masculine in a broken sort of way, and a refreshingly vulgar manner of describing Hollywood, he met a receptive audience among New York show people. His first experience had come, ironically, after four years as a photographer with the British Air Force, ending when his plane crashed during the filming of carrier-aircraft maneuvers off Malta. Contacts made during that early period of his life, plus the publicity of his unfortunate crash and subsequent recovery, brought him to the theater where, after serving as an assistant director for two years, and marriage to Celia Wentworth—a prominent British actress whose father was a member of the peerage—David rose to full director status. He got off with a near hit, followed that with a modest success that was backed by Celia, became involved with the daughter of a wealthy beer magnate—also married—and went through a highly publicized divorce. The woman in the case backed his third play that achieved some success. It was still running in London when she was divorced by her husband, who named David as corespondent. David, realizing now that her intentions were definitely serious toward him, fled London for the United States.

Karen was fascinated by David from the very start, even more so when she discovered he had not come to New York empty-handed. He brought with him an original play he had high hopes for on Broadway and was encouraged by both Karen and Mark, who were receptive to his script. A week later, David received Karen's assurance of her financial support. Within a month, she had it from the Bassetts, Koppels, Lubins, and others who had backed *Penny For Your Thoughts,* with Karen putting up an initial thirty thousand dollars as her share.

The play, *Come Fly With Me*, was concerned with the romantic life of a famous flyer whose career is wrecked when he becomes involved with the young wife of a wealthy middle-aged member of the Royal Household. In many respects it was autobiographical, which—when its plot was partially made known to the theatrical press—created considerable stir and anticipation, since Groley's divorce had received wide attention and press notoriety on both sides of the Atlantic.

Karen became deeply involved with production plans, casting, set designs, and virtually every phase of putting the show together. And, along the way, with David Groley. Tryouts were crowded with aspirants and the *coup* of the season was the acquisition of Paul Calder, fresh from the Broadway triumph, *A Time to Live*. Tami Roberts was signed to co-star as the royal adultress, and rehearsals, under David's sure, firm hand, ripened and matured into the final stages. The first preview showing was scheduled for Boston.

Mark, once the show got under way, found himself relegated to the oblivion of onlooker. With the demands of his job pressing upon him, he missed the familiar activity to which he had given his first devotion and love. He dropped in on night rehearsals, only to remain an observer. Karen, next to David Groley, held the reins tightly in her own hands, acting as co-producer.

In September, the company moved to Boston, and Karen with it. By now, there was little doubt in Mark's mind that Karen and David were having an affair, and by the time the first favorable reviews reached New York, it was common knowledge among the cast. Before the week was over, there were hints in at least two gossip columns, names excluded, and Mark received both columns which had been clipped to a more explicit anonymous note penned in a feminine script on stationery from the hotel where the cast had been staying.

Karen returned to New York that Saturday, but Mark was out that evening on an adventure of his own. Karen replenished her wardrobe and took off at once for Baltimore and the second opening on Monday. After an even more impressive reception there, the show opened in Washington and, thoroughly satisfied with the response in those three cities, David Groley brought *Come Fly With Me* to New York for its grand opening at the Morosco on West Forty-fifth Street.

Karen never looked better or more alive in her life. On the morning following the opening, after the post-theater celebration at Sardi's where they waited for the reviews to appear, and the absolutely wild hysteria of a fresh hit on their hands, Mark did not go to his office. At noon, when Karen rang for her orange juice and coffee, he intercepted

Gerda on her way to the stairs, took the tray from her and brought it to Karen's room.

"Well, Mark," she greeted him with a smile of triumph, "it looks like we're in for a long run. Did you enjoy last night?"

"Considering the fact that I have no part in it, financially or otherwise, and that you were practically welded to David, no."

Sipping orange juice, looking upward at him speculatively, "Do I detect a note of jealousy?"

Mark fumed silently. Karen said, "Don't be difficult, Mark. It's been a busy, tiring time for all of us and I'm honestly glad to be home and in my own bed again."

"And not David's?"

She shot a quick glance at him, eyes flashing angrily, "Mark, I wouldn't start that kind of talk if I were you."

"Why not? Why can't I talk about it? Eeverybody else is."

"What everybody else says or thinks doesn't bother me in the least."

"Or what I think?"

"I can't help what you think, Mark, and I don't want to talk about it."

"I shouldn't think you'd want to, but tell me one thing, if only to satisfy my curiosity. Were you screwing David?"

She put the juice glass down and picked up the coffee cup with a steady hand, not in the least disturbed by the question. "Well," he snarled, "were you?"

"If I said *yes*, what then?"

Mark took some malicious satisfaction in what he took to be a sure admission. "How was it?" he asked.

She said calmly, "I enjoyed every minute of it. In Boston, Baltimore *and* Washington." Her look said, *Now make something of* THAT!

"And now that you're back in New York, are you planning more of the same in your own bed?"

"That depends . . ."

"Or are we supposed to pick up where we left off before you went to Boston?"

". . . on what your plans are," Karen concluded.

There it was. To give up Karen meant giving up job, home, and the new luxury to which he had quickly become accustomed. To continue as they had, sharing her with David Groley and whoever-the-hell else she had had before, or who would follow David, was left for himself to decide. He weighed the one against the other for a moment, then said, "All right, let's play it your way for a while longer, with your goddamned fucking rules."

When she did not answer, he turned and left the room, mind and body heavy with defeat. More frequently than before, more openly, he engaged in a series of affairs with a recklessness that defied logic or reason, even reaching into the cast of *Come Fly With Me* to add the second lead, Kitty Ames, to his list of questionable conquests, knowing that word must surely reach Karen. It was small consolation for Mark.

On a wintry January day, with the show running strongly in its fourth month, an early morning snowfall turned into a veritable blizzard by mid-morning. At noon, after a call from Personnel, Mark dismissed his own staff before traffic would become totally paralyzed. Mrs. Harris brought him the completed specifications for the forty-eight page Annual Report which had been designed by the agency and photo-copied so that various bidders would have copies to use in computing their bids.

When she gave the rough specs to Mark and went back to her office, Mark placed them on his desk, then walked to the window looked down on Forty-second Street for a while. Mrs. Harris, bundled in a heavy outercoat, scarf over her head, galoshes over her shoes, returned to say good-bye and hoped he would have no difficulty getting home. Mark sent her on her way with a smile, then dialed his home number. Max told him Karen had phoned about an hour earlier to say she would probably not be able to get home and would be spending the night with a friend.

"Did she say with whom?" Mark asked. "Or where?"

"I'm sorry. She did not say," Max replied in clipped words. "Only that she would not be able to get home in the storm. You will be home for dinner, sir?"

"I don't know." He hung up, cutting Max off shortly.

Bitch, he ground out in silent anger. How in hell does a man adjust to a marriage with a crazy bitch in heat who can't be satisfied with one man. Well, he told himself placatingly, it isn't as though you didn't know. She spelled it out for you in the clear, and you bought it.

He walked down the long hallway to the other end of the building where he found Reed Steinhorst alone at his desk, sifting through some papers. He knew Steinhorst lived out on Long Island with his wife and four children.

"I thought you'd be gone by now, Reed," Mark said.

Steinhorst looked up with a smile. "In weather like this, I don't even try to get home. I've got too much work here to catch up with and I've made a reservation at the Westbury. I'm in no mood to fight the Long Island Railroad in this weather."

He offered Mark a cup of coffee and the two talked for a few minutes before Steinhorst said, "What about the Annual Report? Are you anywhere near ready to let it out? We're getting pretty close to deadline, aren't we?"

"I just got the specs from Mrs. Harris this morning. They're on my desk now, ready to go."

"Fine. Well . . ."

Mark took the hint and got up, went back to his office and stared at the report. He checked over the specifications lightly and tried to arrive at some rough estimate of its final cost. And having come to a loose, vague figure, he decided to call Pete Channing at Bennington Press.

When Pete answered, Mark said, "I took a gamble I'd find you in today, Pete. How's the snow out on the Island?"

"Man, just take a look outside, wherever you are. It's ass-high to a nine-foot Indian out here. We may have to sleep in the plant tonight. Hey! Long time no hear, no see, Mark. You lock into something somewhere?"

"Sure thing, Pete. A long run this time."

"*Mazeltov*. What is it, and how about a few free tickets?"

"Man, get with it. Don't you keep up with the news? I'm an old married man."

"You're kidding. How long?"

"Almost forever. Would you believe over a year?"

Pete groaned. "Has it been that long since I've seen you? Don't tell me you're out job-hunting, Mark. We're so damned tight right now I couldn't put my own brother-in-law on."

"Forget it. This time I've got something for you. You want to hear about it?"

"If it'll help lift the sales curve even a little notch, yes."

"What I've got in mind could lift the scalp right off your head. Can you get in for lunch tomorrow?"

"Not tomorrow. I've got to spend the day out here shaking up the salesmen, if you can call them that. How about one day next week, if it will hold?"

"Okay. If you think a few hundred thousand bucks or so is worth holding, it'll hold."

"What the hell are you talking about, Mark? You strung out on Mexican alfalfa?"

"Pete, I'm sitting on top of a hell of a good thing, if you're interested."

"Name the place and time and I'll be there if I have to come in on snowshoes. I'll even pick up the check. Where?"

"How about Bouchard's on East Fifty-seventh. You know?"

"I know, I know. One o'clock?"

"One o'clock, and bring your credit cards, you bastard."

"I'll have to ease you into the picture, Pete," Mark said over lunch. "There are five or six outfits who've been getting fat on this account for a long time, but every time this job changes hands, a new printer isn't too hard to slip in. If we can work out some arrangement between us, you're next on the list."

"Come on, come on, Mark. I can work out anything if it means business. Tell me more."

"It's big stuff, the packaging division alone. You think you can handle it?"

"Can we? Christ Almighty, we've got presses dying of starvation, just waiting for something like this."

"Okay. I'm in the catbird seat and I've got this assistant who'll roll over and play dead for me, but you'll have to grease her quietly after you're in. I'll start you off with this Annual Report and feed you some of the smaller stuff, forms, letterheads, some ad reprints and so forth, until you're established as a supplier. Then, after a while . . ."

"Where does the agency fit into this?"

"That's the beauty of it. Nowhere. They do the design layout, art, and pasteups, then turn the camera-ready material over to the printer we select. I hand out the contracts on competitive bidding. I also open the bids and make the decisions. You hold on to yours until I can give you the bottom figure, which you underbid by a few . . ."

"Oh, for Christ's sake, Mark, are you going to teach me how to suck eggs?"

Mark laughed. "Okay. If anybody knows the tricks of the trade, you should."

"The big question. What's your cut?"

"A straight fifteen percent off the top."

"You're too far out, old buddy. There isn't enough of a spread for a fifteen percent kickback."

"Bullshit, old buddy. Now who's trying to teach who to suck eggs? With quantities running into the multimillions, you're telling me you don't know how to handle short runs, to shortship a customer? Particularly when you're shipping to four out-of-state plants, and with me inside to cover for you? Come on, Pete, this is Mark you're talking to."

"Well, let's see how it works out, but don't hold me to that fifteen override. Ten would be more like it, and I'd be stretching it a few points at that."

"Fiteen, Pete. What the hell, with printers handing out color television sets, gift certificates, cases of liquor, and other fringe stuff, you're not kidding me one bit. What's more, with Valerie Harris eating out of my hand, you'll be safer than a nun in a convent."

Pete sipped his beer thoughtfully for a moment. "Okay, Mark, it's a deal. Fifteen percent. I'm sure we can work it out. When do we start?'

"We've already started." He opened the slim leather envelope he had brought along and took out the forty-eight page layout and specifications for the company's annual report. "This is a photocopy of the job, black and white, with the colors indicated on tissue overlays. Get your bid set and hold it until I tell you what price to fill in. When you've got it, drop it off to me so I can introduce you to Mrs. Harris. Once you're in, I'll have her call you in to bid on some of the other stuff until you're in line for the bigger jobs when the contracts come up. You can take it from there."

It took over a year of careful handling before Bennington Press became one of the major suppliers of printing to GFP. If Valerie Harris had any suspicion that she was being used, or that Mark was the beneficiary of some outside financial reward for his friendship with Pete Channing, she said nothing. She had already received a color television set (delivered to her home), spent a three-week vacation on a cruise with her daughter at Bennington's expense, and was the recipient of small packages of perfume, and expensive lingerie and hose, none of which she reported to Mark.

With most of the work flowing through her desk, Mark soon became bored with his job and began looking around for something more promising and exciting. Eventually, he ran into Sid Roth's department and the thought of testing his strength against Karen's ex-father-in-law grew more and more tempting. It wouldn't be easy, he knew, but Mark had learned quickly how to rise to a given challenge, spurred on now by an earlier remark of Karen's, a warning not to meddle with Sid Roth. "You won't win," she had said then.

Sid Roth had now been on the job for almost fifteen years. At fifty-one, he was looking forward to at least another fourteen years before retirement; but when Herschel Goodwin called him to the New Jersey plant one day to discuss the matter of Mark Lawson becoming his assistant in Advertising, Sid began to see a fairly accurate facsimile of someone's handwriting on the wall. Mark's? Karen's? And yet, how could he say *no* to Herschel? Unhappily, he agreed to take Mark on.

Herschel, at least, was pleased with Mark's choice, having known from the start that he would one day be faced with the fact that Mark would outgrow his job in Purchasing, which was no permanent position for Karen's husband. In Advertising, with the Leary Agency to backstop him, the chance for a major error to occur was miniscule with a team of experts, and an entire agency staff, if necessary, to run interference for him. And there was, of course, Sid Roth.

Although Sid had given in with apparent graciousness, Mark soon began to realize that his new department head was doing his professional utmost to see that Herschel's relative-by-marriage, the man who had replaced Julian as Karen's husband, would learn as little as possible; which opened a quiet, yet earnest feud between them. Mark tread cautiously at first, playing a waiting game.

He had settled his problem with Valerie Harris by asking Steinhorst to promote her into his old job with a raise in salary, and status, once he was certain that Channing's contact was firm and would not be broken, thus collecting a handsome bonus in addition to his normal salary, now raised to twenty-five thousand dollars.

Mark planned his campaign against Sid so meticulously that within six months, Sid realized he was losing the battle. Gradually, yet determinedly, Mark had wooed the key members of the GFP advertising staff with lunches, dinners, and occasionally, tickets to popular shows.

He won over Bernie Jacobson, whom he had displaced as Sid's knowledgeable assistant, by introducing him to a succession of young actresses, and romanced Sid's not very attractive secretary into submission. He handled the Leary Agency men with the finesse of a diplomat, using guile and flattery, agreeing with them each time Sid Roth disagreed.

Sid, hampered as he was by Mark's relationship to Herschel Goodwin, was finally needled into admitting that blood, even when transfused by marriage, was thicker than the waters of loyalty. At Dora Roth's suggestion he finally took the problem directly to Herschel, who tried his best to smooth Sid's ruffled feelings. He suggested separating sales promotion from advertising, with Sid in charge of that division; but Sid argued that this would reduce his effectiveness and only prolong the inevitable. It all came down to Sid and Mark.

In the end, Sid resigned with a generous bonus and a company party that would have done honor to a retiring United States Senator, complete with generous gifts and testimonials. Within a month, Sid accepted a position as assistant advertising director with Singleton Mills, which supplied much of GFP's flour, a job that Herschel had quietly promoted for him.

Mark, now unhampered, took over with rare zest. He had learned the routines of the department fairly well, with Bernie Jacobson to guide him, even though he lacked the creative talent, originality and initiative his job called for. More and more, he abdicated those prerogatives to the agency men, taking on the mantle of supreme critic. When Bernie Jacobson protested that the GFP staff were being reduced to mere spectators instead of activists, Mark fired him for insubordination. Sid's secretary and Bernie's resigned together on the same day. Mark called a meeting of his staff and let it be known in the clearest of terms that he was The Man In Charge. Two of the staff resigned on the spot. The others gave in quietly.

Mark held the assistant spot open and replaced the secretary and two recalcitrant men with outsiders and the new pattern was set. Slowly, he weeded out anyone whom he believed was still loyal to Sid Roth's memory and replaced them from outside the organization.

To those he felt were "on my team," he was generous in his praise. Others soon discovered that Mark was possessed of a dangerous combination of characteristics, to the point of paranoia. He was stubbornly independent and strongly determined to have his own way. Ideas submitted to him, with minor changes here or there, became his own. The Leary Agency specialists began to feel the give at the seams and it took all of their ingenuity to hold the account together. Mark became notorious for sudden outbursts of rage, and demands that were most unreasonable.

Soon, both Mr. Leary and Wade Barrett adopted another, and altogether revolutionary practice. When Cliff Sorensen, then the account executive on GFP, reported an impossible situation, either or both would take a quiet trip to the Harrison plant to "visit" with Herschel Goodwin. Within a few days, they found that Lawson's earlier reluctance to accept a particular presentation had diminished or evaporated completely. However, with each such visit to Herschel, the personal relationship between the Barrett-Sorensen team and Mark Lawson became a little more eroded.

From the agency's point of view, although it was seldom voiced openly, survival of the GFP account depended on Herschel Goodwin remaining in good health.

The change in Mark over the next two-year period was remarkable. Having tasted a certain power for the first time in his life, Mark felt the need, the urge, to use it. Yet there were dangers he was wise enough to recognize. His strength and power lay in his marriage to Karen. Without that, he would be back on the streets again, with no need for Pete Channing to maintain their present relationship. It was, indeed, Pete, who brought Bob Davies to Mark's attention, and Bob became Mark's assistant.

In April of 1959, when Wm. B. Leary died, his son, Wm. B. Leary, Jr. found himself in the unique position of heading an advertising agency that, until now, he had never taken seriously.

After graduating from Harvard in 1946, Bill, Jr. had spent two years abroad. The first year was a gift from his father, a promise made in Bill's sophomore year with the condition that he straighten out, bring his grades up to a respectable standard and, hopefully, receive his B.A. degree. The second year was taken against his father's express wishes, financed from a small fund inherited from his mother. On his eventual return to New York, Bill used the Leary Agency for little more than a mailing address, content with living at home to cut his expenses, spending most of his time enjoying life among friends whose hedonistic pleasures matched his own.

Came the day when Bill's private funds ran out and he was faced with an ultimatum: buckle down and take his rightful place in the agency, or go his own way. Bill's capitulation was total and immediate.

With more reluctance than enthusiasm he reported for work as any other new employee was required to do and received no special privileges or treatment. He checked in with Personnel, filled out the required application forms, was advised of his employee benefits, given a booklet of rules to study, and informed that he would receive a trainee's salary until he passed his probationary period six months hence.

Eventually, he was assigned to small writing tasks, but his skills in copywriting were considerably less than spectacular. He was moved into the administration section, for which he had a better feel and to which he devoted far more interest and attention. Having scored some measure of competence during his year in that department, he was assigned to Keith Allard, who instructed him in the duties of an account executive without portfolio. It was Allard who brought Bill, Jr. through his trying apprenticeship into full maturity in the agency he would one day inherit, a period that had run for eleven years when his father died. Whereupon, Bill dropped the "Jr." after his name and took over full command.

In addition to the agency, Bill inherited the Leary home, somewhat grand and ancient, which he put up for sale at once, moving into a modern apartment. He learned that his wise, conservative father had, over many years, invested in the stock of his client companies and thus had served on the boards of directors of half a dozen corporations. Wm. B. Leary's portfolio of stocks at the time of his death was worth between ten and twelve million dollars alone. At the reading of his will, Keith Allard became the owner of a fifteen percent interest in the agency, along with five thousand shares of GFP stock, "an interest Mr. Allard shared with me." On that day, GFP closed at forty-two and, apart from the value of his interest in the agency, which was Wm. Sr.'s way of insuring that Allard would be there to manage it, he was worth the respectable amount of $210,000.

Bill, Jr. was in his thirty-fifth year then, and seven

months later, he slipped away and married Donna Carpenter, an attractive girl of twenty-six, whom he had met during a party in Old Lyme, Connecticut, and who worked as a researcher for a New York weekly magazine. On their return from a lengthy honeymoon, Donna's first act was to find them a new home. She chose a cooperative duplex on Sixty-third Street, just east of Fifth Avenue. Her second act was to redecorate the office Bill had taken over from his father, a rather small, musty room crowded with memorabilia of a lifetime in advertising; books, clients' samples, framed reprints of ads, plaques, awards, autographed photographs, and membership certificates in many and various professional and charitable organizations, and silver cups won in earlier times for his prowess on the squash courts of the New York Athletic Club.

The wall between Bill's office and a small conference room was removed and the two rooms merged into one. Carpenters, plasterers, electricians, glaziers, and painters labored for weeks, after which the decorators were brought in. A new desk, cabinets, sofas, chairs, a bar, paintings, and sectional furniture converted the huge room into one in which any visitor could imagine himself in a private home. Recessed into one wall and hidden by paneling were high fidelity and stereo equipment, tape recorders, a color television, and a pull-down screen for viewing filmed commercials, all operated from the desk by an elaborate pushbutton system. Donna also had a voice in choosing a mature woman, Mrs. Lucille Kimbrough, as Bill's secretary.

To Bill, by right of direct inheritance, fell the responsibility of maintaining the GFP account, although Wade Barrett remained in charge as account executive. On Bill's first visit to the New Jersey plant he went alone, approaching the task of meeting Mr. Goodwin with considerable apprehension. Herschel Goodwin made him feel welcome and put him completely at ease at once.

"Ah, yes," Herschel said with sadness arising from his own memories, "it is as it should be, the son follows in the father's footsteps. A wonderful thing." Then, with a quick smile, "You know how much your father did to help us grow, he and Mr. Barrett and Mr. Allard, no? He came to see me when we were just beginning in one of the buildings you see here. Now there are nineteen buildings here for manufacture and storage alone, others for receiving, warehousing and shipping, aside from this office building.

And there are—I guess you know—the plants in Elgin, Syracuse and Canton. You have seen them?"

"No, sir, but I hope to."

"You will, you will. Some day I would like to put up a bigger building here and move everybody out of the Forty-second Street offices. The problem is to find houses for the people to live in and to replace those who wouldn't want to move from New York. I talked about this to your father *alov hasholem* many times, but. . . .

"A fine man, your father. A good friend and a real gentleman. Believe me, Mr. Leary, when he died, I mourned him like my own. Ah, the times we had then, when it was a struggle, your father, Mr. Barrett, and Mr. Allard, always with new ideas, thing I never heard of and still don't understand. Consumer psychology, motiv—motiv—"

"Motivational research," Bill offered.

"Yes. Yes." Herschel laughed. "Long before I heard of this motivation research—that's it?—my Anna knew that women would want ready-to-bake mixes for cakes, biscuits, pancakes, and cookies. She put Goody in the icing and topping business. After all, what is a cake without it? So, Mr. Leary, never tell me about consumer reaction or this motivation thing, whatever it is. My expert on such things lives with me in Wyecliffe."

He asked Bill a number of questions about how the agency was getting along and was evidently satisfied with the answers he received. Bill recognized in Herschel a man who saw himself trapped in a business without a son to succeed him, one whose place in the world of commerce and finance had gone far beyond expectations. He said diplomatically, "If you, from what you have learned in your many years of experience, were impelled to offer me some advice, Mr. Goodwin, what would you say to me?"

Herschel thought for a moment. "I would say, don't try to get too big too soon. Have sons who will work beside you and take charge when you feel the time has come to let go."

"I'll try to remember that," Bill said.

"Remember this, too, Mr. Leary. I am no longer a person, an individual. People look at me and see a corporation, but in my heart I am still the East Side baker nobody remembers. My brother Zalman, *alov hasholem*, and I sold a bakery-shop chain for $180,000. Today GFP spends maybe five times that much every month for advertising, almost nine million dollars a year, yes?"

"That's correct, sir," Bill acknowledged.

"And next year, more, yes?"

"According to the new budget projection, yes."

"So, Mr. Leary, if this is what you came to hear, go ahead and spend my money carefully, the way your father spent it, and we will get along tomorrow the same way we did yesterday. Give my regards to Mr. Barrett and Mr. Allard."

Bill left, feeling as though he were bringing his first major account into the agency.

Above all, he was determined that GFP would remain his primary responsibility.

BOOK THREE

Chapter 8

1

With the mail cleared away and the Work Progress Chart before him, Steve made several notations to check out with Chuck Baldasarian, then got out the California memoranda and began organizing his report for Bill Leary. At eleven-thirty he was ready to write the first rough draft but decided to allow it to cool until after lunch. He dialed Chuck's extension and asked him to come in.

"Chuck, what about this latest thirty-second commercial storyboard? The chart shows it was due this morning with production scheduled for Thursday or Friday. I don't see it checked off here."

Chuck grinned sourly. "A slight screwup I was saving until you were free. Back in December, somewhere around the fifteenth, Arnie Cook came down with a virus and we got jammed up in the art section. I asked Lex Kent to give me somebody from the bullpen to fill in, but he was all jammed up and drafted Lennie Hawkins from Bryce's department and he's been filling in on storyboards for us ever since. This last commercial was due and I put a rush on it. Lennie took it with him to do at home on Friday so we could have it for pre-production discussion this morning or tomorrow.

"He didn't show up this morning and then Eth Loomis called about an hour ago to tell us he'd brought Lennie home from Saint Vincent's hospital last night."

"Hospital? What's wrong with Lennie?" It was Peggy who asked the question.

"Seems like Lennie had finished everything but lettering in the audio late Saturday night and went out to get a bite to eat and a breath of air. On his way home, two of his soul brothers tried to mug him and . . ."

"How bad is it?" Steve asked.

"Suspicion of concussion, not too serious. Lennie knocked one of them out but the other guy slugged him from behind and took off. The cops picked up the one Lennie cut down and took both of them to Saint Vincent's, then called Eth. Last night Lennie refused to stay put, and Eth took him home."

"I'll be damned. Is he all right?"

"Aside from a splitting headache, Eth thinks he's okay. He wanted to take the storyboard with him, but Lennie insisted he could finish it."

Peggy said, "If tomorrow is all right, I can stop by on my way home this evening and see if it's ready. My place is only a short walk from there."

"Okay, Chuck?"

"Sure. That'll give us enough time to kick it around and if we can get set on it, Bryce can start shooting on Thursday. Friday at the latest."

"You don't mind, Peggy?" Steve said.

"No, of course not. I'll be glad to do it."

"Okay. Give Lennie my best and find out if there's anything we can do for him."

During the next few minutes, Steve stared at his work chart, concentrating on the most recent changes that concerned the spring-into-summer campaign. Most of the items he had initiated before leaving for California had been completed and scratched through, replaced by others totally unfamiliar to him, and for a moment he felt a sudden absence of control; as though the direction had been taken from his hands.

It was noon. He felt wearied by his first full morning back in harness and decided to regenerate his flagging spirits with lunch at Emil's, known loosely as the Third Avenue Ad Club because it catered to many of the advertising, newspaper, and magazine men and women in the area. Dressed warmly against the biting cold, he walked briskly to Third Avenue, then half a block north to Emil's.

At 12:20 the bar was packed three deep, the air crackling with loud voices and shrill explosions of goodnatured laughter and banter. Steve handed over his hat and coat to Bobbie, the hatcheck girl, glanced toward the crowded bar, and decided against it. He went directly to the entrance to the dining room. He smiled and nodded to Wilma over the heads of a knot of men and women waiting to be seated. Wilma, guarding the grilled doorway, arms cradling a dozen leather-covered menus that were limp from overuse, signaled him forward. "Glad to see you back, Mr. Gilman Are you alone?"

"Yes, Wilma."

"There's room at the Leary table. Mr. Kent and Mr. Baker left a few minutes ago. Mr. Bryce and Mr. Adrian are still there." She craned her head around a group of four who blocked her view. "Mrs. Berton and Mr. Hayden and that new young what's-his-name—"

"That's fine, Wilma. I see them."

He glided through the narrow aisle that parted for him and entered the noisy room, taking and returning greetings from several regulars, most of them from nearby agencies. Midway down the center aisle, he turned right, squeezed past two tray-laden waiters and a bus boy to the large round table in a booth next to the wall. Larry Holman, the new what's-his-name from Don Bryce's Television-Radio department, saw him approaching and needlessly raised an arm to guide him. Norm Adrian squirmed over to make room for Steve on the leather settee.

"Hi, clansmen," he greeted, as he slid into his seat.

They all responded variously. Frank Hayden grinned and said nothing. Bryce said, "Have you seen or talked to your buddy Lawson yet?"

"No, why? Has Mark been pushing the panic button?"

Bryce's reply was a low snarl. "That bastard. All of a sudden he's bugging me. He and that flake of his, Davies."

Elizabeth Berton, Leary's media director, looked up from her dessert and said, "I thought we had a gentlemen's agreement not to discuss business at lunch. My analyst tells me . . ."

Bryce snorted. "Tell your analyst that my analyst tells me it's very healthy to divest oneself of one's aggressiveness at any time, any place, at lunch, in the shower, on the john, or in bed." As Adrian grinned broadly, Bryce turned back to Steve. "What the hell is Lawson up to, anyway?"

"How in hell would I know if you don't tell me?"

Bryce glared. "First of all, the sonofabitch gave me a long telephone lecture on programming last week, then turned your legman, Baldasarian, loose on me, then Parris, then his ape, Davies, complaining about our spots on the Wally Greer Show. Not about the spots, but the show itself. Now I know, and you know, that Greer is no daytime Johnny Carson or Merv Griffin, but . . ."

"Don't say I didn't warn you, Don. I told you from the

start that Lawson is strictly a movie lover and hates comedy or talk shows. Give him Any Night at the Movies and your problems are solved."

"In *daytime*, for Christ's sake?"

"They do run movies in the daytime, don't they?"

"Man, all our daytime scheduling is divided between game shows and soap operas."

"Take it easy, Don. I'll talk to him about it."

But Bryce couldn't let it rest. "Knocking Wally Greer's variety show is like knocking the space program, Medicare, and Motherhood. Doesn't that jerk know that Greer's Neilson is a good four points up?"

Norm Adrian said, "Does any client honestly care about Neilson, ARB, Trendex or any other of those phony polls, Don? All he knows is what *he* likes, what his wife and kids watch. That's where he wants his money spent."

Bryce ignored him. Liz reached over and took one of Adrian's Chevaliers and Larry Holman alertly lighted it for her. Bryce said, "I went to a hell of a lot of trouble to get participation on one of the hottest daytime network shows and now, four weeks later, that dingaling wants to cancel."

"Forget it, Don," Steve said. "Lawson knows he committed for at least nine more weeks." With a nod toward Adrian, "At the end of thirteen, maybe you can get McCreery to peddle it to Chevalier."

Adrian's laugh was a minor explosion. "Over his dead body." A pause, then, "Hey, that's not such a bad idea."

No one amplified that remark. Adrian's problems with McCreery were something in which few at the agency wanted participation. A waiter broke the momentary silence, appearing with a goblet of water, silverware, and a fresh napkin. "You ready to order, Mr. Gilman? Something from the bar? The special is a cup of onion soup, shrimp scampi, salad, dessert. You been on vacation or something?"

"Yes, Armand. A vodka martini, double, on the rocks, and the special."

Frank Hayden picked up his check, waved, and left, saying, "See you back at the factory, Steve."

Adrian said, "So what's new out on the coast, Steve? How was Larry Price?"

"Price?" Bryce cracked. "Is he still dead?"

"I don't want to eat your hearts out, so I'll skip the weather report. Larry was fine and sends his regards to everyone at the shop." He added to Adrian, "How's everything in your world, Norm?"

"Quiet for the moment, but something must be up. I haven't had a memo from the Genius since last Wednesday. Could be he's getting mellow. Or getting ready to jump with the account."

Bryce said, "You hear about Lennie Hawkins?"

"This morning. Anything newer than that?"

"Only what Eth told us. He's got one of your storyboards at home that Chuck's been pushing us for."

"I know. We'll have it by tomorrow morning. I'm having somebody stop by his place tonight to pick it up. Keep the shooting schedule open for Thursday or Friday, will you?"

The waiter brought the martini and onion soup together, and placed a saucer over the cup of soup to keep it hot. "Sorry, Mr. Gilman," he apologized, "so busy in the kitchen, if I don't bring 'em together it'll be three o'clock before you get outta here."

Bryce stood up. "See you. I'm due over at General for a taping session on Prestige Fashions. Steve, get Lawson off my back, will you? Come along, Larry." Liz Berton stubbed out her cigarette and left with them. Adrian, unusually quiet, sat toying with his coffee spoon while Steve attacked his meal.

"Anything wrong, Norm?"

Adrian looked up, then shifted his heavy body on the settee. He had a large head, thick with graying hair that always looked unkempt. His eyes were small and piercing under thick lids, giving him the impression of a man half asleep. Even when he sat or stood erect, his huge shoulders hunched forward, the result of years bent over a typewriter. For a big man, his voice and manner were gentle, those of an inherently kind person. With the exception of several bouts with the short-fused McCreery, Steve couldn't remember a time when he had heard Adrian's voice raised in anger.

"No more than usual," Adrian said.

"You seem so preoccupied."

The big man smiled. "A few things on my mind."

"Anything I can help with?"

"Thanks, Steve, but no, I don't think so."

Probably not, Steve thought. What a shame for a man like Adrian to be at the mercy of an opportunistic no-talent like McCreery. And for no apparent reason except the mysterious human chemistry that, from the very start, determines who shall become friends and who shall remain enemies.

Steve recalled a long-ago conversation he had had with Norm's secretary, Shirley Coombes, shortly before she resigned to marry Bert Shearer, a CBS producer. Shirley, a six-year veteran at Leary, had access to the gossip transmission belt and knew up from down at the agency. McCreery, she told Steve, would never be happy until he "got" Adrian.

"Why, for God's sake?" Steve had asked. "Where would McCreery be without Norm?"

"Why? You don't understand, Steve. You don't belong to our club."

"That's stupid, Shirley. You Jews are so goddamned overly sensitive. What about Marty Elkins, Sam Abrams, and a dozen or more others I can mention."

"With a name like Gilman, you skip a lot of the problems, although I'll admit that at Leary, it doesn't matter much except to people like McCreery. To get back to your question, Marty Elkins is an account supervisor. Sam Abrams is an account executive. They're as big or bigger than McCreery and know how to fight back. Me and the others, he doesn't come in close contact with, so we don't even exist in his world. Norm is a goodnatured *schlemiel* and he works *for* McCreery. On the same account. It makes a big difference." Her final prediction to Steve, "If Norm lasts the year out, I'll name my first son Norman Adrian Shearer."

It had come as little consolation that Norm had managed to outlive Shirley's gloomy prediction.

Question: What about *this* year?

They paid their separate checks and walked back to the agency together.

2

Frank Hayden and Reed Baker were in Peggy's office kidding around easily, obviously waiting for Steve to return from lunch. Both were young and personable, Hayden with the makings of a brilliant advertising executive. He was married and more formal in manner than Baker, who was Frank's age, twenty-six, a free-swinging bachelor and reputedly a heavy scorer in the womanizing department, although cautious enough to operate away from the agency area.

"Hi, boss," Reed greeted.

"Hi, men. I take it all goes well if you can afford the time to entertain Miss Cowles."

Hayden, smiling, said, "Well, discipline *has* been shot to hell while you were gone. Going to be mighty tough getting back to our normal dull routines."

"Peggy," Steve said, "if you're through with these two pigeons, I'll take them off your hands now."

"Be my guest." It was all said in goodnatured geniality that indicated the friendliness of their association. In Steve's office, Hayden sprawled on the sofa while Baker took the chair beside the desk.

"Well, gentlemen," Steve said when they were settled, "I assume something is on your alleged and collective minds, so let's get down to the bitching hour. Reed?"

"Steve," Baker said, "coming to you singly, this sort of thing could be misconstrued as sniping, which, in fact, is what it really is. Together, we figured it would look more like a minor demonstration without the picketing, rock-throwing or fire-bombing . . ."

"A very sound and beautiful opening, Reed," Steve interrupted, "and you've no idea how well your introductory point is being taken. What has Chuck been up to now?"

"Well, as Frank has already indicated to you, we like it here at Leary, particularly working for you . . ."

"I'm deeply gratified, gentlemen."

Hayden laughed and sat up erectly on the sofa. "Steve," he said, "can you get that brown-nosing bastard off our backs? He's impossible to work with, to the point where Reed and I have been talking about checking in with a placement agency."

Baker said, "We've had a good relationship at GFP with Dan Tyson, Tom Jewell, and Bob Davies, as you know, Steve. Couldn't be much better. We even get an occasional smile from the Great One himself in passing, but while you were away, Chuck did his damnedest to undercut us with just about everybody, including the clerks down there. We have equal status with Chuck as account execs, and our paychecks tell us that. But Chuck has gone out of his way to give everybody there the impression that we're a couple of high-priced errand boys."

"How," Steve asked, "did he accomplish that miracle?"

"For one thing, he informed us that only he, on your express orders, was to contact Mr. Lawson, no matter what. Later, when Frank and I were working with Tyson and Jewell, Chuck would break in like a warlord checking on the disposition of his troops and take over. If Dan or Tom questioned anything we were discussing, Chuck invariably sided with them against us. Every time."

Hayden said, "It got so embarrassing, both of us were looking for reasons not to go down there."

"Tell him about . . ." Baker started.

"I'm coming to that. One day I was outside Lawson's office with a color proof he'd asked for specifically. I'd picked it up from Eth Loomis and taken it to him. Charlotte came out of Lawson's office and left the door open. Sitting next to it, I couldn't help overhear Chuck's discussion with him.

"I know, because you've often made the point, that GFP has never been involved in any kind of premium or giveaway gimmick, but Chuck sat there openly discussing premiums with Lawson and agreeing with him down the line, great idea, marvelous promotion possibilities . . ."

"You couldn't have misunderstood?" Steve asked.

Hayden shook his head negatively. "No way, Steve. Lawson was for it and Chuck was pushing it like hash or acid to an addict, you know?, the greatest thing since sliced bread."

Steve studied both men for a moment, then said, "I appreciate your telling me this and I know your motives are more than purely personal. I'm sure you know that Chuck was more or less forced on me, a topside political decision, which makes this a very touchy problem. I can't confront him with this without his knowing it came from you, which would make matters much worse. Let's just sit on it until something breaks, either from Lawson or Chuck. At that time, I promise you I'll handle it. Meanwhile, as a personal favor to me, how about forgetting this business about a placement service. Okay?"

Baker and Hayden stood up. Baker said, "Okay for now, Steve, but get the bastard off our necks and back on the track, will you?"

Moments after they left, Chuck came in with several rough layouts, copy attached to each, waiting for Steve to check them over before taking them to Lawson. After a cursory examination of the material, without indicating approval or disapproval, he said, "This is what came out of the last discussion you and Wade had with Mark?"

"And Davies. There are a couple more out back, but I thought you'd want to see what we have in the preliminary stages, the new approach."

"I see. All right, Chuck, hold onto all of this until I get my report out for Mr. Leary. I'll want to talk to Wade before we go ahead with any of this."

"Okay, Steve. I'll pass the word along."

When Chuck left, Steve returned to the California notes and began searching for an orderly format to present his thoughts on why GFP should make the effort to acquire B & B Coffee. From the accumulation of statistical data and rough notations, he listed the most cogent points:

1) Addition of a prime item to the existing line without having to start from scratch;

2) Logical approaches to use on Perry Bond and his mother to encourage them to divest themselves of a company whose sales, gross and net profits were slipping badly;

3) Comparative prices of the company's stock today with that of its peak, in John Bond's time; passing of dividends for the first time in the company's history;

4) Need to check out tangible net worth or book value, indicated value of goodwill (if any still exists), earnings for the past year, arrive at approximate purchase price (this by GFP people);

5) To be outlined in detail: Recommend specific goals, creative strategy, size and scope of advertising program, attitude of campaign, copy platform, art treatment, media, suggested schedules for print and electronic media, point of sale and outdoor material;

6) Approximate costs of introductory campaign nationwide.

To these items he appended a supplement of the most recent factual figures available: Sales: $87,056,695; Income: $3,642,114; Assets: $31,794,641, including goodwill and intangibles; Employees: 1262; Advertising Budget: $3,232,185 (now reduced by nearly $750,000); Advertising percentage of sales: 3.73%; Stock Value: 24½; Dividend: $2.20 (Stock now at 19¾, last Dividend passed). Common Shares outstanding, an even 1,000,000.

From this skeleton outline, Steve began expanding his thoughts under each separate heading skipping over No. 4, broadening No. 5 in far greater detail, which included the marriage of the names GOODY and B&B to bring the latter, known only in the Far West, southwest and portions of the Mid-West, into national prominence; the ease with which GFP would be able to distribute the new item through outlets presently distributing the full GFP line.

By late afternoon he turned the completed rough draft over to Peggy for a clean copy with triple spacing and wide margins to allow room for corrections, additions, deletions, and the final polishing.

Peggy said, "Will tomorrow be okay, Steve? I have to stop by Lennie's place to pick up that storyboard, you know. I can have it finished sometime during the afternoon."

"Sure, Peg, and take a cab to Lennie's if you can find one, and turn in an expense tab for it."

"Thanks. See you in the morning."

Steve stayed on after the others were gone and made a number of notes for the copy-art conference he intended to call after his talk with Barrett. At seven-fifteen weariness brought him to a halt. It had stopped snowing, the streets were clear and wet, some slush remaining in the gutters and along the inner edges of the pavements. He stood at the window, staring out into the near-deserted street below. For no good reason, he found it difficult to pick up where he had left off. The ease and smoothness he had known before going to California, was somehow missing, the fluidity of rhythm broken; and not since he had first come to the agency had he felt this utter lack of confidence in himself; a sense of uneasiness about his work. The changes in the spring campaign ordered by Lawson, he told himself, were less worrisome than Barrett's and Baldasarian's acceptance of those changes without protest. And overall, the memory of Larry Price came back to haunt him.

He moved away from the window, went to the closet and got out his overcoat and hat, then remembered his promise to George Maczerak. He gathered up two dozen packages of GFP mixes, found a shopping bag beside Peggy's desk, left a note for her to order in more samples and went out. He walked for five blocks until he picked up a cruising cab. At home, he rang the Maczeraks' bell, handed over the shopping bag to an appreciative Inga, but refused George's offer of a drink, pleading weariness.

In his own apartment, he fixed a light dinner of eggs, bacon, toast, and coffee, then showered, and got into bed. Moments later he was sound asleep.

3

When Peggy left shortly before five o'clock, first having gotten Lennie Hawkins's address from Personnel, the city was submerged in darkness. Cold wind bit into the four inches of exposed thighs and kneecaps between the bottom edge of her coat and the tops of her shiny snowboots. A cab, she knew, would be impossible to find at that hour. Even an empty cab wouldn't stop for a girl alone when the driver could count on a heavier tip from a man or a group. She turned north on Lexington toward the subway station at Fifty-third. Lennie's place was on Perry Street just west of Seventh, which meant getting off at Eighth and Fourteenth.

This was a part of New York living Peggy detested, had never liked, and would probably never like; the crowds, traffic, tumult, hemmed in between towering concrete and glass slabs that resembled a gigantic Grand Canyon fallen victim to over-population. Buildings that were pointed out proudly to sightseers as signs of man's progress, she saw as gravestones dedicated to man's self-destruction in his everlasting defiance of Nature's continual battle to maintain a proper ecological balance.

Peggy had been born and raised in Omaha, and graduated from the University of Nebraska at Lincoln, a liberal arts major. Several of her poems and two short stories had been published in obscure magazines and with that modest success behind her, she had decided to take on New York with four hundred dollars and a new portable typewriter, a gift from her parents. After three months of job-hunting by day, pounding out reams of wordage by night, skimping on meals, and missing much needed sleep, she was prepared to admit defeat and return to Omaha when, by a stroke of good fortune, she found a job in one of the employment agencies at which she had registered.

In the year that followed she wrote less poetry, no short stories, read fewer books, saw an occasional movie, and concentrated on bringing her shorthand and typing up to a more respectable level of acceptance. Attractive, she had no problems getting dates, only in fending off aggressive offers to share a variety of beds. And in that year, she fell in love with a young accountant, fell out of love, moved up to become secretary to Bob Larch, who owned the Larch Employment Service, got drunk at the office Christmas party and woke up next morning in a midtown hotel with Bob, who was married and lived in New Rochelle with his wife and three children. Remorse overwhelmed her and for a while she debated seriously on which method of suicide would be least painful in the event that she became pregnant.

In January, while she was working hard at avoiding Bob Larch's further advances, yet needing her job, a call came in from the Leary Advertising Agency for a competent secretary. She at once resigned her position with Larch, called on the Leary personnel director, took a shorthand and typing test that put her at the top of the list of applicants with one hundred and twenty words per minute in shorthand and close to one hundred in typing. She filled out the required forms and was temporarily assigned to the secretarial pool. When, to her immense relief her normal period occurred, Peggy felt a certain new appreciation for life.

The atmosphere at Leary was far more to her liking, the pay much better, and the people friendlier, although much more competitive. A month later, she was invited to move into an apartment shared by Nikki Overholt and Lois Royce, sister members of the pool, on Twelfth Street just east of Seventh Avenue in a rent-controlled building, this when the third member of their establishment moved back to North Carolina. Thus, for her share of $58.50 a month plus the cost of food, transportation, and other incidentals, she gave up her single room for the companionship her new move offered.

It wasn't long before she left the pool to take the assignment as secretary to Steve Gilman, whose secretary had resigned to be married. Six months later, the assignment was made permanent and her salary increased to six hundred and fifty dollars a month, so she was able now to afford a small apartment of her own, but unwilling to leave the security she felt with Nikki and Lois. Not to be discounted were the savings that accrued from living *à trois*.

Her one unhappy experience with Bob Larch, beyond waking up to the terror of finding herself in bed with a man almost twenty years her senior, began to grow dim with the passing of time. Now twenty-four, she began double- and triple-dating with Nikki and Lois, had friends in for small parties, and kept aloof of the extracurricular affairs in which she suspected her roommates were involved, since these were kept outside the apartment and seldom discussed. At times, Peggy was certain she was in love with Steve Gilman. At others, she speculated on how it would be with him. And, aware of his previous marriage and divorce, overhearing bits and pieces of his telephone conversations with a miscellany of women, she experienced mild fits of jealousy and decided he wasn't worth the effort.

Now, caught up in the crowd surging toward the exit door as they approached her stop, she felt an anonymous hand stroking her buttock, but the offender was impossible to detect among the gallery of tired, anxious, harassed faces. The door parted and she was pushed out onto the platform, the incident—which happened frequently—forgotten.

Braced against the cold, she paused to get her bearings, then walked along Greenwich Avenue, swung into Seventh to Perry and finally found the narrow, three-storied house where Lennie Hawkins lived. She mounted the steps and in the dark vestibule saw six mailboxes. She struck a match. Only three boxes had name-cards and as she made out the name L. HAWKINS, neatly lettered on the last box, a white man, preceded by a black woman who was carrying a light-colored child, said, "Lookin' for somebody, Sis?"

"Mr. Hawkins," Peggy replied.

"Lennie? Top floor back," the man said and followed the woman up the stairs to the second floor. In the hallway above, lighted by a single bare bulb of low wattage, she found his door, marked by an 8 x 10-inch sheet of stiff drawing board that displayed an amazingly accurate caricature of Lennie, his name lettered beneath it. She knocked, heard no response, and rapped her knuckles against a panel again, more energetically.

"Door's open," she heard his voice call out. She stepped

into a large room and a wall of cooking odors. At the far end, in a small, open kitchen. Lennie was engaged at the oven. To the left of the kitchen, an open door disclosed a small bathroom. The large central room, its walls and ceilings scarred by peeling paint, held the most battered collection of furniture Peggy had even seen. Next to the kitchen stood a round table and four chairs that were unrelated to each other or the table. In the center was a pull-down bed, rumpled with a tangle of sheets and blankets, a pillow lying on the floor. There were a wardrobe and two dissimilar cabinets against the far wall, a battered sofa and lounge chair, an ottoman. Facing the chair was a small television-set on a metal stand. A color set, she noted. Against the wall looking out on Perry Street was a large drawing table and a Formica-topped, ten-drawer art cabinet with all the tools of an artist's craft. And on that wall were thumbtacked dozens of sketches, cartoons, and caricatures, some of the latter familiar, most of them strange. One section contained a series of combat drawings and color sketches, the location easily identifiable as Vietnam.

His back was toward her when she entered, busy with a frying pan that sizzled. adding fresh layers of smoke to the room. "Who is it?" he called out.

"Peggy," she called back. "Peggy Cowles."

He turned, carrying the frying pan with him. His forehead was plastered with a wide bandage, held by four strips of white tape. He came toward her, still holding the pan, his mouth partly open with surprise. In a low-ceilinged room he looked much taller than in the cleaner, grander atmosphere of the agency, more muscular in the tight blue shirt and equally tight khaki-colored slacks; wiry, broad-shouldered, slim-hipped. So clean, he seemed to be as out of place here as she felt. Then he smiled broadly. "Hey! Where'd you come from, Miss Cowles?"

"Peggy," she insisted. "Steve asked if I would stop by to pick up the new storyboard. I told him I lived over on Twelfth just east of Seventh."

"Hey, you didn't have to bother. I'll bring it in myself in the morning."

"With that head?"

"Nothing," he said deprecatingly. "Solid rock."

"I've seen rocks split into pieces."

"Yeah? Well, not this one. The board's not finished yet.

Got some lettering to finish up. I was going to do that after supper."

"You don't have to do that, Lennie. I can take it in and have Lex get somebody in the bullpen to finish it."

"No, ma'am," Lennie said emphatically. "I got a job to do, I don't let anybody else mess around with my work."

"Well—I don't think you should try to come in tomorrow. That looks like quite a thing, your head. Was it bad?"

"Been only one of 'em, it wouldn't amount to anything. The other one, the guy who got away, he clobbered me from behind while I was busy with the first one. Funny thing is, I knew the one got caught. Lester Goodby. Whole thing lasted only a few minutes—seconds, I mean."

"Lennie, Steve said . . ."

"Got to get back to my supper." The pan he held was filled with thin slices of potato he had been frying. She followed him as he returned to the kitchen area, replaced the pan on the burner and turned to the small oven, opened it, and removed an aluminum pan in which a commercially prepared fish dinner was heating. "Fish and chips," Lennie said, "except that the chips are pan-fried. You had your supper? Plenty here for two."

She gulped down the lump that had risen in the back of her throat. "I'm sorry," she said, "but my roommates are expecting me for din—supper. But thanks."

"Well—I'm going to eat, then finish up that pasteup and lettering. Tomorrow, I'll bring it in, usual time." He said it with an air of finality, dismissing her.

"Look, Lennie," she said, "why don't you finish it up after you've had your supper. When I've had mine, I'll come back and get it. Then you can stay home and rest for another day."

He turned and said, "Hey, what's with you? Why're you so concerned about me? What difference does it make?"

"I'd be concerned about anybody who'd been attacked and hurt . . ."

"A dog, too?"

"A dog, too, but more important, a human being and a talented artist."

"You really dig what I do?" he said with a widening grin.

"I dig and admire what you do, yes. I think you turn out some of the best work I've ever seen."

Lennie exhaled slowly, seeing her as though for the first time; more than just pretty, coat open, nyloned legs reaching up out of her boots to where her short skirt ended some four inches above her knees. Her face, lips parted slightly, delicate features, eyes large and blue, black bangs drifting over her smooth forehead. He turned away and said abruptly, almost sullenly, "Okay, if you want to come back. Take me about an hour after I finish eating. Maybe an hour and a half. Say about nine o'clock."

"I'll be back around nine."

On her way out, she paused for a moment to look at the display of caricatures again and saw among them explicit likenesses of Bill Leary, Lex Kent, Ethan Loomis, Don Bryce . . . . And among them, set off in a neat black frame, the one that could easily be of herself, more a portrait than a caricature.

When she returned at a few minutes past nine, Lennie was at his drawing table, lettering the last of the audio on the storyboard. Again, she looked over the collection of caricatures and saw that the one of herself was missing. She made no comment and asked, "All finished?"

"Just about. Another fifteen minutes. Pour yourself some coffee."

She was about to refuse, then sensed that it would be a mistake to allow him to think she was too stuffy to drink from a black man's cup although, she thought, during the summer my skin is almost as dark as his. In the kitchen, she found a coffee mug and poured the black liquid, savoring its warmth and flavor, sipping at it to drive out the chill of winter that still lingered on her flesh.

She came back and watched over his shoulder as he completed the lettering in the white box beneath the last cutout which represented the television screen, used a square of kneaded rubber to erase the light pencil marks. "I'll put these in an envelope for you—hey, why don't you take your coat off and sit while you drink your coffee. That's pneumonia weather outside."

She motioned the cup upward. "This is delicious."

"I make the best," he said pridefully as he began searching for a large envelope. "Anything that's mine, I want the best. This art table, cabinet, the color TV, they're mine. All the rest of this junk is the landlord's taste, comes with the apartment."

She looked about her again, the question in her eyes unasked, yet caught by the observant Lennie. "You wondering why, if I like the best, I live in a dump like this?"

"The thought did pass through my mind."

"Well, when I'm ready, I'll have it. Meanwhile, I'll save for it." When she did not reply, "Listen, I started with Leary for a hundred a week. I'm getting two hundred now, ten thousand a year before taxes, more'n I ever made in my whole life. I'd like to live out on Long Island, maybe up in Connecticut, a place where I could have a real studio of my own. A car. A lot of things I never had or thought I'd ever have. I've lived in slums, shacks, slept in rice paddies and tents in Vietnam—"

"Then why live here now? You can afford something better with what you earn."

"So far, I can't make it past the Whiteys who say, 'Sorry, no vacancies' and mean 'Nigger, crawl back in your hole and don't bother me.' "

"Oh, come on now."

"You going to tell me all white people aren't like that; I know that, but to me all white landlords *are* like that and I say fuck 'em all."

He saw the shock reaction to his obscene phrasing in her eyes, in the sudden stiffening of her body as she sought to ignore it, but he offered no apology.

"Uh—do you always express yourself so colorfully?" she said.

"When it's applicable. When I'm up to here with it."

Peggy sipped the coffee, unwilling to carry the subject any farther. Lennie said, "Tell me, what kind of a guy is your boss?"

"Steve? The best. The very best."

"Oh? I hear he's kind of tough on the hired help."

"I don't agree with that. He knows what he wants. If that's being what you call tough, yes, but he's even tougher on himself. The group respects that. He gets the job done."

"Sounds like he gets more'n the job done," Lennie said, grinning.

His oblique reference annoyed her and she said bitingly, "Listen, Mr. Hawkins, whatever I sound like is my business. I'll tell you this much, though, you do your job as professionally as he does his and you'll go a long way a lot faster."

"Thankee, missy," Lennie replied, touching two fingers

to his forehead in a mock salute, caricaturing an Uncle Tom.

"And you can skip the minstrel act, too. No one at our agency is pushing any special color this season, or any other. If you don't believe me, ask Marcy Thompson, Lew Brown, Ethan Loomis . . ."

"I don't have to ask that fat cat. He's been preaching color balance and harmony to me for a long time. In fact, he got me the job. He's my uncle."

"Well, bully for you. He's another man who has everybody's respect at the agency."

"Well," Lennie said, "the Leary Agency may be every black's security blanket, but what about the great big outside, the rest of the establishment?"

"If you despise the establishment so much, why join it? Why not burn it down?"

"Baby, ain't you heard it's a lot easier to start a fire inside the furnace than outside?"

"My God, a revolutionary!" Peggy exclaimed. "That's a great attitude for someone it supports."

"I get paid for what I do, not for my attitude."

"Well, Lennie, it's too bad you feel that way about it. You've still got a lot to learn."

"You get any extra time on your hands, how about moonlighting to teach me?"

She glared at him, then stood up, picked up the large envelope with the storyboard in it. "Goodnight," she said stiffly, and went out.

4

On arrival at his office the following morning, partially refreshed from a full night's sleep, Steve found Peggy ready with coffee, the mail opened and sorted by category, the storyboard for the new commercial spread out on his desk. "How was Lennie?" he asked as he handed over his coat and hat.

"A little the worse for wear, but I'm sure he'll be in tomorrow morning, well, sick, dead, or alive."

Examing the storyboard more closely, Steve said, "This is great. That boy is one hell of an improvement over Charlie Walls. Gets maximum feeling into every sketch."

"He's very talented. He filled in beautifully while Arnie was virused out of action."

"Peggy, virus isn't a verb."

"So I'm inventive. And you should see the caricatures and war sketches on his wall. Beautiful."

"Well, maybe with that fantastic recommendation I'll talk to Don and see if we can't keep him in our group permanently. I think he could work well with Gary Parris. What do you think?"

"I think he'd make a great addition and I'm sure he'd feel he could get farther on GFP than in Mr. Bryce's department."

"I'll talk to Don about it. Give this to Chuck to check out against the original script, then have Gary turn it over to Bryce's people. They'll want to start setting it up for shooting as soon as possible. How is the report coming?"

"I'll get onto it as soon as I give this to Chuck. I'll have it sometime this afternoon. You're scheduled for lunch with Mr. Barrett. Vanessa called a few minutes ago and confirmed."

"Fine. You stay with it and I'll take a walk around and say 'Hello' to those I missed yesterday."

He went through the working area of the section and stopped at each cubicle for a few words, then came back to his desk and picked up the copies of the Call Sheets he had asked Peggy to get out for him, visits to Lawson's office by Chuck and Wade, made together, and separately. The calls Chuck made alone were merely routine, but the one by Chuck and Wade together was more illuminating, not so much for what it reported, but for what had been omitted. He studied it carefully. It would become the principal subject-matter of his luncheon discussion with Barrett.

He sat at his desk thinking about the upcoming spring campaign, wondering what new approach he could come up with that would inject GFP into the vortex of today, now. Something vital was happening in the country and could not, should not, be ignored. Added to growing consumer discontent, campus unrest, increasing militancy on the part of hawks and doves alike, the market situation was creating more concern, business and industry were alarmed by high interest rates, inflation, rising unemployment, with unions demanding more money and benefits along with a shorter work week. Taxpayers seemed on the verge of revolt and everything that was happening contributed to the higher cost of living. Particularly in the area of GFP's prime interest—the household food bill.

This is the time, Steve thought, to gear our advertising to the times.

Question: How?

He made notes on a pad of copy paper, scratched through some, retained others. Come what may, the American housewife was less interested in Mark Lawson's idea of something spring-y, flowery, and more concerned with how to keep her weekly marketing bills down.

At eleven-forty, Peggy rang to remind him of his luncheon date. He put his notes in the top drawer of his desk, got his hat and coat and went to the floor above to meet Barrett. They cabbed to the Colonade where they could enjoy their meal in relative quiet and after ordering drinks, gave the waiter their food orders.

"Well, Steve," Barrett said as they were getting zeroed in on their first martini, "how does it feel to be back in full harness?"

"So far, so good, but nothing is official until I see Mark."

"You talk with him yet?"

"No. He was snowed in at Wyecliffe yesterday. His office knows I called in. I'm sure he'll phone me when he gets my message." He paused for a moment, then added, "I read through your last Call Sheet, Wade."

"And?"

"I think Mark is being unrealistic as hell. This light, airy, feminine approach he's talking about . . ."

Barrett smiled negligently. "You know Lawson, Steve. Arbitrary as hell. I didn't want to start any kind of a hassle for you to inherit, so Chuck and I just listened and let it go at that."

"Except that it was left at that. My people were up to their asses in this new theme, discarding a program that was well set before I left for the coast. You know that's only going to make it so much harder to unsell him on the idea now that he thinks it's in the works."

"Maybe, but I think you can handle him. We've got other things to talk about that are a lot more important."

"I happen to think this is very important, Wade . . ." Steve began, but Barrett said suddenly, "This B & B Coffee thing, Steve. That was one hell of a stroke of genius, your idea for GFP to buy them out."

"Did Bill tell you about it?"

"No, it was Keith. I've been thinking about it all night.

It's exciting, isn't it, and I've got some ideas I'd like to discuss with you."

"Wade, you're jumping the gun. Mr. Goodwin hasn't even heard about it yet and I've got enough work to keep me busy from here to yon between now and any decision to buy, or the Bonds' decision to sell. Then there'll be a time lag to find or build the necessary facilities, and install equipment before the project can begin rolling."

"I know, I know, but this thing excites me, just thinking about it. Christ, it could mean another five or six million in billings. Even more."

"I realize that, too, but I don't want to put too much time into something that may not materialize. And besides, I've got to come up with a whole new concept for this spring campaign that's been shot out from under us."

But Barrett seemed not to be listening and said, "I understand, Steve. Jesus, we'll have a ball with this one. It's like bringing in an entirely new account."

"As far as we're concerned, if it does come in, it will *be* an entirely new account, a different score to play under GFP. I'd like to handle it as a separate item until we've saturated the market enough to include it into the general line . . ."

"Yes, of course," Barrett agreed, "that's the way we'll do it." Forking more veal piccata into his mouth, "How do you think Larry Price will come out of this, Steve?"

"I don't know. What did Keith tell you?"

"We didn't discuss that, but I know Bill is goddamned unhappy and will probably take some kind of action, make some changes out there."

"Possibly, but that will be Bill's decision to make. I've no idea what's on his mind."

Barrett nodded, chewing on his food. "Larry's really blown it this time, hasn't he?"

"I'm in no position to evaluate that, Wade. In this case, I think he was a victim of circumstances. If John Bond hadn't died and . . ."

"Oh, for Christ's sake, Steve, you're covering for him. I *know* Larry Price. Let him break a fingernail or lose a filling out of a tooth and he runs for the bottle the way a baby goes for a tit."

"Wade, that's out of my province. I'm just a little ol' country boy who . . ."

"I know all about that turd-kicking country boy act of

yours. After all, I got you your first job with Leary, remember?"

It was the first time Barrett had ever reminded Steve of that event and he felt a sense of annoyance, as though Wade was now expecting some sort of payment in return. It also occurred to Steve that while Barrett had been instrumental on that occasion, it was Keith Allard who had actually hired him. He laid down his knife and fork on the plate, and waited.

He did not have to wait long. Barrett said, "Steve, what if Bill decides to let Larry go?"

Steve shrugged. "If he does, that's it."

"There's no one out there who could replace him as branch manager, is there?"

So that was it. "I don't know, Wade. Dave Chesler seems knowledgeable and capable enough to take over. He's had ten or twelve years out there under Donnelly and Larry, knows all the accounts well, and sits in on every major decision. Also, there are a couple of good men in Chicago and here, as well. I hadn't given that any thought."

"Well—Steve, if it comes up for grabs, I want it. Back when Bill, Sr. was alive, it was a tossup between Larry and me, but the old man didn't want me off the GFP account at that time, so Larry backed into the job. I'd like to take a crack at it this time. I can talk to Keith, of course, but I'll need help."

"What about B & B if Mr. Goodwin decides to go for it?"

"That shouldn't matter too much. Hell, the company has always been based out there. We could still handle it from the West Coast."

Steve studied Barrett for a moment, knowing that his idea about headquartering the B & B account in Los Angeles was no more than wishful thinking. Bill Leary would never agree to it, nor would Allard. Or Mark Lawson. Wade said, "Can I count on you, Steve?"

Steve squirmed. "I doubt that in this case, Bill or Keith would even consult me, Wade. Anything about GFP, yes, sure, but a decision to replace a branch manager?"

"I've got a hunch you'll be called in on it by Keith or Bill, or both. For your opinion. They respect your judgment."

"Why don't we wait and see what happens? I hate like hell to jump the gun on anything."

"Sure, Steve. Just remember, though, I want it."

Privately, Steve had no intention of speaking up for or against Barrett. His sins of omission with GFP, recognizable in his unwillingness to tackle Lawson on this most recent issue was a good enough example of Wade's way of evading responsibility. His problems with Ted McCreery and Norm Adrian were others he would avoid if he were sent to Los Angeles.

Steve spent the next hour with Arthur Thalberg in Marketing, going over economic and buying trend reports, searching for some angle by which he could connect his own reactions to the mood of the buying public. Back in his own office, he decided to hold his group meeting without involving Barrett. He took the offensive Call Sheet from his desk drawer, then dialed Allard's office. Gail Kingsley checked and said that Keith could give him twenty minutes. He made it to the upper floor in two, and dropped the beige sheet on Keith's desk. Keith glanced at the heading and said "I've seen this. As a matter of fact, I've been waiting for your reaction."

"All right, here it is. It smells bad for all the perfume, spring flowers and bride's bouquets, no matter from which angle I look at it. In short, it stinks."

"If it will make you happier, I've been waiting to see what comes through on this. I can assure you it wouldn't have gotten past me or out of this office."

"Well, that shoots down the original concept and gives me a dead loss of time to make up."

"I agree. So there's only one thing to do. Get a new concept. You can do it, can't you?"

"Sure I can, but that's evading the issue. You know what I'm talking about."

"I'm afraid I do and I don't like the idea of Wade sitting back and taking this sort of thing without voicing his objections strenuously. Frankly, and don't let this go any further, I think he's lost contact with the account. That happens, you know."

"I also know that Wade brought the account into the agency, years ago."

"Yes, he made the initial contact and that's what makes the situation a sticky one."

"Well—I'll see Lawson as soon as possible and try to get this squared away. Meanwhile, I'll get the group together and try to come up with a fresh concept."

Allard nodded approvingly. "Do that and keep me posted."

Peggy was busy finishing the report when Steve returned to his office. She looked up and said, "There's a note on your desk to call Mr. Lawson as soon as you can. Shall I get him for you?"

"Yes. then get the group in for a conference. Chuck, all the copy and art people, plus Gary."

"Will you want me there to take notes?"

"No, this will be strictly an informal bullshooting session. They'll take their own notes. You stay with the report."

When he answered Peggy's ring, Mark Lawson greeted him with a booming, "Well, you lucky bastard, how was California?" then Steve had to listen to a lengthy account of Mark's having been snowed in at his uncle-in-law's home in Wyecliffe the day before.

"When are you coming down to see me?"

"I was planning that for later this week, Mark. I understand Bill is setting up a meeting when it will be convenient for Mr. Goodwin."

"Yeah. The old man just phoned from the plant and told me to pass the word along to Leary. Friday at 2:30. How about clueing me in on it?"

"It's just an idea we've run across, Mark, one I think you'll buy."

"About what?"

"I think I'd better wait for Bill to work out the final details first. With the little I know, I could easily louse it up by talking too soon."

"Cautious bastard, aren't you. You coming down with Bill?"

"Yes, and I think Keith and Wade will be there, too."

"The first team, eh? It must be pretty big if it can shake the brass loose from that ivory tower."

"It could be important, Mark, or nothing at all."

"That tells me a hell of a lot, doesn't it."

"About as much as I know right now."

"Well, with the old man coming in from Harrison, Leary must have done a good selling job. Okay, I'll look for you on Friday. Pass the word along, will you? And I'm glad you're back."

"Thanks, Mark. I'll give the word to Mr. Leary and see

you on Friday." Steve hung up, then dialed Allard's extension and gave him the message.

"Fine," Allard said. "I'll alert Bill and Wade. We'll probably have lunch together and go on from there. Keep yourself free. How's the report coming?"

"It should be ready later this afternoon."

"Send Bill's and Wade's copies to me. I'll see they get them. Keep one copy for yourself, no file copy, and tell Peggy to forget what she's seen or heard."

"Will do."

As he cradled the receiver, Chuck knocked on the communicating door, opened it, and peered in. "Ready for the troops, Steve?"

"Bring 'em in."

Other than Frank Hayden, who was out at the time, they entered in a pattern of twos, as they generally worked together, with Chuck and Reed Baker leading the way; Alan Grant and Don Berman, Randy Ellis and Arnold Cook, Benn Archer and Lyle Keller, Jon Hartman and Norris Bardo, copywriters and art directors. Absent at other duties were Gary Parris, the Television-Radio producer, Lew Kann, production liaison, and Lennie Hawkins. Chuck stood the visual layouts on an easel for all to see and Steve took over.

"I've been reviewing these new spring ads very carefully," he began, "as far as you've taken them, and after discussing the theme Mr. Lawson suggested with Mr. Allard, we've decided not to go any farther with them until I've had an opportunity to talk with Lawson. In its place, I'd like all of you to think about an angle I intend to persuade Lawson and Davies to consider."

Reed Baker's hand shot up. "Steve—?"

"Yes, Reed."

"I'd like to tell you that as a group, we've been discussing this approach and none of us could see it . . ."

"All right, Reed. For one thing, I'm not blaming anyone here for going along with a client's request or demand. Let me tell you how I feel about it, then we'll get into a general discussion."

Steve outlined his thoughts on general conditions, the sense of growing uncertainty about the national economy. "I feel that our advertising should, and must, mirror the mood of the consumer, knock out the frills, the gimmicks, the fun-and-games attitudes, and place a heavier, more sober emphasis on values. We know the housewife has already become more cautious and is getting more and more selective in her spending and shopping habits. In short, she's getting damned tired of being shortchanged and kicked around.

"What I'm reaching for is some way to let our readers and listeners and viewers know that they are getting more for their money with GFP than with our competitors. I want them to know that GFP is just as concerned with high prices and rising food costs as they are. I want to focus our effort on economy in the weekly food bill, even if we have to point out the low cost of each individual serving, x-pennies per portion. Emphasis on quality is still important, but we want to stress the economy factor along with it. I want the kind of ads I don't have to apologize to my friends for. Any questions?"

Randy Ellis said, "What about Mr. Lawson's idea? From the Call Sheets, it looked like a positive directive."

"Let me worry about that, Randy. What I'm interested in at the moment is your gut-feelings and thoughts on this new approach."

"I'm all for it," Hartman said. "The beating I take at home is more than enough to convince me. Between trading stamps, grocery bingo, premiums and all the other gimmicks that run our food bills up, I wouldn't be a damned bit surprised if a national consumer revolt doesn't spring up to make student demonstrations look like kindergarten picnics."

Steve shot a quick glance at Chuck, who seemed ready with a retort, then decided not to go ahead. Baker smiled knowingly at Steve. Hartman's opinion started a round of lively discussion that included Arnie Cook's remark that the biggest business in the country was consumer fraud, and for a few minutes it appeared as though a minor demonstration of sorts might begin there in Steve's office. He allowed the discussion to continue its stimulating course for several minutes before calling the group to order.

"All right, I think the point has been made and well taken. I like your reactions, but we're not here to solve the economic problems of the country. Not at this session. Maybe we can set an example of some kind for others to follow. Just get this into your minds. I'm not as concerned with art treatment as I am about getting our message across forcefully. If you want a better name for it, it's hard sell."

Don Berman said, "You want us art directors to take a vacation, Steve?"

Steve smiled and said, "No, not at all, Don. What I mean is that I don't want the art treatment to compete with the message. Your job is to project that message graphically and forcefully, see that the words leap out at the reader. Okay? For now, let's forget the present theme. I'm seeing the client on Friday and I'll give you a firsthand progress report on Monday. Meanwhile, readjust your thoughts to the premise of this discussion. Make notes, very rough layouts, or whatever, and be ready to run with the ball when you get it, probably on Monday morning. I think that's all for now."

The meeting had lasted until four-thirty. Peggy brought the final draft of the California report to Steve and after he had checked it carefully, he had the original and two copies sealed in an envelope for Peggy to take to Mr. Allard and place into his hands. He tucked his own copy in his jacket pocket and destroyed the file copy.

Peggy returned to close out her day—the sight of her giving him a needed lift—dressed in a brief plaid jumper dress over a long-sleeved and high-collared black shirt, nyloned legs flashing as she came toward him carrying several letters and memos he had dictated earlier. He glanced at them with approval and signed each, watching as she picked them up and arranged them in orderly fashion. Of the secretaries he had known at Leary, Peggy was not only the most attractive, but the most careful and accurate as well as the swiftest. He had often wondered how long she would last before someone tapped her for marriage and he would be sampling the pool talent for a replacement.

"Everything all right, Peg?" he asked, as he signed the last memo.

"What? Oh, sure. Everything's just fine."

"Good."

She stared at him for a moment in curiosity, then said, "Why?"

"Nothing. For some reason I can't define, I just remembered when you first came to work with the group."

She broke into a little laugh and said, "How well I remember it. For a while, I never thought I'd have a chance. You told me I was a secretary and if I had any ambitions to become a copywriter, to forget it."

"And you didn't like that, did you?"

"Since I'd never had that ambition, I thought you were a horrible, presumptuous, and smug man."

"A bastard, is what you mean."

"Well, no, not that extreme, but I thought you'd be terrible to work for."

"And now?"

"After all of four years, are you trying to squeeze a compliment out of me, Steve? Somebody been putting you down?"

He returned her smile easily. "Beat it, before I find myself tempted."

"Oh, no, not Steve Gilman."

"And why not Steve Gilman?"

"Because everybody knows Steve Gilman wants no entanglements with Leary girls. Too close to home."

Ah, how little you know about how close to home and doom I've been, Miss Cowles. Aloud, "That's how the water-cooler crowd rates me?"

"Don't knock it, Steve. Your ego would soar through the roof if you knew what other things they say about you."

"Like what?"

"Uh-uh. Try somebody else. All I am is a secretary, remember?"

"Okay, coward, take your letters and run."

"Goodnight, Steve."

"Goodnight, Peg."

He watched the rhythmic rise and fall of her firm, smooth buttocks as she retreated toward her own office, recalling again the day he first interviewed her as a replacement for the girl who had resigned to marry an aeronautical engineer and move to Seattle. Peggy had come up from the secretarial pool on probation and even before he had dictated his first letter, he had asked, "By the way, Miss Cowles, are you engaged?"

"No," she replied.

"Any romantic attachments?"

She hesitated for a moment, studying him coolly. "I thought I was trying out for a secretarial job, Mr. Gilman."

"You are, Miss Cowles. In the past year, I've lost two very attractive secretaries and I'm trying to get a small idea about how long you intend to stay here before announcing your engagement or marriage."

She said, "I'm not planning to resign in the foreseeable future. That's as close as I can come to an answer."

"Well, let's skip over that for the moment. Do you have any higher ambitions beyond secretarial work?"

"I'd like to learn more than just my job."

"How much more would you like to learn?"

She began showing signs of exasperation. "As much as I can in order to qualify as an efficient secretary. I know that GFP is the agency's largest account and I feel that the more I learn about its operation, the more helpful I can be to you."

"Possibly by becoming a copywriter?"

"Mr. Gilman," she said, "I'd like to be a writer one day, a real writer, not particularly a writer of commercial fiction."

"Is that how you see advertising?"

"I'm not competent enough to discuss the philosophy of advertising. I leave that to the theoreticians."

He smiled at that. "What would you like to write?"

"Poetry. Short stories."

"Not novels, plays for television?"

"Well . . ."

"If that's it, I'd suggest you forget it while you're working for me."

"Does that include my nights, weekends and holidays?"

"What you do with your free time, Miss Cowles, is your affair. I am primarily concerned with your daytime efforts."

"And my remaining single and unattached?"

"There are no rules about that, of course . . ."

"Mr. Gilman," she said boldly, "I'll make a deal with you. I'm twenty-three years old, single, and unattached at the moment. If you won't offer to marry me sooner, I'll stay at least five years, getting over my great disappointment. Shall I report back to the pool now?"

Her display of mild temper caused him to laugh. "No. No, Miss Cowles. You've just signed on for five years. Welcome aboard. I'll phone Personnel in the morning. Is that satisfactory with you?"

She smiled slyly. "Then I take it I'll also be safe from a proposal of marriage?"

"You know," Steve said, "I think you and I are going to get along just fine."

Alone, he pondered the eccentric manifestations of life in general, and his own in particular, delving into the vagaries of cause and truth. By purist standards, he saw himself as a copout. Thirty years old, divorced, running from nothing to nowhere without having left a real mark anywhere. Only a smudge.

In his work, he was above average—he conceded immodestly—having reached a plateau of competence for which he was well rewarded financially, and envied by many in his profession. On the deficit side of his personal ledger, a broken marriage, a considerable number of encounters of no importance whatever, and few real or lasting friendships. Zero. He tried to avoid thinking of Libby, who belonged in the past, yet was conscious of her ethereal presence; knowing she would remain a part of him until something—or someone—stronger came along to drive her out of his mind and life permanently.

What? Certainly not his job.

Then, *Who*?

That, as Mr. Shakespeare had put it so succinctly, was the question. Until the day when the *who* came along, Libby would continue as the dark symbol of his personal failure. Just as his father had failed before him.

A very poor balance sheet to comtemplate.

5

By mid-morning on Thursday, Steve had had separate sessions with Bill Leary and Keith Allard to clarify certain points made in his report. Late on Wednesday there had been a joint meeting with Bill, Keith, and Wade, at which time Bill had given them a run-through of the additions he had made to the report, with copies for each to study. On this Thursday morning, Steve was reading through his copy again when Peggy rang him. "Can you spare a few minutes for Mr. Abrams, Steve?"

"My office or his?"

"Yours. He's here with me now."

"Sure. Show him in."

Modishly dressed, limping slightly, Sam Abrams came in and sat in the visitor's chair. Sam, as account executive on the Prestige Fashions account, had nothing in common with GFP and had never before dropped in for either business or social reasons, which now increased Steve's curiosity.

"Sam, what brings you among the laborers in the vineyard?"

Sam grinned infectiously. "My expense account is running light so I thought I'd take a peasant to lunch today. I don't want the front office getting any idea they ought to cut down on me. How about it, sport?"

They weren't exactly lunch-buddies, except by the accident of running into each other occasionally, and Steve knew this was no simple gesture of friendliness. "What about a raincheck, chum? I'm up to my gluteus maximus with work."

"Look out the window, Steve. It's not even threatening, a nice day to get outside for a breath. Besides, sending out for a dried-up drugstore sandwich is ulcer bait. I've already called Emil's and Wilma is holding a table for two in a quiet corner."

"Sam," Steve said, "I'm beginning to get a small hunch . . ."

"That's good. If your hunch is right, it'll save the long preliminaries." He limped over to the closet, got Steve's coat and hat, and grinning impishly, said, "Come on, sport, get off your gluteus whatchamacallit, you intellectual bastard. If we had time, I'd take you down to Katz's on the East Side and fill you up with food, you'd hibernate for a month."

Abrams was too persuasive to be denied. He was a short, slender man of thirty-eight, with the lean, hungry look of a ferret, possessed of a cocky self-assurance that was often as annoying and disconcerting as it was refreshing at other times. He was known as a tough infighter when it came to protecting client and agency, between which he divided his loyalties with equal zest and fire.

At sixteen, in 1948, he had passed himself off for eighteen and worked on the detail desk at the *Times* as a proof-runner. Within a year, he knew every department head by name, from mechanical to editorial, and most of the leading writers and columnists. Even more important, they knew Sam Abrams by name, and gave him passes to movies, Broadway shows, and sporting events, which Sam immediately peddled for cash.

Delivering proofs to agency production departments, he was swift, careful, and dependable. In 1949, when an opening developed at Leary, Norman Adrian recommended him to Ethan Loomis, who offered him a job in Production, which Sam accepted eagerly. Quick and intuitive, his absorbent mind eager to learn, he filed cuts, artwork, and plates, collected okayed proofs, ran from office to client and back, and scurried out on innumerable personal errands. In 1951, the draft caught up with him, and later that year, after his initial training period, Sam shipped out to Korea.

All during those months, he wrote of his experiences to Ethan Loomis and Norm Adrian, who circulated his letters among Sam's Production friends, then posted them on the Employees' Bulletin Board.

Sam saw less than a year of action before he was airlifted back to Tokyo, then to the United States, minus a foot that had been blown off at the ankle while on night patrol, when the man closest to him stepped on a land mine. Sam was one of the luckier ones. Two others died and three were wounded. Sam Abrams's running days were over.

After months in an Army hospital, he worked feverishly to master the artificial replacement for the limb he had lost. He won that battle, but now began to ponder his future. He had been a runner all his life. Now, slowed down to a walk, or limp, he wiped Leary from his mind.

It was Norm Adrian who brought the word to Eth Loomis that Sam was back, for Sam had stopped writing when he learned his foot was gone. An avid reader of Sam's letters, Norm had written to the Army Adjutant General inquiring as to Sam's whereabouts. When he showed Eth the reply he'd gotten from the Department of Defense, Eth went at once to see Sam and offered him a job.

"Thanks, Eth," Sam replied with some despair, "but I can't run no more for you. I swapped my foot for a Purple Heart."

"You don't have to run for me, Sam. I need a fast thinker to help me herd the rest of my crew around. See you on Monday, you understand? And Sam, I'm not doing you the favor. You're doing me one."

Back at Leary, Sam knew that if he was going to make it up the ladder, he would have to walk, and reconciled himself to certain other changes, important ones. His friend Norm talked with him at great length, encouraging him to take night courses to improve his English and to study advertising. With a pension—and veteran's G.I. Bill privileges—Sam worked by day and struggled with his studies by night, helped over the rough spots by Adrian, with whom he had been spending much of his free time. Three years passed before Adrian showed some of Sam's better efforts to Allard and persuaded him to allow Sam to try his hand at copywriting.

Allard agreed, with reservations. Sam's work was no better, no worse, than the average new trainee and when it appeared he would not get to the top of his craft, Allard discovered that Sam was basically an idea man, promotion-minded, interested in that important phase of advertising. He gambled, throwing Sam in with Adrian for a brief period of indoctrination, then moved him permanently over to Walt Ferren's Prestige Fashions account. It was here that Sam, as he put it later, found himself a home.

Not too long after, Ferren took Sam over to meet Max Zweig and his son, Manny. In another year, Sam was spending most of his time at Prestige and when Walt eventually accepted an offer from the Mason & Stanton Agency, Sam maneuvered Max Zweig into asking Bill to offer the spot to Adrian; but it was Adrian himself who recommended Sam Abrams instead. After a period of probation, Sam reached full account executive status, and in the years that passed, had lapped the field and broken across the finish line while Norm was still cruising along as senior writer for the Chevalier account.

At Emil's, they stood at the bar while Benny mixed a martini for Steve, and a bourbon over ice for Sam. They were greeted by a number of familiar faces, several of whom invited them to their tables, but they turned down the invitations and soon were ushered to their own private table by Wilma, Sam finishing a story he had begun at the bar. "—so in this Chinese joint where I've been going for years, suddenly they've got these pretty, new menus, shiny, plastic covers, you know. So I open the menu. On the left side, all Chinese dishes. On the right side is something new. All kinds of pizzas, a whole pageful. I call Quong over and say, 'Hey, Quong, what the hell? What's with this pizza jazz in a Chinese restaurant, hey?' Old Quong, he looks me straight in the eye and says, 'What the hell else can I do, Sam? I'm in a Jewish neighborhood!' "

Steve laughed, although he had heard the story before—as a matter of fact, he recalled when, during a rehearsal of the very first Wally Greer show under GFP's sponsorship—a story Don Bryce had ruled out for obvious reasons.

"Okay, hey, Steve?"

"A goody, Sam. Let's start talking, shall we?"

"Okay, sport. What's this I hear about Leary picking up a very juicy new account out on the West Coast?"

"Christ!" Steve exclaimed with genuine dismay. "That one sure as hell got out fast. Where'd you pick it up, Sam?"

Sam's face cracked into a knowing grin. "What the hell, we're no different from an Army message center, where the privates know before the generals what's going on. Since Monday, Allard's had his secretary digging in our library for anything on coffee. Also, she's hit the Fifth Avenue library two days in a row for everything *they*'ve got on coffee. Also, my secretary and the broad in our own library are close friends. You want more?"

"No. I just don't think we ought to be discussing this, Sam."

"Well, it's not that exactly. Something else."

"What?"

"Norm Adrian."

"How does he fit into the picture?"

"Well, I was just thinking that maybe you'd be a nice guy and talk Bill and Keith into letting him take over that part of GFP if they pick up this B & B outfit."

"Norm? Jesus, Sam, he'd be great on it, but what about Chevalier? And another thing, Norm had a lot to do with breaking me into this screwed-up business . . ."

"Me, too. So what?"

". . . and the idea of him working for me would be an insult to him."

"You're dead wrong, Steve. If we could get him off Chevalier and away from that louse, McCreery, we could maybe save Norm *and* Chevalier. It's getting rough, what goes on between those two."

"So I keep hearing, but . . ."

"No buts, Steve. Add it up for yourself. If Norm was a pusher type like me, for instance, McCreery could easily use that angle to get rid of him, but you know Norm. He's a nice, easygoing, gentle guy, and to a bastard like McCreery, that spells weakness, and he can't resist shoving a weaker guy around, no more than a kid with a stick in his hand can resist a picket fence."

The waiter saved Steve from commenting on that bit of analysis by placing their food before them, but Steve knew the lapse was only momentary. When the waiter left, Sam continued. "Norm is an old and good friend, Steve. I can't begin to tell you how much he helped me get where I am right now, where he ought to be. He's done more for that Chevalier account than anybody else who ever touched it. I've watched him tear himself apart to do an even better job, and watched McCreery take all the credit. And still that sonofabitch treats Norm like a dog. You know the old saying, In order to destroy a man you need only give his work the character of uselessness. That's what McCreery's been trying to do."

"Sam, believe me, I'm on Norm's side, but how does a man like Norm take a thing like that for so long?"

"How?" Sam shrugged. "I don't know, except that he's been on the account so much longer than McCreery. Still, that's no excuse. Me, I'm a kind of modern version of my old man, who was a pushcart peddler on the lower East Side. Except that my pushcart is a sixty dollar attaché case loaded with ideas from our creative department and the classy phrases you genius word-merchants punch out on your fancy electric typewriters, instead of bolts of yard-goods and cheap cotton dresses and rayon stockings. Norm's father was a rabbi who raised his son to be a *melamed*. A student. Maybe it would have been a lot better if he'd had to be a streetfighter like me, instead of a scholar. If you don't have to fight when you're a kid, where the hell do you get the fight you need when you get to Norm's age?"

"What you're saying, Sam, is that McCreery is anti-Semitic, isn't it?"

"Right on, man. Like I said before, add it up yourself. Ask yourself what did Norm ever do to McCreery, who started this war between them? You ought to know better than anybody else because you worked on the damned account a few years ago. I just don't want to see Norm get hurt. He needs his job. He's got a wife, and two growing kids, and at his age, a copywriter looking for a job in this jungle, you know what his chances are. He's a leper, a pariah. Something you look at out of the corner of one eye like a hunchback, a cripple, or a beggar."

Steve said quietly, "Sam, I like Norm as a person and respect his ability. I'll fight for him, not because he's a Jew and not because McCreery doesn't like him. But maybe there's another way out of this hassle."

"Show me."

"How about your Prestige account? Is there room for him there?"

"Don't think I haven't thought about that, but you know what Prestige bills a year. It can't support a senior writer of Norm's earning stature. I've even thought of talking to Max and Manny Zweig and get them to put him on their payroll, but they've never had an inside advertising manager. They use us for that. Even if they did, Norm couldn't get anywhere near what he's making now. I know it's better than being out of a job, but I don't like to think what it would do to his self-respect, even if it could work out that way. A sensitive guy like that, it could kill him."

Steve nodded. "Sam, I can't give you a commitment, but don't give up on it. I promise I'll do everything I can to try to keep Norm in a top writing spot."

"Thanks, Steve. I knew I had you figured right. Let's skip it for now and enjoy the food."

The subject did not come up again during the meal. Instead, Sam entertained Steve with a number of stories about Max Zweig that had made him a legend in the garment center.

"Old Max," Sam was saying as they walked back, "couldn't care less about the crap we spout about Prestige Fashions. All he knows is what it's done for him and that he's got to have it, and pay for it. Max can hardly read, but he's got a head for dozens and grosses and balance sheets that would knock a certified public accountant off his feet. He likes the pretty pictures and sexy broads in his ads, and models around the place. Models wiggling their diet-skinny asses into a new number, standing around in the near-raw, smiling, dimpling, taking a pat on the cheek from a hand that has skin like the bark of a tree. But don't underestimate Max. If the orders don't come back in the mail, or from his salesmen, you couldn't sell him a snowball in the middle of a *schvitzbud*—that's Latin for a Turkish bath, Russian style."

"And Manny?"

"Manny couldn't care less about anything except playing the field and figuring out his *Morning Telegraph* or Daily *Racing Form*. Anyway, as long as Max is around. One day he'll have to take over, and that's my ace in the hole. He'll need me a hell of a lot more than ever, more than Old Max needs me now. I'm saving Manny for my old age security."

As they entered the reception foyer of the agency, Steve said again, "Try not to worry about it, Sam. Let's play it cool and see what happens. As far as I'm concerned, if nothing else works, I'll still want Norm as my Number One man."

"Thanks, Steve. I—uh—I know I don't have to tell you . . ."

"Norm will never know you mentioned it to me."

"Thanks. If I can help in any way, you know . . ."

"I'll count on it, Sam. And thanks for the lunch."

"Hell, Leary paid for it. On my expense account for today you'll be listed as Manny Zweig."

6

On Friday, Bill Leary, Keith Allard, Wade Barrett, and Steve lunched at Bill's club and cabbed to East Forty-second Street. Bill had the new report in his pocket for reference, and the key points, which they again rehearsed, firmly in his mind.

They were ushered into the office reserved for Herschel Goodwin's rare appearances at the city headquarters of GFP, a large room with comfortable leather chairs that looked strangely unused. Present were Mr. Goodwin—looking older and much smaller in the large chair behind the polished walnut desk—with Mark Lawson sitting on his right, and Ward Hardwick, the GFP general sales manager on his left. On the long sofa sat Curtis Fitzjohn, the comptroller, and Lee Rogers, GFP's "in house" attorney; which had sparked the humorous reference to Russell Charles as the firm's "outhouse" attorney, not present today. After hands had been shaken all around, Mr. Goodwin asked Bill Leary to take over and explain the reason for the meeting.

Bill, as in any presentation to a client, was at his very best. He gave Steve full and due credit for having uncovered the situation with B & B without divulging the circumstances that involved the West Coast agency branch. Steve glanced toward Mark Lawson and saw him draw a deep breath and smile—and at once recognized this as the possessive expresson of a football coach taking quiet pride (and credit) for one of his rookies who had performed with distinction on the field.

In his quiet soft-sell manner, Bill outlined the reason why he believed the acquisition of B & B would benefit GFP and how, if the matter were concluded successfully, B & B could be smoothly integrated into the GFP line and brought from sectional to national prominence and public acceptance with minimal effort and cost.

Steve's eyes moved from Herschel Goodwin—who received Bill's outline with little reaction—to Lawson—showing cool restraint with interest—to Curt Fitzjohn, whose reaction was indefinable; and to Lee Rogers, pad on lap, pencil busy making notes, his face showing only bland attention. Finally, Bill was finished. He sat down and waited.

Herschel Goodwin looked around as though checking the faces of his own people for their reactions, then cleared his throat. "Thank you, Mr. Leary, and you, Mr. Gilman, Mr. Barrett, and Mr. Allard. I am sure your interest in us prompted this interesting report on B & B Coffee." He paused, poured a glass of water from the carafe and sipped at it. "But," he continued, "I kept wondering, as you talked, if we should go into an item that could be so costly to acquire and would require us to spend so much more to bring it out nationally. This would require more construction, equipment, personnel, and administrative help on our part, maybe a year or more before we could get into full production. I know you realize that this isn't similar to any item we are already producing that can be manufactured and packaged on our present equipment in facilities already standing and operating, eh?"

"Also, in today's marketplace, we are facing certain economic situations that throw some doubt over my mind. As you already know, we have three or four marginal items in test markets and we are keeping them there in order to reduce the cost of breaking them nationally."

He smiled somewhat ruefully. "If I were twenty, even ten years younger, maybe I wouldn't even hesitate. Like when we went into margarine, mayonnaise, and peanut butter. I think if I had to make those decisions today, I might think twice."

Ward Hardwick, crestfallen, said, "Is that a final decision, Mr. Goodwin?"

Herschel grinned. "You ought to know, after all these

years, Ward, that no business decision I make is final until I talk it over with Anna." To the others, "I know Ward wants it, this new item. Ward came to us years ago from Atlantic Foods who, as everybody knows, has always had a popular coffee item in their line. Ward has always missed that in our line, haven't you, Ward?"

Hardwick pursed his lips, then said, "I can't deny that. It's a tough, competitive item, but with the GFP name on it, I think we can give any competition a good run. As Mr. Leary has reminded us, we've got a ready-made and immediate entree into the outlets. The same people who sell and distribute the GFP line can add this to their lists without any trouble at all. Accounting is the same . . ."

"*Nu, nu,*" Herschel interjected, cutting Hardwick off. "Of course, I agree with Ward that coffee is a special class in itself, far different from the rest of our line." He stopped there, turned to Lawson, and said, "Mark?"

"I like the idea very much. I think we could do a great job with it."

"Curt?"

Curtis Fitzjohn, solemn and conservative, said, "I would prefer to reserve judgment until I have a clearer picture of the financing we would have to undertake, assuming the present owners are willing to sell."

"And you, Mr. Rogers?"

The young lawyer looked up, flustered at having been drawn into the matter for other than legal reasons. "Uh—before I—uh—can project an opinion on whether it would be a worthwhile operation, I would like to—uh explore the possibilities Mr. Leary mentioned of presenting an offer to the Bond family and uh—prepare to enter into negotiations. Other than that, I can see no point in . . ."

"Well said," Herschel interrupted, saving Rogers from further participation. "And you, Mr. Allard, Mr. Barrett?"

Allard took the pipe from his mouth and held it firmly in one hand, using its short stem to direct his words at Mr. Goodwin. "I think, in this case, I can speak for Wade and myself. Our very presence here answers that question, Mr. Goodwin. If the purchase of the B & B company is feasible, I am convinced we can do for GFP's B & B Coffee what we have done in the past for its other products. I agree with Mr. Rogers, however, that first steps come first."

"And of course, Mr. Gilman, I don't need to ask you that same question," Goodwin said when Keith concluded. When Steve did not reply, "I thank all of you for your thoughts and opinions. I will think the matter over very carefully, talk it over with Anna and Mr. Russell Charles, our company attorney, and let you know what I have decided, maybe in another week or ten days. If there is nothing else, gentlemen . . ." he glanced at the wall clock, "I have a long ride back to Harrison."

The meeting ended on that note. It was exactly 3:30. Leary, Allard, and Barrett, after exchanging general pleasantries with their hosts, left to return to the agency. Steve and Mark were walking down the long corridor toward the stairs that led to Mark's office on the floor below, when Ward Hardwick overtook them. He placed a hand on Steve's shoulder and said, "Leaving now, Steve?"

Mark said, "No. He's coming to my office for a meeting with me. Something you wanted, Ward?"

"Just a question." To Steve, "You really think the Bonds would entertain an offer to sell?"

Steve said, "I can't know that for certain, Ward, but I have a strong feeling that if we go at it tactfully, there's a very good possibility."

"I hope you're right. I'd like to see that item in our line."

"Well, the next move will be up to Mr. Goodwin."

"Yes. I only hope he makes it before someone else gets wind of it and makes the Bonds an offer. Have you seen the sales figures for the past quarter?"

"No. All I know is that they were way off."

Hardwick laughed. "I don't mean B & B. I mean ours."

"Not yet."

"Get Mark to show them to you. See you." He turned toward his own office and Mark said, "He's got a lot to smile about. They were up nearly five-and-a-half percent over the same period for last year."

"That's promising."

"He won't be as happy at the end of this next quarter. The usual fall-off after the holidays when the bills come rolling in, taxes due, watching the pennies."

"I know, and we've anticipated that with a heavier shot in the arm for TV during the next two months."

Mark looked at him quizzically and said nothing. In Mark's office, Steve took the chair beside the large uncluttered desk. Mark said, "Didn't you bring anything along to show me on the new spring lineup?"

"I'm afraid not, Mark. That's what I wanted to discuss with you. The changes you suggested to Wade and Chuck were so far out in left field compared with what we'd decided on before I left that it all came as a complete surprise to me. I've seen some partial layouts and copy, but I thought we'd better talk about it more thoroughly before we get along too far with it."

The temperature of Mark's earlier warmth dipped several degrees. "What about it?" he asked coolly.

"Frankly, I don't like it, Mark. I don't think it works,"—and as Mark began an objection—"Hear me out before you start knocking what I have to say."

"All right, go ahead. I'm listening," Mark said with easily recognizable resentment edging his words.

Steve took a deep breath and let it out slowly. "Thanks. In the meeting we just left, we heard Mr. Goodwin mention certain facts about today's marketplace and economic conditions. I'm basing my objections to the present campaign on those same factors. I am convinced the market is in for a drastic change and I'm talking about the consumer market, not Wall Street, which is also showing signs of nervousness. The unemployment figure is rising, while wages and prices are on the upswing . . ."

"I read the papers, too, Steve. I don't need a crystal ball to tell me what's going on in the world."

"Then how can you afford to ignore the facts?"

"What facts? For Christ's sake, this is all off the top of your head, from what the old man said in the meeting, isn't it? Another excuse to knock an idea because it didn't come from the agency?"

"No, Mark, it isn't that, and you know I don't play that game. I've listened to people on the West Coast, and gone into the matter with our merchandising and marketing staffs. The consumer is thinking twice about things he and she would have bought on pure impulse only a short while ago, particularly in luxury and hard goods; automobiles, travel, furniture, jewelry, and clothing feel it first, but when it reaches the everyday food level, the noise will burst your eardrums. I'm for moving in that direction before the big explosion occurs."

For a moment, Mark stared at Steve, framing a reply, then, "Goddamn it, Steve, I never know when you're conning me into something or . . ."

"Mark, believe me, I couldn't be more serious about this. All the signs are there. Talk to your own marketing and merchandising people and have them show you the retail sales breakdowns for the last quarter in other fields. You'll see a general slowdown all along the line. Everything I've heard and checked out indicates we'll be facing resistance to a campaign that is fanciful and without meaning or substance. I'm convinced that we've got to sell *value* to women who are becoming increasingly conscious of rising food costs."

"What you're saying is, you want to switch to hard sell."

"Call it that if you want, but if we refuse to recognize a revolution of sorts in the making, GFP will suffer for it in the long run. I wouldn't want that kind of responsibility on my head."

"And if you're wrong?"

"Even if I am, I can't see the harm in selling value along with quality as long as it's in good taste."

"When can you have something to show me?"

"Within a week or ten days I can show you enough to give you a clear, concise picture of what I have in mind."

"Well—okay. Ten days at the most." Mark smiled suddenly and said, "Let's talk about this coffee thing."

"I don't know what there is to talk about at the moment, Mark. Why don't we hold that up until I get this present project under way, at least until we get Mr. Goodwin's decision to go ahead with the suggestion to buy."

Mark shifted in his chair and swung around to face Steve more directly. "We're going to have a lot to talk about when we get it, won't we?"

"*If* we get it," Steve amended. "Do you think he'll really spring for it, Mark? I had the feeling he was very cool toward the whole idea."

"I think you caught him by surprise and he wants some time to think it over. He'll talk it over with Anna and Russ Charles, just as he said. I'd guess Russ will go for it if the price is right. What the hell, the old man can't turn a good thing down because he's getting on in years. When he goes, the business will still be functioning, won't it? Anyway, we'll see. By the way . . ."

Mark reached down, pulled out a lower drawer and came up with a small oblong package that was wrapped in blue foil, tied with a gold ribbon and bow. "Catch." He threw the package to Steve, who caught it, held it for a moment, then looked into Lawson's smiling face. "Merry belated Christmas, Steve. You'd have gotten it last month if you hadn't been screwing around out on the West Coast."

It was the first gift Mark had ever given him and Steve found words hard to come by. Mark said insistently, "Go ahead, open it. I had Karen pick it out for you."

Steve slipped the ribbon off, removed the foil, and saw the Tiffany name impressed in gold on the dark blue box. He opened it, and stared down in awe at the most exquisite gold watch and chain-link bracelet he had ever seen.

"Like it?" Mark asked.

"It's—a beauty. Magnificent."

"For eight bills, it should be."

Discomfort mounted at this reminder of its cost, but this lay beneath the surface of his stunning surprise, unconsciously wondering how much Mark would expect, even demand, in return. "Thank you, Mark, and Mrs. Lawson. I've never seen anything as lovely."

"Compliments of GFP. You stick with me, Steve boy, and you'll be wearing diamonds for shirt studs someday. Slip it on and remember who your friends are. If this coffee thing goes through, you deserve it more than ever."

"Thank you, Mark, and please thank Mrs. Lawson for me. Her taste is superb."

"Okay, enjoy it. Anything else we have to talk about?"

"I don't think so at the moment. I'd like to get back and look into a few things before everyone gets away for the weekend. I'll check in with you during the week."

"Okay. Karen stayed on in Wyecliffe to visit with her aunt. I'm driving up in the morning to bring her back on Sunday. I'll get a few licks in with the old man while I'm there. See you next week."

Back in his office, Steve checked with WPC and learned the new commercial was in production. Chuck had left early. Frank Hayden had a few questions for him, which he answered quickly. Jon Hartman had some initial copy ideas he wanted to discuss, which Steve put off until Monday. He signed what mail Peggy had for him and, knowing she was anxious to get away for a dinner date, said, "All right, Peggy, beat it, and have a good weekend."

"You, too. See you Monday morning." She left, and Steve dropped into his chair, fatigued, trying to decide about dinner; whether to have it alone and get a good night's sleep, or call someone and make a night of it.

Allard came into his office then, dressed for outdoors. "Anything more with the genius after we left?" he asked.

"Not much, Keith. He's all steamed up with the coffee thing. He and Mrs. Lawson are spending the weekend with the Goodwins and I think he'll work out on Mr. Goodwin when he gets the chance."

"I think it will be a hell of a shot in the arm for GFP," Keith said, "but I doubt the value of any pressure Mark can exert on the old man. I'd put my chips on Mrs. Goodwin and Russell Charles."

"Well, at least he won't try to kill it."

"I doubt if he could do that, either. Incidentally, what about the change in theme for the spring campaign?"

"Mark bought my suggestion for changing it, and for the time being, I've got a green light. But if we don't have some kind of a recession by April or May to back me up, he'll be screaming for my head."

"You'll get around him somehow."

"I know. As you keep reminding me, I'm Mark's boy."

Allard laughed. "Hell, you've had the Indian sign on him for a long time. If I didn't know you better I'd think you were sleeping with him."

"A suggestion like that could give me nightmares. What do you think about Mr. Goodwin, Keith? Will he go for it, or not? He's too cagy for me to read."

"I think he'll buy it unless he's farther over the hill than I think. You know, that 'Who needs it?' kind of thing. Well, we'll wait and hope. Goodnight, Steve, and have a nice weekend."

"You, too, Keith, and love to Louise."

Waiting beside the bank of elevators later, he heard soft footsteps behind him, turned and saw it was Lex Kent, the VP executive art director. Lex, with neatly trimmed, swept-back hair that turned up over the edge of his mod overcoat, mustached and goateed, had added years to his appearance with the additional hirsute growth, sporting a flaming red Ascot around his throat, ends trailing outside, and skin-tight slacks that flared out at his ankles in the mod manner of today. "Hey, man," he called, "long time no see."

"Hi, Lex. Still grooving it?"

"You'd better believe it, man. What else?"

"How about me stealing Lennie Hawkins away from

Don Bryce permanently? I expect to have enough to keep him busy full time."

"Sure, if it's okay with Don. I can get a replacement easily enough. I hope you can handle him. Too goddamned temperamental for me. Great on those storyboards, though. Listen, you free tonight, how about dropping by the pad? Got some beautiful cats coming over for a weekend shakedown. Free everything. Booze, broads, food, pot. Dig?"

Lex, during business hours, couldn't be more circumspect in behavior or choice of language in serious pursuit of his work, but from Friday afternoon until Monday morning, in his own words, "That's my own time, baby, my time and my life, uncluttered by the goddamned establishment and its fucked-up clients."

"Thanks, Lex, but I've got my own shakedown this weekend."

"Gotcha, man. If it runs out of gas, you know where the old pad is. We'll be in high gear until Monday morning."

"I'll keep it in mind."

7

Saturday was clear, sunny, and cold. It was Peggy's turn to do the marketing for the week and she started out immediately after doing some ironing in order to be free for an afternoon of purely creative effort, a poem she had been toying with, *Winter City*. Nikki had left for Westport for a weekend houseparty the night before, and Lois was preparing for a lunch-matinee date.

On the edge of the Village, carrying two heavy bags of groceries, she felt a hand reach out for one of the paper bags and heard Lennie Hawkins's baritone voice beside her. "Here, let me give you a hand with that."

"Oh. Hi, Lennie. It's nothing . . ."

"Nothing? Must be a fortune in chow in there. Give me the other one, too."

"No, I can handle this one, thanks."

"Which way?"

"Twelfth Street. I'm taking you out of your way."

"Nope. Just walking. Looking."

"For what?"

"Not what. At. People. Just people. Observation of

homo sapiens at large. *Homunculi quanti sunt*," he quoted.

"Huh?"

"What insignificant creatures we men are," he translated.

"A cheerful thought for a beautiful day?"

Lennie grinned with self-satisfaction. "Try this one on for size. *Homo sum; humani nihil a me alienum puto*."

"I pass. I was always lousy in Latin."

"I am a man; nothing that relates to man do I deem alien to me."

"Curious," she said.

"How do you mean, curious."

"Like, if you mean that, how do you relate to things like Vietnam, Laos and Cambodia."

"War? Hell, I was in it. I accept it because it's there. That doesn't mean I approve of it, but since it was man-made and deals with men, it isn't alien to me."

"And you don't have a solution for it?"

"Of course I have. The simplest of solutions. If there must be wars, let the men who cause or declare them be forced to lead their troops into battle, and put the politicians who vote for war in the front lines, where leaders should be. That would end all thoughts of future wars."

They walked along, talking easily until they reached Peggy's apartment building and when Lennie hesitated at the entrance, she said, "Come on up," and led the way to the elevator. On the fourth floor, he held both bags while she got her keys out and unlocked the door. The groceries distributed on shelves and in bins, the meat, eggs, milk, and butter in the refrigerator, Peggy said, "Thank you, Lennie. Will you have a drink in payment?"

He said, "I don't accept payment for . . ."

"I didn't mean it that way."

"Thanks, no. Too early for me."

"Then how about lunch? I'm dying for a sandwich and some coffee. Do you mind if it's reheated?"

"No-o, but . . ." He looked around as though expecting someone to come from one of the other rooms."

"Let me fix something. Nikki and Lois are out—you know them, don't you? They work at Leary, too."

"I guess I've seen them around."

She made two cold roast beef sandwiches, heated some leftover beans, brought out pickles, opened a can of tomatoes that had been cooling in the refrigerator, and set the table in the kitchen. When the coffee was heated, they sat down to eat, and she took note of some uneasiness on Lennie's part and guided the conversation toward his work, then to art in general, but found him unresponsive.

"You've got a nice place here," Lennie said finally.

"We like it. It's convenient and rent-controlled, so we make out very well, splitting expenses three ways. The furniture is Nikki's, left over from her divorce."

"You do anything besides your work?" Lennie asked.

"Like what?"

"Like write. Most people in agencies get the bug sooner or later, don't they, a writing thing?"

"Some do, I guess. My thing, away from the office, is poetry."

"Anything published?"

"A few little things in college. Some poems, two short stories. Nothing commercial."

"Beats hell out of me. Why poetry?"

"Why anything? Don't you dig poetry?"

"It's all crap to me. Mystical crap with no bread attached, like nothing."

Peggy flushed, resentment rising. "Does everything have to have a dollar sign attached to it? Poetry is good discipline for the mind, for someone who hopes to do it seriously some day."

"Maybe as a copywriter?"

"Why not serious poetry? Or short stories? Even a novel."

"The Great American Bag?" he said, the scorn coming through.

She was annoyed and showed it. "Man, you've really got a mad on, haven't you? Writing, the Establishment, is that it?"

"Maybe. And maybe it's just my own thing. I'm an artist."

"Does that affect your attitude toward poetry, or any other form of creativity? And what good is your particular art if you haven't any faith in anything else, in the future?"

"My faith," Lennie said, "is in me, and to me, the future is today, here, now, this minute."

"No tomorrows?"

"Only when they become today. One day at a time."

"And what about your yesterdays. Don't they add up to anything?"

"Baby," he said slowly, "when today becomes yesterday, it's done, over, gone forever."

"Leaving no memories to live with?"

"The kind of memories you're talking about are for old people, something to warm shriveling bodies. Dreams." Then in a sudden burst, "Dreams are shit."

She was shocked into silence, lips forming a rebuke that never came. He said, "You don't like that word, do you? Why, because it's real?"

"I don't like crude words or crude people."

Lennie stood up. "Remember that when you write your poetry, or your novel. Or do you expect to get past reality with asterisks and dashes, the way most people live their lives?"

She said nothing and Lennie began picking up the plates, carrying them to the sink.

"You don't have to do that," Peggy said.

"I know I don't. I'm doing it because I want to do it."

"Then please don't. You're my guest and my guests don't pay for their food."

"Okay, okay, but don't get so uptight about it."

"I'm not uptight."

"Sure you are. You're bugged, like I get bugged sometimes."

"Do you really? About what?"

He stood with his back resting against the sink ledge, feeling the sarcasm in her question. "Things," he said. "Just things."

"What things?"

"Oh, lots of things. Like the way people accept what's dished out to them without thinking. A world filled with brainwashed sheep who take the crap of life without even opening their mouths."

"You're very good at making statements that show anger, but you give no reasons."

"Let me spell it out for you. I mean, like damned near everything we touch, or that touches us. Like lying politicians who live by expediency. Like the frauds that are practiced on us every day of our lives by industry and commerce, all in the name of sacred free enterprise. Like the bullshit spoonfed us from the cradle to the grave, by Washington, by state and city governments, by the press, in the name of their own private freedom to slant the news. Like being jerked around by religionists, made to feel guilty by belief in superstition, voodooism and witchcraft. Like . . ."

Peggy had gotten up and begun to rinse the dishes. "You've lost me, man, way past my stop."

"Oh, shit! You're like the rest of the stupid, fucked-up people who get screwed every time they go into a store, buy a car, go to church . . ."

The plate she was holding fell and crashed on the enameled ledge and shattered into small pieces. Lennie, shaking his head apologetically, began gathering up the shards of china. "Done it again," he said.

"Well, you do have a unique way of expressing yourself."

"I'm sorry if I offended you. I get mad as hell and pop off. Can't control it most of the time. Maybe our different cultures . . ."

"Oh, I know the words. Even out in Nebraska, we've heard them before. I'm not a child. Let's get back to religion, heaven, and hell."

"Okay. You believe in some kind of life after death, don't you?"

"Yes, of course."

"Why?"

"Because . . ." she began haltingly.

"Because you've been brainwashed since childhood to believe it. Where's the proof? Who ever came back to tell about it? *How do you know?* From the Bible? For Christ's sake, ninety percent of it is fiction and the other ten percent is fairy tales and legends handed down for thousands of years. Organized religion was the first *Lost Horizon,* the *Shangri-La* fantasy people need to dream about. Like every guy likes to dream he's the best stud in the world, and every woman the greatest lay. It's all bullshit."

"And *that's* what your world is made of?" Peggy said softly. "If it is, I feel terribly sorry for you, Lennie."

"Don't waste your sympathy. I can't see how your world is any different or better than mine. Thing is, you see yours through sunglasses and with blinders on."

She was finished with the dishes. Lennie said, "I've got to go now. Thanks for the lunch."

8

An hour before the first of the GFP group arrived on Monday morning, Steve was at his desk transferring copy notes he had made over the weekend onto the rough layout on his drawing board. Penciled in at the top was the headline:

A Statement from
the President of
GOODY FOOD PRODUCTS
to the
HOUSEWIVES OF AMERICA

Below that, the hastily lettered copy read:

> In these days of rising food costs it isn't where the Buck stops, so much as how it can put More into your shopping cart.
>
> GFP recognizes the problem, whatever the causes, and we don't like it any more than you do. But not liking it isn't enough, and this is what we are DOING about it:

The balance of the copy, legibly written, was the proposition, or intent; and an immediate across-the-board reduction of from five to ten cents on every item in the GFP line, using refund coupons attached to each package and bottle, redeemable at the checkout counter at time of purchase.

A special copy block, illustrated, and enclosed by rules, offered the 175-page soft cover *Goody Famous Recipe Book* free, with any six Goody labels, formerly available for seventy-five cents and any three GFP labels.

In the center of the ad were two charts. The first showed an upward spiral with the legend: *'As the Cost of Living Rises* . . . and beside it, a similar chart showing a downward spiral, its legend reading: *This Is What GFP Is Doing to Lower Your Food Bills. . . .*

Pencil lines indicated the closing statement over the written signature of Herschel Goodwin as President, beneath which was a list of all GFP items; each cake, biscuit, pancake, and muffin mix, toppings, margarine, mayonnaise, peanut butter, salad dressings, and instant puddings.

It was rough, but it was there; the bare outline of a new campaign. The challenge. Headings were bold to capture attention and add emphasis to the core of the message, yet the ad was generous with white space so that when reduced to magazine-page size, the important elements would remain uncluttered and legible. The final signal to go ahead would be approval of GFP to institute the first price reduction ever offered in its history, and which must be authorized by Herschel Goodwin himself, which would necessarily require a round of discussions with Curtis Fitzjohn and Ward Hardwick. So far, so good.

Peggy looked in on Steve at nine o'clock, saw him deeply engrossed, and brought him a cup of coffee, but withheld the mail. Chuck came in and asked, "What time?" and Steve, without looking up, replied, "Ten o'clock."

When the account executives and creative group entered promptly at ten, the roughly penciled ad, rubber-cemented to a stiff cardboard backing, stood on an easel facing them. Peggy wheeled the coffee cart in and each helped himself to a cup. Cigarettes were lighted and, after examining the ad close up for a few moments, those present found seats on the leather sofa and extra chairs were brought in by Lew Kann, Gary Parris and the messenger-trainee. Peggy took the chair beside the desk, notebook poised, ready to record any pertinent remarks or observations Steve might require for future reference.

"Okay," Steve said when they were settled. "You've seen it, and you know the direction I want to take. Any comments before we open the general discussion? And let's show no mercy. Shoot the hell out of it if you feel that way. There will be no reprisals."

Alan Grant, the senior writer, said, "What the hell, Steve, it's obvious you intend this for openers. What comes next?"

"I'll answer that after the comments are in, Al. What I want now are your gut reactions to this kickoff theme."

Grant started a reply, but Frank Hayden, nodding firm approval, said, "I'm for it, all the way. This lays it on the line and I think the public will spring for it."

Chuck Baldasarian said, "Hell, it's always easy to give something away. The question is, will the client buy it?"

Before Steve could reply, Reed Baker said, "Why shouldn't he? I think I could sell this to Lawson myself."

Chuck, sharpness accelerating his voice, snapped, "You're out of order, Reed. Don't start flying too high."

"It's the only way I can get past you without stomping on your toes, Chuck," Reed replied with excessive sweetness.

"Let's knock off the sniping and start talking," Steve admonished the entire group. To Don Berman, his hand half-raised, "Don?"

"Well," the senior art director said, "Except for the lousy layout technique, I think you've got an interesting proposition there, Steve."

Steve laughed, and replied, "I had to leave something for you art directors to contribute. Coming from the old school, I realize there's a considerable generation gap to overcome and I don't intend to tell you young geniuses how to do your jobs, so let's get back to the basic premise and theme.

"What I want are several layouts with copy, followups that will reflect this identical message and give continuing prominence to the refund coupon idea and free recipe book offer. How we combine these features in the follow-up ads will be your baby, Don. Yours, Randy, will be to remind our readers that the GFP is the *Value Line*. You might even consider using that phrase as a tagline to tie in with the logo."

Steve let that sink in for a moment, sipping at his cup of coffee. Chuck said, "Steve, don't you think we should have one or two more general rap sessions before we start working on definite layouts and copy?"

A small groan went up from the assembly and Steve said, "Chuck, I don't think so. For one thing, there's the time element. For another, those big creative conferences are nothing more than exercises in futility and turn out to be nothing more than group therapy for noncreative minds. I'd a hell of a lot rather let our copy-art teams do their own brainstorming between themselves, nothing forced. This is the pattern we want to follow, so let each team pick up the ball and run with it."

"Hooray," Al Grant said softly.

"All right, are there any other questions you want answered?"

Berman asked, "What about this hearts and flowers jazz we've been holding back on?"

"Forget it. Go your own route with the new approach."

Parris ventured, "What about the tube?"

"I want you and Lennie Hawkins in for another session on TV and Radio later this afternoon."

Then Cook, "Can we take this rough of yours with us?"

"Yes," Steve said, "and have photostats made for everyone here."

Grant wanted to know the deadline.

Steve answered, "I want at least two ads like this one in visual form, one this size, one reduced to magazine size. Also, one followup in both sizes, newspaper in black-and-white, the other for magazine in color, no later than Friday noon. I'll show them to Lawson for what is laughingly known as consideration and approval. Copy and layout. The final decision on the price reductions will have to come from topside. Friday noon is both D-Day and H-Hour."

"Can do."

"If that's all—" Steve began, but Chuck cut in:

"Steve, I take it that none of this has been cleared with Lawson, the price thing, the free recipe book?"

"I thought I'd made that clear, Chuck. Let me repeat it for all of you. They have no idea what we're coming up with. It will go to Lawson first. If he approves, and I hope he will, he'll have to clear it with the decision-makers. If that's all, let's get with it, top priority."

They filed out in a talking mood, one that, to Steve, indicated eagerness to move out of the monotony of a going campaign into something newer, fresher, different. Chuck remained behind. Peggy closed her book and said, "Another feather in our collective caps?"

"So far," Steve said, looking questioningly at Baldasarian. "Something else, Chuck?"

"Yes. What happens if Lawson turns it down?"

"Why don't we wait and see what he does?"

"Well, since you seem to be in a giveaway mood, have you given any thought to a premium program, something GFP has never had?"

Steve eyed Chuck curiously for a moment. "Chuck, the reasons why GFP has never had a premium program are too many and too old to take up here and now. For the record, once and for all times, we will not suggest premiums in a program designed to cut the household food bill."

"I hate to bug you again, but suppose he *does* turn it down?"

"That comes under the head of persuasive salesmanship—my job."

Slyly, "I thought that was Barrett's end of the load to carry."

"Normally, yes, but every account has its own characteristics and peculiarities, Chuck. Sometimes it's easier for an account man to sway the client where the supervisor, creative director, even the Big Man himself might fall on his face."

"While drawing sixty or seventy-five thou a year against your thirty?" Chuck said with a grin.

Steve returned the grin without enthusiasm. "Why don't we just forget the goddamned office politics, Chuck? We've got work to do and a lot of it. Just remember, creative men build agencies, but businessmen run them. Okay?"

"Okay, if you like it that way." When he went out, Peggy said, "In a way, he's right, you know."

"You can knock it off, too, Peggy. That's what starts corporate dissatisfaction and industrial unhappiness."

"Well, it isn't fair for Mr. Barrett to draw twice as much as you while you're doing his job, is it?"

"That's heresy."

"I know very well what it is. Establishmentarianism. Lennie says . . ."

"Whoa! Since when this 'Lennie says' bit?"

Peggy's face crimsoned. "A lot of what he says makes sense."

"Well I'll be damned. Are you spending company time getting instruction in antiestablishmentarianism from Lennie Hawkins?"

"No, of course not. I run into him occasionally on the subway. We don't live that far apart."

"Well, I don't intend to interfere with your personal life, naturally, but I'd suggest that you and Mr. Hawkins keep your opinions on the establishment between yourselves."

Peggy reacted sharply. "You're making a lot out of nothing, Steve, and it's not what you think. I'm not *seeing* him. We just *happen* to run into each other on the subway, around the Village area, shopping . . ."

"I'm not talking about that, only ideas. I'm a part of what Lennie calls the establishment. There's even the possibility of a distant intellectual gap between us. Inside these walls, I don't want to discuss politics, religion, the senselessness of war, campus unrest, sex, *or* the establishment."

"And outside these hallowed walls?"

"We enjoy the freedoms, liberties and pursuit of individual happiness we see fit to enjoy, such as they may be. If that makes me out a stuffy bastard, I'm sorry, but this is a workshop and my responsibility . . ."

She turned to go, then turned back. "Steve, don't read anything wrong into Lennie and me. He's a great talent and I admire talent. His, Lex Kent's, Don Berman's. And yours."

"Thank you. Can we forget it now and get back to work?"

"I hate to spike you, but that's your privilege, too." When she reached the door, he said, "Peg?"

"Yes, boss."

"And you can knock that off, too. Bring some coffee in with the mail, will you? This stuff is cold."

With the morning mail was a letter from a Myron Haywood, a vice-president of the C & H Sales Merchandising Corporation of Chicago, referring to an earlier letter, requesting an appointment "at your earliest convenience," about which Steve had no recollection. Peggy said, "You saw the letter your first day back from the Coast. You said to put him off, and I did."

"What did you tell him?"

"That you'd just gotten back from a month-long field trip and suggested he get in touch with you at a later date."

"Stall him. I don't want him making a special trip to New York just to get turned down on some premium deal he has in mind." He took up the next letter, dictated a reply, and went on to the next until the batch was disposed of.

"What else is on the schedule, Peg?"

"Mr. Bryce would like to have you look at some tapes in the screening room this afternoon at three, if you're free. Lunch with Mr. Allard at one, schedule review in Traffic at four-thirty. That's it for today."

Chapter 9

1

On the following Wednesday, after sitting through an hour of video-taped commercials in the viewing room with Don Bryce, his top director, Colin Ferris, Gary Parris, and Peggy, Steve was summoned to Bill Leary's office. He found Keith Allard with Bill and was informed that Herschel Goodwin had invited them to his home in Wyecliffe on Saturday to discuss the B & B matter. The news gave Steve a heightened feeling of encouragement, and sensing that same gratification in Bill and Keith, he assumed that if Herschel Goodwin had been inclined to turn the proposal down, it would have been done in a letter to Bill.

"Will Wade be there?" Steve asked.

"Yes," Bill replied. "Keith is driving me up. Wade has a morning meeting with his attorney and I'll have him pick you up at your apartment around noon. Besides ourselves, there'll be Mark Lawson and Russell Charles, so I'd safely guess Herschel is ready to give us an affirmative answer. I'll want you to answer any questions Mr. Charles may ask which my report may not cover."

Steve had planned a skiing weekend with Barbara O'Connell, a fashion designer, and another couple, but was now forced to cancel out, a disappointment to both. A tough business, Allard had warned him long ago. It was sometimes tougher on a man's social life Steve had learned long ago from experience, knowing how bitterly the married executives took these sudden directives to keep the Almighty Client happy.

On Friday, he made the planned trip to Lawson's office to present the basic idea for the new spring campaign. With the first ad set up on the bottom ledge of Mark's blackboard, he could sense immediately a mood of reluctance. Finally, Mark turned to him and said, "Just what the hell are you guys trying to pull off here, Steve?"

"We're not trying to pull off anything, Mark, only doing

our best to conform to the conditions of today, just as you and I discussed them last week."

"Okay, so you preached doom and gloom and you want me to believe we can solve it all by giving away our profits?"

"We won't solve the problem, Mark, but we can help build confidence in the GFP name and image. The practice of giving discounts isn't new except to us. GFP has never offered one . . ."

"Why the hell should we, when we've always been a few cents under any of our competitors?"

"And the public knows that, but the added impact of a further cost cut could put us in on top of the biggest of our competitors."

"And the free cook book with it?"

"I checked that out with Mrs. Harris. There are close to seven hundred thousand of those recipe books in your warehouse and they're moving at a snail's pace. What's more, it's long overdue for a revision of cover, recipes, and menus. This is a sure way to get rid of the old ones before the new book comes out to make what we have obsolete, ready for the trash can."

"Okay, so you win a few points on the book deal, but this other thing, the coupon refund, you know goddamned well I can't give you a green light on that. Hardwick and Fitzjohn are involved—the old man himself."

"Which is why I'm bringing it to you first, Mark. I thought it would be more effective if the whole idea came from you, the means for boosting sales while the competition is screaming because they've been caught with tight shoes. You present it to your board and recommend it. That gives you the edge on Sales, Marketing, and Merchandising, all the way down the line."

A soft grin began to play over Mark's mouth. "You cagy sonofabitch. You're a real smarty, aren't you, setting me up to pull your goddamned chestnuts out of the fire."

"Mark, it's a good, sound business move, and you know it. If they don't approve it upstairs, we've still got time to go another route. Why not take the chance they'll agree with you?"

Mark thought for a moment, then said, "All right, smart boy. I'll go your way for now. What's next?"

Steve brought out the followup ads, which were more conventional, showing the full line of items in a double-page spread, incorporating the Value Line theme. "Hey, now!" Mark exclaimed. "That's got balls. I like it."

"I thought you would. Hard sell and soft sell combined in one ad. What follows will be the single-page ads, but there wasn't enough time to get the layouts through by today."

Mark was at the blackboard examining both ads, expressing his admiration by running his fingertips over the cellophane covering, pointing out various elements that pleased him. "Okay, Steve, I'll spring for this. I'll take it up with Fitzjohn and Hardwick on Monday and see if it pumps any adrenalin through their veins. Curt won't be easy to sell, you know that."

"I'm sure you and Ward can convince him, Mark."

There was a knock on the door and it opened slightly. Mark turned toward it, his face registering annoyance at the interruption, but it cleared when he saw the girl who stood there; young, smiling shyly, wide-eyed, and beautiful. "I hope I'm not intruding, Mr. Lawson," she said. "Charlotte isn't at her desk, and I knew you wanted to see the sales figures on the new . . ."

"Yes, of course, Jerri. Come in and say hello to Mr. Gilman, our advertising agency man. Steve, this is Jerri Davis, took Sue Garvey's place last month."

"How do you do, Miss Davis," Steve said.

"I'm fine, thank you," Jerri replied, smiling, tilting her head to one side. "Will that be all, Mr. Lawson?" She was placing too much emphasis on the *Mr.*, as though this formality was purely for Steven's benefit.

"For now, yes, Jerri, but be sure to check with me before you leave for the day."

"Of course. Nice meeting you, Mr. Gilman." She turned and walked out. The look on Lawson's face was sheer bliss as he said to Steve, "Nice?"

"Very nice," Steve agreed, wondering about Robin Ford and whether Sue Garvey, Jerri's predecessor, had suffered Robin's fate.

"You said it," Lawson beamed with special emphasis. "And fills the job beautifully."

"I'd already assumed that."

Lawson's grin broadened with self-satisfaction. He winked one eye and said, "Stick with me, Steve, and you'll hit the big leagues yet."

Steve stood up. "If that's all for now, Mark, I'll leave

these with you. Will you call me as soon as you've gotten a decision?"

"Sure. You coming up to Wyecliffe with Leary and Allard tomorrow?"

"Yes. Bill and Keith are driving up together. I'll be coming up with Wade."

"You don't have a car, do you?"

"No. I wouldn't know what to do with one in the city."

"If you'd like to drive up with Karen and me—oh, sorry, we'll be going up tonight, but I'm sure we can make room for you if you can stay over. How about it?"

Steve was not even mildly tempted. "I'm sorry, Mark, but I have plans for tonight that I can't possibly cancel."

"Then we'll see you there tomorrow."

"Yes. Of course."

2

Barrett picked Steve up at his apartment at a little past one o'clock the following day, apologizing briefly for being late, grumbling over "these goddamned lawyers, wrangling and killing time at Christ only knows how much an hour," grumbling about his missed lunch, and the rented Ford he was forced to drive because Sylvia had kept the Cadillac and given the Buick to their daughter Carol. When Steve suggested they stop so Wade could have a sandwich and coffee, he refused.

They took 9-A to the George Washington Bridge, then into Route 4, with heavy Saturday traffic all the way, despite a gloomy, threatening overcast. The radio was on, and in Houston there was a post-season football game in progress, the announcer ecstatic in Astrodome comfort while rotted ice and snow rimmed the New Jersey roadside and landscape, causing Steve's mind to drift back momentarily to Los Angeles and, inevitably, the problem of Larry Price; wondering if Bill had come to a decision, almost certain that whether the Goody–B & B deal came off or failed to materialize, Price's days with Leary were already numbered.

"You want to hear this game?" Barrett asked suddenly.

"Not particularly."

Wade shut the radio off. "You ever met Sylvia?" he asked.

Steve was somewhat startled by the question, hoping he would not be drawn into Wade's personal problem to any greater degree. "Of course," he replied. "Don't you remember? I had dinner with you and Sylvia sometime ago."

"Yes, sure, I remember now. This damned thing has me so upset, I can't even think straight." The road flashed by for another quarter of a mile before Wade spoke again. "You didn't like her, did you? I don't blame you. She always looked down at anybody I brought home from the agency, the damned snob."

It was a question and statement and Steve felt no reply was required. Another uncomfortable mile went by. The air, like the dirty crust that lined both sides of the road, seemed frozen, and despite the warmth given off by the car heater, Steve felt a chill.

"Goddamn her!" The words burst from Wade's mouth like an explosion. "She's trying her goddamnedest to take me for everything I've got. House, the boat, even the Buick for Carol, and took the Caddy for herself. Left me on foot, tied up my cash, stocks, the works, until those fucking lawyers work out a settlement. Christ!" He threw a side glance at Steve. "You have anything like this mess in your divorce from—from what's her name—Elizabeth, wasn't it?"

"No," Steve said shortly. "Ours was an amicable divorce."

"Lucky you. You don't know what you're missing. Well, thank God, Carol's on her own. Twenty-seven years shot to hell. That bitch was never satisfied, no matter how well things were going. Always sniping for something new, bigger house, more jewelry, trips to Europe, first class all the way. Christ, the money she pissed away on clothes alone. Then she suddenly gets this new kick, wants a life of her own, her own friends, a higher cultural level of life, what the hell ever that means. Agency people were never good enough for her . . ."

Wade rambled on compulsively, spewing hate and bitterness, more for his own need than for Steve's benefit, who began running the tip of his tongue over the edge of his teeth out of sheer nervousness, knowing no way to turn off the steady waterfall of complaint and self-pity; remembering the deterioration of his own marriage, reliving the aloneness of Libby's departure, the months of desperate emptiness she had left behind.

Wade turned off onto Paramus Road and continued north until they came into the village of Wyecliffe, passed through the busy commercial section and stopped at a filling station to check the road map Keith had sketched from memory. They found Thorpe Road and drove through a section of pleasant private homes and larger estates, came to a wide crossroad with the uninspired name of Four Corners, then continued on for another winding two miles before they reached the Goodwin estate.

Although snow covered the ground, the inner road had been cleared. Ice-laden tree branches dipped low with weight and white fence rails were almost invisible against the misty backdrop of a natural valley. To one side Steve could see a wide stretch of river, and on the other, the upright posts between which, come spring, tennis nets would be stretched. The house had a mildly pitched roof that showed several small patches of heavy shake shingles where the interior warmth had melted the snow away. As they drew closer to the U-shaped structure, he could see a small caretaker's house with smoke spiraling upward from its chimney. Beyond the house was a long, low building that could only be a horse barn.

Keith Allard's Lincoln stood in the driveway near the entranceway, a sparkling white Mercedes sedan behind it. As they emerged from the Ford, the front door opened, and a tall black man smiled invitingly.

"Mr. Barrett, Mr. Gilman? Come inside, gentlemen."

He took their hats and coats just as a woman entered the wide hallway from a room on the right, and advanced slowly, smiling, one hand extended toward Wade. "I remember Mr. Barrett," she said, then turned to Steve, "and you must be Mr. Gilman. Welcome to Wyecliffe. I'm Anna Goodwin. The others are in the study." To the black man, "Eric, tell Leona I'll be with her in a moment."

Her voice was low and melodic. She was tall, but bent slightly forward, and wore a brocaded ankle-length housecoat, her features difficult to make out in the dimly lighted hallway, although Steve at once saw the resemblance to the photograph he remembered in Herschel Goodwin's office in the Harrison plant during his first visit.

She led them along the carpeted hallway past several rooms to a large, cozy study with a head-high fireplace in which two huge logs blazed merrily. Seated around a low marble-topped coffee table, Herschel Goodwin, Keith Allard, and Bill Leary were in conversation over drinks.

They exchanged greetings with the new arrivals, Bill Leary glancing at his wrist watch in a manner that indicated they were late. Then Anna Goodwin excused herself and went out. Wade turned toward the bar and called out, "Hello, Russ. Good to see you again," and dropped into a chair between Bill and Keith.

At the bar, Steve saw a tall, balding man, dressed in rich country tweeds with leather patches on the elbows of his jacket, a black turtleneck pullover beneath it. The one-word impression Steve had of him was *distinguished*. Somehow drawn toward him, Steve went to the bar where the man was mixing a drink and said, "I'm Steve Gilman. You must be Mr. Charles."

"Russ," the man replied. "If you're a Scotch-and-water man, take this." He slid the drink across the bar and began pouring another for himself. Russell Charles said, "I understand you're the chap who will be entitled to a finder's fee if this buyout jells."

"We'll be well rewarded without a finder's fee if the deal goes through," Steve replied.

Charles' eyes crinkled into a half-smile. "Amazing," he said softly, "amazing. Well, here's to success."

They sipped their drinks and drifted back to the table and joined the others, Steve wondering why Mark wasn't there to take part in the discussion that would certainly begin at any moment; but the talk seemed to be touching on every subject except the one in which he had come to participate. Bill was talking about the abysmal stock market situation, which brought out Herschel's thoughts on the relative merits of President Nixon's efforts to stem the inflationary trend, a possible lowering of interest rates, new and outrageous union demands, and threatened strikes. Steve gathered, through his quiet contributions to the general conversation, that Russell Charles dealt in corporate law, with offices in Manhattan and associates in numerous cities from which he drew much of his background information. Again, Steve wondered about Mark's absence, then remembered the football game and assumed he would be elsewhere in the house, glued to a television set.

Anna Goodwin returned, followed by a coffee-colored maid, obviously Leona, who carried a large tray of hot canapés. Eric came in and began gathering up glasses for refills. In the brighter light, Steve's eyes were on Anna and he guessed she was in her middle sixties. Her hair was a soft gray-brown, her eyes languid, and there was a telltale softening of the flesh along her jawline and neck. She held her hands in a manner that suggested brittleness, perhaps a mild arthritis, but her facial expression was lively, her smile bright with good humor. She stayed only long enough to make certain the men were served, then left the room.

A moment later, Karen Goodwin entered, and Steve, rising with the others, recognized her at once from the color photograph on the cabinet behind Mark's desk. She wore a pair of black form-fitting slacks and a Chinese red topper, and moved with the suppleness of a ballet dancer, effortlessly, and gracefully. Raven-black hair fell smoothly until it curled gently in a soft wave at the base of her neck, a tiny red bow affixed above her left ear. She offered her hand to Steve, warm and firm. "I've heard so much about you, Mr. Gilman, I thought you must surely be a much older man."

He knew it was intended as a compliment, and murmured, "Thank you, Mrs. Lawson," then remembered he must find an opportunity to thank her for the watch she had chosen for Mark to give him. She moved past him, bending her ripe, elegant body to pick up a small frankfurter encased in a flaky roll, then sat in a chair just outside the circle of men, sipping the drink Eric had brought her.

Herschel swiveled his body around in his chair and said, "Where is Mark, Karen?"

"I left him in the small study watching the football game."

"What was the score?" Russell Charles asked.

"Twenty-four to fourteen, when I left."

"Who was winning?"

She smiled impishly. "Twenty-four, I assume," and everyone laughed.

Herschel said to Eric, "Ask Mr. Mark to join us, please."

The maid returned with a silver coffee service, placed it on the table, went out, and came back with a second tray of cups and saucers. Then Mark entered the room, greeting the agency men with brief nods as he dropped into a chair at the table, reached for a cigarette, and lighted it.

The meeting opened with a statement from Herschel Goodwin. "Gentlemen, I thank you all for coming here today. I know I have inconvenienced you, but I also know you were interested in getting this word as soon as possible. I have discussed this idea with Mr. Charles during the past week, after talking it over with my financial advisers. I will say that at first I was not completely sold on going into a new venture at this time, but I have been outvoted and my objections overridden. Anna likes it, my comptroller and treasurer like it, Mark, Mr. Hardwick, and others want it. Mr. Charles is also in favor of it." Grinning, he added, "Also, my advertising agency, whose advice has seldom failed me over the years—many of them—wants it.

"I have given Mr. Charles the go-ahead signal to begin preliminary negotiations with the Bond family. On Monday, he will fly to the West Coast and set up a meeting with Mr. Bond and his mother. Russ?"

Russell Charles put his drink down, crossed his legs, and said, "There is really very little I can add at this point. I have drawn reports on B & B and—with some additional intelligence I have gained from my West Coast associates—find the information substantially the same as that contained in Mr. Gilman's report to Mr. Leary. I have talked with my Los Angeles people who, in a matter of a few days, have acquired a remarkable amount of data for me. Arrangements are now being made for me to meet privately with Mrs. Bond and her son, Perry, at her home in Santa Barbara. I have reason to believe no one else has made them a similar offer at this point.

"Naturally, I can make no predictions until I have met with these two principals. The question of cost will rest on numerous factors, such as tangible net worth, or book value, earnings during the preceding year and as of the present, plus that intangible of intangibles, the value of goodwill, such as it may be, and the price the Bonds place upon it. I hope we may come to an equitable agreement to purchase before further deterioration of the company—through internal neglect—occurs.

"If we are successful in reaching some level of agreement in Santa Barbara, a willingness to entertain our proposal to buy, I will offer the Bonds a letter of intention to buy based on our examination of all books and records, and the value of their stock and assets. That is all I can say to you gentlemen at this time, except for the need of the utmost secrecy during the period of negotiation."

But Herschel, now that the decision had been made, wanted to explore in greater depth and detail the plan by which B & B would be absorbed into the GFP line, the steps to be taken to construct additional facilities, and acquire necessary equipment and personnel in order to expose the item to other than the western states and the—as yet untapped—markets of Alaska and Hawaii. And finally, the method GFP would utilize to introduce B & B to the national market.

Barrett, to whom he seemed to be addressing this last question, looked somewhat perplexed, the man who had evidently been left out of the preliminary discussions held between Bill and Keith. He looked toward Keith helplessly and showed great relief when Keith smoothly took over. For the next forty-five minutes, Keith articulated a step-by-step program that would bring Goody–B & B Coffee into national prominence via media, sales promotion, marketing and merchandising, all wrapped up into one package. Herschel Goodwin listened carefully, nodding his approval as each point was made.

Mark said then, "What about testing markets? How much time do you think we should allocate to that phase, and in how many markets outside the West Coast area?"

Bill Leary answered. "At the present time, we've given no detailed thought to the testing program, Mark. We'll have plenty of time for that during the period of actual acquisition and the time that follows, when GFP is getting organized to produce coffee on a national, rather than sectional, basis."

Mark started to reply to Bill, then decided not to. Steve had been watching Mark to see how deeply he would enter into the discussion and now, having asked this single question, he fell back into silence, just as he had during the meeting in the Forty-second Street office. There was more talk that dealt with financing, new construction, equipment, and personnel, most of which was of little interest to Steve, whose mind was concentrating on the intricate maneuverings Allard had outlined; making a mental note to dig deeper into the test-market question which, until now, had been bypassed.

What was most remarkable, Steve thought, was Mark's attitude throughout the rest of the meeting. Not once, beyond his initial question, had he spoken up to voice an opinion. Mark, always ready with suggestions, judgments, evaluations, criticisms, and majestic pronouncements—logical or illogical—sat silently in the presence of Herschel, Russell Charles, Bill, Keith, Wade and Steve, for all the world like a judge waiting to hear the total evidence before rendering the final decision. Which, of course, never came.

At any moment, Steve had expected Mark to break out and become a part of the proceedings, yet he sat in his chair and uttered not a single word; lighting a cigarette from time to time, toying with a pocket knife or a gold pencil, pouring and drinking a cup of coffee, listening to each speaker in turn; no longer the man who considered everyone around him as bit players supporting his star performance.

Later, Russell Charles called on Steve to amplify certain statements in his report, his reasons for feeling that Perry Bond would not object too strenuously to ridding himself of the company. In reply, Steve cited numerous instances to substantiate his remarks in his original report. During this recital, Mark's eyes were fastened upon him, an odd smile on his lips, but again he had no comments to offer.

The meeting came to an end at 5:30. Russell Charles left at once, pleading a dinner engagement at the club. Dinner had been set for six o'clock because Bill had announced their intention to return to the city as early as possible. Eric showed the four agency men to a guest room and bath so they might refresh themselves before dinner, and Wade Barrett, once Eric left them, said petulantly, "Somewhere along the line, Bill, I was left out on a limb."

"Well, Wade," Bill said smoothly, "you've been so preoccupied this past week, what with Chevalier and personal matters, and Keith and I felt we couldn't delay our discussions."

"I think you might have kept me posted by memo."

"Two reasons, Wade," Keith said. "One, there wasn't time. Two, the more memos, the less chance we have of keeping this thing under wraps."

Steve suddenly thought of Sam Abrams and wondered just how well the whole thing was being kept "under wraps." Bill then said, "You getting any closer to some solution to the Chevalier problem, Wade?" When Wade did not reply, "Or do you think it's time I stepped in?"

"No to both questions," Wade, feeling the prick of the needle, answered sullenly.

"We've got a lot at stake there . . ." Bill began, when Wade exclaimed, "Hell, don't you think I know that, Bill?

For Christ's sake, I haven't got my eyes closed to what's going on around me."

"Then what are you doing about it?" Keith asked, coming from the bathroom, wiping his hands on a guest towel.

Barrett glared at Allard. "My best, goddamn it, but it gets fouled up more and more every day. Not only are McCreery and Adrian at each other's throats, but . . ."

Steve moved into the bathroom, running the water slowly in order to hear what lay beyond that fatal word, 'but'. . . .

"I—it's gotten jammed up a hell of a lot worse," Wade concluded.

"Since when?" Bill asked quietly.

"Since yesterday. I had lunch with Hugh Benson. We've got more than a personality clash to deal with now."

"Go ahead, Wade."

"Well, our contract is up on July 15. On June 1, Frank Abbott reaches the mandatory retirement age of seventy. When he leaves, Hugh Benson will take over as president of Chevalier and who do you think steps into his shoes as advertising director?"

"Let me guess," Allard said, "Theodore H. McCreery."

"On the nose. J. P. Dandridge's favorite nephew. And if that isn't enough, his engagement to Benson's daughter, Nancy, will be announced sometime during the next week or two. It looks like who will be getting the Chevalier account on July 15 will undoubtedly be Ted McCreery's decision."

"And why in hell didn't you resolve the situation between Ted and Adrian long before now, Wade?" Bill asked with remarkable calm.

"There was only one way to do that, Bill, and that was to fire Adrian."

"Then why didn't you?"

"You know that as well as I. Because I didn't want to lose the best cigarette man we've ever had because of a snotty, spoiled prick like McCreery."

"Let me ask you this. If we let Adrian go now, do you think Ted would be inclined to renew the contract with us on July 15?"

"I don't know. I just don't know that, Bill."

"Well, let's explore it on the way home."

"I drove Steve up in a rented car."

"Then let Steve drive it back to town and you'll ride

back with Keith and me. There's not a hell of a lot of time left between now and doomsday."

Karen opened the table conversation with a remark about a recent Broadway opening. Keith had seen it with Louise, and this began a lively exchange of comment and criticism. Bill entered into it, discussing a musical Karen had seen which evoked a goodnatured difference of opinion. At one point, Karen said, "The man I saw it with is a reviewer . . ." and at that moment, Steve, his eyes on Mark, saw him flush with restrained anger. And again, curiously, Mark did not join in the conversation despite his obvious interest in the theater. Anna and Herschel sat through it all with interest, offering brief comments now and then.

Suddenly, Karen turned to Steve and said, "I'm so happy to have finally met you, Steve. I've been hearing about you off and on and you'd become some sort of ghostly figure in my imagination. Tell me, are you really the driving force behind all those millions of dollars of advertising for GFP?"

Almost blushing at this extravagance in the presence of Bill and Keith, Steve said, "I'd call that the exaggeration of the year. I'm only one of eighteen people directly involved in producing what you've seen in print and on television, with a hundred others backstopping us."

Karen turned to Keith. "I didn't think such modesty was possible in this day and age, did you, Mr. Allard?"

Keith said, "As group head, Steve has to take his share of credits as well as the knocks, but there are others who contribute toward the overall success of the GFP programs. Including Mark."

"I keep forgetting about Mark. I always see him as the man to whom the finished work is brought for his signature. What I mean is, the actual creation of the basic ideas, the decision that one concept will be more effective than another, and the development process, all that must be terribly fascinating and a tremendous responsibility."

Steve said, "If you really mean that, Mrs. Lawson, I'd be delighted to show you through our agency and let you see the work in various stages of progress."

"I'd love that, I really would," Karen replied. "I haven't the faintest idea how it all begins. That part interests me because I find myself in the same situation when I start a painting, staring at a blank canvas for hours at a time.

Advertising people can't afford that luxury, can they?"

"It may surprise you to learn that writers and commercial artists are no less prone to mental blocks," Steve said, "but we have the advantage of communication that most fine arts artists refuse to recognize. More than often a discussion between an artist and a copywriter is all the spark either needs to set the machinery in motion." He added, "I'd like to see some of your work when it is convenient."

"I'm sure that as a professional you wouldn't be interested in the work of an amateur."

Anna broke in then. "She does beautiful work, Steve," and to Karen, "Why don't you show Steve some of the things you did here . . ."

Deprecatingly, "Oh, those," and after second thoughts, "there are one or two things I like. I'll show them to you after dinner, but I think you'll be bored."

"No, really. I'd enjoy seeing them."

"Then after dinner?"

"I'll hold you to that."

Karen beamed a glowing smile at him and the subject was dropped when Herschel answered a question from Bill, one that involved land values in and around Wyecliffe. Herschel told him of buying their parcel of land at the suggestion of the Charleses, of building the house, of the old McComb house that dated back to the early eighteen hundreds and which he hoped, one day, to restore. But there was never time—

Thus, by piecing together certain dates that were mentioned, Steve guessed that Karen was thirty-five, five years older than himself although she looked to be no more than twenty-five. Again he looked at Mark, toying with his gold cigarette lighter, almost totally detached, seeming to be there on sufferance.

It was half past seven when Bill, Keith, and Wade made their apologies for bringing the pleasant evening to a close. When Eric, assuming that Steve was leaving with them, brought his hat and coat, Karen said, "Not Mr. Gilman's, Eric. He's staying a while."

Anna excused herself and went to the rear of the house. Herschel, Mark, Karen, and Steve returned to the study where Eric served more coffee and brought a tray of after-dinner drinks.

Mark said, "How long do you think it will take to get into this coffee thing?" and Herschel replied, "Don't be in too big a hurry, Mark. By the time Russell talks to the Bonds, and later on when the word gets out, there will be other bidders trying to buy them out. If the big competitors can pick up B & B, they'll be cutting out a newcomer in the field, so it all depends on the Bonds. If we do get it, there are many other important problems we'll have to face, so we'll take it one step at a time, eh?"

"Okay." Mark turned to Karen and said, "If you're going to show Steve your gallery, I think I'll read a little and turn in early. I want to get back to the city in the morning. I'm leaving for Detroit and Chicago on Monday morning."

"How long will you be gone?" Karen asked.

"About a week. We're running some special promotions and I want to make sure we're all set with our distributors out there."

"Then why don't you run along," Karen said.

Mark stood up. "See you when I get back, Steve," he said, and with a "Goodnight," to the room in general, left.

"So," Herschel said, "you show Mr. Gilman your paintings, darling, and I'll look over some papers I brought home with me. Goodnight, Mr. Gilman. I hope you enjoyed your day here."

"I did indeed, Mr. Goodwin, and thank you for inviting me."

Karen said, "Come along, Steve. My best pieces are in the library," and when they reached it, she added, "My earlier work is in the guest house on the other side of the pool, the kind of things I'd like to burn, but Aunt Anna would have a fit if I even suggested it. These were done here, one or two at college. Some I brought out from the city."

The room was large and square with head-high shelves of books on two walls. The exposed hand-pegged floorboards, of random width, were polished to a dark gleam, and were covered with several imported rugs in various sizes. On the other two walls were several recognizable works that had no doubt come from important galleries; and here and there were interspersed the works of Karen Goodwin: two landscapes, a picture of a blond nude about to immerse herself in a river, and a portrait that could have been the same young blond woman. Beside it was another that could have been a younger Karen Lawson. His eyes were held by those of the bare-breasted girl who stared back at him from the canvas and completely overshadowed the other work.

"Like it?" Karen said after several moments of silence.

"Like it? It's marvelous."

"Thank you."

"Yours?" Steve asked in honest surprise.

"I painted that quite some time ago. Mark didn't like it, so I gave it to Aunt Anna as an anniversary gift. Of course, they'd like to have seen it covered up a little more, but . . ."

"It's beautiful. What do you call it?"

"Portrait of Clymene. She was a sea nymph who was believed to be the mother of Prometheus."

But the face and body are yours, Steve thought in silence. It was a hauntingly beautiful face, the body nude to the waist, emerging from a sea of color that raged across the broad canvas in bold, angry strokes, forming a whirlpool; arms upraised, either in welcome or pleading for help, suggesting possible danger or entrapment. It gave Steve a curious feeling of reverence, a feeling that it should be hanging in a museum or in the private gallery of a palatial mansion. No single color could be isolated or defined. Long, heavy masses flowed and swirled toward the bright core that was Clymene, viable, alluring, yet unquestionably related to the storm of tumultuous billows that surrounded her.

"That's one I'd like to own," Steve said, more to himself than to Karen.

"Thank you, but I don't think Anna would part with it. Still, if you don't mind, I'll accept that as the rarest compliment an artist can ever receive."

There were others of her works hanging, but Steve's eyes and mind returned to Clymene. "I have dozens more at our house in the city," Karen said. "I'd like you to see those some time."

"I'd enjoy that very much."

"Then you shall," she promised. "One day, you'll see them all."

"Thank you." He checked the time. "I think I should be going now."

"Why don't you stay over, and drive in tomorrow after breakfast," Karen suggested. "I hate traveling at night in the winter."

He thought of Mark then and said, "I'm afraid I can't

do that. I've got a lot of material at my apartment that needs study for a conference on Monday morning."

Steve saw Herschel and Anna before he left, again urged by them to stay over, Herschel observing that snow had begun falling again. Steve was tempted, but felt a peculiar need to be gone from Mark's presence. He bade them goodnight and went out to the rented Ford. It was nine-thirty and with luck, he guessed he would be home and in bed sometime after midnight.

As he turned from the Goodwin estate into Thorpe Road, the snow became mixed with a drizzling rain. The wind turned colder, biting at his ankles. He moved the heater lever from medium to high, now beginning to feel its first warmth, then turned his attention to the defroster to kill the fog that edged the windshield and rear window.

Thorpe Road was now wet and slick with a thin coating of ice beginning to form. Steve stopped the car and checked the trunk, but the rental agency had neglected to provide a set of chains. Within minutes, the snow became heavier, wet and gluey, sticking to the windshield. However, there was no traffic coming from ahead or behind as he drove at reduced speed, peering through the flashing wipers as he tried to recall his bearings, now beginning to doubt his wisdom in having refused to stay over. After a mile of concentrating on the road ahead and the thick snowflakes driving toward him, he felt almost hypnotized by the rhythm of the wipers. He turned on the radio, lit a cigarette, and opened the window a crack on the driver's side to allow the smoke to escape. Then he saw his first remembered landmark, a single light that marked Four Corners, the halfway mark into the village of Wyecliffe. To his right, waiting for him to pass, he saw a pair of bright headlights.

He crossed the side road that was marked with an arrow pointing to the left and a sign which read: WYECLIFFE VILLAGE, 1 MI. and had reached out to flick the ash from his cigarette into the tray when he saw the burst of light coming up suddenly from behind, and realized that the car at the crossing had turned into the main road and was now attempting to pass. Steve held his course, aware that the road had little or no shoulder. The car came abreast of him, started to pass, skidded, and swerved sharply to the right, as though the driver had misjudged the length of Steve's car, cutting sharply in front of him.

He heard the grinding crunch of metal against metal as

the other car, a pickup truck—as he saw in a split second—forced him over to the right. His front right wheel went into the soft shoulder. He tried to turn it back onto the road and felt the car skid, sliding into the ditch as he struggled with the steering wheel, then hit the brake hard, hoping that this would stop the sliding action. There was another bump as the rear of the car hit the edge of the shoulder and he knew then that he was out of control. The pickup truck was ahead of him now, sliding from side to side from the impact, as he felt the Ford go over on its side, falling into the ditch. He was thrown to the right side, hard against the door, and as he reached out to break his fall, felt a sharp pain in his wrist, trailing upward into his shoulder. At that moment, his head hit the steel doorpost. He stared in disoriented awe at the explosion of light that burst in front of his eyes, then everything went black.

3

When he came to, he was in a bed in what he recognized at once as a hospital. No other room anywhere could be so sterile, so small, so medically, antiseptically clean. Through a vague blur he saw a figure in white hovering over him and as his eyes came into focus, made it out to be a nurse. Almost at once, he heard her say, "Doctor?"

A portly man came toward the bed, stethoscope dangling from his neck, peering at him through black-rimmed glasses. He felt Steve's pulse, then said softly, "Well, Mr. Gilman, it seems you've had a little run of bad luck."

"Where am I, Doctor, and how bad is it?" Steve asked.

"The Wyecliffe Community Hospital. Two men in a pickup truck brought you in . . ."

"They ran me off the road."

"Yes. They told us their truck skidded into your car after making a turn into Thorpe Road at Four Corners. Should be a traffic light there, but— Anyway, they turned in a report to the Wyecliffe police and went on to Ridgefield."

"How bad is the damage?"

"I think not too bad. We'll know more about that by morning. You have a badly sprained wrist, and your forehead required several stitches, but we're holding you for further observation, possible concussion. What I'm going to do right now is give you something that will put you to sleep. Rest is very important. Is there anyone we can notify? The identification card in your wallet doesn't give a next of kin. We have your business card, but I'm sure there's no one at your office late on Saturday night, almost Sunday morning."

"No," Steve said, "it can wait."

"Were you visiting someone in the area, Mr. Gilman?"

He had almost dozed off again, hearing the question but feeling too dizzy and nauseated to reply. "Mr. Gilman, do you have friends nearby?" the doctor asked again in a voice that seemed to be coming at him from miles away.

"Mr.—ah—Good—win. Mr. Herschel Good . . ."

The doctor smiled. "Of course. I know the Goodwins well. I'll notify them."

"No—don't disturb—please—"

And then a glutinous mass formed and rose in his throat, gagging him. The nurse was ready with a curved pan and caught the vomit as he expelled it, then wiped his mouth and chin. The nausea left him, but he still felt dizzy, hearing the doctor's voice faintly, unable to understand the words. The nurse handed the doctor a syringe, but Steve felt nothing as the needle was inserted into his arm. A moment later he was fast asleep.

On Sunday afternoon he awoke with an aching head, but with clearer vision, the nausea and dizziness completely gone. An elderly nurse was leaning over him, starchily white, smiling pleasantly. "How do you feel this afternoon, Mr. Gilman?"

"A bit banged up. You tell me."

"Dr. Lindstrom has been in to see you twice since this morning. He didn't seem to be too worried. You'll be up and out of here in a few days I think."

"A few *days?*"

"Oh, yes. Please don't be in too big a hurry, Mr. Gilman. Some pure rest never hurt anybody."

"Is today Sunday?"

"Yes. Sunday, two-fifteen, afternoon."

"I've got to be in New York by morning. I've got a million things to do."

"Relax," the smiling nurse said. "Mr. Goodwin was here this morning. He's already called New York, a Mr. Leary. Mr. Leary said that you're to have the best care and everything else will be taken care of. You're not to worry."

Later, the doctor returned. "Well, Mr. Gilman, you look one hundred per cent better. Color's returned and"—examining his eyes and face more closely—"eyes bright and clear. How do you feel otherwise?"

"Very stiff. My wrist . . ."

"A bad sprain, no more. In another week or ten days you won't even remember it. The cut on your forehead won't show a scar. I'll want you here to check out that possible concussion, but I don't think it will amount to anything. Only a precaution. I understood from Mr. Goodwin that everything in the city, your job, and so on, will be taken care of. Mr. Petrakis, the owner of the truck that hit you, has assumed all financial responsibility, so there isn't a thing in the world that should worry you for the moment."

The nurse brought him some broth and a soft-boiled egg, at which he picked lightly, then fell asleep again. When he woke next, night had fallen, and he felt a terrible restlessness, but knew he would not be allowed out of bed, nor did he feel like making the effort. Through the windows he could see snow falling. From the corridor came the voices of visitors, and he felt desperately alone. A new nurse came into his room half an hour later and gave him a capsule. He fell asleep at once.

On Monday morning, yet another nurse awakened him, and after a light breakfast and bed-bath, brought his first visitor: Karen Lawson.

She was in a hooded fur coat, glistening with melting snow, a large puff of dark hair like a waterfall over her forehead as far as her eyebrows, and he thought he had never seen a lovelier sight. Or smile. She carried a large bouquet covered with glazed paper and a second package, which the nurse took from her as she shrugged off hood and coat and said, "Steve, how are you feeling?"

"Fine, now, Karen, and very stupid for not taking you up on your invitation to stay over. I've been like a man in a prison cell until this minute. Thank you for coming."

"Oh, Steve, I can't tell you how worried we were when Dr. Lindstrom called. Dad came in yesterday morning, but I had to stay until Mark drove back to the city. He wanted to get back before the weather got worse and found himself snowed in again."

"And you're staying on?"

"Yes. There's no real reason for me to risk the trip in this awful weather. Aunt Anna and Uncle Herschel insisted I wait until it clears up and the roads are cleaned. A day or two at the most."

"Mark's loss, my gain."

She laughed and said, "I've brought you two books, just in case you're up to reading. And two pairs of Mark's pajamas, and some bedroom slippers, and a robe. Sometime this afternoon I'll bring some shaving things, toothbrushes, and paste. Which brand do you prefer?"

"Karen, please don't bother."

"No bother. I love to get out in the snow. I've got to do some shopping for Aunt Anna in any case."

"You're much too kind. Did Mr. Goodwin go in to the plant today?"

"Yes. Eric drove him in shortly after breakfast. The road to Harrison has been plowed clear. Are you feeling more comfortable this morning?"

"Very. Other than this"—raising his bandaged wrist, fingertips brushing the taped bandage on his forehead—"I feel fine, well enough to get started back to town."

"Not according to Dr. Lindstrom. It's only a few days, Steve. Enjoy your holiday."

"I don't know what else I can do. What about the car?"

"All taken care of. Uncle Herschel had it towed into Wyecliffe and turned over to a garage that will see that it gets back to the rental agency. Mr. Petrakis's insurance will cover the damage. The flowers are from Petrakis & Son, the florist from Ridgefield who ran you off the road."

"Another of life's little coincidences."

Karen stayed until noon, but did not return that afternoon. At nine that night the nurse on duty brought him a yellow capsule to take, and that carried him through the night.

Next morning, he ate a full breakfast, and then listened to Dr. Lindstrom's optimistic report on his X-rays. "When can I leave, Doctor?" Steve asked.

"I'd say by Thursday, if nothing else shows up."

"What might show up that hasn't already?"

"Whiplash, for one thing."

Oh, Christ! Steve muttered under his breath. "Can I get up and walk around?"

"Ask me that tomorrow morning. Meanwhile, stay in bed and rest. I'll look in on you later."

At nine-thirty he called New York, spoke with Bill Leary, and was assured that the agency was still alive, well, and operating. Bill switched him to Chuck and was again reassured, but Peggy was practically in tears with relief at hearing his voice. "Switch me over to Mr. Allard, Peggy?"

"If he were in, Mr. Leary would have transferred the call to him. He's out of the office. I'll leave word with Gail that you called."

At eleven-thirty Keith called, cautioning him to take it easy, that all was under control in the world of advertising. Not too long after, Louise Allard phoned to ask if she could drive up to bring him home on Thursday. Steve told her he had already made other arrangements, a lie that shut off her protests.

It was still snowing when Karen arrived with razor, shaving cream, lotion, two toothbrushes, and a tube of toothpaste, the local paper, *The New York Times,* and two magazines. And an apology for not having returned the afternoon before. "It's so lovely out in the snow," she exclaimed, happy as a child with a sled on a hill. "The plows are out on the side roads, but ten minutes later, the roads are covered again."

"Karen, that road . . ."

"I've driven it for years, and the station wagon has snow tires. My, you look so much better in pajamas than in a hospital gown."

"I feel a lot safer too, not so damned exposed."

She opened the packages and arranged the toilet articles on his bedstand, then held up the can of shaving cream and razor. "Are you a man of courage, Steve?" she asked.

"I've never run from a mouse yet."

"Then I'm going to shave you."

"Shave me? My God, Karen, I'm not that helpless." He held up his right hand, tried to clench his fingers into a fist, and winced as the shock of pain ran up his arm.

"See?" she said in triumph. "And this hospital isn't large enough to have a staff barber. Come on, Steve, be a sport. I've always wanted to shave a man and you really are in need."

Looking at the child-eagerness in her face, he wanted so much to feel her hands on him, even in so prosaic a matter as a shave, that he muttered, "All right. Do you know how?"

"How do you think my legs get shaved?" she said, removing her jacket and rolling up her sleeves. She busied herself with filling a small basin of water, humming all the while, enjoying herself. She applied a soapy washcloth to soften his stiff bristles, and inserted a fresh blade into the razor. Steve wondered idly if she had ever shaved Mark. And doubted that she had.

She washed the soap from his face gently, avoiding the bandage on his forehead, then sprayed a large glob of lather from the aerosol can onto her fingertips and carefully applied it to his cheeks, chin, and upper lip. "Now don't wince or pull back," she cautioned. "I'm very good at this. I think," she added.

She was indeed. She sat on the edge of the bed and used the razor deftly, the way an artist would stroke a brush upon canvas he thought, watching her eyes, and the way she bit her lower lip and moved her mouth as he moved his to give her a better working surface. She trimmed his sideburns, and was finished.

"There," she said, "no cuts, no need for post-shaving first aid," then removed the excess lather with the washcloth, applied some lotion, rinsed the razor, and put everything back in its place.

"Thank you, Karen. I'd like to call on you to perform that service for me again."

"Anytime, sir. Tomorrow?"

"That's a date."

The nurse returned and, reassured that her patient was in extraordinarily good hands and spirits, left again. Karen rolled her sleeves down and put on her jacket. Steve said, "Don't go, Karen. Stay awhile."

She stopped in the act of buttoning the jacket and stared at him with a small smile. "I wasn't going to leave."

"Sit and talk with me."

Then her expression changed and something seemed to draw her away from him, a distant vagueness in her eyes as she looked toward, but through him, as though making a definite effort to seem attentive. Her face became a mask, hardly alive to her surroundings as she sat in the armchair beside the bed.

"What are you thinking?" he asked.

She turned toward him and said, "Steve, do you enjoy your work? Is it everything you want?"

"Not everything, Karen. It's a good job and I do well in it. I don't think I can ask for much more than that."

"Did you ever want to write anything besides advertising?"

"Yes. Yes, I did, very much. I once wanted desperately

to become a newspaperman. A journalist. But—well, things happened, other things didn't happen, and I had to abandon that plan. At Columbia, I wrote several dozen short stories, a very pretentious novella and an outline for a historical novel that might have had a chance if I'd gotten around to finishing it. Unfortunately, none of it was up to professional standards and didn't get past the agents I submitted it to."

"You were too young then, perhaps. Wouldn't you like to try it again?"

"I've thought about it many times, off and on. Yes, I would, but advertising is a jealous mistress. If I were anything but a creative planner and writer by day I might be able to work at it by night, but after a full day in advertising I'm too bushed mentally to consider writing fiction by night."

"What a pity. You'd be so good at it."

"What makes you think that?"

"I can't say exactly. A feeling I have. I think you have a certain compassion for people, for life, locked inside you, that wants to come out. I sense that in you."

"Like what you feel when you paint." It wasn't a question, but a flat statement. and after a few moments Karen said, "I think that's true. When I paint I have a tremendous pull toward what I'm doing, so terribly involved, almost a compulsion to feel . . ."

"What you felt when you painted Clymene?"

She smiled. "Yes. Exactly."

He knew then that Clymene was Karen, feeling turmoil, storm, rage, spilling it all out on canvas with paints and brushes. A troubled Karen, sad, arms extended—not inviting, but in supplication—pleading for help. He put out his left hand and she touched it, then grasped it firmly, and stood up. "I've got to run now, Steve."

"Tomorrow?" he said.

"If I can make it," she replied, without turning back.

She returned the next day, Wednesday. Dr. Lindstrom came in while she was there and was less evasive than he had been the day before, but gave Steve no definite word. Karen left, promising to return during the afternoon, and it was the longest day Steve could remember in a long time, despite calls from Keith and Peggy. None came from Wade Barrett. Flowers arrived from Louise and Keith, from Bill and Donna Leary, from the combined GFP group, and again from the Goodwins.

Karen returned in the afternoon, bringing Anna, laden down with two dishes she had cooked especially for him; and Anna forced him to sample each one before giving them to the nurse to keep until later. Dr. Lindstrom dropped in, all smiles as he removed the bandage from Steve's forehead and replaced it with two small pads of medicated tape. "All right, Mr. Gilman," he said. "I've cleared you to leave anytime tomorrow after breakfast. Just take it easy on that wrist and don't go back to work until Monday. For the rest of today, you can practice being on your feet until you get tired. Don't overdo it."

Lindstrom left, and the nurse helped Steve into the robe—Mark's robe over Mark's pajamas. He tested his weight on his feet and was soon pacing the room.

"What time do you want to leave tomorrow?" Karen asked.

"As soon as I can check the schedules and make arrangements to catch the first bus into the city," he said.

"You see, Karen," Anna said, "Mr. Gilman doesn't like our suburban hospitality."

"Ah, no. You've all been wonderful, but I must get back to my work." *To my own pajamas and robe, and my own bed,* he added to himself. "There's so much to be done."

"Very well," Karen said, "but the bus is out and the arrangements are all set. Mark called last night. He's going on to Saint Louis and will be away until Monday. I'm going into the city and I'll drive you in. That is, if you can trust me behind the wheel."

It had stopped snowing the night before, so the roads would be clear. He said, "Anyone I trust with a razor, I'll trust behind the wheel of a car. After all, I didn't do too well in that department last Saturday night."

Anna looked puzzled and Karen laughed. "I shaved Steve yesterday morning," she said.

"You shaved Steve?" Anna shook her head. "Good Lord, the talents you have that your uncle and I never suspected."

4

On Thursday morning, the sun broke through the heavy overcast like a good omen. Outside his windows the hospital grounds glittered like the white frosting on a wedding cake, decorated with hanging icicles. He breakfasted with a new zest, and shaved, testing the awkwardness of his left hand, then he showered and dressed, and made up two packages; one of Mark's pajamas, robe, and the two books, the other of the toilet articles Karen had brought him. He checked with the cashier and learned that his bill had been guaranteed by Mr. Petrakis's insurance company. He was free to leave. He returned to his room and at nine o'clock Karen arrived.

She handled the station wagon expertly and once through Wyecliffe, Steve settled down to a pleasant drive at moderate speed. The snow-covered countryside was a beautiful vista after his confinement, traffic was light at that hour, and it was a bright new world. His wrist pained only when he forgot to restrain its use, the only apparent after-effect of his misadventure. After a while, Karen threw him a brief side glance and said, "You're not nervous, are you, Steve?"

"Why should I be? You're a much better driver than I."

"Are you always so generous to the weaker sex?" she asked slyly.

"Are you always so defensive about your own sex?"

"Touché." She changed the subject immediately. "Dr. Lindstrom thinks you shouldn't go back to work for the rest of the week. He also seemed to think I would have more influence on you than he."

"Considering the alternatives, I think he was perfectly right."

"Then you'll take his advice?"

"I'll give the suggestion every consideration."

After a few moments of silence, she said, "You get along very well with Mark, don't you?"

"I assume so. He's never complained about the quality of my work."

"I mean personally, aside from work. You've made some business trips with him and I can't remember that he ever did that with the other agency men." A pause, then, "I know that men get to know each other much better when they're together outside of their work."

My God, he thought, *is she going to try to pump me about Mark?* and said aloud, "We get along reasonably well, Karen."

"I'm surprised. You're the only Leary man I've never heard him rant about. There aren't many men Mark really likes."

"I should think Mark would have lots of friends."

"Not really. Some acquaintances, yes, show people he once worked with, but hardly what one would call close friends. Essentially, Mark is a woman's man. Or didn't you know that."

Her tone was light, even teasing, and he wondered what had caused her to make that particular point, even in levity. There was no question mark tagged to the end of the sentence, seeming not to call for an answer. In the silence that ensued he felt an urge to look at her, and did so. In profile, her expression was indefinable, lips turned upward yet unsmiling, eyes on the road ahead, gloved hands on the wheel with a light, sure touch, maneuvering the car expertly now, in heavier traffic.

Her head turned toward him momentarily and he caught a glimpse of her quizzical expression, lips parted to show a fine line of white. Trapped in the act of staring, Steve looked away, concentrating on the road.

"You remind me very much of someone," Karen said finally.

"Oh?"

"Someone from long ago, when I was much younger." She paused and said, "Anna noticed it, too. He was very dear to me. He was killed in Korea."

"Then he was quite a lot older than you."

"Not that much older. He was—have you ever heard of Zalman Goodwin?"

"I've heard of him. From your uncle, and from Keith Allard. He was your father, wasn't he?"

"My stepfather. Uncle Herschel's brother. I was a child when my mother married Zalman Goodwin. She was a widow and our name was Hartog. Zalman adopted me, so I became Herschel's and Anna's niece indirectly. They had a son, Robert, with whom I practically grew up. Robert was at Princeton when he enlisted in the Marine Corps and was—killed. His body was never recovered. We were deeply attached to each other."

Why, Steve wondered, *can't she say she was deeply in love with him?* Aloud he said, "I'm sorry." He got out his cigarettes from his left jacket pocket and shook one loose for her, but she refused with a quick shake of her head, and pushed the dashboard lighter in for him.

He puzzled over her obvious closeness to Robert, wondering how, and if, Mark had been any part of that era of her life; and thinking of Mark caused him to recall Mark's repeated infidelities, full-fledged affairs with Robin Ford, with Sue, and most assuredly—if he could read the signs—with Jerri Davis. His one-night stands with the Sherrys and Jo-Anns of his travels. How could Karen not know? Or did she, and didn't she give a damn? And somehow, this train of thought brought him back to the emptiness of the lives of Grady and Jenny Gilman. Of his own life with Libby. *Oh, Christ, get off it!*

And yet he was reminded at every turn of similar broken lives. Don and Edith Bryce, separated. Marty and Lorraine Elkins, divorced. Lew and Patricia Kann, divorced. Alan Grant working on his third marriage. Wade and Sylvia Barrett split. And more of the same. He came alert when Karen's next question penetrated his thought, startling him. "Have you met Miss Davis, Steve?"

Warily, "I'm sorry. Who?"

"Miss Davis, the latest in the succession of girls who followed Miss Ford when she left."

"Oh, Jerri. Yes, I've met her at GFP."

"What is she like?"

"I only saw her for a few moments on one occasion. Young, attractive." He saw Karen smile then, a curious twist of her lips as though she had scored a small victory, and somehow he connected it with her earlier remark that Mark was essentially a woman's man. He braced himself for a continued questioning about Jerri, but it never came. As suddenly as she had introduced the subject, she dropped it. But he knew that Karen knew. She could have asked him about any one of a dozen women at GFP, Charlotte, his secretary, Mrs. Harris, Miss Platt, Miss Ostrow, Miss Riggs, but she had chosen Mark's latest acquisition, Jerri Davis.

It was past noon when they reached his apartment. Karen parked at the curbside, shut the motor off, and started to get out. Steve said, "Thank you for everything, Karen. You've been very kind."

"I'm coming up to make sure you have everything you need."

"You've done more than enough already. Please don't bother."

"On orders from Dr. Lindstrom. You're to go to bed and rest and not go in to work until Monday. No arguments, Steve. Let's get on with it."

He remembered that his cleaning woman had been due on Wednesday, and that the apartment would be in order. He also discovered, in trying to use his left hand to get his keys out of his right pocket, how much he was temporarily disabled for the smallest necessities of everyday living. Karen extracted the leather keycase from his right pocket and unlocked the door. They entered, and she put the package of toiletries on the table in the foyer. She helped him out of his overcoat, then removed her own fur coat and said, "Where is the kitchen? I'm going to fix lunch for us."

Protest was useless. He showed her into the small kitchen. "Pots and pans in this cabinet, dishes and glasses in this one, silver. . . . I'll set the table."

"You'll do nothing of the kind. I'll take care of this part of it. You march yourself into the bedroom and get your pajamas and robe on. You're to stay here through the weekend."

"Yes, ma'am," he replied with mock meekness. "If you need anything, sing out."

In the bedroom, he undressed slowly, again realizing the importance of his injured wrist, wondering how long before he could manage a layout pencil, a pen to sign letters and checks, initial a memo or a proof, or use a typewriter. He slipped into pajamas, robe, and slippers, and checked the mail on the table in the foyer, but found nothing more than a few bills and the usual complement of junk mail.

Karen seemed happy, her face aglow as she ladled out two bowls of canned soup. The table in the dining nook had been set and he was hungry. They had tomato juice, the soup, an omelet, and coffee. When they had finished, Karen cleared the table while Steve went into the living room to look over the copies of the *Times* that had piled up in his absence. *Life*, *Newsweek*, *Harper's*, and *The Saturday Review* also awaited his attention, but he was too conscious of Karen moving around in his kitchen to do more than glance at headlines. Later, she came out and sat in the chair beside the sofa where he lay. "Comfortable?" she said.

"Very. And thank you, Karen. I can't tell you how much I appreciate everything you've done for me."

"I'm sure you would have done as much for me."

"Bet on it."

"You're a very nice person, Steve."

"Like Robert?"

She began to reply, then stopped, stood up, and went out into the foyer. He followed, and saw she was putting on her coat, then her gloves. At the door she turned and said, "Would you like to come for brunch on Sunday and see my other paintings?"

She had opened the door and the backlighting from the hallway shaded her face, adding to its loveliness, destroying his will to let it come to an end here and now. "You promised," she said.

"I'd like that. Very much."

"I'll phone you. You aren't unlisted, are you?"

"I'm in the book."

"Until Sunday, then." She turned, closed the door behind her, and was gone.

In his small study he removed the telephone receiver from its cradle, placed it on the desk, and dialed the agency number with his left index finger, then spent the next half hour being successively reassured by Peggy and Keith that everything was going well and that there was no need for him to come in until Monday.

The doorbell rang. He answered it and Inga Maczerak stood there wearing her customary little girl outfit with its brief skirt. "You are sick, Steve?" she asked, staring at the bandaged wrist, then at the strips of tape on his forehead. "What happened?"

"A little accident over in New Jersey last Saturday night. Nothing serious. How are you and George? Is he in town?"

"Yes. Today is my day off. I came in before and saw the lady was leaving. I wondered, this time of day, you should be having visitors."

"It's really nothing, Inga."

"Your hand. You will have supper with us."

"I think not—"

"You will," she insisted firmly. "I will send George to make you come."

"Inga . . ."

"Steve, you cannot do things with one hand. Half-past six. George will come for you."

He gave in. "All right, and thank you."

George came for him at six-thirty as promised, and over an excellent meal, Steve told them about his accident and stay at the Wyecliffe hospital. Inga was curious about the woman who had brought him home and Steve passed over this lightly, giving her little satisfaction. He was back in his apartment and in bed by ten o'clock, asleep with the aid of the container of yellow capsules Dr. Lindstrom had given him.

He remained at home on Friday, this time on orders from Keith. At noon, Louise came to visit, bringing flowers. She fixed lunch, which they shared, and they had coffee in the living room.

"I'm not used to being pampered this way, Louise. Keith threatened to fire me if I showed up at the office."

"And you know Keith would do just that," Louise said with a short laugh. "He's the gentlest villain in the whole world."

"Sometimes I don't know how he manages to remain so damned calm when everyone else goes into panic."

"He's that way around the house and sometimes I could kill him for it, but luckily, that's Keith's greatest asset. He's one of the quiet, confident, resourceful types. Like you."

"I? Lord, Louise, if you only knew how panicky I can get at times."

"I'm sure that under that cool exterior, so does Keith, but he doesn't show it and that prevents the feeling from spreading. Take Larry Price, or Wade Barrett. They're enough alike temperamentally to be twins. Keith was the cool head that kept them in place for years."

"Didn't Mr. Leary, Sr. know about Larry when he sent him out to L.A. to second Tom Donnelly?"

"Of course he did. Keith's choice at the time was Wade, but I think it was Mr. Leary's way of getting Larry out of New York. He never really approved of Larry, but hated to fire anyone. There'd been some strong feeling of competition between Larry and Wade, and at that time Wade was a lot more stable than Larry. The idea was to let Larry have the benefit of Tom's long experience in a more casual atmosphere."

"So Larry was kicked upstairs."

"Well, that happens often. You get rid of someone by promoting him out of your sight. In that respect, I don't suppose private industry is too different from the government, or military service."

Steve said, "I wish they hadn't sent me to Los Angeles. I feel like an executioner, partly responsible for what I think will happen to Larry Price."

"That's nonsense, but understandable. Keith didn't want to send someone who would try to cover up for Larry. He trusts you implicitly, but I don't have to tell you that. And if the B & B deal goes through, there's the possibility that it might somehow save Larry's neck."

"You don't really believe that, do you? He's muffed other accounts besides B & B."

"Keith has talked about that. Maybe there'll be something back here for him." She stubbed out her cigarette. "Did you know Wade is bucking for Larry's job?"

"Yes, I got that impression from him."

"What do you think?"

"I—just between us, Louise?"

"Promise."

"It won't work. I think Wade is as far over the hill as Larry. He's a frightened man and his upcoming divorce from Sylvia isn't going to do much to help him."

Louise sighed. "What happens to people in this business, Steve? Wade and Keith were college classmates. They practically started out in advertising at the same time. If it hadn't been for Keith's loyalty, Bill would have fired Wade years ago. The one thing that stopped him was Keith's reminder that Wade bird-dogged the GFP account for Bill's father over thirty years ago."

"I don't know what happens, Louise. Wade may have been a real hotshot in those days, but he's afflicted with adman's disease—fear. He's afraid of Ted McCreery, afraid he's going to lose Chevalier, afraid to speak up to Mark Lawson. He believes a new scene will change all that, but all he'll accomplish will be to take his fears with him to California and infect the people out there with them."

"Is that what bothers you?"

Steve said slowly, "I think I've paid off any debts I owe Wade a long time ago. What does bother me is that someday, when I'm riding a seventy-five thousand dollar job like Wade's, I'll come down with the same disease."

"Not you, Steve, never," Louise said firmly.

"Maybe not, but like Keith, I'm still surrounded by it. My own fears or someone else's. Mark Lawson may one day decide he doesn't like the way I part my hair or a tie I'm wearing, and everything I've put into GFP will lose its importance. Where do I go then?"

"I can't answer that," Louise said quietly. "In over thirty years, I've seen all kinds come and go. Marty Elkins came out of the mail room. Sam Abrams out of the production department. Marty Link was a thirty-dollar-a-week copywriter when I first knew him. They—the others

—are still in the batting box. So are you. You'll all be there long enough to retire voluntarily, I'm sure. The others? There are always psychological cripples in every business or profession."

"Thanks for the vote of confidence. You've made my day. Remember . . ."

"I know. Not a word to Keith, and I've got to run now. Shall I shop for you tomorrow?"

"No, thanks. I'm breaking out tomorrow, come hell, high water, snow, or the bomb. I'm up to here with prison."

"The air will do you good. It might even blow away some of the morbid thoughts I'm leaving behind with you."

On Saturday, Peggy came with her own contribution of flowers, catching an unshaven Steve having his breakfast, and insisting she was going to spend the day as a nurse's aide. She had coffee with him, then aired out the bedroom, washed dishes, made the bed, dusted, took linens and his soiled laundry to the basement, and returned to do the ironing, all over his weak protests.

"I met half a dozen of your tenant neighbors," she exclaimed proudly. "By now, they know you have a brand new mistress, namely, me!"

"Peggy, I've got to go on living here."

"Oh, it's all right. They not only expect it of you, but secretly think it's a great idea. I had the feeling you've been pretty secretive about the girls you bring home, but now they're happy to know you've found one you can be open about."

"Peggy . . ."

"In fact, one little doll, Mrs. Maczerak, loaned me some bleach and told me how lucky I am to find such a wonderful man. I even suspect she was a little envious."

"Goddamn it, Peggy—you—you're fired."

"You can't fire me, Steve. I've still got a year to work out on our five-year pact, remember?"

"All right, but stop riding me."

"Okay. While I finish the ironing, think pleasant thoughts. Like what you need from the grocer."

"I'm going to get dressed and do that myself."

"And I'll be right beside you. Or behind you. We can't have you doing anything that will damage your precious wrist."

They shopped together and talked about the office. Everything was in order, she told him, except for waiting out the decision from Lawson to go ahead with the new spring campaign. "Don, Arnie, and Lennie have come up with some beautiful layouts. Alan, Randy, Benn, and Jon are working like mad on their copy assignments and Mr. Allard is keeping a close watch on the scene. Even Chuck is behaving himself. I think they're going to come up with some of the best material you've ever seen, and most of it will be ready for you on Monday. They love the new concept. You've never seen such high enthusiasm."

"Great. Now if Lawson or the higher-ups nix it, we can all go back and start from scratch."

"My, what a foul mood you're in today."

"Sweetie, there's a hell of a lot in this world to feel foul about."

"Not today, with me here to bring a little ray of sunshine into your life. Hey, do you like zucchini? These look marvelous."

"I hate zucchini."

"Not the way I fix it, crisp, succulent . . ."

"Where in hell have you found time to learn this housework and cooking bit?"

"Didn't I ever tell you I was the middle child of five? On a dairy farm just outside of Omaha, every kid learns to pull his own wagon and there weren't any streets or alleys to wander off into. We grew up *en famille,* a way of life that's rapidly disappearing from the American scene."

"I'm just beginning to realize there's an idiotic charm about you."

"I knew you'd discover my finer qualities sooner or later." She put the zucchini into the shopping cart without further discussion. They finished shopping by three-thirty. Peggy put on a small roast, prepared the vegetables—including the zucchini—sliced in long, thin strips, dipped into a tempura batter, and fried lightly. "In the revised *Goody Recipe Book,*" Steve said, after a first taste, "let's include this one."

"Thanks for the left-handed compliment," Peggy acknowledged.

"And let's finish up quickly. I'm going to reward you with your choice of movies."

"Is that how you're planning to get rid of me?"

"You weren't thinking of moving in with me, were you?"

"Well, the thought might have occurred to me once or twice during the past three or four years."

"What would your friend Lennie say about that?"

"That's your nasty streak coming to the surface again. He'd probably say the establishment had won out again over the miserable downtrodden lower classes."

"Do you perform this service for him, too?"

"If you weren't a temporary invalid, I could slap you for that remark. I don't perform *services.* I'm a nice, well-mannered girl who treats people as human beings and finds that people who are treated like people respond in kind. Except you."

"Your Nebraska upbringing is showing again."

"If I could wave it like a flag, I'd do it. Now let me clean up while you pick the movie."

They saw a French picture, Peggy's choice, because she enjoyed ignoring the English subtitles. "My own very special snobbery," she explained.

When the movie was over, they had coffee at a nearby restaurant and argued about how she would get home, ending with her insistence on taking a cab alone. To Steve, spirits uplifted by Peggy's natural exuberance, it concluded a surprisingly enjoyable day.

5

When Karen phoned at eleven on Sunday, Steve was waiting. "I'm sending the car for you," she said.

"Please, no. I'll catch a cab outside."

"Are you sure you don't want the car?"

"Yes, of course."

"Is your wrist better?"

"Much better. I'm using it more every day."

She gave him the Eighty-fifth Street address. "In an hour?"

"I'll be there."

He had shaved and bathed earlier, a most awkward business requiring infinite patience, holding the razor in his left hand. He had removed the bandage pads from the stitched area on his forehead, then replaced them with two small strips to hide the ugly ski tracks left by the stitches. He dressed carefully and had to ring the Maczerak apartment to ask George to knot his tie for him. The doorman whistled up a passing cab, and he reached the house at the appointed time, to be greeted at the door by a short, rotund man dressed in severe black, with a striped vest, who showed him into a large formal living room.

"Mrs. Lawson will be with you directly, Mr. Gilman. May I bring you a drink?"

"No, thank you."

When the man left, he looked around the room and saw nothing he could identify as Karen's among the paintings. He examined a rosewood cabinet of carved ivory figures; men, women, animals, and birds, all neatly arranged on six glass shelves with mirrored backs. A duplicate cabinet contained several small bronze pieces. On a nearby table stood a bronze portrait of Herschel Goodwin.

"Hello, Steve." He turned and saw her walking toward him, smiling, warm, and lovely, in a long black housecoat that made her seem more mature than the slacks and mini-length dresses he had seen her in before. "I'm so glad you could make it."

"I've been looking forward to it," he replied.

She led the way into the dining room where the table had been immaculately set for two, with a low floral arrangement between them. They discussed the progress of his injuries and the weather before she said, "Mark phoned last night. He'll be coming in late tonight instead of tomorrow. He asked about you."

"What did you tell him?"

She smiled and said, "That you'd received the best of care and would probably be back at work on Monday."

He assumed that she hadn't told Mark the full story; that she had called on him several times at the hospital, driven him back to New York, that he would be sitting across this table from her today; and he had mixed feelings about the deception by omission—if his assumption were correct. Karen had turned the subject back to painting and he became aware that her knowledge of the arts was more professional than amateur. She had had a gallery showing and had been urged to display more of her work, but pleaded laziness and other pursuits and interests that caused her to procrastinate.

After the meal, Karen showed him to her studio on the third floor. "My only real privacy in this entire house," and he found this, too, a strange remark.

He hadn't been prepared for the extravagant spaciousness of the room, an entire floor given over to a single purpose; open, yet broken by several six-foot screens that gave the impression of sectional privacy, with one area set apart by one long, and two short sofas, set in a U-shape around a six-foot-square coffee table. Framed and unframed canvases hung on the wall, some standing against easels, each of which held a canvas in a finished or near finished state. There was an art cabinet beside each easel with its own tubes of paint, bowl or vase of brushes, palettes and other necessary tools, and drawers pulled out showing pastel and charcoal sticks. A special cabinet held rolls and sheets of virgin canvas and heavy drawing papers and, beside it, empty canvases on raw frames were stacked against the wall. In one screened-off section was a three-legged modeling stand, sculptor's tools, several cartons of plasteline clay, a workbench that contained a full set of carpenter's tools, squares of inch-thick wood, and coils of plastic-covered wire for making armatures.

Steve's impression, after one of initial surprise, was of sloppy clutter; then, as it grew on him, of comfortable disarray he could associate with Karen, not unlike the careful disorder in which he himself preferred to work. It was a completely personal workroom few outsiders would ever see, a place to paint, sculpt, read, and shut out the rest of the world for a few hours at a time, and not be concerned that everything must be put away out of sight and kept in fastidious order.

"These are all yours, I assume," Steve said, when his eyes had taken in the full expanse.

"All mine. Look around, Steve, while I get out of this housecoat. I don't want to get it paint-smeared."

She went to the dressing room and returned moments later wearing a pair of close-fitting gray slacks with a black turtlenecked slipover, her feet encased in black sandals; all of which seemed to fit the picture more properly. And strongly emphasized her sexuality. She stood just beside and behind him as he moved from one painting to the next. Most were fully detailed, yet only half a dozen were finished, and none were signed.

"Do you like them?" Karen asked when the full turn had been made.

"Very much. With the exception of Clymene, these are a great improvement over what I saw in Wyecliffe."

"Ah, Clymene," Karen said softly. "She is my all-time favorite."

"If you love her so much, why is she there and not here?"

She shrugged and smiled. "She should hang only where she is appreciated."

He wondered how much that remark had to do with Mark, then walked to an easel that held a canvas which had been covered with a cloth. He touched one end of the covering and asked, "May I?"

"Yes. I particularly want you to see that one."

He raised the cloth and draped it over the back of the crude frame, then stepped back to take a better look. It was the portrait of a young man, about twenty or twenty-one. And seeing it, he knew at once who it was, and why she had wanted him to see it. The same head and jaw structure, the nose a trifle longer, eyes staring back at him as though through a mirror. And yet, had she not made this special point of it, he would under no circumstances have identified it with himself, ten years earlier.

"Robert Goodwin?" he said.

"Yes. Robert. I'd been painting it from snapshots, a photograph, and memory. Then he was killed in Korea and I stopped working on it."

"A beautiful rendering."

Karen said nothing.

"You were very much in love with him, weren't you?"

She said, "I loved him very much, yes."

"I'm sorry. This must be a painful reminder."

"No. Not at all. It helps me to remember. I want to remember him, always."

Steve stepped in and covered the portrait and when he turned back to Karen, saw the merest trace of tears that had welled up in her eyes. He moved to another easel, but she remained standing there for a few moments, staring at the cloth covering. Moments later, he felt rather than saw her standing beside him, then heard her voice saying throatily, "I get the distinct feeling you don't care for abstract art."

The painting was a flood of cubes and diamond shapes against a background of broad, bold splashes of color.

"How can you tell?"

"The way you stand. The way most people stand and stare who come upon it suddenly. Shocked."

"I'm not shocked, but I really don't understand it, Karen, except as an exercise in balance and color. That sounds narrow, even close-minded I know, but I've seen so many amateurish attempts, muddy colors with so little sense of values, hardly any depth or feeling, not to mention the most outrageous titles, even in our finest museums. Sometimes I get the feeling I'm being put on by some third-rate, tongue-in-cheek artists."

"At least you're honest about how you feel. Most people gape and say, 'My four-year-old daughter can do better than that.' "

Steve grinned self-consciously. "Maybe you can make me understand it. Most artists seem to resent the question and refuse to explain. Or—more likely—they can't explain."

Karen laughed. "It's a form of artistic snobbery to some. I don't know if I can explain it any more clearly, but I'll try. Abstract is something most artists come around to trying sooner or later. I'm not apologizing for it, understand."

"That doesn't help much. I simply don't accept it in the conventional sense."

"Let me try. Children discover abstract in the imaginative stories they try to tell without any semblance of reality. But when they talk about the giant, the dwarf, the faun, the prince or princess, none of whom are even remotely apparent, they actually *see* them there, doing what they're supposed to be doing.

"The adult viewer looks at an abstract, then at the title, and exclaims in horror, 'My God! *That's* a bowl of *apples?*' and insofar as the painting in no way resembles a bowl of apples as the normal eye sees it, he's right.

"To the artist who painted it, a person with greater sensitivity and perception, perhaps, the knowledge that there is more to an apple than the outer skin, the stem with a leaf or two clinging to it, persists strongly.

"He also sees the creamy white of the flesh beneath the skin, the brown seeds, the small sacs that hold the seeds. He visualizes the tree that bore the fruit, the branch from which the apple hangs, the earth that contributed to its life and growth, the various stages of coloring during the ripening period. Then there is the sky above the tree, the clouds that bring the necessary rain. He sees all of this with a certain inner sense of order that can only become total confusion in the mind of the casual observer, and as he paints its components, he has not only painted an apple but the story of its magical birth and life. Exactly how it all comes out on canvas is the essence of the abstract."

Steve, impressed with this dissertation, nodded his acceptance. "You make it sound clearer than I can see it."

"It may not be the accepted explanation, but that's my version."

"I think you should be teaching art, or art appreciation."

"You know, I once wanted to do just that."

"Why didn't you?"

"Because I—oh, I don't know. Why is it we most often never do the things we've always wanted to do, dreamed about doing? The way you started out to be a writer and wound up in an advertising agency."

"Probably because only the lucky ones ever manage to do what they enjoy doing in life." He turned away from the abstract and walked to a smaller canvas, unframed, and examined it; a woman bent over the bed of her child, looking down upon him with love. He was again conscious that Karen had moved over to stand beside him as he said softly, "And dream only happy dreams, son. On the morrow a bright new world will await thee."

"That's a lovely quotation," she said. "Whose is it?"

"My father's. He used to put me to bed with it every night until I was about six or seven years old."

"What a nice thought to sleep with. Would you allow me to use a part of it as a title for this painting?"

"Of course. Shall I write it down for you?"

"No. I'll remember it. It's so beautiful."

He stared at her for a moment and she looked squarely at him and he was momentarily disconcerted. He walked to the sofa and sat there, reaching for a cigarette from the box on the low table. She came to him, struck a light, then took another cigarette for herself. "I'm so glad you came, Steve," she said. "Your flattery has been good for my ego."

"It wasn't flattery. I think your work is as professional as any I've ever seen."

"Oh, Steve," she said with a light laugh, "I'm hardly in that class."

"You are, really. You've already had one showing and Clymene is a perfect example . . ."

"I couldn't sell her," she said quickly. "It would be like—like selling a part of myself." She was beside him now and he could feel her closeness, the perfume and touch of her body so close to his own. He turned toward her, felt himself moving toward her and saw her eyes widen, her lips part, the thin line of white teeth showing.

He drew back, and she said, "Steve . . ." then turned away.

He was tempted, almost driven to take her into his arms, suddenly aware that if he did, he would become Robert Goodwin. He looked at his watch and said, "I think I'd better go now."

"Don't, Steve," she said in a low voice. "It wasn't you—"

He knew then that he could move in, hold, and kiss her, but the vision of Robert returned vividly, with Mark somewhere in the distant background. He forced himself to stand up. "Thank you, Karen. I enjoyed the breakfast and the art lesson very much."

"Stay for dinner, won't you?"

"I don't think I'd better."

She stood up and he moved toward the stairway door with Karen following. "Don't you want to?" she said.

"I really can't. I've a number of things to think out clearly for tomorrow, when I get back to my desk. I've GFP's spring campaign to organize."

"Steve?" She put one hand out and touched his arm, staying him.

"What, Karen?"

"Kiss me. Please."

Command, or request? She was standing close to him when he turned to her, so close that the perfume of her hair and body permeated his nostrils, exciting him enormously. He leaned down and kissed her lips lightly, then hard enough to cause them to part, feeling the naked body beneath the thin wool pullover, and experiencing a tremendous urge to possess her in a way—for that single moment in time—that had nothing to do with Mark, Robert, or with anything or anyone but themselves.

"Stay, Steve," she murmured.

He pulled back. "I'm sorry, Karen. I can't."

She let him go then. They returned to the first floor where Max materialized out of nowhere to hand him his hat, hold his overcoat. Outside, he walked without any sense of direction, recalling the time he had rejected Libby here in New York, and spent an entire year of regret; but this was no boy-girl high school romance. This was Karen Goodwin Lawson, wife of *The Client*. And remembering Mark, he was reminded of the curious remark Mark had made during the episode with Jo-Ann in Chicago. *You think I've got it made, don't you? Big job, fine house, beautiful wife, everything a guy could want. Yeah, man. Solid. And a goddamned ring through my fucking nose with a steel leash on it.*

Christ, he thought now, *what am I getting into this time? First Robin. Now, Karen. How close does a man get to the fire before he gets burnt? How many different ways ARE there to blow an account?*

He walked on until he found himself in front of the Blue Baron on Fifty-third Street, west of Madison, where on weekdays, many ad men could be found taking an alcohol "fix" to unwind from momentary pressures, sound out friends about making a job change, or pick up the daily gossip concerning shifting accounts; but on Sunday the Blue Baron was virtually deserted. A pair of elderly men on stools at the bar, hunched over their drinks in serious conversation. A young man, three stools away, nursing a drink apparently waiting for someone, checked his wristwatch frequently. Two men and two women were at a table, one waiter leaning against the wall.

The barman looked up from his newsmagazine in mild surprise. "Hello, Mr. Gilman, you working today?"

"No, Charlie. Just out for a walk."

"Martini?"

"A double."

Working on it, Charlie commented, "Cold day for a walk. Must be freezing out there."

Steve didn't answer. Charlie took the hint and remained silent. Steve took a deep gulp at his drink and Charlie went back to his magazine.

What am I? Steve asked himself. *Where am I? Where am I headed?*

More than ever, he began to appreciate Grady Gilman, a man with many problems to face each day, yet never losing his cool. Grady had carried the burdens of an entire community on top of the stresses of his personal life, all without showing any sign of inner panic, as Steve was showing now. Keith Allard, the true guiding spirit and strong hand of the Leary Agency, had that same remarkable quality of coolness in the face of adversity.

Why am I so fouled up? Am I another Larry Price, a Wade Barrett, heading for destruction by my own hand?

In one brief moment, Karen had given him a choice, and despite the overpowering urge to take it, expediency had conquered desire. Or was it cowardice? And yet he felt that it was not over between them, only a beginning, and certainly more reckless than his affair with Robin.

Curiously, he cared little about Mark, softening his own guilt with the knowledge of Mark's infidelities. He had more concern for Herschel and Anna Goodwin at that moment than for Mark; he worried about what effect such an affair, when it inevitably became known, would have upon them. But then again, was it purely for the sake of his job that he had thought of them?

He heard some of Grady's words again. *When you take an important step in your life, Steve, you've got to accept the responsibilities that go with it, whether you succeed or fail.* And, *You run across a problem, work out your solution, and ask yourself, 'Is this the right way to go? Will anyone suffer by what I am doing?' The answers to those questions will answer the big one: When I've done it, will I be proud of what I've done?*

He drew little comfort from the memory of advice given him as a callow youth. After all, what great joys had Grady derived from his oft-spoken philosophical homilies and platitudes? Why had he failed in his own marriage? *And even in that, I've stepped into his footsteps.*

What was it that he really felt for Karen? At this moment, it was as strong as any pull he had felt toward Libby. Love, or pure sexual attraction?

The word *love* nagged at him and he tried desperately to give it substance, human feeling, a clear definition. It was one of the most over-abused words in man's vocabulary, too often related to material possessions: a pet, clothing, furniture, jewelry, a car, or a house. Love of a job could become total devotion, often far and beyond love for another human being, wife or children. How many marriages each year broke apart because the job was placed above all other considerations?

Was it love, this kind of love, he felt for Karen? And if so, what kind of love, if any, did Karen feel for him? How, in so brief a period of time could either know? On his part, the stakes were high—job and career—which could, he had little doubt, be replaced or restored in most top agencies in New York. Or somewhere else. How much or how little would it mean to a woman like Karen; an affair in a moment of unhappiness, or the dissolution of her marriage?

He finished his second drink, paid the check, and left, walking westward toward his apartment. Dusk had come early and swiftly. Lights had come alive and people became, like himself, passing shadows. He reached home at a little past six o'clock, chilled to the bone, his wrist aching. He heated what was left of the morning coffee, drank two cups, then poured himself a stiff Scotch, and savored its warmth gratefully. He poured a second drink, and when it was gone, a third, beginning to feel a sense of having purged himself of his earlier evil mood. Stretched out on the sofa, he turned his thoughts toward the coming week.

Mark was due back late tonight. In the morning, he would press for a decision on the coupon refund offer, and when and if it were approved, give the group a full green light. He must work more closely with Gary Parris and Bryce's people to develop the television and radio spots, thus far virtually ignored.

He closed his eyes and dozed, then awoke. It was seven-thirty and he hadn't had dinner, yet he felt no hunger. He decided to call a halt to his drinking, go into the study, and make a few notes for the morning meeting he intended to call.

The doorbell rang. He thought it would be George or Inga Maczerak looking in on him to see that he was eating properly. He went to the door, opened it, and found Karen standing there, the hood of her fur coat held by one edge to partially shield her face.

"Are you alone, Steve?" she said.

"Yes."

"Aren't you going to invite me in?"

"Of course. I'm sorry."

She came in quickly, almost furtively, stepping into his arms so that it was impossible for him not to kiss her, a brief brushing of lips, yet so warm and eager that he wanted to linger over it; but she had drawn back to remove her hood, shaking her head so that her hair swirled and fell back into place with that single swing of motion. She turned and allowed him to help her out of her coat, and in his eagerness he felt a mild shock of pain shoot through his right wrist and forearm.

She was wearing a soft beige wool dress that hugged her upper body closely and showed several inches of thigh and sensual nyloned legs as she crossed into the living room and sat on the sofa, took a cigarette from her gold-and-leather case, lit it with a matching lighter, and leaned back in perfect relaxation. To hide his momentary feeling of awkwardness, Steve picked up a cigarette from an enameled box on the coffee table and accepted the light she held for him. "Drink?" he said.

"Yes, thank you. Let me make them." He followed her into the kitchen, and got out a bottle of Scotch and two glasses, while Karen removed a tray of ice cubes, dropped two cubes into each glass, and poured the Scotch, adding water from the tap. She turned toward him, her smile gone, eyes widened, lips parted in anticipation, body touching his. And then she drew back, still staring at him. "Steve—" she began.

"I'm sorry, Karen. I apologize . . ."

"There's nothing to apologize for. I knew you didn't really want to leave this afternoon. That's why I came."

"Karen, we shouldn't—can't . . ."

"Why not? Because of Mark? Steve, you know him as well as I do, the kind of man he is, even better than I do in some ways."

"Does knowing make it less wrong for either of us?"

"Does anyone know what is right and what is wrong any more? There aren't any rigid moral codes left to live by in today's world, are there? Why can't we do what we want, have what we want while we can, and not waste so much of our lives waiting and wanting?"

He said, "I often wonder how we ever really know what we want. We're born out of someone else's want or need, raised by their moral and religious codes until they say *no* to something we want, and then find ourselves having to make a choice."

"You sound terribly pontifical. Are you worried about me being here? Shall I leave?"

Had his life depended on it, he could not have said *yes* at that moment. "No, of course not. I want you to stay. Very much."

He kissed her parted lips and felt the pattern of her intermittent breathing as he held her in his arms, felt and measured the length of her body against his own, the delicacy of her mouth, and found it impossible to differentiate between the pounding of his own heart and Karen's.

She drew back after a few moments, picked up her drink, sipped at it, and replaced the glass on the counter, conscious of his hungry stare, then went into the living room and through it to the short hallway. She stopped to look back, to see if he was following her, then walked past his study into the bedroom. When he entered a few moments later, her shoes were off and, her back toward him, she was unzipping her dress. Beneath the minuscule slip he could see the outline of her panties, the shadow of her hose which she unhooked and stripped off, draping them carelessly over the dress that lay on a chair; then she removed the lacy, almost transparent bra.

The effect on Steve was electric, almost psychedelic, as he stood motionless, dazed by the perfection of her body, which was transformed by nakedness from mature womanhood into yielding youthfulness. He stood as though the slightest movement on his part would destroy the illusion and cause her to vanish into thin air.

With only the brief slip covering her from waist to mid-thigh, she came toward him, eyes bright, hair tousled attractively. "Do you like me, Steve?"

"You—you're beautiful. Perfect," he breathed.

"Here, let me help you." She held the jacket while he maneuvered his arms out of it, undid his tie and removed it, unbuttoned his shirt, and slipped it down over shoulders and right arm. He got out of his trousers while she turned the lights off, stepped out of her slip, drew back the covers, and slipped into bed. Steve went to the window, but she said, "Don't draw the curtains, please." The light from outside was minimal so that only little more than outlines were discernible in the room.

Lying beside her, feeling her flesh against his own, lips pressed together, everything else was forgotten beyond recall. "Steve," she whispered. "Oh, Steve . . ."

"What, Karen?"

"I want you so much."

He held her, kissing her throat and cheek, then sought her tensed lips, fondling her breasts and feeling the strain of her body, her fingers gripping him tightly as she worked herself closer to him, repeating his name until it became a term of endearment.

"You're too tense, Karen," he said. "Relax."

"I'm trying . . ."

He soothed and prepared her and she received him expectantly and easily, then, with a violent shudder, she enveloped him and raged upward in a series of spasmodic thrusts. "Take it easy, Karen," Steve said, slowing her down by pressing his hands down on her shoulders firmly, "we're not competing with each other."

"I can't—help it, Steve. It's been so long . . ."

"Let me guide you." He began pacing himself smoothly,

carefully, pausing to kiss her. Their bodies began to dampen with perspiration and he could feel the tightened muscles in her arms and shoulders; and then, reacting to his own pace, Karen's writhings became less violent as he took over control, her movements measured to his even rhythm, moving in concert. "Better?" he asked.

"Much—much . . ."

For once, Karen realized, she was allowing her partner to take the lead, attuning herself to him, rather than asserting her need to dominate. Steve made love to her gently, as though she were something—or someone—precious, delicate, and breakable, yet thoroughly, passionately involved. The act, once a contest in which one lost or won, had become tender, sweet, and without thought of sin. She began to feel a new sense of communion, a mutuality of sharing, natural, and beautiful.

She was reaching her peak and knew that Steve was ready; and suddenly, she became the aggressor again, driving upward with demented fury, attacking as he drove downward, probing deeper. She cried out, "Now, oh, now!" sobbing as she reached a shuddering climax. Steve held her, caressed her as she glided slowly down from the mountain top, then subsided, allowing him to pursue his own conclusion.

"Oh, God, God," she gasped as relief came. "Thank you, Steve, thank you."

"Don't thank me. You were magnificent."

"I could stay here with you forever, sleep for days, weeks."

"Aren't you picking Mark up at the airport?" he reminded her.

"No. Max will do that. His plane doesn't get in until 11:55."

"Would you like to nap for an hour?"

"With you, yes."

She slept in the curve of his left arm, holding his bandaged right wrist between her hands, and once settled peacefully, Steve closed his eyes and slept too. Happily, dreamlessly.

She woke first and nudged him. The illuminated hands of the clock showed 10:25. "How do you feel?" he asked.

She drew closer, arms around him, one leg pressing between his thighs. "Wonderful. I'm still floating on a cloud. You?"

"Merely sensational."

"Darling?"
"What?"
"You won't be worrying about this—us—will you?"
"You don't think I have anything to worry about?"
"I don't want you to. I don't want you to feel guilt."
He laughed lightly, wryly. "I can't ignore the fact that this has to have some effect on both of us. You're married to Mark, my client . . ."
"Oh, Mark," she said deprecatingly.
"Karen, Mark may be everything you think he is, but you're still his wife, and technically at least, I'm his employee. Doesn't that add up to something in your pretty head?"
"Mark," she said, "is not an insurmountable obstacle. We can't hurt each other any more than we have already."
"You realize, of course, that I'm not in that position. He can hurt me with a single telephone call."
"I know it isn't as simple as I'm making it sound, but I'm willing to take it one step at a time."
"That's fine, but how do I resolve tomorrow, the next time, the time after that?"
"We'll work it out. I know we can, Steve. Don't you want there to be a next time, a tomorrow?"
"Of course. You know I do."
"Then why waste what time there is left?"
He kissed her breasts, then her mouth and neck as she moved closer to him, guiding him smoothly between her thighs. There was little of the earlier tension in her as he sank down upon her and she felt him securely inside her. "Am I better this time?" she asked.
"Much, much better."
"Kiss me."
He did, and felt her tongue caressing his own with the full confidence of success behind her. "Easy," Steve said. "The idea is to make it last as long as possible."
"Show me. Lead me. I want you, I want you so much—"
Pacing, stroking slowly, awakening and stimulating her, feeling her move under him, the rhythm increased as she rose to peak, then forcing her to relax and allow the tension to recede, and pick up again, he orchestrated the act as though he were directing a symphony; then coming into the conclusive climax, he heard her half-scream rising in her throat as they reached the end simultaneously.
"Let's stay this way forever," she said.

"Ah, if that were only possible."

"Do you think we're in love, Steve?"

The question startled him. "Don't jump to conclusions too quickly. So far, it's sex, and very lovely sex."

"It's more than that. It's got to be, else why hasn't it been this good for me before?"

"What it is, is more likely chemistry."

"And what is this kind of chemistry but love? What it's all about, what we read about, see on the screen, watch and envy in others, and seldom in ourselves."

"Karen, do I need to remind you again that you're a married woman?"

"No, you needn't. The question it, what do we do about us, you and me?"

"That's what bothers me. Not only about myself. I'm more concerned about you."

She laughed then. "Haven't you ever heard that when your concern for someone else becomes greater than for yourself, that's love?"

"Regardless, I'm still concerned."

"Try not to be." She reached up and kissed him again, then said, "Steve, have you ever been in love, truly in love?"

The question, asked so abruptly, nettled him; as though she were probing in an all-to-private area. "Yes, Karen. A long time ago, back in Lancaster."

"Who was she?"

"A girl I grew up with as neighbors. We went through our high school years together. Then I went off to Columbia and she went to a college in Virginia."

"What happened?"

"I married her. She came to New York to live and couldn't stand the city. We were divorced a little over a year later."

"And she went back to Lancaster?"

"Yes. And married one of the old crowd. Her father ran him for Congress from our district and he was elected, then re-elected. They're living in Washington."

"Think of that. You might have become a congressman. Any regrets?"

"That all happened a million years ago."

"But you've never forgotten her, have you?"

"There are many things I haven't forgotten."

"I'm sorry. I shouldn't have reminded you. I have a first marriage of my own to bury."

Steve switched on the bed lamp. "It's nearly eleven."

She sighed, reluctant to leave the warmth and comfort of the bed. "Put some coffee on while I dress, will you, darling?"

"Won't that be cutting it a bit thin?"

"Because of Mark? Nonsense. That won't make any difference. We don't account to each other for our time."

"Karen?"

"What, darling?" She was out of bed, reaching for the slip, standing there naked, holding the flimsy garment in the act of putting it on.

"There's so much I don't understand about you. And Mark. Neither of you acts as though the other exists."

"That bothers you?"

"Of course it does."

"Don't let it, darling. What you and I have together has nothing to do with Mark."

"The hell it hasn't! I can't see a man by day and his wife by night and not feel that it hasn't something to do with all three of us."

She studied him for a moment, then said, "Steve, I've found something with you I've seldom had in my life before. I don't want to lose it. We'll work it out, but it will take a little time. Be patient for a while. Please."

"And what about Mark?"

"Mark and I are in something like a convenient cold war. We're seen together at occasional social events, we dine out, go to an opening, spend an infrequent weekend in Wyecliffe with my uncle and aunt, but it's mostly for appearance's sake. It's not an uncommon arrangement."

"Nor too common, is it?"

"I'm not up on the statistics, but that's how it is between us. Mark has his own life and you know that as well as I do. Let me ask you this: Did you enjoy tonight, bringing me to life with your body, your strength, and will? Do you realize what you've done for me, given me? Can you honestly say you want it to end when I walk out of here tonight?"

Steve knew the answers. He had admittedly created in Karen a certain viability and *no,* he didn't want it to end when she left tonight. He said, "How do we live with this, Karen?"

"We'll work it out together, Steve. We're not in a unique situation. Everywhere else in this world, people are living in this very same way, and happily. We're entitled to that happiness. We're mature human beings and have seen marriages break up, and no one dies because of it. One out of every three or four marriages ends in divorce. Why should we think of institutional marriage as something holier than honest love?"

Again he thought of Grady's and Jenny's miscast alliance, the emptiness of the years they had lived together as virtual strangers. "All right, Karen," he said. "We'll work it out. Somehow."

She dropped the slip on the bed and moved into his hard embrace. He held and kissed her, luxuriating in the touch of her flesh against his own, rousing him. "Is it important for you to be home when Mark gets there?" he asked.

"Of course not."

"Can you spend the night here?"

"I wouldn't want it any other way."

"What about that coffee?"

"We'll have it for breakfast," Karen said. She kissed him and added, "You make love so beautifully, Steve."

Chapter 10

1

New York Office
WM. B. LEARY ADVERTISING
Report of Interview with Client

No. 73
Representing Client: Mr. Mark Lawson, Mr. R. Davies
Representing Agency: S. Gilman
Meeting held at: GFP, Forty-second Street
Subject: Spring Campaign

Route to: Wm. B. Leary, K. Allard, W. Barrett, S. Gilman; Hayden, Baker, Berton, Thalberg, Castle, Baldasarian, Bryce, Parris, Kann, Traffic Control.

PRINT, ELECTRONIC MEDIA PROPOSAL TRANSMITTED: Attached herewith Xerox copies of list of six (6) ads, copy, and layouts submitted to Mr. Lawson and Mr. Davies for approval.

Related material, Point of Purchase, Display Units, Window Strips, Store Banners, etc. also left with Client for consideration and approval.

In preliminary discussion of media planning, Mr. Lawson indicated the probability of running proposed campaign through July, perhaps August, ending prior to breaking of Fall Campaign in September. Discussed need for increase in television budget levels to gain maximum exposure in least possible time. Mr. Lawson will discuss this further with Mr. Fitzjohn and Mr. Hardwick and keep us advised.

TRAFFIC/MEDIA: Please Note: On approval, it will be necessary to establish deadline dates.

S. GILMAN

2

As with every campaign, it was a new ballgame. After a series of high-level conferences at GFP, the spring campaign was approved, with Steve's coupon refund and the free recipe book offer intact. Sales objectives were projected, advertising goals outlined, media selected, the overall budget approved, and space and time ordered. Basic copy and art strategies were moved from the initial presentation stage and expanded, and purposes and goals were defined in a series of group conferences and individual meetings as the work progressed.

And finally, the copy was written, visuals created, examined and discussed, and changes made and approved. Television and radio copy and storyboards were labored over, sweated out, revised, and finalized for production. Traffic Control and Production sent memos to Steve when copy was due at the composition houses, art for the engravers, camera-ready copy for printers, plates for magazines. Point-of-Purchase material, billboards, special store displays and banners were completed, and readied to go. A new tagline, GOODY . . . *To Be Sure*, was adopted for the length of the campaign.

During this press of work, Larry Price flew in from Los Angeles one Friday afternoon, spent two hours with Bill and Keith at the office, and the next two days with either or both, at their homes and at Larry's hotel. Late on Monday he flew back to the West Coast. Steve learned through Peggy's contacts with the office grapevine that Price was in town, but hadn't caught the merest glimpse of him during his visit, about which he felt some mixture of relief and guilt. Neither Keith, Bill, nor Wade, mentioned the fact to him and Steve decided not to ask questions at that time, hoping for the best for Larry.

Days blended into weeks and the Work Progress Chart began to resemble the logistics charts for an invasion plan. By the latter part of April, GFP's troops in the field were armed and ready, backed up by a complete advertising and sales promotion plan. The Leary men and women, exhausted by the strenuous tempo, began to relax, and there was little more for Steve to do but wait for the campaign to break. But not for long.

"Good job, Steve," Keith said at lunch one day as the kick-off-date approached.

"Thanks, Keith. It ain't been easy."

"Nervous?"

"No more than usual. The pressure's been terrific. Anxious, I'd say, and hopefully expectant. With inflation, and the cost of living index pushing upward, I'd say we've got a good chance."

"I agree."

"How does Bill feel about it?"

"Can't say. I haven't seen too much of him lately. He's been spending more time with his stockbroker than with clients." After a moment devoted to his second martini, "Seen much of Wade lately?"

"He's been looking in on us. I understand he's having his hands full with Chevalier."

"Not as full as he should have. It's gotten to the point where he and Ted are hardly speaking to each other."

"Um-m. Are we going to blow it with Chevalier, Keith?"

"Unless we come up with a full scale miracle by July 15th, when the contract comes up for renewal. Right now, I'd say the prognosis is very bad, with little chance for recovery."

"What about B & B?"

"Thank God that seems safe. Russ Charles's people have been over the outfit with a fine tooth comb and sent the Bonds a formal letter of intention. He's waiting for their reply, which he expects to have by the end of next week if something doesn't happen to upset the applecart. There have been other offers, but Russ is confident that GFP has the inside track."

"What about Larry Price?"

Keith squirmed in his chair. "Bill and I had some long talks about that after Larry came in that weekend. We're still in the hashing-over stages."

"No decisions?"

"Yes, I think so." Keith looked up from his drink and into Steve's eyes. "No use pulling punches with you, Steve, but keep this to yourself. He's out as of the moment Russ confirms the sale of B & B to GFP."

Now it was Steve's turn to squirm uncomfortably, remembering that last morning with Larry back in January. "Does Bill give him a bullet to bite on before he gets the good news?"

"Oh, shit, Steve, don't get so damned uptight and bitter about it. It happens, and when it does, the swifter you get it over with, the better." The waiter appeared and placed their food before them. Keith said, "Larry will be offered the opportunity to resign because of ill health or whatever other reason he chooses for himself. Six months' leave with full pay, and full retirement benefits. There's no other way, Steve. We can't bring him back here and Marty Link doesn't want him in Chicago. A vice-president branch manager in a lesser job can only undermine the whole goddamned structure."

"Poor bastard," Steve said with deep feeling.

"It's tough, sure, but at least he'll make out financially. If he can stay off the bottle."

"Any decision on who replaces him?"

"Wade." Keith said it quickly, and saw Steve's sharp reaction.

"Wade?"

Keith nodded. "Sylvia's been in Las Vegas for the past seven weeks. His divorce came through the other day. It just about broke him. I know it sounds like we're kicking him upstairs, but he made the initial contact with GFP years ago, and he's had an otherwise good record. Until a few years ago. Until he fouled up with Sylvia he was a good, capable man, but when personal predicaments begin to overshadow a man's ability to perform, he becomes a detriment."

When Steve withheld comment, Keith continued, "We discussed Wade for hours on end and we think that if we give him a change of scenery out of range of his personal difficulties, we can salvage a lot of good in him."

"Well," Steve said, "it can't be all bad. He wanted L.A."

"It's a good out for him, as well as for us. Chancey, I know, but we think that Larry's unfortunate experience dangling in front of him will make him realize that he's getting a good chance. If he blows it, Larry has pointed the way."

"And what about Chevalier? The McCreery-Adrian battle won't go away because Wade leaves."

"No, it won't, and that bothers me. Any suggestions, Steve?" Keith said with a slow smile.

By that familiar, all-knowing smile, Steve guessed that Keith already had an answer, but was leaving it to Steve to suggest so that it would not appear as something being forced upon him. "There's one I can make, Keith," he said, "if you and Bill will go along with it."

Keith, still smiling, waited with upraised eyebrows. "What if when Wade goes, I put in a strong bid for Norm Adrian as senior writer on the B & B division of GFP?"

"You're sure you want him?"

"Damned sure," Steve said with emphasis. "We'll have to form a separate B & B group and I don't know of anyone who could organize and run it better than Norm."

"Under your supervision, of course."

"I don't think Norm will resent that. And the pressure will be off Ted and Chevalier."

"That part remains to be seen, but if you can handle it that way, fine. That leaves us with the problem of replacing him on Chevalier."

"I'd go outside to do that, bring someone in who will meet with Ted's fullest approval."

"You would?" Again that certain smile. "Why not from inside?"

"Any account man from within will have two strikes on him to start off with, and the rest of the group would blow their stacks. Maybe out of Chicago, if Marty Link will turn loose a good man, but not from this office."

"You may be right."

"I'd like to make another suggestion."

"What?"

"How about convincing Wade to take Chuck Baldasarian with him to L.A.?"

"Chuck giving you any trouble?"

"Not as much me, as some of the others. Frankly, he's getting in my way too often, tripping Hayden and Baker whenever he can and making a general pain in the ass of himself. I think a transfer would be in order."

"Not now, Steve. The way things are, I wouldn't want to offend Marty Link or McCandless. But I'll say this to you—if it ever becomes serious, you've got the right to fire him and I'll back you up every inch of the way."

"Thanks, Keith. I don't think we're even close to that point."

"Good. Ready?"

When they returned to the Hungerford Trust Building, Keith pressed the elevator button for the thirty-fifth floor. "Come up to my office with me, Steve. I've got something for you."

When they arrived there, Steve saw several piles of material spread out on the table that stood against the far wall. Keith pointed to it. "There's your next assignment."

"What is it?"

"I've been doing some of your homework for you. For weeks. I've had Marketing, Merchandising, and Research, our own people, and outside experts, digging up everything they could find on the subject of coffee. Where and how it's planted, grown, harvested, shipped, blended, roasted, packaged, merchandised, and sold, the whole bloody works. In this stack, you'll find competitive ad clippings from all over—including foreign language papers and magazines—translations clipped to each ad. This third pile contains national economic and marketing reports and trends. Everything here has been gone through by our researchers, who've weeded out the useless material and reduced it to basic essentials."

"And which, I assume, you will turn over to me for study in my spare time?"

"For familiarization. I've got a great feeling that B & B is in the bag. Even if the deal is signed, sealed, and delivered this or next week, it will still take quite some time before GFP takes over and gets set up to operate."

"And if the deal falls through?"

"You're being pessimistic," Allard grinned. "Think positive, man. But," he added, "if it does, you'll still have a well-founded education in coffee advertising and merchandising that won't hurt you one damned bit."

"Okay, Keith. I'll try not to let it interfere with my other work. Or vice versa."

"Don't let it. Everything else is rolling well, so start yourself on a personal orientation program. By now everybody knows about it and it's just a matter of that final *yes* or *no,* and I think it will be *yes."*

"How will Wade fit into this?"

"Exactly nowhere. Out West, he'll only be a part of the general service function, just as Chicago will operate. We'll be in full charge here."

"One thing more. Lawson has been at me like a dog with a bone over this, and I suspect he'll want to play a heroic part in the B & B division."

"Don't worry about Lawson now. At worst, he'll want to start an opening campaign going long before production is ready. Just keep a few jumps ahead of him. Come up with an introductory theme or campaign, and we'll handle it through Herschel Goodwin if Mark gets too tough or in your way. This is too big, too important to play around with, so screw Lawson."

"When do we go with Norm?"

"As soon as we get the final word from Russell Charles that the deal is set. On the other hand, I think I'll hold onto this material until then. Instead, I'll give you the folder of condensed notes I've made, a sort of general guideline to go by. We'll know for sure within a few days."

In his own office a few minutes later, everything was proceeding quietly and in an orderly fashion. The WPC had become a battle map of green, red, blue, black, and orange lines indicating the various stages of work from initiation to completion, with only a few openings to be filled in. Peggy came in and closed off two more of those blocks. "What's new from topside?" she asked.

"Not a lot, Peg. Everything is hinging on the news we're waiting for from the Coast."

"We'll be getting a new group in, I hear."

"Okay," Steve said with a smile, "let's have it. What's the word from the water-cooler crowd?"

"Well, Personnel has been interviewing copywriters and art directors for a whole week now, strictly with food experience, and I know it can't be for GFP, so it can't be for anything else but B & B, even though they aren't saying much about that. That'll give us at least four more people. We'll need more space, desks, everything."

Four. So the word about Adrian, at least, was still secret. "We'll find it, Peg. Once the word comes in and we're all set, we'll move Paul Jenkins and his electronics gang out of their space, break through the walls, and spread out. If Personnel is on the job, we'll be doing some interviewing on our own among the finals, but not for a while yet. Any coffee left out there?"

She went out, returned with a cup of coffee and left him alone.

During the past two months, Steve had been seeing Karen on an average of two times each week, stimulated by each surreptitious meeting, reveling in the excitement and pleasure each brought to the other in each encounter. And yet he despised the need for caution and secrecy.

He waited on edge for her call to say she would meet him at his apartment, and once when Mark was out of town, she sent Max and Gerda off for a weekend holiday so Steve could spend an entire Saturday and Sunday alone with her at the house on Eighty-fifth Street. Another weekend, they drove into the Connecticut countryside, registered at a small hotel, walked through woods and along narrow lanes, ate in small, quaint restaurants, and shared the same bed, his toilet articles beside her cosmetics in intimate arrangement on the bathroom shelf. They bathed together, and Karen not only shaved him, but trimmed his hair. And seldom, during those idyllic hours, did either mention Mark's name; as though by refusing to do so they could wish him out of existence.

Steve's guilt over Mark was at first deep and incisive, but as he and Karen continued their relationship, he rationalized, justified, and eventually surrendered to the pure enjoyment of uninhibited sex and the absolute release that Karen's physical presence provided. Each visit became more prolonged, each departure heightening the expectancy of their next meeting. There was an ease and naturalness about them that had once seemed impossible to Steve, and Karen became more alive than ever, renewed each time they shared his or her bed.

At work, he drew a curtain over his mind to block out the image of Karen. When he called on Mark, even though her photograph smiled up at him from behind Mark's desk, it became the photograph of Mark Lawson's wife and had nothing to do with the Karen he knew. That same curtain, he discovered, also helped block out the memory of Libby. Since Karen, he had thought of her perhaps once or twice, but not for very long.

Karen telephoned him once or twice a week at his office, using the name "Miss Stafford," which had begun to draw questioning looks from Peggy, and which disturbed Steve for only a short period. Over weekends when they could not meet, Steve pondered his part in this adventure—or misadventure—in adultery, recalling to mind an old aphorism: *When stretched out too long, adultery has as many disadvantages as marriage, plus the additional complications.* Thus far, there were few disadvantages, and no complications.

How, he wondered, would it be resolved? He was not convinced he was in love with Karen, but readily admitted she filled a need; that she, on the other hand, showed signs of being in love with him. They had discussed love in general terms, peripherally, yet neither could directly speak those words to the other: *I love you.* And if one cannot say it, can one truly feel it, he wondered? Like Grady before him, he was sipping honey without having to cultivate the flower or pay for the upkeep of the bee, except that Grady's women were paid whores and his conscience had no doubt been clearer than Steve's. Yet, Steve reasoned, why should I be so bothered about Mark, knowing him as I do, living his life apart from Karen. The answer became simple then.

And so, in Keith Allard's words, screw Larson.

3

Shortly after three o'clock on the following Friday, Steve began the ritual of clearing his desk of odds and ends in preparation for the weekend, for which he had definite plans. Routinely, he checked the Work Progress Chart with Chuck Baldasarian, then dictated several memos to Peggy for Monday morning. The phone rang and Peggy took the call. "Mr. Lawson," she said laconically.

Steve took the receiver from her with little joy, visualizing some last-minute crisis that might in some way interfere with his weekend. Even before he spoke, he heard Mark's impatient voice, charged with galvanic excitement. "Steve? Hey, Steve—"

"Hello, Mark. What's up?"

"Steve! Hey, boy! We've got it locked in!"

Now with matching exuberance, "B & B?"

"What else? Russ closed the deal in Santa Barbara a couple of hours ago. The old man called us and the trade paper boys have had Fitzjohn, Hardwick, and me cornered, asking for confirmation. It'll be in tomorrow's *Times* and *Journal* as well."

"Congratulations, Mark. Looks like we'll have our work cut out for us."

Mark's exhiliaration was in full flight. "You bet your sweet ass we will. We're going to swing high and wide with this one. Old Hardwick's even sent out for champagne and Fitzjohn's actually got a grin on his face from ear to ear. When can we get together?"

"What's the rush, Mark? We've got plenty of time and I don't want to go off half-cocked."

"What the hell have you got in your veins, ice water? Jesus, get excited for once, can't you? Listen, how about dinner tonight? I'll phone Karen . . ."

Steve broke in quickly. "Mark, I'd love to, believe me, but I can't make it tonight. I'm wired in for dinner with the Allards and they've got theater tickets. How about early next week?"

It took several minutes more before Steve could get off the phone, and as he began dialing Keith's extension to relay the news, Allard walked into his office. "Your phone off the hook?" he asked. "I've been trying to get you for the past twenty minutes." From his craggy smile and goodhumored tone, Steve knew he was the bearer of the same news.

"I've been talking with Mark."

"Then you know. Congratulations. We got the word from Herschel Goodwin half an hour ago. Most of the credit goes to you."

"Thanks, Keith. It's great news."

Keith sat on the sofa, legs extended fully, ankles crossed.

"It's a lot better than that, even better than bringing in a brand new account. Instead of staring at a three-and-a-quarter-million loss, we'll be picking up a five- or six-million shot in the arm. Maybe more later on."

"Well, that's the name of the game, isn't it. I'm beginning to feel a little uptight about it, now that it's finally here."

"You can handle it," Keith said confidently. "Right now, let's go up to Bill's office. He wants to announce it officially."

Just as gloom and despair can envelop an agency with the word that an important account has gone astray, so swiftly will the news of a major coup infect it with elation and jubilation. On their way to the thirty-fifth floor, it was obvious that the interoffice wireless system had spread the word of GFP's (and Leary's) acquisition, reflected in the smiling faces and waves of silent congratulation that greeted them en route.

In Bill's office, the bar had been thrown open, Mrs. Kimbrough, and Allard's secretary, Gail Kingsley, were serving drinks to the dozen members of the executive and administrative staffs who had gathered to share in the celebration. Bill Leary, his face a full moon of pure joy, waved a free hand toward Steve and Keith as he spoke into the telephone, confirming the story to an advertising journal. Marty Elkins and Elizabeth Berton formed one group, with Sam Abrams, Frank Castle and Ellis Thornton, while Arthur Thalberg, Charlie Taft, Lex Kent and Morris Tweed milled around the bar. The "anonymous three," James Fanning, Hartwell Woodward, and André Chalfonte, as usual, looked wise, drank together, and spoke only to Bill Leary and Keith Allard. Don Bryce and Ethan Loomis came in together and headed for the bar. Two waiters from a nearby restaurant suddenly materialized, carrying a cloth-covered table which they put down beside the bar and began serving hot canapés. Others began streaming in.

Off the phone, a drink in one hand, Bill called for attention and made the formal announcement, "which, as you all probably know, will result in a substantial increase in our billings. And," he added, "full credit is due Steve Gilman, who recognized the means to turn a very probable loss into a positive gain, for which he will be duly rewarded."

There was the expected applause, along with some back-slapping and congratulations for Steve. The two waiters were behind the bar now, working feverishly to keep the supply equal to the demand. Sam Abrams cornered Steve for a moment. "Well, sport, you pulled it off, didn't you?" he said happily.

"Thanks, Sam. I won't forget my promise."

"Anything I can do for you, Steve, anytime . . ."

"Don't go into hock to me, Sam. I want Norm with me. I need him very much right now."

"Any way you look at it, I take it as a personal favor."

At four-thirty, with the weekend coming up, the celebrants took their final drinks and started drifting out. Noticeably absent were Wade Barrett and Ted McCreery. As Steve began to walk out with Ethan Loomis and Greg Barnes, Bill called out, "Wait up, Steve, please," and Steve returned to the bar. The waiters moved most of the debris out along with the table. Lucy Kimbrough and Gail Kingsley were dismissed for the day and Bill, Keith and Steve settled down in leather chairs in Bill's favorite conversation corner.

"I usually hate these things," Bill said, "but this one has been a distinct pleasure." Keith smiled, tamping fresh tobacco into the bowl of his pipe. Bill turned to Steve. "As of Monday, Steve, you will be in complete control of both the GFP and B & B divisions. We have a dozen or so prospects for you to look over and make your choice of the copy and art people you'll need. Personnel has come up with some exceptional talent, but the final decision will be yours."

Nothing from Keith but a small grin. "Thanks, Bill," Steve said. "I intend to build the new group around Norm Adrian, if there aren't any objections."

"If that's what you want, fine. That will relieve some of

the pressure on Chevalier, which pleases me. We'll find an adequate replacement for Norm, one that will meet with Ted's approval."

"Thank you, Bill. I'd like to spend some time with Norm this evening and get him set up for talks on Monday morning. I think our account execs are sufficient for now, but we'll need at least two copy and two art people to start with. We can use our present TV, production, and clerical help until the work load increases. Also, we'll need more space. If we can move Paul Jenkins and his group out, and break through the walls, we'll have access to those offices and keep our two groups close together."

"No problems there," Bill agreed. "More important to you—since we will consider GFP and B & B as separate accounts for the time being—is that, technically, you'll have account supervisor status, and with it, a vice-presidency. Keith and I arrived at that decision the moment the word came in this afternoon. With the promotion, of course you will be entitled to the raise that goes with it, forty-five thousand. With your bonus, that will bring you up into the neighborhood of between sixty thousand and sixty-five thousand."

I've made it. I've made it.

Keith said, "Well, Steve?"

The suddenness of change, with the increase in income, robbed Steve of immediate speech. He swallowed twice and was reignited by Keith's own grin of pleasure. "I—I can't tell you—how much I appreciate all of this. Thank you both."

Bill said, "Nonsense. You deserve it, Steve. I want you to clear matters up downstairs so you can move up to this floor where you now belong. You'll take over Wade's suite. When do you think you can be ready to make the change?"

He recovered then. "Bill, I don't want to make that move yet, if you don't mind. I think that for the present, I belong where I am, with my group. We've become a closely knit unit and I don't think it will help matters if I suddenly isolate myself from them. I don't want to offend my people by forcing them to make appointments to see me, or have them trooping upstairs for conferences. I'm very comfortable where I am."

Bill shot a quick glance at Keith, whose own expression easily spelled out *I told you so.* "All right, Steve," Bill said, "work that part of it out any way you want. The suite will be there for your use anytime you require it. Also, we'll have building maintenance work out the problem of expanding your space for the new B & B group." Bill sipped at his drink and added, "As you no doubt know already, Larry Price has asked for retirement. On Monday morning, Wade leaves for L.A. to take over from him."

Asked for retirement! Here's the loaded gun, Larry. You know what to do with it. Just don't mess up the carpeting in your office. And be sure to leave a properly signed suicide note.

So, Steve thought, the wheel turns. Larry Price was moved to Los Angeles because Bill Leary, Sr. didn't want him in New York. Wade Barrett strikes out in New York and is kicked upstairs to branch managership of the Los Angeles office, pushing Price off the ladder. Steve Gilman becomes the beneficiary.

What happens on the next spin of the wheel?

4

The dinner engagement he had used to beg off from Mark's invitation had not, of course, been with the Allards, but with Karen, at his apartment. On the way there, he stopped off for flowers and six bottles of champagne, two of which he began icing as soon as he reached home. He showered and dressed casually, removed two steaks from the refrigerator, and assembled the salad vegetables, fruits, and cheeses for dessert, his mind filled with thoughts of the future. And some very definite plans. A new apartment somewhere on the East Side, in the sixties or seventies, decorated with Karen's help for Karen's pleasure and comfort as well as his own. Something with an underground garage so that he could keep a car of his own.

Until now, he had given little thought to how he would—if he reached that level—live on sixty-thousand-plus a year, what his everyday life would be like, how his tastes and habits in food, manner of dress, entertainment, vacations might change. And the man himself, would he become another person?

And how much could it all matter, psychologically manacled as he was to Mark Lawson, client, and husband of his mistress? How quickly would the agency cut him loose if his affair with Karen were discovered?

She arrived promptly at seven, her glowing smile telegraphing knowledge of the acquisition. "Congratulations, darling. I've already heard the good news from Aunt Anna."

"How does your uncle feel about it?"

"The way someone feels when the biopsy has been performed and the doctor says, "Benign." During the negotiations he was actually ambivalent about the whole thing, but since Russ called from Santa Barbara he's like a child with a new toy. Aunt Anna says he couldn't be more delighted. Incidentally, he feels terribly grateful to you."

"And I to him." He told her of his elevation to supervisor status, and his increase in salary. "But mostly, I feel more indebted to you, for giving me the gift of you."

"Thank you, darling, you're sweet, Is that cham*pagne* I see under the towel in that ice bucket?"

"It is. A celebration is due and it occurred to me that we've never had champagne together. Do you like it?"

"I *adore* it."

The bottles were thoroughly chilled. They drank a toast, then went into the kitchen to prepare dinner, at which Steve was far more expert than Karen. Watching as he tended the steaks, "I owe you so much for everything you've given me," she said suddenly.

"Hey, what brought that on?"

"I don't know. The good news, I suppose, that makes you so happy. And other things. I'm beginning to feel a stronger awareness about us, our situation. There's so much more to life than sneaking around in the shadows."

"And Mark?"

"Mark," she said, "is Mark's problem. I want to enjoy peace of mind with you."

He forked the steaks onto the plates and shut off the broiler. Karen added the vegetables and carried the plates to the table. Steve poured the champagne, and the meal began on that somber note. After a few moments, Steve said, "Would you consider divorcing Mark?"

"I would if I didn't have to answer to my conscience for Aunt Anna and Uncle Herschel. I've had one divorce and it hurt them far more deeply than it did me. They're much older now, and more vulnerable."

"Then what peace of mind can either of us enjoy as long as Mark is there between us?"

"Please, darling, be patient and let me work it out my

own way. When the time is right, I'll have it out with Mark. You won't enter into it at all."

"Do you think Mark would give up what he has without one hell of a fight?"

"Steve, all Mark has is his job, and the thousand shares of GFP Uncle Herschel gave him the day we were married. I'll give Mark a fair settlement and he'll take it."

"And I'll take Mark's place."

"Not the way you make it sound, darling. Mark never really had a place. Only a job."

"Karen, it won't be much different. What I have can't possibly come close to matching your personal wealth. All I have is a job that was raised to sixty thousand a year only this afternoon. I own a piece of property in Lancaster, a few hundred shares of stock, and about six thousand dollars in the bank."

Karen laughed. "If all marriages were based on an equal financial basis, the system would never have gotten off the ground. And there wouldn't have been a Julian or a Mark in my life. Steve, we have each other. How much does the rest really matter? This is what counts, you and me, and what we have to give each other of ourselves. Will you open the second bottle?"

They finished the meal and the second bottle of champagne, then fell into a half-drunken ecstasy, exploring, tantalizing, finally consummating the act, with Karen crying, "To think what I've missed for so long, so long!"

They slept, awoke, loved each other again, and when they woke next, the sun was streaming in upon them through windows they had forgotten to curtain. For an hour they lay awake in the euphoria of each other's arms, then got up, showered, and had breakfast. While Karen read the morning paper, Steve dressed, and went shopping. When he returned, Karen had put the apartment in order. They put away the groceries and laughed over Steve's extravagance in buying up a number of expensive delicacies befitting an executive in the sixty-thousand-a-year bracket.

When everything was in place, they made love again. And when night fell, they dressed, and went to a small restaurant on the lower West Side where they could feel safe from scrutiny while enjoying Viennese food. Later, they walked along a maze of unlighted streets in the Village, then taxied back to Steve's apartment for more champagne. At one o'clock they fell into bed and made love again, then slept in peaceful contentment.

5

On Monday morning Peggy greeted Steve with a ceremonial bow and an elfish grin. "Congratulations, oh, master. You were so long at the party on Friday, I had to get the scoop from the usual reliable sources. When do we move upstairs?"

"I hate to shatter your dreams of glory, sweetie, but we don't. Not for the present."

"You mean that beautiful suite of Mr. Barrett's will be going to waste?" she asked, showing her disappointment keenly.

"Only until B & B is safely underway. Fear not, it will wait for us. How's the mail?"

"Light. I've got the notes you gave me on Friday . . ."

"Bring them in with the coffee."

At his desk, he remembered he hadn't been able to talk to Norm Adrian after the Friday afternoon session in Leary's office and jotted a note to himself to call Norm and invite him to lunch. Peggy came in with the coffee and memos, reading them back to him while he sipped, names and contents recorded in his mind. "Okay, let's get Chuck in first, then call Mr. Adrian and ask him if he can have lunch with me . . ."

The phone rang. Peggy picked up the receiver. "Mr. Gilman's office," she said, then, "One moment, operator, I'll see if he's in." Covering the mouthpiece, "It's long distance. Mr. Haywood."

"Haywood?"

"Chicago, C & H, the premium house man who wrote you a letter a while back asking for an appointment. You told me to put him off."

He hesitated for a moment, then said, "I'll take it."

Mr. Haywood came on and Peggy handed the receiver over.

"Steve Gilman here, Mr. Haywood. I'm sorry I haven't been able to get back to you."

"That's quite all right, Mr. Gilman. I was about to write you again when I learned I have to be in New York this week and wondered if it would be possible to see you, say on Friday?"

"I'd like to say yes, Mr. Haywood, but I'm up against a very tight schedule. Could you give me an idea of what you have in mind?"

"Well, yes. We've developed a comprehensive premium plan we think you'll be interested in for your GFP account and I'd like to explore it with you at your convenience."

"For GFP? Are you aware that GFP has never entered into the premium race?"

"I'm fully aware of that, Mr. Gilman, but in the case of an entirely new item to be introduced nationally . . ."

"Word gets around fast, doesn't it?"

Haywood laughed and said, "We do read the trade papers here in Chicago, Mr. Gilman."

"I'm sure you do, but since the acquisition was made just three days ago, and your letter was written quite some time before that . . ."

There was a moment of silence, then Haywood said, "Oh, come now, Mr. Gilman, it's no secret that GFP has been negotiating for B & B as far back as January."

Regaining his composure, Steve returned, "I congratulate you on your resourcefulness, Mr. Haywood, but I am in no position to discuss any plans for B & B at this early stage."

"I'm not doing this entirely out of the blue," Haywood said. "In fact, my first approach was made to Mr. Lawson several months ago. It was at his suggestion that I wrote you. What we are proposing . . ""

"I'm sorry," Steve cut in abruptly, "but I can't discuss your proposal at this time, Mr. Haywood, except to suggest that a meeting between us would be a complete waste of your time and mine."

"Shall I phone Mr. Lawson and tell him that?"

Now thoroughly angered, Steve said, "Frankly, I don't care what you do or who you call. I might add that GFP's long-standing no-premium policy meets with full approval of this agency, and my own, and I will be inclined to veto any such proposal."

"Well"— Haywood began—"thanks for the tip on where you stand." There was a sharp *click!* as the connection was broken. Steve stared at the receiver in his hand with tightened lips.

"Problems?" Peggy said, as she took the receiver from him and cradled it.

"Lawson," Steve muttered. "The first fly in the new jar of ointment."

The look on Peggy's face was a combination of sympathy and resignation. "What's he up to now?"

"Who ever knows what in hell Lawson is up to?" Steve replied morosely. "Get him on the phone and ask him if he can see me around two-thirty." When Peggy went out, he dialed Keith's office and spent the next hour there gathering ammunition to use on Mark.

When he returned, Peggy said, "Mr. Adrian dropped by to see you. He can't have lunch, something about a school problem with his son, but he can see you before he leaves at noon."

"Ask him if he can make it now."

Norm Adrian came lumbering in a few minutes later, sleeves rolled up, clothing somewhat disheveled as usual. "Nice going, Steve. I'm glad to see you making it to the top ten in your class."

"Thanks, Norm. Breaking in with you on Chevalier helped. Get comfortable. Coffee?"

"No, thanks." He dropped his huge body into the sofa and lit a cigarette. "I like the atmosphere a lot better here than where I am. More relaxing than the pressure cooker."

"That's pretty much what this is all about, Norm . . ."

"I even suspected a little of that. Sam caught me as I was leaving on Friday and did some hinting. Of course, I knew the B & B thing was in the wind, everybody did. I'm glad it came through for you. You deserve it and I know it will be in good hands."

"Your hands, Norm, if you want it."

"With the blessings of the brass?"

"It's already been cleared with Bill and Keith. I want you to head up the new group."

"Well—I'd like it fine, Steve, and I know I can do a good job once I divorce myself from tobacco and adjust my tastes and mind to coffee."

"I know you can do it and I've got plenty of backup material to help you make the switchover. I don't know how much Sam told you, Norm, but I really need a man like you on top of this. I'll feel a hell of a lot more comfortable with you alongside me."

Adrian nodded, smiling. "Thanks, Steve. I appreciate it."

"The thanks go to you, Norm." He stood up and

walked to where Adrian sat, looking down on him. "You knew me as a raw trainee when I first broke in. With a new account like B & B, I'm beginning to feel the way I did back then."

"Why the hell should you?"

"Because B & B is going to be handled like a new, separate account and I've never worked on one from the very beginning."

"It won't be much different from what you're doing now."

"Norm, I took GFP over after it was a going concern. What we're going to do with B & B is treat it as something apart from GFP until it has established a track record of its own, then we'll see how we go about integrating it with the rest of the line."

Adrian shrugged his massive shoulders. "No sweat. We'll get along and we'll do the job. And a good one. That's a promise."

"Great, Norm. You realize, I'm sure, that Mark Lawson is no great prize to work with."

Adrian grinned. "After McCreery, Lawson won't be much of a problem at all. Besides, that will be your department, yours and your account execs. When do we go with this?"

"As soon as McCreery picks your successor."

"And good luck to him, whoever he is. Can I have some of your material to look over in the meantime?"

"Any time you want it, feel free."

"Maybe tomorrow. I've got to get up to my boy's school. A social problem."

"Nothing serious, I hope."

"In this modern age, no. Merely an inconvenience of the moment. He's two months away from his thirteenth birthday and he and three other kids got picked up smoking hash in the gym locker room. This afternoon, after we try to close the generation gap a little, he's going to get his first haircut in almost a year. Maybe," Norm added inconclusively.

Lawson welcomed Steve eagerly and, as he had long suspected, was immediately made aware that Mark would not sit quietly on the sidelines waiting for a completed campaign to be presented for his approval or disapproval. He wanted in on it at the start, and pacing back and forth, he said, "Steve, we've got to have something to make every housewife think she's just discovered coffee for the first time in her life when she takes her first sip of B & B."

"Big order, Mark," Steve countered. "Coffee is one of the most staple items in her daily household needs. No amount of advertising can push her into an abrupt change of habit overnight. Our first job is to convince her to *try* B & B. If we can do just that much, we'll have done the toughest part of the job. After that, we'll concentrate on holding her. What I have in mind at the moment is using the refund coupon in the West, to recapture the lost market out there, then feature it prominently when we break nationally . . ."

"Refund coupons!" Mark snorted. "Hell, what's so new about that? Just because we're doing it with the rest of the line? We don't even know if it will work for us, and besides, everybody else has been doing it for years. I want more than that, a hell of a lot more."

"So do I. That's what we're searching for."

"Premiums," Mark said flatly. "Not the usual run of the mill thing, something good, big enough to attract her attention, grab her. Hold her."

Blandly, with a half-smile, Steve asked, "What did you have in mind, Mark, a car, boat, furs, a diamond tiara to wear in her kitchen?"

Mark slapped a palm angrily down on his desk. "Listen, you screwed-up word jockey, I'm not cracking jokes. I want something to make the eyes bug out of her head when she sees it. Important enough to start her buying wheels in motion. I want . . ."

"Mark," Steve said evenly, "the success of B & B means as much to me, to the agency, as it does to GFP, and to you. I'll have a group of experienced people sweating this one out, including myself. Why don't you give us a chance to come up with something, to show you what we can do? What can we offer the housewife that she can't already get with trading stamps? What you're talking about is not only costly and time-consuming, but adds to the food bill, directly or indirectly, and at a time when the housewife is concerned about dimes and nickels in her weekly budget. Why . . ."

"Why in hell, Mr. Know-it-all Gilman, does it always have to be *your* way? What the hell is so wrong with an idea coming from the client, for Christ's sake? Haven't you guys ever been wrong?"

"Of course we have, but our track record is as clean as any you've ever seen. All we're asking for is a chance to come up with something that will serve our purpose and do the job we both want, the one that's best for GFP."

"You're stalling, Steve. You don't want this premium thing because you didn't suggest it first. Hell, even your own boy, Chuck . . ." Lawson caught himself, then added, "I'm warning you, if you, Leary, or Allard go running to the old man with the idea you're going to kill this, I'm going to be one tough sonofabitch to live with. And you can pass that along to your agency."

"And," Steve said calmly, "I'm only saying we shouldn't try to cross bridges before they're built. Let's get a viable program going first and if it isn't working, we can talk premiums at that time. The point is, why get into something of that sort if we don't have to?"

"Bullshit, Gilman, pure bullshit. Our competition has been in premiums for years. Some of them are ten times our size and what's good enough for them is good enough for GFP. Top that one if you can."

After a moment of silence, Steve said, "Mark, I've grown with this account and I've always done my very best for it. If you want to write me off, all you have to do is call Bill or Keith and say you want a new man on the job. Maybe someone else can take your abuse, but I've just about had all I want."

The change in Lawson was as remarkable as it was swift. He plopped down in the chair behind his desk and leaned forward with a sudden explosion. "Well, for Christ's sake, are you pulling temperament on me after all these years? What the hell are you so touchy about today? I'm the guy who always bragged how receptive and open-minded you were."

Not mollified in the least by Mark's sudden reversal of attitude, Steve replied with controlled coolness, "Mark, there's nothing new, exciting, or different about premiums, except that GFP has never used them in its entire history. Mr. Goodwin has always resisted the idea . . ."

"Only because whenever the subject came up, the agency was right there pouring cold water on it."

"And for good cause, apparently. For myself, I don't like them for the same reasons Mr. Goodwin has opposed them for years. In GFP's case, I don't like trading stamps, bingo games, auto license lotteries, and similar gimmicks. Free or not, they all have to be paid for by someone and the cost always manages to wind up on the housewife's food bill. I'll take any other way out I can find, and that's what we're going to dig for. I don't object to giving someone something as long as we're just giving, and not charging for it elsewhere."

Mark shook his head from side to side. "You guys are something else. You with your goddamned classroom solutions for everything. Okay, bright boy, you do your digging. Find the way and I'll buy it. But if you can't, we'll reopen the subject and you'll damned well buy it my way. Okay?"

"That's good enough for now," Steve conceded with a measure of temporary relief. "Just keep your Mr. Haywood off my back."

"Haywood? Hell, he's only a guy with a job to do, just like the rest of us. Don't blame him. He's an innocent bystander."

"For an innocent bystander, he seemed to have the inside track long before the news hit the papers."

"Well," Mark said with a smile, "those guys have their own special sources of information. They're the CIA of industry. If you haven't anything else for now . . ."

"Not at the moment." Steve started to get up, and reached for his attaché case.

"Hold it. I'm not through yet. How about a drink?"

Another first. Nowhere in the GFP corporate offices had there ever been a bar, nor had Steve ever been offered a drink there during working hours. His reply, as Mark rose from his chair, was a silent lifting of eyebrows. What next? Mark started for the door, halted, and said, "Talk to Charlotte for a few minutes. I've got to make a call first."

Outside Mark's office, Charlotte, who was dialing a number, nodded, and smiled, "Hi," to Steve, then into the phone, "Miss Anthony, please." After a few moments, she rang Mark's phone and hung up. Steve sat down and thumbed through a trade journal, not even mildly interested in Charlotte's violet eyes or the svelte figure that was uniquely displayed to show off its every advantage. What stuck in his mind, turning over and over, was Mark's indiscreet broken sentence, *"Hell, even your boy Chuck . . ."*

A few minutes later Mark came out, a smile lighting his face. "Let's go," he said to Steve, and to Charlotte, "I won't be back today."

Charlotte nodded, giving both of them her automatic

smile. In front of the building, they caught a vacant cab. Mark gave the address, "Warwick Hotel," and said to Steve, "I've got something to discuss with you. It's important to me, and just between us, okay?"

"Okay," Steve said, not at all sure it was. "Business?" he inquired.

"Sure," Mark replied with a little laugh, "all business."

"I'm all ears. Tell me more."

"Don't get so smart-assy. This is something I want, and you're going to get it for me."

"Don't get me wrong, Mark. I'm interested, really. What is it?"

"Television. Our commercials for B & B Coffee."

"What about them?"

"Your people haven't done anything about that end of it yet, have they?"

"All we've done so far is set up a tentative budget, just as we have for the rest of any campaign we'll be thinking about, but nothing definite so far."

"That's fine. Just fine."

A few blocks later, Steve said, "What's the point, Mark?"

"The point is, I'm getting tired of watching the frumpy broads you and Bryce have been casting in our GFP commercials, and I'm just as sick of the phony neighbors who always drop in with some of our mixes or other items at the psychological moment to get our stupid characters out of a mess that a child making mud pies couldn't get into even accidentally. Hell, they could just as well be discussing deodorants, suppositories, sleeping pills, or the miracle floor wax that machine-gun bullets can't hurt."

It was clearly an over-exaggeration, Steve knew. He swallowed, and said, "Miss Anthony, I take it, is the solution to that problem."

Mark turned, startled. "Where in hell . . . ?"

"Don't be alarmed. I heard the name when Charlotte asked for her, and I assume we're on our way to meet her."

Mark relaxed. "What big ears you have, grandma. You're right, but don't jump to any conclusions until you've seen her."

The cab drew up to the hotel entrance. They got out and Mark paid the fare. "Let's go to the bar."

Margo Anthony joined them there a few minutes later. Steve and Mark rose to greet her and Mark ordered two Scotches and water, and a stinger for Margo. Even in the dim, intimate lighting, Steve could appreciate her perfectly immaculate beauty. She was perhaps twenty-four or -five and looked like a teenager, dressed in a white-trimmed black dress that was in exquisite taste, and a black hat with downswept brim that added a certain quality of mysterious shading to her classical features.

"Tony," Mark said, "Steve is our advertising agent." She acknowledged this with a low-voiced, "How nice."

"Tony's been in a number of shows, Steve," Mark added. "The last was off-Broadway . . ."

Margo laughed prettily and said, "And folded after three whole days. Three evening performances and one matinee."

"Are you doing another, Miss Anthony?" Steve asked.

"There's little around at this time of year. I've been thinking of going back to modeling."

"Are you with an agency?"

"Not at the moment." Again that smile. "I've had offers, but the show, rehearsals and all, tired me out. I'm not a very strenuous person."

It was Steve's turn to smile. "Have you ever done anything in television?"

"No, but I'd like to. Very much." She finished her drink and said, "Mark, I've got to run now. You'll forgive me, I know."

They all rose, said good-bye, and she left. Steve instinctively noted her height, elegant walk, and long legs encased in honey-colored nylon that matched her hair. Mark and Steve sat down again and Mark ordered another round of drinks. "Well," he said, "what do you think?"

Steve nodded. "Spectacular, of course, but I don't think she's what Everyman expects to find in his kitchen. She's not exactly the kitchen-type housewife."

"The hell she's not," Mark exclaimed. "You guys all have the sick idea that every housewife has to look like a bundle of dirty laundry, like a hungover bag, the kind that makes a guy bury his nose inside his newspaper at the breakfast table. A face and body like Tony's are what he puts himself to sleep with at night, for Christ's sake."

"I'll buy that, but I'm more concerned with what the guy's real wife will think when she sees somebody like Tony making her husband's coffee."

"Your goddamned classroom theories again," Mark sputtered. "Let me tell you something, buddy, seeing Tony in the kitchen may even give every housewife the idea that

that's what *she* should look like. Think of what *that* would do for millions of husbands!"

"Okay, Mark, the point has been made and well taken. You want Margo, or Tony, to become that fresh new personality image for Goody's B & B Coffee."

"Well, you're kind of slow on the trigger today, but you've finally caught on."

"All right, suppose we give her the usual test for voice and . . ."

Mark exploded. "Usual, my ass. That's a copout and you know it. I don't want a kissoff, Steve. I want her *in,* and I'm serious about this."

"So I gather, but we don't know if she can act her way out of a paper bag, or what her voice will sound like on-mike."

"I'll vouch for her acting ability, and whatever her voice sounds like on-mike, can be doctored, can't it? Looping, or dubbing, or whatever the hell you call it."

"All we can do is shoot it and run it. That's where the test stands up or falls on its face."

"Well, I want this one to stand up. Period."

A piece of early Allard wisdom came into Steve's mind then, dating back to when he first began contacting Lawson. *Whenever you're faced with compromise, give in on the lesser evils. That makes it a lot easier to fight for the bigger issues. It's the only way you can come out of it without total defeat.* "All right, Mark," he said, "we'll give it everything we've got."

"Give her the best, Steve. Producer, director, technicians. Bury the extra cost somewhere along with the other mistakes and waste that get hidden in the agency's bills."

"I could challenge that remark," Steve said, remembering vividly the arrangement between GFP and Pete Channing.

"Oh, balls. We do it, you do it, everybody does it. Let's get back to Tony."

"Let me talk to Don Bryce and get something scheduled. But it won't be until we come up with the B & B program."

"Good enough. Just don't forget it, buddy, because I sure as hell won't."

6

The GFP spring campaign broke and the response to its anti-inflation message, carried over Herschel Goodwin's signature, brought a surprising flood of letters from housewives and wage-earners, all soundly applauding GFP's policy statement. Followed by the series of ads promoting, for the first time in GFP's history, refund coupons and the free *Recipe Book* offer, sales reaction was immediate and sufficient in volume to require a substantial reprint order to keep up with the expected demand. It also brought laudatory praise from Herschel Goodwin and Ward Hardwick.

Meanwhile, as GFP moved to organize its B & B Coffee division so that operations could commence on a national scale by a September or October target date, Ward Hardwick, accompanied by Steve, flew West to look over the situation. Steve quickly surveyed the current advertising program and influenced Wade Barrett and Dave Chesler to shift a more considerable portion of its B & B budget from print media into television and radio spots to gain instant maximum exposure, then devoted the balance of his time to redesigning magazine and newspaper ads to give pictorial emphasis to the ten-cent coupon refund, hoping to regain the portion of the West Coast public lost over the past year.

Response was weak and disappointing. Thus far, other than the original trade paper releases, there had been little mention in any advertising of GFP's takeover, which would be scheduled for later in the year.

Ward Hardwick, however, was faced with the more difficult task of trying to rebuild the weakened B & B Coffee sales force and regaining the outlets lost by Perry Bond's mismanagement. For a while that job looked hopeless, until something of a minor miracle occurred to turn disaster into success. One night during his second week in Los Angeles, he was contacted at his hotel by Harlan Weschler, the former B & B sales manager under John Bond. Weschler made it patently clear that he was unhappy at Cal-General and would entertain an offer to return to B & B under the new management. Hardwick was more than eager to offer him the position, with a free hand in the western area, and Weschler accepted. In turn, he assured Hardwick that he would be able to bring with him those key salesmen who had followed him to Cal-General.

Steve's three weeks in Los Angeles with Barrett and Chesler were fully rewarding. When he returned to New York, the current GFP campaign was in full swing and progressing satisfactorily on schedule. His first concern now would be an all-out effort to produce a dramatic presentation of the Goody–B & B marriage.

In his absence. Karen had located a two-bedroom apartment in a modern high-rise building on East Seventy-third Street just west of Third Avenue. Although it cost more than twice what he was paying for his West Side apartment, he signed the two-year lease without hesitation. He moved his study over intact, but permitted Karen to choose most of the rest of the new furniture, carpeting, and draperies, and arrange it all to her satisfaction.

For Karen, it had been a labor of love. She brought four of her own unsigned paintings and hung them in the living room on facing walls, scattering Steve's own modest collection of oils, water colors, and line drawings throughout the other rooms, hallway, and foyer.

At the agency, Steve noted with some gratification that Chuck had not repeated his earlier violation of moving into the larger, more spacious office. Generally, the GFP situation, he found, was in that pleasant, exhilarating state known as "orderly chaos," the steady followup activity that always proceeded in the wake of a successful opening campaign. With the basic pattern set, the work flowed smoothly from creative hands into production, its progress carefully monitored by the WPC and Traffic Control. Most of the contact work, as usual, had been the responsibility of Chuck, Frank Hayden, and Reed Baker, Chuck calling on Lawson and Davies, and Frank and Reed on the brand managers, Tyson and Jewell.

All, however, was not wine and roses. On his first day back, Steve sensed from the over-effusive welcome of the group that something resembling a near-revolt had been forming in his absence, although the workload had not suffered. A secretary, two clerks, and the group's messenger-trainee had resigned and been replaced. Baker and Hayden had submitted their resignations to Peggy, to be forwarded to Keith Allard, but she had persuaded both to wait for Steve's return. Benn Archer and Norris Bardo, Peggy suspected, were showing their "books" around.

"All right, Peggy, what the hell's been going on around here?" Steve asked when they finally had a moment of privacy together.

"That man," Peggy replied, referring to Chuck, "is probably the last living descendant of Captain Bligh. A real, practicing bastard. He rode herd over everybody like an old-time plantation owner. All he needed was a whip in his hand, but he used his snotty tongue instead."

"How much of a bad time did he give you?"

"He gave it his best effort, but that wasn't good enough," she said with a smile and knowing wink, "but you'd better circulate among the troops and hand out a few Purple Hearts and Bronze Stars to the walking wounded. Before somebody throws him out of a window, and that wouldn't be a bad idea."

"Someday," Steve said reflectively, "I'm going to have to rectify that mistake I inherited."

"Can't you get rid of him the same way we got him, move him over to another account?"

"I would, but I don't know who I can convince to take him. He's been on at least half a dozen accounts that I know of."

"What about a little talk with The Axe?"

"It won't work with Chuck. Others have tried and failed."

"Just who is his patron saint around here?"

"For a gatherer of miscellaneous useful information, I'm surprised you don't know the answer to that one. Old Chuck is George McCandless's only nephew, and a close relation to Marty Link."

"Thank God there's only one of him. Who is George McCandless?"

"Are you kidding?" He saw from her expression that she wasn't. "George McCandless is responsible for about twenty-five per cent of Marty Link's billings in Chicago. Lux Plywood, Brandon Electronics, Egan Chemicals, Arcturus Airlines, most of them involved in government contracts."

"I've never heard of him. He's not listed anywhere . . ."

"Of course not. Like our mystery men up on Cloud thirty-five, Fanning, Woodward and Chalfonte. George McCandless and God work in mysterious ways. He's Marty's brother-in-law for one thing, and has his hand, both hands, in local and Washington politics. Very big in the influence peddling profession."

"Then why isn't Chuck in Chicago?"

"Because he was too hot for Marty or George to handle there and Chuck wanted New York. Obviously, what Chuck wants, Chuck gets."

"Oh, boy. Well, Frank wants to see you, probably with his resignation clutched in his hot, trembling hands."

"Send him in, and ring me in ten minutes."

Frank Hayden, medium build and height, thin blond hair and bespectacled, Penn State *magna cum laude,* with one year on the *Philadelphia Inquirer*, three with the Ernst, Wellborn Agency and a little over two with Leary, was in no mood to be cajoled, as evidenced by his unsmiling expression. "Frank," Steve greeted him, "How are you?"

"Good and somewhat depressed, Steve. I wanted to break the news to you personally before I send my resignation upstairs."

"Chuck?"

Frank nodded. "Ordinarily, I wouldn't let him get to me, but that uncouth ape has finally discovered my breaking point and I've had it with him."

"What happened?"

"I'll just give you the most recent incident. Chuck was out one day and Mr. Lawson called in and asked for an explanation of some details in one of the followup ads. He wanted it, like, yesterday, so I got out the necessary proofs and took them down to Forty-second Street. While I was explaining its *modus operandi,* Chuck marched in and took over, dismissing me as though I were a messenger boy who'd been sent out for coffee. Later, when he returned to the office, he gave me one hell of a bloody working over for having dared to contact Lawson without his, *Chuck's*, permission. I simply dictated my resignation to Annie, but Peggy got a look at it and talked me into holding it up until you got back. I felt I owed you that much."

"What about Reed?"

"I'd prefer that you ask Reed about that, but you'll find that pretty much the same thing happened to him in Bob Davies's office. I won't mention the disturbances he has created in the back room. I'm sure you'll hear about those sooner or later. I know I promised you I'd hang on, but I've had my say and I want out."

Steve said, "Frank, I want you in. I need you, Baker, and the others as well, at this particularly vulnerable point in the overall program. Will you leave it to me to square things away?"

Hayden squirmed. "Look, Steve, I like my job and I think I'm doing damned well at it, but we've been through this before, after your last trip to the Coast. I don't want another repeat of this sort of thing because I don't particularly relish the idea of being called down to the District Attorney's office on a homicide or manslaughter charge."

"Give me one more chance, will you, Frank? If I blow it this time, I won't stand in your way."

The phone rang, Peggy's signal. Steve reached for the receiver and said, "Will you do that much for me, Frank? And talk to Reed for me?"

"Of course, Steve, but get him to hell off our backs, will you?" He left, feeling the same sense of relief Steve was experiencing. Into the phone, "Is Chuck in, Peg?"

"No, he's on his daily visit to GFP to bask in the glory of Caesar."

"I want to see him the minute he gets back."

He made a quick tour of the group, his very presence offering some reassurance. He found Reed Baker in Hayden's office and it was evident that Baker, too, would hold up his resignation. Steve took particular pains to talk with Benn Archer and Norris Bardo, but neither gave any hint of plans to defect. For the moment, Steve felt in control again.

In the new B & B section, he found that Norm Adrian, to whom he had left the final decisions, had formed his initial group. The space vacated by the Jenkins group was more than adequate, with room for further expansion if it became necessary. Released from Ted McCreery's continual criticism and carping, Norm had taken on the appearance of a free, uninhibited soul, divested of Chevalier not only in fact, but in spirit and memory as well.

So far, so good.

An ebullient Chuck returned from GFP after lunch, which, he informed Steve, he had enjoyed with Mark Lawson. The Man Himself. "Everything in good shape there?" Steve asked quietly.

"You bet. Couldn't be better," Chuck replied, giving the A-OK signal with thumb and index finger. "Got along great with Mark." So now it was Mark, not Mr. Lawson. Progress.

"That's fine, Chuck. I'll take over from here on in." Chuck's smile dissolved quickly, his fists balled up. "And I want to discuss a few changes I want to make within the group."

"Changes?"

"Yes. With two groups functioning at full blast, we're going to be swamped with a million added details and I'm going to need you here to take some of them off my hands." As Chuck started to reply, Steve waved the interruption aside, "Because it's going to happen so fast," he continued evenly, "I can't rely entirely on Traffic Control to help me juggle two accounts at once."

"What do you have in mind?" Chuck asked.

"I need someone in here to act as my administrative assistant, to work more closely with the heavy traffic flow. Someone to work hand in hand with Production . . ."

"What the hell, Steve, that's Lew Kann's job, isn't it?"

"It's *our* job as well. Also, you'll work with Gary on Radio and TV, and with Media and Marketing. I want you to take over full responsibility for the WPC, keep it up to the minute on GFP and B & B. Mr. Leary and Mr. Allard want to be informed daily on our progress for the next month or so and that will be your responsibility. I'll be busy with Norm and both groups as well as contacting Mr. Lawson, while Frank and Reed are doing their jobs with Bob Davies, Tyson, and Jewell."

He saw Chuck's face turn slightly red, trying to come up with a reasonable objection against being removed from the action arena. "I promised Mark I'd bring . . ." he started.

"Whatever it is," Steve cut him off abruptly, "either I, Frank, or Reed will handle it. I've told you, Chuck, we're in a crucial period, which is why I find it necessary to relieve you of all contact work for the time being."

Chuck got the message and was decidedly unhappy about it. The next move was up to him and he stood up sullenly as if to go, then turned back. "Are you cutting me down, Steve?" he asked.

"Chuck, you've been my assistant and you're still my assistant, but the character of the account has changed, and so have your duties for the time being. You're here to do what I tell you to do to make this job easier for me to handle. If that's too much to ask of you, I'd suggest you have a talk with Mr. Allard and ask for a change of assignment."

"Or possibly Mr. Axelrod?"

"If you prefer it that way. I've never yet stood in the way

of any man or woman who wanted to move up in his or her work."

"Or out."

"Or out."

"It was Hayden, wasn't it? Or Baker?"

"Why, Chuck," Steve asked with affected innocence, "have you been having problems with them?"

The heat went out of Chuck. "Anything else?" he asked.

"That's all for now."

The confrontation had been trying, and he sank into his chair and stared at his blotter pad. Then the door opened and Peggy stuck her head into his office. "What is it, Peg?" he asked.

"I think I love you very much, Mr. Gilman," she said.

He stared at her for a moment, then said, "That war has only just begun, Miss Cowles."

The daily conferences with Keith and Adrian were a thing of the past now, moving the Goody–B & B project from the pre-planning talk stage into the actual work of preparing copy and visuals. Never before had Steve experienced the impatience he felt now, facing a vital part of the campaign, yet holding back in order to avoid taking the ball out of Adrian's hands; although every final decision, along with the full responsibility, must be borne by himself.

Adrian was quick to recognize Steve's anxiety and found numerous excuses to confer with him, usually at the start of the day's work, often in midafternoon. On frequent occasions they lunched together in order to exchange ideas without interference to Norm's normal work schedule.

On Steve's return from Los Angeles, Mark had insisted on thrice-weekly meetings, but these ended when, at Hardwick's request, Mark began spending more time in the field to keep distributor interest in the coffee item stimulated. The other obvious advantages to Steve were Karen's accessibility during those absences.

With Adrian as the nucleus, the B & B team was now composed of Byron Johns, a writer brought on from Chicago; Dan Thaw, writer, from the Kemp & Thomason Agency; Christine Galbertson and Barry Haas, art directors, from placement agencies. All were well experienced in food advertising and eager to start rolling on their new assignments.

On June 1, George Lang, hired away from Kinston & Cooper to replace Adrian on Chevalier, took over as account executive when Ted McCreery moved over to Chevalier's Park Avenue offices, where he replaced Hugh Benson as advertising director. Lang had been McCreery's personal choice, a Dartmouth man, one year ahead of Ted's class. With that move, Bill and Keith were hopeful that Ted's injured feelings would be healed sufficiently to renew the Chevalier contract with the Leary Agency on D-Day, July 15.

It was a lot to hope for.

The Johns-Thaw-Galbertson-Haas team, under Adrian's guidance, had been turning in copy and layout ideas that showed excellent potential, but were without a true central theme or direction. Some of the submissions were catalogued as "possibles," some were immediately discarded. Galbertson and Haas were experimenting with new art techniques, but until the central core theme was firmly established, these, too, were held in abeyance.

It was a trying time for Steve. Potential ads would not get the job done and Steve began to feel the pressure mounting within, not so much from what was being said as from what was being left unsaid by Keith Allard. At this stage, he was still in full control, the initiative his own to take.

Between them, Steve and Adrian had come up with the basic introductory ads, the dramatic announcement linking GFP with B & B. Next, a new package and label design, the first such change since the B & B company was founded in 1906, in order to incorporate the Goody name. After much discussion with Adrian, the group was turned loose to develop the followup ads and now they were searching with quiet desperation for the positive theme, the concept, the *thing* to hang the first major campaign on.

And again, Steve and Adrian were both faced with the Number One stumbling block: what could be said about coffee that was new and fresh, that hadn't been said in millions of words before? How did one present coffee in a way never shown before? How can words and illustrations project taste and flavor alone, and give the reader and viewer sufficient reason to induce him or her to switch from a brand long in use? Or even *try* it?

7

Don Bryce listened to Steve with a cold glint of rising distaste in his eyes. A perfectionist of the first order, Don had come to the Leary Agency in 1965 from the Intercontinental Broadcasting Network to become vice-president in charge of TV Radio operations, and had run his department successfully enough to warrant a gallery of award plaques that adorned the walls of his plush office. Seldom abrupt, never patronizing, he generally handled account executives and clients with patient diplomacy and usually managed to get his own way with miles and hours of commercials that passed through the hands of his staff of competent producers and directors. There were, however, occasional exceptions, and Mark Lawson was one of those.

When Steve finished, Bryce said, "Steve, do you know what a thing like this involves, the cost of casting an amateur into an important role, building her up over a period of time?"

"I know better than most, Don, but in this case it's a matter of necessity."

"Sure, necessary for Lawson, who's probably balling hell out of this broad. Who the hell is Margo Anthony, anyway? What's she done before, and where, except in bed with Lawson? We can pour a million bucks into making her a star image, then have her walk out on us because she and Mark have a blowup. Or, we build her into a national image and she begins to hold out for Johnny Carson's or Dave Frost's take-home pay. That jerk is fooling around with dynamite. Just how important is all of this to the agency?"

"Well, I don't think we'd lose the account, Don, but life could get pretty damned sticky. My life."

"He's married, isn't he?"

"Yes."

"Well, his wife is either the world's biggest *schnook* or else she's got something of her own going for her."

"Don, let's not probe that deeply. The question is, what do we do about our problem?"

"One of two things. I can give her an audition that will kill her off inside of the first seven seconds, or give her every technical break we can find and have her come on like Gunga Din. What's she look like?"

"Something just a little less than spectacular. I'd guess she has photogenic quality. She's everyman's dream of the girl next door he'd like to get his hooks into. Makeup and wardrobe can tone the glamour down somewhat, even age her a little, but I'm not too sure of her voice. It's all guesswork, anyway, until she's been exposed to camera and mike."

"Well, hell, our engineers can overcome a bullfrog as far as voice is concerned. What about personality, her presence? Does she have anything there, look like she belongs in a kitchen instead of a bed?"

Steve shrugged. "I've never seen her in either setting. What do most successful models and actresses have that they didn't get from a good director?"

"Not a hell of a lot, except for a rare few. Just for the record, I don't like this at all, but I'll reserve judgment until I see how she tests out. How do you want to handle it, stick her in front of a camera as is and see how the ball bounces?"

"I don't think so, Don. Lawson will swear we did a knife job on her. Let's give her the full treatment. Script, rehearsals, makeup, the whole works."

"Okay, if you say so. Who's going to do the script?"

"I will, while you're scheduling it. What about timing?"

Don checked his current production schedules. "How about Tuesday morning, ten o'clock? That gives us a full week. Think she can make it?"

"Sure. One week from today, 10:00 A.M. She'll be here."

He decided on a thirty-second script, and before settling down to work on it, phoned Mark and told him the arrangements had been made with Bryce.

"Now you're talking, boy. Remember, she's going first class, not tourist. Just level with me on that," Mark said.

"Mark, I'm doing the script myself. Don Bryce will personally produce, and Colin Ferris will direct. The man behind the camera and every technician will be top grade."

"Okay. What do you want Tony to do meanwhile?"

"I'll need a couple of days with the script, then I'd like to have her study it and walk her through it. I'll keep the first one as simple as possible, but she'll have to go through rehearsals before we put her in front of the camera."

"When and where?"

"Let's say Saturday, tentatively. How about here at the agency where we have our own test kitchen. The place will be empty except for a skeleton staff, but no one else will be in on it. I don't want any rumors spreading. Two in the afternoon?"

"I'll check it out and have Tony call you. And let's keep this whole thing under the rug, you understand."

"I understand perfectly, Mark."

Steve's usual procedure, when involved in planning a new project or developing an idea, was to work with pencil at his drawing table until he reached a point of certainty, then switch over to his typewriter. The knot that faced him was to write a craftsmanlike script, and still keep Tony performing with a professional air.

Visualizing her as he had seen her last, he re-dressed her in his mind and placed her in one of the two kitchen sets used in the GFP commercials. Transforming her into a young housewife was not too difficult a task. He jotted down some rough sketches on a storyboard form; Tony taking up a fresh can of the regular ground coffee, smiling expectantly, enjoying the aroma of its contents as she opened it, measuring out the required amount, filling the percolator with water, inserting the stem and basket, and placing it on the burner. Up to that point, no dialogue. He made a note to have Tony hum a pleasant tune to herself, barely audible.

As Tony places the percolator on the stove and turns the flame up—CUT—music rising, then back to the same scene, the coffee finished, perking, ready to be poured. Medium and closeup shots only. Cup and saucer handy. Pours a cup, sips it, her face reflecting contentment, a rich smile that tells the world, Ah-h-h, now *that's* a cup of coffee! CUT—Announcer's voice (if Tony's can't make the grade): *And that's how easy it is to make the finest cup of brewed coffee you've tasted in many years. Goody's–B & B. You'll find it at your favorite food market.* CUT to closeup of package. FADE OUT.

There would be a retake using instant freeze-dried coffee, but essentially, this would be it, as far as the test was concerned. If he could get her through it successfully, other settings would follow, with others brought into the scene; a husband, a husband and one small child; a friend;

at breakfast, lunch, dinner, party, but with Tony always as the principle repeat character. The Image.

He was pleased with the minimum use of audio so that Tony and the coffee can or jar would be on camera ninety percent of the time, giving both maximum exposure until the closing seconds, when the product would be featured.

It would, he knew, please Mark, eliminating everyone from the first test who might compete with Tony or require exact timing or cue-ing. Perfect for a first test. No bugs, no traps. It was a performer's dream, on camera almost a full thirty seconds, written for a client who must be kept happy.

He swung back to his typewriter and began to type a clean, fresh draft of the script to turn over to Don, unwilling to ask Peggy to do this one, suspecting that she might discover just exactly what he was up to.

Tony arrived promptly at two on Saturday, dressed more appropriately for the part than Steve had expected. Her solid gray suit skirt ended just above her kneecaps, the blue blouse she wore under her jacket was unfrilled, the merest trace of color added to her lips, her hair combed neatly with a toss of bangs that ended about an inch above her eyebrows. After greeting her and complimenting her on her appearance, Steve handed her a copy of the script, in the standard leatherette binder with the agency name embossed in gold.

"This is strictly a warmup for Tuesday, Tony," he told her reassuringly. "I'll walk you through the part a few times to familiarize you with the set, and for timing. I'll mark the floor with tape to keep you locked into camera range at all times. When you're on camera, you'll be restricted to your movements, with no deviation allowed. Step out of range, make a false move, and we'll need a retake. That means consuming time for everyone involved and costs a lot of money."

She nodded without replying, showing no sign of nervousness. "Our commercials run anywhere from ten to fifty thousand dollars, depending on time and length—" he saw her eyebrows arch upward, duly impressed, "and you are the principal key to that cost. Blow a line or a move, and up goes that cost. You understand?"

She smiled engagingly. "I understand, Steve. I've done some acting and modeling, nothing very much or very successful, except for the modeling a few years ago, but I know the importance of timing and movement, although I've never done anything for television."

"That experience will help a lot. In this test, you'll hum a little tune at the start and have a closing line, something to give us a voice check. All of what I'm saying now is important only as a preliminary test. In the actual test, you'll have one of the best directors in the business guiding you. Colin Ferris."

"That sounds lovely, Steve. Thank you. I want so much to have this work out."

"All right then, let's get over to the set. You can read through the script while I lay down the floor tapes."

Next to the kitchen set was a small dining room setting where Tony sat and read through the script while Steve put down the tapes. When he called to her, she was ready.

The first few walk-throughs, timed with a stop watch, were stiff and awkward, not much more than Steve had expected. After the fifth attempt Steve said, "How about a coffee break?"

Tony agreed. Steve opened a fresh can of B & B. Tony filled the percolator and went through the motions as though she were doing it from the script. Steve smiled and said, "That's exactly what I'm trying for, just the way you did it then, naturally, forgetting you're being watched and timed."

"I'm a little tense," Tony said. "This is so new to me, this form of acting."

"That's normal, your first time out in television. It's different from the stage, where the set is much broader and deeper and considerably less restricted. You're keeping your eyes on the tape instead of where they belong, on what you're doing. What you've got to do is forget me, the camera, and people who will be all around you on the set on Tuesday. But you're doing fine. You'll get used to it and it will become second nature to you. It takes just a little time."

"You're marvelous to work for, Steve," she said. "I hope Mr. Ferris will be as lenient."

"Colin will help you a lot more than I can, if you're serious about your work and pay close attention to him. He doesn't bark or bite, but he's very conscious of time and costs. He's a purse-minded Scot, and maybe that's why he's so good at his job. He can't stand waste."

"I'll try very hard, I promise."

"Good. If you're finished with your coffee, let's have another shot at it, shall we?"

By six, both were tired and Steve's nerves were stretched to a fine edge, but he was satisfied that four hours of indoctrination to the set were enough to prepare Tony for what would confront her on Tuesday.

Outside, the sky was overcast and there was the merest trace of fine mist in the air. "Can I drop you off, Tony?" Steve asked.

"I'm going home to do some more rehearsing, then to bed. Would you like to come up for dinner? That kitchen set gives me ideas."

"Such as?"

"Well, nothing elaborate, but once in a while I turn out a very tasty spaghetti sauce. Does that appeal to you?"

He hesitated for a moment, then said, "I think you'll probably practice much better without me."

Tony smiled. "Or are you concerned with what Mark might think."

He returned the smile. "Not in the very least."

"You don't like me very much, do you?"

"What makes you think that?"

"Something—I don't know what it is. Perhaps *approve* would be a better word. You don't approve of me." She said it with a lightness of tone he found irritating, that of a young, beautiful girl, always in total command of a situation, using her looks and body the way a jockey uses his whip. He said it crudely, intending it just that way, eyes meeting hers. "Everybody has his own hustle, Tony, and in our world of hustlers, you'll probably come out on top whether I approve, disapprove, like, or dislike."

"Is it because of Mark using his influence about this?"

"Are you suggesting this is all Mark's idea?"

"Not entirely, but he didn't oppose the idea."

Steve smiled. "I can't imagine Mark opposing anything you wanted."

"So that's it. I'm not your choice, so you don't like the idea. Well, Steve, I suppose the man with the upper hand wins, doesn't he?"

"Those are your words, not mine."

"All right, so you know about Mark and me. Is that what you want to hear me say?"

"Until now, I'd say it was no more than an educated guess on my part, based on past performance."

"Look, Mr. Everybody's Conscience, I know Mark is

married and I know there have been others before me, but it's a job and why shouldn't I have it?"

"Why not, Tony? That's it, and that's all. Shall I walk you over to the Summit for a cab?"

"No, thank you," she replied shortly. "I'm perfectly capable of doing that much for myself. Goodnight."

He had no plans for the weekend. Karen was spending the two days in Wyecliffe and he assumed Mark would either be with her or off on his own somewhere else, possibly with Tony. The prospect of dining alone at his apartment suddenly palled on him and he turned toward Third Avenue and O'Malley's, where he ordered a beer and a steak, and then toyed with an after-dinner brandy and a cigarette. It was early, but on a Saturday there was always an overflow of the afternoon crowd and numerous singles had already gathered and joined up into pairs and foursomes. At a table nearby he caught sight of a back that tantalized him with the memory of Libby, but when she turned so that her profile was visible, it turned out to be a total stranger. The girl who sat opposite her had caught him in the act of staring and smiled a tentative invitation. He returned the smile but made no move to join them.

He ordered another brandy and reflected on Karen and Mark and himself. Mark's reckless arrogance, when his entire future could come to a sudden end through a single swift decision from Karen. Karen's and his own reckless affair, heading—where?—and which, if discovered by Mark, would spell certain doom to his career at Leary regardless of the cost to Mark. The Goodwins, no matter how strong their love or familial ties to Karen, couldn't condone a public scandal, nor would Bill or Keith be able to bail him out. He knew now what had driven Mark to his Sherrys, Jo-Anns, Robins, and Tonys to support a strong sexual drive that Karen was unwilling, or unable to satisfy.

And what, Steve wondered, drives me? What kind of a whore am I, pandering to Lawson's appetite for power by day, sleeping with his wife by night, paving the way for the success of his most recent mistress, Tony; hoping that in some way this affair might destroy him? What difference is there in our moral positions?

After a lonely and restless Sunday, broken only by a

call from Karen made from a public telephone booth in Wyecliffe Village which left him hungering for her, the following morning found Steve, Adrian, and Allard in Keith's office, determined to hammer out a definite course the agency would recommend to open the Goody-B & B campaign. The meeting began with a discussion of the standard methods, breaking in certain key cities or areas in order to test consumer reaction to different themes; discarding the weak, and choosing from among the strongest responses the one which showed the most positive, productive results.

"If we're going to go with the normal test route," Keith said finally, "we've got to get the show on the road, and fast."

Adrian shook his head from side to side, frowning. "The time element is bad. We'd have to come up with at least four different and complete campaigns, test each of them before September . . ."

"The logistics alone," Steve suggested, "and even overlooking the additional costs, will damn near cripple our budget."

"How do you propose to overcome that situation?" Allard said.

"I think we're overlooking our best bet, Keith," Steve said. "We've already got the item in the Western market where the GFP line is as well known as it is in any other test market we choose. Why not cash in on that by exerting more effort to regain the audience B & B lost through negligence, or whatever? If we can do that and move a notch or two above B & B's best ranking out there, we'll have all the answers we need in time to break nationally by September."

"Norm?"

"I'll have to go along with Steve, Keith," Adrian agreed. "We would be able to concentrate in one large area instead of dividing our efforts in four separate directions."

Keith said, "We'll have to do more than that. We can't simply go into a known territory and give it a shot of adrenalin in order to beef up sales for a brief period. Apart from identifying B & B with GFP, we've got to have something to sustain consumer attention, to hold, and keep them. I'll buy the West Coast idea, but only if it can be the forerunner for the national campaign. Keep in mind that when we break in Minneapolis, Chicago, Denver, New Orleans, Miami, and Philadelphia, it will be coming out as an entirely new item, an addition to the regular GFP line."

"I think we can handle it on that basis, Keith," Steve said, "and still move B & B into close contention."

"Norm?"

"I like it a hell of a lot better than spreading ourselves thin. I vote to go along with Steve's suggestion."

"All right, let's get on with it. I want nothing less than a full, concentrated effort on this presentation, something with a hook in it to sustain interest."

Back in Adrian's section, the word had been passed on to the Johns-Galbertson-Thaw-Haas team which had already been testing various themes and art techniques under Adrian's guidance. In Norm's office, the corkboard-lined wall had been partitioned off with masking tape into three four-foot-wide sections. In the first, were half-a-dozen layout possibilities for the introductory ads, as well as all formal announcements of the Goody-B & B marriage, using various treatments, conventional, unique, and mod.

In the second section were four suggestions for followups, thanking the public for its magnificent response, one full page of testimonial excerpts, coupon refund offers, and one calling attention to the new package design for a tried and true old brand name (this latter for the West Coast area only).

The third section remained empty.

The examples in the first two sections were set. Adrian would go with these. The third section—the followups which he and Steve sought—was the stumbling block.

After a brief, tense session with his group, Adrian sat at his desk poring over notes, pounding out new suggestions on his typewriter. He made quick, rough sketches on a layout pad, poked through stacks of research material and market reports, and scribbled more notes; all with the patient demeanor of a beast of burden.

Occasionally, he got up and paced the floor, went out to confer with Johns or Thaw, Christine Galbertson or Haas, all of whom were laboring with equal dedication over typewriters and drawing boards to come up with that single clincher idea that would start them in motion in the same direction.

On Tuesday, Steve remained away from Bryce's department, engrossed in the subject of coffee, drinking much of it, searching for a better, newer way to say what had been said tens of thousands of times before.

The old standby clichés: ANNOUNCING! INTRODUCING! IT'S HERE! NEW! DIFFERENT! STARTLING DISCOVERY! AMAZING! and REMARKABLE! were too old, worn, tired, and fragile to even enter consideration. Nothing about the product was new, different, startling, amazing, or remarkable. B & B was an excellent brand of coffee which, when properly brewed, provided a tasty, flavorful beverage, day or night; one that had been pleasing consumers on the West Coast and in surrounding states since 1906. It contained no special additives to beat the drum for; no flouride, no lanolin, no LT-40, no XP-70, no enzymes to shout about.

Shortly after five o'clock, Bryce dropped in to see him, his expression telling Steve nothing. He dropped into the chair beside Steve's desk with a grunt. "Well, chum, aren't you interested in the test?"

"What did you get?"

"A two-take commercial. That girl is pretty damned good. Even remarkable. Came on like Patton charging across Europe at the head of his whole goddamned tank corps, guns blazing."

"What about her voice?"

"You'll never recognize it when you hear it. Comes through like raindrops on a lilypad. What's next?"

"I guess we've got ourselves a new Goody girl to image in on the waiting public."

"Well, not yet, Steve. She's got quality, but one test never made a superstar that I ever heard of. Remember, this was a solo shot. We don't know what will come out of the mangle when she's working with others, although I'd guess from what I've seen that she can do it. Question is, do you want to show this to Lawson and make him happy or do we louse her up in the lab, which we can do easily enough."

Steve looked back at Bryce with mixed feelings. "She didn't see the tape?"

"We didn't tape it. You wanted the best, so we shot it on film. I told her it wouldn't be ready until sometime tomorrow, but I know it's good. So does Colin, who's wild about it. It's up to you, now or never."

"I'll run it for Lawson as is. Tomorrow. What time can I have it?"

"It's at the lab now. You can have Gary screen it for you by ten o'clock tomorrow morning."

"Thanks, Don. And let's keep this on the q.t. . . ."

"Sure. See you."

Steve phoned Lawson at once and caught him as he was leaving for the day. Mark agreed eagerly to the appointment for eleven the next morning at the agency. "How does it look, Steve?"

"I haven't seen it, Mark, but Don and Colin think you'll like it."

"Great. I'll want Tony there when you screen it."

"Yes, of course. Goodnight, Mark."

Steve dropped in on Adrian, sitting hunched wearily over his typewriter. "You look like a stock market prophet after the Dow has dropped fifteen points, Norm."

Adrian smiled wryly. "I must be getting old. I've been on Chevalier so damned long, I can't remember how to start an entirely new campaign. I've hundreds of ads on paper and in mind, once we get over the first leap, but this kickoff thing's got my back to the wall. Look." He dredged up sheets of headlines, copy leads and taglines. "Take a look, Steve. I've even stolen the one we once used for Chevalier, '*The Only Extravagance is in its Flavor.*' If I remember correctly, that was one of yours, wasn't it?"

Steve laughed and said, "Sooner or later, we all start stealing from ourselves." He nodded toward the first and second sections of corkboard. "Some nice things there, Norm."

"But not what we need for the hook once these have run. I don't usually like gimmicks, but I think I'd go for one in this case, if I run across the right thing."

"Hell, Norm, don't fight it. You've been through too many campaigns and presentations to let this one throw you. Why don't we check out for a fix at the Blue Baron? Do us both good."

"Don't try to corrupt me, man. The day I have to get stoned in order to get an idea will be my last one on the job. Coffee, yes. Booze, no. Hey, I've got a couple of good TV ideas here somewhere. You mind if I draft your boy Hawkins to do a storyboard or two?"

"If he's free, be my guest. If he's tied up, I'll get somebody from Lex's bullpen for you."

"I'd rather have Hawkins. And thanks, Steve."

"For what?"

"For getting me off the hook with Chevalier."

"Forget it, Norm. I'm just grateful we're on this one together."

"What's the word from topside, are we still in the danger zone with Chevalier?"

"I'm not sure, but I think that situation has eased up a little."

"Funny, isn't it? After all I put into that account, I lost out because of office politics."

"Don't let it put you down. It happens in the best of families. If I can give you any help, Norm, holler."

Talking with Norm had eased Steve's own tensions for the moment. Every creative writer and art director, as he knew from personal experience, had his temporary mental blocks and lapses, more often when there was too much time to think of alternatives, but when the chips were down, the professionals came through every time. If nothing else, Adrian was a tough pro.

8

At five thirty the Hungerford Trust elevators became express cars for Leary employees, arriving empty at the Thirty-fifth floor, making one stop at the Thirty-fourth, dropping swiftly to the ground level to disgorge human cargoes and send them on their separate ways home, and shooting upward again until all but the stragglers had been transported and ejected back into the human jungle outside.

Lennie Hawkins was pressed against the back wall of the car, clutching a thin leatherette envelope bearing the Leary insignia. He looked over half a dozen heads to single out the one that had become important to him. Peggy Cowles. In the weeks that had passed from the bleakness of winter into the balminess of early spring, two major events had occurred in his life. He had won a permanent spot in the GFP group, teaming with Jon Hartman, and had won it through pure merit and accomplishment without reference to color. And, as a member of the group, he had been drawn closer to the orbit of Peggy Cowles, so close, that for the first time in his life he had begun to feel a true sense of belonging.

Peggy's influence on Lennie was marked. His manner of

dress changed first, then his mode of living. He had asked her to help him choose some pieces of furniture to replace the scarred, battered collection of landlord junk in his apartment, and she had agreed. They had shopped together for a used breakfast set, a new sofa, two cabinets bought at an auction, and some other pieces that had been advertised for sale by private owners. There wasn't much to be done about the wall-bed, but that was made up every morning now, and out of sight until he was ready to go to sleep.

One weekend toward the end of March, Peggy suggested they buy a pair of rollers and paint the apartment. Lennie bought the paint, rollers, pans, and a plastic filler to eliminate the cracks. It was done on a Saturday and Sunday, and later, they went to an Italian restaurant and gorged themselves on antipasto, veal parmigiana, and wine.

In return, Lennie did several serious water colors, Village scenes, which he had framed, and gave to Peggy; and he watched carefully as their relationship gradually progressed from fellow employees into something akin to friendship.

There was, of course, the very strong and ever-present color question in Lennie's mind. He continued to see his black friends in the Village, ate, and drank with them in his free time, listened to their talk of revolution, absolute freedom, the eventual world organization of blacks against whites, the commonality of black establishment as opposed to white establishment. But that talk seemed useless now and began to bore him. He could no longer see profit or benefit in destroying, by bomb or fire, with no plan formulated beyond tearing down. Out of physical need, he brought a girl to his apartment occasionally, used her, and sent her on her way the next morning. White girl, black girl. It seemed to make no difference. Until he began to think of Peggy during copulation and realized how very much she had intruded into his life and changed his outlook; even to reaching out for the possibility of a future he was still not willing or able to define.

Reaching ground level, some thirty Leary men and women emerged into the lobby and headed for the street. Peggy walked north toward Fifty-third, Lennie about twenty-five or thirty feet behind her, in no hurry to catch up. Not until they were on the subway platform awaiting the arrival of the next train did Peggy become aware of him. Eyes widening, she smiled broadly, "Hi, Lennie. I haven't seen you all day."

"Busy." He tapped the leatherette envelope. "Homework."

"B & B?"

"Yes. A storyboard for Norm Adrian."

"Anything interesting?"

"The usual stuff. Clean script, but the same old tired jazz."

The train came and they were rammed inside, huddled together in the aisle. "Christ," Lennie said in a low voice, "even in Vietnam, shoved into trucks, it was better than in this cattle car."

"The price of living in Fun City."

"Almost makes me yearn to go back to the Army."

"I'll bet."

He laughed. "There've been times."

They swayed back and forth with the motion of the car, jammed against each other as passengers thrust past them, Lennie grimacing at the impact, yet consciously aware of Peggy's body so close to his own, the urge in him rising with each contact. Her head topped off just above his chin and the faint odor of her perfume, or hair set, stimulated him to unbelievable heights of want; and he wondered how it was possible for her not to know what he felt.

"You tied up for dinner?" he asked suddenly.

"No."

"Night like this, I hate the thought of that place of mine, all the cooking smells. How does Jeremiah's grab you?"

"What about your homework?"

"I'm not going to do more than study the script a little more closely and think about it tonight. I can do that in bed."

"Okay," Peggy said agreeably, "Jeremiah's it is. I'll phone the girls from there and tell them not to wait for me."

They exited at Eighth Avenue and Fourteenth Street and walked in the warm, humid air along Greenwich to Jeremiah's, an unpretentious restaurant-bar just off McDougal Alley, that featured good food without music. It was crowded, but the volume of conversation, punctuated by the clatter of dishes and the movement of waiters, lent a certain privacy in that no one could possibly overhear the talk that passed between diners at the next table.

"How's the B & B thing going?" Lennie asked after they had ordered a drink and their food.

"Still in the preliminary stages at the moment. Some nice things are coming through, but what they're looking for is the followup to the kickoff."

"I'd like to sit in on one of those, right from the start."

"Anything in mind?"

"Nope, but I've never been in on anything from the beginning. You know, watch it grow from the seed. On my end, everything's been decided and long under way before it ever reaches me."

"Lennie . . ." Peggy put down her drink and looked up at him, eyes suddenly wide open and bright.

"Oh-oh."

"What oh-oh?"

"You're onto something. I can see it from here."

"Well, you can't be around a thing like this as long as I have and not catch on fire once in a while."

"You got something, why don't you take it to our leader? Or Adrian? He's the boss-cat on this deal, isn't he?"

"Because I haven't anything to show on paper. It's just an idea. Not even a very original idea, but I think that with some imagination, it could come up different enough to catch on."

"And you need an art treatment to make those stupid cats see what a clever thing you've got, right?"

Petulantly, "You're putting me down."

"No, but I recognize that I-got-it, I-got-it look."

"All right, if you don't want to help . . ."

"Hey, come on now. I didn't say I wouldn't help you. Only thing is, I don't want to see you drown in your tears if it all comes tumbling down around your shoulders."

"You will, Lennie, really?"

"I'll give it the old college try. What've you got rattling around in your mind?"

Peggy leaned forward, eyes bright, speaking animatedly, outlining her idea. Lennie listened, frowning with concentration, seeing no great merit hook upon which to hang a hat. And then, suddenly, Peggy stopped, deflated by what she interpreted as his lack of interest. "You don't like it, do you?"

"I'm still listening."

"Well, what do you think?"

"Hell, Peggy, I'm no copy or creative chief, but I haven't heard anything new or original to flip over."

"I didn't say it was new or original, but the way I see it . . ."

"You've just made a point. *You* can see it, but you haven't made *me* see it."

"And that's exactly *my* point. If I tell it to Steve or Norm and *they* can't see it, it won't have any chance at all."

"That's because you're seeing it in your mind. Why don't you put something down on paper, like a piece of copy, or script, so *I* can see it and find some way to illustrate it for you?"

"If I do, will you work on it with me?"

"Sure. I said I would. What comes after that?"

"Then I'll walk in, put it on Steve's desk and he'll leap at it. I know he will."

"No way, baby. Not Steve Gilman. This is Adrian's flap. You give it to him first. That's protocol. If he likes it, you've got more than an even chance with Steve."

"All right then, Norm."

"Okay. When will you have something to show me?"

"No later than the end of the week."

"Good. I'll work on it this weekend."

"Will you mind if I come over and watch?"

Lennie grinned. "You'll have to if you want to see it come out just exactly the way you see it in your own mind."

Dinner was over. Lennie paid the check and they went out into the busy street, now thronged with the usual sightseers and local characters. Peggy said, "Do you mind if I run now, Lennie? I want to get home, do my hair, and start putting something down on paper."

"Sure, go ahead. I'll wander around a bit, then go home and look this script over."

He sauntered along happily, envisioning himself a co-conspirator in Peggy's secret, although he saw little or no hope for her dream. Advertising didn't happen that way, he knew. Art directors, copywriters and creative chiefs, yes. Secretaries, no. There was very low tolerance by the elite professionals toward the outsiders. Even artists were generally looked upon as mere mechanics who followed a specific layout supplied by the a.d. *You do it my way, boy, and keep your kinky ideas to yourself. If I want your suggestions, I'll ask for them.* Words seldom spoken, but implied. But that was something Peggy would have to learn for herself. Working along with her on the project, however, would be. . . . *Hey! Don't go working yourself up to something, boy. You're way out of your league.*

"Hey, man!"

Lennie turned and saw Big Tom approaching from behind. Big Tom, gaunt, goateed, and turbaned, had chosen an X for his last name, the self-styled black leader of a small group of Village militant hoodlums who managed to subsist by minor extortions.

"Hey, Big Tom, how you making it?"

"Passable, brother, passable. Where you been hidin' out?"

"Been busy."

"Man, you do look square, like you done signed up with the honky establishment."

"It supplies the bread, man, and I like to eat regularly since I got used to it."

"Shit, man, we all eat, don't we? I'm meetin' some of the boys over to Beanie's. C'mon along."

"Can't, Big Tom." Holding up the leatherette envelope. "Got to skip home and study a script."

"Yeah. I seen you with the white chick back a piece, comin' out of Jeremiah's."

"A girl from the office where I work."

"Yeah, sure." Big Tom leered, clutching Lennie's arm. "C'mon, man, boys'll be glad to rap with you a little. We kinda short of bread right now. We need some dues to pay for the coffee."

Lennie grinned. "I can let you have a couple of . . ."

"I'n askin' for no handout from a brother, man. C'mon sit with us, an' we let you pick up the tab."

Lennie allowed himself to be led the half block to Beanie's, a small, dimly lit restaurant-coffee house that was Big Tom's unofficial headquarters. At a round table, Gypsy Augie, Rajah Smith, and Fat Joe X lounged, thick white Army mess-hall cups of coffee before them. They greeted Big Tom and Lennie with raised, clenched fists and Raj Smith hooked a chair from the next table with his foot and dragged it over for Lennie. He sat down, greeting each man individually. Big Tom held up two fingers toward the counterman, who brought two cups of coffee to the table.

"Well, how you guys makin' it?" Lennie asked.

"Okay," Rajah Smith replied.

"Where you been keepin' yourself, man?" Gypsy asked.

"Working. I've got a job, remember?"

"Workin'. You so busy workin' foah Whitey you got no time for your own anymore," Rajah said.

"Raj, I'm what you all been preaching since I've known you, a free soul. I don't have to answer to you or anybody else about my time or how I spend it."

"Shit, man, you even beginnin' to sound like them white mothers."

"Cool it, Raj," Big Tom interjected. "No way to talk to a brother."

The whole scene and atmosphere was depressing to Lennie; the mug-rimmed wetness of the clothless table, fetid body and cooking odors mingled with the aroma of smoke and nonedible hash, bad lighting, oddly dressed characters at the surrounding tables, the loud voices and general disorder. His mind was on Peggy Cowles, her freshness, the pleasant feeling about his cubbyhole at the agency, the recently acquired personal possessions in his apartment, the new way of life with a goal as yet undefined, but surely miles apart from that of these unkempt dropouts who had begun their usual rapping about power to the masses, power that would be in their own disorganized minds and hands.

Listening, not hearing, yet familiar with the words, Lennie's mind slipped back to an earlier time, his first days in the Village, when he was fresh from the Army and more ready to respond to this sort of conversation, made to feel a part of it out of sheer need to be with someone; to listen, nod, accept, laugh, do whatever was called for in response. But tonight he was suddenly angered by these stupid shitheads and in no mood for amiability. These sad, sorry bastards were nothings, and were going to make no points with him. Not even one. Fuck 'em. Let 'em try something. Anything. Action. Reaction. Their anger had become his anger.

Big Tom was expounding his stale, overworked theories of takeover, emphasizing his demands by pushing a spatulate finger into Gypsy Augie's chest, punctuating his remark with, "Right, Gyp?, Right, Raj?" Fat Joe X, out of Big Tom's reach, stammered, "R-r-right on, B-b-b-big T-T-Tom," with all three echoing approval.

"Right, Lennie?" Big Tom demanded.

Lennie, completely turned off, not wanting any part of

it, his coffee still untouched, stared back at Big Tom without replying.

"Right, Lennie?" Big Tom repeated louder.

Lennie said, "I can't see it, Big Tom."

"What can't you see, brother?"

"Big Tom, that's the goddamndest hogwash I ever heard. Pure garbage."

"Takin' our homes, our women, our businesses for three hundred years is *garbage?*"

"Man," Lennie said, "three hundred years ago, your people, my people, didn't have any estates, houses, or businesses confiscated from them. What they lost was freedom and equal opportunity to free education, to jobs, to live decent lives. Everything else is too far in the past and if they were here to collect, I'd say, sure, they're entitled to it and let's by God go get it back. What we ought to be fighting for here and now is that freedom, education, and equal opportunity to decent living I'm talkin' about, but you're not going to get it handed to you on a silver platter or by tearing things down and pulling them apart."

Big Tom looked aghast, stunned. "Well, looka here! Listen to Little Black Sambo talkin' white, would you?"

"Tom," Lennie said, "I don't know about you, but if you think this country's banks are going to empty their cash drawers to fill your pockets, forget it. And forget your cockeyed dreams about a world coalition of blacks. It hasn't worked in Africa, it won't work anywhere else."

"I think," Gypsy Augie said, "we done lost us a brother."

"You keep spreading that kind of trash and you'll lose a hell of a lot more than your brothers," Lennie said.

"Now just a goddam minute," Big Tom spat angrily. "Just because you done sold out an' turned white, you ain't talkin' for nobody else but you."

"And you're not speaking for me, brother. You don't want rights or freedoms; you want hard, cold cash. Somebody else's cash. Okay, give it to those that are hollering loudest for it, and damned few others—the deserving—will ever see a dime of it. You'd become the antithesis of your black power dreams. Your new slogan will become 'Hooray for me and screw you, brother. I got mine, go get yours.' That's your whole philosophy, and it's as phony as a three-dollar bill." He stood up, dropped two dollars on the table, and said, "Good-bye, brothers."

As he turned, he heard Big Tom say, "You're dead, man. You're dead."

He came out onto the sidewalk trembling with rage, more for himself than for the three misfits he had left behind, for having allowed himself ever to have become a part of them. And as he moved away, he realized that he had finally cut himself off from the past. So much of his twenty-six years of life were now inexorably private, incommunicable, unshareable.

Except, perhaps, with one person. Peggy Cowles.

9

In the agency viewing room, Larry Holman, in the projection booth, threaded the leader through the projector, then said into the microphone, "All set here, Mr. Gilman."

"Okay, Mark?" Steve asked.

Tony put down the coffee cup, stubbed out her cigarette, and leaned back in the comfortable leather armchair, smiling nervously. Mark looked at her quickly, smiled reassuringly, and said, "Roll it."

Steve spoke into his microphone and Larry hit the switches to darken the room. Besides Larry, only Tony, Mark, and Steve were present. Blinding light streaked across the room and struck the screen on the far side, then came a series of identifying symbols that gave way to the first shot of Tony, with a soft musical background, a new theme written especially for the upcoming television campaign.

And now, everyman's dream of what he would like to see on arising in the morning came into view. Tony, in full, glorious color, the young housewife (or fantasy mistress), only minutes out of bed, wearing a knee-length robe that added allure to her exquisite body, hair cunningly touseled, sleepy eyes coming alert with expectancy.

Opening the cabinet, removing a new can of Goody's-B & B Coffee, opening it, CLOSEUP as she caught its fresh aroma, her slow smile of anticipation widening. There was no deviation from Steve's script and in the final seconds, as she sipped the steaming fluid with obvious relish she looked directly into the viewer's eyes and said, "And that's how easy it is to make the finest cup of brewed coffee you've tasted in years. Goody's B & B. Try it." CUT to

CLOSEUP of LABEL, full screen. ANNOUNCER'S VOICE in the background, "Now—at your favorite food store." FADE OUT as MUSIC comes up.

Lawson was on his feet. "Great! Great! That's the best damned commercial we've ever produced, Steve! Tony, you were sensational!"

Tony said, "May we see it again, Steve?"

He signaled Larry to run it again. It wasn't sensational, not even great, Steve thought, but it was good. Effective. Tony's beauty and aliveness made it good, better than most. There was a quality of freshness about her looks, a warmth in color that made it more acceptable than the usual run of commercials and gave it an uncommercial level of credibility. Yet he made a mental note to have the glamour aspect toned down a little to avoid irritating the women viewers. When it had run through the second time and the lights were turned on, Lawson said, "How about it, Steve, she's got it, hasn't she?"

Steve said, "Yes, Mark, she has. She comes through like a charm."

Tony said, "I think I should have worn a wedding band."

Lawson laughed delightedly. "How about that? A good thought. Make a note of it, Steve." And after a brief pause, "Well, how about it?"

"You saw the same thing I saw," Steve said. "She gets my vote, if that's necessary."

Tony stood up and, looking directly at Steve, said, "Let's give credit where credit is due. It was a perfect script, and the director was great. Thank you, Steve."

"Without you, Tony . . ." he began, when Lawson interrupted impatiently. "Where do we go now?"

"First," Steve said, "do you have an agent, Tony?"

"No, not at the moment."

To Mark, "I think Tony should get herself someone to handle her schedules, which will come thick and fast once we get into full production. Also, someone to take care of her financial affairs, the checks and residuals and everything that goes with it. I can send her to someone like Duane Charlton, he's one of the best in town, with a small, select clientele . . ."

"I know the Charlton Agency," Tony said with a quiet smile. "Do you think he would handle me?"

"With a client like GFP backing you," Steve said, "the

door will be wide open. I'll talk to Charlton personally, if you'd like that."

"Yes, I'd like that very much."

"Mark?"

Mark put an arm around Tony's waist possessively. "Do it Tony's way, Steve, and let's get things all set up and squared away."

"I'd suggest Tony make herself available to us until we're ready to go into full scale production."

"She'll be available, won't you, Tony?"

"Of course. I'll need to put a new wardrobe together to match my new image."

"Yes," Steve agreed. "We'll want more than morning shots. Daytime, outdoor, indoor, entertaining at lunch, dining out, family supper, party wear, vacation and summertime iced coffee scenes . . ."

"She'll have everything she needs," Mark said. "Okay, Tony, that's it for now. Why don't you run along? Steve and I have other things to discuss."

Tony said, "Thank you again, Steve. I know how much you helped. I appreciate that very much and I promise I'll be very cooperative."

"I'm sure you will. We'll be in touch and I'll set you up with Charlton within the next couple of days. By the way, don't forget to leave your address and telephone number with my secretary."

"I'll do that on my way out, and thank you." She turned, and Mark's hand trailed down from her waist across her smooth, round buttocks, then she was gone. Steve and Mark remained in the comfortable viewing room.

"I owe you an apology, Steve," Mark said. "I thought you and Bryce were going to pitch me a curve on this one."

"Why would we do that, Mark? Hell, she's got everything going for her. Looks, personality appeal, camera presence, and her voice is a lot more natural on sound track than it is in person. If she works out, we'll have a real find on our hands."

"She'll work out. That kid's got class all the way."

There was the matter of the B & B budget that needed some discussion. Curtis Fitzjohn wanted more definite details before he would commit funds for the year, but since the campaign was in its infancy, the agency required more time before a more explicit breakdown could be furnished.

"Okay, I can hold Fitzjohn off for a while. Where do we stand with the kickoff on B & B?"

"So far, we have the introductory ads going into the visual stage, plus some followup ads. What we're shooting for is the established campaign that follows, something to keep the consumers interested once our first major shot has been fired."

"And you still won't consider the premium offer?"

"Not at this stage, Mark. If we need it later, we can always fall back on that, but for now, I'm interested in something that, frankly, will eliminate the need for premiums. Even a good reason to give a few thousand pounds of B & B away—just to get it into people's kitchens and let them try it—would be better than kitchen clocks or appliances."

"Okay. I told you I'd give you a chance, Steve, but if you don't come up with something that will do the trick—and soon—we're going into premiums whether you, Allard, or Leary like it, or not. I'm not going to let us blow this one because you're so goddamned hard-nosed about premiums, and you can count on that, for sure."

"Then there's no use squabbling over it now, is there? Just give us that chance you promised, that's all we're asking."

"Okay. And call that agency guy and set Tony up for an interview, will you?"

"I'll do that as soon as I get back to my office."

"He's not in, Steve," Peggy told him. "Will you speak with Miss Tracy or Mr. Webb?"

"No. Have Charlton call me when he gets in. You have Miss Anthony's address and phone number?"

"Yes, she left it with me."

Duane Charlton called back at four o'clock. "Ah, Steve, dear boy. Sorry I couldn't get back to you sooner. What can I do to make you happy today?"

"A special case, Duey. I want to arrange an interview appointment for a young lady . . ."

"Ah, ah, Steve . . ."

"Nothing like that, you dirty-minded old man. This is already in the bag and has the client's okay."

"GFP?" Charlton's voice went into high gear with anticipation.

"GFP. And possibly for a long run. Interested?"

"Indeed, yes."

"Okay. Name, Margo Anthony, also known as Tony. She . . ."

"Margo Anthony," Charlton repeated. "That name rings a bell. She was something of a minor sensation a few years back, modeling for a youth magazine, a protégé of Benn Schwill if I remember correctly, wasn't she?"

"She may have been, but I wouldn't know about that."

"I'll get in touch with her personally."

"Fine. Take this phone number down. It's unlisted." He gave it to Charlton, along with Tony's address on West End Avenue.

"I'll call her at once, Steve, and thank you."

"Okay, Duey, and handle with care. This girl is going to be our superstar image."

10

On Saturday, Peggy was up and out early. By ten, the weekend food shopping completed, she had a second cup of coffee with Nikki and Lois while they discussed arrangements and menus for the week, then gathered up her manila envelope of notes, and her purse, and walked briskly to Perry Street. Lennie had left the door slightly open, but she rapped her knuckles against a paint-scarred panel, heard him call out, "Door's open," and went inside.

The windows were wide open, the small apartment in neat order, the bed folded back into its closet. Lennie sat at his drawing table sketching light figures into the oval-cornered white panels of a black storyboard pad. There were twelve such panels, each in the shape of a television tube, with an oblong space for dialogue beneath each panel. Two completed sheets were thumbtacked to the wall and he was working on the tenth panel of the third sheet. The coffee pot sat on an electrically heated trivet on the cabinet beside the table.

"Good morning, Lennie," she called out.

"Hi," he replied without looking up. "Pour yourself some coffee while I finish this thing up. Fifteen minutes."

She found a mug, poured the coffee, then went to the bookcase and quietly examined his hoard of art books, some new, most of them picked up at used bookstores, all well-thumbed. There were two shelves of classics, published in paperback, weighty in history, philosophy, the great religions of the world, the *Columbia Encyclopaedia,* a thesaurus, Bartlett's, as well as English, French, Spanish, and German dictionaries. The rest of his collection were novels, short stories, and the nonfiction and fiction of Wright, Baldwin, Malcolm X, Carmichael, King, Wilkins, and other black writers and leaders.

Lennie swung away from the table, and pinned the third and last sheet next to the other two, placing the script he had been working from in an envelope similar to the one Peggy had brought with her. She went to him and stood beside the table, examining the lightly penciled sketches.

"Hey, man, these are great."

"They'll look a lot better when I lay the color on." He stepped back and said, "Well, you look pretty feisty this morning. Got your stuff down on paper?"

"Yes. A start, anyway." She began to open the envelope.

"Get it out while I wash this crud off my hands."

He came back within minutes, wiping his hands on a towel. Peggy had the notes clutched in her hand and as he reached to take them, she said, "No, wait a minute. I want to explain what I have in mind and you keep quiet until I'm finished."

"Okay. Sit down and start talking."

"No, you sit down and listen. I'll stand."

"Just like our leader, hey, pacing back and forth while he talks out an idea?"

"Shut up and leave Steve out of this."

"For now, you mean."

"For now, just pay attention."

The idea, she explained again, was not new, not original, not even exciting, perhaps, except in how it could be presented in layout, art treatment, and type arrangement: big, bold, yet with plenty of white space, the way size and appearance gave an ad a sense of vitality and importance.

"Check," Lennie said. "I'm with you so far."

"All right. What I see is this jingle contest—don't laugh—jingle contest open to the public, two cartoon blocks prominently displayed. GFP runs these ads, with say, half-a-dozen sample cartoons illustrating the jingles and offering a cash prize, maybe one hundred or two hundred fifty dollars for each jingle that will appear in a future ad, plus a certain amount of Goody's B & B Coffee in cans and jars to every contestant whose jingle is accepted. Each loser-contestant receives a one-pound can of B & B for entering the contest."

She paused and waited. "So far," Lennie said, "nothing new, nothing original, nothing exciting. Quoting you, of course."

"I *know* that. Except that when I got the idea, I checked out some figures with Research and discovered that the response to these jingle contests is fan*tastic*, a lot higher than the response to those 'Complete this sentence in twenty-five words or less' things that begin with 'I like Jazzbo Detergent because. . . .' All right? I think that if we make ours appealing, there are tens of thousands of women who'll try out their repressed writing ambitions . . ."

"Like yours?"

"Lennie . . ." she said warningly.

"Ok-ay, ok-ay. Go ahead."

"And we'll get a terrific response, which is what I think Steve and Norm are looking for. This way, a handful of women will receive cash and coffee prizes, but the majority will get the pound can of coffee to use for as long as it lasts, which might convert them from the coffee they're using now. At least it gets the product into the house, even though it's being given to them free."

"Hey, not bad, baby, not bad. But that's one hell of a lot of coffee to give away for no bread, isn't it?"

"So what if it's added to the cost of advertising? At cost, it's a lot cheaper than the time and space cost, isn't it? Or some premium thing that they have to put out cash to get."

"Well, I'm only an artist. That part belongs to the brain boys upstairs. Is that it?"

"No. The idea is to make them submit each entry on an official blank they can pick up free at their food market, as many as they want, but only one cash winner to a family. Now, only those grocers or food markets that handle B & B will have the official blanks, so if people ask for them and the merchant doesn't have them to hand out, he'll have to put in a stock of B & B in order to get the blanks. Therefore, we pick up some outlets we've never had before along with the new customers. Does that make sense to you?"

"It does so far. You been doing a lot of digging into this thing, haven't you?"

"Score yourself an A+ for that. What I'm thinking is

that it could be the followup to the introductory announcements, don't you?"

"Baby, what I think adds up to a Zero-minus. I still don't see why you don't walk this thing past Adrian, or Steve, the way you're doing it now for me? Hell, that's where the action is going to be, the big *yes* or *no*."

"Lennie, that's the part I'm getting to now, and where I need your help. I can't talk to Steve or Norm about a thing like this the way I can to you. I'm a secretary. I take notes, dictation, type letters, file letters, make coffee. Period. I'm not supposed to make like a copywriter, an art director, or a creative being. I want a visual, full page newspaper size, to put on Norm's easel, and let him walk in on it, and see it there; the art, the type matter, all spelled out."

Lennie grinned. "You're coming on strong. Okay, let's have the jingle thing."

"I've got half-a-dozen, so we'll pick out the one you like best for illustration purposes. Just one. I'll type the others as followups to fit the same blocks . . ."

The first, she explained, was a courtroom scene, the judge on the bench, a seedy prisoner before him standing next to a uniformed officer.

First Box. JUDGE: *It's 60 days in jail for you,*
Two months, no liberty!

Second Box. PRISONER: *That's okay, Judge, as long as they serve* GOODY'S B & B.

In the second, two maids are in head-to-head discussion over a back fence as the happy employer of one passes by, briefcase swinging merrily in hand, whistling as he heads for his car.

First Box: FIRST MAID: *Whatever's happened to your boss,*
He's acting mighty gay.

Second Box: SECOND MAID: *He's changed since we've been serving* GOODY'S B & B *each day.*

For her third effort, the notes read, *Desert scene, a cowboy with his horse in the foreground.*

First Box. COWBOY: *A cowboy's life's a dreary life*
Out on the lone prair-ee-ee.

Second Box. HORSE: *To make it swing we always pack*
GOODY'S B & B *on me.*

Lennie perused the other three jingles carefully. "I hope you're a better poet then you are a jingleer," he said.

"Let's not confuse the two, and enough with the smart cracks, okay? If I gave this an all-out shot of intellectuality, how many housewives do you think would give it a second look?"

Lennie laughed. "Sure, baby. Well, let's go with the cowboy. I'm great with horses."

He got out a large sheet of heavy illustration board and taped it to the drawing table, ruled off a fourteen-and-a-half by twenty-three-inch space, penciled in the margins, and then inked in a half-inch border. Allowing space at the top for the headlines, he next ruled off two large blocks for the cartoon illustrations and began sketching figures lightly with a soft pencil. Peggy, watching over his shoulder, disturbed him. He paused for a moment, then said, "Here's some money. Go out and pick up something to make lunch for us. This kind of stuff gives me an appetite."

She refused the money, saying, "This is my treat," and left, knowing she was in the way and that Lennie was only being polite. She took her time and returned an hour later with cold cuts, potato salad, cole slaw, fresh rye bread, and a small lemon meringue pie. She put on a pot of fresh coffee and set the table. When the aroma of the coffee reached him, Lennie threw down his pencil and came to the table. "All roughed in," he announced. "Soon's we finish lunch, I'll ink it in."

"Why not leave it rough, in pencil?"

"Because, lady, when you want to really sell something, you dress it up in the best package you can find. That's lesson number one in this racket."

"Mr. Allard would hand you your head if he ever heard you say that."

"Hell, Peggy, it's just a racket, a hustle, like any other racket or hustle."

"Why not a business, like any other business?"

"Where's the real product in advertising except what

comes out of somebody's mind? Brainwashing, is what it is."

"Oh, come on now, Lennie, you know better than that."

"All I know is that it's brainwashing that the public accepts, buys, and pays for."

"And that's what you think you get paid for?"

"I get paid for doing my share, contributing to the delinquency of the gullible consumer. And what you're doing is playing around with semantics. Next, you'll be waving a flag and giving me that 'free enterprise' jazz."

"And what in the world is wrong with free enterprise?"

"One thing, it's not free except to the manipulators at the top who control it, fix prices, jerk the consumer around, and buy protection from the politicians and legislators who write laws the way they're told by the lobbyists and wheeler-dealers who put 'em in office and own 'em. Does that spell it out for you?"

He was suddenly angry again, remembering old injustices, humiliations, violations of his personal dignity, all hammering at his brain and nerves, mouth drawn in a tight line, muscles rigid. Peggy said, "Lennie, don't try to fight the world singlehanded."

He stared at her for a moment and said, "Lady, I'm not fighting the world. I'm only a pawn in a game I can't beat, the same game you're in, but I don't see it with rose-colored glasses the way you do. You keep trying to elevate advertising into something holy, like the legal profession, or medicine, which isn't much better."

"Is that how you really see advertising?"

He said, "Peggy, don't you know that advertising violates the human system of values? It exalts materialism at the expense of traditional spiritual values in what American life was, and should be. It is corrupt because it is all-powerful, just as America is corrupt because it is the most powerful nation in the world."

"And among its other virtues, doesn't it create employment, and feed thousands and thousands of people?"

"Are you talking about virtue or decadence? We're a consumption-oriented people whose standard of living is the highest, the most envied in the world, all at the expense of the poverty-stricken millions, the hungry, the enslaved, who yearn for those virtues and employment they don't have and can't have, because we spend billions on unnecessary wars and so much else that is useless and costly. Let me ask you: does advertising preach love, brotherhood, happiness, or the joys of living except when it profits the advertiser? Does it really make anyone happier except the seller and his stooge, the ad man?"

Peggy said, "Lennie, I've never heard anything so idiotic in my whole life."

He threw down his fork, angry now. "Oh, shit. You're like all the rest of them, got this America Beautiful thing. My ass! We're living in a goddamned cesspool of pollution, poverty, and corruption, and you think if we ignore it, it'll go away, disappear, the same slave-oriented attitude my people had for hundreds of years until enough of 'em got mad enough to break the iron chains. So where are there enough people now to break the rest of the chains, the hate chains, the segregation chains, the psychological chains that are still choking most of us to death? I know you'll say, 'Wait, give it time,' but how much time have I got left to forget I'm just another nigger, not fit to be with white people?"

Peggy felt a terrible hurt, as though she were the direct target for his accusations. "Lennie," she said, "you work with white people every day of your life. I'm white. I'm here across the table from you. Could we have done this thirty, twenty, even ten years ago?"

"And how long will it take before we can have more than just sitting across a table, talking? Another ten, twenty, thirty years?"

She said calmly, "What more do you want, Lennie?"

And he replied heatedly. "The one big thing I can't have. You. You're what I want. Goddamn it, I can't sleep nights, thinking about you. Half the time I can't even think straight thinking of you. That's what I want. You. Does that answer your question?" He pushed himself away from the table and stalked back to the drawing board, threw himself into the chair and began to work.

Peggy sat at the table for a while, her eyes blurred. Stunned by his sudden outburst, she could think of no answer because there were no words to answer his question, only some action on her part.

With eyes welled up, she lit a cigarette and smoked it down to the final inch before she could bring herself to get up and begin slowly to clear the table. She washed the dishes and put them away. When she was finished, she sat in the reading chair she had helped Lennie buy, picked up a book of Chagall drawings, and sat turning pages listlessly, scarcely seeing the black-and-white illustrations.

She was not frightened by his angry outcry against the world, knowing how much he loved what he was doing; the results of his efforts alone proved that much. It was his inadvertent accusation that she was the cause of his misery that was disturbing, his yearning for the unattainable white girl for whom he was willing to pour out pure talent—or love—on paper.

Lennie worked on, his back to her, while she held the book in her lap and thought, *Why does it have to be this way, this anger? Why can't we be as we are—friends—without the need for whatever he hopes will come between us?* And she pondered the thought of sex with Lennie, that strong, forceful body in motion, their bodies engaged, feeling his weight upon her, thrusting, filling her emptiness . . .

"Peggy? You all right?"

She came out of the dream with a gasp, embarrassed. "Wh—what?"

"I said, you all right?"

"Yes. Yes, why?"

"I thought I heard you call me."

"No. I was just dozing. What time is it?"

"Past four-thirty. You want to see this as far as I've gone?"

"Yes." She went to him, and stood at his shoulder. The ad was nearly completed and he had been right. Inked in, it was a hundred times more effective. The heading announced the contest in two lines of strong gothic type, the two boxes centered beneath, the art in his own free-flowing style. Below, two blocks of meticulously lettered copy outlined the rules, and finally, the can of Goody's B & B drawn in, a jar of freeze-dried beside it, standing together on a white field, unobstructed, acting as the signature for the entire page.

"That's beautiful, Lennie! I love it!"

"Give me another ten minutes and it's all yours."

She went back to the chair again and sat there, staring at her thighs, legs, the tips of her shoes. What would it matter, after all, she thought? I did it with that horrible old Bob Larch without ever knowing about it until next morning. I've wanted to do it with Steve and given him every chance, even going to his apartment when he was hurt, but he couldn't see me except as a secretary. A thing. I've thought about it, read about it, heard about it most of my life, and now I'm twenty-seven and still don't know as much as some fifteen- or sixteen-year-old kids. Lennie, at least, is honest about it. He wants me, but he's never pushed himself at me the way others have, never even mentioned it until now. What can I lose? Why do I hold back? Not because he's black. I've never even thought of him as being black . . .

"All done." Lennie brought it to her, holding it up from about four feet away.

"That's—perfect, Lennie. It's the best visual I've seen in a long time."

"Best one I've ever done." His good mood had returned. "A labor of love, lady . . ." He caught himself and said, "I mean, I loved doing it. I'll wrap it for you." He took it back to the table, ripped off a long piece of brown paper, wrapped the stiff sheet of art board carefully, then taped its edges tight with masking tape. When he turned to give it back to her, she was standing beside the chair, eyes locked onto his, unsmiling. He reached toward her, package in hand, but she made no move to take it from him and continued to stare. "Here," he said, "take it. It's all yours."

She said, "You do want me, don't you, Lennie?"

His eyes closed down to mere slits. "Listen, I was a damned fool. I'm sorry . . ."

"You do, don't you?"

"You don't know what you're saying, Peggy. Listen—listen to me. You don't have to pay me for this."

"It's not in payment for anything."

His head rolled and rocked from side to side. "Christ Almighty," he whispered. "Oh, Jesus Christ Almighty."

"Well?" She moved then, kicking off her shoes, bending slightly as though to pull the bottom edge of her dress up; then hesitated, waiting for some response from him.

"Look," he said, "I'm fouled up enough as it is. I don't want to foul you up, too." His hands loosened their grip on the package and it slipped to the floor. "Look," he said again, "take the damned thing and get to hell out of here before we both get loused up."

"Lennie . . ."

"Go on. Get out!" He turned away swiftly, stopped momentarily, then ran out of the apartment. She heard his footsteps clattering down the wooden steps, and finally the sound disappeared and she heard nothing, felt an iciness in herself that replaced the warmth of expectancy that had been there only moments before.

Slowly she slipped her shoes on, picked up the brown-wrapped labor of love, and went out. On Perry Street, there was no sign of Lennie Hawkins.

11

On Monday morning, Peggy slid the wrapped art board between her desk and the wall, removed her jacket, placed her purse in the bottom drawer, then went through the coffee-making ritual. By the time she had opened and separated the mail, glanced through the letters, and arranged them in order of importance, the coffee was ready. She poured herself a cup, hearing the voices and noises of the other members of the group beyond her wall as they entered from the main hallway, calling their "Good morning's" and "Hi's" as they prepared to face the new day and week. She heard a knock on her door and opened it. Lennie stood there, his expression one of enigmatic doubt, shy, undecided whether to come in or turn away. "Good morning, Lennie," Peggy greeted. "Come in. How are you?"

He came in and stood near the door. "Okay, I guess. Listen, I'm sorry as hell about Saturday."

"It's all right, Lennie. I was a fool. Silly."

"No. No," he protested. "If anybody was a fool, it was me, and a damned big one."

"I don't think so. I think you were the wiser of . . . Lennie, let's forget it, shall we? If it had happened, we'd both be feeling our guilt so badly this morning we'd probably be unable to face each other."

"Okay. It never happened." He grinned weakly. "We still friends?"

She returned the smile. "Of course."

"You got the thing with you?"

"I've got it."

"How are you going to give it to Norm?"

"I don't know yet. I'll wait until the right moment."

"Well, good luck, you hear?" He started out, reaching the door just as Steve arrived. "Hi, Lennie. Something you wanted?"

"Hi, man," Lennie improvised glibly. "Just checking to see if a letter I was expecting came in. I gave this address." He pushed past Steve and walked down the hallway.

"Good morning, Peg."

Peggy picked up the phone and checked Steve in with the receptionist, then said, "Hi. Coffee's ready."

"I can use some. Any messages?"

"Not even one so far."

"Maybe this is one of my luckier days. What's in the mail?"

"Nothing personal or important. Oh, there's a checklist from Traffic Control with a red flag on it."

"Bring it in with the coffee."

A few moments later she went into Steve's office with the checklist and a cup of coffee. Steve checked the Traffic memo with the WPC, then removed his jacket. Peggy hung it in the closet, waiting for any instructions he might have for her. Baldasarian tapped on the door and poked his head inside, and Steve nodded him in. They conferred on some current material for GFP and when he left a few minutes later, Norm Adrian came in carrying a full newspaper layout and a photostatic copy that reduced it to the size of a *McCall*'s page. They exchanged greetings and Norm laid the ads on Steve's desk. Peggy moved over behind the desk to examine it from beside Steve.

There were four bold lines of type just above center, reading:

What!
You *still* haven't tried
GOODY'S B & B COFFEE
Well, Lady. . . .

Beneath that was a block of twelve-point copy in bold face, neatly spaced and leaded:

Clip this ad, take it to your nearest
food market and exchange it for a FREE
4-OZ. SAMPLE. That's all there is to enjoying
a new, exciting taste thrill every
morning, noon, and night. No obligation whatever,
just GFP's way of introducing you to
what Coffee *should* taste like! Good
only during the month of September.
Do it today, now.

and finally, the signature, a can of Goody-B & B, bracketed between two jars of freeze-dried, all wearing their new, distinctive labels. Under the illustration was the legend:

GOODY'S . . . . *to be Sure!*

Adrian waited, saw no excitement rising in Steve or Peggy, and said, "Well, I wasn't that wild about it, either. It lacks something, the grab, the punch. We can write reams about carefully selected beans, perfect roasting, smoother blending, but like cigarettes, it's all been said and done before in a thousand different ways. This is a giveaway, sure, but four ounces never changed a habit any more than a four-cigarette sample pack ever changed a smoker's habit."

"Well, Norm, we can't give a full pound to every housewife in the country, can we?"

"No, but I wish we could. So where do we get the hooker to make them curious enough to try it?"

"I don't know, but if we don't come up with something, I'm going to be fighting Lawson's premium gimmick before very long."

"What about a teaser campaign, blind, no names, keep it running for a week or two, then come out with it like an A-bomb?"

"No, Norm. I gave it some thought, but the teaser campaigns always burn up a hell of a lot of money we can use more effectively in other ways."

"How much more time do we have?"

Steve pointed to the word September in the ad. "Use that for the time being, which doesn't give us a hell of a lot of room to breathe or stretch."

"Well, we'll keep on it."

"Okay, Norm. I know you can do it, if anybody can."

Adrian lumbered out with the ads. Steve sat down and picked up his coffee cup, but it had turned cold. Peggy said, "Another cup?"

"Not right now."

She said, "Steve, do ideas care who has them?"

He looked up and smiled. "Now that's as cryptic a remark as ever I've heard."

"I mean, it doesn't necessarily go that ideas can come only from what you call the pros in this business, does it?"

"Speaking academically, which I'm sure you're not,

ideas can hit anybody, anywhere, not unlike a meteor falling out of the sky. Now, what's bugging your pretty mind?"

"I mean, if somebody walked in and had an idea you could use, say the man who runs the elevator, or a janitor, or a . . ."

"Space pilot? Or maybe a secretary, is what you really mean, isn't it? Come on, Peggy, get it off your chest and let's get down to work."

"Give me a minute?"

"Take two, and come back with your notebook."

She went out and returned with the wrapped art board, removed the tape, then placed the visual flat on his desk. To hell with protocol. "That's what I've got on my mind," she said.

Steve stared first at the ad, then back at Peggy, and returned to the ad, eyes moving across, then down, quickly. He shot another glance at Peggy, then read the body copy Lennie had painstakingly lettered in. "Where did this come from?" he asked.

"That's what I mean. Does it make any difference? It's there. Is it any good?"

"I recognize Lennie's fine Italian hand, but I know somebody had to put him up to it, and it's not that hard to guess just who that somebody is."

"You're not angry, are you?"

"No, but if you don't start talking, I'm going to be angry as hell."

"All right. It was my idea, but I didn't want to just *tell* you about it. I wanted you to *see* the whole picture for yourself, so I asked Lennie to do the visual for me."

"I see."

"Well?"

"Get Norm back in here, will you?"

She picked up the receiver, dialed Adrian's extension, and hung up after speaking to him. "He's on his way. Do you think it will work, Steve?"

"Let's see what Norm has to say about it."

A moment later, Adrian came in and Steve motioned him behind the desk to look at the ad. After a few moments, Adrian looked up and said, "Where did this come from?"

"Aside from that, what do you think?"

"Right now, it's a damned sight better than anything we've got. There's the appeal to the housewife to make a few bucks for herself, money and free coffee to the winners, coffee for everybody who submits a jingle, and some extra clout with the distributor and grocer, all in one package. I think we can make it stick, Steve. Whose is this? You been holding out on me? I know it's from the inside. That's Lennie's artwork."

Steve pointed a finger toward Peggy. "The genius poet here. She kept it under wraps because I once told her I'd fire her if she showed any ambition to become anything but a good secretary."

Norm, almost as though he hadn't heard Steve, said, "We'll need a few more of these jingles as starters to push our public into participating, Peggy. You got any more of these?"

"I've got five more in reserve, and I can do as many as you want."

"Well, bless you, my child." To Steve, "Anytime you want to fire her as your secretary, I'll take her on as our Edna Saint Vincent Millay in residence." And to Peggy, "Can you let me have the others?"

"I've got them in my purse."

"Again, bless you. What do you think, Steve, okay to go with this?"

"Let's give it a try. Get me a photostat of that, full size and magazine page size first, then turn your people loose on it. I'll want to show them to Allard as soon as they're ready."

Adrian nodded. To Peggy, he said, "Let me have the rest of them, will you, darling."

"Right away." Adrian picked up the visual and went out. Peggy said, "Steve—thanks."

"Mine to you, Peg. If we can sell this to Lawson, I'll see you get a bonus. Maybe even a raise."

"What about Lennie? He had a lot to do with this."

"I'll take that into consideration."

Impulsively, Peggy threw her arms around Steve and kissed him. "That's for being very tolerant about secretaries who break your rules," she said.

"Don't let it go to your head, sweetie, and keep remembering, you're still my secretary," he said.

"That's all I've ever wanted to be. The best secretary you've ever had."

Chapter 11

1

She sat quietly in the comfortable red leather armchair in the reception room of the Duane Charlton Modeling Agency, turning the pages of the most recent issue of the *New Yorker*, through which she had just thumbed for the third time. The atmosphere was elegant, delightfully perfumed, with handsome furniture and appointments. The soft, pink-tinted walls were liberally sprinkled with framed 11 x 14-inch black-and-white and color photographs of beautiful models, head-shot closeups, head and shoulder shots, and full-lengths, in a variety of indoor and outdoor settings; teenage fashions, hair, and cosmetics; housewife type, and glamour stylists; some bland, some exotic, others totally sensual. Something for everybody. Beside each photograph, laminated between sheets of clear plastic, with its own spotlight directed upon it from the ceiling, was a reproduction of the advertisement in which that face or body had appeared; and for which the user-client had paid anywhere from sixty to one hundred dollars for an hour of the model's time.

Outwardly calm, blood pounded through her veins as Margo Anthony, born Mary Angela Emiliani, waited. Arriving early, she had been waiting for half an hour for her appointment with Duane Charlton. During those thirty minutes she had counted nine marvelous examples of feminine charm and beauty enter the reception room and speak to the astonishing beauty who presided over the center desk and telephone console, watching as she consulted her appointment chart and sent each caller through the door on the right or left to meet her Charlton representative and discuss the business or personal matter at hand. Two other callers never got past the receptionist, probably seeking an interview without an appointment, a lost cause with an agency of Charlton stature.

Margo Anthony—having an appointment—waited, pondering the future. She was twenty-four, with jet-black hair, green-eyed, five feet five inches tall, and weighed one hundred fourteen pounds, perfectly proportioned from head to bosom, waist, hips, thighs, calves, and ankles. The weight problem she had endured and anguished over during her early teen years had been brought under effective control long ago with strict exercises and a careful diet regime.

But there was more to Margo than mere statistics could project. There was a marked aliveness in her exotic, oval face and sensual body that demanded a second or third look; it attracted desire from men, envy from women, and appreciation from both. There was that strong temptation in people to go beyond mere staring, a need to talk with her, touch her beauty, and thus become some part—however small or vague—of her vital personality.

Margo had first become aware of the commercial possibilities of her beauty when the photographer who had taken her portrait for the Brookhurst graduation class book on Long Island sought her out later and asked if she would consider posing for a commercial project he had in mind, for which he was willing to pay fifty dollars for a release. At eighteen, with a summer vacation coming up, Margo agreed.

On the following Saturday afternoon she appeared at the photographer's studio, and after the man had outlined the project so near and dear to his heart, walked out when it dawned upon her that he had expected to shoot her in the nude. But the idea of modeling was firmly implanted in her mind and remained even after she had enrolled in a secretarial school and, at twenty, found herself working as secretary to an editor on *Allure*, a magazine dedicated to the youth, beauty, and fashion market.

Made aware of her desirability, she took all the male byplay lightly, amused by the various techniques used by young, adult, middle-aged, and even old men to bring her to bed, emotionally unmoved, and physically unattracted. Until she met Ben Schwill.

Ben had provided nine of the last twenty-four covers for *Allure*, more than any other outside photographer. In a discussion with Margo's editor-employer one day, Margo was asked to pass judgment on four photographs Schwill had submitted for a June cover. Suddenly, Schwill's interest turned from the job at hand to Margo. On his way out later, Ben handed Margo his card and said, "Any time you're interested in changing your career, sweetheart, call me."

Margo, taking in Ben's swingy manner, mod jacket, skin-tight trousers, and long, yet neat, hair style with bushy mustache, replied, "No, thanks, Mr. Schwill. I don't pose in the nude."

Ben smiled tolerantly. "You goddamned uppity dames. All you've got on your mind is rape. Forget I asked."

"Exactly what *did* you have in mind?" Margo asked quickly.

"Not what you have in yours, baby. All I want from you is a cover. No bra or girdle jazz, no calender art, no center spreads. I want a certain quality, and I think you've got it. What you're thinking about I've got at home, and I do all my homework there. Okay?"

"Okay. Saturday is the only day I have off."

"Saturday is fine. Ten in the morning. Don't worry about makeup. I'll have my wife there to coach you. She's an ex-model and until the kids came, was one of the best."

On Saturday morning, after Diana Schwill helped prepare her, Ben took medium and closeup shots for two hours, using a Hasselblad, while she moved from one pose to another, smiled, laughed, became sober, smoky-eyed, somber, and plaintive, on cue; looking over Ben's head, left, right, front, up, down. He reloaded, readjusted lights, and shot her sitting, standing, kneeling, lying on a carpet of bogus grass, drinking coffee, playing with Diana's toy terrier, doing her nails, and applying makeup.

In payment, Ben promised her a complete set of color and black-and-white blowups which she could make into a model's book to show around at various modeling agencies; but the competition was unbelievable and nothing came of her futile efforts in that direction.

The miracle occurred when one of the photographs of Margo was submitted for consideration and was chosen by the art director of *Allure* for the October cover. On the day of publication, Margo's life style changed. *Allure* was inundated with calls asking for her name, her agent, and her phone number. On Ben Schwill's advice, she changed her name from Mary Angela Emiliani and signed on with the Halverson-Kraag Agency whose clients were primarily interested in the teenage beauty and fashion markets, and where she would not have to compete with older, more experienced models.

In that year of her greatest financial success, she also became Ben Schwill's mistress and—incautiously—pregnant. Ben arranged and paid for the abortion, but there were complications brought on by internal infection that required a hysterectomy; which ended her relationship with Ben and what had begun as an outstanding career as a magazine model. She wanted no more of either.

With more than a fair cash reserve to see her through, she enrolled in a school for acting, took voice-coaching and spent weeks readjusting from teenage photography, makeup, and hair styling, to studying scripts, attending rehearsals, and appearing with other students in plays that had been successes in London and on Broadway many years before. Jobs, however, were few and far between. She tried modeling for awhile, but found it too strenuous, and was too humiliated to call on agencies with dozens of others trying out for a job, only to be rejected. She moved from her apartment into a room, and ate sparingly, conserving her wardrobe as much as possible in order to stretch out her funds; and at a point when her bank account dipped below the one thousand dollar limit she had set for herself, another break came her way.

Through Ann Lucas, an actress she had met, she read for a small role in an off-Broadway comedy that lasted through nineteen performances. But the experience had been important, the exposure vital. She was picked up for another part that lasted three months, and from that one, stepped into a third that was responsible for a two-month role on Broadway as a minor character. When that closed, she returned to an off-Broadway production for nine weeks.

Five years passed, and Margo was barely holding her own, still hovering around the thousand dollar bank balance limit, when she found a part in another off-Broadway production that lasted six weeks. During the backstage farewell party, she met Mark Lawson, who had been one of the play's financial backers. He was, Margo learned, more than just a wealthy theater buff who used his position as backer to supply himself with girls. Or so she thought.

Lawson was immediately attracted to her, but she refused to accept his invitations to go out on the town; however, after several months of seeking a job without results, her bank balance hit a new dangerous low and she gave in. She started dating Lawson. Within three months she was chosen for a play in which Mark Lawson was a backer. Later, she moved into an apartment on West End Avenue, leased and paid for by her new sponsor.

The beauty at the desk-console looked up and said, "Miss Anthony? Mr. Charlton will see you now." She aimed a pencil at the door on Margo's right. "All the way down the corridor to the office with the double doors."

"Thank you."

The girl smiled, and said, "Good luck."

Duane Charlton was forty-five, no more than an inch taller than Margo, paunchy, and pink. He wore a neat toupee and was dressed expensively in a greenish-beige silk suit, bright orange shirt, orange and blue-striped tie, and loafers that were actually tiny. Despite his androgynous appearance, Charlton's hand was firm and hard, and his smile disarming. He apologized for keeping her waiting, ordered coffee from a statuesque secretary, and showed her to a conversation corner in his huge office, yards away from his desk.

"Ah, Miss Anthony. So happy we could get in touch with you."

"I'm happy about that, too."

"I understand you were with Halverson-Kraag at one time, quite a fine record there, Kraag tells me."

"That was ages and ages ago."

"Yes. Well. I see you haven't lost the charm for which you were justly famous."

"Thank you."

"Ah, I understand you are free at the moment?"

"If I weren't, Mr. Charlton, I could hardly be here, wasting my time and yours."

"Ah, yes. Yes. I think we may have something very desirable that might interest you. Television commercials. That is, if you can fit the needs of the agency and client."

Tony smiled and said, "Mr. Charlton, suppose I said I am not interested."

Charlton's eyes blinked owlishly, his mouth opening and closing twice before he could catch his breath. "My dear girl, why on earth would you not be interested? This isn't one of the usual opportunities I'm talking about. If you are acceptable . . ."

She said, "Mr. Charlton, let's not play games, shall we? I've already tested for the part, the client is agreeable, and the agency that made this appointment is ready to sign me on. If your agreement is ready, I'll take it with me and read it. If I find it satisfactory, I will sign it. Is that agreeable with you?"

Charlton looked like a startled bird for a moment, then relaxed, and smiled. "My dear child, you are way out in front of me. I can have the agreement ready by this afternoon and placed in the mail. And I hope we shall enjoy a happy relationship together."

"We will, Mr. Charlton, as long as the contract you draw up between me and the client-agency is strong and gives them as few escape clauses as possible, with a heavy bonus if there is a termination."

"Ah, yes, yes, indeed, Miss Anthony," Charlton said agreeably.

2

Once the jingle contest idea had been tentatively approved by Keith, Steve and Norm set up the campaign to follow a prescribed order:

a) Introductory ads
b) Jingle contest announcements
c) Winning contestant ads, featuring the winners by name and photographs
d) Full-scale followup campaign

From that point on, Steve's most difficult task was to control the impulse to inject himself into the daily workings of the B & B group, knowing that his continual presence could only inhibit the workers in the vineyard; and to keep Chuck, Frank, and Reed from putting pressure on the copy-art teams. Anxiety was contagious, easily transmitted by a nervous gesture, smile, frown, or unintentional comment at the wrong moment.

From time to time, Norm showed his gratitude by checking in with Steve to keep him posted on the group's progress, and inform him that Byron Johns, Christine Galbertson, Dan Thaw, and Barry Haas were coming up with some excellent material, promising, "we'll have something definite to show you for the presentation in a short time."

Not that Steve and his three assistants didn't have enough to keep them busy. The regular GFP line had its own problems and Steve served not only as group head but as chaplain-arbitrator to the Grant-Berman, Ellis-Cook, Archer-Bardo, Hartman-Hawkins teams, settling disputes, arguments, differences of opinion, and occasional cases of simple tantrums, or just plain sulking.

On several occasions he heard Chuck's abrasive critical carping over a layout or piece of artwork he felt was not up to standard, or a piece of copy he thought needed "more beefing up." Since it was generally accepted that approval or disapproval of copy and art was now Steve's exclusive province, Chuck's invasion into this area caused added friction and required Steve to remind Chuck to limit his duties to production needs. But in the main, despite the wildness that often attacks creative people during the frenetic period of campaign incubation when the pressure is on, the work came through with professional capability.

The action in the B & B group was far more intense. Rap sessions took up most early morning hours, with Norm acting as moderator. Byron Johns was a shouter. Dan Thaw, during these conferences, became deadly cold, pressing his points of view with the drive and finesse of a fencer. Chris Galbertson, when she disagreed with Haas, Johns, or Thaw, had a way of developing migraine headaches or some mysterious internal feminine disorder not yet recognized by the medical fraternity, and would retire to the ladies' room until she regained her composure. Garry Parris, functioning as television-radio producer for both groups, escaped by visiting Don Bryce's area of control, and Lew Kann, always placid in this vortex of emotional turmoil, took on the role of peacemaker, pleading, "Aw, come on, fellows. Traffic Control is on my neck . . "

Norm, however, was enjoying the whole affair immensely now that the campaign was finally in progress measuring the exact amount of permissible temperament, coercing, cajoling gently, persuading his people to get back on the main line. In good time print ads and commercials began to pour out, while outdoor and display material was completed and ready for inspection.

Allard had ruled out a formal presentation for the B & B campaign to the Agency Plan Board in favor of a searching review by Bill Leary and himself, with Steve and Adrian making the presentation pitch, the entire session taped, in order to later extract the salient points to be made to GFP.

Bill at once expressed his full satisfaction and approval of the material content and Keith finally added his own blessings. Norm excused himself to break the good news to his group, the signal to relax and blow off steam. Byron, Chris, Dan, and Barry at once took the rest of the day off to hoist a few at a nearby bar in celebration.

"Well, Steve," Bill said after Adrian's departure, "you're the only one not jumping for joy. Anything on your mind we should know?"

"I'm a little concerned about Lawson's reaction," Steve admitted.

"Because you cold-watered his premium thing?"

"Yes. He was so damned set on it, he'll be sure to cloud up and rain all over this. He could set us back three months if he kills this presentation. You know how arbitrary he can be."

"Keith?"

Allard knocked the dottle from his pipe, talking as he pulled out a pocket tool to scrape the crusty bowl. "Well, there's always that possibility, but there's a way out." Bill and Steve waited silently. "We haven't made a full-scale pitch to GFP since the Year One. Usually, it's been more or less a one-to-one presentation to Mark, and we take it from there. I think we should treat this B & B thing as an entirely new, separate account we're going for, and give it the big treatment. Us against Them. Blue Team versus Red Team."

Bill came alert. "Of course. We'll hit them with the first team. Me, you, Steve, Castle, Thalberg, and Berton, against Herschel Goodwin, Lawson, Davies, Fitzjohn, and Hardwick, and anybody else they want to bring in on it. If Herschel and the others go for it, what can Lawson do if he's been outvoted? We'll cut off Mark's water before he can turn the faucet on. He can't shoot us all down."

"No," Keith said, "but we've got to remember that when it's all over, Steve will be the one who has to live with him."

"Steve?"

Steve had already considered choice and alternative and said, "Once we get over this first hump I can live with it. This is much more important than catering to the ego and whims of one man. I buy it."

"I'll phone Herschel Goodwin in the morning and sell it

to him," Bill said. "We'll need a full two weeks to get our marketing, merchandising, and media data in order, flip charts, slides, tapes, and a full dress rehearsal. The works. Suppose I shoot for two weeks from today, say Friday at 10:00 A.M. Or is that cutting it too thin?"

Keith and Steve agreed on the two-week period. Bill said to Steve, "By the way, where'd you find that fresh new face for those commercials?"

Evading a direct link between Tony and Lawson, Steve said, "She came from the Charlton Agency. No problems there. Mark's already seen the test we ran on her and okayed it. As a matter of fact, he suggested we use her on a regular basis and include her in the print media after the contest period is over."

Bill shot a quizzical glance at Steve. "Some kind of payoff there, do you think?"

Steve shrugged, repressing a grin. "No point fishing in strange waters, Bill." Keith merely smiled and said nothing.

"I suppose not. If Lawson wants to make her a rich girl, that's his business as long as she works out to your satisfaction. I'll put in that call to Herschel and let you know how it comes out."

In those last frenzied moments, Peggy Cowles had become an integral part of the campaign. The first three jingles had been illustrated by Lennie and incorporated into individual announcement ads, each a full page in size. For presentation purposes, Norm wanted a two-page spread, one page representing winning illustrated entries, the other listing nonwinners who would receive a one-pound can of ground coffee and an eight-ounce jar of freeze-dried coffee for their submissions.

On various departmental bulletin boards Peggy had posted an announcement:

SITUATIONS WANTED

explaining the need for ideas that could be translated into jingles for the campaign. The responses came from every division of the agency, including the noncreative, administrative, accounting, and executive offices; in itself an indication of the public response that might be expected. Suggestions covered every field; space pilots, sales manager quizzing salesmen, restaurant, domestic science class, shipboard, doctor and patient, author and wife, Hollywood studio, newspaper office, boardroom, firehouse, gas station, advice to the lovelorn, and other adaptable situations. Peggy chose twelve within four days, and by the end of the week had turned in her completed jingles.

At once, a problem arose with Lennie Hawkins. Adrian, eager to conserve time, divided the dozen chosen jingles among his two art directors and Lennie; but Lennie, who had illustrated the first three, at once adopted a possessive attitude toward this phase of the campaign and objected strenuously to the changes in art style. Norm argued that the change would add impact to the presentation but Lennie insisted that the basic technique should be retained for reader identification and, while Norm agreed in principle, time was of the essence and his decision remained firm. A chastened Lennie returned to his drawing board and went into a monumental sulk. Throughout the next week, he accepted his assignments without a word of comment, despite Adrian's positive assurances that when the public entries came in, Lennie would be their sole illustrator.

3

In Steve's office that Friday, the entire print media presentation for B & B's West Coast campaign had been placed against the wall in the order in which it would appear in newspapers and magazines. On his desk lay the television commercials ready for screening, tapes of the radio spots, and rough visuals of outdoor and point-of-purchase material. From a leather folder containing an outline of OBJECTIVES, Steve studied the data that would be copied, placed in similar folders, and presented to each of those who would be present at the joint meeting with the client.

Despite the mysterious and high sales figure that had been projected by the agency wizards charged with producing magical numbers, the budget for that initial three-month campaign, by any standards, was high, generally tapering off when and if expected initial goals would be reached. On a national scale, the overall figures for the first year were more reasonable, running to an approximate six million dollars. But for the moment, it remained for the initial campaign to be sold to GFP.

Norm, Chuck, Frank, Reed, Peggy, and Steve sat staring at the two introductory announcements and the six newspaper ads promoting the jingle portion that would follow. Viewed, heard, and approved by Bill Leary and Keith Allard earlier, all that remained was to pack the acetate-covered sheets of art board in proper sequence to take to GFP's Forty-second Street office for the client presentation on the following Friday morning at ten o'clock.

Steve said, "Well, Norm, anything else you can think of before we pack it in?"

Adrian shook his massive graying head, removed his glasses, and said, "It's all there, except for the dressing up and the outdoor and point-of-purchase finals, and we'll have that completed by Wednesday, or no later than Thursday morning. We'll pack the flip charts in with that, and you'll be all set. What about easels?"

"No problem. GFP has plenty in the conference room."

Peggy said, "I've got the copies of Mr. Leary's talk ready. All I have to do is put them into their binders as soon as I get them from Lex."

"Good enough. Let's be sure we've got everything ready to leave here no later than nine o'clock on Friday morning. You'll see to that, won't you, Chuck?"

"I'll check it out personally and have it set up in their conference room in plenty of time."

To Peggy, Steve said, "Usually, Keith's secretary comes along to take reaction notes. If you'd like, I'll arrange to have you take her place."

"I'd like that very much, Steve, but I'm not sure I'm up to Gail's speed."

"That's no problem. Everything will be taped. Your job will be to keep an eye on the GFP people and make notes of their visual reactions, something that can't be picked up on tape. Just forget the actual word-for-word dialogue. All we want is some specific visual reaction, the tone, that sort of thing."

"I'm nervous about it."

"It's as much your baby as it is ours, Peg. You might as well be in on its birth. Or death."

"Bite your tongue," Peggy said. "I'll be glad to be there."

"Well," Adrian said as he levered himself upward out of the chair, "we'll know by Friday night. I'm going out to make sure we've got everything that's listed on the schedule." He nodded to Steve, smiled at Peggy and the others, and left. Frank, and Reed Baker went out, then Chuck. Lex Kent came in.

"Hey, man, I hear you got a real show going in here." With a quick sweep that took in all the ads, "I think this is one of the best packages I've ever seen put together in this joint."

"What counts is whether the client buys it or not. Any predictions, Lex?"

"I'll bet five bucks across the board. This has got to be real *in,* man."

He stood staring at the loose grouping of newspaper and magazine ads for a while, then said, "Hey, I've got some interesting cats dropping in for a thing tonight. How about you guys making the scene, like anytime after eight?"

Peggy, included in the invitation, looked at Steve before answering. Steve said, "It's been a rough go all week, Lex. How about a raincheck? Maybe when we get this one behind us." Peggy looked disappointed.

"I've been giving you nothing but rainchecks, man. Hey, you remember Jack Orion?"

"No. Should I?"

"If you're with it. He kicked around in our bullpen for six months or so a couple of years ago, then quit to direct an off-Broadway thing, took off for the Coast for his first shot at a movie. We're going to screen it at my place tonight. A new breed thing, you know."

"What you mean is, it's a sexploitation nudie, don't you?"

"What I mean, man, it tells it like it is, today, now."

"Let me check with you later."

"Okay. How about you, Peggy?"

"I've got a kind of date . . ."

"So bring him along, okay?"

"I'll see."

To Steve, "You know my pad on East Ninth, don't you?" When Steve looked blank, Lex picked up a pencil and jotted the address on a sheet of memo paper. "Don't miss it," he added. "It could wake up your mangled corpuscles."

When he left, Steve called Chuck back in. "Let's get a couple of Eth's boys in here and start packing this up. Have them check with Norm for the rest of the material." To Peggy, "Get those folders made up for Mr. Leary, Allard, and the others so they can study the material during the next week. Let's have a few more copies Xeroxed in case there are more GFP people present than we've anticipated."

At three o'clock Peggy rang to tell him Miss Stafford was on the line. The call from Karen was unexpected since they had planned to meet at his apartment for dinner and spend the night, if not the weekend, together. He picked up the receiver and said, "I'm on, Peggy," her cue to hang up, and when he heard her reply, "Go ahead," and click off, he said, "Karen?"

"Steve, I'm terribly sorry. I've got to cancel out. Aunt Anna just phoned. Uncle Herschel came home from the plant after lunch and he's not feeling well."

"I'm sorry to hear it. Nothing serious, I hope?"

"Probably not, but he's being very difficult. He won't let Aunt Anna call the doctor and she wants me to come to Wyecliffe to see what I can do with him. He's hardly ever been sick before, other than a slight cold, and she's worried. I'll probably be there all weekend."

"I'll miss you," he said, "and I hope your uncle's in no danger. We're expecting him in town next Friday for the big presentation."

"I'm sure it's nothing terribly serious, Steve. I'll phone you tomorrow or Sunday."

Moments later, Peggy rang to tell him Mark was calling. He spoke with Mark for ten minutes, carefully evasive about the presentation except that he was sure Mark would like it.

"Don't be so damned sure about that, boy. I still don't like the idea of you people bringing in everybody from the old man down to the janitor on this one."

"Mark, that decision was out of my hands. This isn't one of those one-to-one presentations. It's something entirely new, and we've got a couple of million dollars riding on this breakout . . ."

"Don't snow me, Steve. I know how Leary operates when he wants to bypass me. A goddamned three-ring circus . . ."

"Mark, be reasonable . . ."

"Reasonable, my ass. I know the score, so don't put yourself in the win column too soon."

"All right, Mark," Steve said with a weary sigh. "We'll see you next Friday morning."

Mark slammed the receiver down without replying and Steve wondered if Tony was giving him a rough time of it. For a while he sat at his desk, flipping over the pages of his personal copy of Bill Leary's talk, copy that had already been condensed into headlines and lettered on flip charts, not unlike television cue cards, to refresh Bill's memory as he made the presentation. Apart from these, there would be color slides to illustrate his talk, then the video tapes to back up the print media: an expensive, yet important and necessary tool for selling a campaign.

At five, Peggy came in with four letters to be signed, and with those cleared away, he asked, "Everything set, Peg?"

"All A-OK. Production has it and after you and Norm check it all out on Thursday, we'll have two men deliver it to GFP to be set up in their conference room by 9:30 on Friday. All the folders have been distributed and I'll have three new steno books and a dozen sharpened pencils with me."

"Keep your fingers crossed, and you may win yourself a raise."

"If Lawson louses me up, I'll shoot him," Peggy said.

"That's against the law, isn't it, even in Nebraska?"

"Well, they shoot horses, don't they?" she quipped.

"Lawson is a horse?"

"Maybe," she said thoughtfully, "we could have him reclassified."

"Beat it, girl. Go make yourself beautiful for your date."

"I don't really have one. I mean, it's an iffy thing."

"Then why don't you go to Lex's party and see what new promise Hollywood is spewing forth?"

"I may at that. I haven't been to a good orgy in ages. How about you?"

"I had other plans, but they've been canceled. No, I don't think so. I'm not much for Lex's type of diversion."

"Sometimes they can be fun, you know. Different. Zen addicts who stand on their heads and meditate, sitar players, truth seekers, God-is-deaders, art freaks, gurus . . ."

"I didn't know you swung with Lex's crowd?"

"Oh, once in a long, long while. How can we know how the other half lives if our half won't look in on them?"

"Your liberal attitude is commendable. Maybe I'm getting too old for that kind of sandbox activity. Well, goodnight, Peg."

"Goodnight, Steve. Have a nice weekend and I'll see you on Monday."

By five-thirty the GFP groups, like the rest of the agency, had cleared away the debris of the week, covered their typewriters, locked their desks, and were gone to their homes, apartments, and beach and mountain resorts to escape the warm, humid city. With Karen away in Wyecliffe and Steve's own plans collapsed, he felt an overwhelming dullness in his mind, a weariness throughout his body. And he was lonely. It had been a physically exacting week, driving himself to complete the presentation, and although it was finished, he was well aware of the danger of Mark's feelings of resentment toward Bill, Keith, and himself for having gone behind his back to bring GFP's top echelon into the picture.

From his windows, Fifty-second Street was a moving portrait of shadowed canyons with faint beams of sunlight streaming down between tall buildings to pick up tiny figures and miniature cars battling their way out of the downtown area. A green-and-white patrol car, lights flashing, brought traffic to a momentary standstill, then the flow began again, an endless line moving eastward, halting at Lexington, then continuing on.

Karen came into his mind, and he felt disturbed by the impact she had made upon his life in so short a period of time. It seemed that everything he did now was done with the thought of whether Karen would approve or disapprove. And yet, when they were together, they seldom touched on the subject of his work. Or Mark.

Even with the added workload thrust upon him, he still found time to slip away from the office at least twice a week to spend an hour or two with her at his apartment. Between those afternoons, and an evening or two, or an occasional weekend, there was hardly time left for reading, or for the writing he had promised himself to get back to. He had even allowed his physical exercises to go, and had begun to cut down on lunchtime drink and food intake in order to lose the few pounds he had recently taken on.

He decided not to go home and spend the evening alone and shortly after six, walked over to Third Avenue and had a drink at O'Malley's, pondering over his lengthening affair with Karen and the possible dangers in discovery. The bar became crowded, and he moved to a table where Fred Eberle, Jack Shepherd, and Tom Olivero—all from

Soames, Kirk, & Calder—were unwinding from their own week of labors. Eberle was married, Shepherd divorced, and Olivero separated, and living with a television pop singer who had announced to the press that she was joyfully pregnant and had no intention of marrying.

After a third drink, they had dinner, discussed the usual street rumors of client and personnel changes. Eberle missed his seven-thirty train to Scarsdale and refused Shepherd's proposal to pick up the two girls at a nearby table who were flirting with them. Olivero was depressed by the falling stock market and, as he poured alcohol on the flames of his discontent with the world, loudly abused the administration for not taking effective measures to stem the creeping inflation he insisted was the cause of the market's collapse. At eight-thirty, Fred and Jack moved in on the two girls, and Steve, bored with Tom Olivero, paid his check, and left. After a few minutes of self-debate, he signaled a cab and gave the driver Lex Kent's address.

4

Lennie refused to go to Lex Kent's party. "They're all a lot of finks and Lex is the finkiest," he told Peggy.

"Have you ever been to one of his parties?" she asked.

"I don't have to go there," Lennie insisted. "I know his crowd. The Village is full of the same kind of freaks, everybody with some kind of kinky bag who thinks he invented it."

"I want to go."

"Then don't bug me and go. I've had it with creeps."

"I don't know what's wrong with you. I feel like celebrating. We've got this B & B thing going for us next Friday . . ."

"Look, baby, I've told you before. It's *your* thing, *your* idea. I was only the mechanic on the job. Any artist could have done that visual for you. If you don't believe me, ask Adrian."

"And I've told you over and over again, it was your illustration that really sold it to Steve and Norm."

"Don't give me that jazz. It's yours. And Norm's. Leave me out of the goddamned thing, will you?"

Peggy sighed. "You're a hard-nosed, violent man. A throwback."

"And you don't know up from down if you believe that."

"And you're the genius who has the whole world figured out, aren't you? You stand alone, waving your own flag, an army of one against everybody?"

"And you're so damned conformist you can't see beyond the end of your nose. You're in love with life as you see it, and all I see is shit."

"What I can't understand is why anybody who thinks the way you do would even want to go on living."

"Maybe because I've got no choice except suicide, and I haven't got the guts for that. So I live, but without the blinders you wear in order to see only what you want to see."

"I see you, Lennie."

"So what do you see in me?"

"A sad, unhappy, angry man."

"Oh, Jesus. Why don't you go to your goddamned party and leave me to hell alone?"

"All right, if that's the way you want it."

Lennie had caught up with her after work and they had ridden the subway together. Ever since Steve and Adrian had decided to go with Peggy's jingle contest idea, she had felt the change in him, at first subtly happy, then enthusiastically interested. He had worked out the drawings for the courtroom scene, the two maids over the backyard fence, a cooking class for housewives, doctor and patient, customer and waiter situations, all included in the presentation as examples for entrants to go by.

Then had come the burst of anger and resentment when Norm assigned Christine and Barry to do the next six illustrations, using Lennie's first illustrations as their guides. Lennie made no effort to disguise his injured feelings. He wanted to do them all. They were his illustrations and he didn't want Chris or Barry messing around with them, trying to imitate his technique. And because he felt that Peggy had sided with Adrian, he had turned sullen.

Peggy went to Lex's party alone.

It was a party Steve hadn't particularly wanted to go to, and under ordinary circumstances he wouldn't have given it another thought; but with Karen canceling out their date he felt adrift and rudderless, with too much time to think about things he didn't want to remember.

Besides, he had been working closely with Lex recently and didn't want to offend him.

There were half a dozen Leary people present, art directors mostly, and a copywriter he recognized but whose name he couldn't recall. The others were total strangers, more than a few in weird *now* dress, long-haired, bearded, unkempt, displaying various symbols of peace and freedom, and cultism of various kinds.

There was considerable drinking, boisterous conversation, a profusion of pseudo-intellectual protest between the *today* people and the squares (in which latter group Steve categorized himself), badgering each other with pro and con opinions on the political, industrial, and professional establishments, civil rights, campus rights, bombing rights, and the right of everyone to do as he damned well pleased. In one corner, a small group had already turned off, and were turning on in a world in which grass was a way of life rather than something with which to beautify lawns and parkways.

Steve found Lex behind the bar with a black artist from his bullpen, both working at supplying the clamor for liquid refreshment. A huge bearded man took over from Lex and sent him from behind the bar to take up his duties as host. Steve got a tall glass of Scotch and ice a d moved back to the large living room. It was an attractive apartment in a modern building on the periphery of the Village, decorated in excellent taste, its walls hung with a profusion of pop art oils and watercolors. At the small piano, a young girl played some Dylan while a hairy guitarist strummed and sang.

More people were coming in, crowding the large room so that the overflow began spreading into the bedroom, the kitchen, and Lex's studio, where another guitarist and sitar player, accompanied by a turbaned Oriental girl on a pair of bongo drums, played and chanted. Another girl, wearing a lavendar sari and nothing else, gyrated sinuously, eyes closed, arms twisting above her head to the strange, complicated rhythm.

Moving back toward the bar, Steve caught a glimpse of Peggy as she arrived, alone, wearing a short-skirted one-piece black dress with a deep plunging V-neck, outlined with tiny pearls. He had never seen her dressed for an evening out, her hair combed up instead of the soft, flowing style she wore at work, and he found himself warming to the sight of her creamy complexion, tomato-reddened lips, and faint trace of eye-shadow.

One of the Leary art directors greeted her, handed her his drink, and lighted a cigarette for her. Lex came up from behind, embraced her, kissed her cheek, and began introducing her to several other newcomers. Steve waited his turn at the crowded bar, watching as Peggy drew away, entered the living room, saw him, and made her way through the crowd toward him.

"Hi," she called above the conversational clamor.

"Hi, yourself. Where's your date?"

"He couldn't make it. Where's yours?"

"She came down with a mild case of bubonic plague."

"Then I guess we're stuck with each other. Okay?"

"My pleasure, princess. You look very elegant."

"Only because I'm a very elegant person away from the office."

"And modest, too."

"Of course. Do you think we've observed enough of the amenities so I can get rid of this awful drink and get some decent Scotch over ice?"

"Your slightest wish, princess."

He managed the drinks and led Peggy away to a far corner of the room where they found two unoccupied pillows and sat on the floor, backs against the wall, following what seemed to be the normal seating custom. Peggy, forced to bend her knees upward in order to pull her short skirt down, found the process of sitting an awkward one. "Is this something like a police drunk tank I've read about?" she asked.

"Except for the booze, the hash, and the pillows, it can't be a lot different, and I speak from a definite lack of personal experience with police drunk tanks."

"What?"

"Forget it, and drink your Scotch." The decibel level had risen considerably and private conversation had become almost impossible. They sipped their drinks and Steve got up for refills. He returned ten minutes later to find a bearded man trying to wrestle Steve's pillow from Peggy's grasp.

"Hold it, brother," Steve said. "That's my girl you're poaching on."

The giant smiled affably. "Sorry. I thought it was a come-on."

Steve handed Peggy her drink. "Take it easy. Transportation is rough and these are triples."

She said somewhat thickly, "If I didn't know you so damned well, Mr. Gilman, I'd think you were trying to get me drunk and . . ."

"And?"

"Reduce me."

"You mean *se*duce you."

"That's what I said."

"You know, Miss Cowles, you're getting to be a pretty fresh broad for a cleancut Nebraska wolverine."

"Husker. In Nebraska, we're cornhuskers."

"Imagine. All that going on behind my back."

"And that's not all."

"Now let's not start getting mystic."

"Well, you ought to look behind you once in a while and catch up to all that goes on behind your back."

Before he could reply, Lex had made his way to the center of the room. Standing on a chair, calling for attention, one hand clutching the arm of the bearded giant who had tried to move in on Peggy earlier, he announced, "Listen! Listen, everybody! Jack Orion is just back from the Coast where he shot this absolutely fantastic picture. Jack's going to run it for us in the first public viewing before he shows it to a group of art house exhibitors. Why don't you all find seats where you can, the rest of you sit on the floor as soon as we get the projector and screen set up."

There was a scrambling for seats and floor space while Orion arranged the projector on one end of the bar and Lex rigged the screen against the opposite wall. There was some minor difficulty in threading the film, and over the buzz and hum of voices, the guests finally managed to get settled down. Lights were turned off and Peggy sat on the floor between Steve's legs, leaning back against him, sipping at her drink.

The film began to roll. It was in color, but the interiors were poorly lighted, the sound scratchy and indistinct, and the photographic quality amateurishly bad and jerky in movement. However, as the first hundred feet rolled, neither sound nor quality seemed to be important. It was another of a spate of pornographic movies that passed for Art, excessively preoccupied with orgasmic exhibitionism from the earliest pictorial frames. The story line—if there was one—was eclipsed by overt action that ran the gamut of teenage experimentation with sex, strongly implied (and often overt) fellatio and cunnilingus, to summer colony girl-swapping, lesbianism, homosexuality, and general perversion. None of the participants was over the age of eighteen.

Steve, in close contact with Peggy, could feel the reaction in certain movements of her body, flexing, tensing, later relaxing, then turning away from a scene of sadistic sexuality between a white girl and a muscular black boy.

As the second reel came to an end and the next was being threaded, Steve said, "Had enough?"

"Yes," she replied quickly.

Hardly anyone noticed as they got up and made their way over seated and supine figures, some in most intimate embrace, others calling for faster action to the rethreading process. They made it to the front door and down the elevator, then walked westward. Steve said, "It's just a little after ten o'clock. You don't want to go home this early, do you?"

"I couldn't if I wanted to. Lois and Nikki are entertaining tonight and I promised not to get home until after midnight."

"Uptown for a drink?"

"That sounds like a good deal."

"How about O'Malley's?"

"I've never been there."

"Time you were introduced."

A cab came along and Steve flagged it down. Inside, heading north, Steve said, "Hairy, wasn't it?"

Peggy laughed. "That's the understatement of the year. If that represents today, here and now, I'm an ancient crone living in the deep, dark past."

"Maybe you're not alone."

"I keep wondering about this heavy, exaggerated emphasis on—on . . ."

"Sex?"

"Not sex *per se*. It's as though it were being discovered for the first time. Hallelujah! Let's bring it out of the bedroom into the open sunlight, worship it on the beaches, in the parks, streets . . ."

"You're not knocking it, are you, Peg?" Steve asked, smiling.

"No, of course not, but I can't understand the need to degrade a natural act by making it so—unnatural."

"Would you be surprised to learn that with thousands of

people it's by no means an easy, natural act, that their hangups and tensions won't allow them to function naturally?"

"I've heard that, too, but I still can't understand why something so personal and private has to be brought out into the open and made public, the sex act itself, I mean."

He wondered then if Peggy knew that Lex Kent was a homosexual, that there were, or had been, at least a dozen or more homosexuals and lesbians present. He assumed she did. In the small, tight world in which they lived, advertising men and women were often more discerning and less critical of each other than in most working societies except, perhaps, the theater. In that atmosphere, the phony, or the mediocre, were soon ferreted out; similarly, the talented were just as quickly discovered and set apart. Steve had long ago learned there were a number of homosexuals and practicing lesbians among the employees in the New York office of Leary alone, probably more than he knew, although there was little that would distinguish these from other Leary personnel. To change the subject, he said, "How do you feel about next Friday?"

"Excited," Peggy said, "and nervous. It's something like waiting for the baby to be born."

"Or the bomb to be dropped. I've got the firm feeling that we're going to hit the greatest female audience in the country with that idea of yours."

"Lennie's, too."

He said then what Lennie had said earlier. "Hell, Peggy, Lennie was only the artist, and I'm not knocking his talent. It was *your* idea, and the idea is what counts."

"I think the other is important, too, how it's presented to the public. If it hadn't been for Lennie, I could never have gotten the idea across to you, could I?"

"That's true, but dozens of artists could have illustrated those ads. The idea came from you, so that's where the credit belongs."

"Anyway, I still think Lennie deserves a share of it."

"Peg, you're confusing your sense of values—hey, what *is* this? You have some kind of hangup about Lennie?"

She was grateful for the darkness that hid the crimson blush she felt on her cheeks. "Of course not, but we did it together and I think he deserves an equal share of the credit, that's all."

"All right, but we can't let him sign the illustrations, so he'll have to be satisfied with another form of reward."

"Money," Peggy said shortly, making it sound as though financial compensation was worth far less than public recognition.

The cab braked in front of O'Malley's and Steve handed the driver a five-dollar bill. "Gonna rain soon," the man observed as he made change.

Peering up at the sky, Steve said, "Doesn't look like it."

"Take my word for it, friend. I got a bum foot, it ain't been wrong in twenty years."

O'Malley's was cheerfully noisy. They found a table, ordered Scotch on the rocks, then a second round, then steak sandwiches and coffee, and topped that off with brandy. Several people stopped by for a moment or two, and lo and behold! there were Fred Eberle and Jack Shepherd at a back table much the worse for wear, still operating with the same two girls. Luckily, Fred and Jack were too absorbed to notice the world around them.

They stayed on until one o'clock, interrupted or momentarily distracted by some of the regulars Steve knew, exchanging introductions, until Peggy said, "My God, this place is as private as Grand Central."

"Ready to leave?"

"If you are."

There were no cabs out in front. They walked north, hoping for a cruising empty to come along. Four blocks later, Steve remembered the cabby's earlier prediction when mist began to fall. Midway between Fifty-sixth and Fifty-seventh streets, brilliant streaks of lightning split the skies, thunder rumbled, and rain began falling in torrents. They ran for the nearest doorway, drenched by the first onslaught, huddling together to ward off the wind-driven spray that followed.

"My God!" Peggy exclaimed. "A cloudburst. We'll be lucky if we don't drown!"

"We will if we don't get the hell out of here."

"If we could rent a boat . . ."

"Let's try to make it to Fifty-seventh. We might be able to pick up something there."

"Pneumonia, maybe?"

"We're wet as trouts now."

"Well, let's try, and pray."

Running, keeping close to the building line, they reached Fifty-seventh Street and found another entranceway that afforded less protection than the first. After a few minutes, Steve sighted a cab heading north along

Third Avenue, and leaped out in front of it, arms waving. As the cab stopped, he signaled Peggy to join him, opened the door for her, and jumped in behind her. "Jesus," the cab driver muttered. "The chances you guys take. Where to?"

"Peggy?"

She gave the address. The driver turned and shook his head. "No dice, lady. I'm off duty in ten minutes an' I'm makin' no trip alla way downtown. If you ain't goin' within five minutes of here, get another cab."

"Where would you suggest we find one?" Steve asked.

"Look, mister; that's your problem. It's tough everywhere. The garage is only eight blocks from here an' I'm on my way home. I had a long day. I'll take you to the subway . . ."

"Can you make it to Seventy-third and Third?"

"Okay."

"Let's go."

Peggy offered no objections and the cab headed north. Steve said, "I hope you don't mind. If we don't get you under cover and dried out . . ."

"I don't mind in the least. My teeth are beginning to chatter."

Inside his apartment, he led Peggy to the bathroom, handing her a warm robe. "Get into this and spread your things out to dry. I'll change and put some coffee on."

In his room, Steve stripped off his outer clothes and underwear, and got into pajamas and a wool robe. He found another pair of pajamas, knocked on the bathroom door, and when Peggy poked her head through the narrow opening she said, "I'm stark naked." He thrust the pajamas at her. In the kitchen he opened a fresh can of B & B and put the pot on, took a drink of straight Scotch, and lit a cigarette.

Peggy came out a few minutes later, swimming in his pajamas and robe, barefooted. "I don't know which is worse, drowning in the rain or in this burnoose. Give me a cigarette, please."

He lit one for her, poured some Scotch over two ice cubes, and said, "Luxuriate in Oriental splendor, princess, while I get the coffee."

"Ah, heaven." Lying on the sofa, she called out, "Hey, I love this."

"What?"

"Your new apartment. My first time here."

"A big improvement over the old one, isn't it?" He brought the coffee, cups, saucers, cream, and sugar on a tray. Sitting up, Peggy said, "She did a nice job for you."

"She?"

"Your Miss Stafford. She did the apartment for you, didn't she?"

"Peggy, are you on a fishing expedition?"

"Of course not. Two or three times, she left messages when you were out. 'Have him call Miss Stafford, his decorator.' "

"Oh. Yes. Miss Stafford, the decorator." He sipped his coffee. "How about your things?"

"Soaked through. They'll take forever to dry."

"We'll see about that in the morning. I think there's a steam iron in the kitchen somewhere."

Peggy put the cup and saucer down, curled her legs up under her, and pushed the sleeves of the robe up over her elbows. "Very cozy," she said, "and very expensive."

"And very late. Suppose you take the bedroom. I'll get some things and make up this sofa."

"I wouldn't think of it. I'll take the sofa. I'm shorter than you."

"Don't be noble or difficult. It's a very comfortable sofa. I've slept on it any number of times."

"Who was in your bed those times?"

"Peggy . . ."

"All right." He started toward her and she said, "That's your office voice. Don't you dare use it on me here."

He bent over, lifted her, carried her into the bedroom and dropped her onto the bed. She bounced and sat up, laughing. "The last time anyone did that to me, I was eight, and my father was angry because I wanted to stay up for the finish of a prize fight on radio."

"Who won?"

"Sugar Ray Robinson. He was my favorite."

Steve got out some sheets, a blanket, and pillow from a shelf in the closet. "If you're a good girl and take the spread off, fold it, and get to sleep, someday I'll introduce you to Sugar Ray."

"You mean it? You know him?"

"I've met him twice. He's my all-time favorite, too."

"Will you, really?"

"Promise. Sleep well."

"You, too. Goodnight, Steve."

"Goodnight."

He went out, closing the door behind him. He spread the single sheet over the sofa, doubled it over, laid the blanket over it, and turned the lights off. Lying there he thought of Karen, longing for her warmth and comfort, again caught up with the complexity of their precarious positions.

And in his bedroom, Peggy—having stripped off the robe and pajamas—lay awake wondering why Steve could not see her as more than a machine programmed to perform the duties of a secretary.

She awoke a little past nine next morning, took her almost-dry clothes from the bathroom into the kitchen, found the steam iron, and worked quietly so as not to disturb Steve. Finished and dressed, she began preparing breakfast; sausage, bacon, biscuits, eggs, and coffee. In the midst of her preparations, Steve came in, eyes squinting sleepily. "You bucking for a raise or something?" he said.

"Or something," Peggy smiled brightly, "and you've got no more than five minutes to brush your teeth and get to the table before I put the eggs on. And don't use the blue toothbrush. I did. You may want to sterilize it or throw it away."

He yawned. "You got any special diseases I might catch?"

"Leprosy, but only in the early stages."

"That all? You had me worried for a moment."

He came back after a quick wash, hair still damp. The table was set, the food ready, and they fell to like a pair of lumberjacks. "Do all Nebraska girls learn to cook like this?" he asked.

"All Nebraska girls who had mothers like mine. In our household the males worked to support the females, who cooked, sewed, laundered, and kept house in return."

"Fair enough."

"Not fair at all. Until I went to Lincoln to college, I didn't know what peonage meant. And until I came to New York and went to work, I never understood the meaning of personal freedom."

"And that's important to you?"

"Isn't it to you?"

"Well . . ."

"Of course it is, except for women, no? The old, rapidly disappearing double standard. Man invented it, lived by it, and saddled his women with it. You'll miss it, won't you?"

"Don't be so damned feminist. You've got more free-

dom today than your mother ever imagined was possible."
"But not on an equal basis."
"Okay, the change is in progress and it will come. Just don't bend too far backward and try to burn it down. It's the only world we have."
"If men were as understanding as they'd like the world to believe, they'd help women achieve full freedom."
"Peggy, I don't know what you've been reading lately, but I didn't ask you to cook breakfast for us. I'm capable of doing that for myself. Even for you. And to prove it, I'll do the dishes."
"Big concession."
But Peggy insisted on doing the dishes while Steve showered, shaved, and dressed. The rain had stoppped falling earlier, but the skies were ominously gray, and the streets still wet. "You have any special plans for today, Peggy?"
"None at all."
"I've got some shopping to do."
"I'm good at that."
"I remember that last time. And while we're out, I'll put you in a cab and send you home."
"Like a discarded mistress?"
"You make a lot of big talk for a little girl."
"I'm not a little girl. I'm twenty-six years old, I have a good job, and I talk like what I am. A woman."
"And getting to be a dangerous one. Get your purse. We're leaving."
But as they left, she became suddenly conscious of the fact that she was hardly dressed for grocery shopping, and did not protest when Steve put her in a cab, paid the driver, and sent her on her way, wondering why her job in a glamorous advertising agency wasn't as glamorous as she had come to believe.

Karen phoned at six o'clock. She had persuaded Herschel to have Dr. Lindstrom look in, but he refused to go to the hospital for observation. Lindstrom had given him a shot to relieve the pain in his chest and left some pills. Herschel was asleep, but she intended to remain in Wyecliffe until Monday.

In her West End apartment, Tony said, "Mark, are you going to buy the campaign next Friday?"
Lying in bed, watching Tony as she stroked her luxuri-

ant hair with a brush, Mark said, "I don't know yet. I may, or I may not."

"If you don't, what happens to the commercials I've been making?"

"They go out with the campaign and you'll make some new ones. Either way, you're in."

"And what happens if Karen finds out about us?"

Mark laughed. "We've been through this before. I've told you, she couldn't care less. She has her own thing going, all her very own."

"And that doesn't bother you?"

"Why the hell should it? She wrote the rules."

"And that's all right with you?"

"Why not?"

Tony shrugged and Mark said, "Tony, I believe in live and let live. I married Karen because she wanted the protection of a name, not a husband. Her thing is her own, so what the hell. She lives her life, I live mine."

"You sound so sure of yourself."

"What's so hard for you to understand?"

"Because it's the queerest thing I've ever heard. Spooky."

"Don't let it throw you, baby. I get what I want, she gets what she wants. What's so spooky about that?"

Another shrug. "All right, if that's the way you want it."

"That's exactly the way I want it. Now put the damned brush down and come here."

Chapter 12

1

Since Friday night when he had refused Peggy's invitation to take her to Lex's party, it appeared to Lennie that she had been avoiding him. Despite the additional workload thrust upon the B & B group, Lennie began to feel old aggressions of persecution returning, mounting inside him. He still felt put upon by Norm's division of the new jingle illustrations between Chris and Barry, only partially accepting Norm's explanation of the need to speed up the operation, reasoning that Lennie's work on storyboards was more important than conformity in the jingle art technique.

But by Lennie's reasoning, the jingles were his by prior right and he wanted to complete the units himself. His resentment increased when Adrian gave Barry another assignment he felt should be his—to work up a full page layout showing an aggregation of winning jingles with head-and-shoulders photographs of the two hundred fifty dollar winners—which would run after the winning entries had been selected.

Coldly furious, he had vented his silent rage on Johns, Thaw, Chris, and Barry during the days that followed. He had rebuffed Peggy's attempts to assuage his injured feelings and restore peace; and now, alone and brooding, he wanted—needed—very much to be alone with her, to accept her reassurances, and narrow the gap that had widened between them. If they could have dinner together, return to his apartment and just talk, perhaps. . . . One more chance, please.

Since meeting Peggy, having fallen into some curious, exciting association with her, he had changed in many ways he could not himself explain. Or even understand. At first, she represented the unattainable, but that had been no real sweat then, because so many things in his life that had had special meaning for him had been unattainable. Until now.

There had been a few white girls in his college years in California, but they were the kind of pigs anybody could ball; ragbags who thought they were solving the white-black problem by zonking out on grass and screwing a black boy now and then. Kicky. Groovy. Let me prove to the world that I'm a true liberal in the most liberal sense. But that kind of shit didn't mean a goddamned thing to him, no more than getting off his charge into the broad to let her ease her white-black guilt; and maybe because it was their way of saying, "Fuck you," to their materialistic parents who supplied the cash-in-pocket, cars, credit cards, food, booze, and grass. Down the Establishment and Up Yours!

But Peggy represented a hell of a lot more than those beaded, stringy haired, skinny, fat, hard, soft, pseudo-intellectual, and stupid cats who preached violent revolution and wanted to remake the world, but couldn't come up with anything but destruction as the way out of their own dilemma. In Peggy, he saw a certain quiet stability, and understanding of himself as a talented artist. In her, he had found a totality of reassurance he had never known before. Perhaps it was her Nebraska background in which there had never been blacks and which therefore provided no festering white-black question to bring from childhood into maturity.

She respected him as an artist and a human being, for his ability; and as a result, had become more than a reasonable influence upon him, a positive deterrent to the violent tempest of hate that had once surged through his veins. Social acceptance by one—*the* one—had become the breath that sustained him. He had, in recent months, forsaken old haunts, and militant companions with whom he had drunk, discussed, argued, debated, and whose ideas of revolution he had finally come to accept. No more. No way. Unconsciously, almost everything he did now—the clothes he wore, even the food he ate—was done with the thought that Peggy Cowles would approve.

When she asked him to go to Lex's party with her, he was disappointed that his own plans to spend the evening alone with her at his place were doomed. He could see she wanted very much to go to the party, but even his refusal was, in a sense, for her own protection. Apart from Lex, whose attitude toward him had always been passive and cool, there would be other Leary people present. Coming in with Peggy could start the rumor mill going among those fucking long-tongued tattlers at the agency and might possibly result in a sign-off between them. Peggy hadn't realized that he was being protective of her and they had parted with considerably less than normal cordiality.

All right. So she'd stayed in her office, not walking through the group area as she usually did, punishing him; and he had made no effort to impose himself upon her. Monday, Tuesday, and Wednesday passed without a single exchange of words between them. He had seen her twice, both times with Steve, smiling, and laughing. Everything he wanted was wrapped up in that five-foot, five-inch body, so easy for Whitey Gilman, so unreachable for Lennie Hawkins.

On Thursday, he waited outside the Hungerford Trust Building until he saw her emerge on Fifty-second Street, walk to the corner of Lexington, and turn left toward Fifty-third Street and the subway station. He followed at a safe distance, saw her disappear into the cavern below and onto the crowded platform, then got into the car behind hers. At their destination, they left the cars, and he caught up with her as they came up the steps into daylight.

"Hi," he called from behind her.

"Hello, Lennie," she replied without any particular warmth.

"You still sore at me for last Friday?"

"I'm not sore at you for last Friday, or anything else."

"You sure been scarce for the past four days."

"I've been very busy typing schedules, letters, reports to Mr. Leary and Mr. Allard, a ton of memos to Traffic Control . . ."

"Look, Peggy, I'm sorry about Lex's party."

"There's no need to be. I had a marvelous time."

"How about some dinner together? I'd like to . . ."

"I'm sorry. I'm busy tonight."

"Just tonight, or just busy?"

"Lennie, you're still being childish. I'm busy, and if you want to read something more into that simple statement, I can't help it."

"If you're not sore about me putting you down, it's got to be something else. Or somebody else. What's happened, Peggy?"

She was annoyed by his insistence and it showed in her tone. "For one thing, you've been acting like a spoiled child about your work. I don't think you know the meaning of team effort, but that's something else again. The other thing, which you won't accept, is that with a big new presentation coming up tomorrow morning at which I've got to take notes, I've been busy with a thousand details, and I'm simply busy tonight."

"So why don't I cut out, split, and leave you alone. Is that what you're saying?"

"Lennie, don't push me. I don't like it when you take your aggressions out on me the way you've been doing on the whole group all week long."

"Okay, Whitey," he spat out angrily, "forget it. Just forget the whole thing." He swung away from her, eyes flashing brightly with anger. Increasing his stride, he reached the corner, and turned off into a side street, walking swiftly until he reached the heart of the crowded Village, coming alive now.

With flower children, curious tourists, hard faces, innocent faces, stoned faces. Black, brown, white, and yellow faces. The honkytonk carnival of the city. Pizza parlors, malodorous eating places, book and art shops. Long hair, beards, headbands, tinkling beads, belled belts, and sandals, and cult signs. Littered pavements, filthy pot-holed streets, the debris of life not yet camouflaged by the protective coloration of night and its artificial illuminations. McLuhanland—Warholville—with modern wandering minstrels and weirdos emerging from daylight retreats to gather and become part of the night action that lay ahead. The scene. Winos, moochers, strange animals making their way through the forest to favorite watering holes.

In front of Traynor's Bar, Big Tom X, Gypsie Augie, Rajah Smith, and Fat Joe X lounged against the rough brick wall near a doorway, adjacent to another that led to second-floor rooms. All were dressed in their usual castoff crazy-quilt garments, turbans, and berets. Big Tom X smiled at Lennie insolently and called out, "Hey, brother, how's for springin' for a brew?"

"Bug off," Lennie snarled.

Gypsie Augie, a brass loop dangling from the lobe of his left ear, cackled, "You heard the man, brothers, bug off. He got no time fo' us now he's makin' it with that white piece of ass he been ballin'."

Rajah Smith, turbaned in purple and lavender, a wide belt of the same material around his waist, closed in.

"Shit, man, he ain't ballin' that white chick. He goin' down on her, ain't you, brother?"

"Listen, you bastards," Lennie ground out between gritted teeth, "I got no fuckups for brothers. I'm not asking for trouble from nobody, but if you want it, just start something. Here. Right now." And to Fat Joe X, "You, too, you lousy fag."

Fat Joe X, weighing over two hundred pounds, chest-high to Lennie, completed the circle around him, as they moved toward the wall, forcing Lennie to move with them, their voices low, incisive, hate-filled, toying with him. People passing by, coming from two directions, were oblivious to the five blacks who huddled between the two doorways, concerned only with their own conversations and destinations.

"L-l-listen, m-m-man," Fat Joe stuttered, "y-y-you got no c-c-call t-t-talkin' 'at way to me an' th' b-b-brothers."

"Brother, shit!" Augie exclaimed. "This ain't no brother, Fat Joe. He just another establishment nigger, takin' Whitey's bread, suckin' up to his white tail, what kinda brother is 'at?"

Rajah said, "An' what kinda brother turns one of his own over to the pigs? Lester Goodby doin' one-to-five 'cause this brother rapped on him."

Lennie braced himself, uptight, sweat beads rolling down his face and neck, turning his shirt black. Muscles in his legs and arms tightened, telling him he was in trouble. They were facing him, and behind him. No Vietnam now, only the jungle of the city. But in his present mood, there seemed to be no difference. "Lester Goodby tried to mug me and got what he had coming to him . . ."

They weren't listening. Big Tom said, "Say somethin' nice, brother. Like, 'You cats need some bread, sure, he'p yo'selfs.' Then we part the sea fo' you an' you free from Pharaohland, go do your own thing. How about that?"

"I told you crumbs to bug off," Lennie said in a brittle voice. "I work for my bread and I'll do what the hell ever I want with it. You put a hand on me, somebody dies. Which one of you shitheads wants to be the one?"

"I do," Big Tom said with a lightning thrust of a hamlike fist that he sunk into Lennie's gut, doubling him over. "Inside, quick!"

Big Tom, Fat Joe, Rajah, and Gypsie Augie surrounded Lennie in a flash and drag-carried him into the vestibule and up the stairs to a squalid room, the door slammed shut and bolted in seconds. Augie pulled a cord and a bare bulb came on, yellowing the room. Fat Joe and Rajah held him by the arms, and on signal from Big Tom, threw him down on one of the four bare mattresses that littered the floor. Lennie started up, but a kick from Rajah's booted foot caught him alongside the neck and he went down again.

"Let's see what this white nigger got on him," Big Tom ordered.

Augie and Fat Joe kneeled over Lennie and emptied his pockets. Sixty-two dollars in cash, keys, cigarettes, lighter, loose change, knife, two mechanical pencils, ballpoint pen, checkbook, pocket sketchbook. Big Tom scooped up the cash, counted, and pocketed it. "Take 'em clo'es off'n him. Ought to bring in some bread fo' our poverty program."

As Fat Joe kneeled again, Lennie rolled over and sprang to his feet. He rammed a knee viciously into Fat Joe's stomach, smashed a fist into Augie's face, and backed off, ready to spring at Rajah who was coming for him. Rajah's knees bent, surging in slowly, twisting from side to side to evade fist or foot. "Come on, you bastard," Lennie snarled, "come on. You want these clothes, come and take 'em off me."

Augie joined Rajah, and they came at Lennie from two sides. Then Big Tom inched in, hands spread wide to grab hold of him. Slowly, they moved in until Lennie's back was against the far wall.

"G-g-git 'at m-m-mother-fucker," Fat Joe gasped. "G-g-git 'im!"

They lunged forward together. Big Tom caught a hard right on the chin that staggered him momentarily, but before Lennie could recover his balance, Augie and Rajah were upon him, arms encircling him, legs spread and back to avoid his flailing feet, their combined weight dragging him to the floor. Big Tom threw himself into the thrashing bodies and hit Lennie again and again, crushing blows on his body and face. Big Tom's mouth dripped blood on Lennie and Lennie's own blood began to choke him. Then, finding an opening, Fat Joe literally hurled himself upon Lennie's chest, crushing him into submission.

They stripped him naked, and Lennie, lying on the bare floor, stared up with glazed, half-conscious eyes at the swaying bare bulb hanging from the ceiling. The four brothers divided the money and distributed the other loot among themselves. Big Tom sent Gypsy Augie out with

Lennie's suit to peddle, taking Lennie's shoes because his were the only feet they would fit.

"Wh-wh-what we gone d-d-do with him?" Fat Joe asked.

"What'd you like to do with him?" Big Tom asked, winking lewdly at Rajah. "Or to him?"

"N-n-no use w-w-wastin' th' m-m-man, is they?" Fat Joe asked.

"No use in the world," Big Tom agreed. "Tha's the trouble in this fucked-up society today, waste. You think you c'n handle him, Fat Joe?"

"Sh-sh-shure, m-m-man. He c-c-can't hurt me none."

"Okay. Raj an' me, we'll wait fo' you downstairs." He went to the wall where an assortment of odd, filthy garments hung on nails, took a pair of denim pants and a shirt from a nail and threw them at Lennie where he lay. "That'll git him home. You finish your thing, Fat Joe. Jus' don't take too long."

They went out and Fat Joe removed his clothes and went to where Lennie lay helpless on the floor, one eye closed by massive swelling, the other a mere slit. Lennie saw Fat Joe's ponderous bulk looming over him, fondling his tumescent growth in one hand, sweat gleaming on his hairless body, expectancy written on his moon face.

"Fat Joe," Lennie whispered, "don't do it."

"B-b-boy, I'n goin' d-d-do nothin' else."

"I'll kill you, you fag sonofabitch. So help me Christ, I'll cut you down an inch at a time."

"Sh-sh-shit, man. I'll k-k-kill you first. Y-y-you can't even g-g-go to th' pigs. They l-l-laugh at you."

"Fat Joe . . ."

"Roll over, man."

"Fat Joe . . ."

"I'll he'p y-y-you." With one arm, Fat Joe rolled Lennie over on his belly and Lennie screamed with pain. "W-w-won't do you n-n-no good, b-b-boy."

Lennie wept and cursed as he felt the obscene flesh of Fat Joe upon his naked buttocks, heard the joyful sibilant hiss of satisfaction as Fat Joe lowered himself, felt the crushing weight of the man and the searing pain in his chest and ribs and prayed for unconsciousness that refused to come.

2

On Friday morning, Chuck, Frank, and Reed were first to arrive at GFP to unpack and arrange the presentation material. Easels were placed beside the podium so that the flip charts would be within easy sight of Bill Leary as he addressed the assembled group. Reed Baker would remain to turn the pages for him on cue. The projector and screen were set up, sound was tested, leatherette folders, yellow legal pads, white memo pads, a red and black ballpoint pen, water goblet, and ashtray were placed at each seat around the conference table, with water carafes between each two seats.

At ten o'clock the principals of the firm began to drift in with their agency counterparts. Curtis Fitzjohn and Elias Gordon the company treasurer, led the way, followed by Keith Allard, Arthur Thalberg, and Frank Castle. Then Hardwick, Killian, Cardell, and Benziger, with Elisabeth Berton and Bob Davies. Next came the two brand managers, Tyson and Jewell, with Harry French, the GFP corporation secretary. Then Steve Gilman, Mark Lawson, Bill Leary, and Peggy Cowles.

There were twenty chairs around the oval table and the men and Liz Berton found their places by checking name cards, then began arranging their own notes, examining the contents of their folders, lighting cigarettes, and pouring water. There were two small desks for the secretaries and Peggy put her purse on the floor beside one and set out her steno notebooks and pencils. A tall, angular woman came in, smiled briefly at Peggy, and took her place at the second desk, then went to a table next to the podium to check out the tape recorder.

Mark's attitude was one of indifferent coolness during these preliminaries. There had been no time for a premeeting conversation with Steve, and his greeting to Leary and Allard had been glacial, no more than a brief nod, and a flinty smile for Steve, who now went to the three easels and checked the covered ads, to make sure they were in proper order. Bill Leary shuffled through a sheaf of 3 x 5-inch cards that duplicated the copy on the larger flip-chart sheets. The conversation that hummed between the GFP people and Leary personnel was light and cordial, much like the beginning of a luncheon or cocktail party.

Almost all had met before under varying circumstances and were reacquainting themselves before the more serious part of the business started.

At ten-fifteen the double doors parted and Herschel Goodwin entered, with Russell Charles and one of his associates, Austin Delevie, along with Lee Rogers, the GFP "in house" attorney. Smiling, Herschel looked gaunt, almost skeletal, no doubt the after-effects of his recent illness. He spoke a few words to Bill and Keith, who shook hands with the two attorneys, then went to his chair between Mark and Mr. Fitzjohn.

Herschel Goodwin opened the meeting by introducing Charles and Delevie as "the two gentlemen who handled the negotiations between ourselves and the Bonds and are here at my invitation to sit in on the first action we will be taking to launch our new product.

"I think everybody here knows everybody else now, so I will turn the meeting over to Mr. Leary."

Bill stood up and described briefly how the presentation they were about to see had been put together: the basic research of the product itself, the innumerable conferences between agency and GFP personnel, between Leary and B & B people in California, the outside expertise employed to give counsel in marketing, media and merchandising problems, the intense, all-out effort of the agency's creative staff to produce an effective, appealing campaign that would be acceptable to the buying public.

From there he went to the podium, and Baker began uncovering a series of demographic charts dealing with territorial breakdowns, share of market percentages, population densities, marketing outlets, and other statistical data, while Bill explained each chart, speaking into a microphone for the benefit of all present as well as for the tape recorder.

Next, he briefly discussed certain advertising theories and philosophies before signaling Baker to uncover the introductory announcement ads, which had been blown up photostatically to twice the size of full newspaper and magazine pages. When these were accepted with favorable comments from the GFP audience, Bill went into the followup ads, also oversized to lend more dramatic effect. Baker then unveiled the ads that had been placed on the wall, normal newspaper full-page size, the magazine ads in full color.

"I would like everyone present to see these close up,"

Bill said, "and read the copy as though you were seeing it in your favorite newspaper or magazine. Then I shall discuss the strategy that led to this approach."

Mark was the first one on his feet and Steve followed him, watching Mark as he inspected each ad, and glanced over the headlines, illustrations, and copy. There was no reaction he could define on Mark's face, which did not change its phlegmatic expression. The others, Peggy noted in her book, not only expressed approval by facial expression and voice, but were delighted with the jingles, reading the rhymes aloud.

When they returned to their seats, Keith and Steve exchanged brief smiles of satisfaction, but Steve's private opinion was one of reservation. No matter if the campaign were accepted, he would still have to face Mark when the others were gone—unless Mark decided to voice his objections here and now.

As Bill returned to the podium and began discussing strategy, Mark was scribbling notes on his yellow pad. He wrote another on the smaller white pad and passed it to Steve. It read:

"See me when we're through here."

"So," Bill was saying, "we not only have an appealing approach to our readers and viewers, which we will project for you shortly, but an interesting way to involve those retailers and distributors who at present do not handle the GFP lines. We feel that outside pressure—however subtle—from our public audience seeking the free blanks on which they must submit their jingles, will give us entry into areas in which these products have not heretofore enjoyed shelf space.

"Also, there is the positive indication that thousands of homes outside the present marketing area of B & B Coffee will now, at no cost to themselves, be sampling Goody's B & B Coffee in an amount sufficient to break previous coffee-drinking habits."

Ward Hardwick's head was nodding approval, Steve noted, along with smiles from Cardell, Benziger, Killian, Tyson, and Jewell. Mark remained impassive, Herschel Goodwin relaxed and at ease, Charles and Delevie were visibly impressed by the proceedings.

On signal, Baker moved to the projector. Peggy went to the light switch panel and threw the room into semidarkness. A brilliant beam of light shot across the length of the room to the screen built into the wall, and the film began to roll.

Margo Anthony's photogenic face and smile captivated the audience. Under Colin Ferris's direction, she moved gracefully about the kitchen setting, introducing the product she had discovered by participating in the jingle contest, becoming converted to its flavorful taste and richness. When it was brewed, she served it to her "husband" at breakfast, and sent him happily on his way to work before settling down to her second cup.

There were six such commercials, interspersed with others that pointed up the contest, with two hundred and fifty dollars offered for each jingle published, plus the offer of free coffee for each entry submitted. When they came to an end and the lights came on, Baker and Hayden had brought in the replicas of billboard and point-of-purchase material to make the presentation complete.

"On the subject of Marketing . . ." This was the signal for Thalberg to take over for the next fifteen minutes. He was followed by Castle, who gave a scholarly discourse on Merchandising, then Liz Berton outlined Me[illegible] plans, which all could follow in their individual folders. Bill closed the presentation with a few brief remarks.

It had been a well-planned, erudite performance, and when Bill finally thanked his audience for their attention, he was applauded by the GFP personnel. Herschel stood up and asked, "Are there any comments before Mr. Leary and his people leave?"

Ward Hardwick said, "I think this has been one of the finest presentations I have ever witnessed and I would like to compliment everyone who played a part in it."

"Thank you, Ward," Herschel said with a smile. "We will count your vote later in executive session, eh? But I think you have expressed our general sentiments for the time and effort given to prepare this excellent presentation. Now if Mr. Leary will excuse us, we will have our own discussion and give him our findings when we reach a decision."

Bill and the Leary people rose, thanked their hosts, and filed out, leaving Baker and Hayden to gather up the material to bring back to the agency. When the others reached the street, seeking cabs to take them back to the Hungerford Trust Building, Bill, Keith, and Steve walked slowly toward Vanderbilt Avenue. Keith said, "We're in, Bill. That was a marvelous selling job."

Bill said, "I think it went well. Mark looked sour all the way through it, but Hardwick and the others will vote favorably. Steve, it looks like we'll have to leave Mark to you."

Steve held up a folded slip of paper. "Mark wants me to call him around four o'clock. If they've arrived at a decision, he wants to see me in his office."

"Well—you do that, Steve. If it's as solid as I think, he can't reverse the majority decision."

"What about lunch?" Keith asked.

"Sorry," Bill said. "I've got to see my broker before the market closes. It's been playing nine kinds of hell with me. I'll see you at the office when I'm finished there."

In the cab they caught at Grand Central, Keith said, "Are you anticipating any trouble with Mark?"

Steve shrugged. "Depends on what happens in the executive session. I'm sure we've got the votes in our favor, but Mark is something else again. If he's a holdout, Davies will throw in with him, and all I foresee is a rough time for a while."

"Well, you've been through a couple of those with him before. To give you the strength to face your ordeal, I'm going to throw at least two drinks and a hearty lunch into you. Cheers."

Promptly at four, Steve phoned Mark. "How did it go, Mark?" he asked.

"Get down here right away," Mark replied curtly and hung up.

Forewarned but unarmed, Steve braced himself for a sullen, angry tirade born of defeat and disappointment. Instead, Mark welcomed him with a smile. The blue leatherette folder outlining the entire program lay open on the desk, a yellow pad filled with notations and doodles beside it. Steve sat in the visitor's chair and wondered which role Mark had decided to play out for him.

Mark picked up his phone and said, "Hold all my calls until I ring you back, Charlotte." He leaned back in his chair, still smiling, but there was little warmth behind it, nor in his eyes. "You and your boys really sandbagged me, didn't you?" he said.

"No one sandbagged anyone, Mark. This whole thing was treated the way any new account coming into the agency would and should be handled. The trouble is that the client never knows how much effort really goes into the comparatively small amount of work he sees at the formal presentation: the research, copy, and art conferences . . ."

Mark was flagging him down with a waving hand. "Spare me the hearts and flowers, friend. For what you people do, you're paid damned well. What I want to know is, why did you switch my premium idea to an outright giveaway with this goddamned childish jingle contest? Jingles, for Christ's sake!"

"Mark, the premium idea was given full discussion and consideration, but it was ruled out as being nothing more than a 'Me, too' thing that isn't exciting, stimulating, or different."

"And jingles are exciting, stimulating, and different?"

"Ordinarily, no, except in how we are presenting this to the public, with cash and merchandising prizes and the strong effect of full-page ads, and TV and radio promotion to stimulate action and participation."

"So much for opposing opinions," Mark said. "Okay, I think you've guessed by now that I was outvoted by the others, but I still think the whole idea stinks. What's more, I don't like this borax type of ad. We're not selling discount furniture."

"Mark, I agree that these first introductory ads are heavy, but they're clean, neat attention-grabbers. Once we're past the contest phase, we'll be back into our normal program until B & B has been fully absorbed into the regular line. Bill spelled that out fully and made it perfectly clear at the presentation."

"All right," Mark said in a slightly subdued voice, "let's put this aside for the moment." The tinge of menace evaporated and caught Steve off guard, wondering what would be coming next. Mark was staring at him quizzically, like a child making up its mind whether to pull the wings off a fly it had trapped. Even more disconcerting was the indefinable smirk playing at the corners of his mouth.

"You and I go back a long way, Steve, longer than any account man I've dealt with. Joe Childs, Wally Norris, Cliff Sorensen, Jack Henderson, Andy Makyrios, Jim Whipple, everybody except Leary, Allard, and Barrett. I once told you that if you played with my side . . ."

"I remember very well, Mark," Steve interrupted.

". . . you'd come out on top. Until this morning I was pretty happy with you. Right now, you feel like a winner, putting me down by calling the old man, Fitzjohn, Hardwick, and everybody except the janitor in to back you up. Just remember this, though, if you blow this campaign, or the next, or the one after that, you could be out—through —. Or I could step that up by calling Leary and tell him I can't get along with you—a personality conflict—to assign a new man to the account. I've done it before, and I've still got enough muscle to do it again."

"All right, Mark, I get the message and the threat. What comes next? The call to Leary, or do you want me to carry the message to him for you?"

"You're still a cocky bastard, aren't you? You think you're home safe because you bird-dogged the B & B item, don't you? Well, if it comes to a showdown between you and me . . ."

"Mark," Steve said suddenly, "I'm not looking for showdowns and I don't think you want one, either. I think you've got your own reasons for riding me and we could save a lot of time if you'd get down to specific cases. For one thing, I'm not anxious to hurt or lose the GFP account. For another, I've got enough of a track record to take to any one of a number of top agencies. I'm doing my job, and damned well, but I'm not paid to take insults or your harassment. Pick up your phone right now and call Bill or Keith if you want someone else to contact you, but I've taken all the abuse I'm going to take for one day."

Mark smiled again, but his eyes were steely and cold. "I can do that anytime I want, you know?"

"I'll make a special effort to remember that."

"You do that . . ." Mark broke off suddenly and began to laugh. "Okay, he said, "I guess we've both had enough for today. Why don't you just shove off?"

It was 5:20 when Steve returned to his office, anger searing his brain like all the furies of hell. It was Friday, and with the success of the campaign assured, the groups had taken off to enjoy the weekend much earlier. On his desk were several telephone messages, spaced out and weighted down by Peggy so he would not miss them. The first two were from Bill and Keith. He dialed Bill first, but Lucy Kimbrough told him he was three minutes too late, that Donna had called for Bill and they were on their way to Old Lyme for the weekend. He dialed Keith, who was waiting.

"You sound beat," Keith said.

"I am. Mark worked me over and put me through his wringer. Shall I come up?"

"No. I'll pick you up on my way out. Louise wants you for dinner."

"I could very well turn out to be lousy company tonight."

"All the more reason for coming home with me."

"Let me make one call before I decide."

"Okay. Ten minutes?"

Steve dialed Karen's number and was told by Max that Mrs. Lawson had driven back to Wyecliffe with Mr. Goodwin. Steve then phoned the desk of his apartment house and was told that a Miss Stafford had left word she had been called out of town for the weekend. When Keith came by moments later, he was ready.

Louise had the martinis chilling and after a second round, shut off the supply, and bustled them in to dinner. She made no effort to discourage the business talk between them, and after coffee, disappeared to give them privacy. "You're not really worried about blowing the account, are you, Steve?" Keith asked.

"The account, no. I'm more sure of this campaign than I've been about most that I've worked on. Norm, Bill, and you went for it. The client bought it. What I'm worried about is Mark's hurt feelings, he's like an actor who got a third-rate role instead of the lead."

"So if we show results, and sales, which will be more than enough to please the powers that be, what can he do?"

Steve had decided from the outset to skip the more pertinent details of his confrontation with Mark, which could only lead to a lengthening of the problem and perhaps some move, or strategy, that might further deteriorate their relationship, already hanging by a thread. "I don't know, Keith, but Mark is a vicious, vindictive sonofabitch and it doesn't do to underestimate him."

Keith laughed. "One of the reasons we've survived with GFP is because we not only do not underestimate Mark, but we anticipate him. And we'll do it again, Steve."

"I hope we can. I'd hate like hell to have him become the reason for me blowing my first major opportunity."

"No more than we can afford to lose the account."

How long, Steve wondered, could he keep up his juggling act? As long as he continued to perform within the area of his responsibility, as long as the results could be measured in sales, he would not only have the backing of the agency but, he felt sure, of Herschel Goodwin, Fitzjohn, and Hardwick.

But what would happen if it became known that he was involved with Karen?

Alone in his apartment later, sleep evaded him. He tossed restlessly in bed for an hour, got up and fixed a stiff Scotch, turned on the television to an ancient movie, turned it off again, chain-smoked, and had another drink. Without relief from his thoughts.

What meaning was there to his life? Growing up in Lancaster, and during his first two years at Columbia, he had leaned heavily on the wisdom of Grady Gilman, always so ready with an answer to every problem; at least, he had given Steve a sounding board to work out his own solutions; but those words of wisdom had done little for Grady's own life or happiness. With maturity, they had become trite, insipid platitudes, uttered by a man too weak to live his personal life by his own utterances, no matter how much comfort they had brought to others.

Life should be more than a sentence imposed by the past, yet man's own weaknesses and fears led him down dark, unknown paths to self-destruction. Larry Price. Wade Barrett. And now, Steve Gilman?

He had read that man's personal conflict comes from his refusal to face the truth of his own being. What *was* his own being? How does one separate a strong psychological block from one's everyday life in order to examine what and who one is?

He poured another drink, finding only questions and no answers. By the time he felt drowsy enough to fall asleep, he was too tired, weary, or drunk to make it to the bedroom again. He spent the rest of the night on the sofa.

3

The phone woke him at ten the next morning and it was moments before he was able to recognize the voice, garbled, and verging on hysteria. "Peggy? Is that you, Peg? What is it? What's wrong?"

"Oh, Steve, Steve, it's terrible, my God, so awful . . ."

"Peggy, for God's sake, get hold of yourself!" He sat up, swung his feet around to the floor, and heard her say, —"just took him away"—

"Who? Took who away?"

"Lennie!" The name came across the line in a shriek. "Oh, Steve, they—oh, wait—wait . . ." Her voice trailed off in a sob and someone else said, "Steve?"

"Yes. Who . . ."

"Eth Loomis, Steve. Peggy's all upset. The police are here and the ambulance just took Lennie's body to the morgue . . ."

"Lennie? Morgue? Eth, what the hell are you talking about?"

"He committed suicide, Steve. Left a note and shot himself with the .45 he brought back from Vietnam."

"My God, Eth! Why—why?"

Eth's voice was the calm in the center of the storm. "Don't make sense to me, Steve. He was pretty badly beaten up. The police took the note, but it looks like suicide. Something about not being able to live with—with his—violated body—in a world he can't adjust to."

"Jesus, Eth, I don't know what—who found him?"

"I did. I'm talking from his place now. He didn't show up for work yesterday, and Norm called me to ask if I knew why. I tried to get him on the phone, but no answer. It kind of bothered me, but I didn't get a chance to go down there. Tried to reach him all of last night, but he still didn't answer. Oh, Lord. This morning, it still nagged me, so I came on down. I had to bust the door in, and there he was. I called the police to send an ambulance, and while they were here looking things over, Peggy came in. They're all gone now, but I don't know what to do about Peggy, she's so tore up about it."

"What about you?"

"I called my wife and told her about it. I'm about to leave here now."

"Could you drop Peggy off here on your way up, Eth?"

"Let me ask her. Hold on." He came back a minute later. "Okay, Steve. She don't want to go back to her place right now."

"Thanks, Eth."

Steve showered, shaved, and dressed quickly, put a pot of coffee on, rummaged through the medicine cabinet for something with which to sedate Peggy, and came up with the plastic container of Nembutal capsules Dr. Lindstrom had given him before he left Wyecliffe Memorial. He fixed a light breakfast and had just finished when Eth and a visibly shaken, but more coherent Peggy arrived. Steve gave them coffee, and Eth, moist-eyed and sad, talked about Lennie.

"You know, I really didn't know him well. His mother was my sister, younger than me. She ran away from home with a man when she was no more'n fifteen or sixteen. He took her to California and we didn't hear from her until Lennie was born, and she was living with another man who married her. She ran out on this Hawkins fellow, who raised Lennie, put him through school, then college. He died while Lennie was in Vietnam. The first time I ever laid eyes on him was after he got back, finished college on the G.I. Bill, and then came East. That's when I asked you about a job for him. He was getting along fine, too, and now, this. We'll bury him, poor boy, soon's the medical examiner is through with him."

Peggy, crying into a handkerchief, said, "He left a note to his Uncle Eth. In it, he—he . . ."

"Well," Eth said, "he left a savings account book with the note. Nine hundred dollars in it. After expenses are paid, he wants Peggy to have what's left . . ."

"I don't want it! I don't want it!" Peggy cried.

". . . and any or all the drawings and books, and anything else she wants."

"What did the police say?"

"Well, they got some suspicions. He was beat up real bad, around the face, body all bruised. The ambulance doctors thinks some ribs were broken. It's not clear whatall happened. Detectives came by to go over the place before we left. They'll be asking questions later."

Eth was anxious to leave, now that Steve had no more questions to put to him. He saw Eth to the door, poured more hot coffee for Peggy, and let her sit quietly for a while, then gave her two of the capsules and, twenty minutes later, she stretched out and fell asleep on the sofa. Steve carried her into the bedroom, placed her on the bed, and closed the door, then cleared the table, rinsed the dishes, and looked in on Peggy. She was fast asleep, muttering under her breath. He made up his usual Saturday shopping list and went out, returning an hour later to find Peggy had kicked the light cover off and lay curled up on one side, head resting on one arm. He drew the summer blanket up over her upper body and set the air-conditioning controls on LOW.

In his study, Steve re-examined the data he had brought home the day before, checking the timing of the campaign and its length of run before the contest would be over, and the normal ad program would begin. By that time, he hoped, the results would more than vindicate the agency's chosen approach and kill off any further attempt by Mark to invoke his premium plan.

For the moment, Lennie Hawkins was forgotten. Peggy too. He began jotting down random thoughts that might be useful to Norm for the followup, toying with an idea that might catch the public fancy and hold it. Travel was an alluring, fascinating subject, and the Far West was a romantic, intriguing place to America. Why not try to combine the two by giving the national campaign a Western flavor?

His layout pad became a mass of penciled scrawls, words, sentences, and half-paragraphs, interspersed with doodles of ranch brand marks. *Remember your last trip West? Apart from the scenic wonders, do you recall the marvelous flavor of Western coffee? Chances are you were drinking B & B, one of the most popular coffees served by the better hotels, motels, and restaurants there. It's the same flavor and aroma you'll find in* GOODY'S B & B *at your nearest supermarket or food store.*

And, *The coffee that won the West is now available in all fifty States.*

A random headline asked: *When was the last time you said* WOW! *to a cup of coffee?*

Headlines, copy angles, and thumbnail sketches flowed from his pencil until several pages of the pad had been filled. Much of it, he knew, would be discarded, but there was enough to stimulate the art and copy group into improving what he had here, and to provide the nucleus for several discussion conferences.

He became suddenly aware that the sun had gone down, and turned on the desk lamp. It was a few minutes past five and threatening clouds darkened the sky prematurely. Steve went to the bedroom and peeked in. Peggy, hair tousled, eyes slightly puffed, lay in a halfway state between sleeping and waking.

"How are you feeling, Peg?"

"Numb. Oh, God . . ." Shaking her head to clear away the fog.

"How about taking a shower, and rejoining the world?"

"May I have some coffee first?"

"Sure thing. I'll heat some up and bring it to you."

"Don't bother. I think I'll feel better if I get up." She threw aside the cover, stood up somewhat shakily, and smoothed out her dress, running her fingers through her hair, and looking completely detached from reality. At the table, he waited for her to reintroduce the subject of Lennie, but she sat hollow-eyed and dejected, not speaking, staring down at the woven place mat. He poured the coffee when it was ready, lit two cigarettes, and gave her one. She drew on it, sipping the black coffee with relish as her color began to return.

"I'm sorry I've been such a bother to you, Steve," she said contritely.

"Nonsense. You've never been a bother to me, Peg. In the four years we've known each other you've always been indispensable to me."

She nodded, unsmiling. "Like a pencil sharpener."

"Stop it, Peggy. We're more than that and you know it."

"Just what are we, Steve?"

"Well, for one thing, we're friends, whether you realize it or not. Good friends. And friends are for leaning on when the going gets rough."

"So I lean on you. Tell me, who do you lean on when things get out of hand?"

He smiled and said, "On you. On whoever is handiest."

"Keith Allard?"

"Keith among others." He thought for a moment and said, "Why did you especially single out Keith?"

"I don't know. Maybe because I'm more careful about my choice of people to lean on."

"You don't like Keith?"

"It isn't a matter of like or dislike. More like trust or mistrust."

"As one friend to another, I'd like you to tell me why."

"I—well, Wade Barrett didn't find him a very substantial leaning post, did he?"

"Peg, Wade Barrett was a special case and I know a little more about it than you do."

"And Mr. Price?"

"Larry Price had a special problem, too."

"That's the point, isn't it, Steve? Everybody's problem is

special to himself, don't you see? Lennie had a special problem, too, and now he's dead."

"Lennie took his own life, Peg. Are you assuming guilt for that because you were his leaning post, and you feel you failed him?"

"Steve, Lennie was hurt. The night before last, before the presentation, he asked me to have dinner with him. He thought I'd been avoiding him because I'd asked him to go to Lex's party with me and he refused. I was busy all of last week and he thought I was angry. I wasn't, but I was tired, and wanted to get a full night's sleep so I'd be on my toes for the presentation yesterday.

"That was the night—night before last—according to the police, that someone beat him up. Sometime yesterday, it got to him in some way, and he killed himself."

"And you believe none of it would have happened if you'd gone to dinner with him?"

"I think so, yes."

"Peggy, you're whipping yourself for no good reason. I know you'd been working out your jingle idea with him—tell me, why did you go to his apartment this morning?"

"He didn't come to work yesterday. I thought he might be sick, but he didn't answer his phone last night when I called to tell him it looked like the campaign was in. So I went around this morning and found Eth and the others there—oh, Steve, it was so damned *awful,* so damned scary, seeing someone you know . . ."

"All right, Peggy." He touched her hand across the table and felt the trembling in it. "Why don't you take your shower now, then get dressed? I'll whip up some dinner and . . ."

"I don't want anything, Steve. I couldn't touch a thing."

"Take your shower. It may change your outlook. You know where to find a robe and whatever else you need. And take your time."

She stood up, and smiling weakly, kissed his cheek. "Thank you, Steve. I couldn't have faced Lois and Nikki's questions. You're a great, comfortable leaning post."

While she showered, Steve prepared a stew. He was adding a can of tomato sauce to the meat, onions, and other vegetables when she came into the kitchen, fully dressed, hair properly combed, a touch of lipstick to give her added color. "Smells wonderful. Anything I can do?" she asked.

"Inhale, enjoy, then set the table while I put the salad together. Fruit for dessert?"

"Fine." She was in a better mood, more alive now, bustling about. He watched her come back to near-normal, enjoying her presence, feeling a sense of deep affection—or was it protectiveness?—for her. He had pondered over her evaluation of Keith as a reliable friend and found her judgment faulty, yet he could not help wondering if Peggy's was a purely personal assessment or a consensus among her co-workers. It hadn't occurred to him that employees at the secretarial level would be concerned with high level interagency politics; but then, why not? Barrett and Price, scarcely known to most of them except by name, reputation, legend, rumor, and only occasional sight, had apparently become symbols over which to take sides. Curious, he had never considered the feelings of others on their behalf; only his own, Bill's, and Keith's.

Peggy had little appetite for the tempting dish, but made a gallant effort to please Steve. Later, she insisted on doing the dishes while Steve turned on a news program, as much interested in the thirty-second GFP commercial as he was in the news of Cambodia and its effect on South Vietnam and Laos. There was no news of Lennie Hawkins, probably run with the local news he had missed.

Peggy, finished with her kitchen chores, came into the living room just as the news program signed off. "Anytime you're ready to throw me out," she began, when the doorbell rang. "Shall I answer it?" she asked.

For the merest fraction of a second, the thought of Karen occurred to him, then he said, "Sure."

When she opened the door, two men stood there. One was young, his hair cut almost militarily short, neatly dressed, and with the body lines of an athlete. The second man was older, more weathered, wearing a dark blue suit that showed age. He introduced himself as Detective Sergeant Fredericks and his partner as Detective Walsh, out of Centre Street, investigating the case of Leonard Hawkins. "We've been in touch with Mr. Loomis, the deceased's uncle, who told us we might find Miss Cowles at this address. You are Miss Cowles?"

"Yes."

"May we come in?"

From behind her, Steve said, "Yes, please do."

They came into the living room and after glancing

around casually, sat beside each other on the sofa. Walsh had a pocket notebook in his hand, flipping pages. Fredericks said, "You're Mr. Steve—Steven Gilman?"

"Yes."

"Mr. Hawkins worked for you?"

"Mr. Hawkins worked for the Leary Agency and in the creative group I head up."

Fredericks nodded, then turned to Peggy. "Miss Cowles, I understand you were a friend of Mr. Hawkins?"

"That's right."

"A close friend?"

"Sergeant," Steve said, "Miss Cowles is also a member of the same group. All of us work very closely together in our daily work. In that frame of reference, we are all close friends."

Fredericks threw Steve an annoyed look, then turned back to Peggy. "What I meant was," he said, "did you see this Hawkins outside of your work, Miss Cowles?"

She snapped the answer back with resentment rising in her voice. "Yes. I did see Mr. Hawkins outside my work." It was unnecessary, from her tone, to add, *"Now make something out of that!"*

"When did you see him last? Before this morning, I mean."

"The night before last, Thursday, about ten minutes past six."

"Can you tell us the circumstances?"

She described leaving the office, the subway ride home, Lennie coming up from behind after she had reached ground level, his invitation to her to have dinner with him, her refusal because she had work to do.

"Can you describe what Hawkins was wearing at the time?"

"*Mister* Hawkins was wearing a black-and-white checked suit, very small checks, with a thin line of red forming blocks about three inches square. His shirt was dark blue, a knit, I think, and open at the throat."

"No tie?" The question came from Walsh, his pencil busy recording the description.

"Not a conventional tie," Peggy said. "It was a scarflike thing he wore around his throat, with a brass or gold ring at the neck. The ends flowed out over the jacket. It had a white and blue pattern."

"Shoes?"

"I didn't notice particularly, but I'm certain he was wearing a pair of shoes."

Fredericks ignored her sarcasm. "Watch, or ring?"

"A watch, yes, I'm sure, but I don't remember a ring. I think not."

"He wasn't marked in any way, was he? I mean, as though he'd been in a scrap recently?"

"No. Lennie wasn't a violent type at all. Aggressive, but not violent. As a matter of fact, he'd cut himself off from a group of former friends because he didn't believe that violence was the way to achieve equality."

"Yes, miss. Did you know any of those friends or acquaintances?"

"No, he never introduced any of them formally by name. By the time I knew Lennie fairly well, he'd given most of them up."

"But you saw some of them, heard their names?"

"I saw a few of them when we were in the Village together on one or two occasions. Sometimes they would approach him, but he seldom spoke more than a simple greeting."

"Can you remember what any of them looked like, or a name that was spoken?"

She concentrated, frowning, trying to remember. "One," she said, "was a grossly fat man, short, epicene . . ."

"Excuse me, Miss Cowles," Walsh interposed, "what was that last word? Epi—something?"

"Epicene. E-p-i-c-e-n-e. It means someone who, well, in this case, a male who has certain effeminate characteristics. Am I correct, Steve?"

"For your intended meaning, yes."

Fredericks said, "A homosexual, you mean. A fag."

"I wouldn't know that, Sergeant," Peggy said stiffly. "I think Lennie called him Fat Joe."

"Any others?"

"There were others, but I can't recall them all. I wasn't really interested, or paying close attention. Oh, one man, a man with a turban and a goatee, very tall. I think Lennie called him Tom. Big Tom. They weren't like Lennie at all. Hustlers, he called them, men who refused to work and got by on their wits. Some were addicted to marijuana or heroin, I believe."

"Was Hawkins an addict?" Fredericks interjected quickly.

"Of course not," Peggy snapped back with indignation.

"Lennie Hawkins was a very decent man who had a tremendous art talent, a good job with a promise, and was just beginning to find his place in the world. He had no reason to resort to drugs."

"You'd be surprised, Miss Cowles, to learn how many people who have no reason to resort to drugs are picked up every day for resorting to drugs," Fredericks said dryly.

"Will that be all, Sergeant?" Steve asked politely.

"We'll be through soon," the sergeant said, and turning once again to Peggy, "Miss Cowles, we're looking for some reason why someone, anyone, would want to beat Hawkins up so badly. We don't believe, we're pretty sure, that is, that it didn't happen in his apartment on Perry Street, but somewhere else. You were there this morning. You didn't see any signs of that kind of disorder. If we can determine where, or by whom, we're sure to come up with the why."

"How can I help you with that?"

"In a roundabout way, maybe you can." Fredericks paused, then said, "We've got to look into every possible angle. Robbery is one, the first. He had no money on him, no watch, keys, wallet, the usual things a man carries on him. Another reason is—well, could anybody, friends or acquaintances of Hawkins, have had some reason to be—uh—jealous of him?"

"If you mean because of me," Peggy said, "I think your question is in bad taste and insulting. There was nothing intimate between Lennie and me. We worked together at the agency and were working on an advertising idea for a client. I admired Lennie as an artist and I think our friendship helped him in his personal adjustment in—well—in living. If you're trying to make more of it than that, you're very wrong. And stupid!" She stood up and ran out of the room into the bedroom, and closed the door.

"Anything more, Sergeant?" Steve asked, rising.

"I guess not. I'm sorry Miss Cowles got upset, Mr. Gilman, but we've got a job to do and sometimes people get offended at questions we have to ask."

"I understand," Steve said, "but unfortunately, the timing is bad. I'll say this for Miss Cowles, however. She is a very honest, truthful person."

"Yeah. Well, thanks. We'll take it from here." Fredericks and Walsh picked up their hats and Steve showed them to the door.

He went to the bedroom and knocked. Peggy came out, her face still flushed with anger. "Have they gone?"

"Yes. How about a drink?"

"Yes, please." Steve poured two stiff Scotches, added ice cubes, and gave her the drink. She sipped at it and began slowly to relax. "Those filthy implications," she said.

"Peg, in a case of this kind, an investigator is forced to frame questions so he can get answers. If someone robbed and beat Lennie, or did something to cause his suicide, the police want to know the facts so they can apprehend and prosecute the violators."

"Violators." The word struck a chord in her memory. "Steve, what did Lennie mean in his note to Eth, something about not being able to live with his violated body."

"I don't know, Peg. Maybe we should wait for the medical examiner's report."

"Do you think it means . . . ?"

"All anyone can do is guess. He was beaten into helplessness and robbed. It isn't too remote a possibility that he was finally assaulted criminally by a homosexual."

"Oh, Steve! How disgustingly awful!"

"And, sensitive as Lennie was, it could well have preyed on his mind and caused his suicide. That's only a guess, of course."

"God! How sick, how degradingly sick, sick, *sick!* What kind of world do we live in?"

Grady's words, *It's your world, my world, And Miss Lormond's world, too,* came back into his mind.

It had begun to rain and Peggy went to the window and looked down into the street, now dark and wet. After a while she said, "Lennie was in love with me. I know that much. I wonder, if I had let myself love him, would he be alive now?"

"I think your reasoning is wrong, Peggy," Steve said. "We don't *let* ourselves love or not love. We love because we want to, wholeheartedly and without question or reservation. We don't love when there's no spark, no chemistry to allow us to love."

"Then why do some women love many men and why are some men always chasing after new faces?"

"You're confusing love with sex."

"And the only happy combination is love *and* sex?"

"That's as close as anybody has ever been able to come

to it. Love *and* sex *and* companionship *and* understanding *and* an awareness of someone other than self."

Still staring through the window, "Then how does it happen that an attractive male like Steven Gilman, about thirty, financially secure, once-divorced, is married only to his job? Unless he isn't looking for love *and* sex *and* companionship *and* that special awareness of someone other than self?"

"I should have added that very often there are certain circumstances beyond one's control that prevent those factors from falling into proper place at the proper time."

"And that's too bad, isn't it?"

"I'd say so, wouldn't you?"

"What I'd say is that I think it's too much for me to think about."

"Then perhaps I should think about getting you home."

"It's pouring."

"Maybe it's a good night for being alone to think things out for oneself."

"I'm susceptible to colds, flu, even pneumonia."

"Were you planning to stay here tonight?"

"May I, Steve? I don't think I can face the quiz show Nikki and Lois will put me through. Besides, those two detectives must have been there asking questions about me. I'll take the sofa this time."

"I don't think you'd better, Peggy. If you want to avoid Lois and Nikki, I'll get you a room at a hotel."

"I don't want to be by myself in a hotel room."

"Peg . . ." It came out as a warning.

"I want to, Steve, please. I want it to be with you."

"Without love or understanding?"

"There's still sex, companionship, and awareness of someone other than self. That can add up to a lot."

"Why now, Peggy?"

"Because tomorrow," she said slowly, "I could be as dead as poor Lennie. And I'd have died ignorant of what it's all about."

"You've never known?"

"Someone else knew, but I didn't." She told him of her misadventure with Bob Larch, all but his name. The humiliation, anxiety, and shame without ever having experienced the delight. "I promise I'll never make a single claim on you, Steve."

And so on that rainy night, Peggy Cowles went to bed with Steve Gilman, this time wholly conscious of the man with her, inside her, achieving the reality that had been no more than fantasy in her previous lifetime, weeping without knowing why; partially with regret for the wasted life that lay in the morgue with a tag tied to its toe bearing the name Leonard Hawkins, an identifying number beneath it.

4

Frantic and disorganized as it might seem to the uninitiated onlooker, the work flow progressed in an orderly manner through normal channels, monitored at key points by Traffic Control, Production, and the Work Progress Chart, every eye and mind keenly attuned to the all-important Target Date.

Print ads were scheduled, art completed, type set, camera-ready copy sent to engravers and plate-makers, proofs carefully scanned, read, okayed, and plates and mats shipped to publication destinations. Television scripts had been written, re-written, cast, directed, translated onto film, viewed, scored, parts re-shot, and then distributed. Point-of-purchase displays and banners were sent into the field, and billboards readied. Trade ads and direct mail broadsides were prepared and shipped to distributors while GFP's marketing-merchandising-sales-promotion people fanned out to follow up with personal calls. Traffic Control memos flew between Media and Production and the WPC on Chuck Baldasarian's desk reflected each progressive step as Goody's B & B campaign approached launch date in the Western area.

In Los Angeles, Wade Barrett's staff were standing by to give as much aid locally as possible. In the New York office, Leary's Marketing-Merchandising division heads, Thalberg and Castle, had been out in the field working with their GFP counterparts, to make the trade aware of the upcoming campaign, acquaint them with the promotion possibilities of the new coffee item added to the regular GFP line, and arrange for the redemption of coupons turned in by retailers who would exchange coffee for contest-winning certificates. Showing advance proofs and miniature display kits, they gathered orders, assigned shipping dates, and called on retailers to arrange for special displays and demonstrators.

Meanwhile, Lennie's body was released for burial by the Medical Examiner and Ethan Loomis made the necessary arrangements in a Harlem mortuary chapel for the funeral service, which was attended by Steve, Peggy, and others of the GFP and B & B groups who had worked closely with Lennie. The agency sent a large blanket of white and red carnations which covered the casket during the brief ceremony. According to instructions in his note to Eth, Lennie's body would be cremated.

Detectives Fredericks and Walsh, among others, worked patiently with no deadlines, locating the suit Lennie had worn on the night he was attacked. The description given by the store owner who had paid six dollars for the suit, fit that of one August Thomas, nailed down by the ring he wore through his left ear. The used-clothing merchant identified Augie's mug shots from a group of twelve, and Augie was picked up two nights later. He remained close-mouthed for four days, until his need for a fix became so great that he would have sold out friends, family, and country to get the blessed relief he needed. He didn't exactly talk, he babbled.

Fat Joe, however, who had been picked up first through Peggy's description, a nonaddict, refused to acknowledge his acquaintanceship with any human being alive. His rap sheet was lengthy, including several charges of homosexual attacks on juvenile males.

Big Tom X and Rajah Smith were brought in after Augie talked. They at once charged police brutality and discrimination, then challenged the right of the authorities to make an illegal arrest upon two citizens of something they called the World State of Free Africa. But the oversized blue denim pants Lennie had worn home that night had Rajah's name printed in India ink inside the waistband; and Lennie's loafers, checked out with the store clerk who had sold them to him, were on Big Tom's feet.

The four were arraigned, indicted, and sent to the Tombs to await trial. Lennie Hawkins, who would never in his life have given the police credit for much more than writing traffic tickets, might have changed his mind. Had he been alive.

5

GFP's Western campaign broke with the full page introductory announcements in the leading newspapers of that area, Sunday magazine supplements, and local magazines. During this initial period, exposure on television and radio was massive, coordinated with billboard, transit, and point-of-purchase advertising. The immediate response, however, was considerably less than spectacular. It was, in fact, disappointing. Like cigarettes, the public coffee taste was too deeply set to be quickly changed by the written or spoken word. In major supermarkets and food stores, the item was being displayed on shelves and special aisle displays with a large corps of demonstrators available to offer shoppers a coffee break, but one cup of coffee was hardly enough to break an ingrained habit.

Then, on the heels of the introductory ads came the Goody–B & B Jingle Contest with its money and free coffee offer. The action began to pick up during the first week and swelled each week thereafter. Entry blanks disappeared at an extraordinary rate. Distributors reported new outlet placements and put in calls for more entry blanks to meet the demand. Day after day, week after week, the jingles poured in. A special staff was hired by Barrett to cull through the mass of entries to weed out the obviously bad material and the balance was air-mailed to New York, where Peggy and three other judges selected winners and awarded the cash prizes, with certificates to the runners-up which could be redeemed at their food stores.

The winning jingles were quickly illustrated, photographs of the winners were obtained, and appeared in print—some on television commercials—and their names were announced on radio. In the weeks that followed, the repeat orders began flowing in. Coming in swiftly, the competition began stepping up their own advertising and sales promotion efforts, but GFP had not only outdistanced them, they had lapped the field. Sales were up beyond initial projections and Ward Hardwick, with a winner on his hands, was ecstatic. Even Curtis Fitzjohn, the man who carefully guarded GFP's purse strings, beamed with anticipation, eager now to see the campaign break nationwide.

During this tense period, Mark Lawson remained an enigma. As the only dissenter to the initial program, he could not now take full credit for its success, although the advertising press mentioned his name prominently in connection with the hard-hitting campaign. The rising weekly sales figures hardly gave him the joy they gave to Ward Hardwick.

Since so much of the campaign had already been prepared and approved, there was no pressing need for frequent contact with the agency, and for two months, the only exchange between Steve and Mark had been conducted mainly by telephone, usually when Steve phoned to "touch bases" with Mark.

Norm Adrian was now in his element, spearheading the group which brought forth a generous stockpile of ideas for future consideration. Byron Johns came up with the suggestion to give added meaning to B & B, translating it to read "Better Blended." Dan Thaw proposed a group of ten-second I.D.'s for television based on the single sentence, *For that moment of pure enjoyment in your day. Or night.* Chris Galbertson contributed a series of striking layouts showing Tony in Western garb, adapted from Steve's suggested theme. Norm added a light touch with, *Have yourself a love affair with a cup of Goody's B & B.*

Early success had a remarkably stimulating effect on the entire agency and suggestions came in from almost every copywriter and art director who felt the need to become a part of the overall success story. Brainstorming sessions within their own group brought the most rewarding results and after numerous copy and art conferences, a theme was chosen by Steve and Norm, and the group settled down to present it in its most acceptable form. Roughs were translated into visuals, microscopically perfect in detail, since Lawson would be looking for any possible excuse to reject the offerings. Every success paved the way for breaking the campaign nationally in the months to come.

Chapter 13

1

Early in June, some of the pressure on Steve was lifted when Karen announced that Anna Goodwin, who had not been feeling well, had taken a cottage at Harwich Port, on Cape Cod, for the month, providing Karen would accompany her. With Herschel urging them to go, Karen agreed.

Within a week of her departure, Peggy became a frequent guest at Steve's apartment and spent one entire weekend there with him. During the third week, he became aware not only of her physical presence, but of her cosmetics in his bathroom, and the intimate nightwear and one or two changes of clothes that hung in the bedroom closet.

The atmosphere became charged with her presence and personality. Peggy, he discovered away from the office, was completely charming, pleasant, and delightfully comfortable to be with. She was witty, warm in love, and happy with life; and obviously with Steve. They dined out frequently and openly, and at other times, Peggy surprised him with her versatility and inventiveness in the kitchen. Suddenly, new and previously unfamiliar items began appearing on the weekly grocery list and in menus. And, when it became necessary to bring his work home, Peggy allowed him full freedom in his study while she listened to stereo music in the living room, tuned low to avoid disturbing him; or served as a sounding board for ideas he wanted to talk out with her.

With Karen's imminent return at the end of the month, however, Steve suggested that they were getting in a little too deep for Peggy's good (!), that it was inevitable that office gossip would catch up with them. "I'm afraid it has already," Peggy said quietly.

"Who. . . ?"

"Last week, Chuck hinted . . ."

"Chuck isn't that subtle. He's never hinted at anything

in his life that he could blurt out. What did he say? Did he make a pass at you?"

"It's nothing, Steve. I may have misunderstood him."

"That's moronic. No one misunderstands Chuck. What was it?"

Hesitantly, "If you make a big thing out of it, I—I'll have to resign."

"That's even more idiotic. Are you going to tell me or will I have to get it from him?"

"If you promise not to make a mountain out of a molehill . . ." Steve waited. "It was an inference—or an implication—I can never get the two straight . . ."

"What did he imply or infer?"

"That we were having an affair. Period."

"And he wanted to buy in?"

"I don't know exactly. Maybe something of that kind. He asked me to go away with him for the weekend."

"That conniving bastard . . ."

"You promised."

"Okay, but let me handle this."

"Just don't precipitate anything, please. I don't want to be caught in the middle. And I think you're right. I'd better move my things back to the apartment."

"What about Nikki and Lois?"

"There's nothing to worry about. We have a sort of working agreement. No questions, no confidences exchanged."

Deliberately, Steve didn't call Chuck in for their usual fifteen-minute morning review to establish the normal working order of their day, which usually consisted of checking the WPC and issuing necessary instructions or orders to the group. Nor did Chuck intrude on Steve all that morning. It was sometime well after lunch, around three-thirty, when Chuck knocked on the communicating door and came in. Steve looked up from his typewriter inquiringly. "What is it, Chuck?"

"Been kind of busy all day, haven't you? I've got a few items to check out with you." He came toward the desk with three memo slips in his hand, and offered them to Steve, who read them and merely nodded. "Okay, is that it?"

"You sore about something, Steve?" Chuck said.

Steve pushed the three memos toward Chuck. "Why? Is your alleged conscience bothering you?"

"She blew the whistle on me, didn't she?"

"Who are you talking about?"

"Peggy. She told you . . ."

"Chuck, I've told you before to keep away from Peggy except for purely business reasons. If you haven't got the sense to realize I meant it . . ."

"Big deal."

"Chuck, I've warned you before. I'm not going to put up with that sort of thing in my office, with my secretary. This is the last time. Lay off or it's over, Marty Link or George McCandless notwithstanding."

The old, well-known look of insolence returned in Chuck. "You think *you* can fire *me?* You actually think you can get away with it?" he asked incredulously.

"Off the job and out of the agency. Bet on it."

"Well, I'll be damned. I had it figured right, didn't I, that she was putting out for you?"

"Listen, trashmouth, if you want to bring this to a head right here and now . . ."

"Jesus, no. It's not worth it."

"Then we understand each other. Now get the hell back to your work and make sure you remember it."

Chuck turned, a cold smile on his lips. "Okay, boss. I leave the field vanquished. She's all yours, but I still think you're taking a wet deck from Hawkins . . ."

Steve held himself in check and allowed Chuck to exit without further comment.

On the following day, Keith called him to say that Herschel and Anna were giving a small victory party celebration at the Lawson home on the following Saturday evening. From the agency, Bill and Donna Leary, Keith and Louise, Steve and a companion of his choice were invited. GFP executives Ward Hardwick, Curtis Fitzjohn would be there, and, of course, the Mark Lawsons would be present.

There was no escape, no way he could beg off. An invitation from the head of GFP, the super-client, superceded any previous engagement and could not be turned aside. Now, two dilemmas presented themselves: a face-to-face meeting with Karen in Mark's presence, their first since the affair had begun; and his choice of a partner to accompany him to Karen's home.

Preoccupied with the problem, Peggy rang to tell him that Miss Stafford was on the line. When Peggy rang off, he said, "Karen?"

"Hello, darling, how are you?"

"Fine. And you?"

"Marvelous. It was a wonderful month and did both of us world of good. I've got a piece of news for you."

"I think I've had it already."

"Saturday night?"

"Yes. Keith just told me."

"You don't sound too happy about it."

"Should I?"

"I don't know why not. I am. It's been ages since I've seen you. A whole month."

"Isn't that shaving things just a little too close?"

Her short laugh trilled with amusement. "I think it could be interesting."

"I can't say I share your feelings about this at all."

"Be a sport, Steve. You'll bring a date, won't you?"

"I don't know. I haven't even begun to consider that part of it."

"You'd better start soon. I—may I make a suggestion?"

"I don't think that would be wise."

"Why not? She's attractive enough, and she's not exactly a Leary employee, is she?"

"Who are you talking about?"

"Margo Anthony."

The suggestion caught him by surprise. "No, Margo is under contract to GFP and I don't think I'm up to exposure to all that glamour."

"Then if you won't, someone else will bring her, I'm sure. I've just invited her. I'm interested in seeing her off-screen."

"You're due for an eyeful."

"You sound like—are you holding something back, Steve?"

"No, and I don't want to discuss it on the phone. I have another call waiting," he lied.

"Then I'll see you Saturday night. Nine o'clock?"

"Yes, of course."

He hung up. The phone rang immediately and he picked it up again. It was Peggy with a call from Louise Allard, who wanted Steve and his Saturday night date for dinner before going on to the Goodwin party.

"I haven't settled on a choice yet, Louise," he said.

"If you're planning on going alone, Steve, I have . . ."

"Oh, no you don't! As soon as I've made my decision I'll phone you."

Peggy came in with a memo that had been sent in by

Traffic Control. He glanced at it, initialed it, and gave it back to her. As she started to leave, he said, "Busy?"

"Not for the moment."

"Sit down for a minute."

"Problems?" When Steve smiled, she said, "For some reason, you look like an unhanged pirate."

"You're getting to be a very discerning woman, Peggy."

"After four years, it's not hard to interpret your moods. You look as though you were afraid something has happened that you've been afraid would happen."

"That's what I need right now, a mystic with a crystal ball. I'm not afraid of anything."

"No? My father always taught us to be afraid of people who are never afraid when they should be."

"Of what should I be afraid? Or of whom?"

"Of Mark Lawson, for one. He's been too quiet lately. I think he's lying behind a bush with a hatchet in his hand."

"That's nonsense. He's merely disturbed because he was opposed to a campaign that—fortunately for us—happens to be working."

"I've never thought of him as the forgiving type."

"Well, to prove you're wrong, Mr. and Mrs. Goodwin are throwing a little party this Saturday night to celebrate the initial success of B & B on the West Coast, and that party will be at Mr. Lawson's house."

"Well, hallelujah!"

"Would you like to go? As a major contributor to that success, I think you're entitled to share in the commencement exercises."

"With you?"

"With me. And Bill Leary, Keith Allard, plus the top GFP brass."

Peggy's face came alive, then faded slowly. "I haven't anything decently formal enough for that."

"You've got until Saturday night to make up for that. I want you to go out and get something pretty and not overly formal. Dress, shoes, purse, everything you need. I'll put the cost through as a necessary agency expense, a bonus over and above the salary increase I've put through for you. And don't be skimpy about it. I want you to look and feel your very best."

"Steve, now I *am* afraid. The Learys, the Allards—I've never been at that level."

"It's no different than any other level."

"There could be talk . . "

"There's always talk. In this case, you're entitled to a slice of the cake. Don't you want to go?"

"Of course I do!"

"Then that's settled. Take off, and attend to your shopping."

By Friday, having spent two afternoons shopping, Peggy finally decided to go back to the first dress that had captured her eye at Bonwit's. What had made her hesitate was the price, one hundred and eighty dollars, the most she had ever spent for a dress; but when she put it on and inspected herself in the three-way mirror, its very elegant simplicity told her it was *right.* To ease her conscience, she had shopped at Lord & Taylor, and Saks Fifth Avenue, and peeked into Bergdorf's, but the little black dress with its sparse white accents and short standing collar completely overshadowed anything else she had seen. With her smooth tan complexion that almost matched the color of her hair, new black shoes and matching purse, confidence grew.

The dress was ready by mid-morning on Saturday. She had lunch, and spent the next two hours having her hair done, and nails manicured, then taxied home for a revitalizing bath and rest. Steve phoned to ask what time she would be ready for him to pick her up, but she told him she would meet him at his apartment at seven o'clock and spare him the double ride.

She arrived promptly at seven. Steve, opening the door, gave her his immediate approval in two words. "You're adorable."

"Thank you. I'm also a little nervous. I hope I haven't wrecked the GFP budget."

"Whatever the cost, it's well worth it," he said, feasting his eyes on the subtle slenderizing effect of the dress, the accent of the swell of her breasts, its just-above-knee-length that complemented her longish legs. "I almost wish we weren't going out."

"The dress alone cost a hundred and eighty dollars. It's not for staying in on a beautiful night like this."

"We can discuss that later. Time for one drink before we're due at the Allards. Martini?"

"Perfect."

Louise, meeting Peggy for the first time, extended herself to put her at ease, signaling her approval with a secret wink for Steve. Keith exuded pure charm over pre-dinner drinks and by the time dinner was over and the car brought around, they had become an amiable foursome on their way out to a pleasant evening. The agency had hardly been mentioned, stifled by Louise's uncanny ability to lead the conversation along more entertaining lines.

2

They reached the Lawson home at nine-thirty. Max showed them into the formal living room, where the Hardwicks, Fitzjohns, and Russell Charleses stood in a close group with Herschel and Anna Goodwin. Herschel, looking pale beside Anna's magnificent Cape Cod tan, was smiling at one of Russell's anecdotes. Karen came in directly behind them, stunning in a brief white dress with dark blue piping. Introductions, hardly necessary except for Peggy's benefit, were made while a Negro couple served drinks and canapés and took orders for the new arrivals.

The conversation, quite naturally, fell into the agency-client pattern, bearing particularly on the marked success of the B & B program in the Western states and its possibilities in the rest of the country when it would break nationwide in the fall. Peggy became the center of attention when Steve credited her with authorship of the jingle idea.

"I loved it," Anna Goodwin said, one arm around Peggy's waist. "I already have four entries to send in under an assumed name when the contest runs in the East."

"Please let us know which name you use," Keith said with a smile. "Our policy is to keep the client happy at any cost."

Karen said, "How clever of you, Miss Cowles. I wish I could do something as worthwhile as that."

"I've seen a few paintings here with your signature, Mrs. Lawson. I envy your talent. They're beautiful."

"Thank you. You must see the others," Karen said with a beaming smile. "Later, I'll take you for a tour of my studio."

"I'd love that."

"You must be a great help to Steve."

"I'm not really a writer, Mrs. Lawson, only a secretary."

"I'm just as sure you're more than 'only a secretary,' and please call me Karen."

"Thank you."

Steve, observing the two as he stood in a group with the others, saw no cause for alarm. Karen and Peggy, so opposite in coloring, were of nearly equal height and similar build, both radiant. He wondered with some small concern if he had been less than wise to bring them together; and it suddenly occurred to him that Peggy might in some way be able to identify Karen's voice as that of Miss Stafford; a thought that had not, until now, entered his mind. Yet, among the names that had blown through his mind when Keith told him of the party, none would have been as suitable for an agency-client gathering as Peggy. Not until now had he even considered it a gamble.

Bill and Donna Leary arrived, and more introductions followed, more drinks served, more canapés passed. Herschel displayed a genuine fondness for Bill and began a nostalgic remembrance of his first meeting with Wm. B. Leary, Sr., at which Keith and Wade Barrett had been present. And Steve noticed suddenly that Mark Lawson had come in quietly to join them.

"Hello, Mark," Steve said.

Mark smiled, exuding genial charm. He shook hands with Steve, then with Bill and Keith, and nodded smiles to the others. Karen brought Peggy back to the group and introduced her to Mark.

"So this is our pretty little jingle expert," Mark said, holding her hand between both of his own. "Steve, I've got a notion to hire this lady away from you."

"I'm afraid I couldn't get along without her, Mark," Steve replied lightly, "and besides, I don't think she could do as much for you as she can for us." He glanced at Karen, whose face showed an enigmatic, unnatural smile. Mark released Peggy's hand in the moment of silence that followed and turned to signal the waiter for a drink.

Russell and Faith Charles were engaged in "neighbor talk" with Anna and Herschel. The Fitzjohns, Hardwicks, and Learys had formed their own group, leaving Mark, Karen, Steve, and Peggy to themselves, when Austin Delevie, Russell Charles's associate, arrived with his wife, Eleanor and, on their heels, Margo Anthony with Don Bryce's key director, Colin Ferris.

All attention was focused on Tony, flawlessly beautiful in shimmering blue-black mini dress with matching hose sheathing her spectacular legs. Almost at once, the air became charged with subtle electricity as Mark moved in and bestowed a fleeting familial kiss on her proffered cheek and assumed the duty of introducing her to the other guests.

Colin Ferris, his face flushed red with the effects of alcohol, bristled, and Karen looked mildly annoyed with Mark's act of possessiveness, but the others warmed to Tony as they would have to a popular stage or screen personality. Peggy whispered to Steve, "Do we ask for autographs?"

Introductions over, Herschel Goodwin said, "I think we are all here now, no?" and when Karen nodded affirmatively, "Anna and I are not party-givers as a rule, but I thought some kind of celebration would be in order to show you our gratitude for your contributions to the success of the newest and biggest item GFP has undertaken since the business began almost thirty-five years ago.

"Among my own people, our agency people and our attorneys who negotiated this deal, it would be very hard to single out any one person for special mention because everyone did his part to put us into this new market. Mr. Fitzjohn, who has watched over our finances ever since we went public, has begun walking around with a smile instead of a frown, which is an even better yardstick to go by than his financial reports. To Mr. Gilman, who first brought B & B to our attention, goes a special thanks, and to all of you, Anna and I would like to give a personal token—Curt, you won't find this in the expense figures to argue about—and, well, Anna?"

Max entered the room and placed a carton on the table before Anna. She picked up the first package and read the name: Louise Allard. Next, Ward Hardwick. And so on down to the last package, until each person except Anna and Herschel, Mark and Karen, held an oblong or square package in his or her hand.

"Open them, open them," Herschel called out.

Bows and ribbons came off, and gold paper was tossed into the empty carton. The men had received gold watches, the ladies gazed in open admiration at the gold-and-diamond pins. The back of each watch and pin was engraved with the recipient's name, "with our deepest appreciation, Anna and Herschel Goodwin."

The caterer's people came in to serve champagne, toasts were tendered, and the buzz of delighted conversation rose to a mild roar. The watches were similar, but the pins were individual pieces. Peggy had received a gold sunburst with slender rays, each tipped with a small diamond. She refused to allow Steve to pin it to her dress until she had had her fill of enjoyment in handling and admiring it. "How did they know?" she asked. "Did you tell them in advance?"

"I told Keith and Louise. They must have passed your name along."

In the dining room, a buffet had been arranged, and Anna ordered everyone in to enjoy the lobster, rare roast beef, Maryland crab puffs, salads, molds, a plentitude of desserts, and not surprisingly, the star of the evening, B & B Coffee.

Karen and Anna circulated among the guests to make sure everyone had enough to eat. Colin Ferris was drinking quite heavily, never more than inches away from Tony, refusing to permit Mark a moment alone with her. Steve watched over Peggy protectively, and when the food had been consumed, reluctantly gave her over to Karen for the studio tour.

Like most agency-client parties, there was a distinct pairing off; the Fitzjohns and Hardwick, in their own corporate huddle, the Learys, Allards, and Steve in their own group, the Charleses and Delevies in quiet conversation with Herschel, while Anna moved among them in a dispirited effort to bring the separate groups together. Colin Ferris, beginning to show the effects of his alcoholic intake, was devoting rapt attention to Tony, who threw an occasional helpless glance at a glowering Mark, as if to say, "But what can I do?" and Mark, after several unsuccessful attempts to break in, wandered out of the room.

What had begun as a celebration party became a somewhat dull, listless endurance contest. When Karen and Peggy returned from the upstairs studio, the hour was approaching midnight. Russell and Faith made the first move to leave, claiming the long drive back to Wyecliffe as their excuse. The Delevies left with them, and the Hardwicks and Fitzjohns followed. Ferris and Tony left next, and then Steve and Peggy, turning down an offer from Keith to drive them.

Outside in the balmy, starlit night, Peggy and Steve strolled south on Fifth Avenue, the street virtually empty of pedestrian traffic. Steve attempted to hail two passing cabs, but both were carrying passengers and passed them by. Peggy said, "I don't mind walking for a while. It's nice out."

"All right, you healthy Nebraskan, but not for too long. I've been neglecting my exercise lately."

"Thank you for asking me to the party tonight, Steve. It was very enlightening."

"In any particular way?"

"Oh—I love my pin. I think it was awfully sweet of the Goodwins to give me a present along with the others. I didn't know clients were that thoughtful."

"It was a gesture of appreciation for a good job well done. Each of us played a part in it and this was the Goodwins' way of saying, 'Thank you.'"

"And," she said, "I enjoyed seeing Karen's studio. She's a very talented person."

"Yes, she is."

"Steve . . ."

"What?"

"Those paintings in your living room. They're Karen's, aren't they? They aren't signed, but the technique is unmistakable."

"You're very observant."

"Most efficient secretaries are."

"And most efficient secretaries are discreet."

"*Touché*. I made the mistake of thinking that outside the office we could drop the secretary-supervisor roles."

"That isn't the mistake, Peggy. Prying into certain areas of another person's life . . ."

She stopped short, and removed her arm from the crook of his elbow. He turned toward her, and saw tears of anger welling up in her eyes. "Peggy . . ."

"You're so—so damned smart, aren't you?" she said bitingly. "Just how smug and secure do you think you're being, having an affair with a client's wife, hiding her under the name of 'Miss Stafford'? How dumb do you think I am? And if I can figure it out, don't you think someone else will?"

"What did Karen tell you up in her studio?"

"Nothing."

"What, Peggy?"

"Nothing. Just—little hints. Not even that much. How brilliant you are as an advertising man, how dedicated you were, bringing in the B & B deal, how charming it must be for me, how exciting, working for a man with such a marvelous future."

"And you put two and two together from that?"

"And the fact that her voice is too obviously the voice of your Miss Stafford."

They had resumed walking, separated physically, strangers. "Peggy," he said finally, "I'm not going to attempt to explain how it happened, or why I let it happen."

"You don't owe me any explanations, Steve, any more than I owe you an explanation why I went to bed with you. I let that happen because I wanted it to happen. I assume it was the same with you and Karen."

"Why don't we go back to my apartment and talk it out."

"No," she said shortly. "That won't solve anything."

"Not talking about it can't solve anything, either. Peggy, I'm trying to say something to you, but it isn't coming through."

"I don't know what you're trying to say, Steve. All I know is, you're deeply involved with a married woman—more importantly—a client's wife. You're the only one who can solve that."

An empty cab slowed down, and Steve signaled him to the curb. They got in, and Steve said, "Peggy?"

"I want to go home," she said.

Steve gave the man Peggy's address.

3

When the last guest left, Mark poured a stiff drink, took it into the study, sat in his favorite chair, and used the remote control device to switch on the television set. He changed channels from one late movie to another, and finally settled for an old Western, staring at the tube without watching or feeling the action. Tony and that bastard Ferris. Seeing them together, Ferris pawing drunkenly at her, hardly able to wait until he could get her home to the apartment and into the bed Mark was paying for.

If there were only some plausible excuse he could dream up to leave—but with Herschel and Anna spending the night, there was no way. He gulped at his drink and squirmed in helpless anger. In the morning, as soon as they left for Wyecliffe, he would—goddamn it, if he found

Ferris there with Tony, he'd kill the sonofabitch, strangle him.

In the living room, Herschel and Anna thanked Karen for the party she had arranged, kissed her, and went up to their room, leaving Karen to give Max and Gerda some final instructions for the caterer's people.

Herschel came out of the bathroom, buttoning his pajama jacket over his spare upper body. Anna was already in bed, the lamp on her side turned off. Herschel came around and sat on the edge of the bed beside her. After a moment he emitted a deep sigh.

"You feel all right, Herschel?" Anna asked with concern.

"Sure, sure."

"Then let's go to sleep. I want to leave for home as soon as we've had breakfast."

"You don't like it here, either, do you, Anna?"

"I didn't say that."

"I know, I know. I don't say it to you, you don't say it to me. Why is it we can talk about anything except Karen and Mark and this house, eh?"

"Please, Herschel . . ."

"It's no good . . . the whole thing . . . this marriage. They're like strangers, polite, but from far away. *Guttenu,* this is the way married people live today?"

"Herschel, please. If Karen didn't want it this way, she would change it. It didn't take her long to divorce Julian, did it? Nobody ever made her do anything she didn't want to do, even when she was a child, remember? She's a grown woman, in her second marriage. What can you or I do or say to make her change now?"

"Ah, yes. You're right, Anna. You're always right."

Herschel stood up, walked around to the other side of the bed and got in, but left his lamp on. Anna said, "Herschel . . ."

"It wasn't a good party, was it, Anna?"

"I think they enjoyed it for what it was. After all, they aren't exactly close friends, only business acquaintances. They ate, drank, enjoyed the presents. You can't expect much more from a company party. Don't aggravate yourself or you'll never get to sleep. Turn off your light."

He did, plunging the room into darkness and silence, but sleep eluded him, the only comfort the familiar presence of Anna beside him.

The mystery of Karen and Mark pressed heavily on his

mind at times like this. A curious thing it was, this marriage that showed no visible signs of love or affection; no children to carry the name forward, to take over GFP one day. No one but an *aüslander* who married Zalman's daughter—step-daughter, he caught himself—although he and Anna had always considered her their own since Sophie and Zalman were drowned; Mark, a man whose competence was seriously in doubt. But he had, for whatever reason, been Karen's choice and Karen had always gotten what Karen wanted.

Crazy, Herschel thought. Crazy. For a long time, despite occasional hints from Russell Charles, he had procrastinated updating his old will, which left everything to Anna to be held in trust for Karen and her children, made before she married Julian Roth and unchanged since that time. Placing Mark in a position of control, considering his gratuitous position as advertising director, was unthinkable. And to bypass him would surely create problems for Karen.

The only alternative left to him was equally distressing. He and Zalman had begun the business together so many years ago. To destroy it would be like destroying Zalman's gravestone. If only Robert had lived. . . . But Zalman and Robert were gone.

McFadden Industries, during the past three years, had approached Russell Charles on two separate occasions with tentative feelers to buy out GFP. He had never mentioned this to Anna because the thought of selling out and retiring had been farthest from his mind. After all, it was only money the McFadden people were offering and at his age, what need was there for more money? Karen was independently wealthy, plus all that would accrue to her at his death. Mark had his safe job, and was now drawing seventy-five thousand a year for what little he contributed to the company.

If he could only talk to Karen, he might be able to come up with some acceptable decision, perhaps move Mark into one of the plants, give him more authority against the day when—when—maybe he could even—maybe—even—he—

His head began to ache and he felt a harsh, bitter taste rising in his throat, then a slow burning in his chest. A nondrinker, he wondered what he could have eaten to upset him. He tried to lie still so that he would not disturb Anna, but the burning in his chest became more painfully pronounced, and he twisted his body and rolled over on one side, hoping to relieve the pressure; but it was becoming more constant. He gasped aloud, and Anna was instantly awake. "Herschel? What is it?"

"In—indi—gestion—I think . . ." he gasped. "Ah—h . . ."

Now the pain had moved across his chest into his left arm and he began slowly to realize what was happening, remembering an article he had read some time ago; a commuter on a train, the same symptoms . . .

The light came on and he saw Anna's face as though through a piece of gauze, staring down at him in alarm. He wanted to say something to allay her anxiety, but the words refused to come. She touched his forehead with the palm of her hand, and felt the beads of sweat. She ran to the bathroom and returned with a wet washcloth to cool him. He heard her frightened voice, "Herschel, Herschel, tell me, what is it?" and saw her face drifting out of his vision, growing fainter, through eyes that were totally disoriented. And then he was alone in the growing darkness, hearing Anna's voice coming from far away, calling faintly, "Karen—Karen—doctor . . ."

"I can't tell you any more at present, Mrs. Goodwin," Dr. Danzig said somberly. "Your husband has had a heart attack. I can't tell how serious it is, nor will I attempt to minimize the danger. At the moment, he is alive, that's the important thing, to keep him alive. I've ordered an ambulance so I can take him to Columbia Presbyterian where we have the finest facilities in the world. It will take a little time before I can give you any kind of reasonable prognosis."

"Thank you, Doctor." Anna sat in the chair clutching Karen's hand tightly, wisps of dampened hair falling across her forehead, eyes staring starkly from deepened sockets, weeping silently, rocking back and forth as though in ritual prayer.

"Aunt Anna, please let me help you get dressed. We'll want to be ready to go to the hospital." To Dr. Danzig, "Will that be allowed, Doctor?"

"Of course. I can assure you Mr. Goodwin is in no pain."

"His eyes are open," Anna said.

"He is not awake, Mrs. Goodwin. He can feel nothing."

"He is unconscious," Anna said bleakly.

"In a manner of speaking, yes."

Mark was downstairs awaiting the arrival of the ambulance, Max with him to render what assistance he might be called upon to give. Karen and Gerda began helping Anna to get dressed, and a moment later the ambulance growled up to the door.

4

After a few hours of restless sleep, Steve felt dull and worn. He had gone to bed angry with himself, with Peggy, with Karen, with the world, and had awakened in the same angry mood. He lit a cigarette, went into the kitchen, and made a fresh pot of coffee, then started toward the front door to get his copy of the Sunday *Times* when the phone rang.

It was Karen. "Steve?"

Her voice was a mere whisper, coming from miles away. "Karen? What is it? Where are you?"

"At Columbia Presbyterian . . ."

"What's happened?"

"My uncle. He had a heart attack last night shortly after everyone left."

"God! How bad is it, Karen?"

"All we've been told is that it's serious. He's still unconscious. He—he's in an oxygen tent—they're doing everything possible . . ."

"Karen, is there anything I can do, anything at all?"

"There's nothing anyone can do but wait. They say if he gets through the next week or ten days, there's hope."

"What about you, your aunt?"

"Dr. Danzig gave her a strong sedative. She's asleep now, here at the hospital. Mark went home a little while ago."

"Karen, I'm sorry, terribly sorry. I don't know what to say."

"Nothing, Steve. God, I'm so tired, but I don't want to sleep, dream . . ."

"Karen, let the doctor give you something. You can't do without sleep at a time like this."

"I'll be all right. There's so much to do. Mark is calling the people at the office, and I thought I should call you. Would you mind telling Mr. Leary?"

"Of course. I'll phone." The phone went dead. He

decided he would call Keith, and got the houseman on the line, who told him the Allards were still asleep. Steve told him to awaken Keith, that it was an emergency. Minutes later, Keith's sleep-filled voice came on. "Steve? What time is it? I feel as though I'd just gotten to bed."

"It's twenty minutes to seven."

"Jesus, has somebody dropped the Bomb?"

"Keith, it's Mr. Goodwin. Sometime after we left last night he had a heart attack. It's serious. He's at Columbia Presbyterian, unconscious, under sedatives, and oxygen."

"Oh, God! Have you called Bill?"

"No. Karen Lawson phoned only a few moments ago and I thought I'd call you first."

"Okay, Steve. I'll phone Bill, but I'll wait awhile. I want to think about it first. Stay put. I'll get back to you a little later."

Steve rang off. He went to the door to get his paper, and glanced over the front page, knowing there could be no word about Herschel Goodwin this soon. The coffee was ready and he drank two cups while he pondered the effects of this new, unforeseen crisis. He recalled vaguely an earlier notion, expressed by one of his predecessors, that the GFP account woud be safe with the Leary Agency only as long as Herschel Goodwin remained in good health. What now?

Who would be in command? Mark, the professional relative? Curtis Fitzjohn, by virtue of seniority and his thorough knowledge of corporate affairs, was Herschel's logical successor as president, but there was Mark waiting in the wings, husband of Herschel's only living relative other than Anna. Stock control would undoubtedly fall to Anna Goodwin, but Mark's role in the business, in these unexpected circumstances, could hardly be overlooked. No matter how the wheel of chance turned, Mark would still be a positive factor as far as the GFP advertising account was concerned.

And what about the X-factor, Karen?

Waiting, he became impatient to be doing something, talking with someone. Bill, Keith, anyone. He had a fourth cup of coffee, lit another cigarette, then decided to shave. The phone remained silent. He showered and dressed, then prepared a light breakfast but left most of it on his plate, drank another cup of coffee, and leafed idly through the *Times*.

At ten-thirty, the phone rang. Bill Leary. "Steve, Keith

called me about an hour ago. I haven't had time to give this any very deep thought, but Keith and I are going to my office for a talk. Can you meet us there?"

"Of course. When?"

"I'm ready to leave now."

"I'll get there as soon as I can."

He walked to the corner of Third Avenue, then south to Sixty-ninth Street before he could flag an empty cab. Going directly to the Thirty-fifth floor, he found Keith and Bill in the latter's office, their discussion well underway. Steve at once diagnosed the look on Bill's face as one of repressed concern. Keith, the stubby pipestem gripped tightly between his teeth, said calmly, "Steve, as our resident expert on the subject, do you think you can operate that damned coffeemaker of Mrs. Kimbrough's?"

"Sure." In Lucy's office, Steve got the coffee going, then returned to Bill's office.

"Depends, of course, on who will be picking up the loose ends," Bill was saying. "I don't know of anyone over in Harrison who . . ."

"Fitzjohn," Keith said. "He's the only man who's had his nose and fingers in every corporate department. Outside of the manufacturing end, Curt originally organized the rest of the setup."

"As far as we are concerned, where will Lawson fit into this thing?" Bill gestured to Steve. "Any ideas on that score, Steve?"

"I'm as far out in left field as you are, Bill. This whole thing could be a temporary crisis. It could blow away with the first good report from the doctors."

"Be realistic, Steve. Herschel Goodwin is at least seventy years old, probably more. Even if he comes out of it with a fairly whole skin, he'll never be one hundred percent active again. At his age, another attack, however slight, could finish him off, if this one doesn't."

What the hell are we doing here, burying the man prematurely? Steve thought. *Not one of us has even expressed grief for the man, only the possible loss of the goddamned account. We're writing him off before he actually dies and nobody gives a damn for the man, the human being. The only reason we seem to want him alive is for the account, the goddamned account is all that's important.*

"Is the coffee ready, Steve?" Keith asked.

He got up without a word and went to get the coffee,

two cups, foregoing his own in some infantile display of silent protest.

Then Bill said it, and his implication was clear. "Steve, how did it happen that Mrs. Lawson phoned *you* this morning?"

Steve caught the special emphasis on the word "you" at once. He checked the first angry retort that leaped into his mind. "I don't know, Bill. Maybe it was pure impulse on her part. She knows I handle the account with Mark."

"Strange," Bill said. "I should think her more natural impulse, after last night, would have been to call me, as head of the agency, wouldn't you?"

"I can't answer a rhetorical question, Bill. I have no way of knowing what Mrs. Lawson's emotional feelings were at the time."

"I see. Well, to get back to an earlier question, how do you see our chances with Mark Lawson in the event of Herschel Goodwin's death?"

"I'm afraid I can't make any evaluation, Bill. Only time and Mark can answer that."

"Is there any suggestion you can make that might further our chances? This is now an $18,000,000-plus account we're discussing, with over $3,000,000 in gross profits at stake. If I seem concerned, it's only because I am."

"I'll have to pass that one. All I can suggest is that we go on servicing the account as best we can, and see what happens."

"You know that Lawson has made some veiled threats to move the account if he ever got the chance, don't you?"

"I've heard that from Bill Makyrios and Jim Whipple. Mark has even hinted the same to me in moments of pique, but I still feel he'd have a rough time convincing Ward and Mr. Fitzjohn. And, if it came to a showdown, Mrs. Goodwin."

"And Mrs. Lawson?"

Steve stared back at Leary with anger. "Bill, are you making some point that I don't seem to be getting?"

Bill remained perfectly calm, his words even. "No, of course not. I simply don't want to exclude any possible source we can count on for support if it ever becomes necessary."

"I don't think I can add any more to what I've already said." Steve stood up. "Do you mind if I leave now?"

"No, and thank you for coming down. I'm sorry to have burdened you with this on a Sunday."

"I'll see you in the morning, Steve," Keith added.

On Monday morning, other than the buzzing of the office grapevine, there was no further word. Steve phoned Mark's office, but Mark, as Steve had suspected, was not there. A call to the hospital brought only the floor nurse's reply that Mr. Goodwin was resting quietly and doing as well as could be expected. He heard nothing from Karen.

A week passed, and it was another Monday, and there was still no word of improvement in Herschel's condition, no contact with either Karen or Mark. Tuesday was July 14. Imprinted beneath the date on his calendar was a line devoted to the information that this was Bastille Day in France. Beneath that, for some reason, now obscure, he had made a notation some months ago that the next day, the fifteenth, was *D-Day—Chevalier*. It also occurred to him that since the night of Herschel Goodwin's attack, his relationship with Peggy had grown very cool, if not icy.

July 14. Ten years and a month since he had sat in Allard's office hearing the words, "I'll go along with Oscar Sterling's and Wade Barrett's judgment, and my own first impressions ... report to Mr. Kelso in Personnel next Monday morning at nine o'clock. . . ." That day in 1960 had been indelibly engraved on his memory, along with the warning, "If you haven't made it to a top spot by the time you're thirty-five. . . ."

He had made it, with almost five years to spare, but the foundation upon which his success rested had become too shaky for comfort, tilting the sense of security that should have come with the self-satisfaction of achievement. It rested, as with all account men, on his ability to maintain a healthy, firm relationship with The Client. Mark Lawson. Or, as Bill Leary seemed to have divined, with Karen Lawson.

Bill's questions about Karen on that Sunday had thrown him off balance, and although his first impulse had been to challenge Bill openly, he knew that frank disclosure would have been the end. With an $18,000,000 account at stake, Bill—and Keith—*must* write him off, in favor of a client the agency had kept on its roster for over thirty years.

The client comes first. Before Flag, Motherhood, Country.

Name of the game.

Steve stared at the Chevalier notation again. Another case of skating on very thin ice. Ted McCreery had moved over to Chevalier's Park Avenue offices to become advertising director, succeeding Hugh Benson, his prospective father-in-law, now Chevalier's president. George Long, who had replaced Ted as account executive, had developed the renewal campaign for Chevalier. Bill Leary and George had made the presentation to Ted, Hugh Benson, and the Chevalier staff, and the final decision was due tomorrow.

If Ted—as Steve privately suspected he would—decided to throw the account to the Weatherford Agency (since Charlie Weatherford and Ted had been seen lunching openly recently), $3,800,000 in billings would fly out the window. Enough reason for Bill to be edgy. If—to add insult to injury—the GFP account went down the drain, the loss of over $22,000,000 in billings would inflict irreparable damage, and could possibly wreck the agency. Other clients might easily become suspicious and nervous when the word began spreading that Leary was losing prime accounts, that its top writers and art directors were out looking for new connections. It was not unknown nor unusual in advertising. Back in 1964, the Wade Agency in Chicago closed its doors and sent one hundred fifty employees searching for new homes when the Alka Seltzer and Toni accounts moved some $14,000,000 in billings to another agency.

One day to go.

Meanwhile, the chill between Steve and Peggy had become decidedly noticeable. She made the morning coffee as usual, opened and sorted the mail, said "Good morning" when he arrived, brought the mail, messages, and memos with his coffee, but the former easy pattern between them had been reduced to matters of formal business routine. She had not as yet submitted the bills for her Saturday outfit and in his preoccupation with the work and other problems at hand, the status of Herschel Goodwin's condition, and Karen, he had overlooked the matter.

He dictated several letters, and replies to the interoffice memos, held an art-copy conference with the regular GFP group, had a review session with Adrian, viewed some television commercials with Gary Parris and Don Bryce, and Tuesday passed without his having seen Bill or Keith, who were at that moment primarily concerned with the fate of the Chevalier renewal.

Bill had seen Hugh Benson once since the presentation, but Benson, involved in higher levels of decision brought on by his ascendancy to the presidency, made it clear he had no knowledge that another agency was involved, and had every confidence in Ted McCreery's judgment. Bill had no such confidence, and two attempts to reach Ted by telephone met with failure.

At three-thirty on Wednesday, all hope of retaining the Chevalier account was shattered when Peggy brought Steve a General Office Memorandum, addressed to the "A" distribution list, which included all department heads and account supervisors. One glance at Peggy's face telegraphed the bad news.

> I regret to inform you that as of this date, this Agency has relinquished control of the Chevalier Cigarette account. Turnover will be effected by 15 August. There will be certain changes and job shifting among the present Chevalier group. Let me assure everyone concerned that every effort will be exerted to fit as many of this group as possible into other positions within our organization.
>
> WM. B. LEARY
> *President*

Steve read the memo twice. "Does Norm know about this?" he asked Peggy.

"I don't know for sure, but it would be a miracle if he didn't. The floor has been buzzing for the past half hour."

"Ask him to come in if he's free."

Norm lumbered into Steve's office and unfolded his bulk into the visitor's chair like a deflated balloon, forehead creased in a thoughtful frown. "Just heard the official crash of the bomb," he said. "That sonofabitch McCreery has a long and nasty memory."

"Well, at least it's over with," Steve said. "How many people do you think we'll lose?"

"Out of twenty-two, I'd guess at least half, give or take a few. Who got the account, Weatherford?"

"Probably. The street talk had Charlie locked in on it over a month ago."

Norm nodded. "Well, I guess Lang will move over to Charlie's stable. Probably take a dozen or more of our people with him. We'll lose Jack Freeman, Ken Nichols, and Kay Berry. The rest—who knows? They'll hit the placement agencies with their books before nightfall. I just hope our other clients don't start getting any ideas."

"I doubt it, even though it's enough to give the brass around here some nervous moments. Do you think we could use a couple of the Chevalier people, Norm?"

"How fat are we?"

"If B & B keeps rolling, I think we'll have to add a couple of copy-art teams, plus another typist and clerk. I may even have to put on an assistant for Lew Kann, and another for Gary Parris."

Thoughtfully, Norm said, "I think we can get first crack at anybody we want, if we move fast enough. I'd like to have Artie Fane and Carl Marvin, for sure, maybe Danny Rossi and Jim Cooley for the second team. No problem with the others."

"I'll suggest them to Keith if you'll back up my recommendations."

"My recommendations, under the circumstances, might not amount to a hell of a lot. After all, I could be the reason . . ."

Keith Allard came in at that moment. Norm struggled to his feet and went out. "Checking for fallout, Keith?" Steve said.

"In a way. You know how restless the troops get when something like this happens. Anybody in your section doing a Chicken Little?"

"No. I've just been discussing it with Norm. I'd like to have Fane and Marvin, maybe Rossi and Cooley, a production and TV assistant, and a couple of clerks and typists."

"I've already got one request for Fane, but I think I can work it out for you."

"What about George Lang?"

"Don't worry about George. He's already told us he's going with Weatherford and given us a fairly good idea how many he'll be taking with him, but we'll have first crack at them. We'll shift some, and lose the rest."

"Anything on the horizon to replace Chevalier?"

"A possibility or two, if Bill can forget the stock market long enough to dig in. Luckily, we've got B & B to take some of the slack up. What's more worrisome, though, is the GFP situation we were discussing Sunday a week ago. Have you been in touch with Mark this week?"

"No. I've tried to reach him several times and left word for him to call me, but he's been spending most of his time over in Harrison with Mr. Fitzjohn, looking into the production situation there."

Keith grimaced, then said, "And Karen Lawson?"

Steve again felt anger rising as Keith busied himself with his pipe, tamping and lighting it. As he sat on the sofa across from Steve's desk, Steve said, "This makes the second time Karen Lawson's name has come up in our discussions about GFP. First Bill, now you. I'd love to have you spell it out for me, if you don't mind, Keith."

"All right, Steve, I'll level with you if you promise to keep your cool. What we don't need right now is an internal eruption to split us wide apart. Gentleman's agreement?"

Steve nodded.

"All right. First of all," Keith resumed, "we both know what's at stake here and we can't afford to overlook any possible means of saving the account if anything should happen to Herschel Goodwin."

"I understand that clearly."

"Good. When an agency of this size has an account of that magnitude at stake, you can also understand the importance of keeping it healthy by whatever means are necessary. Anything that affects it adversely becomes vital to management.

"Which brings us to the cogent point. When you moved into your new apartment, Karen Lawson wasn't as careful as she might have been when she set out to decorate and furnish your place. Donna Leary ran into her at Albrecht's, where most of your new furniture came from. Mrs. Lawson didn't recognize Donna, which was fortunate. Donna was curious, however, and as a long-time customer, Mr. Albrecht supplied the answers to a few questions and learned that the chairs, table, and sofa were going to your new address.

"If you had been a little more perceptive, you may have noticed that the Oriental vase Bill and Donna sent you as a housewarming gift also came from Albrecht's. Mind you, this isn't an accusation, Steve, but when Bill heard that the apartment of his newest account supervisor was being furnished by the client's wife, you can understand that he could have a few misgivings."

"Thanks, Keith." Steve's voice was rimmed with the choler of inadequacy, even stupidity. "I appreciate Bill's and your concern . . ."

"What aggravated the situation was when Mrs. Lawson

carelessly made the slip of phoning you that Sunday morning, instead of Bill, leaving him with the feeling that he was no longer in control. I might add that Bill was prepared to make an issue of it that morning, but I intervened before you got there. Maybe I was wrong, but our friendship goes back too far . . ."

"Oh, come off it, Keith. It's only been a mere ten years and what do ten years mean when there's an account hanging in the balance?"

Keith let a moment pass, then said calmly, "More than you want to believe at this moment, Steve. I told you a long time ago that we're in a tough business. I could have stood aside on several occasions that I can recall and let you and Bill go at each other, but I know what would happen in this latter case and I advised him to use the same caution I'm asking you to use. You and I have been more than working associates, we've been close friends for ten years. I've watched you come up and can take some of the credit for the progress you've made here. I know you've had offers from other agencies during that time, from larger shops than this one, and I've appreciated your loyalty in remaining here. Of course, it has paid off. However, I can't let you dismiss any opportunity to put forth your best effort to save our most important account when, and if, it becomes necessary."

"Which means that you and Bill believe I can still be useful."

"If you want to put it on that basis, I think you owe us that much."

Testily, "Would it make things a little more pleasant all the way around if I offered you my resignation?"

Keith nodded slowly. "I've even expected that, Steve." He shifted his position and said, "Cool it. We're not asking for your resignation."

"And I don't know just what you're asking me to do to save the account."

"Since you're not denying anything, you're obviously doing it already."

"Keith, for Christ's sake, stop talking in riddles, will you? I've worked my goddamned brains and guts out for this agency, taken Lawson's abuse for longer than I like to think about, but I won't lay my personal life on the line for Leary, GFP, or anybody but me, and that's final."

Keith stood up, walked to the desk, and knocked the bowl of his pipe against the rim of an ashtray. "Steve," he said, "in another few years, you could be admitted to a limited partnership in the Leary Agency. Bill and I realize we've got to bring younger men up faster in order to compete with modern trends, and replace some of the dead wood we've been carrying too long. What more can you expect elsewhere?"

When Steve refused to look up and answer the question put to him, Keith said, "Think about it, Steve," and walked out.

A few minutes later Peggy came in with several letters to be signed, cool, reserved as she had been since the aftermath of the Goodwin party, waiting quietly as he penned his name, and picking up each letter as he signed it. Handing her the last one, he said, "What's the latest scoop from the water-cooler crowd?"

Offhandedly, "Very little. Just some speculation about who will be leaving."

"Accounts change every day, you know."

"Anybody who reads *Ad Age* or *Daily* knows that it's that kind of business."

Struggling to keep the conversation going, "It's not too different from other businesses, is it? They all have their own special hazards."

"I'm beginning to find that out."

"Peg . . ."

"It's past 5:30. I'd like to leave now, if I may."

He sat at his desk nursing his own fury, angry with Peggy, and with himself. With Bill, and Keith. With Karen and Mark. With the whole goddamned screwed-up business . . . his job . . . the world. But more than anything else, with himself.

He heard the outer door close with force, as though Peggy had slammed it shut to let him know she was leaving, and it was minutes before he was able to take his eyes off the door that separated his office from hers. Alone now, he got out the master control folder and reviewed the portion of B & B's budget projection again. He had already reduced the general magazine and newspaper figures, throwing the additional money into more heavily expanded television exposure. Every such change required revisions in space- and time-buying estimates, and re-allocation of schedules, as well as manipulating creative personnel from print to electronic media, plus outlining his justification for the changes.

Studying the figures, it suddenly occurred to him how

far he had divorced himself from his original goal in life. In the beginning he had wanted only to follow in Grady's footsteps and become a newspaperman. Later, he decided that after a few years in newspaper work, he would become a novelist, with the freedom to work where and as he pleased. But Grady's untimely death, and debts, had forced him into advertising as a means to support himself, and there he had experienced an even greater sense of creativity than newspaper work had ever given him.

And now, ten years later, moving progressively up the ladder, he had become an administrator, supervising the creative efforts of his two groups, periodically visiting the client, generally removing himself from the truly creative area where he felt he belonged: formulating ideas, writing copy, conferring with his art director to decide on art techniques . . .

How far, he wondered, do men stray from the goals they set for themselves before they realize that the goal has passed beyond reach? How much do the financial considerations and rewards soften the disappointment, the knowledge that the race toward achievement has become a race for money? And status? And, considering the Larry Prices and Wade Barretts of his world, where now was the security he believed should rightfully be his?

5

On Thursday morning at ten, Peggy relayed the message from Mark Lawson. He wanted to see Steve in his office at once.

"He didn't ask to speak with me?" Steve asked.

"It wasn't Mr. Lawson who called. His secretary gave me the message for you," Peggy told him.

Steve pulled on his jacket and left immediately. Charlotte kept him waiting for a full twenty minutes before Bob Davies emerged from the inner office, exchanged a brief, smiling, "Good morning," with him, and went into his own office. A minute later, Mark's voice said over the intercom, "Send Mr. Gilman in."

Mark's usually clean desk was littered with a dozen or more folders, some spread out and opened, the others stacked in a pile to one side, markers jutting out from their edges. "Sit down, Steve," he said. "I'm pressed for time. This thing with the old man is throwing a lot of extra work on all of us."

"How is Mr. Goodwin?"

"Barely holding his own." There was little compassion in Mark's voice. "He had a rough time last night, but he got through it safely. The doctors have their fingers crossed." He closed a folder that lay before him and put it to one side. "I've been spending a lot of time in Harrison and at some of the other plants, as you know. We've brought Harvey Wayne back from the Elgin plant and made him general superintendent of production, which takes care of that problem for the time being, but there are a hell of a lot of other things I'm working on with Curt and Ward. So, let's get down to some advertising talk."

"We're moving ahead on the September material for the regular line, and the B & B national . . ."

"Never mind that for now," Mark interrupted briskly. "With the old man out, there are going to be a number of changes around here; in personnel, policy, pretty much everything. Curt and Ward and I had a meeting last night and early this morning. Some changes have already been made." Mark looked up with a sudden grin. "Steve, I once told you that if you stick with me . . ."

"I remember, Mark. Diamonds for shirt studs."

"Okay. I'm about to make you a proposition and I want you to hear me out before you say *yes* or *no*."

"I'm listening."

"First, what are you drawing down at Leary?"

Steve shook his head negatively. "I'm sorry, Mark, but that's a little too personal."

"Okay, I'll guess at it. Forty, forty-five thousand dollars a year?"

"It's your guess, Mark."

"I'd say I'm pretty close. Okay, let it pass for now. How would you like to double that, even go to one hundred thousand dollars a year?"

Instinctively, Steve's lips pursed into a silent whistle. He said, "Mark, I don't think I want to go any further with this line of . . ."

"A hundred grand a year, Steve. You'd have to be a goddamned moron to turn your nose up at that." Mark was smiling superciliously, but the look in his eyes was hard and cold with cunning. At a loss for words as the figure of one hundred thousand dollars dangled before him, Steve remained silent. "I'm beginning to get through to you, aren't I?" Mark said.

"You're still talking in circles, Mark. What's on your mind?"

"Okay, the nitty-gritty. According to our latest projections," he tapped one of the folders with a manicured finger, "we're going to be spending about six million dollars for B & B's division alone. Add that to our GFP budget, and we're talking around nineteen-twenty million by next year. A year from then, we could be hitting twenty-two million or better, and I've got some ideas about acquiring additional properties that will boost that figure even higher. Even at twenty million, the agency's cut comes to about three million dollars in outright commissions, plus extra for what you call collateral profits, right?"

"Give or take a little, that's about right." Slowly, two possibilities began forming in Steve's mind. One, Mark was planning to move up in the corporate ranks, and two . . . Mark interrupted that thought. "Say, four million gross. That's a hell of a nice round figure to think about, eh, Steve?"

Steve nodded coolly. "Yes, I'd say so."

"Okay." Mark crossed his legs and swiveled his chair to allow him to face Steve more directly. "Four million," he repeated, impressing the figure deeper into Steve's mind, engraving it there. "I think I can convince Fitzjohn to open an agency of our own to handle nothing but GFP's eighteen-twenty-million advertising account and pick up that four million for the company. Wait . . ." as Steve started to speak, "let me finish.

"I think we could afford to pay the head of the Goodwin Agency—or call it by any other name—a minimum of, say, a hundred thousand dollars a year, plus the salaries of the people he would need to work with him. He could set up an office somewhere near here, buy his creative print and TV material from outside independent organizations and studios, and use our own marketing and merchandising people. We'd show a hell of a profit and nobody ever got hurt taking a profit, did they?"

"You've gone into this house agency thing pretty deeply, haven't you, Mark?"

"There's nothing secret about it, for Christ's sake. Hell, I can name a dozen house agencies that were started by big accounts for the same reason, and with smaller budgets than ours. I know you could name another dozen who have done it successfully. Steve, for God's sake, wake up and look around you. What's the point of working for half of what you can make on your own? One hundred thousand dollars and everything that goes with it, the fringe benefits, running your own shop instead of errands for Leary. Hell, in ten years, by the time you're forty, you could have enough salted away to take care of you no matter what happens, not like that sad bastard, Barrett, or the others who can't get the time of day after they reach forty-five or fifty."

"Are you talking about a ten-year contract?" Steve said suddenly.

"Contract? What kind of contract do you have with Leary? None. And any day he decides to kiss you off, the way he gave it to Price out in L.A., where the hell are you?"

Where am I now? Steve asked himself.

"You're vulnerable, Steve. Anything can happen to you. Blow a campaign, you're up the creek. Louse up with a client, you're out." Grinning, "I could do that to you, and you know it. All I have to do is call Bill and tell him I can't get along with you and I want another man assigned to the account. I did that with Joe Childs and a week later Sorenson took over and Childs was out on his ass looking for a job."

"Why did you knock Childs out, Mark?"

"What difference does that make? He was before your time."

"I'm just curious."

"He offended me. He was another one of those freak intellectual bastards I can't stand, always nit-picking, throwing his goddamned superior Ivy League education around. You and I have gotten along, Steve. We can go a long way together."

Steve shuddered inwardly. "I can't give you a snap answer to a thing like this, Mark . . ."

"I'm not asking for an answer here and now. Just think it over. A hundred grand minimum, to start. And there'll be more to follow."

"Just out of curiosity, have you discussed this with anyone else, Mark? Mr. Fitzjohn or Mr. Hardwick?"

Mark smiled coolly. "Hell, no. Things are happening too fast, but when it's all over, I'm not planning on being advertising director, old buddy. I've got bigger things in mind. Don't worry about Fitz or Ward, either. I'll have 'em eating out of my hand and neither of 'em will be able to look down his nose at a proposition that spells a couple of million pure profit."

I wouldn't bet too much on that, Steve said to himself. *Just one more of life's ironies to complicate an already complicated situation.*

Mark glanced at his watch. "I've got to run now. I'm due at the hospital to meet Karen and Anna. Remember, Steve, you'll be running your own show, with your own people. Nobody breathing down your neck . . ."

Except you.

"And more money than you'll ever make at Leary or any other agency if I decide to pull GFP out. Think about that."

6

Once, long ago, he had puzzled over the expression, "Know thyself" and had asked Grady how a man might really know himself since his own viewpoint could hardly be objective.

"Ah, Steve," Grady had said with a smile, "the inventory of Self is a very trying and painful occupation; exploring, and uncovering the hidden, unwanted portions of one's life. To live with honest thoughts about oneself is an act of bravery that few men possess. If I'm rambling, forgive me. Maybe it's because I can't find the answer you're looking for."

He saw the flash of disappointment on Steve's young, eager face and said, "There are many ways to measure a man, or for a man to measure himself; some do it by their accomplishments, others by their stride, even their shadows. Most, however, are measured by their beliefs, their inner thoughts, and these measurements are taken within the secrecy of their own minds.

"You want to be a writer. Well, I believe the training a writer undergoes better qualifies him to take his own measure than most, because he must accurately examine life and the lives of his characters, and their beliefs, and thoughts. That essential perceptive quality may some day give you the answer to your question."

Introspectively, Steve tried to examine his inner self.

Tempted as he might be by Mark's offer, the hundred thousand dollars looming big in the foreground, the shadow of Karen stood as a barrier before him. His life, thus far, added up to a series of shadow incidents, like beads on a string; weighted heavily, nearing the breaking point.

He had been dishonest with Libby, with Robin, with Mark, with Karen, and with Peggy. Also with himself. Now here was an opportunity to be dishonest with Bill Leary and Keith Allard. Ten years more toward a limited partnership against a month or two and head of his own agency. Correction. GFP's house agency. And a continuing affair with Karen as a plus benefit to his hundred thousand dollar income?

In his thirty years, what had he really accomplished? And when he left it all behind, thirty, perhaps, forty, years from now—if he were that fortunate—what would remain to say that Steve Gilman had once lived on Earth, and here was the mark he had made? Beads. Unwanted, useless beads.

He thought then of the books his father had once collected, read, and re-read. Thomas Paine's *Common Sense,* Thoreau's *Civil Disobedience,* Upton Sinclair, Karl Marx, Dostoyevsky, Hemingway and countless others who had left their legacies for generations yet to come.

In those days, when he had tried to sell his short stories, the novella, the outline for the historical novel, one agent had told him, "You haven't lived long enough to know or evaluate life, and to record it. When you've lived with it, touched, savored, and been beaten by it, you'll be ready to write about it. No man will have to tell you when, and only you will know how. If you leave only one good book behind, you'll have left a mark no one else can ever erase."

He wondered now if he had lived long enough to qualify for that vague prophecy made so long ago. And wondering, he reached back into his mind and thought about the book. Peggy had urged him to get back to it. So had Karen. Instinct told him that he could do it, should do it once and for all. Open up a new career with a dream restored. Get out of the ratrace, out of the jungle, work, with no one looking over his shoulder suggesting changes, demanding changes. Stand or fall by the product of his own mind. . . .

He returned to his office at noon. Peggy was out for lunch, and Chuck getting ready to leave. "Anything new from Forty-second Street?" Chuck asked.

"No. And no word from the hospital."

"Well—how about some lunch?"

"Not now. I've got some things to clear up first."

"Okay. I hear Wade Barrett is flying in tomorrow for conferences."

"Where did you get that?"

"The jungle telegraph." Chuck was grinning insolently.

"All right, Chuck, get it off your mind. What's the word?"

"Well, I hear the Big Gun called Wade around eleven this morning, that's eight o'clock West Coast time. Seems like some broad answered the phone in Wade's apartment, stoned, and told Bill to go peddle his goddamned aluminum siding or whatever he was selling someplace else. Then Wade got on the phone, bagged to the eyeballs, and Bill read him the riot act."

"Oh, Jesus!"

"It won't be anything like a joyous reunion . . ."

"Who told you about this?"

"My secretary is on the same transmission belt as Peggy. And Lucy Kimbrough's typist. You know Bill always has his long distance calls taped, don't you?"

"That's something else we need to bolster morale, a shakeup on the Coast."

"Well, how about lunch? You look like you could use a fix."

"I could, but it won't solve anything, only prolong the agony. Take off, and try not to spread the glad tidings around. I'll see you later."

He was still at his desk when Peggy returned. "Have you had your lunch?" she asked.

"No."

"Shall I send down for a sandwich?"

"No, thanks. I'm in no mood for throwing up."

"Then you've heard about Mr. Barrett?"

"Yes."

"Oh." Then, "Can you spare a few minutes?"

"Of course. Anything special?"

"Yes. I want to turn in my resignation."

The announcement, coming on top of Mark's proposal and the news about Wade Barrett, was the hard right that followed the left jab. "For God's sake, Peggy, why?"

"For personal reasons."

"Peggy, please . . ."

"I've been thinking about it for sometime. I haven't seen my family for quite a while, and the idea of spending a few months in Omaha gets more and more appealing."

"And it can't be satisfied with a vacation?"

"Not this time."

"Why don't you spell it out for me?"

"Well. . . . I've suddenly discovered I'm not enjoying my job any more. There are plenty of replacements around now that Chevalier's gone . . ."

"I'm not looking for a replacement."

"And I've lived up to my promise. My five years are just about up."

He remembered the promise, made when he first interviewed her, and grinned wryly. "How about an option on another five?"

"No, Steve. I'm serious. It's over, and I'd like to leave on August 15. That will give me almost a month to break in another girl."

"It goes back to the night of the Goodwin party, of course. This has nothing to do with your job. It's just between you and me, isn't it?"

She didn't answer at once. "And Karen," he added.

Peggy said, "Steve, I've enjoyed the five years I've worked with you. I've slept with you and enjoyed that, too. I'm all mixed up, I know, but I can't be a full-time secretary and a part-time whore. I don't know how to—to . . ." She turned away, her eyes brimming with tears.

Steve leaned back toward her, and took her hand into his. "Peggy, please listen to me . . ."

She stood up, her back turned toward him, shaking her head negatively. "I don't want to listen, Steve. You'll just talk me into something I don't want . . . can't understand. Just let me go, please." Before he could reach her, she was gone. When he looked into her office a moment later, she was not there.

Karen called him at 5:30 as he was preparing to leave for the day. Her voice sounded tired, strained with emotion as she told him that Herschel was holding on, but barely. The doctors were giving him no more than an even chance, but her static sentences indicated she was less hopeful than they.

"How is your aunt, Karen?"

"Surprisingly well, once she got over the initial shock. She's strong-willed in certain ways, in emergencies. I wish I could be as strong."

"I saw Mark for a while today."

"Mark?" she said. "I've never seen such a remarkable change in a man." She laughed nervously. "Suddenly he's become all business, holding meetings at Harrison, discussing all sorts of intricate matters with Aunt Anna, Mr. Fitzjohn, the attorneys, calling in plant managers from everywhere for conferences."

"I noticed the difference in him today. Karen, I'm deeply concerned about you . . ."

"Don't be, Steve. I'm all right. Just tired, very tired. I've been spending so much time at the hospital, hoping for some good news, waiting for some change for the better. I've been thinking a lot."

"I'd like to have a few minutes with you, just to talk . . ."

"Not—now—until something—we know something . . ." Her voice broke, and then in a hoarse whisper, "Steve—Steve . . ."

"What, Karen?"

"Aunt Anna wants to see you."

"Me? About what?"

"She's been having discussions with Russ Charles and Mr. Fitzjohn—I don't know—there are decisions that have to be made. She has had Uncle Herschel's power of attorney for a long time—in case—in case . . ."

"I don't know how that would concern me, Karen. If it involves business, why not Mr. Leary or Mr. Allard?"

"She asked specifically for you. Could you call on her tomorrow at eleven?"

"At the hospital?"

"No. My house."

"Will you be there?"

"No. I'm going to Wyecliffe in the morning to bring some clothes and other things back that Aunt Anna needs."

Intuitively, "Karen does your aunt know about us—have you told her anything. . . ?"

"I've got to go now, Steve," she replied. "Eleven o'clock. Aunt Anna will be expecting you." The phone went dead.

7

Considering Bill Leary's querulous attitude because Karen had bypassed him when Herschel Goodwin had been stricken, Steve decided against telling him, or Keith, about his impending visit with Anna Goodwin. With Mark suddenly taking a stronger interest in GFP's internal affairs there was no way of knowing—no indication from Karen—the purpose of Anna's request that he call on her, so he prepared to leave with some apprehension.

At ten-thirty he told Peggy he was going over to Ascon Productions to check out a rehearsal and would go to lunch from there. At 10:55 he arrived at the Eighty-fifth Street house. Max admitted him and showed him up to the second-floor sitting room and a few moments later, Anna Goodwin entered. She looked wan and tired, her eyes sunk deeply into shadowed sockets of weariness, hands clutched together, yet walking erect as she crossed the room to where he was standing. After a brief exchange of greetings she sat in one of a pair of armchairs and indicated the other for Steve.

"I have just spoken to Dr. Danzig and Dr. Lindstrom. They have called in several cardiac specialists and neurologists. They are hopeful. No more."

"At least he isn't suffering."

"Yes. That is a blessing. If he must go, and I pray to God he won't be taken from me, I hope he will go peacefully in sleep."

Steve murmured his concurrence with that hope. "I am sure you are curious about my reason for wanting to talk with you, Mr. Gilman," Anna continued, "and not Mr. Leary. You understand that with the suddenness of my husband's—illness—it has been necessary for me to become involved in the business, not in any particular function except that I have been forced to make certain decisions about who shall have the authority to do what.

"I've been guided by Mr. Fitzjohn, Mr. Charles, and my niece's husband in some of those decisions, Mr. Gilman, and now . . ." with a brittle smile, "I am turning to you."

"If this involves advertising, Mrs. Goodwin, may I suggest that Mr. Leary or Mr. Allard would be better choices to advise you?"

"No, Mr. Gilman, I think not, in this case. If it were

only advertising, I would agree with you, but this conversation is very private between you and myself. It concerns—you may have guessed by now—Karen and Mark. And you."

Steve began to feel the constriction in his throat and chest. In spite of efficient air-conditioning, he felt clammy perspiration beginning to dampen his shirt front. He started to speak, but Anna's words cut across his attempt.

"When this happened, Karen and I were terror-stricken. Later at the hospital, waiting, waiting, we drew closer together than we have been since she was a child, when her mother and stepfather were accidentally drowned and she came to live with us at Wyecliffe. As she may have told you, Karen's first marriage to Julian Roth turned out to be a mistake, a failure. It was a terrible disappointment to us when they divorced. My husband and I felt that Karen's second marriage to Mark was not an ideal one, certainly not what we could or should expect a marriage to be, not what our own had been. There was no—I hate to use the word *togetherness*—no real closeness, or sharing. Herschel and I talked about it often, but never to Karen, because Karen was never the kind of girl who would stand for what she called interference.

"But on that Sunday night, out of guilt or some other emotional reaction or compulsion, Karen began talking to me like a young daughter would to her mother, needing comfort. She cried because she couldn't remember the last time she had said to her uncle, 'I love you.' You are uncomfortable, Mr. Gilman. Shall I ring for Max to bring you a drink?"

"No, thank you. I assume, then, that Karen told you about me. Us."

"About herself and Mark, and about you. But mostly about herself. Long before she met Mark, even before she married Julian. She didn't ask for forgiveness, nothing maudlin. It was a statement of the things she had done in her life without knowing why she did them. I don't want to go into that any deeper, Mr. Gilman. I see no reason to make this more painful for either of us."

Steve nodded, waiting.

"So it all comes down to now, today. And Karen's marriage."

"Yes. Of course."

"You are not married at the moment, are you, Mr.

Gilman? I understand from Karen that you have been divorced. Tell me, how do you feel about marriage?"

"I can't answer that question, Mrs. Goodwin, not at the moment."

She smiled a wintry smile. "I almost suspected you couldn't. Can you answer this for me: do you love Karen enough to marry her if she were to divorce Mark?"

That question, which shouldn't really have surprised him, did; to such an extent that no quick reply was forthcoming. "You can't answer, Mr. Gilman, which is in itself an answer, isn't it?"

"I'm sorry that I've disappointed you," Steve said, "but it isn't an easy question to answer. Let me say this, however. Call it what you will, love, or sexual attraction, what happened between Karen and me was not deliberate on her part nor, I think, on mine. It did happen and there were, of course, obstacles that prevented either of us from bringing the issue to any conclusion."

"You make your living with words, Mr. Gilman, but you aren't saying anything, only talking."

"I am trying to explain . . ."

"Without explaining anything meaningful. I asked you a simple, direct question and you can't answer with a clear *yes* or *no*. Let me remove what you might call another obstacle from your mind. Your position with the Leary Agency or with GFP is not in jeopardy. That is why I asked to see you instead of going directly to Mr. Leary or Mr. Allard. Can you answer the question now, Mr. Gilman? If Karen were to divorce Mark, do you love her enough to marry her?"

"Under certain conditions, if she were willing, yes," Steve replied hesitantly.

Again, Anna smiled her brittle smile. "A gentlemanly answer, Mr. Gilman, but not an honest one, I think. If you were truly honest, the answer would be *yes*, without conditions or qualifications. So. Let me tell you something I think you should know. I have talked to Mark at great length—no, Mr. Gilman, your name never entered into our conversations. I believe that a large part of the blame is Herschel's and mine. Mark should have learned the business from the ground up, in one of the plants, instead of being given a position that was too much for him, the kind an uncle gives his niece's husband to keep him quiet and out of trouble. That was part of Mark's problem with Karen.

"And Karen's problems are there, too, but she is willing now to undergo psychiatric treatment to straighten those problems out. With herself, and with Mark. On the other side of the coin, there is my husband to consider. Do you know what, if he lives, Karen's second divorce would do to him?

"What I want, Mr. Gilman, is to remove as many obstacles as I can so that Mark's and Karen's marriage can be made to work. I don't know if that is possible, but if there is a chance, however slight, I want to help her as much as I can. I intend to move Mark to another position within the company and bring in a new man to become advertising director, someone who understands the business and knows the job. You would continue to work with that man and not see Mark again, ever. When my husband recovers fully, God willing, I am sure he will approve of what I am doing. All I ask is that you never see Karen again."

"And the Leary Agency?" Steve forced himself to ask.

"You needn't worry. At least for the time being. I feel in my heart that my husband will recover, but I don't know if he will ever be active again in the business. It is even possible that the business may be sold to a company that has several times proposed buying it. If that happens, I am sure that one of the conditions of purchase will be that the Leary Agency will continue to handle the advertising for GFP products. My husband's strong sense of loyalty will dictate that.

"I must leave now to go to the hospital. I don't expect a *yes* or *no* answer from you, Mr. Gilman. I know you are an intelligent man and I am sure my judgment in this matter is correct. You will do the right thing."

She stood up, erect as ever, hands gripped tightly in front of her. "Good-bye, Mr. Gilman," Anna said. "I wish you well."

Steve walked west to Fifth Avenue, turned, and headed south. For a while, everything that had transpired between Anna Goodwin and himself replayed itself in his mind, as he sorted out words and meanings, visualizing her every expression as they unreeled like a scene in the viewing room.

Karen had said, *She's strong-willed in certain ways, in emergencies,* and there was no doubt about that assessment now. Even more forceful had been her strength by omission. How much easier it would have been for Anna to have had this talk with Bill Leary, to demand, even merely suggest his dismissal. Or would this have required embarrassing admissions that might later filter through to Mark?

It was a few minutes past one o'clock when he reached the Blue Baron, but the thought of an encounter with the advertising fraternity in his present mood was distasteful to him. He started toward Lexington Avenue and the Hungerford Trust Buidling, and it dawned upon him that there was no special reason or urgency for going back to his office. A cab pulled up at the corner and discharged two men. Steve got in, and gave the driver his home address.

The apartment was quiet and cool. He had no appetite for food and settled for a tall, cold Scotch and water, then dialed the agency. When Peggy answered in her crisp, efficient secretarial voice, he said, "Any messages?"

"Two. One from Mark Lawson. The other was from Mrs. Lawson, in the clear. Do you have her number in Wyecliffe?"

"Yes."

"Then that's all. What time will you be back in case anyone calls?"

"I don't know. Maybe never," he said.

"Are you all right, Steve?"

"I don't even know that."

"Where are you calling from?"

"I'm home in my own apartment with a lovely drink in my hand."

"Steve—are you stoned?"

"Not yet, but I expect I soon will be."

A slight pause, then, "Is there anything I can do to help?"

"For the moment, just cover for me."

He hung up abruptly. And now, he began to feel the keenness of embarrassment as he began again to review that hour with Anna Goodwin, talking, listening, taking her implied, yet gentle, reprimand like a callow schoolboy, unable to articulate answers to her questions, not willing to express his commitment to Karen. He recalled Anna's gracious face-saving escape hatch in allowing him to retain his job under a new GFP advertising director; or was it a simple bribe for agreeing not to see Karen again? And what would her plan for a new advertising director do to

Mark's proposal to take the GFP account out of the Leary Agency into a house agency? Evidently, Mark had no knowledge of Anna's plan . . .

Inevitably, his thoughts returned to himself. *What have I become?*

He poured another drink and sipped it slowly. *Where did I go off the track?*

It was, he decided finally, when he had put aside his writing ambitions and opted for advertising and the security it offered. And where was that highly important security now? Had he continued with his dream, completed his historical novel and gone on to the next, what might he have become in those ten years that had passed? And never having given himself the chance to find out, he would never know now. Was it too late to begin again? He knew so much more about life and living, he could *feel* it. Or did he? If he was so much more knowledgeable, why was his own life so screwed out of shape?

He had become a more than capable advertising man. Sixty thousand dollars a year proved that. What it didn't prove was that he had become a man who could face up to the realities and responsibilities of life.

He thought of Wade Barrett, his shadow following Larry Price. Both had been at the top. Larry had already gone, and Wade was about to follow. What were the odds for and against staying on top? For every Bill Leary who had inherited his agency, for every Keith Allard who remained firmly at the pinnacle, how many bodies—and minds—lay in a broken heap at the bottom, having failed?

It was three o'clock, and the phone was still in his lap. He lifted the receiver and dialed the Goodwins' Wyecliffe number. After four rings, a female voice answered.

"Mrs. Lawson, please."

"Yes, sir. May I tell her who is calling?"

"Mr. Gilman, returning her call," he added.

Moments passed before he heard her voice, strangely low and soft. "Steve?"

"Yes, Karen."

"Steve, I wanted to call you early this morning, before you left to see Aunt Anna, to tell you . . ."

"That you had told her about us?"

"Yes—"

"So that I could change my mind about going to see her?"

"I don't know—if you wanted to—I . . ."

"Karen, I know you're under a heavy emotional strain, but having told her about us, how could I not see her?"

"Oh, Steve . . ." He could hear the tears in her voice and wanted to say something to soothe her, but could find no suitable words.

"It's all over, isn't it, Karen. Is that what you wanted to tell me?"

"Steve, if—if this hadn't happened—Steve, I can't do anything more to hurt Anna. Or Uncle Herschel if, God willing, he lives. I've just begun to realize how much I've hurt them in the past, how much I have meant to them without my caring very much I—Steve—I—so much has happened. I know I need help. I can see that now. I've promised Aunt Anna that I will undergo treatment—analysis . . ." She was sobbing uncontrollably into the phone.

"She told me, Karen. I think your Aunt Anna is a very wise woman. She wants only what is best for you. Let's just let it rest there."

"I'm not doing this for Mark's sake, Steve."

"You won't know why you're doing it until you've undergone analysis. By that time, with greater responsibilities, he may change as well. But whatever happens, Karen, I wish you the best of everything."

"What about you, Steve, will you stay on?"

"I think not. I've some plans to make that will probably take me out of New York. Maybe even to California."

"So far away?"

"Wherever it is, it won't really matter much, will it?"

She said slowly, "No. I don't suppose it will."

"Good-bye, Karen. I hope everything works out."

"Steve, don't hang up yet!" A pause, then, "If it doesn't, will I know where you are?"

"I'm afraid not, Karen. If you do what you are proposing to do, it won't be much good if you hang onto the memory of what we've had. Don't be afraid. You'll know what to do with your life when you've gone through with the treatment."

"I don't know if I can do this alone."

"You won't be alone. You'll have Aunt Anna's strength to lean on. It won't work if I'm there to influence you."

"Steve—oh, Steve . . ."

"Good-bye, Karen. Make a good new life for yourself." He replaced the receiver gently and smiled wryly at the corniness of that last remark. Another bead to add to his growing string of failures.

He poured another drink, feeling little effect as he drank it, yet sensing a lack of control over his life, moving without direction. Where? He tried to concentrate on that *Where,* a future which now seemed dimmer than ever before.

Steve knew what he needed, what all truly dedicated executives need. As supervisor heading two groups, leadership was the prime requisite. To lead without coercion, calmly, with no show of anxiety; to suggest a clear road, then give his creative personnel free rein to articulate and delineate the basic theme of the program; to wring their minds, yet bleed with them in their agony to produce the best within themselves, all the while offering wise counsel and protection during the creative process. He must be father, friend, and confidant, walk the slender tightrope that stretched between the thirty-fifth floor and the thirty-fourth floor; and to the office of the Client.

To achieve that mental and gymnastic feat, he needed confidence, courage, pride, and a dash of what Sam Abrams called *chutzpah.* The respect of others. More important, he needed respect for himself.

At this moment, that was what Steve lacked.

8

When the phone rang, waking him from his dozing, the sky was still light outside. He let the ringing go on and on until the caller gave up. He added more Scotch to the melted ice in his glass and drank it warm. Four-twenty. The only sounds he heard were those that floated up faintly from the street. The phone rang again, more prolonged this time. Only Peggy knew he was here. He decided to risk it. "Hello."

"Steve, are you all right?"

"Sure, Peggy, I'm fine."

"You sound as though you were talking through a mouth full of barbed wire."

"Only a farm girl from Nebraska would come up with something like barbed wire in New York, for Christ's sake."

"Okay, so my early childhood is showing up. Are you fit for a message?"

"Depends."

"Mr. Allard is anxious to talk with you. As soon as I can locate you. Have I?"

"Have you what?"

"Located you."

"Oh, Jesus. Yes, if it's important."

"It may be. Gail called three times. I don't know if I can stall her any longer."

"Okay. Ring her back and say I'll be there before five-thirty."

"Are you sure you're all that sober?"

"I will be." He hung up, lit a cigarette, then went to the bedroom where he stripped and showered. In fresh linen and a fresh suit, he felt better, but the outside heat bore down on him and made him feel more uncomfortable than before. He stopped by his office, only to reassure Peggy that he was sober and fit. "And wait for me. Don't leave until I can talk with you."

"About what?"

"Something about that option to renew."

"I'll think about it while you're gone. You're three minutes overdue."

Keith was dictating a memorandum, but broke it off and asked Gail to close the door and hold all calls except from Mr. Leary. To Steve, "Sit down. I hope you had a good lunch."

"As a matter of fact, I didn't have lunch."

"You beginning to take your work seriously, or are you on a diet?"

"Neither. It's the only way I know how to starve successfully."

"Well, you're always entitled to a meal at Casa Allard, but for the moment, serious business."

"Like?"

"Like Wade Barrett got into town a little while ago. He's with Bill now. I assume you heard about the hassle, the goddamned place is humming with it."

"I've heard it. Is that what this is about?"

"In a way. Bill and I spent a couple of hours discussing Wade and the West Coast office. I know he hasn't been out there long enough to make an accurate evaluation, but this new thing with Wade crumbled what was left of the cookie. When Bill hung up, he put in a call for Dave Chesler and discovered that Wade hadn't been in his office for three days and no one had the slightest idea where he was."

"And so—the firing squad."

"Wade wrote his own ticket this time, Steve."

"I'm glad I wasn't in on this one. It was bad enough watching Larry get shot down."

Keith said, "Steve, how would you like to take a crack at the West Coast branch?"

"You mean, run it?"

"Yes."

"Keith, what in hell do I know about running a branch office?"

"More than you think, Steve. You're a good administrator. You've shown that with GFP, and with B & B. You have a certain talent for picking the right people for the right job, for delegating responsibility and supervising the output. That's all it really takes, and there's no great mystery about it. I did that with you, and you're living proof that it works. All you have to do once you're set up out there, is drop in on the client occasionally for lunch, have him out to dinner, and see that the wheels are properly oiled. In time, you get to meet people, and you pick up an account here and there by showing what you've done for others."

"If it's so simple, how do you explain what happened to Larry and Wade? And why me? Why not Marty Elkins, your senior account supervisor, or someone out of Chicago, even Los Angeles? I saw Dave Chesler on the job out there. I think he'd make a great branch manager."

Keith was smiling, wagging his head from side to side. "Except that Bill, personally, picked you."

"And you went along with him."

"Yes."

"Why, Keith? What about GFP and B & B?"

"All right, we have to get to that sooner or later. Bill feels that change is not only good for the heart and soul, but for the job and the account. You've been on GFP for a long time. Maybe he feels the time is ripe for a shift."

"And I've always heard that in advertising, when you've got a good thing going, you don't screw around with it."

"That may well go for an advertising campaign. It doesn't necessarily hold true as far as the advertising *man* is concerned."

"And, of course, I'm sure Karen Lawson has something to do with this."

"Naturally. Not just something, everything. Let's not start kidding each other, Steve. What you've done, getting involved with the wife of a client, would normally call for immediate dismissal. Neither Bill nor I want that. Why and how it happened is one thing. The important objective now is to eliminate the possibility of Lawson finding it out and jerking the account away from us. Under normal circumstances, where an honest difference of opinon occurs, we could fight him off and have Fitzjohn, Hardwick, even Russell Charles and Mrs. Goodwin on our side. With something like this, however, you stand alone. The agency can't support you in a battle of this kind. The risk is too damned great. The agency can't afford to take your side."

"So it's either the account or me, isn't it?"

"If you were heading this agency, which would you choose?"

"You've made your point, Keith . . ."

"But that doesn't necessarily mean we want to sacrifice a good, talented man, Steve. I'll take over temporarily and with Norm Adrian on the job, I'm sure a commendable job can be done. Moving you out West could be a break for both yourself *and* the agency."

"How much time do I have to give Bill an answer?"

"I wouldn't take too long deciding. Wade will have a few weeks to get himself cleared away. Chesler can handle things out there until you take over."

"And all I have to do is pack my briefcase, unload the lease on my apartment and grab the next plane."

"Of course, we'll pick up any cost of transferring you and your furniture, and we can handle the subleasing of your apartment as well. All we need from you is your decision to accept."

"I don't have much choice, do I?"

"Don't make me answer that, Steve. Believe me, I think this is for your own good. You'll be coming back frequently for conferences. You're not going to Nepal, you know."

"How does Siberia grab you, Keith?"

"You've spent a couple of months out there. You know it can't be all bad."

"All right, then, suppose I let you know in—give me two weeks."

"I'll settle for that. This is strictly between us, Steve, no rumors floating around. Keep things going as they are so that the transition will be smooth."

"I won't breathe a word to anyone, Keith, but these things have a way of getting around."

"In this case, it won't. Bill and I discussed it at lunch. Neither Lucy nor Gail know a word about it."

"Two weeks."

"I'll expect your answer, either way, no later."

Happily, Steve did not encounter Wade Barrett during his return to his office. It was six when he returned to his desk. Peggy had left a note for him in a sealed envelope.

STEVE:

If it has to do with business, you can reach me at my apartment. If it is only the 'option to renew,' I'll be in tomorrow morning at the usual time.

PEGGY

He crumpled the note and threw it into his wastepaper basket.

Chapter 14

1

For Steve, sensing the collapse of his all-too-familiar world, the fortnight that followed was a kaleidoscope of mental dissolves that ranged from stark reality to nightmarish fantasy. He had heard nothing from Karen during that time, nor had he expected he would; and between those times when he missed her physical presence desperately, he could not fully understand the curious sense of relief he experienced that it was over between them. Any word he received about Herschel Goodwin's condition, still hovering in that void between life and death, came to him from Keith Allard.

At work, the restlessness that followed the loss of Chevalier had somewhat diminished, partly because of rumors that Bill and various account supervisors were on the trail of accounts that would replace the $3,800,000 loss; but the space previously occupied by that group remained ominously empty, a constant reminder—even a threat—to former complacency.

The coolness between Steve and Peggy persisted. The ease in their daily contact had degenerated to a synthetic formality with which neither was comfortable. Cautiously, Steve avoided Bill Leary, and felt a sense of relief when Bill left for Detroit to follow up on a lead from Doug Driscoll, the account exec on Post Tool, who had heard that Mercer Drug was having problems with its agency and had arranged a quiet meeting between its president and Bill. From Detroit, Bill had flown on to Los Angeles for the final showdown with Wade Barrett, making it official. On his return, the results of that confrontation became the best known agency secret in years. Not a word filtered down to the normal gossip transmission belt, although a vague rumor persisted on the thirty-fifth floor that Barrett had had it.

All the basic planning for breaking B & B on a nationwide scale had been completed and approved. Physical preparation for all media was moving well ahead of schedule. Twice, when Mark Lawson phoned to ask what progress was being made, Steve sent Frank, Reed, or Chuck to Forty-second Street with layouts, type, and color proofs to show; calls that required no policy-level decisions or actions. Later, examining the detailed Client Interview Report sheets, he felt mildly chagrined that the calls had been handled efficiently and required no action on his part; nor did Mark phone, as he would have done in the past, to complain that a boy had been sent to do a man's job.

Thus, the days passed until a Tuesday morning when Peggy responded to his "Good morning, Peggy," with word that Keith Allard wanted to see him at once.

"Did he indicate what it was about?" Steve asked.

"No, but Gail has called twice." She picked up a copy of *Advertising News* that had been turned to Page Two, where an item in the third column had been outlined in red. "I think you'd better have a look at this before you go up," she said.

Still standing beside her desk, he took the paper from her and scanned the headline:

TIME FOR A CHANGE?

then read the single paragraph beneath it quickly.

> Rumors come and go, perhaps more frequently in advertising than in most other fields. Latest on the Street, according to an unusually reliable source, is that a prominent food products company that recently acquired a West Coast subsidiary, is agency-shopping for its respectable $18,000,000 account after a near-record thirty-four-year residence with a Lex Av house. Coming on top of the loss, last month, of a near-$4,000,000 account, it can be reasonably assumed that the fallout in that area may soon be strongly felt.
>
> E. F.

Steve let the paper drop on Peggy's desk. "What else is new?" he asked, underplaying it deliberately to hide his sharp reaction

"For one thing . . . " she flicked her head in the direction of the working area, "the natives are understandably restless. Norm has looked in twice to see if you were here."

"There's nothing to be alarmed about. These rumors always come up now and then."

"You're taking it very lightly," she said. "Did you have some inkling about this?"

"Not in this form."

"Well, apart from our own groups, there's a lot of nervous reaction among others on the floor and I've already got quite a list of callbacks waiting for you. *Ad Daily*, the *Times*, *Journal*, half a dozen TV and radio people, magazine and newspaper reps, all wanting some kind of confirmation or denial. I can imagine Mr. Allard has had quite a number of calls by now . . ."

"No comment. I'm out and can't be reached. Anything else?"

"Not in the same category. But your boy, Chuck, is walking around looking like the cat that ate the canary. I haven't checked all the mail yet, and Mr. Allard is waiting."

"Okay, I'll be with him, but that's for your information only."

He went out, noticing a few groups knotted up in the corridors that led to the stairway, no doubt discussing this latest break, eyeing him with curious looks as he passed. He knew that they were concerned, as he was, that the word had leaked out. The agency's prime account was in jeopardy and that was cause enough, after the loss of Chevalier, for these and many other informal group discussions. On the thirty-fifth floor, there were other groups in similar discussion.

He found Keith in his office dictating to Gail, who looked a little startled at his sudden appearance. Keith said, "That will be all for now, Gail, we'll finish this later. Bring some coffee for Mr. Gilman and hold my calls except from Mr. Leary. Sit down, Steve." Between the familiar ritual of pipe-filling-tamping-lighting, he indicated the offending *Ad News* article lying on the desk. "You know anything about that?"

"I saw it only a few minutes ago," Steve replied.

Gail knocked, and entered with the coffee for Steve, then went out, and closed the door. Steve said, "What do you want from me, Keith, confirmation? Denial?"

"When did you see Lawson last?"

"Thursday, a week ago. He hasn't been in his office very much lately."

Keith withdrew several beige client interview reports from his desk drawer and slid them toward Steve. "In short, he's been available to Baldasarian, Hayden and Baker, but not to you."

With a mere glance at the forms, Steve said, "Those were only routine matters. A couple of layouts, and some type and color proofs. A messenger could have handled them."

"I see." Keith drew on his pipe slowly. "You have any previous indications from Mark . . ."

"Keith, you know Mark far better than I. He may have made some innocuous remark in anger and someone probably overheard him, picked it up, and passed it along."

"You don't think this is serious?"

"I have no way of knowing positively."

"But you haven't seen him in almost two weeks."

"No. He's been in and out of town and there was no imperative reason . . ."

"I'm suggesting there is one now."

"Of course. I'll phone and try to see him today."

"To lock the barn after the proverbial horse has run off or been stolen?"

"Keith, nothing has been stolen yet, and I think you're placing too much emphasis on an unconfirmed rumor."

"Do you?" Keith drew on his pipe again and said blandly, "What about Mrs. Lawson?"

"If I may be allowed an observation, Keith, Mrs. Lawson is not a client of this agency."

Keith's chair came forward as he sat up very straight. "All right, Steve, let's quit the sparring. There's too damned much at stake here." He aimed the stem of his pipe at the news article. "That piece needs no names named. Can you guess how many people are trying to reach Lawson right now?"

"I'd guess quite a few."

"And that doesn't disturb you?"

"Not too much."

Keith's eyes closed to mere slits. "What do you know that I don't?"

"For one thing, when I last saw Mark he offered me a proposition to pull out with the account and open an in-house agency with a guaranteed one hundred thousand dollars a year in salary, fringe benefits, and choice of my own staff."

The pipe fell out of Keith's mouth, scattering a small cloud of ashes over his tie, cascading down into his lap. He leaped up, brushing sparks and ashes aside, then sat down again. "The sonofabitch! That unmitigated bastard sneak! He actually thinks he can get away with *that,* even before they bury the old man?"

"He's been waiting for my answer and that's why I've been avoiding him. It's my guess that this leak is an effort on his part to make me move."

"What did you tell him when he made the offer?"

"I turned him down, but he refused to accept that. When I left he asked me to weigh the possibilities and think it over carefully. That's why I had Chuck, Frank, and Reed make those calls. You know as well as I do that Mark is doing his damnedest to move into a position of power while Herschel Goodwin is out of the picture. After all, he's a part of the Goodwin family, directly or indirectly, and a possible inheritor. At the moment, there's a crisis. He'll never have a better chance."

"You turned down a hundred thousand dollars a year?"

"Are you so surprised, Keith? After all, Mark will be the key to the whole deal and there was no contract involved. As he put it, a 'gentleman's agreement.' "

Keith hooted at the idea. "With Lawson? He'd sell his mother out for twelve dollars. Or less."

"Then don't give me credit for an overabundance of conscience or loyalty. I couldn't live that close to Lawson for very long."

For the first time since he had known Keith, Steve saw him in a state of thorough agitation. Mark Lawson was on the rampage. Herschel, lying in a semicoma in a hospital bed. Anna too involved in her own personal problems to be of practical use. Fitzjohn? Hardwick? Russell Charles? To whom could he turn? Keith stood up, paced to the window, then came back and dropped disconsolately into his chair, running nervous fingers through his graying hair.

"Sorry, Steve," he apologized, "but you know how it is. The word is out and everybody in this business from mail clerks to presidents know the answers to who and what that damned item refers to. Our own people are jittery, likewise our other clients. I've got a list of callbacks to make to reassure some of them. A bomb goes off and can be the beginning of the end of an otherwise and heretofore perfect ballgame."

"What did Bill say about it?"

"He hasn't seen this yet. He left again for L.A. last night—some last-minute details to clear up out there before Wade leaves. I'm sure that as soon as the word hits out there, he'll be on the phone."

"Well, I don't know what I can do about this rumor."

"If it were nothing *more* than a rumor." He looked up at Steve and said, "One thing is certain. We're not going down without a hell of a fight."

When Steve looked up with a questioning frown, and Keith said, "This may be the time to lower the boom on friend Lawson."

"How do you propose to do that?"

Keith studied him for a moment, then said, "Steve, when there's a misfit sitting on top of an $18,000,000 account, it's a wise investment to do a little homework in order to know where you stand. We've got a dossier on Lawson that could break his back."

"Like what?"

"For the most recent thing, a little lady named Margo Anthony who is occupying a West End Avenue apartment at Lawson's expense. For another, his former affairs with Robin Ford, Sue Garvey, and a list of other indiscretions. For . . ."

"You know about Mark and Robin? And Sue?"

"As I was saying, for a third, Mark's relationship with one Mr. Peter Channing of Bennington Press. Ethan Loomis spelled that one out for us. And if you've been wondering why Mark has been so strong for premiums, I'll bring you up to date on that one. I had Marty Link check out C & H, the premium house in Chicago. It spells out to read 'Channing & Haywood,' with the likelihood that it was Lawson who bankrolled Channing into the company.

"The odds are that Mark, in order to avoid disclosure, has never reported any of his C & H or Bennington Press side income to the Internal Revenue Service, so we've got him coming and going. Herschel Goodwin, even Anna, might stand still for a certain degree of incompetence, knowing the agency was backstopping Mark, but outright theft? And even if Mrs. Goodwin is inclined to be forgiving at a time of desperate crisis, I think Mark can be convinced that Uncle Sam owes him no such family loyalty or consideration. Then there's his somewhat undefined relationship with his wife . . . but you would know more about that than I."

"That's marvelous," Steve said. "I didn't know we were that skilled in espionage. Are we wired in to the CIA, too?"

"In special situations, it becomes necessary, Steve, situations where the protection of three million dollars in revenue are involved."

"I'm impressed."

"Don't look down your nose at it. In our place, you'd do the same thing."

"But it doesn't work in every case, does it? After all, McCreery moved Chevalier over to Weatherford without any difficulty?"

"A different case entirely. Whatever he was, Ted was smart enough to keep his personal life clean."

"Well, you can't win 'em all, can you, Keith."

"The important ones are those that count. And if I interpret the mild sneer in your voice correctly, forget it. It may not be desirable, even laudable, but it works."

"Evidently. But if I may make one suggestion . . ."

"Of course."

"Don't use what you've got on Mark Lawson. You may win, but it will be a temporary victory. In the end, you'll lose GFP."

"Why?"

"Because your dossier isn't complete. Whether Herschel Goodwin lives or dies is the key to your long-shot bet. If he lives, I agree with Bill's expressed opinion that it is unlikely he will ever be fully active again, but he won't dump the agency.

"Let me bring your records up to date, unless through some mysterious source, you already know. Karen Lawson and I are through. That was neatly arranged by Anna Goodwin. Regardless of Karen's feelings for Mark, I'm sure she will go to every length to spare Herschel and Anna the emotionalism and embarrassment of a second divorce, at least until Herschel is clearly and safely out of the woods. That may take quite a long time. And I doubt very much that Anna, as long as Karen and Mark are bound together in marriage, will ever forgive you for exposing Mark.

"Fire him? What excuse can Anna offer without bringing it all out into the open? Send an anonymous letter to

IRS? That would have the same effect; scandal, disgrace, family humiliation, not to mention the effect of making it public in the press. Mark would lose out, no doubt about it, but so would the Leary Agency for having opened up that can of worms."

"Are you suggesting we sit by quietly and let the account slip away from us?"

"I'm suggesting that Anna Goodwin's loyalties to the memory of Bill's father and the agency that put them on the map thirty-four years ago are strong enough to overcome any attempt of Mark's to pull the account away, even into a house agency. Eventually, that decision will have to be approved by Anna, and I think you or Bill can make a strong case with her."

"That's a big gamble, Steve."

"I think it's one you'll have to risk. Don't forget, Keith, Ward Hardwick, with a winning streak going for him, will be strong in your corner. He understands the difficulty of switching accounts, the incubation period before a new staff catches onto how an account like GFP works. From that viewpoint alone, I don't think Mark can pull it off. And Hardwick will have Fitzjohn on his side."

Keith leaned back in his chair again, a smile breaking over his face. "I think," he said, "you'll make a very fine branch manager for Los Angeles, Steve."

"When is Bill due back?"

"In a few days, if this situation can be held in check. He's reviewing the account roster with Dave Chesler, mending fences with each client personally. Chesler will be in charge until you move out and take over."

"Why not Chesler instead of me, Keith?"

"We've been over that ground before. It's even more reasonable now, if we follow your suggestion about Lawson. Assuming it works out your way, you'd be a constant threat to him here, to the account. In L.A. you'll move up to seventy-five thousand dollars a year and in no time should be hitting a hundred thousand dollars to match Mark's offer, with, perhaps, that limited partnership we've already discussed. You can't afford not to accept, Steve. Next to having your own agency, what more can you possibly expect?"

"Nothing, Keith," Steve replied slowly. "Nothing."

2

Back in his own office, he sat at his desk mulling over his conversation with Keith. Two big decisions faced him; Mark's offer which, from the first, he had had no intention of accepting; and Keith's, to replace Wade Barrett in Los Angeles. He started to reach for the phone, but Peggy came in at that moment and told him she would be out for a few minutes on an errand to Traffic Control. When she left, he dialed *Ad News* and asked to speak to Ed Friedman, who had initialed the column that carried the "rumor," and for whom he had written several articles in the past.

"Steve? How are you?"

"Fine, Ed. I need a favor."

"Let me guess . . ."

"You don't need to. I need a name."

"Whose, as if I didn't know?"

"The usually reliable source who gave you the tip on GFP."

"Steve, you know I can't do that."

"Let me see how close you can come."

"Look, Steve, I didn't want to handle the story in the first place, but the front office insisted and I had no choice. It was an opportunity and we had to go with it because it was exclusive. If we refused to print it, someone else would have. What would you have done?"

"I'm not blaming you for running the item, Ed, but it would help me considerably if I knew where it came from, and you have my solemn word that whoever it was, he'll never know it from us."

"Sorry, Steve . . ."

"Okay, Ed, but you realize, of course, you're cutting off the line of communication between yourself and me . . ."

"Come on, Steve, you know damned well I can't divulge a source . . ."

"Ed, don't give me that *Times* routine. All I want to know is this, did it come from GFP?"

"Well—not directly."

"How indirectly?"

"Goddamn it, Steve—listen, just between us?"

"It won't go any further than me."

"Well, that's where it came from, your own office, and

that's my last word on the subject, take it or leave it." The phone clicked in Steve's ear. As he replaced the receiver, his eyes turned unconsciously toward Chuck Baldasarian's door. A moment later, the phone rang and he answered. "Yes?"

"Mr. Gilman?"

"Yes. Who is it, please?"

"Miss Demarest, in Personnel. I have Miss Cowles's resignation before me, but no request for a replacement. I wonder if you can give me your approval to send . . ."

"Let me think about it and call you back, Miss—uh . . ."

"Demarest. Margaret Demarest. If you will be so kind."

He replaced the receiver, and perhaps five minutes later, lifted it again. Peggy came on. "Yes?"

"Come in here, please."

"I'm typing a schedule that needs . . ."

"Forget the schedule. I want to talk to you. Now."

Before she could reply he hung up. A moment later, Peggy came in frowning. "I had a call from a Miss Demarest while you were out," he said.

"I know. She called earlier to ask me if you had any special requirements in mind for my replacement. I told her I had no idea and suggested she call back later and speak to you about it."

"And conveniently found it necessary to carry something to Traffic Control so you wouldn't be here when she called back."

Peggy flushed and said nothing. "Call her back and tell her to forget it. You're not leaving."

"Steve, I am. Please don't make it more difficult for me. My letter of resignation is in. Since you refused to do anything about it, I asked Personnel to send in a replacement, but they told me your authorization was necessary for that. I'm leaving next week. You'll need someone and there's little enough time left if you want me to break her in, the files . . ."

"You're that determined?"

"Yes. There's nothing here that someone else can't do for you. I've already arranged for one of the girls in the typing pool to take my place at the apartment. My family is expecting me a week from Saturday."

"Peggy, don't leave me. Not now."

"I'm sorry, Steve. I can't see any useful purpose in staying."

"Peggy, please . . ."

She dropped into the chair beside his desk, her expression changed from passive detachment to solicitous attention. "I wish there were some reason why I should stay, Steve."

"And I would like—more than anything else—to give you that reason, but all I can tell you is that there are certain changes about to take place very shortly . . ."

"I know. I'd have to be blind to ignore that item in *Ad News*. The word is all over the place that we're going to lose GFP."

"We're not. And the item has no bearing on this whatever."

"Then what is it?'

"I can't tell you in any way that will make sense. It's confused, even in my own mind, at this moment."

"Do those changes include Karen Lawson?"

"That's over, Peggy. I swear it."

"What about her husband, your client? Is that over, too?"

"That's one of the things I can't talk about yet. What's more important to me right now is that you should trust me."

She stared at him with perplexity and doubt. "Peggy, can't you bring yourself to trust me?" he said, touching her hand.

She said, "Steve, you're a free agent and I don't want to impose any strings on you. I can't say I don't care about what has happened between you and Karen, but I was hurt when I discovered I'd become a member of a—a damned *ménage à trois*. I told you about Bob Larch and me and you accepted that. I can accept the Karen situation if, as you say, it's a thing of the past. What I can't accept is your sense of moral responsibility in continuing your relationship with Mark Lawson as if Karen had never existed."

"Peggy, darling, believe me, that part will be straightened out shortly."

She looked up with disbelief in her eyes. "Steve, if you told me you wanted to start all over again, go somewhere and write a novel, dig ditches, drive a truck, anything, I'd leap at the chance to go with you. I'd take a job, do everything in my power to help, but not if you stay on with Leary and GFP."

"Peggy, I've said all I can for now. The rest has got to be on pure trust."

"I don't know—I—I'll—see . . ." She stood up and went to the door, paused there for a moment in indecision, then went out. Moments later, his phone rang and he lifted the receiver hopefully. "Peggy?"

"It's Mr. Lawson," she said simply.

"I'm not in and you don't know where to reach me."

She said, "Very well," and clicked off.

For a moment, he felt relaxed, knowing that Mark was calling to check for the fallout to the item in *Ad News.* It pleased him that his refusal to answer the call would give Mark little satisfaction, also delaying his final answer to the question of the house agency.

3

At five o'clock, when the agency began its end-of-day stirrings, Chuck knocked on the communicating door and opened it slightly, waiting for Steve's invitation to come in. Steve looked up and said, "Something you wanted, Chuck?"

"You've been tied up so much of the day, I thought I'd check with you before I take off."

"Come in." Chuck did so, and closed the door. He dropped into the chair beside the desk and said, "I didn't think you'd be in. Mark called a minute ago and said he'd tried to get you, and that Peggy told him you were out."

"And so he called you?"

"Yes. Nothing important, something about a proof . . ."

Steve reached into his desk, withdrew two copies of Chuck's most recent client interview reports and slid them over to him. "Anything you left off these when you turned them in?"

Chuck stared at the two sheets as though he had never seen them before. "Nothing I can think of," he said. "Just ordinary routine calls."

"Nothing more than that?"

"What are you driving at? If you've got something on your mind, why don't you get to the point?"

"All right, Chuck. I'm suggesting that you and Mark

had a conversation concerning GFP that doesn't appear in either of these reports."

Chuck said, "If there was any conversation other than what I reported, it was purely personal between Mark and me, and didn't require reporting to you or anybody else. For Christ's sake, Steve, what do you want in a report, blood pressure, temperature and bowel movements?"

"I want to know anything and everything that concerns this account. I want to know why you would withhold anything from me that you gave to *Ad News* as a blind item, from, *quote*, an unusually reliable source, *unquote*."

"You're out of your skull if you think I gave that item to Ed—*Ad News*," Chuck said hotly.

Steve laughed at the slip. "You had it right the first time, Chuck. *Ed*, not *Ad*. What kind of a deal did you make for yourself with Lawson?"

"Look, Steve, I'm not going to sit here and take this shit from you. If you're on your way out, you're not going to do anything to louse me up, so forget it."

"I've got an item for you, Chuck. I'm not on my way out, but you are."

"Bullshit, you're not. Mark's up to here with you, stalling, evading him, knocking down his pet ideas, which I happen to agree with. When he pulls the rug out from under you, you'll be out on your ass whistling *Dixie*, and you know it, don't you?"

When Steve only grinned in reply, Chuck became furious.

"Okay, smart guy. Mark asked me to leak that item. What's more, he asked me if I'd go along with you on the new house-agency deal and I told him he could count me in. But you're so goddamned smart, you had to keep him dangling. Well, screw you, Gilman. You've had it and don't know it, and what's more, I'm going to take GFP and B & B right out from under your nose and open the house agency while you're still sucking your thumb." He stood up and went to the door, throwing it open angrily.

"Chuck . . ."

"What?"

"Don't bother to come in tomorrow. I'll see that your salary check and severance pay are mailed to you. Pack your personal belongings tonight and take them with you. It will save you the embarrassment of having to do it in the morning with everybody watching you. And if George McCandless wants to know why, have him call me."

Chuck raised his middle finger and smiled. "Fuck you, Gilman," he said, and went out, slamming the door shut behind him.

4

As she had during the past ten days, Peggy opened the door, poked her head in a few inches, and said, "I'm leaving. Goodnight."

"Goodnight, Peggy," Steve replied. In the next instant she was gone. He sat at his desk immersed in his own thoughts until hunger overtook him at seven o'clock, then he walked through the empty corridors to the elevators. On the street, he caught an empty cab and went directly to his apartment. After a long, cooling drink, he decided to broil a steak and enjoy a solitary dinner. No complications that way. The steak, with a salad, was just right, and he ate them, enjoying the replay of firing Chuck in his mind. Later, he went into the living room and turned on the television set, switching from channel to channel, settling on a movie he hadn't seen before, in the hopes that it would clear his mind of other events of the day that had passed.

At ten o'clock, during the commercial break, it occurred to him that he had no idea of what he had seen during the past hour, and he turned the set off. He started for the bedroom when he heard the doorbell ring, and hesitated. It rang again, then again, then once more, commandingly. He walked to the door, trying to think who it could be. Certainly not Karen. Not Peggy. Each had a distinctive way of ringing his bell that was only too familiar to him. It rang insistently again, and when he opened the door a mere slit, Mark Lawson said, "What the hell. If I can't get you at your office . . ."

Trying hard to mask his surprise, Steve moved to one side and said, "Mark, what . . ."

"Are you going to keep me standing out here in the goddamned hallway, for Christ's sake?"

"I'm sorry. Come in." He opened the door wider and Mark brushed past him, moving into the living room, scanning it from side to side, length to breadth. "Nice pad you've got here."

"It's comfortable."

Mark went to the sofa and sat down. "You wouldn't have a drink to spare a thirsty man, would you?"

"Scotch and water?"

"Scotch, no water."

Steve went to the bar cabinet, opened it, and poured the single drink, emptying a tray of ice cubes into the container and dropping two cubes into the glass, suddenly conscious of how much of the apartment was Karen's. He brought it to Mark, who took a sip, and placed the glass on the coffee table. "You're not having one?"

"No," Steve replied. "I've got an idea I'm going to need all my thinking capabilities."

"Well, then," Mark said, pushing the drink farther away from him, "let's stay even."

"What can I do for you, Mark?"

"For one thing, you can give me a straight answer."

"I thought I gave it to you the last time I saw you."

"And if I remember correctly, I asked you to think it over."

"Before I answer, let me ask you one. Did you leak that item to *Ad News?"*

Mark grinned slowly, evilly. "No."

"All right, I'll buy that." Quickly, "Then why was it necessary to have Chuck Baldasarian do it for you?"

"He told you that?"

"I have my own ways of finding things out. What I'd like to know is, what was behind it?"

"Maybe it was just to get you off your ass and on the ball with an answer. I know you've been ducking me for the past ten days and . . ."

"All right, Mark, I'll give it to you now and for all time. The answer is *no.* I am not interested in opening a house agency for GFP and as far as I'm concerned, I can give you two dozen reasons why it won't work."

"The hell it won't, and a hundred grand a year says it will. That's what you're turning your back on, don't you realize that?"

"More than you do, but no, thank you very much."

"Okay, Mr. Wise Guy, but let me tell you this. With or without you, it'll work, take my word for it. I'll personally see to it." He picked up his drink and sipped at it. "Just how long do you think you'll be dragging your ass before you get another crack at a chance like the one I'm offering you? And how long do you think you'll keep pulling down your lousy forty grand a year from Leary after I pull GFP out of there?"

"For your information, Mark, it's sixty-grand-plus, not forty."

"You just can't help being a smartass, can you?"

"Just keeping the record straight, Mark. Everybody has the right to make his own choices. I've made mine, yours is up to you."

"All right, you smart bastard. You've just slammed the door and locked yourself out." He stood up, still glaring at Steve. "You're not the only genius in this business . . ."

"I've never even remotely considered myself one, Mark, but if you want to go your chosen route, there are plenty of capable advertising men around who will be happy to pick up the ball and run with it." He smiled, "Of course, there's always Chuck Baldasarian. You two should get along very well. He'll roll over and play dead when you tell him to . . ."

"All right, Gilman, I don't need any of your snotty advice and I wouldn't take your errand boy on a silver platter, but I can find someone just as good as you and for a hell of a lot less money. In the morning, I'll call Bill Leary . . ."

"You'd better make that Keith Allard. Bill is in L.A."

"*Or* Allard, and have him put somebody else on the account. That will be the beginning of the end for you . . ."

"Don't let it bother your conscience, Mark. I'll take care of my future without your generous help."

"Let me ask you something, bright boy. Just what the hell do you owe Leary?"

"Something I don't think you'd know much about, Mark, a thing called loyalty."

"Loyalty," Mark said, "is a crock of shit. Oh, I know the old man feels he owes a lot to Bill Leary's old man, but what the hell does he owe Junior? What the hell do I owe him? I'll tell you. Not one goddamned thing. GFP has paid its dues to the Leary Agency a hundred times over in the past thirty-four years, so don't come at me with that loyalty crap. My loyalty is to GFP and to myself . . ."

"But not necessarily in that order."

Mark grinned. "Maybe there's some hope for you yet. Steve, why the hell don't you listen to reason? Big things are going to happen and I'm going to see they do. I'm going to move high up in this firm and I'm still willing to take you with me, but only as long as you play on my team. I've got plans, ideas I've never talked about to anybody else. In time, I want to put GFP in the big leagues, the dry cereals market . . ."

"Mark, Herschel Goodwin vetoed that idea years ago, before either of us were on the scene."

"As you said, that was a long time ago. I'm talking about today, tomorrow, with Herschel on the sidelines and me in the saddle. *If,*" he added with emphasis, "he even makes it."

"Forget it, Mark. Make your call to Keith tomorrow morning and get yourself a new boy."

"You're pretty goddamned sure of yourself, aren't you?

"Not as much in the past as I am right now."

"What makes you so positive right now?"

"Let's say I've recently discovered a few things about myself I never knew before, things that kept getting in my way, tripping me."

Mark said it calmly then, and it came like a knife thrust to the abdomen. "Like Karen, you mean?"

Steve turned to ice, his former aplomb shattered, leaving him open-mouthed, speechless. "Cat got your tongue, you two-faced bastard?" Then, "You just tripped again, didn't you?"

When the denial refused to come, Mark said, "I knew it was somebody. It's always been somebody. But until tonight, when I walked in here and saw those goddamned paintings of hers on your walls, I didn't know it was Steve Gilman. Tell me, how long ago did she give you these?" Gesturing at the two paintings that faced him. Over Mark's head, Steve stared disconsolately at the other two that were behind Mark's back.

He regained his voice then, although the words came weakly. "What difference would that make?"

"Well, for one thing, it will give me an idea how long you've been screwing her."

"Is that so important to you?"

"Let's say I'm curious."

"Oh, for Christ's sake, Mark. You've never given a damn before, why should it make so much difference that it was me?"

"It could have been anybody, but not you, not when I've been paying you . . ."

"The Leary Agency has been paying me for the job I've been doing for GFP."

"You cruddy sonofabitch!"

"All right, Mark, I'm no more a candidate for sainthood than you are. What happened, happened, and it's over. That's the truth. It's over between GFP and myself as well, if that gives you any satisfaction."

Mark stood facing him, indecisive, balancing himself on the balls of his feet, fists clenched tightly, knuckles showing white with strain. And Steve waited—a sense of mind-panic engulfing his nervous system—for Mark's first move, gauging the moment when the first thrust of body and flailing fists would come. He tried to control his own instinctive desire to protect himself from attack and was able to restrain the urge to throw his hands up either to strike the first blow, or ward off Mark's. And then he knew it would never come. Without any sign of movement whatever, Mark had backed down. Inside, Steve felt relief and an insane impulse to laugh; but he remained still and outwardly calm.

Mark's face, contorted with anger, grew coldly placid, stony, and colorless, like that of a man in shock. Along both jawlines, the knots of hard muscle slowly disappeared. His fists became unclenched, his body relaxed, but his eyes remained glittering brightly with the inner rage that was consuming him.

Steve broke the silence then, offering him a final opportunity. "If you have any idea of taking it out on me physically, Mark, okay. We're pretty evenly matched, but I don't think it would be very smart to bring the public or the police in on our personal difficulties. Nor would Karen or Anna appreciate the publicity."

"You've even figured that much out, haven't you, you bastard?"

"Mark, why don't we just call it quits and go our separate ways. That will make it easier for everybody."

"You think you're going to get off that easy, you backbiting sonofabitch?"

"I'm not getting off easy at all. For family reasons, at least, you've got a chance to make it up with Karen and Anna, if you're only smart enough to realize that. Whatever I do, it will have to be a whole new start from the ground up."

"I'll help you that much. As of right now, forget you ever heard of GFP. Within a month, Leary can forget it, too. We'll see if the agency can support what it's paying you without GFP's contribution. But wherever you go . . ."

"Don't waste your time threatening me, Mark. Take your new lease on life and enjoy it. But let me give you one last friendly tip. Don't try to move GFP out of the Leary Agency. If you do, you'll find you've pulled a mountain down over your head."

Mark stared at Steve for a moment, then moved to the door. He opened it, looked back once with a sneer of contempt on his lips, then flounced out. For the moment, it was over, but Steve felt no sense of having been victorious.

Only the emptiness remained.

5

For the first time since his fledgling days at the agency, Steve was at his desk before eight o'clock. He had spent a near-sleepless night, dozing, waking, drinking reheated coffee, smoking heavily, dreading the loneliness. When the brassy dawn crept over the city he roused himself, shaved, showered, drank more coffee, and went to his empty office. Later, he heard a mail clerk enter Peggy's office to deposit the morning mail, but he had little interest in poring over the vari-sized envelopes, knowing there would be little of personal interest to whet his curiosity.

He was still working at his desk when he heard Peggy come in, his ears and mental processes attuned to each sound that came from her office: the snap of the cord that was tied around the bundle of mail, then the lid of the coffeemaker being removed. Minutes later the door opened and he looked up into her startled expression when she saw him at his desk. "Wh—what are you doing here so early?" she asked, regaining her composure.

"I couldn't sleep, and I hated being alone."

She placed some memos and business correspondence on the edge of the desk. "Let me get you some coffee. My God, you look like a reception committee for a disaster that's about to happen."

"You're too late. It's already come and gone."

"What are you talking about?"

"Well, don't look at me as though I were an executioner."

"The other way around, as though you were the execution-ee, to coin a new word."

"In a way, I have been. Executed, I mean."

"Steve—you haven't been drinking this early, have you?"

"No. Perfectly sober. Except that I feel like I'm suspended in mid-air. On a trip. I can't feel the ground under me."

"I'll be back in a second with the coffee."

Other than to light another cigarette, he made no move to reach for the mail and sat waiting for Peggy to return, suddenly more anxious than ever to see her as he had only a few moments ago; fresh and clean in a light blue shirt-blouse, short dark blue skirt with straps that ran from her waist over her shoulders, with sheer blue stockings encasing her legs. He heard a light rap, and when she opened the door, her voice. "Mr. Allard, Steve."

Keith brushed by, still wearing his hat and jacket, evidence that he hadn't yet been to his own office. "Morning, Steve." He stared with curiosity and said, "You been here all night?"

"No. It just feels that way."

"Looks that way, too."

Peggy came in with two cups of coffee and went out again. "Gail tells me Peggy's leaving," Keith said, removing his hat and dropping into the visitor's chair.

"This Saturday," Steve said morosely.

"Too bad. Always liked her. Smart girl."

"Yes. An exceptionally bright girl. You didn't drop in this early to discuss Peggy, did you, Keith?"

Allard put the cup and saucer back on the desk. "I had an early call this morning."

"From Mark Lawson."

Keith nodded. "Woke me up at seven o'clock, calling from the hospital."

"What's the word on Mr. Goodwin?"

"He didn't say. He had more important business on his mind . . ."

"I'm sure of that. Mark wants me replaced on the account."

"He called you?"

"Let's say he got the message across to me. Emphatically."

"Well . . ." Keith reached for the coffee and drained the cup. "That puts us in a tough spot. Frankly, I was hoping this wouldn't come to a head—not right now. I don't think Baldasarian is up to taking charge and . . ."

"Chuck won't be here to fill in, Keith. I fired him yesterday."

"Jesus. Before or after you heard from Lawson?"

"Before. It was Chuck who released that item to *Ad News*, but he did it with Mark's full knowledge. Mark will no doubt try to line Chuck up to join his house agency when he decides to pull GFP out, but Chuck won't head it up. And you'll probably be getting a call from Marty Link or George McCandless sometime soon . . ."

Keith's lips formed the unspoken words, "That bastard!" but Steve added, "I still don't think Mark can get away with it. If I were you, I'd pay a little visit to Anna Goodwin and get things started with her before Lawson makes his big pitch to her. I'd also make it a point to invite Ward Hardwick to lunch and block another avenue."

"What about you, Steve?"

"No problem. You can announce to all concerned that I've resigned . . ."

"Goddamn it, we're not talking about your resignation. What about Los Angeles? I don't like to force the question, but circumstances leave me little alternative. I've got to discuss this with Bill and I want your answer before I call him."

"Keith, I don't know what to say."

Keith's voice returned to its normal level. "You've had a good ten days to think about it, Steve. You know that I—we—would rather have you in New York, but that's impossible as far as GFP is concerned. Los Angeles is certainly a much better opportunity than you'll find anywhere in New York . . ."

"And takes me out of Lawson's sight and hearing."

"That's the least of it, believe me. I want you in L.A. because there's a job to be done there, one I'm confident you can do."

"I feel like I'd be stepping into a dead man's shoes."

"That's childish nonsense. Why the hell do you have to force yourself to assume guilt for which you're not responsible? What happened to Larry and Wade was their own doing. You had nothing to do with their failures."

"It's not that so much as it's the feeling that I'm following an established pattern of failure. Price struck out here, then in L.A. Wade did the same. Now I've struck out here . . ."

Keith sighed loudly, almost a soft groan. "Steve, this

isn't the dark ages of superstition, for God's sake! Where else can you possibly find anything as promising as a branch managership at your age?" He stood up and picked up his hat. "I'm going to phone Bill at five o'clock New York time. I'll expect your answer before then. Give it your most careful thought, Steve. I want you in the Leary organization."

"Thank you, Keith. I promise you'll hear from me in time for your call to Bill."

When Allard left, Peggy returned, picked up the untouched mail, and placed it directly before him. "Most of this is routine," she said. "If you don't want to fool with it, I can handle it."

"Do that, please. And sign your name, for, and in the absence of, etcetera." He wondered idly how much of his conversation with Keith she had overheard, but Peggy's expression gave no indication to give him a clue.

"Are you going out?" she asked.

"Why?"

"Well, the word's out that Chuck either quit or was fired, with most of the bets on the fired side."

"How did that get out so fast?"

"For one thing, there was some talk at the water-cooler that he'd phoned the personnel office earlier about his weekly pay check, and severance pay. And his desk has never been so clean in all the time I've been here."

Steve stood up and said, "A little detail I should have taken care of a long time ago. But you're right, Peggy. I've been thoughtless as hell. I'll make a swing around and talk to some of our people."

He dropped in on Norm first, saw his note of concern, and said, "No matter what you've read or heard, Norm, no matter what you may hear during the next few days or weeks, the sky will remain at its normal height without any chance of falling in. Leary will not lose GFP or B & B."

"You sound pretty sure of yourself, Steve."

"In this, I'm very sure of myself. And something else. Strictly between us?"

"You have my word."

"I'll be leaving New York shortly. Last night, I fired Chuck Baldasarian. That leaves you as the most experienced man in both groups. When I go, I want to make a pitch for you to take over. You may have to operate as an account executive under Keith Allard as your supervisor for a while, but I know you can handle the job without any trouble."

"Steve, I've never . . ."

"Nobody ever has until he's done it. You'll have plenty of help including Hayden and Baker to fill in on the contact end. Also, it's time you were in a top spot instead of giving a leg up to every new man who comes along. Will you take over if Keith offers you the job?"

"If—Christ, I don't know, Steve. If he offers it to me—well—yes. Yes, I'll take it. And Steve, I don't know why you're leaving, but I'll miss you like all hell. And thanks for the chance."

"Just keep it to yourself until it breaks. Don't even tell Sam Abrams or Lisa."

"I'll try not to talk in my sleep."

Leaving Norm on a comfortable cloud, he went among the two groups, making a point of talking with each one, discussing the work on hand, reassuring them that the rumor was no more than a rumor; the account and their jobs were safe. With Norm to back him up later, he was reasonably certain there would be no panic. Temporarily, he chose Frank Hayden to take over Chuck's job until a replacement could be brought in.

When he returned to his office at noon, Peggy was ready to go to lunch and her mention of it reminded him he hadn't had breakfast. "Are you having lunch alone?" he asked.

"Just a quick sandwich at the corner drugstore."

"Let's have it together."

She smiled and said, "Aren't you upsetting a long-standing Gilman tradition?"

"Since neither of us will be here much longer, why not give the water cooler crowd another rumor to monger."

"Neither of us. . . ?"

"I'll tell you about it at lunch. Let's go."

"What about incoming calls?"

"Have Katie take over your office until we get back. With Chuck gone, it will give her something to do."

She did so and they left together. Outside, they walked down Lexington to Bender's where they were able to manage a booth, and ordered lunch for Peggy, and breakfast for Steve.

"What about 'neither of us' being here much longer?" she asked when their orders had been taken.

"Just what I said. I'm through here."

"Through? You're leaving the agency?"

"Not exactly. I've been taken off the GFP and B & B accounts. Lawson phoned Keith this morning at his home and asked to have me replaced."

"After all these years? Who will take over?"

"With Chuck out, I'm going to go to bat for Norm and ask Keith to give him a shot at it. I've moved Frank into Chuck's job temporarily."

"What happened between you and Lawson?"

He told her of the house agency proposition and his firm belief that Mark could never pull it off. And of Mark's visit the night before, omitting many of the more pertinent details. He saw the startled look on her face and said, "What's wrong?"

"Mark came to your apartment? The paintings! He must have seen Karen's paintings. Is that why he asked to have you replaced?"

"Not until after I'd turned down his offer."

She stared at Steve in awe. "There aren't any cuts or bruises on you that I can see."

"It didn't come to physical violence."

"Just a quiet, civilized discussion, huh?"

"Not quite, but conclusive." He sipped at his coffee and said, "Peggy, I know you don't understand this very well, and I can't blame you. Most of it happened before you and I—I'm not offering any excuses for my stupidity in this thing. I could blame it on New York, the pressures of the times we live in, even that perhaps too many things came too soon for me to be able to handle them wisely, but that's over and done with. I wish there were some way I could explain it more plausibly, but I can't. It happened, and it's over."

"Whatever you may think Steve, I'm not a starry eyed child. I understand more than you believe, except for one thing."

"What is that?"

"You've told me you're off GFP and B & B. What happens now?"

"Sometime before five o'clock I'm due to see Keith and tell him whether or not I will leave for Los Angeles to replace Wade Barrett as branch manager."

Peggy's hand shook, rattling cup against saucer. "What are you going to tell him?"

"I've been struggling with that question since the offer was made. Just before I asked you to go to lunch with me, I came to a decision. I'm going to accept and bail out of here."

He saw the flicker of disappointment in her eyes as she said, "A fresh new start in life?"

"Something like that."

"That's what it was going to be for Wade Barrett, wasn't it?"

Steve said nothing, lighting a cigarette to fill the gap.

"Well, good luck in your new job. I hope it works out," Peggy said.

"You don't approve, I take it."

"It isn't for me to approve or disapprove. It was your decision to make and you've made it."

"Since you put it that way . . ." he broke off suddenly, and said in a lighter, more even vein, "Peg, have you ever been to California?"

"No. Only in dreams. Lennie used to talk about it a lot. Poor guy, he never really knew how much he liked it until he came to New York to live. If he'd only stayed there, he'd probably be alive now."

"Would you like to see it, live there?"

"Maybe. Someday . . ."

"Come with me."

"No, Steve. I couldn't."

"Peggy, I love you."

She smiled and said, "I don't want it that way, Steve."

"What way?"

"You don't even know it, but you're on the rebound. You've been doing things, saying things automatically, by reflex action. This whole thing has hit you harder than you know. Yet."

"Peggy, stop being a goddamned amateur psychologist. For the first time in years, maybe in my whole life, I know what I'm talking about, what I want."

"You only think you do. When you wake up, you'll see that all you're doing is following in Larry Price's and Wade Barrett's footsteps. This business has a way of corrupting the best of intentions, purposely or not. It becomes more important than people, takes precedent over lives, marriage, morality, and when that happens, what's left? It ruined your first marriage . . ." She broke off, fighting tears of emotion. "I'm sorry, that wasn't fair. I shouldn't have said that. I'm finished. Shall we go?"

He paid the check and they left, both wordless during the short walk back to the Hungerford Trust Building.

For the next two hours he worked steadily over a fact sheet, jotting down thoughts that could be helpful to Norm after he was gone. He listed the various people at GFP and their relationship to the advertising, sales promotion, merchandising, marketing, and media purchasing program. He got out his personal copy of the Client Facts Book, a three-ring binder filled with various data concerning policy, one that had been passed down to him through a succession of account executives who had preceded him.

Norm Adrian, he thought, could very well be the answer, if Mark Lawson, as it appeared now, would be upgraded, however temporarily, to executive vice-presidency of GFP and a new advertising director appointed to replace him. With Allard, Hayden, and Baker assisting, Norm should be able to pull it off and step into a well-deserved position of responsibility. His B & B group worked well with him and Steve saw no difficulties should Norm take over the GFP group as well.

Then Norm came in and said, "Got a minute, Steve?"

"Sure, Norm. What's on your mind?"

"Everything. And nothing. You talk to Keith yet?"

"No. I'll probably see him around four-thirty."

"You want to think about it again before you do?"

"Norm, I've thought it out very carefully. I can't see one damned reason why you should be having second thoughts about it. I know you'll make it, with room to spare."

"I hope you're right."

"I know I am. You're one of the most experienced men in the agency, next to Keith. The only thing you've got to get used to is the contact end and you'll have Hayden and Baker on your side. Just remember, Norm, the people you'll be calling on know a hell of a lot less than you do about advertising, and that's your edge. They've got all the questions, but you've got something much more important, the answers. Play it cool and you've got it made."

"I wish I could believe that."

"You'll find that out within a month, no more."

Norm shrugged and smiled. "I hear Peggy's leaving, too."

"That's true. You can move your secretary into her office on Monday morning and you're in business without any hangovers. You and Frank will make a good team and you'll have the WPC to keep you honest." He grinned confidently and saw a slow grin break on Norm's face, then explode into a laugh. "Hey," Norm said, "you're beginning to come around again. For a while there, I thought you were planning a quiet suicide."

"When I go out the window, Norm, it won't be quiet. I'll have a brass band playing and the air will be filled with confetti."

"Yeah. The only way to go. I wonder how much of all this the rest of the agency knows?"

"Anybody's guess, Norm. Trying to keep secrets around here is like trying to smuggle an Argentine polo pony through customs under your topcoat. Just keep things quiet and let the official announcements come out of Keith's office."

"I guess I'm committed now."

"You will be after I've discussed it with Keith."

"Yes. Any new word on Mr. Goodwin?"

"It's still a crap game, but I think the odds are improving for him."

Norm got up to go. "Any way you do it, Steve, the best of luck to you."

"Thanks, Norm."

6

Keith said, "Well, Steve, what do I tell Bill?"

"I'll take it, Keith."

"Good," smiling, "I know you won't regret your decision." He picked up the receiver and said, "Lucy, put that call through to Mr. Leary."

"What about my replacement here, Keith?"

"I take it you have a suggestion."

"I have. Norm Adrian."

Keith's lips pursed into a pucker. "I've been toying with the idea of bringing Woody Kirk in from Chicago. Woody's had considerable experience in the food line."

"Most of it has been with soft drinks, and whatever he's got, it can't match Norm's background with Chevalier or B & B. On the merit of that alone, with his people working well with him, all the advantages are on his side as opposed to bringing in a new man."

Keith sucked on his pipe reflectively. "What about the contact end?"

"I'm sure he'll make out if you give him the chance and a little help. Norm's judgment is mature and his patience is fantastic. Even greater than his tremendous capability to think in clutch situations."

"I'll give your suggestion every consideration. I've a strong respect for Norm and I think it might work out. About you, now. Can you leave on Saturday or Sunday?"

"If you'll handle the sublease on my apartment and ship my furniture and other things out when I'm ready for them, yes."

"Good." The phone rang. Bill Leary was on the other end of the line. "Excuse me, Steve?"

Steve nodded and went out.

By Friday, the emptiness was complete. After lunch, when the company paychecks had been distributed, Steve went among the groups and bid each member good-bye; some were solemn, some joking, and a few were moist-eyed. Back in his own office he put together the personal objects he had accumulated over the years; an expensive pen set with a sterling silver and onyx base, a gold embossed memo book, a gold-inlaid scissor-letter-opener in a leather sheath, a gold and silver Dunhill lighter. Much of the accumulation of odds and ends he discarded. Some he left for Norm's use. He removed half a dozen framed and autographed photographs from the wall, and his five award certificates, peeled off the one piece of graffiti he had brought from the very first cubbyhole he had occupied ten years ago: *Too Much Knowledge of the Client's Product Can Be Dangerous* and folded it into the attaché case.

He filled that first, then a handsome, never-used briefcase that had come as a gift from a television network executive. He remembered then, and reached into the rear section of the lower left desk drawer and brought out the outline of the historical novel, wiped the dust from the cover sheet with a piece of Kleenex and flipped through its one hundred and twenty pages quickly, fingering the tabs he had affixed to certain pages to indicate new chapters that waited to be fleshed into completion.

Steve sighed heavily, trying to decide whether to keep dragging it through his life as a reminder of his own procrastinations or to drop it into the wastepaper basket and be done with the impossible dream, once and forever removing this symbol of one more defeat in his life. He hesitated, then shifted a few of the items from the attaché case to the briefcase, put the outline into the former, and locked it. At that point he surveyed the office that had been occupied by himself and his predecessors and saw nothing that would indicate the countless hours he had spent in this room.

In Peggy's office, she had gone through the same procedure and her personal possessions stood on the edge of her desk, wrapped in brown paper, a small package sealed with broad bands of masking tape. She looked up, eyes dampened, and said, "Well, that's that. It's not very much to take with me after five years, is it?"

Steve said, "I've been here twice that long and I'm not taking much more with me."

"It's a little like saying good-bye to someone you—you . . ."

"I know. Have you made your farewell rounds yet?"

She nodded. "They wanted to take me to dinner, but I couldn't. I just couldn't. I'd have made a mess of myself."

He shook his head in agreement. "Since we're in the same lifeboat, why don't we have it together for the last time?"

"Oh, Steve, I'd like that so much . . ." Her head lowered as the tears began to spill over. "I can't," she said. "That would be even worse."

"Peggy, don't."

"I can't help it."

"Come with me. There's still time . . ."

"I couldn't. It would be the same thing all over again. Only the location would be different."

"Then it's a last good-bye?"

Her head bobbed up and down, unable to speak, "Peg—" he began, then turned and went back into his own office.

A few minutes later, his plane tickets were delivered by a messenger. They lay on his desk untouched until he heard Peggy moving about in her office, then he picked them up and put them in his inside jacket pocket. She opened the door only a few inches and said, "I'm going now, Steve."

"When are you leaving for home?"

"Not until next Friday night. I've got some final things to take care of, packing and shipping clothes, other incidentals."

"You won't change your mind about dinner?"

She shook her head negatively. "Good-bye, Steve. I hope you find everything you need to make you happy out there."

"Thanks, Peggy. I wish the same for you. Good-bye."

She closed the door slowly. When he went through her vacated office a few minutes later, it was as though she had never existed.

He went up to the thirty-fifth floor for a final round of good-byes, then to Keith's office. "I've talked with Bill," Keith said. "When you get there tomorrow afternoon, check in at the Beverly Hills Hotel. Bill's staying there and he's delighted you're coming out. He'll stay on for a few days to get you set up, go over the client roster, that sort of thing. Of course, I'll be in close touch with you for a while. So will Bill. Anything you need, you know, you're still only a telephone call away. Drink?"

"Yes, thanks. And I want to thank you for everything you've done for me, Keith."

Keith laughed. "Just protecting our investment in you." He poured two glasses of Scotch, added ice cubes and some water. "Here's to your success, Steve. In another year, possibly two, we'll be talking about that limited partnership."

7

On Saturday morning it rained. The humidity was high, and out on the sidewalk, standing beside the row of luggage, Steve felt as though he were being slowly strangled. He recalled the January morning when he had returned from his first trip to Los Angeles, his joy at the sight of these canyoned streets and avenues he was now leaving perhaps forever; and he had felt this despite the California warmth and casual atmosphere for which he had developed a curious ambivalent attachment during his stay there.

He thought, during the cab ride to JFK International, of many other things he was leaving behind; the memories of his youth in Lancaster with Grady and Jenny, of his first love, Libby; of Columbia and his first days, months, and years at the Leary Agency; of Keith and Louise Allard who, in desperate moments of fantasy, had taken the place of his father and mother.

And he realized that he was using these memories to keep him from thinking about Peggy, who had come to believe, as he had, that he was the final link in a circular chain whose other two links were Larry Price and Wade

Barrett; that he would eventually reach the same ignominious end as they. He thought, too. of Karen and Mark, and wondered if, when Karen completed her course of analysis, she would be able to restore some semblance of normalcy between herself and Mark; or if she would be able to see more clearly that divorce and full freedom were her only salvation.

The rain slowed the heavy flow of traffic but he had given himself ample time. The cab reached JFK with almost an hour to spare. After checking everything but his attaché case, he went to the coffee shop and ordered coffee, barely hearing the clamor of voices around him, the metallic announcements of plane departures, and the shrill roaring of planes taking off. Having spent the trip from town delving into the past, he began thinking of the future; job, associates, an apartment to find, acquaintances to make, the mandatory car he would buy, clubs and restaurants to . . .

There were empty stools on either side of him at the counter and a man was smiling down at him, saying, "I wonder if you would mind moving over one stool so my wife and I . . ."

"Of course." He stood up, and picked up his check. "I was leaving anyway." He left a tip, paid the check, and went out, walking slowly toward the gate number scrawled on the ticket envelope. He passed a bank of telephone booths, hesitated for a moment, then entered one that was vacant. He dropped a coin into the slot and dialed a number, but an operator came on and told him the exact amount required to reach the city. He deposited the exact change and dialed the number again.

"Hello?"

"Peggy?"

"No, this is Lois. Hold a moment, please."

She came on within seconds. "Hello?"

"Steve, Peggy."

"Oh—Steve. Where are you?"

"JFK."

"Is everything all right?"

"Just fine. What are you doing?"

"The dishes. We've just finished breakfast."

"Peggy, listen . . ."

"If it's Los Angeles, Steve, the answer is still the same."

"Will you please just listen. . . ?"

"All right, but please hurry. I can't take much more of this, Steve. I'm terribly upset as it is."

"Then listen carefully. There's only thirty-five minutes to plane time and I've got to tell you this fast, before it takes off."

"What?"

"Peggy, darling, I own a house with six acres of ground around it in Lancaster. It's just occurred to me that Virginia would be a great place to settle down and find out if I can finish that novel of mine that's been bugging me . . ."

"Oh, Steve, how marvelous . . ."

"Shut up and listen to me, will you? I know it will be a gamble for both of us, but we won't starve, not for a few years anyhow. It would be a hell of a place to work in peace, raise children . . ."

"Oh, Steve! It sounds like the answer to a dream. I'll help you. I know I can. I could have a garden of my own, a dog, and a cat . . ." He knew she was crying into her words and said, "Listen, don't unpack anything you've already packed. Just throw everything else into something. While you're on your way here in a cab, I'll pick up two tickets to Washington. I'll have to call Keith and cancel this Los Angeles deal . . ."

"Steve—Steve . . ."

"I've got to run and get my baggage before it's loaded aboard . . ."

"Steve, *wait!*"

"What is it, Peg? Hurry."

"Hey! I love you! I'm on my way . . ."